APR 20 '73

P9-AFI-131

WORLD ENOUGH AND TIME

Robert Penn Warren

RANDOM HOUSE

NEW YORK

World Enough
and Time

A ROMANTIC
NOVEL

To Dixon and Elizabeth Wecter

So oft as I with state of present time
The image of the antique world compare,
When as mans age was in his freshest prime,
And the first blossome of faire vertue bare,
Such oddes I finde twixt those, and these which are,
As that, through long continuance of his course,
Me seemes the world is runne quite out of square
From the first point of his appointed sourse,
And being once amisse, growes daily wourse and wourse.

Let none then blame me, if in discipline
Of vertue and of civill uses lore,
I doe not forme them to the common line
Of present dayes, which are corrupted sore,
But to the antique use which was of yore,
When good was onely for it selfe desyred,
And all men sought their owne, and none no more;
When Justice was not for most meed outhyred,
But simple Truth did rayne, and was of all admyred.

Dread soverayne goddesse, that doest highest sit
In seate of judgement, in th'Almighties stead,
And with magnificke might and wondrous wit
Doest to thy people righteous doome aread,
That furthest nations filles with awfull dread,
Pardon the boldnesse of thy basest thrall,
That dare discourse of so divine a read,
As thy great justice praysed over all:
The instrument whereof, loe! here thy Artegall.

EDMUND SPENSER: *from the Prologue of the Fifth*
Booke of the Faerie Queene Contayning the
Legend of Artegall or of Justice.

WORLD ENOUGH AND TIME

I

I CAN SHOW YOU WHAT IS LEFT. AFTER THE pride, passion, agony, and bemused aspiration, what is left is in our hands. Here are the scraps of newspaper, more than a century old, splotched and yellowed and huddled together in a library, like November leaves abandoned by the wind, damp and leached out, back of the stables or in a fence corner of a vacant lot. Here are the diaries, the documents, and the letters, yellow too, bound in neat bundles with tape so stiffened and tired that it parts almost unresisting at your touch. Here are the records of what happened in that courtroom, all the words taken down. Here is the manuscript he himself wrote, day after day, as he waited in his cell, telling his story. The letters of his script lean forward in their haste. Haste toward what? The bold stroke of the quill catches on the rough paper, fails, resumes, moves on in its race against time, to leave time behind, or in its rush to meet Time at last at the devoted and appointed place. To whom was he writing, rising from his mire or leaning from his flame to tell his story? The answer is easy. He was writing to us.

We have what is left, the lies and half-lies and the truths and half-truths. We do not know that we have the Truth. But we must have it. Puzzling over what is left, we are like the scientist fumbling with a tooth and thigh bone to reconstruct for a museum some great, stupid

3

beast extinct with the ice age. Or we are like the louse-bit nomad who finds, in a fold of land between his desert and the mountains, the ruin of parapets and courts, and marvels what kind of men had held the world before him. But at least we have the record: the tooth and thigh bone, or the kingly ruins.

We have the picture of Jeremiah Beaumont. At least, there is reason to believe that it is his picture, for on the back is written in an old-fashioned hand: *This is the portrait of my brother J.B. who shed human blood but whose sufferings may have merited Divine Mercy and the Hope of Salvation. My Redeemer I cry unto THEE. Laetitia Beaumont Baxter. 1827.* We know that Jeremiah had a sister named Laetitia Beaumont. The name and the date are good evidence.

The portrait is not grand. It is merely a crayon drawing, sixteen by twenty-five inches, done by some nameless frontier artist who perhaps wandered the country, a pack tied with thongs of deerskin on his back, and earned his bread with his crayons, or with ax or sickle if he happened to come at a time of log-raising or at harvest. The colors are faded, but we know from them that Jeremiah Beaumont had dark hair, very heavy, with gray or blue eyes. His jaw is full but the chin is cleft. His mouth is wide, somewhat sullen, with the corners of the lips turned down. His eyes are wide-set and large, slightly protruding, under an erect, square brow. He is wearing a black coat with narrow lapels, and a buff waistcoat with gilt buttons to the throat, where a bit of collar or a white cravat shows.

"When he stands he is not much taller than common," says the letter of a spectator who sat in the hot courtroom at Frankfort, Kentucky, in June, 1826, "but when seated he appears otherwise, for his shoulders are strong-knit and wide, he holds himself straight like a horseman, and his waist is narrow and long to a degree. It is strange to see that for tracts of time he does not seem to attend to what goes on about him while men dispute his life. He sits like a man who thinks inwardly or he looks across the busy room to the wall, but as though the wall were not there, like a strong husbandman who in the hour of ease toward sunset looks distantly over the fields ripening to harvest. But at times he rouses himself, and turns his gaze upon one who speaks and fixes him as though to pluck out the soul, and under his eye I have seen men stammer and lose the order of their discourse, whether they spoke truth or no. If fault he has in bearing, it is some air of self-complaisance which wins regard but not hearts."

The letter continues: "His dress is good and decent, usually pantaloons of pongee, loose at the foot and buttoned down below the boot with straps (but today pantaloons of jean without straps), and a black coat made double-breasted, which he often lets hang open over a plain shirt for reason of the sweating heat. But at any season it is

4

probable from details of manner that he generally affects a genteel untidiness. He is about twenty-eight or -nine years of age, in the green and gristle of his time." Actually, Jeremiah was only twenty-five at the time of his trial—a robust young man, seeming older than his years, sitting erect before eyes unsympathetic at his "self-complaisance," by turns abstracted and acute, sweating in his good clothes, fingering inwardly his fears, his calculations, and his dream.

It was a drama he had prepared, an ambiguous drama which seemed both to affirm and to deny life, to affirm and to deny humanity. But it may have been the drama Jeremiah Beaumont had to prepare in order to live at all, or in order, living, to be human. And it may be that a man cannot live unless he prepares a drama, at least cannot live as a human being against the ruck of the world.

The drama which Jeremiah Beaumont prepared was to be grand, with noble gestures and swelling periods, serious as blood. It was to be a tragedy, like those in the books he read as a boy after coming home from Dr. Les Burnham's Academy (a log cabin set by a spring at a red-clay crossroads) or at night in a rented room, little better than a loft, when he came back from his day in Mr. Harrod's store in Bowling Green, where he measured out calico or ran whisky from a bung into some farmer's Saturday bottle.

But the actors were not well trained. At times even he, the hero, forgot his lines. At times it all was only a farce, though a bloody farce, which, with its comic parody of greatness, struck a desperate doubt into his soul. To us, at this distance, with the blood all dried to powder, it is sometimes the most serious speeches and grand effects which give the farce. And by the same token, we may find the pathos only in those moments when the big speeches are fluffed or the gestures forgotten, when the actor improvises like a lout, when he suffers nakedly from the giggles and the inimical eyes, or flees from the stage. We find the pathos then, for that is the kind of suffering with which we are most fully acquainted. It is not, however, the effect Jeremiah Beaumont had labored to prepare.

He had been a long time preparing his dream. He prepared it in a land on the fringe of the wilderness, where mothers yet remembered to quiet a child by threatening, "Be still, little punkin, or the Shawnees will get you," and where it might be a two-day ride from one town to the next, and the town itself, even the finest, was a random collection of houses, brick, board, log, along a street that was dust or quagmire, according to season. Even at Lexington, where the children of the rich could get lessons in French and polite deportment and where gentlemen in frilled shirts and varnished boots (with mustaches stained with tobacco juice) might meet in Monsieur Terasse's coffee house to gravely read the journals brought over the mountains, or loll in the grape arbor of Vauxhall—even here there was little more than a big village, and in the swelling pastures and hemp fields and ravines around it, the echo of the war whoop still seemed to linger and the names of the dead were still remembered.

Beyond, south and west, were the farms just snatched from the forest, with the black stumps from the slashing and burning still visible before the corn got high, and the shadow of the forest still stunted the corn along the edge of the field. The panther killed a calf in the lot, and in summer the black bear, before his mast grew sweet and hard in the forest in the "lappin season," came down to take a shoat in the open and rip the guts from the settler's hound. In their season the wild pigeons still passed over to black the sky and stun the ear with the roar of their wings, and where they roosted big boughs broke with the innumerable weight and the ground was pale and sticky with droppings. In that world the leather hunting shirt and the broadcloth coat mixed at burgoo, barbecue, market, or hustings, and a man might wear both the coonskin cap and the two-story beaver in his time.

It was a violent and lonely land, and when night came on, the loneliness was equal for the big brick house with the white portico overlooking a meadow or the log hut set at the head of a cove in the knobs. Eastward, cutting off the past, rose the wall of the mountains, and westward the wilderness stretched away forever with its terror and promise. The people had come here to stay, and they would stay. They would possess the wild land, but the wild land possessed them too, and in a secret, ritualistic gluttony they had eaten the heart of every savage killed at the edge of the clearing or in the ambush by the ford. The dirk (of Spanish steel or made from a hunting knife or Revolutionary sword) and the Bible might lie side by side on the table, or Plato and the dueling pistols on the mantel shelf. A man might die for honor or kill for arrogance. In broad daylight the terrible vision of sin might strike him down by the tavern well or back of his own corn crib. It was a land of the fiddle and whisky, sweat and prayer, pride and depravity.

Here a man might plunge into nature as into a black delirious stream and gulp it in and be engulfed. Or he might shudder with horror at the very flesh he wore, at the sound of his guts or the pulse in his blood, because whatever of himself he could touch or feel was natural, too. But he lived as best he could, and left us the land.

That land is the scene of the drama Jeremiah Beaumont devised. Or perhaps the land and the history of the land devised Jeremiah Beaumont and the drama in which he played, and the scene is the action and speaks through the mouth of Jeremiah Beaumont as through a mask. But Jeremiah Beaumont would not have thought so.

6

That idea would have struck him as ridiculous, as worse than ridiculous, for it would rob him of the last shred of pride as the author of his own ruin and leave him alone without identity, staring into the blank face of suffering. The idea would have been ridiculous to him, for in the end he did not ask for pity, at least not human pity. But pity at the price of his self-respect is what we are most ready to give him. For with us pity for others is the price we are anxious to pay for the privilege of our self-pity.

Jeremiah Beaumont was born in 1801 in Glasgow County, Kentucky, on the edge of the section known as the Barrens. That name does not do less than a wrong to the land, for the first settlers who came found a high, shelving and rolling country covered with grass where elk grazed peacefully and where there was no need for the ax to clear a field for the plow. But there was timber, and fruit trees grew along the watercourses. In spring, flowers covered the ground as thick as young grass, and later in the season a man could stoop almost anywhere and gather a handful of wild strawberries. In the story which Jeremiah Beaumont wrote in his "dungeon cell," he speaks of the wild strawberries, how he had gathered them as a boy for a "sweet feast." He continues: "There were still many when I was a child, on the land not yet put to plow or too heavy pastured. I have heard my good old father say that when he came among the first, many years before, it was the season of their full fruit and when he walked across the land to the spot to set his house his boots to the ankle were red and bright with juice as with blood. But I remember from my own time how they were sweet to the tongue."

Jasper Beaumont, the father, came in 1791, among the first to his county. He was a Virginian who had moved young to Pennsylvania and begun to prosper. But he fought in the Revolution as a captain, and war and absence ruined him. So after a few years he joined a party floating down the Ohio on two broadhorns, big flatboats bound for the West.

He spent the winter at Lexington, where because he was literate and clever he got a good position as manager of a rope walk, where he had some contact with people of the better order, and where he attracted favorable notice by promptly and efficiently breaking the jaw of a locally famous bully who annoyed him and a young man of good connection when they were drinking in a tavern. Presumably the blow got him a wife, for the coming spring he married the young man's sister, Hettie Marcher. Her father, Morton Marcher, was a rich planter, but she married the thirty-five-year-old captain, a stranger with no assets beyond the heavy fist that had flattened the bully, a decent suit, a good horse, a few gold pieces, and a Revolutionary sword stuck among the household plunder on his ox cart.

She married him much against her father's will, though apparently with the connivance of her brother. According to Jeremiah Beaumont's story, the brother might have reconciled the choleric old Marcher in the end, but a year or so later the young man was thrown from a horse and killed.

In any case, in May, 1791, Jasper Beaumont and his bride fled Lexington and the father's wrath. Jasper bought a horse for his bride, and a stout Negro to drive the cart, and took the trail southwest to the newer land. He arrived, we know, at the time when the strawberries were at their "full fruit" to stain his boots like blood. He threw up a two-room log cabin, a hut for the slave, and settled. The first several years were hard, and the family lived by the rifle nearly as much as by the plow. Three children were born in those years, all sons, but one was still-born and the other two died within the first year. Then times changed for the better, Jasper Beaumont built a better house, of log, and later added a room of brick in front, for he had hopes and pretensions. The old cabin became the quarters for his four slaves. By this time another child was born, the older sister Laetitia, who was to save the crayon portrait of Jeremiah.

Jeremiah was born in those good years after the brick room was built, a time of cattle on pasture, meal without weevil in the bin, rich hog meat in the smokehouse, killed in the light or the waxing of the moon that it might not shrink on the hook or waste in the barrel, and "sauce and salet" from the green garden or woodland to go with the meat. China joined pewter on the table now and the wood bowls whittled from maple stayed in the kitchen or in the quarters; the mother had a black silk dress and silver tray and six silver spoons, and the father was called Squire Beaumont, for he had served as a magistrate, sitting with a black coat and riding whip behind a table in the Beartooth Tavern to take his jorum and dispense justice.

It was a time of peace and promise, the lull after the first hard years, but the boy heard his father's tales of the war beyond the mountain and knew the old men who talked of other times and places when "the folk was forted" against Indians and you did not trust the owl-whoop at night, or even by daylight the whistle of the "ma-ma-twa," the catbird, in the brush by the spring. So he lay in the woods with a stick for a Decherd rifle and shivered with cold joy when the Shawnee war party footed soft as smoke into the "speckled glade" before him. He remembered that and how, when the shiver left him and there was nothing in the glade, he felt that life was empty and he would live for nothing.

He was a strong child and throve from the first, the source of special pride, born late to a mother almost old enough for those days to put on the white cap and sit with the grannies by the chimney, the compensation for the three sons lost years before and buried at the foot of a big cedar. Where the mother's pride took the form of doting and indulgence, the father's was grim and driving. Jasper Beaumont was near fifty by this time, and his late prosperity, good for the time and place, seemed to give him no joy but to awake in him a black and bitter humor. Perhaps he had dreamed of something bigger and grander, and his name of a "forward and strong-handed farmer" and the respect he got when he sat as a squire at the tavern were nothing but ashes on his tongue. He was lettered, and at night after work or on Sunday, he put his son to a book. It was a book which he himself made, putting on paper the alphabet, big and square, and printing out the easy sentences of a primer, and having his wife stitch the sheets together. "I have kept it preciously," Jeremiah Beaumont wrote, "and esteem it more than a legacy of land and rents which my father did not leave me.

"He was a loving father but he did not bend or swerve and if my childish eye wandered to the burning log on the hearth or to the green fly in the sunlight, the switch on my leg supplied comment. I was sometimes sullen and idle or said the familiar word wrong, from some reason dark even to me, knowing the while how the switch would sting. But the vanity of self which I now see to be the dark reason for deliberate error was also a reason to seek praise, and since my mind was quick and of good apprehension I soon left the poor little hand-writ primer and by my father's side puzzled out Watt's *Hymns for Children*. Then came Aesop's good fables in a pretty book my father caused to be brought from Lexington as a present for my pleasure, and many a summer evening toward sun I lay on the grass with it and left the cows uncalled or water untoted from the spring, thereby earning by an excess of virtue on one hand the punishment for a defect on the other."

We know the books, or at least some of them, of that time. There was *Pilgrim's Progress*, which the boy read "not for the sound instruction and the business of salvation but for the wildness of adventure and the doleful surprises by the way," and the big swamp in Colonel Mead's land "where I went to take frogs I called in secret the Slough of Despond and to the other marks of the country I gave such names as would cast a passion over the commonness of things." When Jeremiah was eight or nine he read Benjamin Franklin's *Autobiography*, "a book to which my father was partial because it gave good lessons how a man might master and use the world." He found his father's copy of Love's *Surveying*, the sort of book which any man in the West who could read and cipher might have at hand in case he decided to become a speculator or run lines for others. Surveying, like

9

law, might lead to wealth or greatness. George Washington had been a surveyor. Jeremiah tells that when his father discovered him with the book, "he tore it from my hands, saying it was his and I had not sought permission, and when I replied that I had found it on a shelf back of some old plunder, his face went black, as was his wont when an unspoken rage came on him, and he crushed it in his hand and went from the room." The book apparently reminded Jasper of old ambitions unfulfilled and the promise of the new land unrealized. But that night the son found the book lying on his cot, a silent apology and perhaps a fatalistic acceptance of the world and of approaching age.

Then there was Guthrie's *Grammar of Geography*— "but how could it be a grammar, I thought?"—which gave the resounding phrases "brazen meridian" and "equinoctial line." He remembered hearing the derelict and lousy old Sam Buttons, an old hunter and Indian fighter from the time of the Long Hunters, speak of the "noction line," and it came on him suddenly that the "equinoctial line" and the phrase in the mouth of the whisky-soaked, dirty old man who had lived out of the savage past were the same phrase. "The thought struck me as I was passing across the big meadow toward Colonel Mead's land on an errand, and I stopped dead still there in the midsummer heat while insects buzzed in the silence, and discovered to myself how wide the world was and how men moved across it for a time and grew old and died and how the ball of the earth revolved on its appointed course and tilted in the awful emptiness of sky, season after season, forever."

There was, of course, the Bible. Jasper Beaumont was not a pious man, but he sat by the son's side and made him read it aloud. And by the Bible on the shelf was "the broken and incomplete book of the Martyrs who died for the true faith against the whorish tyrant of the triple crown." Here over and over again was the story of the one against the many, some stubborn, hard-headed and hard-handed peasant or villager, some preacher sour in pride and righteousness, or some ecstatic female who would take the rack or the flame before the authority of the received opinion. There were pictures here. One in particular he returned to in the end, the picture of a young woman tied cruelly to a post "so that the bonds seemed to crush her sweet flesh and her face lifted up while the flames rose about her." He pored for hours over that picture, which we can visualize as crude, blurred, and splotched on the spongy paper of the ruined book. "Sometimes looking fixedly upon it, my breath almost stopped and my bowels turned to water. Sometimes the strange fancy took me that I might seize her from the flame and escape with her from all the people who crowded about for her death. At other times it seemed that I might

10

throw myself into the fire to perish with her for the very joy. And again, my heart leaping suddenly like a fish and my muscles tight as at the moment when you wait to start a race, I saw her standing there bound, with no fire set, and I myself flung the first flaming faggot and could not wait to see her twist and strive against the tight bond in the great heat and toss her head with the hair falling loose to utter a cry for the first agony. The strangeness of my fancies compelled me and, staring at the picture, I would cling to them. Then of a sudden they would be gone, I could not call them back to mind, and I would feel tired and sad. Or if I had indulged my last and strangest fancy I would be shamed in my own eyes for so mysterious and cruel an imagining and would hate myself. Then when I grew to be a big boy and knew the early stirrings of manhood, it was the picture come alive in my mind which disturbed my slumbers or made me stop bemused by the trail or roadside in broad day.

"I remember the last time I ever looked upon the book. It was on a winter evening before supper, two or three years after the death of my father. I held the old book on my knee and leaned over to study the picture by the light of the fire, for the candle was not yet lit. I stared at the page and felt the heat of the fire make the flesh of my face creep and tingle. So intent was I that I did not hear my mother's step or know her presence till she said, 'Son, what are you looking at so close?' and laid her hand on my shoulder as a mother will and leaned above me to see. 'Oh,' she said, 'just that old book.'

"At her touch and words I felt a hatred for her and for myself, and in my confusion and shame leaped from the chair, almost pushing her back, and flung the book into the fire, and ran from the house into darkness. I ran down the frozen lane until my breath was labored. Then I stopped in the dark and stared up for a long time at the bright-coming stars of the winter night. But at last there was nothing for me to do but go back and take my supper in silence. My mother sat there and said nothing to me, though her eyes were upon me."

Long before that event, however, Jeremiah had been put to school with Dr. Leicester Burnham, who had just come into the section from near Danville to be near a beloved daughter. He was an extraordinarily fat man, "fat as a sow come to farrowing time," with a round face, "the color of the belly of a dead catfish," and with thin gray hair plastered damply on his big skull. He wore moccasins and gaiters, for he could not bear shoes (his great weight had made his feet swell), and the moccasins made a curious combination with his long-tailed black coat, big as a tent. He had been a physician, but had long since given up regular practice because no horse would bear him. Now, however, he still prepared potions and pills which many of his patients survived and which gave him a reputation.

11

Even now we know some of his favorite remedies, for he wrote a book, *The Healthful Man's Vademecum, with Tried Prescriptions and Animadversions upon Morality and the Meaning of Life*. His prescriptions are full of calomel, saltpetre, ground ivy juice, jesuit's bark, pulverized columbo, elixir vitriol in wine, steel dust, beat caster, asafoetida, fat of bacon, sycamore chips, and strong whisky. For a stubborn fever he put a young pullet split open and bound to the sole of the foot, as "warm with life as may be," and for chills he gave pills of cobweb. He had wrought cures, according to his book, and recounted many others, "especially in that kind of suffering called Hypo or Ennui, where mind and body conspire together for our ill." The mystery of the relation of mind and body apparently obsessed him, and he speculated much upon it, and collected medical cases.

For instance, he knew, he says, "of a man who suffered great agony from imagining he had a Cobbler and all his tools in his belly and could absolutely hear him at work mending shoes within. He would cry out and make his wife to lay her ear to his belly to hear and confirm the tap of the mallet on the last. At those times he was in pain, but we must not suppose him mad, for he had made wealth, had fought for his country's sake in the Independence, and wrote a fair and unblotted hand. At length a doctor came after all others had failed, who did not sneer and heard him civilly. Then he brought to the patient's house a set of shoemaker's tools and a naked boy whom he hid behind a door—having administered the patient a grand puke. Before the puke began to operate he caused the patient to be blindfolded, and when the operation of the medicine commenced, he would drop one tool after another into the necessary great pot under the patient's nose, with a clatter. Then at the hardest exertion of the patient, he snatched off the sufferer's blindfold, the naked boy leaped out in front and ran from the door. Then the patient and the doctor prayed and gave thanksgiving together that the Cobbler had fled his mansion in his belly. Thus was the hypo entirely removed. Some other men of my acquaintance have concluded that their legs were of glass and were consequently afraid to walk lest they should break to pieces."

It is easy now to smile at Dr. Burnham's elixir vitriol in wine, his split pullets applied to the feet, the pills of cobweb, the grand and minor pukes, the cobbler's tools and sycamore chips. It is easy to smile at his poems interlarded among the prescriptions and case histories, English poems in chaste couplets in the style of Pope giving advice on diet or explaining God's will in matrimony and procreation, or Latin poems celebrating the natural beauties of Kentucky (for Dr. Burnham showed his softer and more romantic self in the thornier language), the sunset over the Green River, the golden tongues of Colonel Mead's hounds, or the song of the whippoorwill.

But it is even easier to smile at the "animadversions upon morality and the meaning of life," for they strike us as stranger, even, than the cobweb pills or the Latin verses to a whippoorwill, as strange, perhaps, as our own verses or our own animadversions upon the meaning of life and our scientific speculations upon the relation of mind and body may strike some prowler in a library a hundred years from now.

But enough of Dr. Burnham. It is enough that he was the first scholar to come to Glasgow County. He set up his academy in a log structure by a roadside spring, with a great chimney at one end to be stocked in winter by the big boys who cut wood in the fall at recess, and with no windows, just strips of oiled paper between logs to let in the light. In that room, he "spoke familiarly of the famous Romans, as though he had called them by name in their boyhood on the next farm, and to such as would listen he gave patterns of human greatness in devotion to country, appetite for daring deeds, and love of the good beyond flesh or suffering." He was a "stern driver" and kept the scholars in order, the ponderous puffing old lard-tub of a man, who sat on his special chair built wide with props and struts for his weight, and made the boys line up before him for recitation, with a five-foot ash rod in hand to whack shank or knee. His other and happier scholars have left no record of him, but Jeremiah Beaumont wrote: "He opened my mind to the fullness of life, and was ever my friend, even in ways and hours he knew not."

Jeremiah was a little over nine years old when Dr. Burnham opened his school, but he was far ahead of the other boys near his age, and was put immediately to his Latin and history. The first night he brought home the Latin book the teacher lent him, his father sat by his side in the candlelight to look on as usual. But he did not sit there long. Suddenly he rose, and the son looking up into the father's face thought for a moment that his father was in a great rage with him, though he knew no fault. It was not a rage, at least not at the son. The man lifted his arm as though to strike someone, and exclaimed: "God damn, God damn—I didn't get none of it—I didn't get none of it! If I'd a-got it—if—if . . ." Then he let his arm sink, and walked from the room, and the house.

Jeremiah was determined to get what was before him. Study and reading became a passion for him, but a passion crossed now and then by the restlessness of his strong body and the violent willfulness of his nature.

At the school Jeremiah was a "wicked chap to quarrel and fight with the schollars," and beatings only "enfiercened" him, and made him more resolute to have his turn. His quarrelsome nature fostered in him a bent for loneliness, and that bent was not hard to gratify in

13

the lonely land. Since he had no brothers, even his chores were lonely, and when he did his share in the field, he worked apart from the others, at times setting himself some ferocious pace, at times idling with "a head full of fancies or a mouth full of sounding words." He knew the country for miles around, even back into the Knobs and "the devious and lonely wilds," for as soon as his father got him a rifle he became a hunter.

Jasper Beaumont had hunted for meat, at times when the patched pellet in his rifle was the only insurance against a dry gut-rumble that night, but he had no taste for hunting as a sport. He had had bigger dreams than a few coonskins or a bait of bear steak of what he would seize from the land. But Jeremiah knew well all the old men for miles around who had grown up in the days of the great hunting and to whom still four tight walls were unnatural, old Sam Buttons, who was of the time of the Long Hunters, Jake Fairfeather, Solomon Skanks, Jim Runnion, aging men with broken black teeth and hairy faces who had little love for the corn patch or mill, who knew all the hints of weather and lifted the head like a hound when the breeze changed or faltered, and who loved to lie in the sun in front of their tumbled-down cabins, with a jug of whisky at hand, while their leather-faced old wives fetched wood or hoed in the field. Jim Runnion, still hearty and therefore beyond sympathy, was the chief disgrace of the settlements, and the respectable said of him that if "you raked hell with a fine-tooth comb you would not find a more hairy-eared varmint and very butt-cut of sin." Colonel Mead, who was rich and atheistical by report, was his only friend of the better order.

It was Jim Runnion who took Jeremiah when he was thirteen on his first big hunt into the rough country to the northeast. It was past the "gabbling season for wild turkey when the bark slips on the elm, and dogwood time when the she-bear brings out her young, and it was the hour for the hunter to unhouse himself and look to the powder in his horn." With three men in the party, including Colonel Mead, a boy of sixteen, and Jeremiah, they started out. A pony carried their provisions, and on leash were Jim Runnion's bear dogs, Sweetlips, Smoker, and Tear-ear. They went into a country where "cedars hung to the hillsides and streams leaped and rocks were hollowed by the assiduity of time," found a glade with a spring and set up a lean-to camp, as had been the practice of hunters in the early years. By day they ranged over the country, "clambering rock or boguering soft-foot by the cane," making a great kill of meat, including three bear, and at night they gorged on choice bits by the fire and lay on the ground around the embers, if they had not come back to camp, or on the deerskins in the lean-to if they had come back.

14

After the men had fallen asleep and were "grunting and snoring from their surfeit and their pulls on the brown tit of the bottle," Jeremiah would lie awake and watch the stars and "wickedly" wish he had no family to go back to and that he could stay forever in the forest, "shedding blood and feasting on the wild flesh." All other things to come "seemed of no account and I made only for this life in the great silence and the dark shade of trees." He thought, according to his report, that if a man could only stay here he would never grow old and "know the burden of time and things."

But he came back, and that year was sent on his first visit to his grandfather Marcher, who had the fine house to the north on the Kentucky River. The old man had sent a letter to the willful daughter married to Jasper Beaumont. It was his first communication in the twenty years or so since she had defied him. He was ready to forgive now (though he did not say so), for life was closing in, and he asked her crabbedly to come to see him and bring the boy, for he had heard that there was a son. With the warmth of old recollections just stirred, Hettie Beaumont might have gone, but her husband forbade it. He compromised, however, by letting the boy go. The mother had the trump card in the argument; their son should be the old man's heir. The father, in his bitterness and sense of failure, clutching at the last hope beyond himself that his son at least should be rich and grand, gave his consent. Then he mounted his horse and rode off to the tavern, where he got blackly and savagely drunk and quarreled so violently with Colonel Mead that a duel was narrowly averted.

In the summer of his thirteenth year Jeremiah was entrusted to a party heading north to Bardstown, where other respectable and responsible people were to be found to drop the boy at the Marcher place, a day's ride beyond, near Frankfort. At the end of a week he stepped on the land which might some day be his.

Entering between two piles of heaped-up limestone which marked the beginning of a lane, he saw a half mile away, at the top of the slight rise, the establishment of Runnymede. It was a big squarish brick house with broken gables and tall chimneys at the ends and along the ell to the rear, with big trees around it in a great yard surrounded by a stone wall. Within the stone wall were a miscellaneous set of buildings, brick, stone, log, some even in front of the main house. Outside the wall the land fell gently away in a meadow or park as big as a farm, dotted with fine oaks under which cattle grazed. (Jeremiah was to learn that in the years before, the last elk of the region had been in this park, kept for the pleasure of old Marcher, who was a great hunter and loved to run elk with horses. Young Marcher had been killed coursing elk with his father.)

When Jeremiah Beaumont entered the great yard, he saw that

15

the minor buildings were scattered about with no regard for order, thrown up at caprice or convenience, the master's office, log cabins as quarters for house servants, a smithy, a stone coach house, and beyond that a stable, all out of repair. Between the buildings half the grass was worn away, and chickens and guinea fowl and turkeys and a pair of draggled peacocks wandered about, printing the dust. Broken tools, an old broom, chunks of wood, and here and there a stone from the wall cumbered the ground. A cart wheel was propped against a tree with a guinea perched sleepily on it. Under another tree a covey of Negro children were gathered, the older ones playing mumble-the-peg with a broken knife, while the younger ones crawled about naked or wallowed in the dust. Negroes were everywhere. An old Negro man slept propped against a tree with a hat over his face. Others stood there in enormous idleness, staring at him from the shade of the trees. Jeremiah felt that he had stumbled into a kind of drowsy nightmare from which he would never awake, and his feet seemed heavy and his breath slow. For a moment he was tempted to turn and drop his satchel and run back across the park to the road and escape. Certainly, his grandfather did not live here, nobody lived here, and if he entered he would be lost. But his good sense prevailed, and he approached the house.

On the rather narrow porch three hounds dozed. Two good saddles, one new, were piled on a bench, but another saddle with broken girth and crusted, scaling leather was thrown against the wall, and he could see that it had lain there undisturbed for a long time, rotting with the seasons, accumulating dust and chicken dung. The big door was wide open. He walked into the dark interior and stood there in the wide hallway, among great mirrors streaked black and with peeling gold frames, not daring to set his satchel down or call out. He was deadly homesick and wanted to be in the clean room of his mother.

Suddenly, an old Negro woman, very fat but silent on her bare feet, appeared in the gloom and stared at him. He could find nothing to say. Then she took another step at him, leaned, and demanded, "You he grand-boy?"

Jeremiah nodded, and she was reabsorbed into the shadow of the nearest room.

After a little while a door shut deeper in the house, there were steps, and from the room into which the Negro woman had vanished, the grandfather came, burly and wheezing, red-faced and bearded with a wide stained beard, white hair shagging heavily off the sides of his bald, craggy skull, brown eyes blood-shot but acute under jutting, tangled white eyebrows, and solidly in his right hand a heavy stick, much battered but with a gold head. He wore a dark-blue overcoat, cut long with frogs on it, some missing, the cloth streaked and spotted, the coat unbuttoned to show a rumpled shirt not fastened at the top, with no neck band, cravat, or stock to bind the strong crinkled flesh of the throat. He leaned down at the boy as though "peering down a well," and his breath was rank with whisky. Then he prodded the boy with the stick, as he would prod an animal. "Git in the light," he ordered. The boy felt the surge of resentment, but remembering his mother, conquered it, and obeyed. In the light the old man resumed his inspection, then said: "You don't favor Hettie. You must favor that fellow."

The resentment came surging back, stronger than before, and he had to bite his lips to keep hot words back. Then the old man was tapping his leg with the stick, saying, "You look stout. They say he was stout, that fellow. Can you ride?"

Jeremiah said that he could ride. "Huh," the old man grunted, but the boy could not interpret the sound, whether it was satisfaction or skepticism. It may well have been skepticism, for that afternoon the boy was set on a nervous little mare that threw him in five minutes.

"Great God!" the old man roared from his saddle, "ride—you say you can ride! What kind of hosses they got down there in them settlements?"

Jeremiah was thrown twice again that afternoon, and each time the old man ordered grimly, "Git back on."

That was the beginning of the summer. He gradually accustomed himself to the life of the place. It was different from all his expectations of what wealth and grandeur would be, and he tried to imagine what life here had been before, back in his mother's time. There were still the red carpets in the big rooms in front, big tables of shiny dark wood, a big musical instrument with yellow ivory keys in front and a big gilded harp rising in the back from the instrument's interior, portraits on the walls staring severely down into the shadows, the big, black-streaked mirrors with the peeling gold frames, everything covered with dust and marred by neglect. It had been a great house in its time, one of the first of the region, and when Marcher was younger, before his daughter left him or his wife died, the rich and great had come here to feast and dance to the sound of fiddles, to course elk and get drunk and talk politics and horseflesh and wenchflesh and money.

But long since, Marcher had given up most society, interested chiefly in sport, the bottle, and the better-formed and lighter-skinned wenches on the place. But he managed to keep some eye out for his practical interests, and on some mornings he would emerge from the house with great oaths, set all his people by the ears and threaten floggings all around, harangue his drivers, and institute a week or ten days of violent activity. Then some morning it would all be changed again. The Negroes would sniff the air and know from the first light that there was a change of weather, that old Marcher had forgotten them. They came out late from their cabins, took their rich vegetable pleasure in the sunshine, or moved in luxurious, re-tarded indifference about some parody of occupation. Even if the master himself came out and looked straight at them, it made no difference, for they sensed that change in him, and cunningly grinned and bowed and let him pass. Then in the long evenings, down by the cabins, the gourd banjos would sound again and the singing would start. Nobody prevented Jeremiah from getting out of bed and going down there to squat in a ring with them and listen while they hummed and patted juba on the bare earth by starlight.

After the first days Jeremiah put aside his resentment at the old man and grew to like him. No word or sign of affection ever passed between them, but the old man could give grudging praise, and "his words were to me the more precious." Sometimes in the afternoon he would sit out under a tree, a drink by his side, and say to Jeremiah, "Talk to me," or in the evening in the dining room after the dishes were cleared away. And in those long afternoons or evenings Jeremiah had to tell all about his own life, the things he had done and seen, and the way of life at his own house down in Glasgow County. But other days the old man might never come down from his room, or come down only in the evening to supper and sit silently eating, stopping only now and then to throw a bone or morsel to one of five hounds around his chair, or to hand a tidbit to one of the several cats (Jeremiah never knew how many there were, for they came and went) that sat on the old man's shoulder or prowled on the table among platters and cruets.

On those days and nights when the old man withdrew within him-self, Jeremiah was free to follow his own inclinations, to have his mare saddled and ride over the country, or to prowl on foot with some rifle or fowling piece taken from the arsenal in one room of the house. (He learned every weapon in that room and its peculiarities, the long rifles from Pennsylvania, the short, big-bore Yorger that threw a great chunk of lead, the small rifle running sixty pellets to the pound, the great crazy London fowling piece near seven feet long with silver all over the stock, the other fowling pieces that carried twenty-four "blue whistlers" for a buck load or two ounces of small shot for duck.) He never stayed in the house when he could get out. For one thing there was nothing to read here, just a few old almanacs. And nobody ever came any more to Runnymede. Even the word of the new war with England scarcely penetrated here.

Knowing the strange country was Jeremiah's great delight, especially the country along the Kentucky River. He explored the woods and the limestone bluffs and cliffs along the gorge for the distance of a day both up and down, but he recorded only one of his adventures. It fell in his second summer at Runnymede. He had climbed down the bluff to the water to swim, and now lay naked on a sand-and-gravel spit, taking the sun. In his near-drowse he thought he heard music and sat up, "marveling for music in that place." Looking about, he saw nothing but the bluffs and the river, "but the music was now clearer and no dream." Then he saw upstream, emerging around the greenery at the bend, a keelboat making the riffle, the first he had ever seen. The pole-men were heaving to their work, setting the long poles deep to the gravel, making the long boat lurch over the riffle, for the water was low there. On the little deck forward "a fiddler seated on a keg gave forth some sober-sweet music I had never heard and knew not the name for." They got past the riffle into the deep of the main current, and the pole-men trailed their poles in the water to rest and wiped their brows. They came almost even with the boy before one of them saw him and gave a halloo. Then the other men shouted and the fiddler waved his bow in salute, "then fell to fiddling with a fury, making a wild, gay piece I knew, called 'Chicken Pie.' "

Jeremiah leaped to his feet, forgetful of nakedness, and watched the boat pass "with the deliberation of the river." When they had passed a little, he rushed down into the water, as though he might plunge in and follow them to whatever place they were bound, but he stopped and only stood there knee-deep in the stream, watching until they were out of sight around the farthest bend. For a little more he heard the music, then it stopped. Then back up the river, between the walls of the green-gray gorge, came the call of the keelboat's bugle, and "I stood there in the edge of the river that flowed away from me."

Jeremiah Beaumont, years later in the cell at Frankfort, had to recount the incident, for it had meant something, the boat passing steadily by to the sound of music with the deliberation of the river, bound to New Orleans, to a place or port far away and strange, to distance. Then, beyond the last bend of the river out of sight, the bugle had summoned him and he had wanted to plunge in and follow. In the cell, did the recollection of the bright bugle notes come back to him as an image for whatever had summoned him to plunge into a stream stained darker than the Kentucky River ever was at flood?

At the end of the second summer when he got back home, his father died. Jasper Beaumont died of a fever, resisting, bitter, and

19

unreconciled to the end. He had been mistreated, he had missed out somewhere while worse men than he had had the luck, and the fever that burned him up in his strength was just another dirty trick. He summoned his last strength and strove to rise on his pillow, and struck with his big fist, and said, "No, by God, no!" and fell back and died.

The fever had waited cunningly for the right moment to strike him, a moment when he was off-balance. He had borrowed money during the war to buy new land and catch the high market, and the debts were not paid. That summer of 1815 his crop had not been good, the war was over, and men said that prices would fall. It was the last dirty trick, dirtier than all the rest, to catch him now. Within two years the old farm was lost, the farm with the big log house and the fine brick room. Hettie Beaumont and her son and daughter moved to a small tract they had managed to save, where there was a three-room log house. Hettie Beaumont knocked down at vendue five of her seven slaves, and settled in to make the best of the hard times. But Jeremiah continued his schooling. Dr. Burnham insisted on that, telling Mrs. Beaumont that the boy would make a great man, a lawyer and a senator who would bring her "wealth and pride." Dr. Burnham said that he, too, would take pride in the boy and would spare no pain to refine his understanding. So in the afternoons of early autumn, on Saturday when there was no school, Dr. Burnham lay on a bullhide under the big colored maple of the Mason yard, and intoned the noble hexameters to him. Dr. Burnham even hired Jeremiah to help him with the younger boys. For the same reason of wealth or pride for the future, though she needed the boy, now strong as a man, on the farm, Hettie Beaumont sent him back to Runnymede in the summer of 1816, after the corn was laid by. Runnymede should be his.

But it never was. Old Morton Marcher, however, made him the offer. It came in the evening at supper, after one of the black solitary days when he stayed upstairs with his brooding and his bottle. There was no conversation at the table at supper. The only time the old man spoke was to curse the cook because the meat was burned and to send her word by the serving boy that she had better mind or he would have her whipped till there was not a beech bough in the bottom. Then, when one of the cats on the table made to take a morsel from his plate, as was often permitted, he struck it heavily with the back of his hand so that it was knocked from the table and howled pitifully.

After supper, the old man "sat back and smoked his seegar and stared at the flame of the sperm candle in the candlestick before him. Then he said to me he had a mind to make me master of Runnymede when he should be gone. My heart leaped at the thought, for it was a land rich for tillage or pasture and the house had been a great house and could be great again. I confess the vanity of my thought, for I was human to desire the goods of the world and to have an appetite for grandeur. But I shall say that I had a greater happiness for my mother who I knew honed and yearned after the place of her youth, though always a good and uncomplaining wife, and who now suffered the harshness of life. So I replied to my grandfather that I had come to him at his request but that I bore him due devotion and duty in my heart. He said then that I was strong and he hated a weakling who had cold rheum and not hot blood in his vitals and could not master beasts or men, and that before such a one of pule and puke should sit in his chair, he would burn down with his own hand the house he had built in his strength and let his bones rest in the ashes.

"To this I replied that I was happy he could speak well of me. That I had not flattered myself with exorbitant expectation of opinion or property, but that if he thought good to make me his heir I should hope to keep Runnymede a place of respect and honor and to bear myself to be a credit to his memory. At this he uttered some grumping ejaculation, and struck the floor twice or thrice with his stick, and resumed his staring into the candle flame."

The old man stared a long time into the candle flame, while now and again a hound "shifted its lay on the floor and snuffled in the shadow, like a tired man sleeping."

Then he made the boy his proposal. "He told me I was the vessel of his blood and was the son of his dear Hettie, who had left him to follow after a stranger. He said he had wished for a son of his name to live into the later time, but that damned gelding Peacham had faltered at the jump and killed his son, and that he had shot the brute with his own hand and left the carcass to the crows. That I should take his name and be Jeremiah Marcher.

"I could not answer for a time, but looked at the polished wood of the table. Then he said roughly that the name of Marcher was a good name and that stout men had borne it and for no short time as names lived. I replied in all respect, saying that I was proud for the blood of my mother and thanking him for the compliment. I wanted to say, yes, that I would do as he wished, but the word stuck in my throat, like a fish bone that brings red spit.

"Then he roared out at me, 'Will you take it, boy, it is a good name!' and struck the floor with his stick.

"And I said that, begging his pardon, my name was Beaumont, for that was the name of my father."

" 'Your father,' he cried out, 'that rascal!'

21

"I felt the blood rise in my face, but I mastered myself and said that he was my father and no rascal. That had any man dared name him rascal he would have been called to account, had my father lived.

"'Call me to account,' he said, and struck the floor, 'call me to account, that rascal from God knows where!'

"I answered that he was good enough for Hettie Marcher, who had loved him and yet honored his name.

"At that he rose from his seat, and the chair fell to the floor behind him, unseen in his rage. 'He stole her,' he cried, and leaned at me over the table, 'away from her home and proper kind. Had I been in Lexington I had whipped him down the public street.' And he damned her to have left him and dishonored the name of Marcher who had had lands in Virginia for nigh two hundred years and before that were of consideration in England, to follow a man who lived blackguard and died bankrupt.

"'Let the Marchers be of consideration in England or in Hell,' I retorted upon him, and leaped from my chair, 'but no man shall call him blackguard, and were you not old and sottish and my own grandfather, I would show you I am my father's son.'

"At that he leaned and struck me with the gold head of his cane like a club, but I received the strong blow on my left arm and seized the stick and wrenched it from him. He picked up the heavy silver candlestick before him, so that the lighted candle fell from it to the table, and reached as to strike me with that, but I brought the stick down on it just above his hand so that he dropped it.

"'God damn you!' he shouted, 'get out of my house!' I replied that I would leave his house and be happy to go where men were honest to make their living, bankrupt or no, and where old men were not proud to wickedness and did not waste their lands and themselves to lie with a bottle or black wenches, for I had heard them laugh and squeal in the night.

"So I brought the stick down with all my force upon the stone of the dead fireplace behind me, and broke it, and then flung the pieces upon the table before him, and ran from the room. I went to the room where I slept, put my belongings in my satchel, and came down forthwith. As I passed through the hall, I heard no sound from the dining room where I had left the old man, but after I was past the big door and crossing the yard, I heard a voice twice and thought that it called my name. But I could not be sure, and had it been my name, and that name Beaumont, I would not have paused in my pace, for all was past what word could mend."

It took Jeremiah nearly two weeks to get home, walking across the state.

In the late afternoon he approached the house where he now

22

lived, little better than a cabin and seeming worse at the recollection of Runnymede. As he came down the track he saw his mother at the edge of a field toward the house, bending with a hoe, and thought that she must be working the late squash, for that was the place where she had put her green garden.

"I saw her smallness in the wide field under the light of the sun near setting, and thought how heavy the labor must be to her hand at this hour of day and life when she might take her ease in her own house, and how for my pride I had robbed her of what was her own. So I ran down the track, not calling to her. I was almost upon her when she turned and lifted her eyes and spoke my name, which was familiarly Jerry. I did not answer but dropped my satchel and hat, thrust the hoe from her grasp, and held her hands and knelt at her feet weeping for the guilt and perturbation which was in my heart. She stood there and said my name several times, but I could not answer her. Then mastering myself, I began to babble forth the whole event, how I had robbed her and destroyed her hope, not mitigating my fault of violence and pride and praying her forgiveness.

"She made no reply, but leaned and kissed me upon the brow most solemnly, and I remember yet how dry and cracked her lips were upon my flesh, and how sweet in their harshness. Then she lifted me up and said quietly as though nothing had come to pass and I had never left home, 'Come in to your supper, Jerry.'"

So the hope of Runnymede and grandeur was snatched away at the very instant it was certain. But Hettie Beaumont never said a word of complaint to Jeremiah. The old man waited in his whisky-soaked loneliness in the dark house or in the cluttered yard. Then he married a sluttish wench from the inn, who was no better than she should have been. She gave him a son (or perhaps the son was not his), and the name of Marcher survived. After Jeremiah's time a Marcher, a grand-son of old Marcher (or at least a grandson of the sluttish wench) sat in the governor's chair in Kentucky, another grandson, a major of Confederate cavalry, died gallantly with saber in hand in the grand manner, at the battle of Perryville, a great-grandson became presi-dent of a railroad, and a great-great-grandson, with a black cape, was well known in the cafés of Montmartre in the 1920's, wrote an excel-lent little book on François Villon, returned to America to become an associate professor of French in a Middle Western university, and lost his post under the suspicion of pederasty. The house of Runny-mede had been burned by Federal troops in 1862, and only a few heaps of stone and disintegrating brick, not yet engrossed by the blackberry bushes, protrude now from the vigorous blue grass.

As for Jeremiah Beaumont, who might have inherited Runnymede, nothing remained but the dreariness of the cabin and the scrub farm, the grimness of work in the field or at his books, or with the thick skulls of the dull and rebellious boys at Dr. Burnham's school, and the uncertain prospects of his own future. He began, furthermore, to be troubled about the nature of success. "I had seen," he wrote, "my good father die in the bitterness of worldly failure and sick hope, and I had seen my grandfather Marcher live bitterly in the midst of wealth and great place, and I came to see, though in my boyish way, that both were bound to the grossness of nature and the vanity of the world. As time passed, it came to me that I would not wish to live and die thus, and that there must be another way to live and die. Therefore I searched my books for what truth might be beyond the bustle of the hour and the empty lusts of time."

The language Jeremiah used long after in writing of that period echoes the language of the theological tract and the pulpit. His family had gone to church and to meetings, but they had not been pious. Now Hettie Beaumont, in her grief and hardship, began to take consolation in religion, and this new consciousness in the house finds an echo in Jeremiah's account. But for a long time he himself was unmoved by her "gentle reproofs and warm invitations," and continued to search for his hope in his secular books, "in the patterns of famous men, the passions of poems, and the severe thoughts of philosophy." He did, however, go with his mother to church and was touched by the "devotion of the faithful and the joy of the saved," and longed to know their secret. By their example and by the hymns he was "stirred to think on the hour when I should come to death and have nothing in my hand from the journey and labor." At the same time he began to long for death, and the sadder the hymn the better he liked it. As he went about his work he would mutter the words of the hymn that moved him most:

> Oh, lovely appearance of death,
>   What sight upon earth is so fair?
> Not all the gay pageants of breath
>   Can with a dead body compare!
>
> With solemn delight I survey
>   The corpse when the spirit is fled,
> In love with the beautiful clay,
>   And longing to lie in its stead.

About this time there came into the neighborhood a preacher named Corinthian McClardy. He was from North Carolina, but had preached across Alabama, Mississippi and Tennessee, and had even taken the gospel to the wild Indians. He had left across the country a smoking trail of carnage, cold fear in the hearts of men and a sweet shuddering in the loins of women. He belonged to that old race of

Devil-breakers who were a terror and a blessing across the land, men who had been born to be the stomp-and-gouge bully of a tavern, the Indian fighter with warm scalps at his belt, the ice-eyed tubercular duelist of a county courthouse, the half-horse, half-alligator abomination of a keelboat, or a raper of women by the cow pen, but who got their hot prides and cold lusts short-circuited into obsessed hosannas and a ferocious striving for God's sake.

Corinthian McClardy was extremely tall and bony, with coarse red hair, prodigiously ugly, according to all reports, with a freckled and pocked face, twisted mouth, and great yellow eyes, red-rimmed, flashing, and not quite in focus. His common dress was cowhide boots, jean pants tucked in, and a long black coat with tails which tangled with his legs when he strode about or leaped in the heat of exhortation, and flattened on the wind behind him when he rode hell-for-leather across the land seeking the Fiend to try a new fall with Him. The horse was a towering roan, bony of knee and fling-footed, as gaunt and angry and as pitilessly beyond fatigue as the rider. If Corinthian McClardy had any human trait it was pride in the brute that he alone could master, and he had been known to say that if he were not God's man and a hater of show and vanity he would match his Magog against any creature that ever crooked a pastern. Men said of him that he "cared only for God's wrath and that red hellion of a heathen horse."

The tribe to which Corinthian McClardy belonged brought the sweet promise and peace into a land where sweetness and peace were at a premium, but for every ha'penny worth of the more delicate commodity that they handseled out for the price of a sinner's tears, they gave away five shillings worth of hell fire free gratis, and that to all comers. In the easy moments of prinking and sparring they used the love taps of the New Testament, but in the bloody clinches of a real plugmuss they relied on the bone-crushing terror of the "Old Book." They could suffer pain and reviling and could turn the other cheek ninety-nine times, but at the hundredth time the rage of the unregenerate Jehovah might seize on His poor human instrument, as Samson seized the jawbone of an ass, and the instrument might leap down from his platform or up from his chair at the table of an inn, and then the wicked man might tremble not only for his immortal soul but for his mortal brain-pan.

Before Corinthian McClardy came, his "feats were told and his fame norated before him from farm to farm and creek to creek." He had garnered four hundred souls at one meeting, but also, with bare hands, he had wrenched the dirk away from a bully and trod it underfoot. At a great meeting in Alabama an infidel had pestered him past endurance and he had boiled over the edge of his cart and seized the man to lift him by leg and neck high in the air and shout, "What shall we do, oh Israel!" And some unnamed worshipper had yelled, "Stomp the son-of-a-bitch and praise God!" According to report, the notion appeared, for an instant to find favor in the preacher's eyes, but he controlled himself, and, screaming, "Let the dead bough be cast into the fire!" heaved the middle-weight scoffer out of the ring and into bed with a broken arm.

Corinthian McClardy rode his red hellion into Glasgow County at the beginning of a hot August, and awoke some of the enthusiasm of the Great Revival of the beginning of the century. "I had heard," Jeremiah Beaumont wrote, "from the older people how in those times that thousands might gather, coming from the distance of three days' journey, and for days remain together in a great camp praising and worshipping and seeking salvation. I had heard the names of the famous preachers and exhorters of that time and how when they rose to their pitch, the multitude swayed and wept or began the exercise of the jerks and shakes so that a man's head snapped constantly on his neck and all his members flailed about him without ceasing until he fell down like dead. Or the long braids of women were shaken loose and with the aggravated motion flew and snapped like bull-whips. Some might howl like a hound and fall on all fours at the foot of a tree and bay the Devil up there like a cornered painter or coon. Others were taken with the holy laugh, and could not stop. Hearing of those happenings, I had also heard how the unbelievers brought bread soaked in vinegar to stuff in the mouths of those who had fallen to bring them out of their happy trance and to make sport, but how sometimes even this failed until God released a man from His hold.

"I had wondered if the exercises did not pain a man, but those who had undergone them told me there was no pain, only a great joy in God. In my own time I had heard glory-shouts and had seen men and women fall down and twitch on the ground, but in no great number, and by the time I came to the age of memory the great meetings of the thousands had ceased. But the first meeting of Brother McClardy, to which my mother took me, called nearly a thousand together of all ranks and orders.

"He preached on the text, *Warn the people or their blood I will require at your hands.* He told how he had come to us 'in journeyings often, in perils of water, in perils of mine own countrymen, in perils by hand of heathen, perils in the wilderness and perils among false brethren, in weariness and watchings, in hunger and fastings, in cold and nakedness, but oh—but oh!' At that moment he lifted up his arms, then called out: 'But oh, in joy, and the joy of God! I would bring you that joy!' Such were his words, or near that, and many wept for their sweetness."

Day by day Brother McClardy was warming to his work, whip and spur, hell and high water. He had not yet touched his reserves, but he had fully engaged the enemy. August is hot in South Kentucky, the corn is laid by, and in that moment between full effort and harvest there is an interlude of sad idleness in which a man knows that another year is spent and that even if the year is a good year at last, the biggest heap of full-grained ears and the whisky-fun of the corn-husking party will not quite bleach out the stain of vanity from all his labors or fulfill some promise which had seemed to be made long back. Scum gathers on ponds, the water is brackish in the well, the cow goes dry, tempers are short, the husband notices that his old wife has lost her teeth and sags in the tits, the young man had rather cut the guts out of a friend with a dirk than tumble a juicy girl back of the old mill, and all the old meaning of life is lost like water spilled in the ankle-deep dust. The sun boils down all day every day, and at night the Dog Star is baleful and the moon rises the color of blood. It was the right season for Corinthian McClardy, and he knew how to evoke the last wild energy left from aimlessness and unrecognized despair. "Many lay on the ground before him, and many were saved."

Jeremiah knew the terror but he could not be saved. He saw those who were saved and "hated them for their salvation." They had some gift they could bring to God and get His mercy, but he, Jeremiah Beaumont, had nothing in hand to offer for the price of his soul. He felt himself the victim of some gigantic joke or conspiracy. He remembered hearing the tale of a man on trial for his life in one of the Kentucky settlements. "When the Jury was hung, and the hour grown late when men go home to bed, a juror proposed that they should settle the question by a game of Old Sledge, for, as he said, 'We don't know a goldurned thing about this fellow, nohow.' So the cards were fetched and the game commenced between the two champions of the opposed factions of the jury. On the stroke of midnight the score was seven to seven, when the hanging champion threw the jack and won the game. So the gallows was built and on it was nailed the Jack of Spades. When the man was brought forth on the appointed day and stood on his own coffin on the cart, he cursed them all soundly for the injustice that he, being a good man at the cards, had not been allowed to turn even one to save his neck."

So long after, Jeremiah Beaumont, writing in the shadow of the gallows, and feeling again the blindness of man's fate, recalled the story, and how he had long ago felt like that man cursing under the gallows, "how I had wanted to curse God Himself for letting some play a hand for their souls while I was locked up in my damnation and could not throw a single card for luck or justice." For a week he

27

did not attend the meetings. Then his mother persuaded him to go again.

"That time Brother McClardy preached upon the text, *Who shall deliver me from the body of this death?* He said how all men were black and damned from birth and wallowing in the sink of nature, and that no man had a price to give God for his Mercy, which was beyond price, and man had no claim on God. And I saw how I had sinned to make a claim and a bargain with God, even in my misery.

"At that point the preacher paused, and all was so still I heard the breeze passing over the people. Then he said: 'Many before me are familiar to the wood and have striven with savages and with beasts and know the ways of the wilderness. You know how when the lost fawn bleats in the glade, be the doe strayed or dead, the great bear hears and comes forth. His tread is on the green grass and his fangs drip. He takes the fawn and tears the tender throat. Oh, I say to you, lie down in your weakness of sin and bleat. Bleat to call forth the bear. For God is a bear breaking the thickets of the world and the ground shakes to his foot and his fangs drip wrath. They long for your throat and are terrible, but bleat to call them to your throat and let there be sweetness in your terror. Be devoured by the great jaws of God, and rejoice!'

"Thus he exhorted us to lie down, and in my mind I saw how the bear came. I remembered how once I had seen no bear but a painter take a young deer, with a great leap tumbling it over, and how the fallen animal in its very struggle had seemed to offer the throat and how the blood spurted forth. And at the same instant there in the meeting it was also the image of the young female at the stake in the book of the Martyrs, and how in my old fancy I had flung the first lighted faggot and how her head had tossed in the flames. All those things seemed not to be fancy but to be real and present and to be not several but one thing before me and I caught up in them.

"The preacher called and shouted, 'Fall down, oh, fall down, bleat to the bear and fall down!' So some rose from their seats and fell down. There was a great fullness in me, and for an instant I thought some organ in me would break to flood me inwardly with blood. Without knowing, I leaped up and thought I uttered a big cry (though later those watching said I made no sound), and fell upon the earth. The fullness in me seemed to break and flow forth like a great blister. I had the thought that I did bleed and all my blood was coming out upon the ground, but it was a thought of joy, and in the bleeding there was peace. I do not know how long I lay, but I remember I came to know that my mother knelt by me and stroked my hair."

So Jeremiah Beaumont got his religion in the good frontier fashion and all the next year had the reward of it. He watched and prayed and studied the Bible more than the pattern of famous men or the passions of poems, which now seemed to him "vain toys." He was at peace with the world all through the fall and winter, and often "was surprised by untokened joy." The only instance he gives came at the time of a great frost. There had been snow which melted, then rain and sleet, and then, during the night, a heavy freeze. That night he heard trees outside the house crack and groan with the cold, and "sometimes break for the weight of ice with a sound like cannon." Next morning there was brilliant sun that made the whole landscape glitter. Beyond the door of the house was a big beech tree, "all shining and with the wide boughs brought low with ice." He went to the tree and reached to pluck an icicle to put in his mouth. At that instant he thought how God made all things, and "my own strength seemed to pass away through my fingers into the very tree. I seemed to become the tree, and knew how it was to be rooted in the deep dark of earth and bear with my boughs the weight of glittering ice like joy. Then my substance seemed to pass beyond the tree and into all the land around that spread in the sunlight, and into the sunlight itself."

Later, he told this experience to Brother Trotter, who "was learned in doctrine." He was troubled by Brother Trotter's comment. Brother Trotter said that the Devil had "cunning snares and deadfalls for those who took easy joy in their salvation," that though the saved man might be "at peace with nature, were he righteous enough, he should not enter into nature, for the Kingdom is not of this world," and that Jeremiah should pray more devoutly. The doubt planted by Brother Trotter seems to have germinated, for by spring Jeremiah was "overcome by a languor, and though I held fast to my faith I had lost the joy in it."

With September Corinthian McClardy returned to South Kentucky, not to the Beaumont neighborhood, but two counties away, in a rougher country to the northeast. After some days of waiting, and hearing of the great events at the meeting, Jeremiah told his mother that he had to go if he was to be sure of his salvation.

Corinthian McClardy had set up at the edge of a big woods along a ravine, with a sort of rocky meadow before the woods. Even now in that region there is a field with outcroppings of smoothly weathered limestone from the good grass, which is called McClardy's Meadow. The woods have been cut over long back, and only second growth and scrub stuff stands between the field and the ravine. The meetings were much more than a century ago, and Corinthian McClardy is forgotten, but the place—if it is the place—still bears his name. Then back of the meadow trees were turning. Fox-grapes hung in great loops and festoons from the trees behind the rough platform built for the preacher. People who had come a long way camped all over the meadow for days. At night their fires lit the dark like the bivouac of an army, and often "they sang gospel to a late hour." There had been nothing like it since the days of the Great Revival. As many as five thousand attended some of the meetings.

Corinthian McClardy loomed on his platform and waved his gaunt arms against the background of the flaming leaves, under the pagan festoons of grapes, and his powerful voice filled the meadow and swept over the multitude huddled in the sunlight among the outcroppings of gray limestone. The shakes and the jerks returned, and the holy laugh. In the height of the frenzy, exhorters back in the meadow, mounted on limestone or on carts, helped McClardy keep the brew stirred, and, as Jeremiah put it, "the air was filled with the din of anguish and the shout of glory." Each day the people continued "in that way until admonished by the going down of the sun." Jeremiah himself longed to be taken and "transported beyond the self," for he felt that something was missing from his own "experience of God."

Finally it came. He does not tell us the occasion, merely that it was a great day of victory for McClardy and that "many were taken by the various exercises, many shouted and fell down, many embraced and kissed, and some ran howling." The wildness of joy came on him, and he himself was one of those who ran howling into the woods, beyond the screen of flaming leaves and the festoons of grapes. He plunged through the woods, calling and stumbling in the enthusiasm, not seeing the way, tearing clothes and striking against trees. At last he stumbled and fell to his hands and knees, shaken and breathless. He found himself face to face with "another creature" who was crouching there, "close and with her eyes upon my face."

What happened was predictable, and on such occasions no great novelty. It was done without thought and "with violence," but the creature made no resistance, and may even, for that matter, have been lurking in the woods to snare a worshipper. It was Jeremiah Beaumont's first experience with a woman. He tells us that much, and the fact is strange, for on the frontier copulation came early and easy. But we know that he had been a solitary and quarrelsome boy, that his passion for books had set him somewhat apart, and that as he grew older he had spent several summers away from home, up at Runnymede. He had "bussed and toyed" with some girls of his own age, but apparently had not had much share in the life of the young people back in the glades at burgoos and picnics or in the shadows beyond the hullaballoo at the corn-huskings. And after his father's death and loss of the family land, his pride would have worked to set him off even more from the society of his place. So he came a virgin to the "creature" crouching in the woods.

In any case, the deed was done. If Jeremiah Beaumont had had

30

more experience, the sequel might have been different. Or if the unresisting partner had been a buxom, apple-cheeked girl who merely happened to like to stroll apart in the brush, or a clean, pleasant wife of discreeter years who knew what the world was worth, Jeremiah might have lingered agreeably and longer and the deed might have had no consequence for our story.

It was no apple-cheeked girl or pleasant wife, however, and "when the blindness had passed," Jeremiah Beaumont found himself in the embrace of a snaggle-toothed hag whose hair was snarled and greasy against his face and whose odor offended his nostrils. As he recoiled from her and the light fell fully on her face, he saw she was dark and of some mixed breed, largely Indian or Negro or both, but seemingly more of the former. He jerked back roughly, apparently showing his shock and distaste, but the creature scrambled up, too, to a crouching position, and as he rose she clutched him about the knees. He shoved her back, but she still clutched and uttered some "whimper and gabble." So he impulsively struck her across the face with the flat of his hand, "thinking only to be free, and with more force than I knew, enough to knock her back sprawling and bring blood to her lips." Then he fled again through the woods, this time with no wildness of joy but with the horror of contamination and betrayal.

He fled and clambered down the ravine, instinctively toward the sound of water. He came to the water, a brisk stream which even to-day (if McClardy's Meadow is the proper scene) makes its way from pool to pool down the mossy limestone steps of the ravine, with ferns rank at the edges and with light, when the sun is good, flecking the clean gravel of the bottom. The water, even in summer, is cold to touch. Jeremiah stumbled out into a pool, and stood waist-deep with cold water on him, heaving from his exertion like "a wind-broke horse." He stood there till his breathing subsided, then let himself sink back, clothes and all, till the water was over his face. He held his breath and stayed under as long as possible, then brought his face up and gasped for air, then sank again. He did this many times, then lay quietly in the water, with his face just awash, the sunlight red through his closed eyelids, and the motion of the stream upon him.

After a long time he came out and lay on a sun-hot slab of limestone. He was thoroughly chilled now, but the sun was still strong where it broke through the trees to the stone, and gradually he grew warm and his clothes dried stiffly on him. At first, as he lay on the stone, he could hear, now and then, very thin, a distant shout or the sound of singing from the meadow, but by the time the sun had left the stone and the shadow of trees encroached upon it, even that was gone.

Jeremiah did not go back to the encampment. At dusk he came out of the lower end of the ravine and climbed the hill beyond. Looking back, he could see the twinkle of fires in the dark, like fireflies, but he kept on his way. He walked most of the night. At morning he claimed hospitality at a cabin, got a piece of cold corn pone, a slice of fried sow belly, and a "quaff of milk," then resumed the road. The second day he arrived.

He came home as he had come before, from Runnymede, walking with nothing to show for his pains. Then he had gone out to get "an earthly inheritance," now he had gone "to inherit a mansion beyond the sky," but he had got neither the wealth of the world nor the riches not of this world. He was still Jeremiah Beaumont, coming back to the three-room cabin, to the work in the field and in the schoolhouse, and to the world as it was, with which, if he was to live, he would have to make terms.

That winter when Jeremiah was seventeen, Dr. Burnham introduced him to Colonel Cassius Fort, and gave him a new, if more worldly, hope. One day, when the school was over, Dr. Burnham said that "come lately to his daughter's house was his worthy friend Colonel Fort," who had a desire to speak with him, and invited him to come after supper. Jeremiah agreed to come, and all the way home wondered what the famous Colonel, whose name was great in the state, could find to say to him.

That night Jeremiah walked back the three and a half miles, still wondering what Colonel Fort could want with him and what kind of man Colonel Fort might be, who was rich and powerful and who had stood with Andy Jackson at New Orleans. When he entered the big room of the Mason house (for Dr. Burnham's daughter was a Mrs. Mason), he saw a stranger of good height and strong person, standing with his back to the fire, his legs apart and his hands clasped behind, somewhat lifting and spreading the tails of his black coat, "as though to give his arse the benefit of a good warm before being seated." The stranger's head, Jeremiah noted even as he exchanged the compliments with Mrs. Mason, was bowed forward, "as though for the moment a deeper thought had struck him than was happy for the occasion," and in the shadow (for the near candles were on the mantel shelf behind him) his "face was dusky and severe of lineament."

Then Mrs. Mason brought Jeremiah forward and Dr. Burnham came to present him to the guest, saying, "Cassius, this is the thriving lad of whom I spoke. Think well of him for his own parts and for my sake."

At that Colonel Fort offered his hand "without condescension and

32

gave a strong clasp, as of a man used to seize and hold," his face dropped off its graveness, and he said, "My boy, Dr. Burnham speaks better of you than you guess, and who am I to dispute his wisdom?"

Jeremiah stammered something which he feared was graceless and dull, but the kindness took him by surprise and embarrassed him, "for at that time in the heaviness of my lot and the blankness of my prospects I had no opinion of myself and thought that none could speak well of me except in bitter sport."

Jeremiah was flattered and a little overwhelmed by the presence of the great men. He could not see his great men as the world would see them, or as we would see them, one a back-country quack, comic with his big belly and his swollen feet stuck into moccasins, the other a lawyer who probably had little more law than a few Latin tags and a few pages from Coke and Chitty, and a colonel who probably couldn't dress a platoon. If they were great at all, it was with a greatness that Jeremiah could not see. It was because they took their world greatly and were not embarrassed by the accents of greatness, and knew that in study, field, or forum they bore the destiny of men and the judgment of history.

Jeremiah could not recognize the true nature of their greatness, even if they had it, because he belonged to their world, and if we recognize it, we can do so only because we do not belong to their world. If we recognize their greatness, we must do so through the mist of sentimentality or the cracked glass of irony, with self-abasement or self-flattery, and we can take our peculiar pleasure from either. But Jeremiah's pleasure was simple, he knew they were great, and he could not know that what name they would bear to our time would not be because of their greatness but because they stumbled into the drama he was devising.

The glow of the moment when Jeremiah sat with his great men did not prevent him from inspecting Colonel Fort. He saw a man about forty-two or -three years old, with a large, well-formed head which "seemed larger for the full suit of hair combed back long." The hair, black and strong but shot through with streaks of gray, was somewhat unruly, and Colonel Fort had the habit, when thinking or in repose, of leaning his head slightly forward and passing a hand over his hair to put it more in place. His face was large but not "slack of flesh," swarthy but not of an even color, for the blood seemed to come and go beneath the skin, and the flesh was deeply lined and grooved on the brow and on each side of the mouth. The eyes were dark and heavy-lidded, the nose a trifle short and broad in the nostrils, the mouth, "not as wide as might have been expected, but strongly shut and a little bent down at the corners as of one strong to bear the trouble of the world and endure it." Ordinarily, when men's eyes were

33

not upon him, his face was "severe to sadness," but when he spoke he "knew to smile and to lay his inner concerns aside for interest of what a man might say to him, and he practiced to question you that you might discover your mind to him and the depth of your nature." He was strong-handed and thick-thighed, like a man who could bear much labor and fatigue. His whole person, "even though he could indulge the lightness of society, bespoke a solidity rather than a sprightliness of mind and a darkness of mood." That night he wore dark-gray pantaloons of a soft, rich cloth, tight fitted to the full calves, a dark blue waistcoat with a flowery design in black worked into the fabric, and a black tailed coat. He dressed with "reserve and elegance as befitted his station."

Now he was in "the Congress at Washington" and had a reputation for sober thought and considered eloquence. Even back in Kentucky people knew that the great old Jefferson had called Cassius Fort "as intelligent and devoted a man as has come out of the West, whence we may expect in the future most of our best men for reason of the simplicity of manners and the honest life of husbandmen which prevails in those parts." In Congress Colonel Fort had fought well for the good of the linsey-woolsey against the broadcloth, and for the advancement of the West which he called, "the world's grandest amphitheater for clever ingenuity and heroic exertion."

Clever ingenuity and heroic exertion had made him what he was, for he had been born to poor, feckless, unlettered parents, the kind who had lost hope back in Virginia and had drifted across the mountains in the old days by the Wilderness Road, toward a last promise. The fulfillment they got was a hovel in the woods, the nightly terror when the owl hooted or some creature moved in the brush, and at last the Shawnee arrow sent quivering between old Fort's shoulder blades as he stood in the middle of his corn patch. His wife, who had taken the baby and gone into the woods for salet, lay in the brush, her hand over the baby's mouth, and watched the flames of her cabin, then later made her way twelve miles to the stockade. Her mind was touched after that, she soon died, and the child was raised on the rough charity of the frontier till he got old enough to shift for himself.

Cassius Fort had come a long, grim way, but the story had lost some of its grimness in the later days when its advantages became clear on the hustings. To the rapscallion wool-hat and coonskin mob in the inn yard or under the oaks at the barbecue, Cassius Fort would cry out: "Look at me, and you see a child of old Kaintuck, born in a canebrake, rocked in a yellow poplar sugar trough for a cradle, weaned on whisky, fed on hominy and possum fat, and ready to call any man's dare!" So the mob, likkered up from the candidate's whisky barrel and hot from the sound of his fiddles, threw up the wool hats and coonskins, and yelled for Old Cass and Old Kaintuck. Oh, he wore the broadcloth now, but he had earned it, by God, and he was as good as any man and would come to any man's dare. Let any man give him a name, and he would pile right down off that stump, coat tails flying, and you would see the dirk-blade flash out of that fine ruffled shirt, and he would cut his woozen, he would down-dagger him, he would eat the bastard, no salt and blood-raw. Hell, just for sport, he'd whip off that black-tailed coat and wrestle the best bully of any creek, heave and snake-pole, till the sun went down and not a blade of grass was standing for half an acre. Then he would drink him, gourd dipper for dipper, from the whisky barrel and shake his hand.

Cassius Fort knew their lingo and their ways, their names and their condition, and no man was ever shamed at his door or got turned away without hospitality and a full belly. But he knew the names and condition of the better sort, too, and could stand eye to eye with any gentleman, and "match him in manners, honor, or manhood" (to quote from the *Diary* of John Ruffer, who knew him), in friendship or not. It had not always been in friendship, for one fine frosty morning up near Frankfort, Cassius Fort had calmly received Dr. Jameson's fire at ten paces and then put a hot half-ounce of lead in his lung. But if a gentleman came to his house in friendship, he would treat him to the best, give him a good turkey shoot, take him down to the pasture to see the fine cattle, then over the bottle debate politics or read in his rolling voice from a book of poems.

Cassius Fort had made a study of men, and knew how to draw them out. It was a great gift of courtesy and won hearts, and was probably the secret of the charm (as of the power) which he could exercise. Perhaps it had its origin in the brutal circumstances of his early life; the orphan child in the stockade would do well to study human nature and human faces, for his knowledge might mean at any minute the difference between a cuff and a corn pone. Now he knew men, and had something to offer all kinds. He did not offer the time-serving promises of the politician, or the servile flattery of the toady on the make, or the wistful complaisance of the man who cannot live without love and good opinion and whose greatest fear is rejection. No, for Cassius Fort was a strong man who had made his way in a hard world, and he stood steady on his legs and looked any man in the eye. He did not have to offer any of those artificial things—promises, flattery, wistful emptiness—for what he had to offer any man was a true and solid part of himself. He *was* the son of old Kaintuck, he *was* the border brawler with the dirk and the head for likker, he *was* the humorist full of frontier farce and salty humor, he *was* the sober squire who knew the ways of land and animals by science and system, he *was* the soldier with the mark of battle on him, he *was* the gentleman of honor who had faced Dr. Jameson's fire or the courteous companion in a parlor, he *was* the lawyer and statesman bearing the fate of a people, he *was* the retired student who read poetry without apology or discussed the philosophy of Voltaire and Hume without shame.

He was also the man who in the midst of company might be trapped for a moment with the sadness on his face. The painter of the portrait now hanging in the capitol at Frankfort caught that expression. It is intended as the portrait of a masterful man, the right hand laid across the chest, slipped under the lapel of the black coat, the face severe and weighty. But beneath the severity and weight of the official face, there is the dumb melancholy and a blank question; and the shaggy head, the dark, heavy-lidded eyes, the broad, short, rather flat nose, and the grooved, swarthy flesh give the face of a suffering animal that has no words for what it feels.

We do not know why that look is there, any more than we know why the particular look is on the face we meet at morning and evening in the mirror. But we can hazard a guess for the face in the portrait at Frankfort with better evidence than we can for the face we meet in the mirror. We can argue it this way: If Cassius Fort was all the things he was—from border brawler to retired student—what was he in the end? He was so much, but he was so little, and the sadness was the sadness of a man alone with a question which the world could never answer, for the question was the man himself. There is no sadness like the sadness of a man who knows the secrets of the world and of power, for only that man is forced to face the blankness of the last secret.

That night in the Mason house, Jeremiah Beaumont saw only the courteous gentlemen in the parlor, but he saw also the sadness and was puzzled by it, even as he listened to the talk of politics or heard with excitement the great man tell of a poet whose book he had bought in Philadelphia, a new English poet named Byron, who was a lord and brought into poetry, as Cassius Fort put it, "a new lordliness and spirit which both stirs and rebukes the blood." Then Cassius Fort quoted the verses:

> Roll on, thou deep and dark blue Ocean—roll!
> Ten thousand fleets sweep over thee in vain;
> Man marks the earth with ruin—his control
> Stops with the shore. . . .

His eyes flashed as he said the lines, then suddenly he stopped, and slapped his knee with his black-haired, heavy hand, and demanded: "Do you like that, boy?"

36

Jeremiah said that he liked it.

"I will give you a book of his, not with the poem I quote, but others," Cassius Fort said. "I have it in my saddlebags." When Jeremiah protested, he said it was nothing, that he would brook no refusal. But Jeremiah would take it only as a loan.

"All right," the Colonel said, "and you can return it to me when you come to work at the law." And Jeremiah's heart stopped. This was the reason he had been asked.

Colonel Fort said that he did not intend to stand for Congress again, at least not for the present. The great poverty and hard times falling over Kentucky made it his duty to his wife to watch his property at home and to further his law practice and if he came into politics it would be in his home state where men now suffered for bread, and which needed the best efforts of all who owed their birth to her.

Then he broached the business. He needed somebody of unusual intelligence and integrity to bring up in his law office at Bowling Green, and he took the word of his dear friend Dr. Burnham that Jeremiah Beaumont was the man. He would have him go to Bowling Green as soon as might be, and begin the reading of law from his own library there and with the help of Mr. Talbot, who assisted him with his affairs. Then when the next session of Congress was over he himself would return and would do all he could. "Will you do it, boy?" he demanded.

Jeremiah's first impulse was to say that he would go, even to-morrow, but on the very instant that hope and energy rose in him, the dullness and despair of those months came back, and "I felt that nothing good was in this world for me and it would be vanity to reach out my hand." So he said that he did not see how he could leave his mother with the farm, that he was grateful for the kind opinion, but that his fate was not in his hands.

Colonel Fort declared that he knew the circumstances, but that something might be worked out. As for the money, in the few months before his return from Washington, he could promise a place in the store of his good friend James Harrod at Bowling Green, which would leave time for the reading of law. When Jeremiah hesitated, he asked, why not. "You cannot be one who feels that trade bemeans a man. I do not feel so. Trade may become the genius of our people. Whatever a man does is well done if he puts a strong hand to it, and when a man is young he should try many ways and conditions of life to enlarge his experience and ripen his mind."

The boy replied that his duty held him at home.

"Do not give up the idea," Colonel Fort said, "for I can wait. I can wait for the man Dr. Burnham recommends."

The hour was late. Colonel Fort went to get the book. The boy thanked him, took his leave to walk the miles to the cabin. As far as he knew, he would never see Colonel Fort, the great man, again.

But he was to see him. Colonel Fort had already entered the drama, had smiled and spoken his first lines, and then with the characteristic, secret expression of sadness and animal question on his swarthy face, had retired into the wings to wait for the cue that would come. For Dr. Burnham had delivered Cassius Fort into Jeremiah Beaumont's hands, and Jeremiah Beaumont into his. The fat old lard-tub of a man, wheezing and supporting his great weight on the tender arches thrust into moccasins, had awakened the boy's heart "to the fullness of life," and had executed his function of agent or broker or impresario, and could now go back to his poems and his cobweb pills and his speculation on the relation of mind and body.

II

JEREMIAH BEAUMONT DID GO TO BOWL-
ing Green to the study of law. The death of his mother in the spring
removed the impediment.

Looking back on his mother's death, Jeremiah wrote that it had
come in good time to further his prospects. But that thought increased
his grief, and all the next year at Bowling Green this sense of unworthiness and guilt persisted. "I often woke in the night and was
stricken to think how the hand that had tended my infancy was
still at last, and how the lips that had sung by my cradle were
stopped with yellow clay. And in my grief and to my disordered
midnight fancy it seemed that out of consideration for her son she
had taken her departure, as in the past, at night, out of regard for
my studies, she had sometimes gone tiptoe into a farther and colder
room to give me peace."

Guilty or not, he settled into the new routine of his daylight, practical world. Mr. Harrod was an easy taskmaster, and made no complaint if in slack hours Jeremiah propped himself by the stove (or
on the porch after spring had come) with one eye on a book and one
eye out for a customer. At first the store itself was interesting, the
biggest he had ever seen. Bowling Green was a town of some pretensions, and Mr. Harrod was its most flourishing merchant. In the

39

big, dusky cave of his brick building you could find any article in local demand, from plowshares, steel traps, gunpowder and whisky, to dimity and brocade, Bibles, jesuit's bark, and gold-headed canes, a few with a long dagger concealed in the stock. Mr. Harrod, a well-fleshed, ruddy man in a bottle-green, pigeon-tailed coat, would tip his two-story beaver to the prinking ladies and call a clerk, or slap a gaunt-headed woodsman on the back, and say, "Jake, you got a couple of coon skins to spend with me?" Or on a slow afternoon, he would take an hourly tour back to the likker barrel, refresh himself, and return to stand blinking in the middle of his treasures like a "drowsy god of the cave waiting for his worshippers and their votive pence."

That was part of Jeremiah's new world. The other part was the law books from Colonel Fort's library, with their dry language that "crackled like autumn leaves underfoot or thorns lighted under a pot," and their logic that "marched beyond the green confines of human hopes and fears across the sands of a desert toward some far-off mountain of Justice." Two evenings a week he went to Mr. Talbot—"a brittle, bare bean-pole of a man about whom last year's withered tendrils still seemed to cling"—and asked him questions on points in his reading and wrote down the answers in a notebook.

His only friend of this period—the only friend he had ever had except Dr. Burnham, whose friendship was of another order—was a young man named Wilkie Barron, whose mother was a widow with a tidy little house in which Jeremiah rented a "loft-room." The Barrons were genteel poor, with good connections, and total confidence in the world. The old lady was small, brown-faced, and spry, with a fund of good humor and a kind of scatterbrained motherliness that spilled over on her somewhat sullen and self-obsessed roomer. He professes gratitude, but he also confesses that she had the habit of trapping him into long conversations in the evening when he had better been at his books and of embarking on some endless tale which she seemed to find notably humorous, for "she punctuated her discourse with her gay cackle even when the subject could bring no smile to my face, only the grimace of politeness." He records one other fact about her: "The first sound of a fiddle would set her jigging in a chair, and if she rose to dance she shook as neat a foot as any maid."

The son, Wilkie Barron, who was by turns studious and wild, was several years older than Jeremiah. He was studying law, too. He also had a taste for polite letters, and he and Jeremiah sometimes read their verses to each other in the shank of the evening when the law was laid aside. But Wilkie was also a great one for the girls, and as much of a dandy as his purse would permit. He introduced

40

Jeremiah to certain respectable young ladies of his wide acquaintance and to some others who were definitely not respectable. But Jeremiah was dog-poor and threadbare, and even a little later when he could afford to buy better clothes and take some advantage of Wilkie's taste in fashion, he still found himself "short of that small change of gay conversation and pleasant jest indulged by young ladies."

Even when the great Colonel Fort had returned and Jeremiah appeared in the reassuring shadow of his patronage, his silences and awkwardness still prevented his social success. In the second year he did have a sort of love affair with a young lady of charm and good prospects, but though she was more serious-minded than most and gave him some encouragement and let him read his verses to her, she dropped him suddenly to marry a young blood with yellow mustaches, a fat farm, and a stable of good horses.

"She wasn't the girl for you," Wilkie encouraged him. "She just pretends to be intelligent and to have sentiment, and she is really no beauty. What you want is somebody like Rachel Jordan."

"Who is she?"

"Oh, she is the daughter of Timothy Jordan, and he's a big man up on Green River. She is beautiful and she reads poetry and can talk philosophy with you and she rides like an angel on the wing. A thousand men have tried to marry her, but she spurns them all. Perhaps she is waiting just for you, Jerry!"

"Yes," Jeremiah said bitterly, "and she is rich and lives up on Green River."

So he turned from his disappointment to Wilkie's less respectable friends. "I quenched my thirst at more than one dirty puddle and took delight in the mire, but I had not my friend's genial spirit which let him rise from a pallet of foulness with a jest and then turn to the seriousness of the world. As for me, it came about before long that after the fleshly sport I would fall into self-abhorrence and melancholy, and the hotness of concupiscence brought me the coldness of despair. Then when the despair was gone and the desire returned to me, I felt beforehand the pain with which it would be satisfied, and my life would suddenly seem black and empty like a well.

"One evening when I had sat late with Mr. Talbot I returned to find Wilkie on the doorstep just going in. I asked him where he had been and he replied that he had had a piece of 'you know what' with Silly Sal, a young female who was not overly blessed with intellect and who simpered and giggled, but who had a fair soft skin for all her slatternly ways, and was found tasty by many hot boys of the town. Then we entered to find Mrs. Barron by the fire, munching an apple, bright as a cricket. She asked Wilkie where he had been

41

so late, but asked as a sort of joke, or so it seemed to me. Wilkie replied; 'Don't you wish you knew?'

" 'I know you'll swing on a limb, you imp of Satan,' she said, 'if you don't mend your ways.' Then she hopped up, tossed her apple core into the fire, and leaned to kiss her son good night. He seized her and set her on his knee and fell to bussing and tickling her and calling her his mouse, as if she had been one of the loose sluts of his pleasure. She laughed and kicked with her heels, then jerked away from him and gave him a fine slap on the cheek for sport, and laughed to see his face. Then she kissed him quick, and laughed and ran from the room. So Wilkie ruefully wiped his hand where she had struck, and fell to laughing. 'The old lady's got dander,' he said.

"I looked at him, and then overstepped civility by asking if his mother had known where he had been.

" 'She knows I'm a chip off the old block,' he said, and laughed. 'She knew there wasn't but one way to keep my pa indoors after dark before they nailed him up for good. He was a ring-tailed rouser for fair.'

"I said no more, and shortly excused myself for bed. As I lay before sleeping, I thought how his mother had known him returned hot from his pleasure with the half-wit trull and had made a jest of the matter and how she had laughed and bounced on his knee. The thought was horrible to me, and then of a sudden I felt lonely and how I could not take the world as other men for the brightness of the moment and the tickle of the flesh, and how they found what they were seeking but I did not know what I sought. I took no credit for virtue, for my desire was what was common to men, and even as I lay there I suffered a carnal lust and saw Silly Sal as though her naked flesh were bright in the room like light."

In January, 1820, after Jeremiah had been in Bowling Green less than a year, the Colonel returned and suggested that he give up his job in Mr. Harrod's store and come to his office. He could continue his studies, and experience would be as good as study at this stage. And the Colonel would pay him enough to make a respectable life. Jeremiah's joy was so great that he could scarcely utter his thanks.

He was not disappointed in the new state of things. The Colonel himself, "with boundless patience and paternal kindness," supplemented the instruction of Mr. Talbot, who, in comparison with Colonel Fort's full-blooded presence, seemed more than ever the bean-pole wreathed with last year's tendrils. "On Mr. Talbot's instruction, it had seemed that the law existed but for the sake of the law, and that a clean-wrought brief was more precious than the blood of martyrs, but Colonel Fort opened my eyes to the law as mankind's servant, and severe but as a mother may be severe for the child's sake. So the book that had been dull now glowed before my eyes as though it had been a drab, dead coal he leaned to blow upon with his breath and bring to flame."

Colonel Fort also opened his eyes to the world of politics and statecraft. "He said that the health of the state is the measure of men's happiness, for if the state was sick that sickness infected all men. And that from whatever intellect and strength a man possessed he should pay tithe and more to the public good." Having uttered those words, in which no doubt he believed as he believed in the strength of his arm or the blood of a horse, he leaned forward to slap the boy on the knee and unmask with a grin the hero of the hustings, the likker barrel and the burgoo, and say, "Hell, son, and politics is more fun than a coon-hunt or a wrassling match!"

It was a face Jeremiah already knew now, one of the public faces, the face the Colonel showed when he made a speech to the market-day crowd at a settlement or to the half-drunk boys at a barbecue. It was the face of Old Cass who was as stout as the next one. Jeremiah knew that face, but he knew the other public face, too, the one that you saw when he made a speech for Jim Brandow, the poor man's candidate, on the Fourth of July, right in Bowling Green, in front of the big folks who owned the land and the mortgages and the bank notes. He stood up before them, severe as a judge, and said: "It is iniquity for any man to forget that he is not alone and that the good of other men is his duty, and that the state is our life. If your conscience will not awake, let your interest be vigilant, and if a man will not see the truth, I accuse him now of treason and sloth. And I stand on my words." Then he stepped down from the platform as calm as though going to his breakfast table, and walked past savage old Stephen Dunne, who had sworn to have his heart if he talked in Bowling Green. And Jim Brandow was elected.

But Jim Brandow in the Legislature was not enough, and the Colonel knew it. Times were going from bad to worse in Kentucky. It had been panic the year before, in 1819, with wheat and tobacco down to nothing and the United States Bank demanding specie on two and a half million the state owed and with the money of the State Banks and independent banks not worth the paper it was printed on. The loose money issued by the law of the state to stave off the panic had only led to wild speculation and a premium on getting into debt before your money fell again. "And now," the Colonel said, after Brandow's election, "the people are more than twelve million dollars in debt, five million to the Bank of Kentucky, nigh three million to the United States Bank, and nigh five million to New York and Philadelphia, and they haven't got two bits or a coon skin to pay. Folks'll leave this state, they're heading out across the river to Indiana and Missouri like grasshoppers out of a field fire." Then the Colonel added sourly: "Nigger labor—it's getting so cheap that wages to white folks go down." Then he shook his head: "Yeah, I know I own niggers, too. If I didn't own 'em, I couldn't run my place to pay. But they'll ruin this state. They'll drive folks out like a plague of cholera. Oh, I've got niggers—but what's a man to do?"

One thing had been done that the Colonel approved of. The Legislature had legalized a stay of sale for debt up to twelve months, and if the creditor refused notes on the Bank of Kentucky, the debtor could replevy for two years. "Time to breathe," the Colonel said, "time to breathe. Give a man time to breathe and he'll pay out if God lets him. Oh, I've been poor to dirt and back bare to the wind, and I know how a poor man feels, and he'll pay if God will let him. Oh, I've had money owed to me last year, a lot of money for a man no richer than me, and I took Kentucky notes. It was kicking me in the pocketbook, which is nigh as rough as kicking a man in his fun-sack, but I took 'em. I look at it this way, son. If everybody keeps pushing for payment and crying for specie, we will pull down this state on our heads and the whole country with it, and where would you be then, specie or no specie? That's why I've taken re-plevin cases and fought 'em. If a man is so poor he has to replevy, how is he going to pay me for being his lawyer? But I've taken some cases anyway, like you know."

Then the Colonel stared into the fire. "But I don't know where it will end," he said. "You can't replevy everything to the Judgment Day and expect the Angel Gabriel to settle all your debts in gold coin at a discount and all interest waived. You can't fiddle in plow-time and get fat at first frost and corn-pulling." He sank back again into thought, staring into the fire, while the law book lay on the table beside him near Jeremiah's inkpot and idle quill.

Jeremiah noted again the heavy sadness of his face, and for the first time felt a love for him, "not merely the respect and gratitude I owed him for kindness, but love as though he had been a father and good to me. I loved him because I thought I saw the goodness of strength which could give strength to others, and was sad for the weakness of others."

Finally, the Colonel stirred. "No," he said, "you can't fiddle in plow-time. We live in the world, boy, and when the sun is down it is a place of darkness where the foot knoweth not the way." Then, after a silence: "I wish I knew the end."

That was in the fall of 1820, and Jeremiah, six years later leaning over another table in a grimmer room than Colonel Fort's study,

44

wrote: "Nor did I know the end and what would be the burden of our time."

All he knew was that he had come into a time of comfort and respect. That sober-minded gentlemen on the streets of Bowling Green bowed to him and spoke courteously to him of crops and weather and late news. That he listened to the lawyers in the courtroom and knew that he would be a match for any of them, that he himself would some day sit on a bench and listen to their argument and judge them. That his mind ran with a cold joy through the work of the day like a keen knife blade through soft, delicious pine. That Wilkie Barron was a dear friend who could share his dreams and read his verses. That men and books offered him the great patterns of meaning for life. That Colonel Fort, the soldier and statesman, would take him as a guest and hunt with him and drink with him and accord him the dignity due a man and the warmth due a son.

He knew all those things. But he knew that something was missing. But he did not know what it was.

Was she beautiful? There is no picture for us to see, and that is probably just as well, for even if the pictured face was beautiful it could not be beautiful enough to account for the story. It would be only line and color on canvas and would lack the breath and fire. Or perhaps we have lost our faith in beauty, not only on canvas, and know that even in the flesh it is only line and color, after all, and that if there are breath and fire they promise only a hot contact and a poor moment of coupling and that only a supple thigh and not truth would be ungirdled, after all.

We have no picture, but we have the descriptions. They do us little good, however, for there is no agreement among them. Except for the remark of Wilkie Barron (which we have at second-hand through Jeremiah Beaumont), all of the descriptions come after the event, and the face they give us may be taken as a result rather than as a cause of the story.

Some saw nothing but "a woman not more handsome than common, with red hair, features given to heaviness but already marked by time and restlessness, a spot about the size of a man's thumbnail and the color of rust on one cheek, and teeth somewhat uneven, making her slow to smile for vanity. She moved with no special grace."

Others remark her as handsome and dashing and elegant and give her "dignity of bearing sometimes queenly." The smile comes in for comment. One observer says that it possessed a "special charm for its reserve and stirred the heart like a hard-won promise." And Jeremiah Beaumont writes: "In softer mood she had a smile which brought light but at the same time bespoke a sweet and melancholy wisdom as though she knew the worth of joy in the world and for generous pity would not tell you her secret. I cannot do otherwise than limn it as the smile of a sweet and high-souled Sphinx that would not slay the traveler who could not guess her riddle and leave his bones to whiten on the Greek road, but would let him pass on in peace except for the memory of her face."

What made the smile, the high-souled secret or the slightly uneven teeth? We shall never know for sure, and perhaps we do not have to take a choice. Perhaps the uneven teeth made the smile, but once the smile was smiled it made the nature of the smiler and from the dental defect sprang the secret of the Sphinx and her "sweet and melancholy wisdom." But we cannot be sure of that, or of what it would prove if we could be sure of it. What we can be sure of is that Jeremiah Beaumont found in the end the thing he had to find after all the years he had been waiting for that smile.

Rachel Jordan was three years older than Jeremiah Beaumont, having been born in 1798. She had been born in Virginia, in the Tidewater, into a family of some aristocratic pretensions but no great wealth. The Jordans had for a hundred years borrowed money from the greater families around them and married their less attractive daughters. Young ladies named Carter, Randolph, Hopeby, and Pendleton. At least, we can assume that the daughters who married the Jordans were the less attractive ones, and that the Jordans took them off the hands of their grand creditors, in discount of a debt.

In any case, we know that Timothy Jordan, the father of Rachel, had owed a debt to Simon Hopeby, and that the debt was wiped out when he married Maria Hopeby. Timothy Jordan did not thrive in Virginia, even with the debt wiped out, for his land was gutted by a century of abuse. So in 1803 he packed up silver, linen, carpets, books, and the best furniture, loaded those marks of rank and civilization on ox-carts, marshalled his family and slaves, mounted his horse, and found the road west. In 1804 he took up land in Saul County, Kentucky, built a good house, and settled down. Things went better with him here. Fat barns, the elegant silver and furniture, and the shadow of the Tidewater names made him great in the new country, and the Jordan who back home had sat a little below the salt now moved to a chair of honor. He had read some law in his youth, and now he dabbled in politics, went to the Legislature at Frankfort, and served one term as Attorney General of the State.

Maria Jordan, who could never forget that she was a Hopeby, that her liver was bad and her heart palpitated, that her husband was flagrantly unfaithful to her, and that her face was a good deal short of beauty, took what satisfaction she could in life by queening it over the ladies of her own neighborhood and the wives of politicians at Frankfort, and by refreshing herself with the society of her peers in Lexington and at Olympian Springs at the Licks. Her daughter was a belle, and she took what compensation she could for her own plainness of face by counting how many gentlemen in the ballroom or at the racecourse gravitated toward Rachel.

Rachel could have made a good match in those days, but she did not use her chances. Peevish, stupid, nagging Mrs. Jordan could not understand the daughter. At one moment she was the young lady of fashion surrounded by her dandies. At another, she was mooning over a book of philosophy or a book of poems or was scribbling away in her diary and at letters she sent regularly to her cousin Amanda Hopeby, who had visited her for a year but was now back in Virginia. At another, she would fill the parlor with the sad tinkling of her harpsichord or would shut herself in her room, would darken the shutters in the hot, throbbing summer afternoon, would fling herself upon her bed, and with her heavy hair spread loose upon the counterpane would move her head gently from side to side and weep.

The mother's letters of rebuke and admonition (when the daughter was visiting at Frankfort or Olympian Springs), the diary, and the letters to Amanda Hopeby give us this much, or at least enough for us to see this picture of the girl who seemed always to have the world in her hand but who always let it slip away. What came to her hand was not quite what she sought. We can guess that old Mrs. Jordan had something to do with this. There were her dreary, dinning complaints about her husband's unfaithfulness, her reiterated, "For you know what men are and how the better the woman and the more delicately nurtured, the more ready the master of her fate is to neglect and abuse her."

In any case, she poisoned the daughter's natural trust and innocence of heart, so that the young beau who approached her with the highest reverence and the most noble brow was to be suspected on the second instant as a brute and betrayer. At the same time, Maria Jordan, with the hard realism of maturity, prodded the daughter in the direction of whatever available young man had the broadest acres and the grandest name, no matter if he wore a hangman's face and was notoriously diseased. But Rachel could not follow her mother's wisdom here, any more than she could follow her own wisdom with the young man of noble brow. Who could take that hangman's face, corrupt blood, and cold heart, when you knew from all the books and poems and the whispered secrets of other girls that love was a pure flame and a spiritual passion in which pain was joy and joy was sacrament?

Rachel knew, however, that somewhere else in the world, surely somewhere, things were different. Here, again, Maria Jordan had her hand. She had never come to accept the life in Kentucky, and a large part of her conversation concerned itself with the superiority of Virginia, where manners were purer, blood more jealous, life more dignified, and rank more respected, and where, if anywhere, honor and happiness might have been found. Year by year Virginia became more and more the fabulous Land of Cockayne, from which she had been brutally snatched away by that blunt-souled, pot-bellied ogre, Timothy Jordan. She had the art to shrivel every pleasure and tarnish every beauty in the new country. If a ball seemed grand to Rachel it immediately became in the mother's conversation a poor thing, a disorderly huddle of bumpkins tramping to the scratch of fiddles, very unlike a rout in Virginia. If Rachel preened happily before a glass in a new dress, it became a mere rag, but the best that such a failure as Timothy Jordan could buy and good enough, no doubt, for Kentucky. She had the heart to give to everything present and fresh the sad and contemptuous distance with which we now regard the rotted silk, faded ribbon, dusty broadcloth, rusted epaulet, and gimcrack jewelry in a county museum or an attic trunk, finery that was finery only to the ignorant and untraveled.

Rachel's mother told her that in Virginia were prettier dresses, finer manners, and more splendid balls, and her own healthy blood and confident heart told her that somewhere, certainly somewhere, you met a man whose noble brow was not a lie, whose melancholy was not satiety or boredom, and whose energy was not brutal, that somewhere, perhaps Virginia, life was full of meaning and worth. So at times the mother's Cockayne of Virginia and the daughter's Cockayne of the soul coincided like one map traced from another, and girlish vanity, however frivolous, and girlish dreams, however serious, conspired together to define a land beyond the mountains and beyond the present, and to leave her lost and restless in Kentucky. "Ah, if I could come to Virginia!" she wrote Amanda Hopeby. She would never get to Virginia, it was so far away.

As for her father, he told her nothing. He was too busy with his farming, his bottle, his political friends, his yellow wenches or his fancy women of Frankfort, and his little ambitions. He was a short, stocky, ordinary man, who moved in and out of his own house like a somewhat disgraceful and too solid ghost, puffing on the stairs and snoring in bed and picking his teeth after dinner with a quill mounted in gold. Then he died.

His death would have been convenient but for one thing. He took his last revenge on Maria Hopeby and performed his last piece of unfaithfulness by dying at the wrong time. He died in 1820, of locked bowels.

With the easy money recently issued by the Kentucky law, he had been speculating in town lots in Bowling Green, Frankfort, and Versailles, and he died deeply in debt, his holdings over-extended and his affairs tangled and perhaps disreputable. Maria Hopeby was furious, oh, she was furious, she said, and the same day the body was rushed underground, she spat on his picture. At that, the daughter, who had not yet shed a tear, burst into sobs and sank face down across the sofa in the parlor, crumpling her black dress and letting her hair fall loose. It was not grief, for she had not loved her father. It was that she could not bear to think that life was as terrible as this.

The mother leaned over and patted her hair, saying, "Oh, my poor orphan, my poor orphan—the underbred villain, he has ruined you, he has ruined you!"

In the midst of Rachel Jordan's despair, those words struck a truth which she had never recognized, like a cyclone ringing the church bell in the steeple at the moment of destruction. "You—you!" she cried out, and leaped from the sofa and stared at Maria Hopeby. "Oh, I am ruined," she said, "but it is you who ruined me. You ruined me!"

The mother could not, apparently, believe her ears, for she said again, "My poor child, my poor orphan," and tried to lay her hands on her daughter. But the daughter screamed at her, "Don't touch me, don't ever touch me, for you are foul, are foul!" When the mother tried again to touch her and quiet her, the girl shoved her away so hard that she stumbled back against the sofa and fell to her knees on the floor, breathless with shock and rage. With the first breath to come back the mother cried, "You are like him—like *him*—you are no Hopeby—I spit on you both—you are no Hopeby!"

"No," Rachel replied, "no, I'm no Hopeby. I'm—I'm . . . Oh, I'm nothing!" She ran out of the room, leaving the snarling, sick old woman on the floor, crouching as though asking for forgiveness but asking for none, asking for nothing, for she had everything, she was a Hopeby, she was a Hopeby, and even the spit she spat was precious.

Rachel ran out of the house and across the lawn, then stopped. She stood there in her black dress, panting, in the powerful humming July afternoon. Beyond the garden where the yellow roses hung in the heat, the cornfield stretched away on one side, and the corn at that season would be waist-high, savagely green, swelling in stalk and blade from the fat soil and the sun. In the trees behind her the July flies would make their grinding, remorseless, barbaric sound like a nerve twitching in her head. From the stone gateposts the rutted red-clay lane, dusty now, fell away, leading to cabins and houses she could not see, to faces she would never know, to forests, to the wilderness itself, but not to Virginia. At least, not for her.

There was nowhere to go, nothing to do. So she stood there, sweating under the hot sun, in the middle of the brutal, vibrant, tumescent land, which drowsed and throbbed and brooded with its own secret, but cared nothing for her or her secret. In the end there was nothing to do except re-enter the house and face the fact which she had so recently discovered in the dusky parlor.

She resumed the life that had been lived in the house. Maria Hopeby Jordan would never forgive her. She knew that, and knew that she would not forgive the old woman. She could not forgive her for two things, for the fact that she was Maria Hopeby and for the fact that she, Rachel Jordan, was Rachel Jordan. They were crimes past any repentance or expiation.

She had to live with, and suffer from, those crimes, and meet the hate in the old woman's face, day after day, across the table, behind the suddenly opened door, in the dark angle of the hall. Her only strength would be in the hate she could return, and her only comfort in contempt. She thought she could live by that, for there was nothing else to live by.

"We are poor now, poor as trash," the old woman said one day at dinner, not so much in self-pity for the moment as in spite. "You'll have to learn to live different now. You are poor."

"Poor," Rachel said. "I don't care how poor we are. I'd live in a cabin and die in a ditch, if—if . . ."

If what? She did not know.

"You can't have pretty things any more," the old woman said. "You are poor now, poor as dirt."

Rachel did not answer. She sat silent, for she had learned the use of that weapon, and glared at her mother. The mother did not continue, but began to sniffle above her plate. In her diary, Rachel wrote: "I think she is afraid of me. And she does well to be afraid. I am afraid of myself."

She was not afraid of being poor. For one reason, we may cynically suggest, she had never known poverty. It was a dreamland as remote as that other dreamland of Virginia. And she did not have to be poor, at least truly poor.

Colonel Cassius Fort saw to that. He had appeared at the funeral of Timothy Jordan and had paid his respects to the widow and orphan. But some days later he came again, with one of the lawyers, a Mr. Borden, who had to deal with the affairs of the deceased. His appearance was a surprise to Mrs. Jordan, and not entirely a pleasant one. He had been a friend of Timothy Jordan, indeed, and had visited at the house, but she had always been a little less than cordial, despite his greatness, because she knew his origins, he was a nobody, the pauper boy of a stockade.

50

Now he sat in the shadowy parlor, while the widow gave her histrionic sobs and snuffles, and offered his services. Mr. Jordan had employed him in deals in lands, and he wished Mrs. Jordan to have the benefit of his information and of his records. He only wished to be of service. Mr. Carmadoy, the executor of the deceased, had already spoken with him, but he had felt that he had best refer himself directly to Mrs. Jordan.

So Maria Hopeby Jordan accepted the services of the pauper boy of a stockade, and even managed to thank him.

Rachel watched the scene, saying nothing, not really attending to what was going on. She did not really attend when her mother, after the gentlemen had taken leave, said, "It has come to this. To receive a favor from one of Timothy Jordan's common political friends."

"He came as a friend and in humanity," the girl said. "That should be enough. Even for you."

"Oh, he came to make something from the matter. Wait. Mark my words and wait!"

"You fool," Rachel Jordan retorted. "You are as foolish as wicked."

And in the diary she underscored the word *fool*. Then, having recorded the insult to her mother, she added: "The Bible says to honor your father and mother that your days may be long in the land the Lord thy God hath given thee. But what if your father and mother deserve no honor? Then it is a lie to give honor. I shall honor truth and give her no honor. Why should I desire long days in this land?"

So, as another insult to her mother, when Colonel Fort came again she received him with every mark of deference and consideration, beyond the "dictates of mere civility," and was struck by his reserve and dignity "as though knowing his own worth he need presume upon nothing."

Colonel Fort had come to sort out some of the dead man's papers, so he quickly excused himself and was shut up in the library until dinner time. He took dinner with Mrs. Jordan and Rachel. Mrs. Jordan was as silent and sullen as possible within the bounds of politeness. Colonel Fort was not the sort of man to be greatly interested in her account of the manners and amusements of Lexington or in her account of her ill-health and bereaved condition. So, toward the end of the meal, he was discussing with the girl the sad state of the country, and according to the diary, explained well "our perils and our needs." And she added: "I understood perfectly all that he wished to convey."

After dinner he went back to the library and the papers, and worked all the afternoon. He stayed for a cold supper, and rode home by moonlight the ten miles or so to his own place.

51

For a week he did not return, then briefly with Mr. Carmadoy the executor. But a few days later he was back, alone, to do another stint in the library and to talk with the ladies, or rather to listen to Mrs. Jordan's conversation, sour and effusive by turns, and then to respond to Rachel's questions. That day he had brought a book, and read a little to them. We do not know what book he brought, but we do know that Mrs. Jordan yawned almost obviously and fidgeted and picked at her dress, and for her behavior earned another black mark in the diary.

So the new order of things began at Sunderland, the Jordan house. It became apparent that they would probably be able to keep the main part of the place, at least Colonel Fort promised that much, and he might be able, after litigation, to salvage a few of the lots in Bowling Green. But some of the slaves would have to go. The home place had been overstocked to begin with, and now with reduced holdings a culling out was in order. Mrs. Jordan whined at this policy, then assumed an air of Christian resignation. So Colonel Fort inspected the people, and selected those to be put up at vendue. Among those he selected was Gabbo, Mrs. Jordan's coachman, a fine, coal-black buck in the prime of life, handsome in his long blue coat, with the bearing of a senator. Mrs. Jordan wept.

Mrs. Jordan dried her tears but raged in private, saying to Rachel that that fellow out of his commonness and envy took joy in reducing her state and bringing her down to his level.

"It would be a good thing if he could bring you up to his level," Rachel said.

"Oh, he is rich," the old woman replied bitterly, "he could buy and sell us. I am old and poor, but I have my pride, and because he is rich . . ."

"When I said, 'up to his level,' I did not refer to his wealth," Rachel put in, and with those killing words left the room.

She had, by her own admission, begun to enjoy the encounters with the old woman. She always won, and she saw, day by day, the crumbling of confidence, the alternating between hysteria and apathy, the growth of fear. She knew that her pleasure was wicked, but she knew, too, that wickedness was better than nothing and before the death of her father and the great discovery she had been nothing. So she accepted the condition of things and her new role, adding, however, that, "My delight in the ruin of another is the mark of my own ruin."

She had discovered a new power in herself, even in the moment of ruin, and more and more Colonel Fort turned to her to judge a suggestion and to make a decision. He might address the question to the old woman in all respect, but it was for Rachel's answer that he waited. She had begun to help him, too, with the papers when he came to the house with Mr. Carmadoy, or alone.

And when he did not come, she was alone, to prowl the house, to walk alone (against the protests of her mother) in the woods by the river as the fall came on, or to sit by a window with some book, sometimes a book he had brought, and look out over the lawn and garden to the fields where the corn was now browning toward harvest.

In the early fall of 1820 the diary stops. The last entry does not seem important, on the face of it. It was a hot day with a great stillness in the air, and a kind of bright haze lying over the land. She had lain down in her room after dinner, but had not been able to sleep. So then she had gone out to walk in the garden. She stood in the garden, on the moss-grown brick pavement, and inspected the ruinous roses. Then she looked away over the fields to the woods and thought how small the garden was in the wideness of the land and how a garden was a spot made for pleasure but she had never taken pleasure in it. So carrying a rose, from which she tore the petals one by one to crush in her fingers, she moved along the edge of the corn field and entered the woods by the river.

But there was nothing there, only another kind of sadness, with the sun breaking through the high boughs of the hickories to make here on the fallen yellow leaves a glowing spot in the general gloom. "My meditations had long since become solitary and I was accustomed to melancholy thought. I had even come to find what sweetness was in my life of solitariness and melancholy. But in that spot my solitariness and melancholy became different and too great. I could have better supported it, if the sunlight falling on the golden leaves of the hickory strewn on the ground in the glade had not been so bright and sudden in that place. I would have talked with someone to tell what feeling was in me that I might better know myself."

So she came out of the woods, and moved by another way to the spot which had been chosen for the family graves but which was as yet marked by only one, that of Timothy Jordan. She had not visited it since the day of the funeral, and already the place showed the lack of care, as though the dead man had been completely forgotten, or as though his death "but continued the forgetfulness of life." The grave mound was somewhat settled from its first condition and the "rawness of earth was mollified by the leaves fallen from the beech trees standing about."

She stood by the grave and inspected her memories and feelings. She had, she decided, no memory of him any more than of a stranger passed on the road as you drove by. They had never been together. She had never known him. She had known only a name, Timothy Jordan, and now she said that name over several times, to see what it might evoke. But it evoked nothing, that name which was all left of a man who had lived and had been her father.

It might have been different, she thought. He might have taken her hand, like a father, and led her down the path in the garden among roses that were not ruinous. She might have been a child by his side hearing his voice and knowing his wisdom and certainty. They might have sat by the fire in the winter evening while he told her of his own childhood long ago, or read to her from a book of stories. But she had been cheated. She knew it. Cheated again.

So now she stood alone, with dusty shoes, in the merciless light, a twisted rose-stalk, almost denuded of petals, in her hand.

She clutched the stalk and felt the prick of a thorn. Looking down, she saw the tiny globule of blood on her finger. She clutched harder, deliberately harder, and drove the thorns into her flesh. Then, slowly, she opened her hand and saw the marks spring out across the palm and fingers, six bright little drops of the blood which was herself, and in the middle of her palm a detached thorn driven deep into the flesh.

Oh, she had been cheated, and there was no reality left but pain.

Then she thought that, perhaps, Timothy Jordan had been cheated, too. Perhaps he had longed to take her hand and walk in the garden or sit by the fire and tell her of a life he had once lived, but had seen in his house only a willful and selfish girl who was a stranger. So her eyes swam with tears that made all the landscape dance and glitter.

She looked down at the rose stalk. Only three petals remained on it. She plucked them off, one by one, and let them drift, one after another, to the grave mound. Then she flung the bare stalk after them. It was her first and last offering to the father she had never known. It was her first and last meeting with Timothy Jordan. "*Ave atque vale*," she wrote in her diary that night, and closed it for good.

Did she know why she closed it? Did she feel that now, having met her father at last, she now was truly bereaved and alone? That only when you are truly alone, can you begin to live? That when you truly begin to live you must construct your own world and therefore have no need for words written on paper, words that can only give the shadow of a world already lived? In any case, the book was closed.

In the late spring of 1821 Jeremiah Beaumont heard the story. The uncle of Wilkie Barron had a small property up in the Green River section, and Wilkie had visited there just at the time when the gossip began. In the parlors of that section ladies leaned at each other and whispered and glanced covertly across the room at the nubile daughter with the trim little waist. In the tavern the news was passed over a toddy by stout squires wearing boots and spurs, who roared with laughter and winked and lifted their noggins to pledge Old Cassius, for they'd always known he had a good eye for it, even if he was a deep one. By the side of the road, a lanky, snaggle-toothed, whisk-ered, half-hunter-half-farmer, with patched breeches and old hunt-ing shirt, squatted in the dusty mullein and milkweed to listen to his neighbor's tale, then spat on the ground, shifted his quid, and said, "Yeah—yeah—high steppen and frounces and furbelows, but them bitches got the hot itch in the same place." Then spat again, and said: "Wish I had got me some of hit." Then fell silent, squatting there in the heat, feeling lonesome and deprived.

Wilkie Barron brought the tale back to Bowling Green, or at least to his dear friend Jeremiah Beaumont, for he was above passing foul gossip to the vulgar ear. To him it was not a matter for a leer and snicker. It was, rather, a tale of selfless passion, innocent trust, and dark betrayal. At least, that was the way he put it to Jeremiah Beau-mont. It was a tale that "stirred the tenderest sympathy, outraged justice, and provoked the blood in any heart not dead to honor." It was the tale of the beautiful orphan, defenseless and confiding, suf-fering from gaiety cut off and pride brought low, leaning for comfort on one who seemed strong and kind and the soul of rectitude. He saw it all, oh, how clearly he saw it, he said, as he paced the room in the Barron house, the night after his return, and poured out the narrative to Jeremiah Beaumont's ears, stopping now and then in his pacing to vehemently reprehend "the unnamed villain" or to lift his hand as though to "strike down a dastard."

Jeremiah was somewhat surprised by the little scene, by the passion and conviction which his friend brought to it, by the fire and rhetoric. Was this the Wilkie Barron who took his fun with Silly Sal, who loved the quick and salty joke, and who bounced his old mother on his knee like a trollop? Jeremiah knew that his friend had not "proved insen-sible to high sentiment and beauty" in the books and verses they had read together, but the real Wilkie had always seemed to be the young blade who finally leaped up from study or serious discourse and took his hat and left Jeremiah to brood alone. Even now Jeremiah was puzzled to know which was the real Wilkie, and to him the reason and manner of the telling was more than the tale itself. So he leaned and asked: "Did you love her?"

"Love her?" Wilkie Barron demanded, and stopped still in the middle of the floor. "Love her?" he repeated, as though to himself. Then turning to Jeremiah, he said: "I had not aspired so high. Who was I to aspire? The greatest in the country sought her, and what could I bring? So I stifled the first stirrings of passion and never opened my affection to her. But when I saw her last, two summers

55

ago, and took my leave, I had the intimation that she knew all. When I kissed her hand in farewell and then raised my head, she herself had tears in her eyes. I do not know that she returned my affection and was sad to see me go, knowing that I left her forever and for my reason, or that the tears came because she had pity for me. I did not stay to learn, for my mind was made up."

He stood there a moment, then added: "And now—and now . . ." Then he stopped and made a sudden gesture of loss and despair.

Jeremiah demanded: "Do you love her now?"

"I had put it away," Wilkie said.

"You do not love her now?"

"No," Wilkie said, slowly, "no."

"Well, why are you so moved and disordered?"

Wilkie stared at him, "staring in wonderment as though he had never seen me and as though he could not believe what he saw." So Jeremiah described the moment, and his own sense of embarrassment and emptiness in the face of the incredulous stare.

Then Wilkie burst out: "My God, but I knew her! Could any man know her and not feel the disgrace of this? Could any man with a spark of manhood not itch to do justice? Don't you understand? Don't you understand? She has no father and no brother, no one to defend her. She is beautiful and proud and trusting—why, you never saw such a glance of depth and warmth, or a smile so wise and tender— why, man, don't you understand? Why, I'd think any man not full of spleen and water for blood would want to do it. To throttle the villain. To have his heart. For listen to me, he is a villain. He is base and cunning and lying and . . ."

Hearing those words, Jeremiah felt that an indictment was being made against him, an indictment all too true, which he could not deny.

But Wilkie had stopped. He looked straight at Jeremiah and demanded: "Do you know his name? The name of the man?"

Before Jeremiah could reply, he leaned at him, and with a voice lowered in confidential irony, demanded: "Or has he confessed to you, has he boasted to you, and laughed at his cunning?"

"To me?"

"Yes, and is that why you feel no honorable rage? Because you are his friend? Because . . ."

Not quite comprehending, Jeremiah felt a great pain growing in him as though sensation were returning after a blow.

But Wilkie's words went on: ". . . because he pays you? Because he will make you? Because you are his creature?"

At that Jeremiah sprang from his chair and struck Wilkie in the face with his fist. Wilkie fell back a pace, recovered and crouched, with his right hand dropping into his shirt front, where he wore his knife. So Jeremiah made to defend himself and seized a chair. But the hand came from beneath the frill empty, and Wilkie straightened up and licked his puffed lip, and smiled. Jeremiah could not well understand what he meant, unless a duel later, for what he had done could not well be forgiven. So he held the chair and waited.

What came was this: Wilkie stepped to him, thrust out his hand, and said: "Ah, that is my friend. I knew he had blood in him and not spleen and water."

Still not quite understanding, Jeremiah took the hand.

"Forgive me," Wilkie said. "I had not meant to tell you his name. You would have heard it later, but I did not want you to hear it from me. I know how you feel him great and good, and fancy yourself a son to him. I would not have brought you the pain. But—but when I saw you there not sharing my indignation, I spoke before I thought, and in malice. Forgive me."

Jeremiah stood holding the friend's hand, unable to find any words.

"Will you forgive me?" Wilkie asked, and smiled like the frank and honorable friend.

So Jeremiah said, yes, he forgave fully, and asked forgiveness for his blow. He was filled with his own unworthiness in the face of his friend's manhood and generosity. And growing in him was the pain to learn that Colonel Fort, who had been like a father to him, was not the man he, Jeremiah Beaumont, had believed. Colonel Fort had betrayed him as truly as he had betrayed Rachel Jordan. Was he always doomed to betrayal?

That night he lay in his bed and envied Wilkie Barron, who had kissed Rachel Jordan's hand and had seen tears in her eyes, and who, though he had not had her love, could at least have the clean and honorable rage. That was something. That was something, at least. He thought how little he had in the world. His labor at the law was suddenly a dreary and childish routine. How had he ever thought that the law answered the deep cry of the heart? And his glowing prospects, what were they? A few dollars, a few acres, the envious servility of men. And if he should realize those prospects, his success would have been poisoned at the root. For he would owe all to Fort. To Fort, the villain. Ah, where was the greatness of life? Was it only a dream? Could a man not come to some moment when, all dross and meanness of life consumed, he could live in the pure idea? If only for a moment?

He went to sleep thinking how Wilkie Barron had leaned to kiss Rachel Jordan's hand and had looked up to find her eyes bright with tears for him. Then, somehow, it was he, he, Jeremiah Beaumont, who was kissing the hand. He felt the softness of the flesh beneath his lips

57

and breathed the clean perfume. He looked up and saw that the tears were for him.

That was the way Jeremiah Beaumont heard the story of Rachel Jordan, and that was the story he heard. We cannot be entirely sure of the story he did not hear, for the diary of Rachel Jordan is silent, and Jeremiah's account of what she was to tell him later of that period is relatively meager. Furthermore, what Jeremiah Beaumont believed, and what Rachel Jordan had come to believe may be distorted by the intervening events. The experience had been exposed to the light of time and the corrosive influence of a change in the chemistry of Rachel Jordan's own being. Undoubtedly some of the facts she gave Jeremiah Beaumont are true, but she never spoke to him of the deeper *why*. Perhaps she did not know it herself. Perhaps the explanation she came to accept was merely the one necessary for Jeremiah Beaumont's drama. So we have to go back to what we know earlier and try to discover the projection of the secret line of meaning.

We know this much. In the spring of 1821, Rachel Jordan was delivered of a premature and stillborn male child. She was attended by a midwife named Sukie Marlowe, whose affidavit exists, and there are other witnesses who attest to having seen the little grave in the Jordan burying ground with a stone bearing the inscription:

MY SON
Born dead to my sorrow
But to his own happiness
In that he never saw the world.
May 7, 1821

We know, therefore, that in some time in the early fall of 1820 Rachel Jordan took a lover, and that the lover was certainly Colonel Fort. He had come in all the prestige of his greatness, on an errand of chivalrous kindness, in the full strength of his ripe manhood. He came at the time of her despair, when ruin and emptiness seemed to be her final portion, and offered the counterpoise of his certainty and mastery of the world. With nothing, the pauper boy of a stockade, he had seized and molded the world, while she, with everything, had let the world slip through her fingers like water. He had some secret which the very touch of his hand might communicate, some power which might heal her itch and scabs as the touch of the king's hand heals the king's evil.

But with all his force and certainty, he did not come in brashness, but with "reserve and dignity" to "presume upon nothing." And there was, despite his stamp of success, the mysterious sadness of his face. One so sad despite success would know how to sympathize with sadness. You could tell him no secret he would not listen to gravely and understand. You might even lighten his sadness, and do for him what all the gifts of the world had not done. So at some time she took between her hands that heavy, shaggy head and gazed into that grooved, swarthy face and into the dark eyes which wore the expression of a melancholy, questioning animal.

We can be certain that the intimacy between Rachel and Colonel Fort began after the last entry in the diary. Otherwise, some hint would probably have been in the diary, some change of temper, some flash of self-analysis. And besides, the last entry and the sudden breaking off seem to set the stage for a new act. She had discovered Timothy Jordan, her father, and had lost him in the same moment, the man who might have taken her hand and walked in the rose garden or have sat by the fire and read to her from a pretty book.

She had never wanted that before, but on the windless afternoon with its brilliant haze, standing by the grave, she had wanted that more than anything else in the world and the fact that she had never had it seemed her greatest loss. Her father was born for her, and died, in that same moment, and his death left her alone to make her world. So the world she would make, even in her ruin, would be an image of the world she had never had, a little world outside of time, for its natural time was gone, a little garden, breathless with belated roses overblown in the hot, hazy sunshine, lost in the wideness of the violent, throbbing land.

If we must speculate on the love for the father never known, we must speculate also on the hate for the mother too well known. The mother had scorned Colonel Fort, had scarcely been civil to him, and had spoken of him with sneers. The mother's contempt had led to the daughter's reception of him on his second visit with "every mark of deference and consideration beyond the dictates of mere civility." In a kind of shame she made up for the mother's grossness of spirit, and at the same time used her own civility as a weapon against the old woman. By the same token, when Rachel Jordan took into her own flesh the flesh of Cassius Fort, the flesh which Maria Hopeby would have spat on, she would work the greatest revenge on the old woman. For every satisfaction she took in the blunt bulk and grind of his weight she could take a more abiding and deeper satisfaction, because more secret, as though for every pound of that crushing weight which she assumed in pleasure she heaped that much in pain upon the old woman's draggled and sick flesh.

The secret satisfaction could not remain secret forever. At some time in the winter, the fact of Rachel Jordan's pregnancy would have become obvious. Perhaps she never told her mother. Perhaps she merely watched with relish the suspicion growing day by day in her mother's face as the foetus grew in her body. We know, at least that she turned to her mother for nothing. Not only that, she had a last pleasure in defying the old woman. The old woman, gathering her last courage and strength in the face of the impending disgrace, urged Rachel to take the herb tea and calomel to bring it off, to ride horseback (that was the classic treatment), to do anything, anything, to save the shame.

But Rachel followed her own course. She did not think of the future, for long back she had stepped out of time into that belated garden. She considered herself out of the world and held no thought for the world's opinion. She could boast that she was strong enough for that, and she would not grieve for the child, for she would make it as strong as herself. And she was to say later: "Why should my child have had a father, since I had never had one?" So she took her own grim joy in the situation. But the event came to surprise her, and Sukie Marlowe was summoned in haste, in the middle of the night, by the light of a pine flare, across the fields.

We do not know in what way and on what note, she and Colonel Fort parted. But we do know that in the late spring of 1821 Colonel Fort was in Washington and Philadelphia, not in Congress but on private business having to do with lands in Missouri. Perhaps he was thinking of a removal west, despairing that the good times would ever come back to Kentucky. Perhaps he was merely planning a speculation. Or perhaps he was contemplating a flight from the personal difficulties in which he was involved. He must have known that there would be a storm of scandal. There was nothing he could do for Rachel Jordan, for he was married.

In any case, he did not see Rachel Jordan during the last nine weeks of her pregnancy. But, according to Jeremiah's report, Colonel Fort had told Rachel that he would take all responsibility for the child and would settle land upon it. She refused the offer, saying that "she asked nothing from him and would take nothing." Jeremiah was to interpret the words as springing from anger and repudiation, but he heard them long after the event. It may be that they were originally spoken in pride in her own bitter strength, and that later the true motive was forgotten or absorbed into a new temper. This seems probable, for on all evidence she seems to have come to her confinement in confidence and with a kind of joy. The old Negro woman who waited on her and who was obviously attached to her was to tell Jeremiah that she "never seen no woman come to it so stout and gleeful like Missie and Missie tetch herself and say it was hers, it was all hers, and nobody could take it away."

But somebody did take it away. They took it, Sukie Marlowe and the old Negro woman Josie, and wrapped it with a section cut from

60

a fine linen sheet from Virginia, put it into a box made by two Negro men in the farm shop, and buried it. There was no funeral. No preacher was called. It would have been huddled underground like garbage, if Old Jacob, the colored man who had a pair of specs without glass and a Bible he could read in a little and who preached to the hands on Sunday, had not gone with Sukie and Josie and done what he could. "Jacob wore a old black coat Mister Jordan done give him," Sukie Marlowe put in her statement, "and tended he was reading from the Book, but you could tell he wasn, and I wud not be surprized it was helt topsidetuther. Then he sprinkel some dust in the grave and say a prayer like he was a true preacher, it was good praying for a nigger and I wiped my eyes for it, and we all come on back to the big house. Old Josie give me my pay, and I come on home. It was a hot day for sartin and I like to perish coming crost the field."

The day after Jeremiah Beaumont had struck his friend Wilkie Barron and was forgiven the blow, he rose at the usual hour and went to the law office of Colonel Fort. Colonel Fort was still in the East and nobody knew exactly when he would come back, so Jeremiah did not have to worry about facing him. But in the office that morning, he felt as though he had stumbled into a place where he did not belong, as though his first meeting with Colonel Fort, Colonel Fort's kindness, and all the events leading to his own presence here this morning had never come to pass.

That night he returned as late as possible to the Barron house and slipped upstairs without seeing the family. Next morning he went back to the office, into the same emptiness. In the evening he took his supper with the family, for there was nothing else to do, but he went to bed early without conversation or work.

So he entered this new period of his life, a period which reminded him of the dullness and despair of the months before Colonel Fort had first come to him, that time when he had labored without hope. But it was different now. He had had hope and had lost it. He withdrew more and more from the life of the family around him. He never went out any more, except after dark, to escape from the house.

"What the hell is the matter with you?" Wilkie wanted to know. "You're as porely as a kitten with worms."

"Nothing," Jeremiah replied, "nothing's wrong with me."

Nothing was wrong with him which he could properly explain, even to himself. Nothing was wrong except that the world was the way it was.

"Nothing, hell," Wilkie said. "You tear out every night. Nothing, hell. You got some woman you lay with in somebody's barn."

And Jeremiah almost struck him, across the smile.

61

So things went on that way, and Jeremiah felt that they would go on this way forever.

But they did not, for one afternoon Mr. Talbot casually told him that Colonel Fort would be back soon.

He went very early next morning to the office. He gathered his few belongings there together, the books he had bought, a few personal papers, and a homespun jacket he worked in when alone to save his good coat. He left the office and stood in the street.

The street was just beginning to wake to its life, like a buxom young wife, fresh-faced but blowsy with sleep, coming into her kitchen to bang and clatter her pans and yawn against the bright sun. Down the street Mr. Harrod, in his eternal bottle-green coat with brass buttons, was climbing the broad steps of his store in confidence and majesty, "probably belching from breakfast, as was his custom." A respectable woman, wearing calico and a black bonnet, moved down the street with a basket on her arm, leading a child. An old Negro man, draped in rags and with feet bound in sacking, marched beside an ox-cart loaded with stone, muttering and grunting to himself "like a hog at the approach of a shower of rain," and now and then prodded the near ox with a peeled staff he carried. The ungreased high wheels of the cart creaked relentlessly "with the business of the world," and, as the oxen drew nearer, a hairy dog that had been luxuriating in the dust of the street rose and stretched like a lion and yawned in the face of the "sad monsters" and moved to the shade without deigning to bark. Somewhere far away a belated breakfast bell chinked and tinkled. The brilliant light poured down over it all, and over Jeremiah Beaumont, who held the valise in his hand and felt that he did not belong there, or in any sunlit "natural" street. He felt a melancholy at the fact, but at the same time a "freedom and sweetness."

Back at the Barron house, he slipped upstairs and lay on his bed, staring at the ceiling. He lay there and let the future take shape within him. Not that he had a plan. He did not try to plan. He felt that the future was beyond plan, it already existed, he would discover it step by step as he moved toward some flame, some point of light, beyond the murk and mist of things. He need not plan, he need only be himself. Be himself, and not be snared by the world. He had almost been snared, snared by Fort's tawdry glitter, corrupted by his promise of easy greatness, tempted to connive with the world.

He would not connive. At least, not that. He rose from the bed, seized paper and quill, and wrote. He wrote to Fort, saying that he would no longer connive with him in baseness, that he wished nothing Fort could give, that he spat upon false promises, that he would turn from the face of the betrayer, and seek truth in the face of the betrayed. "Truth in the face of the betrayed": he wrote the words down as they sprang into his mind, and knew that we must always turn from the victor to the victim, and all at once his breath stopped.

For now he knew. The mist had shifted for an instant, and he saw the next step. He saw it clear. He had only needed to trust the deep truth of himself. How simple life was if you heeded its most inward voice!

Fort replied to his letter. We do not have the reply, only Jeremiah's paraphrase. "He wrote to say that he was as deeply grieved by my communication as by my departure, that if he had ever wronged me he humbly sought pardon, that he had regarded me with paternal affection, having no son by blood, that he would hope to be able to explain whatever troubled my mind and would attend upon me at my leisure to do so, that he prayed earnestly for my indulgence." But Jeremiah flung the letter aside. He felt that every fair word contaminated him, poisoned the very air.

When Fort's reply reached him, Jeremiah was already in Saul County, at the home of Wilkie's uncle, old Thomas Bartlett Barron. Pleading ill health and the need for retirement, Jeremiah had asked for an introduction from Wilkie. Old Barron had taken him in and would hear no talk of payment.

The Jordan place was in the same county, only a few miles away.

Jeremiah's first sight of the Jordan place was a disappointment. He had scarcely been aware of any precise expectation, until the disappointment struck him. He had assumed without thinking that the place Rachel Jordan inhabited would be somehow worthy of her and would glow with a special beauty and distinction, as "the horn of a lantern glows from the flame within."

As he rode now up the red-clay lane, flanked on one side by a corn field and on the other by a patch of woodland, he saw nothing but a brick house, big for a farmhouse but no mansion, set among good trees on a lawn now streaked unseasonably brown with a drouth of June. The house was only half the size of Runnymede, two-story with a chimney at the end of each of the high gables, and a small portico of one story, painted white, in the middle, facing the lane. He could tell that there was a sort of ell of one story running back. It was not even as fine a house as Colonel Mead's back in Glasgow County, or as half a dozen houses Jeremiah had frequented around Bowling Green. Its pretension consisted in the limestone wall across the front of the yard with the big gateposts, a circular drive of gravel, now somewhat overgrown with grass and weeds to mark the absence of visitors, and a flower garden to one side with hedges and shrubs.

Jeremiah rode up the drive, dismounted, and dropped his reins over the iron hitching post by the carriage block. The big door, under the fanlight, was closed. He hesitated before it. He was struck, he says, by the great quiet, as though no living creature was within or without, not even a dog, a cat, a fowl, a servant or a field hand. There was not even a bird note, or a stir among the leaves. He looked back over the distance, and was struck by the thought that that field of corn would never be harvested and those flowers in the garden would never be plucked. Everybody had gone away, and if Rachel Jordan remained, she lay in the innermost dark of the house, with eyes closed and breast scarcely moving with breath, bewitched and abandoned under a terrible enchantment. He turned back to the door, but did not see how he could lift his hand to the knocker.

Then, behind him, his horse snorted and struck the gravel twice with a hoof. So Jeremiah broke out of his fancy, and lifted his hand to the door.

He waited, but heard no sound within. Then the door opened, and an old Negro woman, tidy and clean, asked him his business. He told his name, said that he was a student of letters and the law now resident in the neighborhood, and that he was an intimate of a friend of Miss Jordan, and solicited the honor of paying his respects. He was invited into the hall, but not beyond, so he stood there, waiting, while the servant went above. The hall, he observed, was wider than he had anticipated from the exterior of the house and the stair curved gracefully "toward the upper region where my interest lay."

The woman returned to say that Miss Rachel thanked him kindly for his attention but was indisposed and did not receive anyone. If, however, he wished to avail himself of her library it was at his pleasure. He told the woman that he would like to take a book, and followed her into a small room back of the parlor where there was a "case of books." He quickly selected a volume, scarcely bothering about the title, thanked the servant, and left. He was not discouraged. He had not expected to be received upon his first visit.

He waited two days before going back. This time he went armed with a letter, that his communication might be more direct. He was received as before by the servant, who took the letter above while he waited impatiently in the hall.

The letter said:

Dear Miss Jordan:
     I beg your forgiveness for the presumption of this communication, and throw myself upon your mercy and that goodness of heart which has been advertised to me. If I am in fault with this, I must take the reprehension. But I cannot do otherwise than write to solicit again the honor of your acquaintance. If your health does not now permit you to accept society, let me assure you that my patience is as great

as my certainty that I could expect no higher reward than your acquaintance, and that I wait the hour when your generosity shall incline to my poor deserts.

As for my reasons, I have none to plead that could count with you the worth of a farthing or the weight of a feather. In my humility, however, I can say that my reasons are great to me, and that each man must live by the truth within him. Some day it is my hope to unfold to you what truth I have. Until that happy moment, and thenceforward to all time,

I am yours to command to anything worthy of honor, as you could command only to honor,

Y'r ob'd't ser't,
Jeremiah Beaumont

P.S. I would thank you for the book.

He had to wait a long time, while the woman, somewhere in the dusky world of repudiation upstairs, pondered the letter coming to her mysteriously from the wide, bright, hot world outside. But finally the servant returned, bringing the reply:

Dear Mr. Beaumont:

I cannot be insensible to the honor you do me with your solicitations. Even if it were possible for me to receive you (as it is not and cannot be), vanity should prompt me to maintain that good opinion you hold of me by not subjecting it to the test of my poor presence. In all kindness to myself and to yourself, I beg you to desist from your attempt, and believe me,

Your unknown friend,
R. Jordan

P.S. You have the full use of my library as long as you reside in this vicinity. But I suggest that you take several books so that you may be spared the labor of returning so soon.

She had seen through his little trick of taking only one book. He knew that immediately, and smiled "sarcastically" to himself that he had been so readily detected. He had one consolation: she had not forbidden him the house. So he returned the book to the library, and got three others. It took him five days to read them, though he read them conscientiously for fear that she might call on him to speak to her about them. Then he waited two days more before carrying them back. This time he sent her no message. He simply got two books, and left.

His studies may have prospered but his project did not. He came and went with the books, choosing them almost at random, reading them under his driving compulsion, sitting into the night with them,

65

doing his service to the woman he did not know and the idea he had not formulated. Then despair struck him.

It struck him one afternoon in the Jordan library. As he stood before the bookcase, reading the titles, he suddenly asked himself what would he have if he read all those books, all those and all the books in the world. He thought of himself locked in the room, in this room, surrounded, walled in, crushed by thousands of books, reading them one after another with "hysterical haste and voracity," fighting through the books and through time to reach some end he would never reach. There would be too many books, and too little time. While all the while, in the room above, where he could never come, lay what he sought, the face, the voice, the word the voice might speak.

Then, quite coldly, he asked himself what word could that voice, or any other voice, speak? What lay upstairs? Might he labor seven years—or seven times seven times seven—and find that he had earned in the end not Rachel, the fair daughter, but Leah? Nothing but Leah, nothing but another woman like all the rest that you need not turn your head to see and who would have nothing to tell him?

"That was my despair, and all my life seemed wasted. So I said out loud, 'I am Jacob, and I am cursed like Jacob, and cheated, and I labor but to be abused in the end.' That fact that her name was Rachel seemed to confirm my fear, and I was Jacob who would sleep with his head on the stone and wrestle with an angel for nought."

At that moment as he looked with "hate and repugnance upon all the lying books" before him, his glance fell on a book that looked familiar and caught him. He reached out and took it. It was a small book, with a blue cover, lined in gold stamping, and with a sudden agitation he read the title, *Poems* by Lord Byron. It was the same book Colonel Fort had loaned him at their first meeting. The same copy of the same book. He was sure of it. He was absolutely sure of it.

He opened the book. The fly-leaf had been torn out, and torn so violently that the title page and the binding were loosened. He had the great desire to know what had been written on that page. That might have told him what he needed to know. Then, all at once, he decided that that did not matter. What did matter was the book in his hand. Not the book itself, but the fact that it was the book given him long back by Colonel Fort in Dr. Burnham's parlor, and later given to Rachel Jordan.

His breath almost stopped with excitement. The despair was gone. For the book came as a sign, the indication of some pattern and logic in things. "I thought how in older days men had opened the pages of the poet Virgil to put down by chance a finger on a line of his verses to find there the wisdom and prophecy they sought in their need. In

66

my need and despair my hand had fallen upon the book that Colonel
Fort had given me and had given Rachel Jordan, and that fact said
that I might wait in serene hope, for our fate was bound together. It
was my *sortes Virgiliana,* from the inwardness of things."

So he continued his life as before, but now in serene hope.

Jeremiah's hope was justified. One late afternoon in July as he rode
between the stone gateposts, he saw in the summer-house or rose
arbor in the garden a glint of white and knew it was a woman's dress
and that the woman was Rachel Jordan. He dismounted immediately,
not even bothering to hitch the horse, and walked across the dry lawn
toward the garden. He had passed into the garden and had nearly
reached the arbor before the woman lifted her head from her book
and saw him. She rose quickly as though to leave, but he blocked the
path. So she stood there, book in hand, in a white dress "of some loose
and filmy stuff, cut low for summer and with the bodice short and
bound close to the small scope of her body not far below the bosom,
from which point the fullness of the skirt began." He noticed the
agitation of her bosom as he approached.

He stopped at the entrance of the arbor and looked searchingly at
her, waiting for some sign. He saw no sign, but saw a young woman
of medium height "with a small and supple waist rising from the richness of her hips, and with a bosom rounded high to beauty. She stood
with quietness and grace, looking directly at me, as I at her. Her face
was not small, but its flesh was moulded firmly with no trace of fat-
ness. Her hair was tawny to the color of leaves of the red oak in
autumn, with a fine luster, and coiled in unusual abundance so that it
seemed ready to break its bonds by its own weight and fall about her
shoulders and breast, or lower yet. Her natural flesh, as I could see
from the throat and exposed part of the bosom, was of great whiteness, but the cheeks gave a glow of color, brighter then for the embarrassment of the meeting, and where the sun had touched were a few
freckles like those of a pear ready to pluck. On the left cheek, on the
cheek bone, was a spot like a freckle for color, the size of a man's
thumb nail or a little smaller, no blemish but a mark toward which
any man might bend his lips, as though it bespoke on that cheek
nearer the heart the inward heat and ripeness of her blood. As she
looked at me, I observed that her eyes were large and of a brownish-
gold color, very deep and bright."

He stood there in the afternoon quiet, waiting under her gaze. Then
he said: "I am Jeremiah Beaumont."

"Yes," she said slowly, still looking at him, "you are Jeremiah Beaumont." Then, after a pause, she added: "And Mr. Beaumont, it was
not honest of you to surprise me thus."

"It *was* honest," he retorted impetuously.

"No, not honest, Mr. Beaumont."

"It was honest to what I am," he said, "and what other honesty can a man have, and I would not come to you except in honesty."

"You play upon words, Mr. Beaumont," she said sternly.

"I would not play upon honesty," he replied, "for that is all I have."

"You know my desires, Mr. Beaumont, how I would have avoided you and kept my privacy. Yet you came on me unawares. Now if you will kindly step aside I shall bid you good-bye, and from henceforth."

At that point Jeremiah Beaumont felt desperation. She would leave the rose arbor where the yellow petals flaked the bricks underfoot, go out of the garden, across the browning grass, and into the house, and he would never see her again, and everything would have been for nothing. He felt the impulse to seize her arms, and hold her, "not in love, for I felt no love, but to make her hear me." He conquered the impulse, but he did not move from the entrance of the arbor.

"Listen to me," he said. "I speak in humility and respect, but I have to speak. I came to this section because you were here and with only the thought that I might see you. I cannot explain to you or to myself why this is true, but it is the truth. I wish nothing from you except the honor of your society. If I were worthy I would offer you my services, but I cannot maintain such ambition. I have waited . . ."

"Mr. Beaumont . . ." she began in anger.

But he continued: "I have waited these weeks because I was certain that in the end I would see you."

"Well, you see me now," she said more in bitterness than anger, "and you see a most miserable woman."

"I see a woman who may command me anything and from whom I ask nothing."

"I have nothing to command you, for I wish nothing of the world. I have put it aside and I have no place for it as it has no place for me. Now if you will return to whatever place is your proper one and permit me . . ."

"This is my place," he said, and stood his ground in the arbor.

"Will you go!" she said impatiently, and made an abrupt gesture of dismissal.

"Yes," he said, "I will go. But I ask a favor for courtesy before I go." "What is it?"

He leaned and took from her hand the book she had been reading, inserting his finger between the pages where she marked her place. "I don't know what this book is," he said, "but will you read me the page you were reading when I came here? Then I will go."

She hesitated, then said, "No."

"May I read it to you, then? Whatever it is?"

She made no answer.

"May I read it, if you will not?"

"Oh, read it," she said, in irritation.

He waited, holding the book.

"Read it, and be done," she said.

"When you are seated," he said. "It will take no longer if you sit down."

She took her seat on the rustic bench of the arbor, sitting erect, with the white drapery of the skirt falling over the bench and the bricks at her feet, and with her hands folded on the lap. (He noticed that the hands, though not larger than one might expect, were "a little squarish and looked strong," and that on the skin of the arms were a few freckles and a light down of golden hair where the sunlight fell through to strike them.)

He sat on the bench, not near her, and opened the book. It was a copy of Plato. "I see you read philosophy," he said.

"I read philosophy," she replied, "to forget what the world is like."

"Philosophy is to tell us the truth of the world."

"I know what the truth of the world is," she said, again with bitterness, "and now if you do not read I will go."

So Jeremiah began to read. What he read was new to him, for, as he records, he had earlier read only the *Republic* of Plato. Now he read a passage from the *Symposium,* that one following the account given Socrates by the wise woman Diotima of how the soul may progress upward by love. "I began to read," he says, "in the middle of a sentence at the top of the left-hand page, and I read of love, and how a man of high soul may use the beauties of earth as a ladder by which he mounts for the sake of higher beauties, resting at last in the single Idea of the absolute Beauty in that life which above all others a man should live to be fully man, the contemplation of the Beauty Absolute."

Suddenly, she stopped him. "Stop," she commanded, "stop. You have read past the place where I was."

"May I read to the end of the passage?"

"No," she said. "Give me the book."

"I will keep my promise, and read no more," he said. "But may I take the book?"

"I was reading the book," she said with some asperity.

He hesitated a moment, studying her. She turned her face away from him, and stared across the garden to the corn fields. "You were reading it," he said quietly, "but I know that you would not deprive me of knowing the end of the passage."

He records that she caught the doubleness of his meaning because her cheek flushed. But she said nothing. So he said: "I must know what the wise man Socrates says will be the end."

"Oh, take the book," she said, not turning to him. "Only go."

He rose. "I'll go," he said, "but I shall bring back the book. After I have read what Socrates says. I hope then to have the privilege of giving it into your hands."

"It is not probable, Mr. Beaumont."

"But is it possible?"

She did not reply, still staring across the fields.

He leaned quickly, took her hand and leaned to kiss it "after the manner of courtesy." When he lifted his eyes from the kiss, he did not meet hers, for her face was still turned away. So without another word, he left the arbor, walked out of the garden, mounted his horse, and rode away.

So he met her at last, and left her sitting there on the rustic bench, a young woman with high bosom showing the great whiteness of her flesh, a slim waist rising from the fine hips, strong freckled hands folded on the flowing white folds of the dress, the head surmounted by the heavy coils of auburn hair, and the brown spot on the flushed cheek. So we see her like an allegorical figure of autumn painted in a sentimental school, sitting under the disintegrating yellow roses of the arbor with the petals scattered at her feet, and with her eyes fixed across the corn fields.

Jeremiah Beaumont tells us that he rode away without once looking back.

III

IN THE SAME ARBOR, ALMOST A MONTH
later, in August, Jeremiah Beaumont asked Rachel Jordan to marry
him.

Sitting with her in the arbor under the ruined roses, in the dead
center of the afternoon, in the great panting silence of the hot land,
without any preparation in words or any calculation or any thought,
he took her hands in his. "I did not immediately speak, for I had not
found my language, but stared into her face as though to read there
the answer to the question not yet put.

"But of a sudden she leaped up, and if I had not held her hands in
a strong grip she had pulled from me.

" 'Let me go!' she commanded, but I who would have heeded any
other command from her lips would not heed that one, but still keeping my place on the bench, gripped her hands the more strongly.

" 'Let me go!' she repeated with a certain wildness, and threw her
weight away from me to jerk free with no thought for grace or genteel
deportment. But in her uncalculated motion for its very awkwardness
there was a kind of wild grace, and in that instant the weight of her
hair slipped its bonds and some fell loose over the neck and the left
cheek.

" 'Let me go!' she said, and tossed her head, and with a sudden

71

stoppage of the heart I saw before my eyes the young female bound to the stake for the flames in the picture in the old book of the Martyrs and how she tossed her head for the first agony of fire, and how I had not known whether my joy was because I would leap in and pluck her free or because I had thrown the first flaming faggot and waited for her to cry out with the pain.

"So I gripped her hard and held on and knew that a great change had come in the instant. In that instant I loved her in a new way. Or to speak truth, before that time I had not thought of love with her as the hotness of passion but as the fulfillment of a necessity within me beyond debate or pleasure. But now the fierceness of passion blotted out that patience in necessity and made me desperate for the moment.

"As she pulled against me, I burst out, 'I love you. I must tell you I love you.'

"At that she drew back so strong that I thought she would break free. Then all at once her arms were limp and her hands limp in my grasp, and her shoulders sagged down. But it was not the limpness of one who surrenders to her lover. It was the limpness and attitude of one who after effort surrenders to tiredness as to a great weight on the shoulders and can scarcely stand. 'Love,' she said, as a kind of late echo to my word, but she said it as though the word was in a language unfamiliar to her and had no meaning beyond the empty sound.

" 'Yes, love,' I repeated, as though by the heat of my own utterance I might teach her the fullness of the word.

" 'Love,' she said again, in a voice that had learned nothing from my own.

"I made a motion as though to take her in my arms, but the look on her face stopped me. I knew she would not resist, but I also knew that I would hold nothing but the empty weight of her flesh. She recognized the moment, and drew her hands from mine.

" 'When I agreed to accept your society,' she said slowly and in a dull voice, 'it was with the understanding that you would not speak on subjects of a close and personal order. And now you have broken your pact, Mr. Beaumont.'

" 'I made no pact but one,' I replied. 'I said that I would undertake to behave honorably.'

" 'Is it honorable to do what you have done, Mr. Beaumont?'

" 'By God, and in reverence,' I retorted, 'it was honorable to say what I have said, and now I honorably ask you if you will give me the happiness of having you as my wife in marriage? And marriage,' I added, 'is an honorable estate.'

" 'It is an honorable estate as the world goes,' she said bitterly, and I knew she took some secret reference from my words to her condition of dishonor, which I had not meant (or had I unwittingly meant it, so curious is the mind?). Then she added: 'But I have withdrawn from the world.'

" 'We will make what world we will,' I said with enthusiasm, and tried to take her hands again.

"But she avoided me and I did not persist. Then she said, 'If there is an impediment to intimate discourse between us, there is the greater impediment for me to accept your protestations and your kind offer, however sincere.'

" 'They are sincere. I swear it!'

" 'The impediment remains,' she said.

" 'There can be no impediment to what I have said in sincereness. Unless it be the impediment of your own heart.'

" 'If there is an impediment, what does my heart matter?'

" 'Look into your heart,' I urged her, and leaned earnestly at her and stared into her face.

" 'My heart,' she began, and paused, '. . . it is—it is as dry as that leaf.' And she pointed at a dead leaf on the pavement at our feet.

"I stooped and picked up the leaf and turned it slowly in my fingers, examining it. 'No,' I said at last, as though I had made a discovery from my examination, 'this is not your heart, though it came from your heart, for your heart is a great tree and with the year will put forth a thousand fresh leaves.' Then looking up from the leaf to her, I added: 'And I will stand in their shade from the heat of the day.'

" 'Oh, stop it,' she said, in the tone of a woman who rebukes a vexing child.

" 'I only spoke the truth.'

" 'Mr. Beaumont,' she said, 'you are a very foolish and fanciful young man, who reads too many books and knows nothing of the world.'

" 'I am old enough to know one thing.'

" 'I am older than you, Mr. Beaumont, in years, and a thousand years older in my suffering, and I tell you that you are foolish.'

" 'Not as foolish as you, begging your pardon.'

" 'So you are rude as well as foolish,' she said, and bit her lip.

" 'I am rude enough to speak the truth, and tell you that there can be no impediment between us except in your heart.'

" 'I have told you once, there is an impediment, and I will not discuss it with you.'

"I took a step toward her, standing close to her and looking down into her face. 'What is it?' I demanded.

"She flushed, but she did not retreat from me, and looked steadily at me. Then she said: 'It is not your affair, Mr. Beaumont.'

" 'What is it?'

73

" 'It is not your affair.'

" 'It is my affair,' I said, 'and it is my only affair.'

"I thought she was about to speak, then I saw that her lips were quivering. Suddenly, she sat down on the bench, with the motion of one whose strength has given way. Then I saw that tears were gathering in her eyes. She made no sound of weeping, and she did not avert her head from me. As I looked, the tears spilled over and ran down her cheeks. She made no effort to wipe them away, but let her hands lie by her sides on the bench on the dark cloth of the dress she wore. I watched how the tears moved down her cheeks, and was astonished at my own lack of compassion in that moment, as though I were a physician and had to observe oddly the symptoms of the patient the better to effect a cure. Then I noticed anew the freckles on her cheeks and for the first time the tiny ones across the bridge of her nose and how the tears moved innocently down her cheeks among them. And despite the heaviness of her hair and the fullness of her bosom, I saw then her face was like the face of a child suffering a grief it cannot understand.

"She looked directly at me, as though she were not weeping, or as though she did not know the tears were there, and said: 'Mr. Beaumont, I accepted your society because I was weak enough in my loneliness to expect some comfort from it. I see that I was mistaken. You have come here to torture me.'

" 'No,' I said, 'not for that.'

" 'For what, then—for what?'

" 'Because . . .' and I stopped, and in that instant I was not sure what answer I could give her or give myself, for I suddenly knew that the passion and the pity had gone from me. 'Because . . .' I said again. Then the answer was clear to me. It was the old answer that in the moment of passion and then in the moment of pity I had almost forgotten and thought lost. But it came back, and I knew it was the answer that would always lie beneath all other answers I should ever give to that question. So I said firmly, 'It is because I must,' and felt a relief and freedom in the answer. And I thought clear as a bell, *ah, I know now that all our freedom is in the necessity within us.* So I repeated: 'It is because I must.'

" 'Oh, must you torture me!' she exclaimed.

" 'I must know what is the impediment.'

" 'Mr. Beaumont . . .' she began, and I saw the anger rising in her face.

"So I lifted my hand quickly, and said: 'Stop. Sooner or later I will know the impediment. You shall tell me. And let me tell you this. There is no impediment I cannot remove.'

" 'Mr. Beaumont . . .' she said in anger.

74

"But I broke in again: 'Unless it is that of your heart.' Then without any delay, even of courtesy, or even another glance at her, I turned from the arbor and quickly left the garden and mounted my horse and gave him the spur."

Then in his narrative he says that that very afternoon in the arbor he had realized one fact. It had come on him like a flash. It had come to him as he looked down into her tear-wet eyes and knew that he felt no compassion. He knew that she must herself tell him the impediment. "I knew her story from the public tongue. But I knew in that moment that I must hear it from her." With that knowledge, seeing the tears among the freckles, he could then feel compassion in the knowledge that he had to torture her to make her say it. "For I knew that once she had named it to me with her own tongue, all would come to pass that had to come to pass, whatever it might be, as the clock hands move when the weight is wound up and released."

When Jeremiah got back late that afternoon to the house of Bartlett Barron, he found Wilkie Barron and another man named Percival Skrogg. They had ridden up from Bowling Green that very day to the house of Wilkie's uncle, and now took their ease on his sagging veranda with a bottle on the floor between them. The bottle was for Wilkie. Percival Skrogg did not drink.

Jeremiah had never met Skrogg, and had not even known that he was a friend of Wilkie. But he knew something of him, that he was the editor of a newspaper at Frankfort, the *Freeman's Advocate,* and that Colonel Fort had once spoken highly of his talents. The *Advocate* had stood firm, the Colonel said, for replevin and the Relief Party and the rights of the poor man to life in the years when the rich man wanted his hard money and would take the house and the land, the cow and the calf, if he did not get it. "He is a man of force," the Colonel had said, "and he fears nothing and will not swerve in the winds of opinions."

The man Jeremiah saw on the veranda looked as though he might swerve in a breeze not strong enough to knock down a single hickory nut in nut-time or flap a pair of dry drawers on the clothes line. He was moderately tall but to his pipestem bones "not enough flesh clung to make a bowl of broth for a man sick with lockjaw," and his brown jacket hung as loose as a dishrag on a nail. His face was narrow and bony, with a sharp-pinched nose as thin as white paper against sunlight. He had very thin lips that barely drew together over a fine set of very clean teeth to give the impression that there was not enough flesh to cover the bone of the face, and when he smiled, "you had the strong impression that the shrinkage away from the teeth was for good and those lips could never be drawn back together for decent concealment." The skin of his face was slick and seemingly hairless, and a pasty-blue-white in color, like buttermilk spilled on a puncheon and trod underfoot. His hair was very black, not too abundant, and "slicked back like the hair of a backwoods dude with bear-grease for Sunday meeting," but Percival Skrogg was above such vanity and the oil was natural. At the slightest exertion, little beads of perspiration appeared at his temples at the edge of the hair. He coughed now and then, sometimes almost to distraction, and when he did so, the drops of moisture came on his temples and on his upper lip. At a bad fit, he would put a piece of sugar in his mouth and suck it.

When Jeremiah shook hands with him he thought how small and bony was the hand he held, and how the whole fellow wasn't much more formidable than the skeleton hung from a rafter in Dr. Burnham's study. Then he noticed the eyes and reconsidered the opinion. Percival Skrogg smiled his smile which was not a smile but a tantalizing exposure of the white skull under the inadequate flesh, and fixed you with eyes that were large and pale blue and very clear, like "ice on a clean pond when the sky is cold and bright." So what life there was in the bag of bones and dry rattle called Percival Skrogg lay in the eyes. But it was life without heat.

"Percy has come home to vote," Wilkie announced.

"Yes," Skrogg admitted.

"I thought you lived in Frankfort," Jeremiah said to Skrogg.

"I got my paper there," he said, "in the midst of the Ammonites. But I vote here."

"And he aims to vote," Wilkie said, "and if any Ammonites around here try to stop him, he is going to vote anyway." Then he laughed, and added, "And I aim to help him." Wilkie took a pistol from his pocket, a pretty little object with silver on it, the weapon of a dandy, and turned it in his hand for admiration.

"If this county is like my county," Jeremiah said, "that thing wouldn't scare any real rouser from up the creek."

Wilkie laughed again. "I scared somebody with it last election down in Bowling Green. A big fellow that tried to stop me from going up to write in my vote."

Jeremiah still looked skeptically at it.

"Well," Wilkie said, and dropped the pistol back into his pocket and reached into his shirt front, "I've always got Little Alfonse." He drew out a Spanish knife with an unusually long blade, toyed with it a moment, and then flicked it cleanly into the unpainted cedar post of the veranda. It stood quivering delicately in the wood.

"What is this?" Jeremiah demanded, "the battle of Waterloo?"

"It will be a friendly argument," Wilkie said gaily, "if anybody wants one."

Skrogg began to cough. He coughed steadily for a minute or so, then rose abruptly and entered the house. Jeremiah looked after him. "He sounds sick," he said.

"He may be sick," Wilkie replied, "but that or nothing else will stop him."

"Who will try to stop him?"

"You been here nigh two months," Wilkie said, "and you might as well have been in China. Don't you know anything?"

"I don't see anybody. But your uncle, and he's not interested in politics."

"No, but he ought to be, for I tell you if the Anti-Relief has their way, they'll ruin us. And they're strong in this county. Why, last year they beat up and cut up and stomped half the people tried to vote Relief. And they'll try it this year. And they're waiting for Skrogg like a painter waiting for a sucking calf in the corner of the barn lot. After the things he has put in the *Advocate*." He stopped, then laughed. "But there won't be any calf meat for 'em this time."

Jeremiah looked at his friend, as he reports, with some sarcasm. "Who will stop them?"

"Me," Wilkie replied.

"You?"

"Yes, and some friends. Oh, we got some boys, some woolly boys that crack hickory nuts with their teeth. And we got . . ." he paused, and stepped to the post of the veranda and drew out the Spanish knife, "and we got Little Alfonse." He tossed the knife in the air, caught it like a juggler, and put it back in its nest in the ruffles. "But that ain't all," he added. "We got somebody else."

"Who?"

Wilkie laughed. "Oh, just somebody," he said. "Somebody right stout."

"Who?"

Wilkie stepped to him, looked him straight in the face, and then clapped him on the shoulder. "We got you," he said.

"No," Jeremiah said.

"Sure," Wilkie said, in perfect confidence, "we got you."

"No," Jeremiah said, "not me," and felt that he was speaking to himself in a great loneliness. He felt a terror. He was not afraid of the fact of violence. He could truthfully say that he had never been afraid of that, and he had always assumed, as it was easy to assume in his world, that some day he would face violence. And he was sure that he would acquit himself as well as the next man. His terror was deeper and more mysterious than the fear of bodily harm. He felt

77

as though all the perspective of his life were suddenly distorted, as "when you wake up in the night and the room where you lie is strange to you, even though you knew the place by day, and you want to call out like a child." He could think of nothing stranger at that moment than a group of men milling and quarreling in the street of a settlement and himself involved with them as in an ignorant dream.

Wilkie was laughing in his face, saying, "Oh, I know you, Jerry, oh, I know you!"

"Know me?" Jeremiah demanded, and the terror increased, and the face before him was vindictive in its laughter and strange as though he had never seen it before.

"Oh, I know you, Jerry. Oh, I know what you've been up to. You're after her like a coon-dog on scent. You're after that girl and . . ."

The expression on Jeremiah Beaumont's face must have stopped him. The laughter vanished from his own face, and he leaned with quick sympathetic seriousness to lay his hand on Jeremiah's shoulder. "And she's worth it," he said. "She's worth whatever a man has to give."

"She is worth it," Jeremiah repeated slowly.

"You love her, Jerry, don't you?"

Jeremiah did not reply, suddenly asking himself the question inwardly, did he love her.

"Oh, I'll tell no one," Wilkie assured him, tightening the hand on his shoulder.

Jeremiah jerked from under the hand. "It is no secret," he declared hotly. "When the time comes I'll publish it to the world." Then he paused: "If I am worthy."

"Don't underrate yourself, my boy," Wilkie said. "The secret of success with the fair sex is never to underrate yourself. I know, my boy." And he drew himself up "in a strutting posture like a swell-breasted pigeon and preened his coat-tails," but with a kind of gay irony and a confidential leer that "allayed the charge of vanity."

Jeremiah was almost moved to smile, but then that gay confidence of Wilkie seemed all at once to belong to a world and a way never to be his own. So he simply repeated, soberly: "If I am worthy."

"Worthy?" Wilkie asked, scrutinizing him. Then he pointed a forefinger at him: "And you know what makes a man most worthy in a woman's eyes? I'll tell you, my boy. A stout heart and nerves of steel and daring deeds. Oh, you come with us tomorrow, and you can show what you've got. You'll be a hero, my boy!"

"I am not interested."

Wilkie laughed. "Oh, yes, you are interested. You want to be worthy. Well, we'll make you a hero and a hero on the right side. Look here," he added, closer and with cunning, "you'll be on the right side. On her side. Don't you know if it hadn't been for replevin the Jordans wouldn't have saved a thing after the old man died? The beauteous Rachel would be living in a shack and eating corn pone. And don't think she doesn't know it. Oh, she reads philosophy but she knows where her bread is buttered. Oh, you'll be on her side, and a hero!"

Jeremiah knew that his friend spoke in jest, and he knew that whatever seriousness lay behind the jest meant nothing to him, to Jeremiah Beaumont. But he felt the old longing he had felt before in the Wilkie household to take the world as other men took it, or as old Mrs. Barron, Wilkie's mother, took it, as a world with Silly Sal in it, with jokes and business and politics and a good appetite. He thought how tomorrow in the settlement there would be fiddles and whisky and ranting and boasts and bullying and perhaps the crack of fists on skulls or the flash of knives, and he thought how it would not be fiddles or whisky or politics that heated men but just a gift for living life as it was. And now he felt not terror at the loss of his old perspective but loneliness that he could not lose it. But he did not agree to go. He only said, indifferently, "We'll see."

"You'll go?" Wilkie demanded.

"We'll see," Jeremiah repeated, and Wilkie apparently sensed that the moment had come to drop the subject.

He looked sharply into Jeremiah's face, then touched him on the arm, and said, "Old friend, whatever you wish." Then without another word, he turned away and quickly entered the house, leaving Jeremiah alone on the veranda, while the sun went down red beyond the cornfields.

When Jeremiah shook hands with Percival Skrogg that afternoon on the veranda of Thomas Bartlett Barron's house, he knew that he was meeting a man unlike anybody he had ever known. He felt the cold certainty that sustained that fragile, awkward frame, but he did not know its history or its meaning, or what its meaning would be for him. No more than Dr. Burnham, or any other physician of the time, could know how Percival Skrogg carried in that bony body and breathed out with every breath the bacillus of tuberculosis, could Jeremiah Beaumont know how Percival Skrogg carried within him another secret life that was as strange and terrible as the bacillus but would never stain a handkerchief with blood or reveal its being on the slide of a microscope.

But we know something of it. We know it because we have the facts of Percival Skrogg's life. We also know it because in the more than a century since Percival Skrogg died on the stairway of the hotel in Frankfort called the Weisiger House his race has multiplied and become the glory and the horror of our time.

79

The family of Skrogg had come early to Pennsylvania, pious Quaker weavers, quiet and happy in God. They prospered, became merchants in Philadelphia, and grew wealthy but not wealthy in the first rank. A younger brother, apparently more restless than the others of his name, moved West in Pennsylvania into a Presbyterian settlement, married a Scotch woman and adopted her religion. That man was the father of Percival.

If the father had remained quietly at home, happy in his shop and in the God of peace, Percival Skrogg as we know him might never have come to be. But the father changed the God of peace for a God more irrational and ferocious, a God who damned his creatures without pity, saved them by whim and a bath of blood, and offered not ease but agony in salvation. The old Skrogg created himself in the image of the God he worshipped and his household in the image of the world his God had created. He had shoulders like a bull, a black beard to his middle, a fist like a rock, and a terrible voice and terrible silences, and his house was a place of darkness. In its shadows avarice masked itself as thrift and egotism as righteousness. A gold coin and God's will were the only realities bright enough to gleam in a dark world damned from birth.

He had two older sons much like himself, powerful, black-browed, and truculent, and he ruled them by terror. The youngest son, Percival, sickly from childhood, he ruled by contempt.

From the older sons he earned the kind of hatred that exists in the face of superior force, the hatred of brute force for more brutish force, a hatred that is instinctive and uncritical and is actually a form of respect that ceases to exist when the superior force is withdrawn, as the scream of the tortured tree stops when the wind stops blowing. So when the older sons got their strength and grew rich and the father was weak, peevish and poor, they could be "good sons" to him. They had that reputation in Kentucky, and we can see why. But from the younger son, the father earned another kind of hatred, the hatred that the mind bears for brute force, a hatred not instinctive and accidental but critical and essential, a hatred that can always mask itself from itself for it exists as a principle of being and when the old occasion passes redoubles its strength for it discovers that the old occasion has a thousand new forms in the world.

Old Skrogg had contempt for his sickly son because he was sickly and could not resist him, but this contempt increased when he discovered that the son had no practical gift and cared nothing for money or goods. In his own crazy piety, old Skrogg had contempt for the pious son, who prayed much and read the Bible, and offered him exemplary obedience. But he was cunning enough to see that the son had intelligence, and he knew that intelligence, too, was a commodity in the world and in the sight of God. So he determined that the boy should be a preacher.

The family had moved to Saul County, Kentucky, about 1800, and when Percival was sixteen his father sent him up to Lexington, to Transylvania University, to prepare for the ministry. We know little about the boy's years there, except that despite his ill health he was a devoted student and a model of piety, famous for his dialectical skill and his nightly vigils at prayer, his contempt for his own flesh and for the minds of other men.

In the middle of his last year he created his scandal. He wrote a letter to the President saying that he had lost his faith. "Candor compels me to state," he wrote in the letter still preserved, "that I feel no regret at this fact, but as though I had come from darkness into light. For I see now that the God you would have me worship, did He exist, would bring nought but suffering and ignominy to man. Rather than worship the Injustice in the sky, I would worship the Justice in my own mind. Thus I state solemnly to you that I swear enmity to you who would darken men's eyes and confound their counsel, to Wealth that would degrade and deprive of bread, and to Power that would bind and break. Make what you will of this, for I make what I will of you."

He did not wait for his expulsion. He had packed his trunk and engaged a room with a poor family in a section of town occupied by low mechanics. He could not go back to his home in Saul County. He knew that, for he had sent to his father a copy of his letter to the President, accompanied, however, with a note to the effect that he would wish to remain a dutiful son and to render what service was due, but that he could come in conscience only when summoned. (And was this last a debater's trick to throw the last burden of guilt on the old man, or a calculated irony to give the last pain?)

Old Skrogg read the letters, and fell to the floor in a fit. Two days later when he was able to sit up in bed, he disinherited Percival, but even he must have known that this was an empty gesture, for you cannot disinherit a son who wants nothing of his patrimony. And it was to become an even emptier gesture, for old Skrogg's health failed and the panic of 1819 wiped out his wealth, leaving him a pensioner on the perfunctory generosity of the "good sons." So the sickly son with hacking cough and cold eyes reached out all the distance from Lexington to Saul County, and then across the years, to strike down in revenge the fleshly father whose face had probably been forgotten in a grander face that peered down from the sky or from any pulpit or mansion portico or passing carriage.

In those years in Lexington Percival Skrogg's life was, to all outward appearances, miserable enough to gratify even the wrath of the father. He lived from one drafty or damp hole to another. His clothing was threadbare. He had to sell his books. He picked up what money he could by copying for lawyers or business men, or by tutoring boys whose fathers would let their sons run the risk of damnation for the sake of a cut rate on instruction. He was often hungry and sometimes ill. He was gawked at by solid citizens. Ladies drew their skirts from him. Now and then some bully would shove him from the sidewalk into the mire in the conscious happiness of defending religion and respectability. He was knocked down in a tavern. He was laughed at by Negroes.

The life seemed miserable enough, but we cannot be sure that he felt misery. It was, more likely, the kind of life he wanted and the first happiness he had found. For now he could forget himself, or could be completely himself. He could forget himself in the poverty he saw around him and sink his misery in the misery of others. He divided his bread with the squatters in a shack five miles from town when the father fell sick. He would chop firewood for them, panting and sweating between each stroke of the ax. He would feed a child hungry on the street. He took in an old man, a derelict with a leg lost in the Revolution, and kept him in his room for a month, in his own bed while he himself slept on a pile of sacks in a corner. Or he could be completely himself, arguing on the street corner or in the tavern with anybody who would listen, rich or poor, lettered or ignorant. He would walk by himself, his lips working in perpetual, soundless monologue, framing the truth that sustained him as he walked. Then, perhaps, he was most completely happy and most completely himself. Wrapped in his shabby coat, he was himself, bigger than the whole world that shriveled to nothing in the blaze of his Justice.

He was thought to be a little mad, and the reputation for madness began to serve as a kind of magic cloak that let him pass unobserved, or at least unmolested, in the midst of the world of avarice and injustice. Then, mixed with the tolerance for madness, grew an awareness of his charities and good works. The madness became a good madness and a scarcely acknowledged rebuke to the churchgoer. In the next phase of his life, the good madness became a wise madness, and the learned men of Lexington began to indulge themselves in debates with him at places of chance meeting. In front of the post office Dr. Spiller, who taught medicine at the University, was seen to stand in argument with him for half of a spring morning. Mr. Madison, who had been a Senator in Washington and who was reported to be a Deist, had him to his table in the tavern all of one evening and listened with respect.

The bad times after the end of the War of 1812 gave Percival Skrogg his chance. He saw the increasing poverty and the corruption of speculation. He became a prophet on the street corner, at first without a disciple for his gospel. But as debt grew in the country, groups began to gather around Percival Skrogg when he deigned to speak. Then, just at the beginning of the panic in 1819, he went home one night and sat up till dawn in his fireless room, using his last candle for light to write a pamphlet. He sold his coat for money to get it printed. Then he gave out copies to those who would swear to read it. Copies passed from hand to hand, in the region around Lexington, then to Louisville and Frankfort, then down to Bowling Green, then back to the outlying settlements. You can find yet a copy, yellow and tattered and gnawed by mice, in the attic of an old house, or neatly bound with other papers in cardboard backs marked, *Pamphlets: Miscellaneous,* on the shelf of a library.

Percival Skrogg began his pamphlet: "To the fool and the hater of wisdom, to the slave who adores servitude and licks spittle, to the rich man who would suck the blood of liberty, I do not address myself. I address myself to any man who is a man and knows the dignity of man, for it is not yet too late to be a man. Though the time grows short and the hour near darkness." He called his pamphlet *A Trumpet Blast for Those Who Would Not Be Devoured.*

A copy came to the hand of Mr. Madison. Mr. Madison was a Deist. Mr. Madison had visited Monticello and sat with Thomas Jefferson. Mr. Madison was in debt. Mr. Madison had lost the political support of the great six years before, and his career had seemed over. Mr. Madison was ambitious. And there is no reason to believe that Mr. Madison was not an intelligent and decent man, with the good of the state at heart. So Percival Skrogg had the money to found a newspaper at Frankfort (where the capitol was and where nobody could remember seeing the mad, hungry infidel scorned on the sidewalk). It was the *Freeman's Advocate,* an organ for the Relief Party.

The *Advocate* was logical, insistent, fearless, violent, eloquent, and scurrilous. The first issue caused a fist-fight in the bar of the Weisiger House at Frankfort. The fifth caused the resignation of one of the directors of the Bank of Kentucky. The fourteenth or fifteenth caused the sudden departure from Frankfort of Granville Snood, a notorious moneylender and land-shark. When the *Advocate* was denounced from a Methodist pulpit, it soon became public knowledge that the brother of the preacher had left an ear nailed to a post in front of the jail in Albemarle County, Virginia.

When one night a few stones were heaved through the window of the newspaper office, it led to a sudden connection between the paper and a couple of ex-keelboat ruffians, brothers, Lilburn and One-eye Sam Jenkins, who took up their nightly quarters there on pallets with the support of a small arsenal and the comfort of a jug of whisky.

Percival Skrogg was famous, but his new fame did not draw him closer to the casual world. It increased, rather, his alienation. He did not stop on street corners now to argue or in taverns to harangue. He wasted no wisdom on the incidental disciple or wit on the young fool brash with his tags of learning. He went down the street, almost respectable in an unpatched coat, looking neither to right nor left, his lips moving in the eternal, soundless monologue, stopping now and then to let a coughing fit wear itself out, then resuming his abstracted pace with his white, spidery fingers moving at his sides, plucking at each other till the blood came, and with the beads of perspiration on his temples at the edge of the black, oily hair. Lilburn or One-eye might follow, lounging along at a discreet distance, his glance roving over the faces of the men Skrogg met, his jacket bulging ominously at the pockets and biceps. But for all the sign Percival Skrogg gave, the ruffian might have been a stray dog. Their presence in the office or on the street behind him was not his doing, or his care. We can assume that Mr. Madison had an investment to protect.

Percival Skrogg's new importance and new prosperity were suddenly augmented when, about this time, much to his surprise, he became a landholder. He had an uncle down in his home county, the brother of his mother, an old man whom he had never known well and never cared for and whom he had all but forgotten. Now the uncle died, and his small place in Saul County he left to Percival. It was not love of Percival that prompted the bequest. It was, apparently, hate for his brother-in-law, old Skrogg. So Percival Skrogg took the bequest, put the land out to rent, and was entered upon the tax and voting rolls of the home county. He began to make trips down to look after his affairs, to vote, and to make speeches on politics. His presence, furthermore, could be no joy to his father.

There was no reason now for Percival Skrogg to argue on the street corners. The things he muttered to himself would appear in the *Advocate*, not addressed to a chance idler but to the world. This was better. If he talked to a man on the street, there was at least the bulk and the face with some reality, however distant and frail. But when the weekly issue of the *Advocate* appeared it would carry his words out into the enormous, faceless emptiness of the world to blaze in that emptiness as they blazed in the cold darkness of his own mind.

That was the man at the moment Jeremiah Beaumont met him on the veranda of the Bartlett Barron house, the editor Wilkie Barron had taken up with, and would defend the next day for reasons best known to himself, the man who had come down to Saul County to vote despite hell and boot-heel and the Anti-Relief. He had come because he was perfectly fearless, and he was perfectly fearless be-

84

cause the world outside himself was not real now. And that unreal world could do no harm to his own body, which was not real, either. What was real was an idea inside himself, and all outside the idea which was his true self—both the wide world and his own meager body—was nothing but chaos which could become real only in so far as it was formed by his idea.

But that was not the last stage of the life of Percival Skrogg. In the end he was to move into the world he had thought unreal. Several years later, when the Relief Party had vanished and the cause for which he had fought was gone, a certain Captain Adams, writing in the *Frankfort Messenger*, referred to the "fantasie and madness of the late Relief and the fulminations of its chief lunatic who yet scribbles in our midst by day and walks alone under the moon by night." This provoked Skrogg's masterpiece of invective, and that in turn a challenge from Captain Adams. To the surprise of all Frankfort, Skrogg accepted the challenge.

The acceptance was a surprise because Skrogg had twice declined a challenge, saying that he was "no fool to brawl with fools." Why did he accept now? Did he recognize that the world was still the world, that chaos still reigned, and that to submit himself to the world and take the bullet would be a last bitter triumph over the world and over his own crazy body which was not himself but was merely part of the world? But he did not take the bullet.

On the morning of February 16, 1828, he faced Captain Adams, at the count lifted his hand with the unfamiliar object in it, and shot Captain Adams dead. It is reported that, after the shot, Skrogg stood for a full minute with the pistol still outstretched while the smoke drifted away in the frosty air from the muzzle of his weapon. Then he slowly lowered his arm. He dropped the weapon to the ground, as though he had forgotten it. Then he walked over to the spot where the surgeon bent over the body of his adversary. "Is he dead?" he demanded of the surgeon, and the surgeon nodded. Skrogg stared down at the body, then leaned and touched his hand to the blood. He straightened up and curiously inspected the smear on his fingers. He stared at it a long time, as though he had just discovered something.

He had just discovered something. Late, almost too late, he had discovered a new and frightful talent, one he had unwittingly carried about with him all the years: his frail, spidery twitching white hand could go suddenly firm as steel, and his pale eyes could see with absolute precision the spot where the slug would enter that unreal body set to face him. Perhaps that was the moment when, after all, he was most fully himself. It was the moment of the pure idea.

Within six weeks after the duel with Captain Adams, Skrogg provoked and accepted another challenge. This time he did not kill his adversary, but he inflicted a serious wound. Within eighteen months in the summer of 1829, he had challenged and killed another man. In 1830, in front of the post office, he shot and killed a certain Charles Grumby. The court of investigation cleared him on grounds of self-defense. Apparently Mr. Grumby had not wanted the risk of a formal duel, but had still underestimated his man. Percival Skrogg now walked down the street of Frankfort as before, alone and muttering, and when he had passed men turned to watch him.

By 1835, Skrogg had fought five formal duels, had killed three men in them, had wounded one, and had been wounded once. He had killed two other men in hot affrays of the street.

In 1836, on November 3, he was shot and killed on the stairway of the Weisiger House, by a John Dabney, a member of the State Senate whom Skrogg had accused in print of taking a bribe. Dabney was standing at the top of the stair, and the slug entered the face of Skrogg, just below the left eye. Dabney was not indicted. Two witnesses swore that Skrogg had fired first, and a bullet was found in the paneling behind Dabney. It was quite wide of the intended mark, however, and there was some wonderment that a marksman of Percival Skrogg's evident skill had made such a bad shot if he had fired before being hit. It was also noted that the two witnesses were on not unfriendly terms with Dabney.

But Frankfort was tired of Percival Skrogg. And the grudging admiration that Skrogg had exacted in those last years of violence disappeared when it was learned that Skrogg wore a beautifully wrought vest of chain mail beneath his cheap, unlaundered shirt. Exploration of his miserable room back of the office of the *Advocate* showed that he slept there with two pistols and a short-barreled fowling piece, all loaded. It had long been known that the one window to the room was sealed up with heavy boards.

So in the last stage, fear had come to Percival Skrogg, and on hot summer nights he had lain sweating in the pitch-black, airless room, little better than a sty, sleepless and listening for a late foot on the street. At some point he had discovered that he was part of the world, after all, and that the pitiful body he wore was part of himself and precious. More precious than any idea.

He had not, however, reached that stage when he sat silent in the evening with Wilkie Barron and Jeremiah Beaumont in the big family room of the Barron house, behind the parlor. It was a room obviously dedicated to the simple and comforting process of life, a room with brown wainscoting and a beamed ceiling, in one corner hanks of yarn hanging from the beams above the spinning wheel, in another corner a bed with a nice canopy of dimity, shelves in an alcove filled with neatly folded linen, a big oak table in the middle of the floor, rush-bottom chairs about, and a couple of long rifles with powder horns and pouches suspended from buck's antlers above the big stone fireplace. Percival Skrogg might have lived out his life in such a room, warmed by the fire, comforted in the bed with the dimity canopy, lulled by the whirr of the wheel where some competent, motherly woman sat, and even his sickness would have seemed but a part of the order of things to be borne without bitterness, even in a modest happiness. But he had already turned his back on that.

Next morning, in the stage of perfect confidence of self and fearlessness, he turned his back on whatever help friends could give him for the day when he would go to the settlement to vote. As they stood in the family room after breakfast, Wilkie turned to Skrogg and said, "Jerry here is going in with us and see you get your voting done." Then to Jeremiah: "Aren't you, Jerry?"

Jeremiah was on the verge of saying, no, he had not decided to go, that he was sorry but it was not his affair and he had an engagement for the day. But he suddenly found the pale gaze of Percival Skrogg upon him, as from a distance, and heard Skrogg say: "It is indifferent to me. If he goes, or anyone else. I intend to go, and I shall vote."

"But I am going," Jeremiah said, for he knew that he would go because this man neither needed nor wanted his help or the help of any other man.

Wilkie clapped Jeremiah on the shoulder. "I knew you'd go!" he exclaimed. "For you are my old friend, and I know the stuff in you."

At that moment, strange to himself, Jeremiah almost repented his decision, but he put the thought from his mind.

When they stood on the porch, waiting for the horses to be brought, Wilkie held a pistol out to Jeremiah. "Take it," he said.

"No," Jeremiah said, shaking his head. "No, thanks. I did not say I was going to fight."

"You might," Wilkie said brightly.

"No," Jeremiah said.

"Better take it."

"No."

"Haven't you even got a knife?"

"No."

"Look here," Wilkie said, "you better take a knife. I'll give you a knife."

"No, thanks," Jeremiah said. "I have never made a practice of wearing one."

They forded a creek, Duck Run according to Wilkie, and climbed the track through a grove, and there was Lumton, the county seat of

Saul County. It was not a big settlement, around six hundred people, and the houses were scattered here and there in a careless way along the track that wound out of the grove along the brow of the hill. A good many were log, some quite comfortable for size, but a few were of board painted white, and there were a couple of brick houses of some solidity and pretension. The track became a kind of street, the clay trodden hard, and at the end of the street was a square, with stores and offices on three sides of it, some of the stores with brick fronts and wooden porches, others of board with wooden canopies hanging over the short stretch of brick pavement. A little brick court-house stood in the middle of the square, with a wooden porch in front, surmounted by a cupola that looked small and squat under the three big oaks of the square. Between the trees, the earth was well trodden with some brown grass showing here and there.

It was early, not much after eight o'clock, before the heat of the August day, when they rode into the square and hitched their horses, but the place was already well populated. The crowd, however, was not yet gathered around the courthouse, but back along the edge of the square, where the gingerbread stalls were set up, and the carts of apples were exposed, and the barrels of whisky, with dipper and spigot, were set on trestles, or stood spigotless on the ground with the head knocked in, ready for business, or still sealed, waited in reserve. Nobody was yet on the porch of the courthouse, not even the officers of the election. For the moment, under the crisp sunlight, the whole place had the air of a picnic or fair, an air of gaiety and friendliness and well-earned pleasure.

Here and there about the square Wilkie greeted somebody, usually a man in young or middle life and with the rough dress of the lower order, linsey-woolsey and wool hat and homemade boots, or hunting shirt and breeches and raw bull-hide sandals or stitch-downs. Once Wilkie turned to Jeremiah and said: "Our boys, and they aim to vote." But Percival Skrogg paid no attention to anybody, and held his slow pace as though walking alone down a country lane.

They halted in a little eddy of the crowd, on the side of the square facing the porch of the courthouse. They stood silent, Skrogg wrapped in himself, Jeremiah now and then stealing a look at his face, Wilkie, with hands in pockets, casting his quick, probing glance here and there. Twice someone came to them. Once a young, dandyish sort of man in tight-fitted blue jacket with brass buttons came lounging up and exchanged compliments with Wilkie and acknowledged most formally the introduction to Skrogg and Jeremiah. "All goes well," he said conspiratorially to Wilkie. Then he twirled his well-oiled brown mustache, flicked dust from the sleeve of his jacket, and strolled away.

Once a fat, slow man of middle age with cavalry boots, much battered, a long square coat, and greasy neck-cloth stopped to say between wheezes that Pollock and his boys were late but they would come. Pollock, Wilkie explained, was the Relief candidate.

Then, from far away, came the sound of music.

Silence fell on the crowd. Each man stopped his talk or business to stand and listen to the thin, gay tune coming over the town. The music grew louder, and the crowd began to stir with a new restlessness, gathering itself. Then a rabble of boys and dogs came pouring down the street, yelling and barking and shouting, big boys all long shanks and windmill arms, little boys puffing and businesslike, black and white all mixed in the same swirling stampede, with a little colored boy whipping along like the breeze out in front, so far ahead he could afford the luxury of a whirl and a cartwheel now and then before the others caught up. "Yip-pee!" they shouted, and "Hurrah!" or gave wild screams of pure joy that drowned out the music and the barking of dogs.

Then, at a dignified pace, the real cavalcade debouched into the square. First, two husky young freeholders with faces scrubbed and proud, carrying banners, one the flag of the country, the other a red square of shiny cloth tied with tassels to a peeled pole. Then the musicians, two fiddlers sweating and sawing and a powerful man with a little fife he seemed strenuously trying to blow apart to the tune of "The Yellow Calf's Eye." Then mounted on a fine bay gelding, the candidate himself, Samuel Sellars, dressed all in black with a gray beaver on his head, red-dyed goose feather in hat band, gloves on his hands, and spurs on his heels. He was a large man, shapeless and slouched, like a sack of meal on the saddle, but as he entered the square he rose in the stirrups, doffed the gray beaver and waved it, and opened his large face in a smile that Jeremiah Beaumont described as glistening with tallow and self-esteem. Behind him rode his most notorious and select supporters.

All but one. Wilkie leaned to Jeremiah and said: "Old Josh Parham isn't there, and he's the king-pin and centerpiece. He owns the county, and he owns Sellars. Body and soul and undershirt. Why, that horse is Parham's horse, or was till a month ago, and if Sellars don't get elected it will be Parham's horse again. If Sellars don't get elected it will be fare-thee-well. Old Parham has no use for a dog won't tree, a nigger won't work, and a candidate won't get elected. He knows what to do with them."

The candidate dismounted in the street in front of the courthouse. One of his retinue took his horse, and as a great cheer went up, two or three men heaved the candidate to the top of a whisky barrel, where he stood and waved his beaver and smiled. "He called us his friends," Jeremiah reported, "and said he was a friend of all true men who loved the flag, believed in the Declaration of Independence, hated the British, and held to the right of every man to make an honest living by the sweat of his brow and have what was his own. For what true man and citizen of Old Kentucky wanted charity, he demanded. And what true man did not trust his own strength to make his way in the world and be beholden to no other for the house he lived in, the dirt he set plow to, and the bread in the mouth of his children? And would any true man snivel and then doff his cap like a nigger and say, Thank you kindly and can you give me a penny? Then he said he was sure no man present was such a weakling as to want Relief or to refuse a drop of good whisky offered in friendship, and that here was whisky free to every man, let him step up and quench his thirst. Whereupon there was a great shouting and a run for the open barrel beside the closed one upon which the candidate stood."

The candidate stood on his barrel, puffing and fanning himself with his beaver while the constituency refreshed itself, while the fiddles and the fife made music and the flags waved.

The first voters were going up now. The magistrate and the clerk of court and the officers of the election were in their chairs on the courthouse porch now, with a jug on the table beside the register of voters and a couple of hounds lying at their feet. A voter would go up and give his name and enter his vote in the book, and turn away to the whisky barrel again, with an air of work well done. "Just Anti-Relief voting now," Wilkie said. "Our boys are holding off."

"Till Pollock comes?" Jeremiah asked.

"No, just holding off," Wilkie said.

Pollock came about ten o'clock, a nondescript, middle-aged man with sad whiskers, riding a fairly good horse, with no fiddles or flags, but with a sizable contingent of backers, mounted and on foot. He climbed on a barrel, made a speech to the effect that he owned three hundred acres of land which he and his four boys worked with their own hands, that he owed no man money, and therefore nobody could say he wanted Relief for himself. He wanted it because it would save the country and give justice. Then he said there was whisky for the drinking, to step up. Then, as Jeremiah reported, if the cheering was less, the drinking was equal. But there was no great movement of voters to the porch of the courthouse.

"Not yet," Wilkie said. "Our boys won't vote till after dinner." Then he nodded at the men who were gathered around the steps of the courthouse porch, talking and pranking and seemingly idle. "They're up there to block off our boys. Let 'em wait. We'll give 'em hell after dinner. Meanwhile, we'll get some fun and they won't."

He started to stroll away toward a circle of standing and squatting men at a corner of the square, and Jeremiah followed him. Percival Skrogg remained where he was, apparently unmindful of their departure.

As they approached the circle a man lifted up a game cock and yelled, "I'm Anti-Relief, my boy's Anti-Relief, my dog's Anti-Relief, and, by God, my cock's Anti-Relief and ain't a Relief cock hatched I won't lay two to one against, and his name is Sam Sellars!"

He fluttered the bird in the air, and the red and yellow and black plumes glittered like metal in the sunlight. Then he held the bird high in the air, with its imperial head turning slow as though surveying the throng. Samuel Sellars pointed at the bird and shouted, "That's me, boys, that's me! And I aim to crow!"

Another man, gaunt and casual, rose and exhibited a cock. "Folks," he said, and spat, "folks, this bird is the breed Andy Jackson fights, and you all knows Ole Andy. He'd kick down the gates of Hell and pee on the fahr. If he blowed on the Mississippi River, it'd backwater uphill. When he walks in the woods, she-painters holes up with rabbits and says, move over and gimme room. If he was a cock you could hear him crow all the way from Nashville to Philadelfy and the hens in ten states would fall on the ground. My bird is the breed Ole Andy fights. He's a Relief bird and his name is Pollock and God help that dunghill he aims to fight."

"Stop talking and name yore bet!" somebody yelled.

The gaunt man looked calmly around, shifted his quid, and said: "I ain't making but one bet. I got a hoss over thar. Third hoss on the rack. I'm bettin my hoss. But I ain't bettin him but agin one man. Against Sam Sellars. My hoss agin his."

"My God, man!" Sellars began, "my hoss is worth . . ." Then he stuttered speechless at the enormity.

"My hoss is half as good," the gaunt man said, "and Anti-Relief was bettin two to one."

"My God!" Sellars said again, red to the ears.

"I owns my hoss," the gaunt man said calmly. "If you owns yores, put him up."

Sombody in the crowd sniggered, and sombody else whistled. Sellars glanced wildly around him for an instant, finding no escape and finding no words.

Then there was a shout from the middle of the square, in front of the courthouse. The magistrate was standing on the steps with a scrap of paper in his hand. "The first count," he announced in a voice that filled the square. He cleared his throat, and continued: "Samuel Sellars, one hundred and four votes! James Pollock twelve!"

There was a roar of cheering, hats flew into the air, the fiddlers

91

made a wild flourish of music, and Sellars suddenly straightened with confidence. "I'll take your bet, sir," he said clearly in the new silence after the last cheer had died.

The other bets were made. The holders of the cocks approached each other in the ring, leaned, and held the birds beak to beak until they showed fight. Then, when the birds had been billed, the holders withdrew to opposite sides of the ring, squatted, and at the word "fight!" from the judge, released the birds. Heads down, the birds rushed at each other, and furiously exploded together three feet off the ground, "like two boards beat flat together and the air full of feathers from a split bolster."

It was a long and bloody fight, very even from the start. But in the end it was for Sellars. The Pollock bird died in the dust, a battered wing spread out on each side, neck outthrust. It made one last effort to lift its head, then the eyes filmed over. Then the big red, yellow and black cock named Sellars, which had been down several times, collapsed again. The owner came to pick it up. It was still alive. The other owner, the gaunt man, stood quietly and looked down at his own bird, then calmly all around him, from face to face, while the Anti-Reliefers yelled and cheered and pocketed their money.

Sam Sellars, on top of a whisky barrel, face flushed to crimson, his hat garnished with the red plume, was flapping his arms and crowing while he lifted first one spurred heel then the other. He seemed about to explode with apoplectic joy. He crowed and flapped and crowed, while some of his men brought him the horse just won. He stopped crowing, waved his arms, yelled "Drink on me, boys!" and was about to get from the barrel to the back of the horse, when the gaunt man whose cock had lost called out: "Sellars!"

"Sellars," the gaunt man called. "You won my hoss fahr and squahr. Hit is yores. But hit is my saddle. You set in that saddle and you won't live till sun."

Sellars still hesitated. Somebody called out: "Git on, Sam, git on!" Others joined the shout, "Git on!" Sellars seemed about to mount.

"Sellars," the gaunt man called.

"Don't let him bluff you, Sam!" they yelled.

"Sellars," the gaunt man called again. "You know me and you know the name I bear. I ain't never tried to bluff no man. Git on if you want, but I done said my say."

Sellars did not get on. He straightened up, smiled benevolently, and said, "Now friends, Mr. Willet is right. It is not my saddle. I would not set in any man's saddle but my own. Take it off, friends, and I'll ride bareback. Yes-sir-ree, bareback, for it is my hoss."

They stripped off the saddle. "Give it to Mr. Willet," Sellars directed, "and thank him kindly."

So they carried the saddle to the gaunt man and laid it on the ground at his feet.

Sellars mounted bareback. The fiddlers and the fifer struck up, the two scrubbed-looking young farmers seized their banners, which had been propped against a tree, and the procession moved slowly around the square to music and cheering. The gaunt man, with the dead cock to one side on the ground, and the saddle dumped at his feet, watched with no emotion, as lonely and distant "as though he stood in his back lot and stared off to the last hill."

Wilkie and Jeremiah walked across the square in the open behind the procession. Wilkie began to hum the tune the fiddles and fife were playing across the square—"Chicken Pie." Jeremiah suddenly remembered that it was the tune the man on the keelboat had fiddled years before, that summer day on the Kentucky River when the boat had drifted past and out of sight and had left him standing naked at the water's edge.

They walked on around the square past the groups of men who played "Old Sledge" and "Brag" on the sidewalk, the groups of women and children munching by the apple carts and gingerbread stalls, and the group of Negroes who sprawled and squatted about a game of thimble-rig, bet pennies, and drank whisky from a gourd flask stoppered with a cob, passing it from hand to hand with a "snickering decorum." As they passed this group, the music ceased across the square, for the procession had come full circuit, and one of the Negroes struck up on his gourd banjo, singing.

> As I was gwine down shin-bone alley
>   Long time ago,
> Dar I meet old Cousin Sally,
>   Jumpin Jim Crow.

So Wilkie began to hum that tune. Suddenly he stopped. "Shin-bone alley," he said, and laughed. "This afternoon," he said, "and it will be shin-bone alley and crack-skull street. Wait till we start our voting."

He laughed again, and "seemed enormously pleased with himself and the world, like a child before the fun begins at a play-party." Jeremiah Beaumont, looking at his friend's laughing, satisfied face, felt all at once a sinking of the heart, and "a sense of the desperation of things and the pitifulness of men, who could sit in the sun and take pleasure together and then rise to strife, one against the other, for reasons obscure to themselves." But he said nothing of this, and they walked on around the "festive square."

It was about two o'clock in the afternoon, after the crowd had had its dinner from packages brought from home and from the gingerbread stalls and applecarts and whisky barrels, that men began to drift up to Wilkie, confer with him, with an air of great casualness, and then drift away to other little groups scattered about the square. The scene was quieter now, the crowd sluggish from digestion and the drowsiness of morning drink. There was not even much excitement when the magistrate again announced the state of the polls, a hundred and eighty for Sellars, twenty-one for Pollock. "Twenty-one," said Wilkie, "twenty-one slipped in they didn't know how they were going to vote."

The magistrate had scarcely returned to his seat on the porch, when Wilkie leaned to Percival Skrogg and said, "All right."

Skrogg walked slowly away from them, without a word. He moved deliberately toward the porch of the courthouse, where the crowd of Anti-Reliefers clustered about the steps, still talking and joking among themselves but giving sidewise glances at the man coming toward them. When he arrived, they paid him no mind, simply blocking the steps. Then he said something to them, but he was too far away for Jeremiah to hear the words. Then Skrogg tried to force his way in. There was a momentary scuffle, then Skrogg bounced out of the group, flat on his back on the ground.

Skrogg lay there for a long moment, amid the cheers and whistles and catcalls. Then, as he rose, there was a quick silence and every eye in the square was fixed on him. He stood there in the open space, paying absolutely no attention to the people around him. He brushed off his coat, turned his back on the gang by the courthouse steps, and walked away.

Skrogg came across the open, almost to where Wilkie and Jeremiah waited, then swerved aside to a barrel, hoisted his rickety frame upon it, and stood there for a moment, oblivious of the crowd, breathing hard, his thin white nostrils twitching and the sweat beading his temples. Then he said: "Listen!"

His voice was not strong, but high-pitched, and in the silence it carried across the space.

"Listen to me!" he called out. "My name is Percival Skrogg. I was born in this county. I own property in this county. Not much but it is all I own and I pay taxes here. I have just been prevented from writing in my vote. Now I am going to vote. And I am going to vote Relief."

Then he climbed down from the barrel, in his comic, creak-bone way, stopped an instant for breath, then began to move again across the open, toward the courthouse steps. As he moved forward the people began to close in from the sides, waiting and watching, very silent. Wilkie began to work his way down the edge of the crowd

94

toward the steps, Jeremiah followed him. Wilkie turned once and whispered: "I got an extra knife. I'll slip it to you."

"No," Jeremiah said. "I'm not in this."

"Don't be afraid," Wilkie said with a touch of contempt. "It's our boys working in from the sides."

"No," Jeremiah said, "it's not that."

Wilkie shrugged and moved on.

By the time Skrogg was ten feet from the steps, the crowd had drawn in to leave only a little semi-circular space, about thirty feet across. The men at the steps had bunched together, looking at Skrogg, waiting for him, but somehow they seemed uncertain, disturbed by his very defenselessness.

Just before Skrogg reached the group, a man stepped out, a husky, lanky fellow, stopped in front of Skrogg, and spat at Skrogg's feet, and said: "Git! And git fast!"

Skrogg took another step forward, his body almost against that man's body. The man struck him, a short, straight, jabbing blow to the chest. Skrogg went down. The man stepped back, and yelled: "You damned Reliefer—I'll kick you crost the square!" He drew back one foot.

At that moment, Jeremiah was on him. It was not a planned attack. He did not even strike the man. He merely flung himself against him, throwing him back, falling with him. Once down, he did not try to take a hold. He simply scrambled up, and in the split second before the other man rose, he marveled to find himself, Jeremiah Beaumont, there ringed around with the eyes, his heart leaping in his tight chest, and the man, a stranger he had never seen, rising at him, drawing together like a panther for the spring.

Then the man came. Jeremiah tried to sidestep, failed, received a blow on a lifted arm, then grappled and went down. As they fell, he heard a burst of shouting and saw the swirl of bodies as the crowd closed in. From that instant, everything blurred out in the pain he felt and the fury of his own effort. Once the man's teeth closed on the flesh of his left shoulder, but he got an ear and pulled loose. Once he felt fingers stab at his left eye, missing the eye but tearing the flesh of his cheek. Once the man managed to jab a fist in his face, bringing a rush of blood from his nose. Jeremiah scarcely knew what damage he himself was doing. Then the hand was on his throat, and he felt his wind cut. He heaved and jerked, and tried to strike the man's face. The man was crowding too close, his face over Jeremiah's shoulder, his free hand clutching Jeremiah's right wrist, his legs grappling his legs. Then Jeremiah was finished. He knew he was finished.

But the fingers were suddenly off his throat. The weight rose from him as he heard a terrible groan. The man was kneeling there, his head thrown back, his face contorted, his arms hanging loose. And there was Wilkie, blood-streaked and dirty with a wild grin on his face, balanced like a dancer, ready to plant another kick in the man's kidneys. The kick came, in the middle of the spine, and the man fell forward over Jeremiah's body, loose as a sack of meal.

Jeremiah managed to roll out from beneath the man, and scrambled up dizzy and half-blind to see the man trying to rise, too, one hand on the ground and one knee up. But Wilkie stepped to him, seized a handful of his long hair, jerked the head back, and for a second, grinning with his lips sucked back and his eyes bulging, stared into the man's face before he planted a thudding blow there. "Ah!" Wilkie uttered, with a sound of luxurious delight.

He did not release the hair, but drew back his fist again.

"Don't!" Jeremiah managed to say.

"Don't what?" Wilkie demanded, and the fist came down on the face, and the elbow smacked across to give a last jolt.

Wilkie flung the man aside and spun around. "For God's sake," he commanded, "don't hug 'em. Fight!"

But with that, a man was coming at Wilkie. Wilkie turned, but Jeremiah did not see the end of that contest, for he suddenly found himself with his own troubles. "Immediately I was set upon by an Anti-Reliefer. I struck him even as he plunged upon me, hitting him below the ear on his left side. It was not a good blow, and did not deter his attack. He hit me in the stomach to hurt and bring vomit in my throat. I gave ground but managed to keep my feet, and then I hit him in the face with all my force and felt a great burst of delight in the act, and the jar and the tingle up my arm filled me with joy. I uttered a cry for the joy of the instant and ran upon him. After that I remember little but the wild pleasure even in the pain I received. I know that at one time he had a knife as we rolled upon the ground, but I managed to set my teeth in his wrist and felt the blood in my mouth as I held on till he dropped it. Meanwhile he was striking my head but I had a hand in his face, which did some damage. I remember beating his head upon the ground till he did not move. Then I fought the other men. Then the fighting was over, and the Relief men were around the porch cheering, while men lay or crawled upon the ground before them, some of their party but most of the adversary. I saw Percival Skrogg on the steps, who called out for all men to come and vote for Relief. He was very pale and dirty and sick-looking that I marveled he could stand. Even as I looked at him and marveled, I had to grasp the rail of the porch to support myself, so weak was I.

"Then I sat on the ground, propped against the porch. I did not feel pain, but a weakness, but with the weakness a kind of joy and peace like a man after his short rows. I remember how distant and bright everything seemed around me and how dim the shouting like children playing a field away.

"After a time Wilkie and Skrogg came to me and stood before me. Wilkie was torn and bloody but he smiled in self-satisfaction. He leaned to put his hand on my shoulder and say, 'My friend, you did well. I knew you had it in you.' I took pleasure in his words and thought them precious. I pulled myself to my feet and leaned on the porch and thanked him for his good opinion. Then he turned to Skrogg and demanded if I had not done well and I remember waiting like a boy for praise from Skrogg. He gave me praise, and said that I had done well, and had fought for Relief and a good cause.

"I did not attend so much to his words as to my own pleasure in them. Then I heard him say, 'I shall tell the men important in our party of your service. I shall tell Mr. Madison in Frankfort, and Colonel Fort.'

"'Colonel Fort?' I stammered forth, as the pleasure in me withered like a green bough in a blaze.

"'Yes,' he replied, 'and soon, for he rides here this afternoon to vote. Mr. Barron and I meet him by arrangement and we shall speak of you.'

"I fixed my gaze upon Wilkie Barron with perturbation and question, and tried to speak but he forestalled me.

"'Listen,' he said to me, 'what you have in mind is another matter. It is a matter of grave import but it is personal. If I deal with Fort now it is for the goodness of a cause in which he is strong. We must put aside personal feelings and criticism for the good of the state and for justice.'

"He took me by the arm and called me friend and continued to speak in the same strain, saying he knew I valued the public good and justice. I could not listen to his words, which seemed to have no meaning to me. I looked beyond him at the people about, some of whom still sat on the ground in their pain, and some of whom drank whisky at the barrels and shouted, and the scene was filthy and odious to me in the instant, and what I had done but the work of a vulgar brawler worthy of shame.

"I drew myself from Wilkie's hand, cutting short his words. 'I want my horse,' I said. 'I want my horse, for I cannot stay here.'

"He was looking into my face with speculation in his eyes. He seemed about to object something, but did not. Then he said: 'You are hurt. I will see that someone rides with you.'

"'No!' I cried vehemently, 'no, I will ride alone!'"

It was near dark when Jeremiah reached the Barron house. He

had to be helped from his horse, and went immediately to bed. Wilkie Barron and Skrogg did not return that night, nor the next day. It was then learned that they had gone to the house of Colonel Fort to ride with him to Frankfort within a day or so.

"Upon reflection," Jeremiah wrote, "I did not blame or judge my friend Wilkie. I recognized the justice of his views. But I felt that each man must live the justice that is deepest in himself. If he can find it."

For two days after the visit to Lumton, Jeremiah Beaumont lay abed to get the ache out of his bones and the bruises out of his muscles. Then the word came that Sellars had won the election after all. Not that it mattered. He was through with all that.

And so, on the afternoon of the third day, he rode to the Jordan place, down lanes that were suddenly and unseasonably mire to the fetlock, and under a sky that sagged gray to the treetops and dripped without ceasing. He arrived just after dark, to be conducted by Old Josie to the little library where candles burned steadily in a twining candelabra. He stared at the flames, and saw how they were reflected below in the rich wood of the little table. Waiting for Rachel, in the comforting brightness and intimacy, he felt a sudden peace, as though after all the violence and mire and dullness of the world he had made his way to the bright, secret center of life.

Then that joy was stabbed to the heart by a sudden shaft of guilt. It was a stolen joy, he had done nothing to earn it, it was not the kind of joy intended for him, it was the trap and the deadfall set in his path, and if he was ever to have this kind of joy it must be long after when he, Jeremiah Beaumont, had fulfilled what was in him. But what was that, what was that, he demanded of himself, and stood there despairing of the answer.

Whereupon Rachel entered, looked at him across the room, and exclaimed, "Oh, you are hurt, you are hurt!"

He lifted a hand to touch the place on his face where the bruises were. He had forgotten them. "No," he said, "it is nothing."

She came across to him, gave him her hand, then sat down. "I heard," she said, "I heard about the trouble. The servants told me. And that you fought."

"Yes," he replied, "I was involved." But even as he admitted the fact, the fact seemed not to be a fact, it was so far away and so much without meaning to him now.

"You might have been hurt. You might have been stabbed, or killed."

"It was not likely," he said, "it was just a courthouse brawl, a lot of kicking and scratching."

"They tell me you fought for Relief?"

"Yes, I was involved with the Reliefers."

"I did not know you were interested in politics."

He paused, inspecting his own mind. Then he said, slowly: "I don't know that I am. I just got involved."

"Relief is probably the right side," she said, then added bitterly: "If there is a right side. If there ever is in those things, out there." And she made a quick gesture which indicated the wet fields, and Lumton, and all the world beyond and everything in it, and set it all off from the ring of candlelight, into which she leaned.

He nodded. "Perhaps that is true," he agreed. "There may not be any right in—in those things. There may just be the interest—what people can get out of it. Or perhaps not even that. Some people who fought for Anti-Relief were poor men, men who owed money, who needed . . ."

"Then why did they fight?"

"Perhaps they were deceived. Perhaps they were flattered. Perhaps they were drunk."

She looked at him curiously, and he detected the disturbing smile, the "slow slight movement of the lips which bespoke more wisdom than the lips could say and yet gave pity." Ill at ease, he waited for what she would say.

"Were you deceived, Mr. Beaumont?" she demanded. "Or flattered? Or drunk?"

"I just got involved."

"You are rude, Mr. Beaumont. Tell me what happened."

"All right," he said harshly, "I'll tell you. I had no intention of fighting. I was not armed, and I do not go armed. But there is a man named Skrogg, who edits a Relief paper at Frankfort, who . . ."

"Yes, I know about him," she interposed.

"He is a weak and sickly man, but a man of determination. He had come to Lumton to vote, and was kept from the book by force. He was struck down. He . . ."

"So, Mr. Beaumont," she said, "you stepped in and fought."

Not looking at her, he nodded.

"Don't you know why you fought, Mr. Beaumont?"

"Does it matter? I fought on an impulse, and . . ." He was about to say that he did not want to talk about it. It was all poisoned for him. Then he heard her voice.

"Mr. Beaumont," she said.

He turned toward her. "I beg your pardon," he said, taking her words for a rebuke. "I am sorry, I . . ."

But she ignored him, saying, "Mr. Beaumont, I know why you fought."

99

He made a gesture of repudiation and dismissal, then saw that she was smiling at him. "You fought for the right," she said.

"I don't care about politics," he burst out. "Just say I fought."

"Oh, I'm not talking about politics," she replied, shaking her head, and he thought he detected an added irony in her smile. "Not that," she added. "Just the right."

"The right?"

"He—that man—he was weak and sickly."

"I fought on impulse," Jeremiah said, "and I"—and he threw courtesy to the winds—"and I do not want to talk about it!"

Then he waited for her rebuke or her anger, bracing himself for it. But it did not come. What she said was: "Do not be angry with me, Mr. Beaumont. I beg you. And do not apologize because you fought for the right."

He was about to speak, but she cut him off with a lifted hand. "You are very young, Mr. Beaumont, and the young feel that to appear older they must apologize for the right. And the old . . ." she paused and the sadness of the smile twisted to bitterness, "and the old, they have nothing to apologize for."

Then she turned from him. He observed how the strong freckled hands lay on her lap, and how the warmth of candlelight touched her face with a glow and ripeness and gave even the whiteness of the throat and breast the hint of gold, and "involved its own color in her rich hair."

He knew that the joy discovered that evening was given him on credit, but he took it and waited. He could afford to wait, in confidence, as a rich man waits untroubled by small debts unpaid. Meanwhile, day by day as the season wore on, he returned. In the bright windless afternoons of September they would sit in the arbor among the ruined roses, or in the evenings, in the first chill of autumn, in the library with lighted candles.

Then the season broke. The heavy frost came, and the world was briefly brilliant. Then the rain set in steady, and all color was washed away. The rains continued, the sodden skies disintegrating into gray, slow rain hour after hour. And if the rain stopped, the air itself was so damp and raw that moisture stood out on cheek or leather or cloth. The earth was so sodden that firm turf quaked underfoot and squelched, and if you stood still you could hear the faint susurrus and hiss of water shifting its place in the spongy earth or being squeezed from the surface by your own motionless weight. At night when it was not raining you could still hear the sound of water dripping from eaves and from the boughs of trees. The streams ran swollen and streaked red and yellow with the earth being borne away, every

gully and ditch was a bleeding wound, and every solid object, tree
or stone or house, seemed to be losing itself in the vast, irremediable
deliquescence. Human strength and human meaning seemed to flow
away, too, to bleed away with the dissolving world.

Night and day were not clearly marked. At noon you could not
locate even the fainter spot in the pervasive gray to mark the point
of the sun. The light of noon was a sad twilight fading away rapidly
to dark. The light itself seemed to drip from the sky and be trodden
underfoot and absorbed into the neutral heaviness of earth. Night
came with a kind of relief, for the dark was absolute and betrayed
no promises.

In the early afternoons of that season Jeremiah Beaumont rode
across that crepuscular world, to the plash of hoofs in mud or the roar
or drip of water, wrapped in a special happiness. The loneliness of
the world, the single sullen traveler on the road, who did not speak,
the sodden horse standing motionless in a field with head down, the
dripping, despairing, soundless bird on a fence, too resigned to twitch
a feather—all of that made more certain and precious the secret toward which he was riding. It made more inviolable the circle of
glowing firelight in which he would soon sit.

And once in the room, when he would be waiting for Rachel Jordan
to come, the mystery of the house which he had not penetrated, the
shadowy rooms beyond and above where he had never set foot and
where things had happened which he would never know, emphasized
the certainty of the bright hearth by which he stood. He had no curiosity about the rest of the house. He preferred to let it belong to the
realm of dampness and shadows.

He was not even curious when he saw the face in the mirror. He
had just been admitted by Old Josie and led to the library, and was
standing on the hearth with his hands to the blaze, when he caught
a slight movement in the mirror above the mantel. In the darkness
of the reflected hall, to one side of the open door and well beyond it,
just peering in as though for secrecy, he saw the face.

When he saw it he did not start. His woodsman's instinct forbade
that, as though the surprise had come from a flicker of leaves or the
crack of a twig. But he registered the mirrored image in the tail of
his eye, calculated it, and never moved his hands from the blaze or
lifted his head.

It was a woman's face, the face of an old woman. The skin hung
slackly from it as though it had once been well fleshed but was now
shrunk to the bone. The nose was sharpened by the skin sagging away
to the sides, past the drawn mouth, to the empty dewlaps. The general
color, as well as he could make out in the shadow, was yellowish,
like old crusted dough, and the eyes were dark. The peering face,

hung back in the shadows as though belonging to no body but float-ing motionless in the medium of the shadows like something drowned, wore an expression of vindictiveness and fear.

He assumed that it was the face of Mrs. Jordan, for he knew that she lived here though Rachel had never even mentioned her. Previ-ously he had thought it strange that he had not been presented to her, but he had assumed that grief or ill health made the mother a recluse. Covertly studying the face in the mirror, he relished the fact that it belonged to the dark house and unexplored rooms and all the twilit world stretching away forever, but not to this room and the bright hearth.

Then at some sound in the house, the face was gone, and in a moment Rachel appeared at the door and moved toward him with a greeting on her lips.

He said nothing to her of the face, neither then nor later. Nor did he speak to her of its subsequent appearances. The subsequent ap-pearances were many. Almost every time he came to the house, he saw the face. As he stood in the hall, it would spy on him from the crack of a door or stare down at him from some region of gloom above the stairs. As he leaned by the bookcase, alone in the room, the face would be in the hall outside, suspended in its shadows. But he never gave a sign of recognition, and never turned his eyes to meet those eyes.

It was a game, precious and obsessive, with cunning and awareness matched against cunning and awareness, a game played for ultimate stakes, like the game that had been played not long back in this land when it was a land of dark forests and beasts and savages, a game of hunter and hunted. But he could not know which he was, the hunter or the hunted, or both, and that ambiguity was, in a way, the source of his final pleasure. "I came to wait for the eyes upon me, and their secret peering," he wrote, "and to know that they were like the eyes of the world which would pry from the shadow upon us in our deep-est solitude and before which we must act in our fear or pride."

Then, finally, one evening Rachel asked him to stay for supper. A real storm had blown up, with driving rain and wind. She had never asked him before, and he had always assumed that some situation in the mystery of the house forbade it. Now he thought, suddenly, that he would meet the mother. He would meet her across a table, across dishes and platters of ordinary food, by the light of ordinary candles, and they would say to each other the things of ordinary civility. His first impulse was one of abrupt refusal, refusal to have that face brought from its swimming shadows and presented to him, with an aging, commonplace body attached, in the common and meaningless light, to violate something that belonged preciously to him.

He did not, however, meet the face. Mrs. Jordan did not appear at the table for supper. "My mother is not well this evening," Rachel said, and offered no further excuses or explanations, not even a perfunctory message of regret. And Jeremiah's own murmured politeness died on his lips.

He was not to meet Mrs. Jordan until much later, and meanwhile the game with the spying face was resumed. And meanwhile he resumed his happiness by the hearth in the library. But with a difference. He knew now that this was only a stage in his journey, a moment in his day, and that this casual joy had almost dulled his purpose and betrayed his deepest self. He had gained nothing.

He was no closer to Rachel Jordan than before. When he had tried to speak to her of love, he had allowed her to shift her ground with innocent ease. When he had tried to make her state the impediment to love, he had not had the courage or brutality to force the issue in the face of her anger or pain. All his little traps had been unavailing. As when, one afternoon, he remembered how she had said she knew of Percival Skrogg, and guessed that she knew of him through Cassius Fort, who was a friend and admirer of Skrogg, and then suddenly, said to her: "You said you knew of Skrogg. How did you know him?"

"Skrogg?" she questioned, and by her voice he detected, or thought he detected, evasion or fear.

"Yes, Percival Skrogg. How did you know of him?"

"I don't remember," she said, looking away from him into the fire.

"Are you sure?"

"I'm sure," she said, and he was certain of the lie in her voice.

He leaned at her, staring at her, trying to make her face him. "Listen," he said, "when I mentioned his name the first time, you recognized it and spoke with confidence. How did you know?"

"Oh, what does it matter?"

He rose abruptly. "It matters a great deal," he affirmed. "You must remember."

"I will not be catechized," she said, still not looking at him.

He noticed that the strong freckled hands, which had been lying loose on her lap, moved, and then clenched, and that her fine waist swayed slightly. He noticed that, with a touch of triumphant cunning. "You must remember," he said severely.

"Would you call me a liar, Mr. Beaumont?" she demanded. And she lifted her face to him, quite steadily but with an obvious effort, and he observed the brightness of her gold-flecked, brown eyes, as though tears were about to start.

He did not have the heart to go on, to press his advantage. It was easier to sink back into his chair, and murmur, "Forgive me," and float luxuriously in the depth of the moment and of her presence.

So all he had gained from the weeks in that room was a more intimate knowledge of her face and the movement of firelight upon it, of the lurking subtleties of brown and bronze and flame in her splendid hair, of the graceful thrust and sway of her waist, and of the strong articulation of her tense hands whose hint of awkwardness somehow stirred him more than any delicacy of modeling would have done. But that knowledge was the knowledge of distance. He had not set his lips to the brown spot on her cheek, "where warmth of firelight seemed to gather." He had not passed a strand of her hair through his fingers or released its mass to fall about her face and his own. He had not encircled the "clean span of her waist." He had not even held her hands in his own, or felt the strong fingers clutch his shoulders to draw him to her.

That, however, was not what he sought. That might come, and he thought much of the time when it would come. He thought too much of that time when it might come, for thinking of that made him forget that that could come and come without meaning. If it came, it must come upon his own terms. Otherwise the hottest breath and most abandoned sigh and most profound latching of members that might take place on the couch in this golden firelight would be nothing more than the bestial horror and sweaty simper of Silly Sal. Then waiting alone in the library one evening when he had been invited to supper, he looked suddenly at the couch and saw as before his very eyes the abomination that he knew must have been there before, in this very room, by firelight or by the last winking coals at night, before this hearth, in this spot.

He sprang from his chair and found himself standing before the couch with his eyes fixed upon it. A groan of agony and rage burst from him, and he lifted his arms as though to strike and kill whatever was before him. If Rachel Jordan had entered at that moment he might have leaped at her and struck her down—he might at least have done that much—and have rushed out into the dark storm. But she did not come. And there was nothing under his gaze, nothing at all but the empty couch, and nothing in him but a kind of nausea "like the slime left on tree trunks and stones when a flood withdraws from the valley."

There was no enemy to strike down. At least, not here. And then he had a strange thought. "There came to me, upon the instant, a fancy which made me see the paradox and doubleness of life. I would have held as enemy and struck down the man who was a betrayer and whose shadow seemed to perform the very act before my jealous and stricken eyes. But was he my enemy? For the very act that made him my enemy had brought me to that room and into the presence of her whom I knew as all my good. For had Rachel Jordan not been

104

betrayed I had never known her. Should I not kiss his hand in gratitude? I stood puzzling that conceit, but suddenly I saw that though it held a truth, the truth itself was but another trap to snare my foot and hold me back from the way I was set upon. As that thought struck me, a servant entered to summon me to supper."

So he went to supper with that thought, and sat almost wordless through the meal, while he ate the food that had no taste for him and rarely lifted his eyes to Rachel Jordan across the candlelight. He would drive on his way. He would make her speak.

The inspiration came as they went back to the library after supper. She had gone to the hearth and taken her accustomed seat. He stopped by the bookcase and laid his hand on a book. "May I read to you?" he asked. "There is something I would read to you."

"Yes," she said.

He drew out the book and held it in his hand. It was the blue book with the name Byron stamped in gold on it, the book Colonel Fort had given him long back. "As I held it in my hand," he wrote, "I felt a great excitement and thought again, as I had thought that afternoon when I first found it there, how the book which he had put both in my hands and hers might be sent as the instrument to fulfill the lives of us all. I went to my seat bearing it preciously as though it might slip from my hands and break.

"I took my seat and pretended to examine the book. 'It is a pretty book,' I said, and looked up at her sharply.

" 'Yes,' she agreed indifferently, but I saw that her eyes were upon it.

"I opened the book to find, as I knew I would find, the leaf torn out at the first and the pages loosened. 'Look,' I said, 'look what somebody has done. They have ruined the book.'

" 'Yes, I know,' she said in her indifference.

" 'Who could have done it?' I demanded.

" 'Oh, I don't know. One of the servants.'

" 'Do servants read books?' I asked.

" 'Oh, I don't know. But it's done. Isn't that enough?'

" 'Is that enough? To tear out the page?'

"She looked quickly at me, and in some agitation: 'What—what do you mean?'

" 'Nothing,' I replied. Then I held the book out for her to see, and added: 'Look, look how it is torn out. Look.'

"She did not look, averting her gaze from me to the fire. 'I am not interested,' she said.

" 'But look—how violently. What could make you tear . . . ?'

" 'But I didn't!' she cried, and again turned away, as to dismiss the matter.

"I regarded her for a moment, and felt sorry for the lies she had told me then and all the times before, for she was the soul of truth, but truth caught in the pain of the world to feel forced to lie and in the lie to compound the pain. But I knew, too, that there was only one salve for that pain. It was the truth. So I leaned toward her as to compel her with my gaze, and demanded: 'Why would one tear it out?'

" 'Oh, I don't want to talk,' she said. 'You said you wanted to read to me.'

"So I turned to the place where a little poem says:

> I speak not, I trace not, I breathe not thy name,
> There is grief in the sound, there is guilt in the fame:
> But the tear which now burns on my cheek may impart
> The deep thoughts that dwell in that silence of heart.
>
> Too brief for our passion, too long for our peace,
> Were those hours—can their joy or their bitterness cease?
> We repent, we abjure, we will break from . . .

"And at that, she rose suddenly from her chair, leaned at me, and said harshly: 'Give me that book!'

"Before I could answer, she had snatched it from me. She straightened up, bent the book wide open so that the seams cracked sharp, and then seized one of the boards and some pages in each hand, at the top of the book. I saw how tight was her grip and how the strong knuckles went white and on the whiteness the freckles started out. Then with the strength of her pain or fury she tore it across, with some leaves falling loose to the hearth. Then she flung it into the fire, and the flames leaped up to take it.

"Then she put a hand to her brow, pushing back the heavy hair, and stared at the new combustion.

" 'Why did you do it?' I demanded.

"She wheeled suddenly at me, and made a wild gesture with the hand that had been at her brow, and tossed her head so that some locks came loose on one cheek almost to the shoulder. 'Oh, I am sick, I am sick of it!'

" 'Sick of what?'

" 'Everything—everything!' she replied and tossed her head.

" 'Everything?'

" 'Oh, I hate it!'

" 'Hate what?'

" 'I hate the book, I hate it!'

" 'So you tore out the leaf!'

" 'I hate it,' she said, 'that's why!' And she flung her arm wide and looked suddenly about and swayed in the light of the fire which was still bright from the burning book. 'That's why,' she repeated. 'I hate it. And I hate—I hate . . .'

"I rose to my feet and stood before her. 'Hate who?' I demanded, and my breath came sharp with expectation.

"She returned her gaze to me, and it was not wild and distracted as before, but steady and searching and cold as though she had just seen me for the first time.

" 'Hate who?' I asked, again.

" 'You,' she said, in a voice like a whisper, and looked into my face, 'you!'

" 'Me?' I asked, but without surprise, for suddenly, at the moment, I knew that it had to be.

" 'You,' she whispered again, with intensity.

" 'Listen,' I said to her. 'Listen to me.' I took a step toward her and looked down into her face. 'Shall I tell you why you hate me?'

"She did not answer, and her lips seemed to grow white and stiff, and her face drawn with fear.

" 'Shall I tell you?' I asked as quietly as might be, and leaned as though to confide a secret.

"Her lips worked without uttering a sound, and then she struck me, on the chest, with both hands, very hard, so hard I was astonished at the force from a woman who was sweetly made. She struck again and again. I stood under the blows, and felt a joy in them, and my heart was big and solid in my chest to strangle breath.

"The blows stopped. Her hands dropped to her side, and her body sagged and swayed from the waist as though she might fall. I did not put forth a hand to stay her, for even if she should fall now, on the hearth before the fire, I knew that I must not touch her. If she fell, and lay there, I must not lean to draw her up.

"But she did not fall. She swayed, and then braced herself with a hand to the mantel shelf. She was not looking at me now. She looked down at the curled and blackened leaves of the book amid the flames now gone small. 'Go away,' she said dully. 'Please go away. Go away, for I hate you.'

"At that I leaned and took the free hand that hung at her side, and kissed it once, but with no considerable pressure of the lips. Then I went from the room."

Jeremiah left the room, into the dark side hall, where he fumbled for his surtout and hat, then into the main hall, which was lighted by one big candle in a stand. As he turned to the outside door, he heard a rustle in the dark side hall. He paused with his hand on the knob, and his awareness of the sound mixed with the elation he felt at the scene just passed.

107

It was the old woman. She had been spying all the time.

He felt no anger at the thought. It was right that she should spy from the dark hall upon them. It was right that as you played the game of love and your dearest hope by the bright hearth, you should play another game with the face of age and envy and hate that stared at you from the shadows.

It was the old woman who, at last, brought an end to that game, and transferred the conflict to another plane. She accomplished it, though presumably it was not what she had intended to accomplish. She accomplished it some ten days after Jeremiah's quarrel with Rachel.

During that period, Jeremiah felt no more the temptation to relax into the "sweet hearthside peace." He knew that when Rachel Jordan's fists struck with their unexpected strength on his chest he had won a victory. "I knew—or rather my heart knew when it grew big in my bosom to strangle breath at the moment of her blows—that I had breached a frontier. I had entered into the territory she would protect, and her violence was the mark of my victory. She was like one who seated in a strong citadel might have defended it forever against assault until the enemy spent his force and withered in the field about, but who had been stung to sally forth without reason from the ramparts and accept unequal battle in the open country."

She retired again, bested and bruised, within that citadel, but she could not man it as strongly now. Her greatest casualty was her judgment, and Jeremiah knew that. Having once been tempted forth, she would succumb more readily to the next provocation, to exposed violence, or if she did not succumb at once she would suffer by the inner struggle to suppress the impulse to venture out to the enemy. "I knew now her secret weakness, and knew that I must press hard. But in my joy at the thought of victory was a kind of sadness at the necessary way, for I could not say to her that I would conquer her country only to love in the end its queen more dearly, as Theseus took the Amazon Hippolyta, and that I would expiate all ravage by becoming not her master but her most devoted slave."

So he returned to her and pressed hard his advantage. We do not have the details of those days, for Jeremiah's record is summary. We do know, however, that more than once she was reduced to tears, that once she swore that she would fling herself into the river rather than live longer in a world where all was against her and she could not find a true friend, and that once in a fury she ordered him from the house not to return. He immediately rose, told her that he took his leave forever, and went away. He could afford this now, for he knew she would summon him. After four days of absence, the note was brought him by one of the Jordan field hands to the Barron house. It said for him to come if he could forgive her hasty words which had been spoken in pain of spirit and could come but as a friend and in mercy. For she needed friendship and mercy.

He came, and there he saw, for the first time face to face, the old woman. He had been admitted into the main hall of the house and been asked by Josie to go into the library while she told Miss Rachel he had come. While Josie went upstairs, he went into the little side hall. Just as he was about to enter the open door of the library, he sensed the presence near him, and slowly turned his head.

She stood just beyond the open door itself, not behind it but beyond it in its shadow. She was, it seemed, making no effort at concealment now, for she must have just stepped from behind the door as he turned to enter the library. She was a rather small woman wearing a black dress—he was aware of that, and of the fact that she was smaller than he had thought, but his gaze fixed on her face. Ah, he knew that face well already, he seemed to have known it forever, he seemed to have met it peering from all the dark corners and secret angles and shadowed doorways of his life. He knew the yellow, drawn face, with the flesh sagging away from the sharpened nose, and he knew the black eyes that glittered at him from the muddy whites in which they floated. He recognized, with the comfort of familiarity, the fear and hate and the terrible curiosity, worse than fear or hate, that the face wore.

She moved a little toward him, seeming to sway toward him without volition or effort as though sustained in the medium of her shadows and borne that little distance by some sluggish shift in their fluidity. She was still again, staring at him.

Then she said: "Go away."

"Are you Mrs. Jordan?" he asked.

"No," she said, "no. And go away."

"Who are you?"

"I am Maria Hopeby, and they—and Timothy Jordan, Timothy Jordan—he brought me here, away from home, away from Virginia—I was a sweet young girl in Virginia—but they brought me here, to this place—and oh, and oh, what they did to me!"

"You are Rachel's mother," he said slowly, examining her.

"And oh, what they did to me," she wailed, more desolate and hideous than before.

"You are Rachel's mother," he repeated in his certainty.

"No," she said, "no—oh, I'm not her mother—if I were her mother she wouldn't treat me this way, she wouldn't do what she did—for she did it—and you must go away, go quickly, go now—for she . . ."

"I cannot go," he said, more to himself than to her, "I cannot go, because I love your daughter."

109

"Love—love?" she whispered, with what he took to be a shudder of horror. "Love—oh, you can't love her, nobody can love her, nobody could—for I'll tell you what she did . . ." She leaned at him, as though the sustaining fluid of shadow had shifted again, and clutched the sleeve of his coat. "I'll tell you," she whispered, enraptured in confidence. "It was a terrible thing—and she did it to spite me, she did it to ruin me—oh, I never did her any harm, but she did a terrible thing, and I'll tell you . . ."

"No," the voice said calmly, and the old woman gave a gasp and stared beyond Jeremiah, and he turned to find Rachel standing just inside the library.

"No," Rachel repeated, "she won't tell you, Mr. Beaumont. She won't tell you. For I will tell you myself." She took a step toward them, and the old woman's hand, which still clutched his sleeve, released its hold and the old woman drew back, with her eyes still fixed on Rachel's face.

"But first," Rachel said, "I must apologize for my spying. Or should I apologize? I have been spied on so long, I have earned the right to spy for once. Though I had not intended to spy. I was simply waiting here in this room and did not declare myself. Perhaps I have been corrupted, too. But I have not waited in corners. I have not stood behind doors in the dark to hear what I should not hear—to see things, things nobody should ever see—to see things people did in the dark. I never spied like that because I was full of envy and hate like . . ." She took a step forward, toward the old woman, and suddenly pointed at her. ". . . like you!"

The old woman retreated, then stopped, and tears began to spill down her cheeks. "Nobody loves me," she said, almost like a whisper to herself. "Nobody loves me. A long time ago—in Virginia—people loved me. They love me in Virginia—but here—but here . . ."

Rachel turned to Jeremiah. "Mr. Beaumont," she said in a level voice, "please feel free to go. To go and not come back. It was my mother's advice, and it is mine."

"No," he said, and shook his head.

"In that case, come with me and I will tell you what my mother calls the terrible thing and would have told you. Then you can go if you like."

Without waiting for an answer she came out of the library, passed between Jeremiah and her mother as though they were posts to a gate, and moved down the side hall and into the main hall, toward the big door. He followed her.

"Wait," he said.

With her hand on the latch, she turned.

"It is cold out," he said. "Very cold. You will need a cloak."

"I need nothing," she replied, and opened the door and went out.

He seized his own coat and followed. By the time he was on the portico she was beyond the drive, on the lawn, moving toward the garden. She was walking quite fast, and he did not overtake her until she had reached the gate to the garden. There, he flung the coat about her shoulders. She did not turn, but continued on the garden path. She held the center, and gave no indication that she wished him to walk beside her. So he let her lead the way to wherever she was going.

She passed through the garden, and over a stile on the low wall beyond. Then there was a kind of lane beside a corn field, with a hedge on one side and the bare field on the other. The stubble stretched away there toward the woods and the river. Overhead the sky was a cold gray with a heatless, hazy sun already westering. The earth of the lane bore a frozen crust, but a crust so thin that at each step it broke into the stiff mud below. Jeremiah noticed that the hem of the skirt just ahead of him was already fouled, and when now and then the skirt flickering with her step showed a heel, he saw that the light shoe designed for carpet or floor was stained and mired like a clod-hopper's brogan.

They came to the end of the hedge, took another stile over a stone wall, and crossed a meadow, where the dead grass was crisp with frost beneath the foot. The meadow sloped gently upward to an open grove on the farther side, a grove of a few cedars and several big beech trees. They approached the grove, in the same order, Jeremiah a pace or two behind, and passed within it. He saw the graves, the small one near at hand, the other beyond, some twenty feet away.

She knelt by the small grave, and passed her hand across the stone at its head.

"Look," she commanded. "Read it."

He leaned to read it:

MY SON
Born dead to my sorrow
But to his own happiness
In that he never saw the world.
May 7, 1821

She looked up at him. "Oh, if he had lived!" she exclaimed. "If he had lived, then I might have lived. There might have been something to live for."

He ignored her words. "Is this—it?" he demanded.

"Yes!" she burst out at him, "and you knew it—you knew it all the time."

He nodded soberly. "But not from your lips," he said.

111

"You were cruel, oh, you were cruel," she cried in accusation, "all those weeks to try to make me say it—say it—when you knew."

"I had to know from your lips."

"You were cruel," she said dully, not looking up at him, the accusation draining away.

"Look," he commanded, and when she lifted her head, he pointed at the stone. "Was I as cruel as—as that—villain?"

"Villain?" she asked, "villain?" and awkwardly kneeling there on the dead beech leaves, she made a wide gesture of despair.

"Yes, villain," Jeremiah asserted.

"Oh, he was no villain, he was no villain. It was just—it was just . . ." She lifted a hand to her brow, palm outward, and looked beyond Jeremiah and around over the emptiness of the meadow and the sky to find her answer. "It was just—it was just something that happened. To him. To me. Something that happened to me. It was nobody's fault, it was . . ."

"Fault?" he demanded.

". . . nobody's fault, and if he had lived, if he had been in my arms —if he had been little and sweet in my arms, then everything—then everything . . ."

He took a step toward her. "Was it Fort?" he demanded.

"But he died," she said. "He was dead—he was dead in me—and I never had him . . ."

"Was it Fort?"

She looked up at him as though hearing the question for the first time.

"What does it matter?" she asked, and sank back upon herself, propping herself with one hand to the ground.

"Was it Fort?"

She nodded, not looking up. "Yes," she said.

"The villain!" he exclaimed.

"I told you—I told you, he was no villain. It was . . ."

He leaned above, not touching her. "Was that the impediment?"

She nodded.

"Do you love him?"

"How do I know?" she demanded. "It was so long ago, and so strange."

"I love you," he said, very earnestly.

"Stop it, stop it," she begged, and lifted her hands as though to ward off a blow.

"I will teach you what love is," he declared, and leaned and took her by each shoulder, looking into her face.

She jerked away, and scrambled to her feet. "It is too late—too late!" she cried.

He pointed at the grave. "Because of that?" he asked. And before she could answer, he added: "If you mean that, I should say that but for your pain I would call it blessed. For it is what first brought me to you." Then he took her in his arms.

For a moment she relaxed in his embrace, letting her head with its loosening hair fall back to one side, and uttering a moan like distress as she took his kiss. He was surprised, even in the joy of his victory, at the reality of her person, at the slack substance and dead weight which seemed about to slip from him to the frozen ground. He experienced an irrational terror, and clutched her strongly to him like a wrestler, so strongly that she gasped in pain and he felt upon his lips the exhalation that the pressure of his grip had forced from her body. Then she returned his kiss.

But all at once she was struggling against him, averting her face and shoving with her hands and wrenching her body. In his astonishment, he let her slip from him.

"No—no!" she said wildly. "It is too late—too late now. Oh, if you had come early, if you had come long ago, long back before they ruined the world—if you had come when I was young and loved the world—if you had come then—but they ruined it, they ruined me—and that is all"—she flung out an arm toward the grave—"that is all they gave me—all he gave me—dead—it was dead . . ."

"Listen!" he commanded, "listen to me." He seized her right hand and held it firmly, though she pulled against him. "Listen," he said, "for I love you!"

"Love," she said bitterly, "how should I know what love is?"

"I know what it is," he declared. "It is that for which a man would do anything. And I—"

"Too late—too late!" she said. "For all the world is ruined."

He gripped her hand more strongly, and leaned at her, speaking rapidly and in a low voice. "One world is ruined," he said, "but we will make another. Do you hear? And to make another we must throw the first away. We must pluck it out and throw it away. We must crush it. Destroy it. Do you hear?" He leaned closer, staring into her eyes. "For there must be justice. You have suffered enough and there must be justice. And when there is justice you will not suffer, and I will do anything . . ."

Rachel jerked back, crying, "Oh, why do you torture me?"

"I do not torture you," Jeremiah said gravely, "for I would bring you peace. Where there is justice there is peace, and I will do anything. Do you hear?"

"What would you drive me to?"

"To peace," he said, and leaned again, his voice almost a whisper. "For when the past is destroyed, when it is plucked out . . ."

"No—no!" And she tugged to be loosed from him.

". . . when there is justice . . ."

"Oh, what do you want of me?" she cried, and tossed her head as in agony.

"To be my wife," he said quietly.

She stared at him, saying nothing.

"For I would redeem all."

She continued to stare at him, slowly, from her distance.

"Will you?" he asked.

She wet her lips. Then, in the middle of the great silence of the frozen land, in a scarcely audible whisper, she said, "Yes."

"Yes?"

"Yes—if . . ."

"If what?" he demanded, and gripped her hand more strongly.

But she was not looking at him. She flung a wide gaze beyond him and the grave and the beech trees and the meadows and frozen fields and sky.

"If what?" he insisted.

"All right, all right!" she cried in a voice that rang suddenly wild and free. "All right . . ."

"What?"

"Kill Fort!" she said.

His heart stopped, big in his breast. Her hand, when he put his lips to it, was cold as ice.

IV

SHE HAD SAID IT. AND IN THE ASTONISH-
ment of the moment his heart stood still. *Astonishment* is the word he
uses. "What she said struck me like the clap of thunder and the flash
of lightning when the bolt rips the summer tree before your face and
unravels all its green, and your blood freezes on the stroke with what
is neither terror nor joy, but both fused in a recognition of magnifi-
cence. It is not surprise. For the true astonishment does but reveal
what you had known most deeply beyond all the words and common
works of life. It reveals what the midnight pulse would say, had we
but ears."

So she had said it, and had laid on him the obligation. Or we may
say more accurately that he had at last succeeded in laying the
obligation on her and thereby on himself, for the obligation sprang
from the depth of his nature, from the "midnight pulse." But the
promptings of the midnight pulse must find their shape in the world,
must find the word and the deed, for otherwise they are nothing.
Jeremiah Beaumont had to create his world or be the victim of a
world he did not create. Out of his emptiness, which he could not
satisfy with any fullness of the world, he had to bring forth whatever
fullness might be his. And in the end must not every man, even the
most committed and adjusted worldling, do the same? If he is to live
past the first gilded promise of youth and the first flush of appetite?

115

"I shall try to be worthy," Jeremiah murmured as he released Rachel's hand, and then she turned away—for she turned and made no answer—and he followed her down the lane toward the house, staring at the crunched tracks her feet left in the frozen mud, and wondering in humility if he could be worthy. Not that he feared to face Colonel Fort's lead. He could take his chance on that, and if the lead found him, he would die in the idea of justice. But was he worthy to die for that idea? Wherein lay worthiness? "I trembled that I was too poor a pot to carry the golden elixir of justice."

Then, staring at the frozen mud, he thought how the world would find him worthy and would applaud his deed: "I had previously considered the case in private justification, but now it came to me that the verdict of all men of honor would favor my enterprise. For how could a man clasp a wife to his bosom when one who had wronged her still breathed the same air?" At the first instant that thought seemed to justify him in his new course, but then he saw that it was an index of his own unworthiness. It was an appeal to the world, and he had repudiated the world when he turned his back on Bowling Green and its fair prospects. No, it was worse than an appeal to the world, for if the act had such a motive, it would be but an act of the world. Any man, however vile, would strike to defend a wronged wife. That was an "interested act" such as the world could understand and applaud. But Jeremiah sought the act "uninterested and pure," and apart from the world's judgment. He would take the wronged woman to wife only after he had defended her, not defend her because she was already, and by the accident of things, his wife.

The gratuitous act: that was what he sought. But why did he seek it, the act outside the motives of the world? The answer is easy. It was the only way he knew to define himself, to create his world. We look back on his story, so confused and comic and pretentious and sad, and it seems very strange to us, for our every effort is to live in the world, to accept its explanations, to do nothing gratuitously. But is his story so strange? Explanations can only explain explanations, and the self is gratuitous in the end.

So Jeremiah discarded the justification of the world and proceeded down the lane and over the garden stile and through the ragged garden. Near the house, Rachel turned. "Do not come with me," she requested. Jeremiah did not answer, but nodded in acquiescence. He leaned to take her hand, but she withdrew from him, suddenly and abruptly as though his touch might bruise or stain. His face must have shown his surprise, for she said, "Forgive me. I would not wound your feelings. But—but not now. Not now."

"Not even your hand?" he questioned.

"Not even my hand," she said.

116

"I am your servant," he said. And added: "In the little as in the great."

She nodded, with the air of a person who is abstracted and can manage only the faintest courtesy.

"I shall not come again until it is done," he said, and turned away and walked toward the stables.

There was nobody at the stables, so he saddled the horse himself, and took the lane that led around the yard of the house to join the approach just outside the stone gateposts of the main entrance. There he looked back. Rachel was still standing where he had left her, on the winter lawn, looking not at him but across the fields, wrapped in her meditation.

As he rode away, he realized, he says, that she was right. She had been right to make him go, and go immediately. "For I saw late what she wisely knew from the first, that our true union now lay in our great Purpose. Further conversation or endearments such as lovers commonly use would but distract us, and even the touch of my lips to her hand, which she had denied on parting, would stain the moment of our resolve and make what we hoped to be no better than any bumpkin Jack and Jill. What had I done as yet to make me worthy?"

Our great Purpose, he called it then, and in subsequent pages of his narrative that phrase, or the word *Purpose,* always capitalized, reappears whenever he speaks of the contemplated act. The real content of the act is almost forgotten, evaporated in the phrase, the word, the idea. What would be the real content of the act? Two men stand up and face each other at a few paces—one a young man in what the letter of the courtroom spectator was to call "the green and gristle of his age," the other a strong man in the strength of his years, the young man ardent, talented, deeply indebted to the other, the other full of fatherly attachment and ripe experience.

They stand at dawn in a glade or clearing, behind them the remaining mass of a dark forest which had once covered the great central valley of a wild continent, before them a muddy track and a corn field ruined by winter, the mark of man's as yet unconquering hand. The other men present—the seconds and the surgeon, a frontier doctor with some wads of lint, a bottle of whisky, and a pair of forceps in a saddlebag—wait with the air of farmers outside a country church waiting for the service to begin. They all wear black coats and their boots are stained with winter mud. A horse tethered under the trees snorts, farts and stamps. At the count, two pistols pop and release their puffs of smoke on the frosty air. One man falls, twitches on the ground, bleeds and gasps. This happens because one of the two men, the older, had done something perfectly natural. He had

117

been in a lonely house with a handsome, young, neurotic, desperate woman, had brought her sympathy, and had, finally, tupped her in a dark parlor. At the time the young woman was not even known to the younger man. Hecuba had been nothing to him and he nothing to Hecuba.

So one of the men dies on the ground. His death is a natural event. Under the given circumstances the heart stops beating. Then the chemistry in that certain mass of flesh alters. Underground in the dark, the hair and nails and beard grow a little longer. Then that growth stops, and the disintegrating chemistry proceeds according to its natural law. That death, which we regard as perfectly silly and unnecessary, is the most real content of the event. Some of our fore-fathers regarded it as silly and unnecessary. In the 1820's, a Frank-fort newspaper comments on a certain duel: "Yesterday morning two dunces stood up and exchanged shots from pistols. One was hit and died. It is a pity that the other dunce did not meet a like fate. We can dispense with a few more such dunces." We are complacent as we look back on those dunces, and we congratulate the newspaper editor in old Frankfort for being so much like ourselves.

But, on second thought, we may be like the dunces. We do not stand up at dawn, but we lie in a scooped-out hole in a tropical jungle and rot in the rain and wait for the steel pellet whipping through the fronds. We go down in the deep sea in a steel casket full of mechanisms like a watch, and wait for the shudder of the depth charge. At five thousand feet in the air we ride a snarling motor into the veil of flak. For Hecuba may be something to us, after all.

For who is Hecuba, who is she, that all the swains adore her? She is whatever we must adore. Or if we adore nothing, she is what we must act as if we adored. And if we adore her, we must do so, not because we know her, but because we do not know her. If before we go out on our great design we lean to kiss her hand, she will always withdraw it and we must ride away to leave her brooding on a winter lawn. Or to regard the matter in a different light, we can never leave Hecuba. She is what we must carry in the breast, though we can never know her. She is our folly and our glory and despair. And if we do not adore her, we can adore nothing or only Silly Sal, who was found tasty in Bowling Green by the hot boys of the town.

The night of his return to the Barron house, after he had left Rachel Jordan alone on the lawn, Jeremiah went to bed early and slept like a baby. It was a deep, dreamless sleep, the kind of sleep a man sleeps "when after long traveling and bad ways he comes home and lies down in his own bed." When he woke up the next morning, the late winter dawn was just coming through his window, and

118

though it was after his usual hour of rising he gave himself the privilege of lying there, wide awake and feeling the course of vigor in his limbs, to relish the new peace which he had found. The recollection of his new obligation merely confirmed the peace, and what he had to do and all that might come after, he saw through the glass of this peace, "as when you sit in a quiet room and look through the glass of a window upon the activity of men beyond in the sunlight and know what they do and see their gestures and the movement of their lips, but hear no sound."

He knew that he would soon go out into that world of action and himself speak words and lift his arm, but he would still remain detached from the self that went out, in the "quiet room" looking out through the glass of the window. For the quiet room might be the reality, and the sunlit hurlyburly outside nothing but the dream. "For it came to me that morning," he writes, "that only if you look out upon your own act as from a window does your act become real to you and take meaning in the world."

But he knew that he had to act, and looked forward to the action as the fulfillment of his peace.

His first act was to write a letter to Wilkie Barron, down in Bowling Green.

> Dear Wilkie:
>
> Since I hold you as my dear friend, I address myself to you for a service. I find myself in a situation which before many days have passed will almost certainly provoke a challenge. I regard this fact with equanimity, indeed with keen complacence, and trust that I am beyond regret for its cause. I also trust that from the affection you bear me and from your kind confidence in my scruple of honor you will see fit to second me upon the occasion. I should of course be deeply indebted, whatever the event. And whatever your decision, be assured that I remain your friend and
>
> Your obedient servant,
Jerry Beaumont

In haste Jeremiah got that letter off to Bowling Green—or a letter similar to it, for this is the version he reconstructs in his narrative. But he only summarizes Wilkie's reply, which came after considerable delay. "I had waited with impatience for my friend's word, feeling that I could not proceed with the Purpose until confirmed by him. The letter apologized for delay, saying that he had been absent on business, and assured me of his willingness to serve me in any way possible, and of his confidence in my judgment. But then Wilkie spoke with alarm, saying he surmised the occasion and begging me to do nothing rash. He pointed to the complexity of the unnamed circumstance, and said that he regretted his own ill-considered words spoken on the subject in his house in Bowling Green. In principle, he said, he retracted nothing, nor would any man of chivalry, nor would he urge me to be less than honorable and keen-hearted. But Justice, too, must be consulted, and therefore evidence, and thereupon he spoke like a lawyer for some space. Most of all, however, he was troubled by the fact that the one whom he did not name but assumed to be my opponent was carrying the fight for the good of the State and for the salvation and very livelihood of thousands. He asked if a private man, under those conditions, should not in all honor put aside the private quarrel and bow to the public need. As for himself, he worked much for it, and in fact was about to go on a journey to Lexington and other towns and would be absent for some time. But he assured me that if I saw fit he would sacrifice what little he could do for his State to the dictates of his friendship, and that a letter might be forwarded to him from his house in Bowling Green. He begged me, however, to think seriously on all he had said, for he wrote from the heart, and to pray on my decision if I retained a Faith in our Religion. He said he knew me to be as just as fearless, and trusted my decision. He ended thus, and I read again the letter which was almost as long as a book."

Jeremiah at first felt nothing but anger and a sense of betrayal. This was not the ardent and generous friend he had known but somebody "full of *buts* and *ifs* and *howevers*." Then his anger passed, and he asked himself what was a friend if not the person whom you had to trust. Had he not seen at Lumton how Wilkie had risked himself for a cause and a man whom he thought to be right?

Jeremiah almost wavered from his purpose. For a day and night he suffered in an agony of doubt. By fits and starts he felt selfish and mean in comparison with Wilkie, who was giving himself for the public good. He remembered Skrogg, and how that rickety form had moved deliberately up to the gang at the steps of the courthouse. He even remembered Colonel Fort.

He had not remembered Colonel Fort for a long time. In one way, Colonel Fort had ceased to exist for Jeremiah the very night when Wilkie had identified him as the betrayer of Rachel Jordan. He had become, as it were, an abstraction, a name only, without face or hands or feet. Even the bestial image that had appeared for a moment on the couch before the hearth in the Jordan library had been nothing but blankness. "I had known it to be Fort," Jeremiah writes, "but its face was turned from me."

Now, however, if only for a moment, Colonel Fort became a reality again, sitting by his fireside, talking like a friend or father, speaking of the law, or with his sad face sadder with the thought of a man's responsibility in the hard times, saying, "We live in the world, boy, and when the sun is down it is a place of darkness and the foot knoweth not the way." At that recollection, which came with sudden vividness like a fleshy presence, Jeremiah felt the old warmth and the old gratitude.

But there was nothing there, except the empty room, with the fire dying on the hearth and the candle guttering in its socket, and the night chill creeping in through the very walls. And he could not think what he might have said had Colonel Fort been there before him.

What would he have said? What would there have been to say? He leaped from his chair, almost in terror. It was terror at the thought that he might have betrayed himself, betrayed the obligation laid upon him, betrayed what was the very meaning of his life. If he betrayed it, he could never go back to face Rachel Jordan. He would have to wander away—where?—somewhere West, somewhere in the wild country, never finding a place to rest, never finding any rest within himself because he would know that he could not trust himself and therefore was nothing.

He had almost fallen into another trap. But he had been saved by the emptiness of the room. It was well to know that such a trap existed. Ah, he was lucky, he was forewarned, he would walk with a cunning foot.

His decision was made. Let Wilkie and Skrogg and Fort be what they were. He, Jeremiah Beaumont, would have to be what he was. And if Fort did good, could that wipe out his evil? "Could it seal my ears to the cry Rachel Jordan had uttered as she knelt by the small grave, 'Too late—too late—for the world is all ruined'?"

Before going to bed that night he wrote to Wilkie to say that he had thought deeply over Wilkie's letter but had found no abiding reason why he should change his own course. That he was honored by Wilkie's expression of confidence and thanked him for his willingness to second him. That if an encounter should develop, he hoped that time and place might be arranged to suit Wilkie's personal convenience and to interfere as little as possible with Wilkie's pursuit of the public good. That he would notify Wilkie immediately of the course of things.

Then he slept.

The next morning he wrote another letter, this to Colonel Fort. He had been informed that Colonel Fort had returned home from Frankfort and would be there for some days. So he gave the letter to a servant at the Barron house with instructions to give the letter only into the Colonel's hands. The letter was simply a request that Colonel Fort might meet him for private conversation at some time in the near future and at some point other than his own home or the Barron house.

The servant did not return until late in the evening, shortly before supper. He still had the letter. Colonel Fort had left home the day before, quite unexpectedly.

The news was, as Jeremiah records, a great vexation to him. His first impulse was to mount a horse, not waiting for supper, and start out upon the roads, asking as he went. But that was crazy, he knew. It was a big country, "and the tracks and trails were many, north and south." He would have to wait for the Colonel's return, or for secure word of his whereabouts. That was his commonsense determination, but everything seemed empty to him and the time of waiting a burden and a horror. It was a burden that he had not anticipated, and he had to brace himself to bear it, "for the burden of the emptiness of time is heavier than any stone."

During this period of waiting he could not go back to Rachel Jordan. He had said that he would return when the deed was done, and the deed had not even been begun. He tried to go back to his books, back to the law, and he did succeed in finding there a kind of relief. It was a relief because it was so far from what he felt to be the flow and fullness of life. He remembered how he had felt this when he first began to read law with Mr. Talbot, but how Colonel Fort had showed the law to be mankind's servant, a vessel for mankind's best hope, and a "glove for the hand of Justice." But now again Jeremiah felt that if the law was mankind's servant, it was "a dull and stuttering one," and if the glove of the hand of Justice it was "a glove so crude and thick that the grasp of Justice would always fumble."

Looking back on that time, he wrote: "I asked myself what might the law say when the heart was struck? I asked where was the voice of Justice but in the heart? And all a man could hope was that his heart was pure and its sentiments corrected and refined. I had read much history and knew how the mass of men lived by the law as by a common pact and accord, but I also knew how we give honor to those men (and to that One greater than man but in man's body) who struck against the Law for Justice's sake and the voice from deep within. The Fathers of our Country had struck against the law they were born to. My own old father had worn his sword as traitor to a law his heart denied, but as servant to Justice. And I asked myself how may we know that Justice is in the heart? There is no one to tell us. It is like a game, I said to myself, in which we place our coin upon a card, then turn the card to see if we win or lose, if on it or no is truly pictured the kingly face of Justice.

"Ah, but—and I put the last sad query to myself—can we ever see the other side of the card? Who will tell us? For if we trust for truth

122

the outcome of the event, and make success our god, wherefore are we better than the vulgar thief who feels himself no thief if he escapes in the dark with the purse? Or if we trust the common opinion and seek general approbation, why trust the heart at all? We had done better to stifle its voice and not stray from the path of practice which wins the nods of old men and the fat prizes of the world. No, I said to myself, we are thrown back to trust the heart at its first whisper, and so I would leap up from my book or tormented thought and ride to the tavern for news that might bear on my obligation and design."

But there was no news for many days, and Jeremiah would return to the house to sit with old Mr. Barron, by the fire in the big family room behind the parlor, where the hanks of yarn hung from the beamed ceiling above the spinning wheel and the firelight gleamed on brass or pewter and a kettle simmered on the crane, to keep water hot for the old man's grog.

Old Mr. Barron had earned his drink with its bit of cinnamon, and the long winter evening by the fire. He had done what men do and had done it well. He had worked, loved, fought, kept his word, given charity, cleared land, raised children, paid his debts, been just to his servants, prayed to his God, read his Bible, feared no man. He had brought light into darkness and civilization to the wild places, as Jeremiah put it, and now he sat before the fire and told a young man, who was his guest, how life had been. He told how the weather had been on a morning long ago in Virginia, "blue frost on the ground and the horses keen." He had once shaken Patrick Henry's hand. He showed the tomahawk scar on his left shoulder. He told how the freshet had flooded his corn in 1780, and what it was like to be hungry in a new country. He named his children, the dead and living, their faults and their virtues, "girls bounden to duty and good boys fair to middlin, and never one to give me shame." He told how he had first seen his wife in North Carolina, the year before he crossed the mountains. She was on her way to church, a young girl riding a fat little pony down a lane in North Carolina, just behind her father and mother, in spring "at the time between blossom and leaf." Barron had stood aside under a tree to let them pass. The girl had not observed him. She looked very sleepy on her pony, not really awake yet, with the drowsy freshness of "a child still abed." Barron, unobserved under the tree, saw her shut her eyes and yawn. He saw how pink her lips were and saw her "little pink tongue curl and how white the little teeth were and even-placed." He had not known her name, he told Jeremiah, but he had known that she was the girl for him. He hadn't been wrong, he said. He had been a smart one, he said, and she had lived with him forty years, and now she was buried on his place.

He had been a smart one, he said. He had been a lucky one, he said. He had no complaints, he said, and he told Jeremiah, evening after evening, what life had been like. It was what life had been like to old Tom Barron, Thomas Bartlett Barron, a series of pictures with their colors faded in time, a series of words in an old man's creaky voice. There had been something else, Jeremiah thought. But where was it? Where was the life of Thomas Bartlett Barron? Wherever it was, it was not the life of Jeremiah Beaumont.

Then the news came.

It was a newspaper, four days old, from Frankfort, a copy of the *Advocate.* Jeremiah saw it at the tavern. It said that Colonel Cassius Fort would address a gathering of patriotic citizens in Frankfort on the burning question of the hour, "Justice and Relief."

The next morning at dawn, Jeremiah set out for Frankfort.

It was after dark on the fourth day when he approached Frankfort. It was by now the season of sugar-making, and long before he saw the few lights of the town, he saw the fires here and there in the woods of the sugar camps. They spotted the country around in the maple groves, getting brighter and brighter as dark came on, then in the full dark like stars far off, for you could not see where the darkness of a hillside left off and the darkness of the sky began. Sometimes Jeremiah could hear singing from the camps, or the sound of a fiddle, thin and far off or close and strong, sad or gay. He passed one camp just off the roadside, and they hailed him in the dark. He drew rein, then moved into the circle of firelight. There were twelve or fifteen people there, a few children red in the face and merry, some young girls and young men in couples holding hands or boldly hugging, laughing and humming, some older people cooking meat over the fire and slicing bread, and one old man with a fiddle, seated on a chunk of wood, plucking the strings softly with one finger, waiting to begin again.

"Git down and eat, good friend," one of the older men ordered Jeremiah.

He refused politely, saying that he was already benighted.

"A man's got to eat," the man said and slapped his good belly, "and you won't find no better meat no where. I raised hit and I know. Git down, good friend!"

He refused again, saying he hoped to give no offense, and picked up his reins.

"Wait, friend," another man said. "Maybe a man don't have to eat, but a man's got to drink." He stepped to the stirrup and held up a bottle. "Here, sir, drink it for friendship!"

Jeremiah took the bottle, drank, wiped his lips, spoke his thanks,

124

and again lifted the reins. But a girl laid hand to his bridle, and held something up to him. She was a big bouncing girl, with yellow hair and full cheeks bright from the heat of the fire and the glow of excitement. "Take it," she said, laughing boldly up at him, "take it, pretty boy, for it's warm sugar!"

He reached down and she pressed it into his hand, her fingers warm and damp to his palm as she gave it to him. "Thank you," he said, and turned away on his road. As he moved away, he heard her laughing. Then the fiddle struck up, then one voice singing, then another, then all the voices. He rode away from the sugar camp and the winter picnic to the tune of the boatman's song of the Ohio, the song of the broadhorns and the keelboats:

> All the way from Shawneetown,
> Long time ago.

As he rode, he ate the sugar bit by bit. It was sweet and crumbly and warm to his tongue, tasting faintly of smoke with its sweetness, yet making him think that sunshine might taste like that "if you could boil it down like sap and hold it warm in your hand."

Then he reached the brow of the hill, saw the lights of Frankfort below him in the valley by the river, a few lights reflected in the black water, and the black mass of hills beyond. The music had stopped now. He abandoned his fancy, and rode down into the town. It was a strange town to him. He had never been here before, to the capital of the State. He met no one in the dark street, but rode on into the middle of town. He was not much impressed with what he saw, but he confesses that later he was to admire, even in his disturbed state of being, the great houses of the town. He mentions one house, Liberty Hall, which "the great Thomas Jefferson had designed for John Brown, the first Senator from our State, and which I regarded with reverence as the work of that mind." Tonight, however, he was merely lost in a strange, dark town, where the lights were going out, a little town of some 2,000 people, on a bend of a river under the hills. He found himself in the middle of town, facing a square in which, well back from the street, he saw a sizable edifice among bare trees. That, he knew, must be the capitol.

Then he saw a man making his way across the square, and hailed him. He asked the way to the Weisiger House. The man told him to ride east a little way and he would see it near the river. At the hotel the barman who showed him up remarked that he was lucky in not having to share a bed with some other guest tonight, for the town was not full. Jeremiah stretched out, and though tired from his long journey, did not go immediately to sleep. He lay there peacefully and "thought on the strangeness of things and how I might have rid-

125

den here into this dark town on a thousand different errands, and no one the wiser, for I lay there in my room and no one of all the hundreds locked up in their houses knew my name and I did not know theirs or what thoughts they slept with."

Then after hearing the watch call twice in the street toward the river, he fell asleep.

He rose early the next morning, breakfasted well in a big room downstairs with a dozen other men, and then went out to stroll the town. He did not want to inquire for Colonel Fort unless that became necessary. He preferred to come upon him suddenly and unexpectedly. This desire was instinctive, he says, and had in it no desire for secrecy, for the duel he intended to fight would be known to the world.

It was late afternoon before he encountered Colonel Fort. Jeremiah recognized him at a distance of some forty paces. The Colonel was standing on the pavement of the Mansion House in earnest discourse with two other men, "gentlemen who looked prosperous and severe like those accustomed to direct great affairs." (He later identified one of the men as Governor John Adair himself.)

Jeremiah did not closely approach the group. He stopped some fifteen paces away, out of range of Colonel Fort's vision, and waited for the conversation to break up. Meanwhile, he inspected Colonel Fort, the blunt, powerful, black-coated figure, the thick legs set wide apart on the pavement, the hands clasped behind holding a beaver hat, the heavy head leaning forward a little with its mane of unruly hair. The hair looked grayer now, but at the distance Jeremiah could not be sure. One of the men (the Governor) made a violent gesture with his hand, at which Colonel Fort shook his head slowly, seeming "to oppose some inner and weighty sureness to the asseveration of the other." That motion of Colonel Fort's head seemed to end the conference. Immediately afterward, the two men took their leave of him, and he moved down the street in Jeremiah's direction.

He did not, however, see Jeremiah. He walked with his head still bowed, his hat still held in the clasped hands over his rump. At his slow pace he came even with Jeremiah before Jeremiah spoke.

"Colonel Fort," Jeremiah said, not loud, and the head lifted slowly and turned toward him.

In that moment Jeremiah was struck by the change on the face. "I had not seen him for many months," he writes, "and had not thought how time might have made its mark. It was the face of the man I had known, but the flesh that had been so strong and full now looked more loose on the bone and drooped to make more pronounced the deep wrinkles on each side of the mouth and to hang at the sides of the chin, and the swarthy color was somewhat streaked with yellow and pasty. The characteristic melancholy of his face in repose was there more strongly, and rested there for the instant he looked at me without recognition. Then he knew me, and smiled, and came toward me and put forth his hand, saying, 'Well, my boy, well met,' and such words to express pleasure. I took his hand without thinking, and immediately regretted the act which had taken me off guard. But at least, then, I gave him no greeting or expression of pleasure.

" 'Colonel Fort,' I said, 'I have come to speak with you on a matter of utmost gravity.'

" 'I would speak with you,' he replied.

" 'Let us walk apart more privately,' I suggested, and he agreed, and we moved down toward the river and then along the river northward in the direction it takes after it makes the second bend. He began to speak, but I said for us to wait. I myself did not feel at the moment prepared to speak. First, I was in some agitation, which I hoped not to show, and second, when I spoke I wished it to be fully and with no interruption by the chance passer. So we moved on down the frozen track beyond the last houses into a place where trees made a grove by the river, though bare now, and dead brush screened us from the world. As we walked into the grove, I stared northward up the river, where the water looked like gray steel in the declining light, and at the rugged hills there. Then I turned to him, and said, 'Colonel Fort, I have something to . . .'

"But he interrupted me: 'My boy, I have something to tell you. I wrote you a letter. Did you receive it?'

"I nodded.

" 'Did you read it?' he asked.

" 'Yes,' I replied.

" 'If I have offended you,' he began, 'if I gave you so little justice . . .'

" 'You gave me justice,' I said bitterly.

" 'Justice,' he echoed. Then continued: 'But, Jerry . . .'

" 'My name is Beaumont,' I exclaimed.

"He looked at me strangely, and shook his head slowly, then smiled again. 'You are Jerry to me,' he said. 'You have been Jerry to me for a long time.' Then he put forth his hand and laid it on my shoulder.

"I trembled with rage and jerked from him. 'I am Beaumont to you,' I cried, 'and I am your enemy!'

" 'My enemy?'

" 'Your enemy,' I said, 'and you know why, and I will not be distracted by pretended kindness and would be to God I had never received any at your hands, nor will I be bought by such as you!'

127

" 'Listen,' Colonel Fort said. 'I don't know what you speak of. I swear I do not.'

" 'Lying should be little to you,' I interrupted, 'after your practice in treachery.'

"He stared at me, and shook his head but so slightly that I scarcely knew it, and he wet his lips as though about to speak but unable to find words.

" 'Are you silent?' I demanded.

"He still did not speak, but continued to regard me.

" 'I have called you a liar,' I said. 'Can you find no words to challenge me?'

" 'I could not challenge you,' he said, very slowly.

" 'But I can challenge you,' I said, 'and will!'

"He stood there, very stolid and heavy, regarding me without answer for a little, so that I repeated my words. Then he said: 'Why should you challenge me?'

"I took a step toward him and stared him in the face. 'I come from Miss Jordan,' I said.

"I saw the blood flee from his face, streaking it more sallow beneath the old swarthiness, and making the skin look thin, and for an instant he seemed to recoil from my words. Then he shook his head like one who would deny what he knows, and spoke, but spoke more to himself than to me, very low. 'So . . .' he said. 'So . . .'

" 'Your conscience should attest that truth,' I replied.

" 'Yes,' he said, still more to himself than to me, 'my conscience.' Then he seemed to sink within himself, denying my presence.

"But I would not have it so, and said: 'I have not come to prick your conscience. That is too late. I have come to fight you.'

" 'Why must you fight me?' he asked. 'What is done is done. And I would to God it had not been.' Then he looked searchingly at me, and asked: 'Can't you understand?'

" 'Will you fight?'

" 'Can't you understand?' he asked again, softly now. Then still looking at me, he burst out: 'My God, can't you understand?'

" 'I understand this much,' I said. 'That I love Miss Jordan, and I will fight you for her. Now will you fight?'

" 'Listen,' he said. 'I cannot fight you. I cannot fight any man on this point. If a man should come at me with a penknife and the name of Rachel Jordan on his lips, and I held a sword, I could not lift it. If he came with a little stick and I held a pistol primed and full, I could not pull the trigger. I could not fight any man. And least of all could I fight you. Not you, my boy.'

" 'You will,' I cried, 'for she has promised to be my wife.'

"At that he reached out his hand to me, as though he would touch

128

me, but I jerked back from it, even as he said, 'Your wife.' And said again: 'Your wife.' Then said: 'She is a woman of goodness and a great heart. She is made to give man happiness. She will give you happiness, for she . . .'

" 'Stop!' I commanded, 'I will not have your tongue foul her by speaking fair. For you have no right.'

" 'No,' he said, heavily, 'no, I have no right.'

" 'For the last time—will you fight me a duel?'

" 'No,' he said.

"So I struck him a smack across the face, and felt his nose go flat beneath the palm of my hand. He winced and his eyes blinked and moisture came to them with the pain. Then, looking at me, he lifted one hand to his face and touched it, and his nose, where I had struck him.

" 'My God,' I demanded, 'won't you fight me a duel now?'

"He shook his head. 'No,' he said, 'I would not hurt you.'

" 'Hurt me!' I cried, and my anger was so great at his words that I did not know what to do. 'Hurt me! Listen, you cannot turn my purpose by any pretended love to me, for I know what your love is worth. I have sworn to kill you. I swore it to her. She said, "Kill Fort," and I swore that I . . .'

"He started at me, and I thought him ready to fight and felt gladness and lifted my arm. Then he stopped. 'She—she . . .' he began, and his face was streaked pasty, and his lips worked without words. Then he said: 'She—she said it? She said—to kill—me?'

" 'Yes, by God,' I said, and found joy in the words. 'She said, "Kill Fort. Kill Fort, for Fort has ruined all the world." '

"He stood heavily, with his arms hanging at his sides, and his lips moving without words, as before. Then he uttered, 'Oh—oh,' twice, deep and tight in his throat, like a man who chokes.

" 'Therefore, I will kill you,' I said, and took a dirk from my shirt.

"He looked at it like a strange thing, and made no move.

" 'Are you armed?' I demanded. 'For if you will not fight a duel, I'll fight you here. Are you armed?'

"He shook his head.

"Then I took out another knife, a Spanish knife, and held them both to him. 'Take your choice,' I ordered him, 'and be damned to you.'

"He did not move.

" 'My God,' I exclaimed, 'I'll make you fight now, duel or no!' So I flung one knife at his feet, and leaped at him and with my left hand seized his throat and raised the dirk and with the dirk still held aloft, tried to force him down. 'Pick it up!' I commanded. 'Pick up the knife or I strike you in the heart.'

"I felt him give at the knees, and his hat fell off, and I leaned with him to be ready if he should seize the knife and make to stab me in the stomach. Suddenly he dropped, so sharply that he almost escaped from my grasp on his throat. He fell heavily to his knees on the ground, but he did not reach for the knife. 'Pick it up!' I commanded. 'Pick it up, or I'll kill you.'

" 'I—have lived'—he said, thick and slow for my hand on his throat—'long enough.'

" 'Pick it up!' I cried in desperation.

" 'Long enough,' he said, 'and I know what—life—is worth!'

" 'Then die!' I cried, and lifted my dirk for the blow.

" 'Kill me—if you will,' he said. 'I do not care—for myself—but my wife—sick . . .'

"Your wife! Oh, you villain,' I said, 'your wife! I'll avenge her too.'

"He was going black in the face from my choking, and his breath was slow and wheezing. I looked down in his face, and thought that I would do it that instant. I thought I would do it the next instant. Then he said: 'Do it—do it—if she said . . .'

" 'She said!' I cried, 'And I will do it.' And I lifted the dirk high again.

"But I did not do it. I was determined to do it, but I could not. It was more than I could do, and in that way. It was not his wheedling or his acting for sympathy, as I took it to be, that deterred me. It was that I could not, with him on the ground before me and his face black with my grip on his throat and his breath making its sound. If he had said one more word I could have done it, but he did not speak again.

"So all at once I thrust him from me, so hard that he fell back on one elbow with his knees bent beneath him. I had thrust him from me without judgment or intention, simply because I could not do otherwise. I stood there and trembled, as though I had been the one to suffer in the encounter.

"Then I took a grip on myself and said: 'Do you think you have escaped. I will horsewhip you in the streets of Frankfort, tomorrow, before the eyes of the town. I will shame you to a duel.'

"He stared up at me and did not speak, his free hand feeling his throat for the soreness.

" 'No,' he said huskily then. 'Do not. Please do not.'

" 'I will! Tomorrow.'

" 'No,' he said. 'Do what you will now, but not in the street.'

" 'In the street,' I said, 'and be prepared.'

" 'I beg you,' he said, 'leave me my good name.'

" 'What good name can you have, you coward and villain?' I demanded, and looked down at him in my contempt. Then I turned

130

from him, leaving him there on the ground, and hurried out of the grove in the direction of the town.

"The sun was setting now, very red and low across the river, as when the weather promises cold. I felt chilled through and walked fast to heat myself. I was well toward the town before I had to stop by a tangle of old blackberry bushes to puke."

The next morning as soon as the stores were open, Jeremiah went out and bought the whip, a strong one with long lash and heavy stock, loaded with lead. Then with a dirk in his shirt and a pistol in his pocket he walked slowly about the square, where the capitol was, then down Washington Street toward the river, then to the Mansion House and back around the square. It was a morning "brisk to bitter," but there was fine sun, which "called many forth on business or to enjoy the cheerfulness." But in the well-populated street, Jeremiah found no Colonel Fort. Then he worked the taverns and resorts of the town.

The next day passed in the same fashion. On the third morning, he learned that after a day of keeping to his room with a fever, Colonel Fort had left and was already a day's ride on the Lexington road. So Jeremiah rushed back to the Weisiger House, packed his saddle bags, paid his score, ordered his horse, and took the eastern road up from the valley of the town.

Colonel Fort was not in Lexington, and Jeremiah got no news by his discreet inquiries in the public places.

But Wilkie Barron was in Lexington. Jeremiah met him in the street, near the Phoenix, easy and elegant in a new dark-blue coat with brass buttons and black varnished boots "so bright you could shave with one for a mirror." He was engaged in familiar conversation with an erect, solid man of upward of fifty years, who wore severe black and carried a gold-headed stick.

When Wilkie saw his friend approach, his face broke into its "quick smile," and he rushed to greet him, holding out his hand with "enthusiasm." He drew Jeremiah to the man in black, and said, "Mr. Madison—Senator Madison—this is my dear friend Jerry Beaumont, the man I told you of, that Skrogg told you of, the man who did such service at Lumton—he hasn't got an ounce of fear in him. Oh, he's a Reliefer at heart!"

"Good," Mr. Madison said. "Good." He regarded Jeremiah with his severe gray eyes, calculating him as a sportsman might calculate a horse or a dog, and Jeremiah was suddenly reminded of the day when he had first met his grandfather Marcher and the old man had looked at him that way and had made him move into the light and had prodded him with his stick. He almost expected Mr. Madison to tap him with the gold-headed stick, and a hint of the boyish shame and anger of years before flickered in him for the instant.

But Mr. Madison was saying that he felt honored to meet him, that he had heard his name with respect from more than one mouth, that they hoped to make a good Reliefer out of him. And meanwhile he had shaken Jeremiah's hand with a firm grip. Then he invited him to join them at dinner, for he and Wilkie were together to discuss affairs of the party and would like to hear his views and a word from Saul County.

Jeremiah mumbled out some thanks and excuses. He had to be on the road, he said. Then, gracelessly, he said that he had to speak with his friend Wilkie if Mr. Madison would indulge him. With "some distance now in his civility," Mr. Madison left them, and Jeremiah turned immediately to Wilkie. "Have you seen Fort?" he demanded.

Wilkie shook his head.

"Do you know where he is?"

Wilkie took Jeremiah closely by the arm. "This is what I feared," he said, leaning intimately to his friend. "I beg you to give up."

"My mind is decided," Jeremiah said.

"It is not too late," Wilkie urged. "All wisdom is against it, and all . . ."

"Wisdom!" Jeremiah broke in. "What wisdom? And what wisdom could alter the fact?"

"The fact?"

"The fact that Rachel Jordan was betrayed. And the fact that she has promised to be my wife."

"Ah," Wilkie exclaimed, "ah," and tightened his grip on Jeremiah's arm. "You are a happy man," he said warmly. "Any man would envy you. Even I"—and he smiled—"could envy you. For you know in what esteem I hold her and how once I . . ."

"Then you understand me," Jeremiah cut him off. "Then you see what I must do."

"Listen to me," Wilkie said. "You are about to marry a woman who is one among the thousands. Your duty is to make her happy. But the course you now pursue is only misery, and most of all, for her. But you can give her happiness and comfort. You have the gifts for success and for . . ."

"Success!" Jeremiah exclaimed. "The success I want is . . ."

"You can have it. Listen, a man like Madison—you impress him, he knows of you, what you have done and the keenness of your mind. You could come to Lexington, to the law, you could be of use in the party"—Wilkie spoke quickly, in a low but commanding voice—"and Madison, he is powerful and great and . . ."

132

Jeremiah looked Wilkie squarely in the face. "Is that why," he asked slowly, "is that why you follow him? Him and Fort?"

Wilkie released his grip on Jeremiah's arm. He stood there before him, shaking his fine-shaped head, wearing a faint, mournful smile on his handsome, smooth face. "Jerry," he asked softly, "do you really think that?"

Jeremiah could not answer.

"Do you think that? Of me?"

Shame flooded over Jeremiah. "No," he said, shaking his head. "No, I couldn't think that." He knew he could not think it. He could not afford to think it. As he had said the words a blankness, a sense of loss, had drained his heart. "No," he repeated, "no."

Wilkie clapped him on the shoulder, and seized the shoulder in a firm grip like a wrestler. "Good!" he said. "That's my old Jerry."

Jeremiah stood there under the hand, in his shame and confusion.

"A drink!" Wilkie exclaimed. "What we need is a drink. A beaker of the best of Old Kaintuck to beat this confounded cold. Come on, my boy!"

Jeremiah shook his head.

"Come on, we'll have a drink. Then dinner with old Madison. Oh, you ought to hear him talk, you . . ."

"Good-bye," Jeremiah said, and turned away.

He had taken two long strides away, before he heard Wilkie call his name. He looked back. "I beg you," Wilkie said, "remember what I have said. I beg you."

"Good-bye," Jeremiah said, and raised the whip in salute, and walked fast down the street, toward the stables. As he turned the corner he caught a glimpse of Wilkie Barron still standing on the pavement, wrapped in his musing.

He went out the Versailles road. He would hunt Fort in Bowling Green. He had not even waited to take food before leaving. He would eat tonight where he found lodging, at some house on the way. But he rode on long past dark. He was now entering the region he had first known when he came to visit his unknown grandfather, Old Marcher, and he thought of his old errand in that part, and how then, as now, he had gone away in the end, heading south, in the dark. But there was one difference between then and now. Then he had gone away, blind, toward nothing, toward a future completely shrouded in darkness. Now, he moved through the dark, and into a dark future, but he felt like a man who sees, far off, a light, a spark, in the middle of the blackness and knows that he will find there what he seeks.

The journey was for nothing. Jeremiah records no details, only that when he reached Bowling Green he learned that Colonel Fort had been there, had showed himself in the streets, had transacted some business regarding lands in litigation to the west, and had left again. So Jeremiah, after giving his horse rest for some thirty-six hours, returned to the Barron house, thinking that Colonel Fort might have gone home and that he, Jeremiah, might catch him sooner or later at the tavern or in the settlement.

The day after his arrival at the Barron house, he wrote a letter to Rachel Jordan, saying that he had failed in his mission because Fort had refused to fight, but that he was determined to provoke him by whipping him in public and with that intention had sought him in both Lexington and Bowling Green. He added that he would not seek her out until he could come with his promise fulfilled. The servant returned with no answer. After the first moment of disappointment, Jeremiah decided that he had no right to expect an answer. There was nothing to be said between them. Only an act could speak.

Three days later, however, he did receive a communication from Rachel Jordan, three words only, "This came yesterday," signed "R." The "this" was a letter from Colonel Fort, dated from Hopkinsville, in the southwest of the state. The letter, which has been preserved for us, runs:

Dear Miss Jordan:

I would I had the privilege of addressing you less formally, but I fear that you will resent that I address you at all. But I beg you to read this for I must vent the distress of spirit which is mine and trust to that nobility of heart which I know to be yours.

There recently came to me at Frankfort the young man Jeremiah Beaumont, whom I have known and for whom I entertain esteem and affection, knowing him to have an ardent and quick spirit, as readily inflamed to high emprize as any Bayard. In his generous chivalry and by his love for you (he told me you have promised to bestow yourself upon him), he has undertaken to avenge your cause against me, and challenged me. I said I would fight him no duel and would not defend myself against him, do what he would. He made to stab me, but stayed his hand. Then he threatened to whip me in the street until I should fight him. Whereupon he left me, but not before he had told me that you commanded my death as a price for happiness.

Miss Jordan, I beg you to believe that I am not afraid of death. That I have exposed my breast in personal quarrel and in the quarrel of my dear country, the public voice will instruct you. I have done so in my greener years when life and ambition were sweet. Should I not do so now with better heart when after forty years I

134

taste the lees of life? Believe me, I do not write you in fear of death. Indeed, when Beaumont told me you willed my death, my last love of life, though of life in the memorized past, fled from me and I could have received steel or lead without repine. When I parted from you, I did not guess such sentiment on your part, and in my own anguish I could perceive your high mind and dignity and feel that in the hopeless case God granted me a glimpse of worth beyond the mortal mark. Do not rob me of that thought and poison what joy I hope to carry with me to the end, in the recollection of your society.

As I do not write in fear I do not write for extenuation. I confess me wrong, and bitterly, for I was weak to take by stealth what was not mine to take. Oh, I was weak and foolish to think that I could have a joy that burst upon my sight so late when I was old and in the toils of life. I betrayed you and betrayed others who trusted me, compounding betrayal by betrayal, and for those months I lived in a dream outside the hard world and its duties. Then I came back into the world, and hope to do my duty still, whatever it may be and bear with fortitude the ills and losses. I speak of myself. But do not think I do not know what you have endured. Could I have made your lot more easy, I had thrust my hand into the fire. You sent me back into the world to play what part in it I could with my poor rags of honor left. That was your great soul and courage, before which I bowed my head. Oh, now do not rob me of that thought, for it is the thought by which I have been able to live.

As I beg this for my own sake, I beg it for your own, and for the sake of the poor boy Beaumont. He is worthy of you in so far as man may be worthy of a woman like yourself. Take happiness with him, and do not stain your heart with hate or his hand with blood —however guilty that blood may be. And it is guilty blood. But it came to guilt, not by coldness and in the calculation of man's vanity, but in hotness and folly, forgetful of the nature of things, and the debt it owed to the world.

I would say one more thing. I will not fight Jeremiah Beaumont a duel, I cannot fight in a bad cause. I will not duel him even if he whip me in the street. But I would, if possible, be spared that shame. I bear, I trust, the name of manhood and hope to bear it still and to the end. It is a vanity, I know, to love the bubble reputation, but leave me what little worth I have. And there is one fear in me. I might—though God forbid—in the heat of the moment and in the weakness of my vanity do what I would regret most bitterly and by a last crime make worse my earlier crimes. This is not a threat. I know that boy to be of mettle beyond such use.

As for the future, I shall go about the country as before, not denying my presence. I am ashamed to say that I fled Frankfort, though not in fear for life. I shall flee no more. "There is a destiny that shapes our ends rough hew them how we may."

Your obedient servant,

Cassius Fort

Jeremiah stood under a bare tree in front of the Barron house, in the middle of a winter afternoon, and read the letter. He read it over and over again, not moving. It shook him. Then he looked again at the single sheet with the three words from Rachel Jordan.

How had she taken the letter? He asked himself that, then thought that the bareness of her words told him all. She had rejected Fort's letter, and was unchanged. Then he asked why he himself should be changed by it. His eyes fell on Fort's sentence, "This is not a threat." And the distress the letter had stirred suddenly crystallized in him as anger. It *was* a threat. And he would not be threatened. By God, he would not be threatened. The letter was Fort's double trick, a threat to him, and to Rachel Jordan a sniveling, flattering, cringing, self-pitiful attempt to play on womanly weakness and softness of heart, to blow up what warmth of feeling might remain for the man she had held in her arms.

And at that thought, there in broad daylight, Jeremiah had the vision again he had had in the firelit library of the Jordan house. "I saw the act which had been performed upon the couch, and knew the horror of it and my jealousy to defend her, and knew how with foul cunning he now tried to stir her blood to save his own, and how she had sent the letter to me to prove that she was above the baseness of his thought. I hardened then my mind."

And Jeremiah had a sudden inspiration. He might combat cunning with cunning. If Fort could stoop, then one might stoop with Fort, and snare him in his own snare. Rachel Jordan might reply, and reply fair, and ask that Fort come to her on a certain day and at a certain hour, after he had returned to his home from the western part. Fort would have to ride through the settlement from his house to the Jordan house, and Jeremiah might lie in wait in the settlement and there call him to account with the whip, before all eyes.

Jeremiah rushed into the house, seized quill and paper and began to write. He finished the letter, outlining his plan, and then stopped to read it over. He paused. What had seemed right and justifiable in his moment of passion just before in the yard, now in the black words on the white paper offended him. Fort had been cunning and had stooped, but he could not stoop. Something would be gone and lost. He tore the sheet into small bits and threw them into the fire. He felt that he had escaped another trap laid in his path. If he had

136

written the letter, if he had sent it to Rachel, she might have resented in horror the baseness of his view of her. He knew that she would have done that. And he would have lost her forever. And he would, too, have lost himself.

So there was nothing to do but wait for his opportunity to execute in his own way the deed which Rachel Jordan had confirmed by sending him Fort's letter and her own terse message.

But had she intended to confirm the deed? Or had Colonel Fort's letter shaken her heart and her resolve, as it shook Jeremiah's? Late in the record, when things had spun themselves nearly out to the end, we find some indication that Rachel herself was shaken. And if she was shaken, why did she send the letter to Jeremiah with no hint as to her own feeling? We can only surmise that she could not resolve her own feelings, that she was torn by their contradictions, and that she passed the decision on to Jeremiah as you flip a coin or draw a card, passing on to him, or to fate, the responsibility. If that is true, then the situation assumes a double irony, for Jeremiah resolved his own conflict of feeling by an appeal to her. He took the bareness of her own note to mean that she had rejected Fort's letter. Suppose they had read Fort's letter, side by side. Then the doubt in her eyes and the doubt in Jeremiah's might have met as they looked up from the sheet, and all would have been different.

Or perhaps not. Perhaps the decision answered Jeremiah's deepest need, after all.

In any case, he now entered up a period of waiting, a period in which "night and day wore the same face." He writes: "I seemed to live outside of time, and nothing about me was real but the thought in me. What was real was the moment I strove toward, which was not yet in time. When that moment should fall into the stream of time, I thought that again time and the world would be real to me. But not before."

And in those weeks, as the winter wore itself out, his passion for Rachel Jordan grew. Not being before his eyes, she obsessed him more than during the time when he had seen her almost daily. The moment when he should strike Fort and the moment when he should at last take her into his arms fused into one moment, the two acts became one act, the secret of life, and all that lay between him and the act was ugly and meaningless. He saw her face constantly before him, "but far off and like something glimmering in the dark." He could not come to her, he knew, until the deed was done.

But he came. He did not come because he was not strong enough to maintain his resolve, but because she called him. One of the Jordan Negroes brought the note. She had to see him, she said. Her mother was very sick, almost at the point of death. She herself was weak

137

enough in her distress to call for the comfort of his presence. There was no one else to whom she could turn. So he went.

He found her pale and cold, wearing a black dress, and a black shawl about her shoulders. Her face had none of its autumnal richness now. The inner warmth and glow had withdrawn or been drained away. The skin looked drawn and strained, and when she spoke, her pale lips seemed stiff as with cold. Her face was so pale that the brown spot on her left cheek, and even the little freckles, which had seemed absorbed into the glow of her flesh and to be the marks of the warm, fecund vitality of her blood, now seemed to be nothing but extrinsic stains sharply marring the pallor of her face.

She was not beautiful now. Jeremiah says as much, but adds, "The fact that her beauty had fled away, as though in the short space time had done its cruel work of half a lifetime, touched my heart so that tears sprung to my eyes and I was caught in the pathos of that fugacity of all we prize."

She stood in the hall, drawing the shawl tight about her shoulders, twisting her hands in the shawl, and he noticed how white the skin was on the knuckles. "Thank you for coming," she said, as stiff and formal as though he were a stranger who had done her a casual courtesy.

He drew her right hand from the shawl, kissed it, and said that he was hers to command. She told him that Mrs. Jordan had been ill for more than a week and had been growing steadily worse. She had been by turns unconscious and delirious for two days. She was now unconscious. The doctor was due to come today, Dr. Thomas, who lived on a farm over near Lumton. She recited this in a cold voice, not even looking at Jeremiah while she spoke.

She had scarcely finished when there was a noise on the porch. Dr. Thomas had arrived. Rachel took him upstairs to the patient, and Jeremiah found his way to the library. The fire there was nearly out, and the room seemed smaller and poorer than before. Jeremiah went to the hearth, and, as he leaned there, he had the old feeling that he was being spied on. But he knew there would be no yellowish drawn face floating beyond in the shadows of the side hall to peer at him. He knew that those secret, vindictive eyes belonged to another time, now past, and that he had moved into a new time.

After a little Rachel came down to him, leaving the doctor above. There was no change, she reported. Then she lapsed into silence, drawing the shawl about her shoulders, clutching it.

There was, finally, the sound of the doctor's tread on the stairs, and Rachel rose and went out. Jeremiah heard the front door close, and she returned to him. Her mother, she said, was no better, perhaps worse. Jeremiah murmured some sort of sympathetic reply, and stepped aside for her to enter the library.

She did not enter. Jeremiah waited, puzzled. Then she said: "I asked you to come. I thank you for coming. But now—now won't you go?"

"But you asked me to come . . ." he began.

But she interrupted, "I did. I asked you to come, but I was weak. I was a fool to think anybody can help me." She twisted the edge of the shawl in her finger.

He said he wanted to be with her, to be of service, but she stopped him. "Go," she said, "go now—get out of this house—you should never have come here, never, it is a terrible place. Go while you can."

Jeremiah felt a cold clutch at his heart. "You talk," he said to her, "you talk like she did. Here in this hall. That day. Like your mother did."

"I speak for myself," she said, "and I say, go now. While you can."

He took her hand. "I'll go now," he said, "since you wish it. But I will return tomorrow."

With that he left. He took his horse and rode away.

He had gone about a mile when he saw ahead of him another horseman, and even at the distance recognized the figure of Dr. Thomas. Dr. Thomas was riding at a slow walk, and in a little Jeremiah overtook him. After renewed greetings, they rode along side by side for a time without conversation. Dr. Thomas, a small man huddled in a big coat, with the skin of his brown old face wrinkled minutely like the skin of an apple that has been kept too long on the shelf, rode with his head bowed a little and his shoulders slumped. A little moisture hung at the tip of his nose, looking cold and ready to freeze there, and now and then he snuffled and twitched his nose, but he did not wipe it away. Finally Jeremiah asked him how the patient was.

"Looks like a goner," Dr. Thomas said.

"She will die?"

"To all prospects," Dr. Thomas replied. "You do what you can. I've done what I know to do, like a man will. But you can't make somebody live."

"Make her live?"

"Not when she don't want to," the doctor said. "Sometimes when I give her medicine, she holds it in her mouth, and then when I turn she'll spit it out. I've seen it on the pillow. That was when she was stronger. Now I can get it down the old lady. But she don't want to live, the old lady don't."

Jeremiah found nothing to say to that. So they rode along in silence for another half mile, until they reached a fork. "I go this way," the doctor said, and turned left. "Good day, sir," he added, but did not seem to hear Jeremiah's farewell.

Riding on to the Barron place, Jeremiah thought of the old woman in the bed with her spying old eyes closed, and the stain of medicine on her pillow, dying because she did not want to live, and thought of Rachel wandering about the house, cold under the black shawl drawn tight about her shoulders, her face pale and not beautiful now. He thought of what she had told him, to go away while he could and never come back.

That was what he thought of that night when he sat with Mr. Barron by the bright fire, and the old man sipped his drink and talked of how things had been long back, the good years and the bad years, and how he'd wager on a good year this year to come, a good crop, for a good year was due now in the Lord's will. "Speaking of that crop to come," Jeremiah writes, "he straightened himself in his chair as though to rise and put his hand to business, and his old bleared eyes brightened like the eyes of one who sees ready before him the good fruit of his labor and knows no regret for sweat spent. But I thought of that other old one, who longed for death, and I was sick at heart with the doubleness of life and with the thought how a man does not know on which path his foot is set. So without premeditation, I leaned at him and the words sprang from my lips without consideration of courtesy: 'But you are old, and you have made many crops,' I said bitterly, 'and does it please you to make another? Just like all the rest?'

"He looked at me as though he thought me somewhat mad or as though I spoke Greek to him and him unlearned, and I waited for his reply. Then he slowly said, 'Son, I made me many a crop. Some good and some poor to starvation. But I aim, under God's hand, to make me one more.' He waited and took a sip from his glass, and then said: 'And this one—it may be the best I ever made.'

" 'But what can it matter to you?' I demanded. 'This other crop? You have prospered, you have land and rent, your sons have prospered, you are old, what can a crop matter now?'

" 'Son,' he said, having looked at me slow, 'you are learned, and in the wisdom of the dead tongues and in the law, and I am nigh unlettered but for reading the Word and ciphering, and I can only say what come to me on the way. It come on me long back that all for a man like me was to set his strength to whatever come to his hand. I come a long way and through bad times and I have seen good men die, and in their strength. I have come over the mountains and in a new land full of wildness. I have done things would shame a man, in wrath and meanness of heart, and I have seen days I cried out against God for the grief laid on me. But what I learned I learned, and we taken this land and it is ours.' At that the old man ceased, and drank, and looked into the good fire. Then he said: 'And son, I aim to make me one more crop. It may be the best I ever made. Under God's hand.'"

Jeremiah said no more, and shortly excused himself for bed. He lay and thought of the old woman dying because she hated life and had peered through crevices, and of the old man whose words he had just heard. He thought how old Thomas Bartlett Barron was certain of life and of death. For a moment, he himself felt that he had stumbled upon a bright secret, "as though you should kick up the dead leaves in your path and see the jewel glitter among that waste of the season," and his heart was so full that he sat upright in his bed, in the cold room.

But that did not last. He was Jeremiah Beaumont. He was not Thomas Bartlett Barron, who could live by the day and the year, from crop to crop. What was another crop? Nothing but taste for the mouth and warm glut in the belly, and the little steaming pile of morning excrement at last.

He felt a terrible wrenching pity, and a tenderness as though he must protect the old man, at any cost, from a truth that might break on him any moment now like a flame to consume all his past life like a dead oak struck by lightning. Old Barron must live out the next month, the next year, and die without knowing. But he, Jeremiah Beaumont, knew, and knew that he was Jeremiah Beaumont, and only himself. With that thought, which was both "desolate and shot with joy," he slept.

The next afternoon, early, he rode to the Jordan place. Rachel received him, without any reference to her words of the day before, how she had urged him to go away and never return. She seemed somewhat more herself now. She had slept some, she said, the night before. Mrs. Jordan had not changed. During the night, according to Josie, she had been wakeful and the fever had been high.

Jeremiah and Rachel spent the afternoon together in the library. They talked scarcely at all. Two or three times Rachel excused herself to go up to the sick room. A young colored girl was watching there, for Old Josie was asleep. A little after dark came on, Jeremiah and Rachel had supper. They ate in the big dining room, by the light of a single candle, facing each other across the great width of dark, polished wood, not talking, eating the cold food.

About nine o'clock, just as Jeremiah had made up his mind to leave, Josie appeared at the library door. Mrs. Jordan, she said, was in a "big sweat." She had been sweating for some time, and the bed was soaked "past what any Christian could lay in." Rachel rose and said that they must change the sheets, and for Josie to go to the quarters to call Dellie to help. But Josie said that changing the sheets would

141

do no good, the mattress was all soaked, too. They would have to change the mattress and it would take somebody strong. In the instant when Rachel hesitated, Jeremiah said, "Let me help. I am strong."

Rachel looked at him, not speaking.

Then Josie said: "Ain't nuthin wrong with that, Missie. Ain't nuthin but a pore old sick lady."

So Rachel nodded, and they went out into the hall, into the main hall, where a solitary candle burned, and up the stairs, into those regions where Jeremiah had never penetrated before.

The bedroom was very large. A fair fire burned on the hearth and wood was stacked at one side. The fire gave more light than the candle on the shelf above. Across the room at one side, was a big tester bed, very high, beside it a table littered with bottles, saucers, glasses and spoons. The body of the old woman scarcely made a hump in the covers of the bed.

Josie took charge. She ordered Jeremiah to step out into the hall while they changed the gown of the patient and moved her to the dry side of the bed. He waited outside, and presently Josie came out, carrying the candle, to conduct him to another room, where they stripped a bed and removed the mattress. Rachel came and held the candle while Jeremiah, with Josie's help, brought back the mattress, and laid it across two chairs next to the bed.

Then Josie turned to Jeremiah: "If you could pick her up. She ain't nuthin but a pore old sick lady."

He nodded, then waited while Josie wrapped Mrs. Jordan in a blanket. He picked her up. She was very light, far lighter than he had expected. He carried her over to the fire, and waited with the form limp across his arms, the head half-propped on his right shoulder. He looked down at the face. The eyes, which had peered at him and spied on him from the shadows, were closed. The game was over, the game of hunter-and-hunted. He had won, after all. He was the hunter, not the hunted. So, looking down into the face of the victim, he felt sorry for her, and the fancy touched his mind that she was not old Mrs. Jordan but any old woman, that she might even have been his own mother "come from the long past and far places to lie dying at last in the arms of a pious son."

Rachel said: "The bed is ready."

He placed her in the bed. He studied the face there on the pillow in the shadows. Then, with a shock, he discovered that the eyes in that face, under half-lowered lids, were watching him. The old game had begun again, he had not won, and fear, for an instant, seized him. The enemy was watching from an ambush deeper and wilder and more secure than any closet or dark hall had ever been, where she had hid, deeper and darker than the thicket or forest, and he—he, Jeremiah

Beaumont—was naked and defenseless in some open spot, like the settler in his corn patch before the arrow twangs.

Then he saw the lips move. What was horrible was that they made
no sound, not even a whisper. It was, he thought, as though a statue
tried to talk. Then the words came, but so faint and dry, like the
slightest shift of dead leaves in a path in a movement of air, that he
had to lean to be sure.

"You"—she was saying—"you—I told you to go—to go . . ."

He leaned closer, trying to catch the words, and he felt Rachel's
fingers gripping his arm so hard that it hurt under the cloth. The old
woman's eyes were suddenly wide open, staring up at him.

"Oh, what they did to me, they brought me here—I was sweet and
young—in Virginia—sweet and young, but, oh . . ."

He saw the wide eyes move in their sockets, fix on Rachel beyond
him, then return to him.

". . . oh, she, she has killed me—and, oh—go away—before she—before she kills you—she killed me and nobody cares and nobody loves
me—nobody . . ."

He felt Rachel's fingers gripping his arm.

". . . loves me—nobody loves—me . . ."

He felt his own voice break from his throat. "I love you," the voice
said harshly, coming from his own throat. And without thinking, he
leaned to kiss the old face, on the brow.

He tasted the salt sweat on her skin and his nostrils were full of the
stale, sour smell of her damp hair. He straightened up quickly, stifling
the clutch of nausea in his vitals. Rachel's fingers still gripped his arm.
He looked down to see that the old woman's eyes were closed. He
thought she was dead, and leaned again to see. The fingers had released his arm, and he heard a movement as Rachel went across the
room.

The old woman was breathing. She seemed to be asleep, or again in
her stupor.

He turned, and saw Rachel crouched on the hearth, as close to the
fire as she could get, clutching her hands together before the blaze.
The light from the candle above fell on her hair, gilding it, but the
light of the fire only defined the pallor of her face. Her shoulders were
shaking as with a chill.

He went to her, and bent to put a hand on her shoulder. She looked
up at him, her stiff lips trembling. "I'm cold," she said.

He took her hands, and began to chafe them for warmth. Then, at
Josie's knock, he straightened up. Josie came directly to Rachel.
"Missie, Missie . . ." she said.

"Oh, I'm cold," Rachel said.

Josie turned to Jeremiah. "Git her out," she commanded. "You git

143

her out a-here. I'll set up here. You git her out a-here. It ain't doen her no good." Then Josie took Rachel's left hand and drew her to her feet, putting an arm about Rachel's shoulder, murmuring and crooning to her, saying, "Baby—baby—baby . . ." That was the only word Jeremiah could distinguish.

Josie led her to the door. Jeremiah followed. Josie, with an arm still about Rachel's shoulder, reached to open the door. Then she turned to Jeremiah again. "You take her," she commanded. "You take my Baby, and git her out a-here." And she shoved Rachel toward him, delivering her over to him.

He took Rachel's hand, and led her out into the hall, which went almost dark as soon as Josie had shut the door. He led her down the stairs, across the hall, into the library, and to the hearth, where the fire was low now. He released her to stir the embers and put on more wood. When he turned to her, she was standing as he had released her, but with her hands clutched together in the shawl.

"I'm cold," Rachel said.

"Come to the fire, come closer," Jeremiah said.

She did not move. So he took her hand and tried to draw her closer. She resisted him, not actively as by will, but as by a deadness and weight that seemed to fix her to the floor and make her sag.

"Come," he commanded softly, "come closer."

"Oh," she breathed, and looked at him. "Oh," she repeated, "oh, she said—she said I killed her."

"Hush," he commanded.

"She said I killed her—she said it."

"You didn't kill her," he replied soberly. "She is just an old woman dying."

"She said it—and, oh, I am wicked."

He took her in his arms. "You are not wicked," he said.

She surrendered to him for an instant, then stiffened. "Yes—yes, I am wicked. But"—and she tried to release herself, shoving against him—"but if I am wicked, she made me wicked, she made me . . ."

"Hush," he said, "hush," trying to quiet her struggle.

". . . and if I killed her, she ruined me, she ruined me—for there's nothing but ruin in this house, nothing but ruin—for nobody ever loved anybody in this house, not here, not here . . ."

He grasped her firmly. "I love you," he said. "And in this house."

"No—no—nobody ever loved anybody here—and, oh, I am lost!"

She struggled to free herself, saying again, "I am lost!" but he exerted his real strength and crushed her quiet.

"You are not lost," he said. "You are not lost, for I love you. Do you hear me? I love you. And in this house."

She leaned back from him in his arms, her hands against his chest.

144

But she was not struggling against him. She was staring intently into his face, as though she had just discovered it and had to learn it feature by feature.

Then she lifted her hands, one on each side of his head, far back and tangled her fingers in his hair, and slowly drew his face toward hers. She kissed him full on the mouth.

That night Jeremiah Beaumont had her, there in the library. From the moment their lips touched he knew it had come to pass. It was an act outside all his preconceptions and decisions. It was beyond any thought he had ever had.

Some hours before dawn, Josie came down the stairs. They heard her even before she reached the library door and knocked. At the knock, their eyes met, and they knew the truth, but neither spoke. Then Rachel rose, went toward the door, and ordered Josie to come in.

Mrs. Jordan, Josie said, was dead. She did not know when she had died. No, she herself had not been asleep. She had been wide awake, before the fire, and there had not been a sound. She had discovered the fact when she happened to go over to the bed. She must have been dead some little time, because by then the body was getting cold.

Without a word or a look, Rachel went upstairs, leaving Jeremiah alone in the library.

Mrs. Jordan was buried in the beech grove beside Timothy Jordan, upon whose picture she had spat, and not far from her nameless grandson. A Presbyterian preacher from Lumton, summoned by Jeremiah, performed the brief service. At the grave were Rachel and Jeremiah, all of the Negroes on the place, and Dr. Thomas. After the occasion, the doctor and the preacher came back to the house and took a glass of whisky against the cold, and rode off together.

A week later Jeremiah again went to Lumton, to the house of the preacher. He had been engaged to Miss Jordan for some time, he explained, but they had not intended to marry for months to come. But the death of Mrs. Jordan had changed everything. Sukie Marlowe, the midwife, who also served sometimes as a sort of nurse, had been staying with Miss Jordan. Miss Jordan had sustained a considerable shock with the death of her mother, and was now alone. Furthermore, the Jordan farm needed a man. Therefore, he and Miss Jordan had decided that, despite the recent death of her mother, they would be married. Would Brother Hillson ride to the Jordan house, on a day and hour of his election, to unite them, bringing such witness as the law demanded?

So they were married, on March 3, 1822.

But Colonel Cassius Fort still lived.

145

V

JEREMIAH HAS TOLD US, ALMOST MOMENT
by moment, how he approached his great resolve. He has not told in
such detail how that resolve weakened and failed in his bosom. But it
did weaken and fail. He slipped gradually and unwittingly into a new
season or a new climate. The ball of his being, to use his own image,
had tilted toward the sun and "fresh plants grew green in regions
where there had been winter."

He moved into the Jordan house. Two days before his marriage he
had told Mr. Barron that he would leave, and why. He had dreaded
the moment, for he knew the kind of loneliness there would be for the
old man after his departure, and felt, obscurely, that he was betraying
an obligation. But he braced himself, and at night as they sat before
the now smoldering fire, he told him. He need not have worried, for
the old man said, "Boy, it is right and good. If it has come in your
heart, let no man say nay. There ain't nothing like a woman by a man's
side, for dark and day, and trust betwixt them."

Jeremiah, in some embarrassment, spoke of his regret at leaving.
"Good Lord, boy," Mr. Barron stopped him. "I can take care of myself,
and have. When my boys took off and my girls married away, I never
peaked and pined. I cared for them and they cared for me, but I
knew they had to go forth and lay hand on the world. For it is right."
He dropped into thought a moment, then added: "Don't worry about

me. I got good niggers here. I done them right, and they done me right. Whatever I ask they do it, and before I ask them."

So that was easier than Jeremiah had expected. But it did not prepare him for what followed. The old man rose from the chair, knocked out his pipe, and went to one of the cupboards set in the far wall. He fumbled there a moment and then returned to the hearth. He had a silver mug in his hand. "My house was never much for vanity and such," he said. "Plain and solid and the best the Lord would give for the strength of my arm. But my wife like a woman liked a pretty, and I wanted her to have them according to her good sense. When my girls left, I give them most. But I kept one or two to remember by. I kept this."

He exhibited the old mug, polished bright in the candlelight.

"I know," he continued, "Miss Jordan has got fine things from over the mountains, and wants for nothing. But you give her this." He leaned and laid the mug in Jeremiah's lap.

Jeremiah looked down at the object, not touching it, and said, "No— no, I could not. I thank you from the heart. But I could not."

"Keep it," the old man urged.

Jeremiah picked up the mug and held it out, shaking his head.

The old man would not reach for it. He stood there on the hearth, grinning down through his whiskers. "It ain't mine," he said, "no more. It is Miss Jordan's. And when she sets lip to it, you take joy in her. Like I did, long back, when Annie smiled acrost it."

The next day when he rode to the Jordan house, Jeremiah took the mug. When he gave it to Rachel she held it indifferently in her hand, scarcely glanced at it, and murmured perfunctory thanks. Then with an increasing sense of disappointment, he told her what the old man had said. At first he thought that she was not listening, for her face was somewhat averted. Then he saw that she was looking down at the mug and that tears coursed down her cheeks.

"What is the matter?" he demanded.

"Nothing," she said.

"What is it?"

"Nothing—nothing—" she said, "—only . . ."

"Only what?"

"Only—" and she rose abrupty, still clasping the mug.

"What—" he began the question, but suddenly he knew what she had meant, and a cold clutch came at his heart. Then, all at once, he saw in his mind the face of the young girl smiling across the mug— a young girl with yellow hair and round cheeks and blue eyes—yes, the eyes would have been blue—and the lips parted above the silver rim to show the little white teeth set so even, as Tom Barron had seen them a lifetime ago when he stood in the budding growth beside the trail in North Carolina and watched the girl yawn as she rode by on the fat, sleepy old pony, riding along on a Sunday morning behind her father and mother, going to the meeting house, and now the girl smiled at him, at Jeremiah Beaumont, across the silver mug, meek and mischievous as though she belonged to him, to him, Jeremiah Beaumont, and not to Tom Barron, no, to Jeremiah Beaumont and invited him to take joy in her, in that innocence of an April morning long ago, long ago in North Carolina, and in that vision a wild despair swelled in Jeremiah, for why should he be deprived, why should Tom Barron have had that joy, Tom Barron who was a wheezing shapeless old man tied to a chair while Jeremiah Beaumont was young and strong! He could have cried out with the anguish.

But even at that instant he saw Rachel standing before him and heard her voice saying: "Only—only that you can never take such joy in me."

"No," he heard his own voice saying, "no, I cannot take that joy in you," and saw the knuckles white with clutching the mug and saw the stricken face above. "No," he repeated, and then it was not compassion he felt for the pain in that face, but a leap and swoop of his being, mysterious and triumphant and abstract. "No, not that joy in you," he said firmly, "but another, a greater joy, for—for . . ."

He could not find the words. He felt the reality straining in him, but he could not find the words. He rose and stood before her. Then he said: "—for you have given me myself."

That night as he rode to the Barron place to spend his last night there, he thought of the episode. He could not understand now that moment of despair when the vision of Annie Barron had come to him smiling across the silver mug. What was she? Nothing but some stupid backwoods girl with her round face and hair the color of straw. Well, young Tom Barron had loved her long ago and there was no quarrel with that if that was what Tom Barron had wanted, a good healthy girl to weave and wash and cook and lie warm at night and drop children as easy as a cow in pasture. And old Thomas Bartlett Barron loved her now. He probably loved her more now than he ever had before, for now that she was dead and rotten at the foot of a cedar tree on the Bartlett farm she could be the memory that justified his life. Well, let her lie and be forgotten, and what joy Tom Barron had had in her, and he, Jeremiah Beaumont, would take his own joy in his own way. And he thought with pitying contempt of the simple joy to be had from Annie Barron. What would she know of the fullness of life?

But "simple joy" came to surprise Jeremiah, too, in his new life with Rachel. "I would look upon her," he writes, "as she sat by the hearthside at night after supper, with embroidery upon her lap, or some other womanly task, and I would see the needle glint in the light and how subtle and sure were her fingers despite that her hands were strong and not formed to the common prettiness of female delicacy. Or when she read to me, as was her custom when I took my ease, I might note how the candlelight pricked out the secret gold or flame of her hair. I remember how upon my departure in the morning to go about the business of the day, she stood on the porch and looked after me and waved with a handkerchief, and especially once, when the day was gusty, how the wind pressed back her garments to define the secret sweetness of her form, which I knew well but which struck me then with such victorious newness that my heart stood still and my tongue clove dry to the roof of my mouth as though I had been Actaeon come suddenly upon the naked goddess by the pool. Or how once in summer when I fell sick of a little fever for two days, she sat the whole of an afternoon by my bed, with no conversation, and I awoke from my drowse toward dusk and saw her face outlined black against the fading light of the window as she looked out upon the fields. I made no stir but she knew and turned to me and held out a glass of water, saying, 'It is fresh, Jerry, and for you.' "

He had discovered what he calls "the bounty of common good which comes with no noise and does not rattle the latch upon the door." But at first he approached the obligations of his new life with reluctance and a kind of half-hidden resentment. Plowing, sowing, and fence-mending seemed dreary and irrelevant before the violence of the passion which he and Rachel Jordan had found. And, at moments even that passion faded before the consciousness of the great "Purpose," the awful commitment he had made.

Fort would come soon. And if Fort did not come, he, Jeremiah, would have to seek him out. So he was more ready now to ride to the settlement and wait for news at the tavern than to see to the roof of a barn or the depth of a furrow. What did an extra bushel of corn count in the face of the greatness of life?

Grudgingly, then, he began to go about the farm. It did not take him long to see that the place had lacked a strong hand. Timothy Jordan had been no farmer and no manager. There was slackness everywhere. Outbuildings unrepaired, land washed, fences down, cattle straying, pastures gone to burdock, milkweed and nettle, brush coming back into good fields, idleness among the hands.

Jeremiah thought how his own father would have sneered at the sight of such ruin of lands and goods. With a twinge of the heart he thought how if old Beaumont had come to this country with half of Timothy Jordan's start, he would not have had to use his last strength to rise in the moment of death in the bitterness of his unfulfillment, and cry out, "No, by God, no!" and then fall back upon the bankrupt's pillow. Old Beaumont would have been rich and great, greater than Colonel Mead or Timothy Jordan or Mr. Madison at Lexington or the arrogant old Morton Marcher up at Runnymede. Greater, by God, than Colonel Fort.

Yes, greater than Colonel Fort. And sitting his horse, looking over the fields bare with winter and ruined by neglect, Jeremiah suddenly saw them covered with corn and oats and rich pasturage and fat cattle on the pasture. He felt the surge of energy in him which would make the vision real.

Then he thought, "Is this my end, to be rich and easy, and heavy as my best sow glutted on oak mast?" For the moment he was sick with self-loathing.

Then he saw again his father's swarthy face wearing the grim smile he used to smile when looking at a rich harvest, and he thought again how he, old Beaumont, would never have let a good field go to pieces or a fat pig stray, and how old Beaumont would have been great, given his chance, greater than Colonel Fort. Then Jeremiah saw the truth. He saw it clearly. He would make the vision of the fat fields come true, and that would be old Beaumont's revenge on all the great whose company he had not been able to join. For old Beaumont had a score to settle, too, just as Rachel Jordan had a score to settle. It was a score with Colonel Fort, one of the great to whom all things came easy, fat land and power and reputation among men and the white, ardent flesh of a young woman in a dark house.

It all fell into order for Jeremiah Beaumont, his pleasure in his wife, his waiting at the tavern for news, his nocturnal brooding over his great purpose, and his daylight energy in the fields.

And as the year wore on to harvest, his imagination began to leap into the future, beyond this harvest. He would buy some Merino sheep, the kind that Colonel Fort had introduced into this section. He would take out the timber on the creek for a new cornland and throw part of the old cornland to pasture to save it from wear and washing. And as he walked by Duck Creek, in the woods, one Sunday afternoon in August, he came upon the place for a mill. So the Merinos, the new cornland, and the mill entered his calculations and his dreams. He could see them before him.

What else could he see before him? He saw Rachel's face waiting for him at the end of every day, speaking to him across the supper table, musing in the dusk as they walked in the garden, smiling up at him from a pillow, from the midst of her unbound hair, as he reached to snuff the candle.

Did he still see Colonel Fort? The solid bulk and sad face beyond the out-thrust pistol pointed at him, at Jeremiah Beaumont? That body or his own lying on the ground by some ritual grove, with the patch of red growing on the breast? He says this much: "I could not forget my obligation and my manhood, but circumstance taught me patience."

He had to be patient, for in the late spring Colonel Fort had gone again to the East, to Philadelphia and New York. He had gone as one of a committee of three to try to work out a system of postponement for debts owed in Kentucky to banks and merchants in those cities. Wilkie Barron had told Jeremiah that.

For in June Wilkie was back at his uncle's house on a visit, as a note brought by a colored boy on a mule informed Jeremiah one evening. The next day Jeremiah rode over to the Barron place.

He found Wilkie prosperous and full of affairs. He was practicing law now in Lexington under the wing of Mr. Madison, writing articles for Skrogg's *Advocate,* speechifying for Relief, consorting with the great, whose names now came easily to his tongue. He was a little heavier than before, but still lithe in carriage and quick in movement. His glistening boots creaked "elegantly" (Jeremiah gives us the word) as he paced old Barron's veranda and gestured with his cigar and expatiated on the wickedness and defect of public spirit and ignorance of law just exhibited by Judge James Clark of Clark County in his decision of May 13, 1822.

A certain Blair, Wilkie explained, had owed one Williams $219.67½. Wilkie dwelt on the half cent. The year before, in 1822, in the August term of the Bourbon County Circuit Court, Williams had received judgment against Blair for the debt and costs. Immediately, according to the replevin law of December 25, 1820, duly passed by the Legislature of the Commonwealth of Kentucky, Blair had gained relief by a replevin bond for two years. But in November Williams had moved to quash the replevin bond and collect. On May 13, Judge Clark had given a decision in favor of the creditor Williams, declaring that the replevin law of Kentucky was void. He had cited Section X of Article I of the United States Constitution which forbade the passing of any *ex post facto* law or any law breaching the obligation of contract, and had then declared that Section XVIII of Article X of the Kentucky Constitution was in full agreement. If Judge Clark's decision stood, it was death to Relief.

But it could not stand, Wilkie declared. By God, it could not.

"It is the law," Jeremiah said. "I remember the Article in the Kentucky Constitution."

"We could change it," Wilkie declared. "For what is our constitution for? It is to protect the people of the state. And when it does not protect, it is not valid. We will change it."

Jeremiah pointed out that the Constitution of the United States would remain.

"Remain!" Wilkie exclaimed. "It will remain where it belongs. On a scrap of sheep's hide in Washington. But not here. For this Commonwealth has its dignity and shall make its own law and its people shall not starve."

He teetered on the edge of the veranda and gestured with his cigar. He seemed not to be speaking so much to Jeremiah as to the empty space of the yard, which might be full of people, people waiting and listening to Wilkie Barron. Then he swung to Jeremiah. "Listen," he said, "I have seen beggary on the streets of Lexington. I have seen men hungry on the road as I came here. And we'll make the law we need."

"The law is . . ." Jeremiah began.

But Wilkie cut him short with a gesture of authority. "Law me no law, sir," Wilkie said, "and split me no hairs, sir. Law is to maintain the right. And when it does not do so . . ."

Wilkie's voice went on, saying things that Jeremiah did not hear, for he was thinking how what Wilkie had just said echoed his own thoughts in those first days after Rachel had laid the obligation upon him. He had then asked himself where was the voice of Justice but in the heart. But what had Wilkie said? He had said: "Where is the voice of Justice but in the belly?" That was what Wilkie had said, all he had said, though in finer words. That was no echo of what he, Jeremiah Beaumont, had said. It was a wicked parody, and he almost started up from his chair in anger like a man who is mocked.

But his friend had not mocked him. His friend was a thousand miles away, talking politics, how this was in confidence but there would be a special session of the Legislature and how the Legislature would assert its sovereign power against Judge Clark and against any man, however great in wealth and place, who stood in the way of Relief. Even against Henry Clay who was turning traitor to the people of Kentucky and to Justice. "For we only want justice," Wilkie was saying. "For that is all a man can live by."

Justice, Jeremiah thought, justice. Justice of the belly. And, by God, justice of the heart.

He rose abruptly from his chair. "You are right," he said.

"Ah," Wilkie said, and looked curiously at him. "Ah, you believe me?"

"Yes," Jeremiah said.

Wilkie laid a hand on his shoulder. "That day at Lumton—you remember, Jerry?"

Jeremiah made no answer, feeling a faint resentment.

"Well," Wilkie said, and his hand clenched on the shoulder, "you will stand by us again."

Jeremiah tells us that his sudden confusion of spirit must have showed in his face, even though he said nothing, for Wilkie grasped his shoulder harder, driving his fingers in, and leaned at him, and said, "If you see the right, if you know we are right, and sit still and do nothing—then—then you . . ."

Wilkie's smooth, brown, handsome face was thrust at him, the dark eyes glittering, the lip curling under the dark mustache to show the even teeth, and it was suddenly strange to Jeremiah, like a face he had never seen before, strange and threatening, and he whiffed the cigar-rich breath that blew out of the curling mouth, over the even teeth. Jeremiah stood motionless for an instant, staring into the face, then recoiled.

But Wilkie was laughing. It was the old, gay, bantering laugh of the days in Bowling Green. He released Jeremiah's shoulder, lifted his hand, and slapped the shoulder with all the warmth in the world. "Oh, you're the bridegroom!" he exclaimed. "And what's the use of talking politics to a bridegroom? Why, damnation, the only politics a bridegroom is concerned with is the politics of the bedchamber. And, oh, the bridegroom—he'll carry his point. Oh, he'll fight for relief!"

Wilkie seemed very pleased with his joke. Again, he slapped Jeremiah on the shoulder, laughing, saying, "Damn it, don't look so doleful. I know I blaspheme against pure love."

Then Wilkie was serious. "Jerry," he said, "I know you are happy. Enjoy your happiness, and may it last forever. But, my boy, when the first blush is past, then you will find that you live in the world."

Jeremiah said nothing.

"Oh, you will find that you live in the world. And then—and then, Jerry . . ."

"Then, what?" Jeremiah demanded, vehemently, almost angrily.

"Then you can join us. Shoulder to shoulder. But now, my boy, I would not disturb your happiness for worlds. But one thing, may I come and see you in your happiness?"

Jeremiah felt the sudden impulse to say, "No—no—you cannot come—nobody can come—and least of all, you." But with the impulse, came the guilt of the impulse. So he said: "You must come. We expect you. Will you come tomorrow? Rachel wants to see you. She told me to ask you. She is very anxious to see you. . . ."

The lies poured out, and each lie, as he became aware that it was a lie, demanded to be compounded with another lie. For Rachel had said nothing, and Rachel would be waiting for him only, for Jeremiah Beaumont only, under the trees on the lawn, in the long summer twilight.

Wilkie cut short the lies. "I can't come tomorrow," he said. "I have letters, urgent letters. Or the next day. But soon. When you come to

153

me again, we'll fix a time. For I must see your happiness." He stopped, shook his head ruefully, and smiled with a sadness half-comic and half-serious, and said, "For you see, Jerry, I have found no happiness. I must see your happiness to keep my faith in happiness."

"You must come!" Jeremiah burst out, and for the first time that day discovered the old warmth and affection. "Drop the letters, and come tomorrow!"

"Not tomorrow," Wilkie said, shaking his head.

"Soon!" Jeremiah exclaimed.

"Soon," Wilkie agreed.

Later Wilkie stood beside Jeremiah, as he prepared to mount. It was the instant just after the farewells had been passed, and Jeremiah's foot was already in the stirrup, and his back to his friend as he made ready to swing up to the saddle. Then he heard Wilkie's voice, very low, saying, "Now that you are happy, Jerry, are you ready to . . . ?"

Foot still in the stirrup, Jeremiah looked over his right shoulder. "Ready to what?" he demanded.

Wilkie was standing close, with a cigar in his mouth, his whole face "looking dark and closed like the outside of a shuttered house," studying Jeremiah from under half-lowered lids.

"Ready to what?" Jeremiah again asked.

Wilkie removed the cigar, tapped off the ash, and replied quite casually, "Ready to drop that old affair? That fool business?"

Jeremiah abruptly turned his head from Wilkie, swung to the saddle, uttered, "No, by God!" and gave his mount the spur.

He was not angry with Wilkie. How could he be angry with Wilkie? For Wilkie only spoke with the tongue of the wise world. For Wilkie only wished his happiness. For Wilkie only spoke as his friend. But he was angry with himself. Angry because he had so far forgot himself and what made him himself that he had to depend on some casual word to remind him of what he was. He drove the spurs in again, savagely, as though he drove them into his own flanks.

It was so easy to forget.

That night, as he lay in the dark, after the act of love, he said to his wife that it was easy to forget, in the midst of happiness, the price of happiness. To this she gave some drowsy response, which made him think she had not heard. He rose on an elbow, and tried to peer at her.

"Did you understand?" he asked.

"You said you are happy," she replied. And added, "Lie down, Jerry. I'm happy, too."

Then she reached out and laid her hand on his.

But he did not respond to her touch. "Listen," he said. "I said it

154

is easy to forget the price of happiness. But you must not think I have forgotten."

"Forgotten?" she echoed, and made some slight stir in the dark.

"My God," he exclaimed, "how could you forget?"

"What? What?" the voice asked, slightly edged with alarm.

"Fort!" he said. "By God, Colonel Cassius Fort. And do you remember who he is?"

There was no answer, but he heard the intake of her breath.

"I'll tell you who he is," he said. "He is the man who laid his foul hands on you." He reached out and laid his own hand on her breast. "And have you forgotten?" he repeated, and jerked his hand back, and rose from the bed and stood in his shirt, saying, "Have you forgotten? What you swore me to?"

There was no sound from the bed, and for an instant he had the wild fear, as he tells us, that there was nobody there, nothing there in the dark, but himself. And that fear made him increase the violence of his words. "Have you forgotten? Answer me!"

Then she answered. "No," the voice said dully from the dark, "no."

"Good," he said. And: "Good. There speaks my wife. For you— you would not"—he leaned toward the darkness where she lay—"for after what he did, you would not let it be said he breathed and lived. To your shame. To my shame."

"Oh, do it," her voice said, but it was like a wail, "do it—and the quicker the better—but for God's sake, for God's sake, let us not speak any more of it! Now or ever!"

He was about to reply, he did not know exactly what, but something in anger to the effect that he would speak of it for it was their dearest bond. But he heard her body shift in the bed, and heard her gasp, and knew that she had buried her head in the bolster to stifle the sound of weeping.

At that, he felt desolate and abandoned, and though the night was hot, he shivered nakedly as he stood there breathing in the darkness of the room.

Somewhat later he crept into bed. He lay there a long time before sleeping. He did not understand himself, he admits—his fury or his fear which had come to surprise him. Nor did he understand her. He could not imagine how it would be tomorrow, in daylight, when they had to face each other across the breach made in the darkness. But at last he slept, and when he woke in the morning, she smiled at him sleepily and reached across to take his hand and kiss it in the palm as though she were giving him a present for him to close his fingers upon and hold.

So it was a day like any other day.

The summer passed. In August, when the crop was laid by, the

155

usual season for a slacking off of work, Jeremiah took his Negroes to a spot on the creek he had located for a mill and began to work on taking out stone for a dam and for the race and foundations. He would be ready when good times came back to the country. Good times would come back. For one thing, as Wilkie had predicted, the Legislature had met in special session and had resolved that Judge James Clark's decision was in contravention of the laws of the Commonwealth, and had appointed a committee to report on his conduct. The committee had reported back that Clark's opinion was subversive of the best interest of the people and shook public confidence in the institutions of government, and Clark had been summoned to defend himself against removal from the bench. If Clark had escaped removal, the Relief sentiment had still been so strong that the necessary two-thirds majority had almost been reached and with the next election there was every promise that Relief would have control of the government.

Meanwhile, Jeremiah's own crop was good. Even with the low prices he would make out. But in addition to that satisfaction, he had had the satisfaction of seeing men stop by the edge of his fields to admire his corn. He felt that he had earned that—"the good opinion of honest and laborious men."

He relished it, too, at the tavern at the crossroads. When he had first begun to go there, he had gone only for news of Colonel Fort's movements, and in his obsession the faces of the men he had listened to had been as meaningless as ghosts. But now, in the fall and winter of 1822, he no longer went there for news. Fort was back in Washington, and a nephew of Mrs. Fort ran the place here and took care of her.

So when Jeremiah went to the tavern now it was for the pleasure that the society there could give. The faces were real now, and the words he heard had meaning. He had the habit of sitting quietly with his whisky (though in that whisky-soaked society he was not much given to drink), and listening to the talk and the arguments. For a long time he took no part. He was not of that world. His world was back at the Jordan house where Rachel waited. But as he sat here, he drew some warmth and strength from the good humor, the brags, and the turbulence of the world beyond him.

Bit by bit, however, he was drawn into it. A man would offer him a drink, and boast of a horse or a cock or a dog, tell some wild tale and slap Jeremiah's shoulder and roar with laughter, or curse the weather and the government. Or in some wrangling argument they would appeal to him, for they knew him to be "learned in the books and the tongues."

He was prevailed upon, too, to go on a hunt in the fall, in the rougher country to the west, where he saw beautiful untouched valleys. He hunted for a week, in the old way, gorging by the fire at night, washing the hot meat down with whisky, lying on a bear skin after the meal and looking at the stars. Late at night, when the others were asleep, he recaptured now and then something of the wild joy of his boyhood, when he had gone on his first hunt and had lain in the dark and "longed to stay forever alone in the free forest, killing and feasting on the beasts." But he knew he would go back, back to Rachel, and the "sweet melancholy of boyhood thought was lost in the peace of manhood's certainty."

He went back, back to Rachel, to his work and projects, to his occasional visit at the tavern, to his pleasure in the respect of men, both the wilder and the graver sort, and his interest in their talk of the world he touched but did not quite belong to.

And in that world that winter the passion increased. The United States District Court had declared the replevin laws of Kentucky contrary to the Constitution of the nation. Wherever the news came it touched off pride and fury. "Shall good men starve now in Kentucky," Skrogg wrote in his *Advocate*, "because sniveling lawyers and the puffed-up rich once wrote down words in a constitution and gave them out to be the voice of God?" And Skrogg's words let blood and broke bones on the streets of Lexington and Frankfort, and in country taverns and crossroads stores.

The sheriff's writ and the pinch of the belly were here and now. The violence, like a tide, washed into the farthest county seat or settlement tavern to release new violence to flood back on the big towns where the great men debated and the rich gave themselves airs and the banker totted up accounts and calculated interest and the fanatic or ambitious man called for justice and uttered the words that, printed on handbills or broadsides or in newspapers, or passed from mouth to mouth, spread over the land to bring blood. This violence washed in and out of Tupper's Tavern, where Jeremiah sat for his ease.

Jeremiah watched the tide lap and swirl at his feet. He did not allow himself to be drawn into arguments or discussion. He was quiet, listening, and if he was addressed or questioned, his courtesy saved him. "For I had never made it a practice," he writes, "to state myself combatively or to insist upon my opinion. I had been spared that vanity, and most of all during that time, when I was saddened to see the waste of manhood and the ruin of prospects wrought by the idle or desperate word, though that word sprang from just grievance."

But it was a dangerous game he played. And it became more dangerous as the supreme court of the Commonwealth, the Kentucky Court of Appeals, considered the old Blair-Williams case, which Blair had carried to that bench after Judge Clark's adverse decision in the Circuit Court.

If Chief Justice John Boyle and his associates Owsley and Mills should rule against the law made by the Legislature of the Commonwealth, they would be nothing less than dividers of the public heart, setters of brother against brother, traitors. But how could John Boyle fail to see the truth, men asked. He had been born in poverty and knew the pinch. He had been brought as a child into Kentucky, in the early days, back in 1782, when men were men to seize the wilderness or died. He was of the blood that had made Kentucky, and would not undo her. No, others said. John Boyle had consorted too long with the great. Prosperity had shriveled his heart like a green gourd plucked and left in the sun. He was the hireling of place and the fugelman of power, and Justice Owsley was his creature. For young Owsley had studied law with Boyle and was his tool. Make no mistake, they would be traitors all—and if they were . . .

There was the broadside:

TO ALL MEN OF KENTUCKY!!
WAKE AND WATCH AND SLEEP NOT!!
WHEN THE COURT SHALL SPEAK
HAVE YOUR ANSWER
READY!!!

Should John Boyle deny his kind, should he forget the gnaw of the belly empty and the brotherhood of the poor, should he take pride in setting lip to the silver cup, should he break faith and foul his sacred oath as the guardian of our good, should he tyrannize over Owsley and Mills, his sworn fellows—

Then—Oh, then—ye men of Kentucky, son of the canebrake or child of the hill, you know the answer and you know the way! Remember how this fair land was ransomed and not without blood. It was the blood of our fathers. Will you be worthy of that blood?

WHAT SHOULD BE DONE
WITH A TRAITOR?
????????????????????????????????
??????????????

The broadside, unsigned, hung on the wall of Tupper's Tavern. It was a late afternoon, in March, 1823. Jeremiah was in his corner, near the hearth, where a little fire smoldered.

Then Squire McFerson came in. That event was unusual, unusual enough to break the interest of the group by the broadside and turn their eyes upon him. For the Squire was deep in his years now, gouty and wheezing and heavy, scarcely able to mount and come to a burgoo

158

or a horse-run or the tavern for the good fellowship he had once loved a little too well for his constitution or estate. His broadcloth was frayed now and his eyes bleared, the color of his red face and hair, and "hearty good will had long since given way to irascibility and despite."

The Squire stumped over to the group by the wall, muttering, "What ha' ye here, what ha' ye here?" The group fell back, watching him.

The Squire stood close to the wall, peering at the broadside with his bad sight. Then he swung round at the men. "What blackguard hung this treason here?" he demanded, and struck the floor with his stick.

There was no answer. So he again struck the floor, and shouted, "Let him speak if he is no coward!"

In the silence, there was no sound, except the measured tap of Mr. Tupper's pipe as he knocked the ash out against the stone of the hearth. Then he rose. He was a small man but broad-shouldered, and he carried his head back with glaring eyes like a game-cock. He was the master of a snug little brick tavern, he knew the arts of the tavern-keeper in that world, long forbearance, measure and civility, then upon necessity the stroke like lightning. He was, for all his small stature and soft voice, a "tight little fistful of man-meanness by common report."

He stood upon his own hearth, with his hands clasped behind him, and said to the Squire: "No blackguard hung it there, sir."

"None but a blackguard," the Squire said.

"I hung it there," Mr. Tupper said calmly, "and recommend you watch your words, sir."

"None but a blackguard," the Squire repeated. Then added: "And a traitor, to boot."

Mr. Tupper rocked on his heels on the hearth, like a man at ease. Then he said: "We have been good friends and neighbors, Squire, for many a year, but if you were not wind-broke with time and swole with dropsy, I'd knock out your last tooth for half of those words."

The Squire was inflamed purple, and for a moment could not speak. Then he uttered something more like a rumble in the throat than like words and advanced a few ponderous steps toward the hearth. Then he stopped, mastered his rage, and said, "I'll fight ye. I'll fight ye, though ye be but a tavern-master and a bottle-washer."

"Tavern-master," Mr. Tupper said, "and I made the tavern with my own hands and my own sweat, and it is mine, and I'll have in it no pus-gutted nigh-bankrupt old waster who better than rail at true words should thank God for Relief to save him a bit of bread for his last days."

Then the old man reached into his coat and drew out a dirk and said, "I'll fight ye no duel, I'll kill ye now!"

Mr. Tupper kept his hands clasped behind him. But there was a big iron poker propped on the hearth, not three feet from him. "I warn you," he said. "This is my house and I have been named blackguard and not lifted a hand, as I call for witness. But if you do not put up that toy . . ."

"Toy!" the old man bellowed, and came lurching at Mr. Tupper.

Jeremiah leaped from his chair and seized the old man's right arm. The old man jerked and then grappled with his free arm, and they swayed together. Jeremiah was surprised at the Squire's great strength, as he almost tore free. At that instant, Jeremiah was aware that the poker had swung into the air. He heaved his weight to one side, stumbled and almost fell. But he jerked old McFerson down on one knee.

The strength was out of McFerson. He was nothing now but a great mass of sagging flesh. His puffed face was red and slick with sweat, his eyes stared wide and blank, and his mouth was open for the painful, rasping gasps. Jeremiah still clung to the right arm. But all at once, the fingers of the hand relaxed, and the dirk fell to the floor.

The poker still hung in the air above them. Jeremiah looked up into Mr. Tupper's face which, streaked white and with glaring eyes, hung there between the uplifted arms holding the poker like an ax. "In God's name!" Jeremiah cried out, looking into the terrible face swinging there in the air, "don't do it!"

"Would you threaten me?" Mr. Tupper demanded, staring down at Jeremiah now. But he let the poker slowly down to one side as though reluctant to forgo the blow.

The weight of McFerson sagged against Jeremiah, as the knee that had supported it gave way. Jeremiah barely braced himself to keep the body from slipping to the floor, getting his left arm around the thick shoulder. The heavy old head rolled back on Jeremiah's shoulder, with the weak surrender of a child or a sick man. But the old man was saying, "You—you—get your hands—off me . . ."

Jeremiah could not release him. If he released him, he would fall back on the floor. But even as the old man let his head lie cradled on Jeremiah's shoulder, he was saying, "Get them off—for you—you're a blackguard—too—a blackguard."

"I did it for your sake," Jeremiah tried to tell him. "To save you. To save you from something you would regret."

Then Jeremiah saw that tears were coming out of the popping, inflamed eyes and running down the puffed cheeks. "I am old—an old man . . ."

Then Mr. Tupper spoke, "Sir, Mr. Beaumont . . ."

Jeremiah looked up to see him leaning on the poker as on a cane and regarding the body. "Will you kindly get him out?" Mr. Tupper said. "I want no such filth on my floor."

"My God," Jeremiah said, "can't you see—can't you see?" And to the loathing he had for that weight in his arms there was the new loathing for the face above.

"I am an old man—an old man . . ." McFerson was saying with his gasps.

"Get him off my floor," Mr. Tupper commanded.

"My God," Jeremiah began, but then other hands began to lift up the body, and Jeremiah scrambled up, too, getting the old man's arm on his shoulder to sustain him. They half-carried, half-dragged the body to the door, for the legs were no good, making feeble motions but supporting no weight.

But just outside the door, the old man seemed to rally his strength for an instant to stand. He looked Jeremiah in the face, and said in a stronger voice, almost like his old voice, "Get your hands off me— you blackguard."

Jeremiah stepped back. He felt the urge to explain, to justify himself, but then he looked straight into the red, puffed face with its gaping, wheezing mouth, and the inflamed eyes that stared straight into his own, and he discovered the nakedness of hate. There was nothing he could ever explain to that face.

So he turned to one of the men. "Get him to a house," he said. "To that house." And he pointed to a house across the road.

He did not wait to watch them go, but turned to re-enter the tavern. He would get his hat and go. He had to get away from the place.

There was a babble of voices in the big room, but as he entered the sound stopped. He found all the eyes on him. He felt stripped and defenseless, accused of some nameless crime. He moved toward the hearth, where his hat lay on the bench, and the eyes followed him.

"And how's the old fool?" one man demanded.

And another: "You should have let him come on, the pride-swole old gobbler."

And Mr. Tupper, leaning on the poker: "And if he had come . . ."

And another voice: ". . . and one Anti-Reliefer the less."

And another: "The son-of-a-bitch of an Anti-Reliefer."

And Jeremiah found himself saying patiently, trying to explain something: "He is just an old man, he is just an old man."

"An old fool!" Mr. Tupper exclaimed, "And he'll come no more to my house."

One of the men had in his hand the broadside which Squire McFerson had snatched from the wall. He held it out toward Jeremiah, shaking it a little as to emphasize what he was about to say. "And how do you stand on this, Mr. Beaumont?" the man demanded.

161

He hated them all, the nasty, vain old bankrupt Scot who would stab one moment and weep like a baby the next, the glare-eyed little tavern-master who leaned on the poker like a victor, the man who held out the broadside in his work-hard hand and was again demanding, "And how do you stand on this?"

He wanted to say, was about to say, "My opinions are my own affair," but the eyes on him forbade that. They would never be satisfied.

"Yeah," a man said, "and how do you stand?"

"Listen," Jeremiah said, "the Court has given no decision. We do not know what it will decide and . . ."

"I know what it had better decide!" the man with the broadside said, and shook the paper in his hand.

"It's our Court," another cut in, "and it better decide what we want or . . ."

"We do not know what the Court will decide," Jeremiah repeated firmly, "and it is unjust to prejudge its decision. Furthermore, a Court that can be threatened is no Court. Law by threat is not law, and if . . ."

"Law!" one of the men said, and turned and spat on the hearth.

"Yes, law," Jeremiah said again. "Law by threat is not law, and if I were a judge and threat were made . . ."

"Yeah, Mr. Beaumont," a voice said, "and what would you do and you a judge?"

"One thing, if I had the strength. I should try to ignore the threat and act by my conscience and oath, and if . . ."

"Conscience and oath!" the man with the broadside exclaimed. "The oath is to defend the people, and, by God . . ."

"And to defend the law!" Jeremiah interrupted, "To defend the people by law and have justice by law . . ."

A big, tall, gangling man who had not spoken—a man like men you saw on the road or lounging in front of a cabin, hairy-faced, wearing homespun and stitched-down shoes, bent in the shoulders, raw-handed—stepped forward and looked straight and slow into Jeremiah's face. "Mister," he said, "mister, you mean you air Anti-Reliefer?"

"I am for Relief," Jeremiah began, "but . . ."

"*But*," the man echoed, "*but* . . ."

"Yeah, he's for Relief," a nasty voice said, "but . . ."

"But he don't need no relief," the gangling man said. Then direct to Jeremiah: "Oh, you got you a place—a fine place . . ."

Then a voice to the rear, the voice of Simpson, a farmer: "Mr. Beaumont has spoke sense. I'm Relief, but to threaten the Court beforehand is to . . ." And the eyes swung to him.

All but the eyes of the gangling man. And he was saying to Jeremiah, leaning at him and squinching his gaze directly into Jeremiah's face: "Oh, yeah, you—you was smart to get you a fine place—you knowed how to get you one—oh, you knowed, all right . . ."

Jeremiah never understood exactly why he did not leap upon the man. For the man's words cut him off from what he had taken to be the central fact of his life, from Rachel Jordan, Rachel Beaumont, his wife, and from all she was to him. But at the same instant that the meaning of the words penetrated to him and inflamed him to rage, they paralyzed him. For the words were not the words of that leaning, squinch-eyed face, but of all the faces, of faces everywhere, over the country, faces leaning at each other leering and winking, saying, "Yeah—yeah—he knowed—he knowed, all right—oh, he was a smart one."

So Jeremiah averted his face, feeling the flush of shame.

Shame for what?

He described the moment: "I was shamed for the weakness that would not let me lift a finger to defend what I knew to be the truth of my actions. But perhaps I was shamed by a deeper shame which it is hard to put into words even now, though I have thought much upon it. If a man lives by what he feels to be the truth in him, and discovers in a single instant that the tongue of the world says differently of him, there comes the fear and shame that what he had held to be the truth in him may not be the truth after all and there may be no truth for him but the terrible truth now given him by the tongue of the world. And if a man is robbed of his truth, and of a sudden, how can he know what he is?

"So I was weak to turn my face, and even weaker to be grateful that none had heard the words of insult addressed to me. For if others had heard, I could not be sure whether even then I might have had strength of manhood. At least I was spared the public shame, for the debate had become general and voices were raised. I took my hat and went toward the door with what dignity is left a man shaken to the marrow of his bones.

"At the door I turned, and tried to save something of my respect, by saying in a voice loud and firm enough to catch the attention that I had spoken my honest opinion and would abide it, and they all looked at me for a moment. And I noticed, even as I spoke, that the tall man whose name I did not know and who had insulted me, wore on his face an expression of mean and sardonic pleasure as though he had surprised a secret to my disgrace."

Jeremiah rode homeward in great distress. He had been appalled by the irrational violence which had involved him. He had tried to save a life and had earned the name of blackguard for his pains. He had tried to speak for reason and justice, and had been told that his whole life was based on the foulest and most prideless self-interest. The injustice done to him smarted like wounds.

He met a man on the road, and to the man's good day muttered something without looking him in the face. He wondered was the man thinking, "There goes that Beaumont—that fellow who married a cast-off trollop because she was rich." Having passed, he had the crazy impulse to turn and pursue and drag the man from his saddle and strangle him and toss the body into a ditch. But the man wasn't the world. You could not strangle the whole world.

But there was Fort. There was Cassius Fort. The blood of Fort would clear him. It would clear him before the world. It would clear him before himself. He would bathe in it and be clean, and the words of the hymn ran through his head, of a fountain filled with blood which would wash away all guilty stains.

He was so preoccupied when he came into his house that he scarcely acknowledged his wife's greeting, and turned coldly from her kiss.

At supper he answered shortly some word she said, and then waited with a cold pleasure for some bitter retort from her. But she made none.

She had never spoken to him in anger, but now he longed for such a word from her. She only looked down at her plate, however, white in the face. He saw how the freckles stood out on the white skin, and how the brown mark was suddenly bold on the left cheek. He thought quite coldly how it was a blemish, and wished it were away. He could not conceive now how once he had longed to set his lips there.

He rose from the table before the meal was over, and went to walk in the yard alone. She did not come out to him. He did not re-enter the house until he saw the light go out in the window of the room they shared.

Lying beside her in the dark, wondering if she was awake, listening for her breath, he felt a terrible remorse, mixed with self-pity. He had been driven to what he had done. It was not his fault. They were victims together. He experienced a surge of his old tenderness for her. He would defend her against all the world. Then the question struck him, did she share the view of the world? Did somewhere, in the unspoken depth of her mind, lurk the notion that he had come to her for her lands?

He had the idea to seize her and wake her and demand the truth, and he actually rose in the bed. But he knew it would do no good to ask. So he sank down again. He would have to prove to her that it was not true, that she wronged him. Ah, there was a way. He would take her and go away, somewhere west, to a new place, a new country, new faces, new names, even he and she with new names. They would go away with nothing, nothing but the clothes on their backs, leaving the land and the house and the stock and the lands for whoever would take them. Ah, that would prove to her that he had come innocently and in honor, that he wanted nothing. As she suffered cold and hunger and the wildness of a new country, she would know him for what he was. Cold and hunger would be a punishment to her for foul suspicion, he thought grimly. Oh, she was gently bred, and she would suffer. As his mother had suffered, who was gently bred. As all those women, all kinds of women, the gentle and the common had suffered who had come to the wild country in fear and poverty. Why shouldn't she suffer? She was no better than they.

But as he relished the picture of her just punishment, he was ashamed of his satisfaction. How did he know that she had ever held that suspicion of him? Why should she suffer? Then he felt like crying out, "And why should I suffer—I who am guiltless?" But was he guiltless? Was not his suffering the punishment for harboring a suspicion against himself? If he had been clear before himself, would the suspicion of the world have mattered? But could you know? Could you know? Was there a way to know?

There was a way. There was Fort.

That was the old circle. Whatever happened, whatever road he took, the circle always closed where it began. There was Fort. There was the perfect act, outside the world, pure and untarnished. Outside the world, the beginning and the end, the perfect justice self-defining and since defining self, defining all else.

Then, clear as a bell, as though the words were spoken in full voice in the dark above him, he heard his own voice as it had spoken that afternoon at the tavern when he looked into the hairy face of the man who held out the broadside. It had said, and said again, now in the dark: "To defend the people and have justice by law." And the voice said again and again in the dark: "Justice by law." And it was his voice snatched out of him that afternoon by all the witless violence he had just been caught in. And to strike Fort down would not be justice by law.

So he began again the old track, treading the old circle, step by step, trying the footing in the dark, fearful that it would give beneath his weight, feeling the quiver of earth beneath each step. But toward dawn, the circle closed where it began, and he slept.

The next day the idea came for a project that would forever stop any mouth from saying, "There is that Beaumont, that fellow that married a woman for her lands and lives on them easy."

He would have lands of his own.

There were still lands in Kentucky, where men would come. On the hunt in the fall he had seen valleys full of strong timber and glades where the grass was waist-high and juicy, soil that would slice to the plow like cheese to the knife and so rich that a grain of corn would explode in it like powder in the chamber of a rifle. There were streams for mills and stone for building. It was waiting for the taking, and a strong hand. And now was the time to take, when times were bad and men made no projects. He would take now, and when things changed, when the settlement began to expand again and men put their minds again on the future and the West, he would be rich.

He wrote to Bowling Green and got a manual of surveying, and every night, no matter how strenuous the day had been, he settled down to study it and stayed with it late, sometimes till long past midnight, till the candle guttered and the first rooster crowed back by the barn. Then he would go upstairs, strip in the dark, and let himself down by Rachel's side to seize a little rest before the horn. He did not tell her what he was doing. He would show her.

He would show the world. Nothing could stop him. He did not want lands and cattle and money to be happy, but you had to show the world in the world's way. And, one night, sitting late by the candle, thinking that, he suddenly remembered his father. "I thought how he had come to the new land with a book on surveying and must have studied it in those hard years before my birth, in a cabin, late at night, by the light of a grease lamp, as I now by a sperm candle set in a silver stick. I thought how in my boyhood I had found the worn copy of Love's *Surveying* hidden with old plunder on a shelf and how my father had come upon me reading it, and had gone black in the face with his anger and had seized it from me, and how later he had left it for me on my bed. Then at once my eyes swam with tears I could not shed, for I knew my father and the bitterness that had struck him when he saw me, a boy, with the old book which was the mark of his hope deferred and brought low, and I knew the nature of that hope, not for lands and wealth, but to show his manhood in the world in the way the world would understand, for a man must find a way to be a man. And I knew the great bitterness in him at his moment of bankrupt death when he strove to rise and struck the bolster and cried out, 'No, by God, no,' meaning to say that he would not be deprived. So in pity and solemnness in a rich house I had not earned, I leaned to kiss the book, as it had been the very same old tattered book on surveying he had left on my bed for apology and in his contrition as a gift for me. With that, I straightened in my chair and put aside fatigue and set anew to my labor, though the hour was late."

As soon as the crop was in, Jeremiah made a trip to Frankfort to study plats of Kentucky land and to learn there what he could of movement to the west. Then almost immediately upon his return, he set out west, taking with him one of his slaves and a strong intelligent white boy, who had had some schooling, the son of a neighbor. He was spying out the land, trying to locate for his first venture in speculation.

He was gone longer than anticipated, and upon his return he found signs of bad season and slackness on the farm. So for the next week he was absorbed in trying to repair the damage of his absence. He did, however, have the evenings with Rachel, and as he turned back toward the house in the late afternoon, he felt a clean lift of the heart, like something glimpsed on the horizon as you top the brow of a hill, the flash of water, the soar of a hawk. He would soon be sitting with her in the garden, in the arbor, in the evening, while the fireflies pricked the deepening dusk over the yard and pastures. He would sit with her, without any conversation. There would be no need for that. He would hold her hand, and she would lean lightly against his shoulder. He would be aware of the faint stir of her breath, less than sound, less than motion, simply part of the throbbing, brimming fullness of the world as dark came on.

But one evening, she said: "When you were away I missed you so I thought how I could not live without you."

He did not answer, but his own thoughts turned to his loneliness on the trip, and he pressed her hand for response.

"You do not understand," she said.

"I understand," he said.

"No," she said, "no, you don't understand."

"I do," he said, and almost began to tell her of lying in the camp, night after night, feeling empty and lost, listening to the boy breathe and the man snore, thinking how they could plunge into sleep as into happiness at the end of the day's labor, envying them because he could not, because he was somehow cut off from that perfect world of effort and repose, because he was alone without Rachel.

But she said again, "No, no," and there stirred faintly in him a resentment which forbade him to speak. If she could not know without his speech, then no speech would do any good. He was almost angry with her because she had spoken at all. But he pressed her hand again, aware of the extra strength he put into the act beyond the pressure of understanding and affection, a strength which must have made her wince.

"Oh, but you don't understand," she said with a sudden vehemence, as though she were answering a new avowal of his own. "Don't you see, don't you see? I was always alone. I never had anybody, not anybody. Not my mother or my father. Nobody ever loved me. I never had anybody. Not anybody. Not anybody . . ."

167

He had the sudden impulse—which shocked him even as it came—to say, "Oh, but you had Fort, you had him," but he suppressed it.

But even as he suppressed it, she was going on as though to catch up his thought about Fort. She was saying: ". . . and after, after that —when I thought I would have a baby—when I thought that that would be mine, that I would have somebody, something. But . . ." She stopped suddenly, and he heard the catch of her breath. "But it was dead," she said evenly. She repeated: "It was dead." Then suddenly: "And oh, I had nothing. And I have nothing but you, and when you were away I thought I would die."

She swung to face him on the bench, and jerked her hand free from his clasp, and put a hand on each of his shoulders, clutching hard, saying, "Don't you understand? I missed you so. I missed you so!"

She released her grip, and turned partly away, letting her hands lie idle in her lap in a sudden helplessness. "I missed you," she said quietly. "But it was almost worse before you went away. When you sat with the book late. When you were in the house but never with me. Oh, that was worse, and I could not sleep. I would lie there, and hear you come in, and you thought I was asleep. But I wasn't. I wasn't asleep."

Hearing her, he felt quite cold. "Listen," he said, "there are things a man has to do. I am engaged in something very important. For you as well as for me. I told you that, before I went away. That I was going on business, important business, and that . . ."

"But you wouldn't tell me what it was."

"No," he replied, "I wanted to surprise you with the fact."

"Is it done?" she asked. "Is it finished? You won't have to go away again?"

"It is only begun," he said.

"Only begun!"

"Only begun," he stated.

"Oh, what is it?" she demanded, and laid her hand on him again.

"I had not meant to tell you," he said. "Not yet."

"What is it?"

"If you must know," he said, "I have been studying surveying."

"But why? Why? You don't have to. You can . . ."

"Can what?" he demanded, and like a flash he thought he had caught her out. "Can what? Can stay here—on *your* land?"

"Oh, it's not my land. You know I didn't mean that. It is your land. I meant, why study surveying? That would take you away. Away from me. You could stay here. You could . . ."

"Stay here," he continued for her, "and be a foreman on your land."

"It is your land!" she said, her voice rising. "Didn't I say it was your land? And you have the law. You have studied law, and you could practice law at Lumton."

"My God," he burst out, rising from his seat. "My God, law at Lumton! Listen," he said, leaning at her in the dark, "there is land to the west. There is money to be made there. When times change, when . . ."

"Speculation?" she demanded. "Speculation? My father—he almost ruined himself. He almost ruined us. If it had not been . . ."

"Been for what?" he demanded, leaning closer, waiting, saying to himself that she would have to say it, would have to say how Fort had come to save them, had come into their house to save them and take his pay. "If it had not been for what?" he repeated.

"Oh, I don't know—I don't know exactly how it was."

"How what was?" he demanded, and steeled himself, and Fort's name rang in his head.

"The law," she said, "the new law. The replevin. But it saved something. It saved this place. But it was almost lost. My father almost lost everything."

"It was because he was a fool," he said, and took relish in the epithet, expecting some protest from her for her father's sake. But none came, so he continued. "He speculated at a time when every fool was speculating. When he had to pay too much, for every fool wanted to buy. But now is the time. You can get land for near nothing. Good land to the west. I have seen it. And then when times change . . ."

"Oh, nothing will ever change," she cried out in anguish. "I'll always be alone. I'll be left alone. You will leave me alone. You will leave me alone, like . . ."

"Like Fort," he finished for her.

And in the dead silence, he added: "That is what you were about to say, isn't it?"

After a moment, she said dully, "No. No. That is not what I was about to say."

"Well, what was it?"

"Whatever it was, it couldn't matter now," she said in the same dull voice, and he was aware even in the shadow that she had turned her face from him and was staring away across the blankness of the garden and the fields.

He waited a moment, then said quietly and in self-possession, "If you will excuse me, I think I had better go in. I have some work to do. To sort the notes I have made on the trip west. Good night, my dear."

He waited for her answer, but there was none. So he turned from the arbor and went out of the garden toward the house, where a

169

candle showed a little light from the open door of the main hall. He went to the study, lighted a candle, and sat at the secretary. So he entered anew upon his work, sorting his notes and checking them by the map. After a while, he heard a motion in the hall. Rachel was going upstairs. He went back to his work with greater concentration, but he was aware of her presence. He knew that she lay alone in the bed upstairs, but his awareness was of more than that fact. From that center, from her physical being, a presence, a massive but impalpable presence as fluid and weightless as dark, flowed out, filling the house, coming down from the region above the stairs which before the last illness of the old woman had been mysterious to him and now, at once, was again mysterious.

The very area of brightness of the candle on the desk before him and in the air around him seemed to contract. He began to concentrate more rigorously upon the writing before him, speaking the words out loud like a spell of exorcism. He clung to each word, trusting it, its look on the page in his calligraphy, its twist to his tongue, its sound in his ear, its vision in his mind of the place far away in the west to which it referred, some valley where the timber stood tall and severe to make a green gloom from which you looked up to catch the dazzling wash of sunlight far above.

He did not know how long he was engaged thus, while the bulb of light contracted around him. Then he knew she was in the room. He had heard nothing, but he knew she was there. He told himself, no, it was not possible, he had deluded himself, he would not turn. But he knew it was true. And finally he turned.

There she was. She stood halfway between the open door and his chair, standing in a white night-dress, with her hair fallen free and with feet bare as though she had surrendered to an overmastering impulse and had not been able to wait, or think, to take slippers. Or, he asked himself, had she taken thought and left the slippers in order to make no noise, to come down as soundlessly and bodilessly as the dark that flowed down from the rooms above and filled the house, to stand in secret behind him? And for an instant he thought he saw beyond her, in the dark of the hall, the old woman's face floating as before to spy on him with its intensity of envy and hate. But it wasn't there. Only the daughter's white figure was there, at the edge of candlelight, her face looking at him, and he thought, ah, how love comes to spy as well as hate, and makes no sound.

"She was looking mournfully at me and as from a great way off, but in her sadness was a dignity which demanded nothing. I could not be sure, for the wavering light of the candle, but it seemed to me that she shook her head slowly from side to side, ever so little, as one who meditates upon what one would wish otherwise but knows

170

one cannot change. She stood so for a time, silent, and I found no word to say, for I could not speak, not knowing what spirit had made her rise and come. When she made a slight motion, I was sure that she would turn away from me, and go as she had come, into the dark hall and beyond. And if she had done so, I might have questioned myself as to the truth of her coming.

"But she came toward me at a slow pace without sound for the bareness of her feet, and stood directly before me. She looked down at me, and I expected her to speak. But she did not. The expression of her face remained mournful, but now with a mournfulness tempered with such sweetness that I felt my heart contract in the bosom. All at once she sank to her knees before me, not taking her eyes from my face. Then she bowed her head upon my lap with a motion which meant submission but a submission seeming aware of the worth of all it gave. Her face lay between my knees and her hair spread over them and hung on each side to the floor, covering them. She did not touch me with her hands, which were quiet at her sides.

"After a little I laid my hands upon her head, and felt how finely it was shaped and thought how much smaller it was than one suspected seeing it bear the mass of her hair. I had thought this before, when taking her head in my hands, with the hair loose, but now it came as new. So I let my fingers slip into the hair that flowed over my knees on each side, and I felt all the pangs of remorse for what I had said and for being unable to take innocently the proffered good of the world. And I thought how my own words had sprung from something in me I did not know the name or meaning for, and how a man moves in the darkness of himself, more trackless than the wild country, toward a light which glimmers far away. But he does not know what the light may be. (And now that all has come to pass, do I know? At this late time I would know, and move toward it, for that is all now left.)

"But that night, with her head on my knee, I looked down at her and thought, too, how she had wandered in her own darkness and toward what glimmer of light. And thought how perhaps she had hoped I might be the way, and might take her hand and guide her and know the name of the light toward which she moved, and how in that hope she had risen from her bed and come to me through the house. Then when I thought how she might have trusted me, who knew nothing, a great pitifulness filled me for her and despair that I could be worthy."

But that night, while he leaned over her bowed head and was filled with pity and despair, the book on surveying and the notes and the map of the country away to the west still lay on the secretary under the candlelight. And we know that Jeremiah went to Frankfort in the late summer of 1823, to investigate certain tracts at the land office there. By this time the western lands had become his chief interest. Fort was in the East, and had even sold his farm on Green River and removed his wife to Pick County, near Frankfort. So the thought of Fort gave way to more pressing concerns. He made the acquaintance of Felix, the son of Josh Parham, a big land-holder and the center of Anti-Relief sentiment.

He attempted to persuade Felix Parham into some sort of partner-ship for the land deal to the west, but this must have been equivalent to persuading the old man, for Felix was young, only a little older than Jeremiah, and was much under his old father's influence. Ex-actly how Jeremiah presented his case, we do not know, for all he says is that he made "no attempt to palliate or apologize for political views which the old gentleman held abhorrent." But the old man, no doubt, put a good business deal on a higher plane than any matter of politics, or being a good practical man, he saw politics as a mere coefficient of business and believed that if Jeremiah was in political error the error was nothing that could not be cured by a sound busi-ness venture. And the venture in the West was one which he at least thought worth considering. Jeremiah must have convinced him of that, and convinced him that he, Jeremiah, had some quality which the son lacked. For the son was known as a sort of ne'er-do-well, a lover of wenches and the bottle, a vain, idle young man, who, accord-ing to popular report, would long since have failed at his farming if the father had not supervised him and made up his deficits.

In any case, in the early fall, before the harvest, Jeremiah and Felix Parham started again west, accompanied by the young neigh-bor boy who had been with Jeremiah before, and the same slave.

The little expedition did not return this time until cold weather had definitely set in, up in November. But despite short rations, hard marches, and bad weather, Jeremiah returned in high spirits. He had found a better location than he had hoped, with excellent town sites. And he had found, also, that he would not have to play second-fiddle to Felix. Decisions had been his, for "Felix, like all men given to pleasure, lacked force of will, and would surrender to the force of another's will if that force was applied in a way not to offend his considerable vanity." It promised to be an ideal partnership. He hoped now to persuade the old man to a final arrangement.

The moment was propitious. The old man was in fine fettle, for "Now, by God," he said, "this country will not be given over to the pot-washings and scum of mankind, an a debt will be a debt again in the face of Hell and replevin, and an honest man can settle down again to make an honest dollar the way All-mighty God intended and none to say nay." For on October 8, the Supreme Court of the Commonwealth had upheld Judge Clark's decision of the Bourbon County Circuit Court that the replevin laws were unconstitutional and void. Williams would now be able to collect from Blair his debt of $219.67½.

Jeremiah already knew the fact. He had heard it in the first tavern they encountered on the way back, in the smoke-filled, stench-filled single room where they ate fat meat scarcely hot through and soggy corn pone and drank whisky out of a mug passed from hand to hand before lying down to sleep, all together, gaunt-faced family and all, on the flea-ridden bearskins.

On their brief stops he had heard all the wild talk. They would hang John Boyle. They would burn Frankfort, every stick of it, and not leave a stone standing, and sow to salt, and piss on the spot. For what was a state for if not to help a man when he was hungry? And by God, it was their state, Court or no Court, lawyers or no lawyers, rich or no rich. Courts and lawyers and sheriffs and rich—all worse than redskins or redcoats, and, like them, mortal when the plug bit in.

We know what they said, in those stinking sties of inns and at the lonely crossroads. Jeremiah does not record it. He does not need to do so, for we know what those men were, and we know the fury of betrayal which swept the country when the Court—their own Court—gave down the decision which seemed to pass a man over, bound hand and foot, to the moneylender and the sheriff, and to the "honest man," as old Parham said, who wanted to make an "honest dollar."

Hearing old Parham say that, Jeremiah suddenly felt that there could be no partnership. What had he to do with these people? The "plump-faced, purse-lipped young dandy on whom the travel-stained garments seemed to hang as a reproach and abomination and not as the mark of honest toil," who knew no woodcraft, no farming, no law, no trade, no book, no way of men or beasts or land or weather—not even a cunning trick of brawl or plugmuss—who could barely spell out the news in the paper, who knew only the heat of whisky in the gullet and the tickle of flesh? Or the hawk-faced old man with the slit-eyes that looked out to calculate you and the world, and the heavy, knotted hands which had seized on the world and still crooked for more? Which was worse, he did not know, the young man's softness or the old man's hardness? He felt like saying good day, and turning his back on them forever.

Old Parham was saying, "Yes, Mr. Beaumont, you go on home and get some rest and fix up your reports. Then you go on up to Frankfort, and check the tracts. You said you were going to Frankfort?"

Jeremiah nodded.

"Well, when you get back, if it's good enough, we can begin to talk business. Yes, sir, business. If that Legislature full of scoundrels don't blow up this country. Looks like they're fixing to try to break the Court. That Legislature," the old man was saying in massive contempt, "that Legislature, up there in Frankfort! They remove the Court and there won't be any business. Not for you and me or nobody."

Well, Jeremiah thought, in that case he would find some other way.

But in Frankfort, his business done at the land office, he was drawn, almost unwillingly, to the capitol where the Legislature now held its session.

"I found myself," he says, "in a most peculiar position. On the one hand, my conviction had been and was for the Relief, and had I not been in the Western parts at the time of the election that year, certainly my sacred ballot had been cast for that faction. On the other hand the defeat of the Relief in the Legislature would make for my private interests insofar as they depended on Mr. Parham. What was the meaning of this fact, I asked myself as I stood in the street of Frankfort that winter day. Was I a double-dealer, in my heart, and with myself? Can a man hold more than one hope in the heart? And I felt like crying out that I had not made the world, and why should I be blamed, and why should I alone be made to suffer for a love of singleness, while others swam like fish with open mouths in the sweet various stream of things? I said to myself that I had never concealed my opinion, that I was clear before men and should therefore be found clear before myself. I said that what the Legislature did, whether for my good or ill, was like the weather that comes and you cannot stop it. Should I blame myself because rain falls on my corn to save it, and ruins the cut hay in my neighbor's field? I would have turned away, gone to the stable, taken my horse, and ridden off from Frankfort, and thus dismissed the whole matter. But I could not bring myself to do this. Instead, I walked toward the room where those men sat who held our fortunes. I could not do otherwise, like a man who must pick his wound to see it bleed and feel the pain."

So he went to the chamber, to twitch his scab. He leaned against the wall, near the door, and listened. A tall, erect man, graceful for all his length of bone and abrupt gesture, was speaking. He wore a black suit, with but a touch of white at the throat. His features, Jeremiah says, were strongly marked to an uncommon degree, not to be called handsome, but his face was such as to hold attention, with a powerful jaw, flashing eyes, and the expression of one born to command. He spoke on the "sacred nature of our human society, with good voice and wide reference, and how the Court of the Com-

174

monwealth had acted but to maintain the trust of man to man, but his remarks were more notable for fire and persuasion than for the close-knit thought."

There was a touch on Jeremiah's shoulder, and he turned to find the face of Wilkie Barron only inches from his, leaning at him, smiling to show the white, even teeth and make the eyes glitter. "Ah," Wilkie whispered, "so you have come to the seats of the mighty!" He took Jeremiah's hand, pressed it warmly, and then laid his arm across Jeremiah's shoulder. "And that," he added, nodding toward the tall man in black who was speaking, "is the mightiest of all. That is the Duke."

Jeremiah looked inquiringly at Wilkie, but before he could frame his question or remember what he had heard in the past, Wilkie said, "Yes, the Duke, my dear country cousin." At the words, he gave Jeremiah's shoulder an affectionate squeeze. "John Wickliffe, and isn't he every inch the Duke?"

Jeremiah nodded.

"The Duke!" Wilkie echoed, with an edge of scorn in his tone. His bright eyes narrowed. "The Duke—and the giant we will slay. Oh, he's the monster and the king-pin of Anti-Relief. He owns half the country, and would take it all! But, look . . ." and he nodded to indicate a man who was across the chamber, a heavy, fattish man in nondescript dress, who strolled in the open space beyond the seats, with bowed head, as though walking alone in the garden or wood to meditate, not hearing the words of the orator, or contemptuous of them.

"But look"—Wilkie repeated, "that is the giant-killer. That is Rowan."

"John Rowan," Jeremiah murmured, and stared curiously at the man who was the founder and father of Relief.

"Yes," Wilkie said, "and he will bring the mighty low. You will see him for yourself, for I sup with him tonight. Will you come?"

Jeremiah was prepared to say no, that he could not, but Wilkie squeezed his shoulder again, and said, "Of course, you'll come. I must go now. I'll see you at the Weisiger House at six."

Then Wilkie was gone, and Duke Wickliffe's elegant height dominated the assembly, his eyes flashed, and his fine voice filled the room. Then Jeremiah thought, "He is speaking for me." And with that thought, that the Duke was his partisan, the words suddenly sounded hollow and false to him. So he left the place, and went to walk in the winter street, deserted now in the dusk, until the clocks struck and it was time to go to join Wilkie at the Weisiger House.

Wilkie was standing in the big room at the Weisiger, talking to two men there, teetering on his heels and gesturing with a cigar.

175

They were laughing at something he had just said. Then he stopped teetering, leaned at them and said something with a confidential smile. At that they laughed louder than before.

Then Wilkie saw Jeremiah, who had stopped some paces away. He excused himself from the men, and came quickly to Jeremiah, taking him by the arm, drawing him toward the bar. When the drinks had been ordered, Wilkie said, "It'll be quite a party. Mr. Madison is coming. You remember him? You met him with me in Lexington."

Jeremiah nodded.

"And Skrogg. He is bringing Davis, Samuel Davis. Davis, now, he is a rare one. He has iron in him. Was a waggoner, and couldn't sign his name. But he has taught himself. The world has been hard on him, and now he'll be hard on the world. But hard in a good cause. He is iron, afraid of no man, Henry Clay or the Duke." Then Wilkie looked up, and said, "Ah, gentlemen!"

And there they were, Mr. Madison and Skrogg, John Rowan and Samuel Davis. With the greetings and the introductions and the first drink, Jeremiah looked at the strangers, and the descriptions he has given are as clear as any that have been preserved to us of the men who for a moment shook the state. There was the giant-killer Rowan, a tall, fattish, shapeless man, with a heavy, sagging, dark, morose face, large of feature, saturnine and abstracted by turns, wearing big spectacles, through which he peered at you with a sudden access of cunning, or behind which his nearsighted eyes would as suddenly veil themselves "as though he found nothing above contempt in what he saw and would turn his gaze inward." Davis, who wore a cheap green blanket overcoat (in which he continued to sweat until they went to the table), was a "short, powerfully built, shambling man, long of arm, with coarse greasy face marked by pertinacity and self-complaisance. When he spoke, which was not often, his voice was harsh and rasping, and he set forth opinion with the dogmatism and bitterness of one who will brook no opposition. He drank much as he stood there, and the sweat dropped from his long hair to the collar of his coat."

At the table, set to one side from the general gathering, the talk turned to Wickliffe's speech of the afternoon defending Judge Boyle and the Supreme Court. Mr. Madison was analyzing what he considered defects of logic in the Duke's argument, when Davis, who had said nothing at the table to that point, suddenly rasped his chair back and exclaimed: "Let him talk. 'Tis the ungreased axle screaks. Let him talk. Talk and flap. A fish flaps most when he's out of water and the hook's in him. Talking don't count. Talking never split no log. It takes a glut and a wedge, and, by God, he's the log we'll split.

It's the vote that counts. Let him talk, and wait for the vote. That's the glut and the wedge, and the oak ain't growed won't split to the shrewd stroke. We'll drive it home."

"But," Mr. Madison replied courteously, "the vote is not yet and . . ."

"They'll vote the way they'll vote," Davis affirmed.

"Yes," Mr. Madison said, "I know that many are already committed, but, for some, the force of argument . . ."

"Argument!" Davis uttered with scorn. "They'll vote the way they are bought. The bastards are bought from birth! What in God's name else is Anti-Relief? But them the rich has bought? And, by God, if they do the buying, we'll do the . . ." He stopped, laid his hands on the white tablecloth. They were great, blunt hands, hairy, calloused and scarred, with fingers that did not flatten out straight.

"And if the removal vote fails, there is one thing . . ." But Rowan stopped, suddenly peering at Jeremiah.

But Wilkie caught the look. "Mr. Rowan," he said, "I can assure you that Mr. Beaumont is our friend. There is no need for reticence, he is the man who fought by our side at Lumton. Isn't that right, Skrogg?"

Skrogg turned his pale, peeled face to Jeremiah, and inspected him as though he had suddenly come upon him for the first time. Then said: "Yes, he fought," but with a tone that seemed to put the cold fact into the air, without commitment.

Mr. Madison, however, was saying, "Of course, Mr. Rowan, you may speak. Mr. Beaumont is one of us, and the friend of justice."

For an instant longer, Rowan's gaze pointed upon Jeremiah, then withdrew. "There is one more step," he said. "If the removal fails. We can change the Constitution of this Commonwealth. We can call a convention."

"Yeah," Davis said, "and if you can't get the vote for removal, how can you get it for a convention? 'Tis all the same, but I know the way. Yeah, I know the way." He stirred heavily in his chair.

But Rowan lifted his hand for silence, and began to explain his view. They might get removal of the judges. It would be a close vote. If not, there was always the good chance of getting some to vote for a convention who could not bring themselves to vote for removal. For, as Rowan explained, a man who voted against removal under compulsion and with grudging and fear could be brought to vote for the convention as a way of washing his hands. Of saying, "Look, I pass the responsibility back to the people. I am an honest man and I trust the people." It would be a way of avoiding the issue. And Rowan added, there were men like that, who in the pinch always sought to avoid the issue. And his own mouth curled on the words

177

with his contempt for, and in knowledge of, the world. And he added, it might even be a way for a bought man to break with his buyer, to think to go direct to the people. For the fool who is bought still longs to be free. If just for one instant. And his mouth curled again, and fell silent, while others took up the debate.

In the middle of the debate, Skrogg, who had taken no part, abruptly rose, saying that he had to finish an article for the *Advocate*. "Wait," Rowan said, "I must go too." And Davis rose with him. They paid their score, said good night, and left the table, and Jeremiah watched them make their way across the big room to the door, Rowan tall and shapeless, Davis, short, long-armed, and powerful, Skrogg between them, thin, stooped and sick, with the high, narrow skull leaning forward and to one side, and pipestem wrists hanging out of his shabby sleeves.

Wilkie was saying, "Mr. Madison, why don't you break now to Beaumont what we lately talked of? What concerns him?"

And Mr. Madison said: "Mr. Beaumont." And when Jeremiah turned to him, said: "From your county, Sellars, as you know, is still in the Legislature. He is a fool and a blackguard. He is the man you fought against that day at Lumton. He was nearly beat by Pollock and could have been beat by a better man, but Pollock, though good and upright, has little intellect and no fire. But Pollock was the best Relief could run in that county. And will be the best next year. Unless . . ." He leaned across the table toward Jeremiah, with courtesy but intensity, looking into his face. "Unless," he repeated, "you will run."

At once the whole scene seemed unreal to Jeremiah. He thought, *I am not here, not in Frankfort, for this, I thought I was here about the lands in the West, but I have been lured here, it is a trap, I have been lured into a trap.*

Almost violently, he shook his head, saying, "No. No."

But Mr. Madison was looking directly at him with his gray, severe eyes, saying earnestly, "But it is your duty. If you can subdue your natural modesty and preference for the private life. It is your duty." Then Mr. Madison suddenly sat back in his chair, and smiled. "Forgive me," he said. "I should not presume to instruct you in your duty. I can only say that, other obligations not forbidding, a man's highest good is to serve the state, and you, Mr. Beaumont . . ."

Jeremiah was thinking, he talks like Fort, the way Fort used to talk, and Fort was a villain.

But you could not think this man a villain, with that direct gray gaze and fine forehead.

And Wilkie was speaking, begging Mr. Madison's pardon, saying: "You could be elected, Jerry. Oh, they remember how you fought at Lumpton for Relief. And what you did at Tupper's tavern that day . . ."

"At Tupper's tavern!" Jeremiah exclaimed, and almost rose from his chair. "What I did—what I did—nobody understood—the old man cursed me—for saving him—and the others, the Relief people—they would have cursed me, too—they said . . ."

"They understand now, Jerry. All think you acted the part of a man."

The gangling man at Tupper's tavern, with the broadside in his hand, stood in the dark of Jeremiah's mind, leaning at him, saying again, "Oh, yeah, you—you was smart to git you a fine place—you knowed how to git you one. . . ." And Jeremiah suddenly felt himself, saw himself on the hustings, speaking to a great crowd, speaking of justice and right, and that hairy face was there before him, calling out, "Oh, yeah, you—you was smart. . . ."

Mr. Madison had risen and come around the table. He stood beside Jeremiah's chair. "I must go now," he said, "but I am happy that I have spoken to you. And you must promise me one thing, or I cannot go."

Jeremiah rose awkwardly, and mumbled his question.

"Promise me," Mr. Madison said, and placed his hand on Jeremiah's shoulder, "that you will think seriously. Before you make a decision against us. I know your heart, my boy. That has been proved. It is a heart of oak, yet sensitive to the slightest breeze of justice. But before you promise, one more word, for I would be honest with you."

"Yes?" Jeremiah said.

"It is this. I am asking you to surrender part of your happiness; that would be the price you would have to pay to serve the state. There is only the happiness there of a good conscience. If"—and he smiled gravely—"you can keep a good conscience in politics." He released his grip on Jeremiah's shoulder, then slapped the shoulder. "But you will promise me," he said in full confidence, and smiled again, but this time with a touch of gaiety that made him look fleetingly boyish for all his dignity and gray hair.

"I promise you," Jeremiah said, though he had not willed that answer.

"Good," Mr. Madison said, and offered his hand. "Your hand upon it."

They shook hands.

"And good night," Mr. Madison said, and turned away.

Jeremiah looked after the departing figure, wondering why he had given the promise. Then he turned to find Wilkie's gaze upon him. "You promised him," Wilkie said, smiling like a man who knows a secret. "Don't forget that you promised him."

"I must go," Jeremiah said.

"One drink more?" Wilkie invited.

"I must ride tomorrow," Jeremiah said.

Jeremiah waited while Wilkie paid, and then they moved toward the door together. Then just as Jeremiah was about to take his leave, Wilkie said, "You must think seriously on what Madison has said. I know it will cut across your plans, but if you will take the advice of a friend, I would think seriously on those, too."

"What do you mean?"

Wilkie looked curiously at him in the half-light. "Your land project in the West," he said finally.

"It is a good project," Jeremiah said hotly. "I have been there."

Wilkie shook his head. "The time is not ripe," he said. "I warrant you could do better to wait. I could tell you when to go ahead."

"How do you know of my plans?" Jeremiah demanded.

"Ah," Wilkie said, and smiled closely, "I know many things, my boy. It is my business to know. For instance, I know"—the smile flickered off his face—"that you are dealing with Felix Parham, or rather with old Parham."

"You know that, too?"

"I know," Wilkie said, "and I know that it is a mistake. You will tie yourself to him, to a hard man, to Anti-Relief, to what you will abhor in the end. Unless," Wilkie added softly, "you are like Sellars, and would lick another man's spit."

"God damn it!" Jeremiah cried out, and jerked from Wilkie's side, and was about to damn him, too, when Wilkie reached out to touch him like a man laying hand on a stung horse.

"Oh, you are not Sellars. You are Jerry Beaumont, and he would not lick spit, and be lackey-boy. No, not to a king!" He wound up with a flourish, drawing himself up as on a platform, and then laughed at his own oratory.

Jeremiah looked at him with some sullenness, but Wilkie said, "Oh, Jerry, Jerry, forgive me if I have my fun. And don't be angry with me, for I am serious underneath, and I speak from the heart and from my old affection. Don't do what you will regret. Don't back the wrong horse."

"I promised Madison I would think it over," Jeremiah said distantly. "That is all I can say."

He thought it over as he walked back that night through the dark streets past the blackened ruins of the capitol to the modest tavern where he was lodging, and later he lay in his bed on a straw tick, thinking. Duty, Mr. Madison had said. Justice, Mr. Madison had said. Yes, Jeremiah told himself, he believed in those things. He believed, for he had a duty, a sworn oath, an obligation taken freely on himself. He believed, for he had sworn an oath to do justice. Yes, he would do his duty and do justice, when the time came. Duty and justice, as they lay in his heart. But what was his duty and justice was not another man's. What led a man to duty and justice?

What led Madison? Skrogg? Davis? Rowan? He had a sudden longing to see into the being of those men and know the secret springs of their action. Madison—there was no whisper against him. The worst men said was that he was a politician, and loved power. But there were the steady, gray eyes, full of strength and candor, and the voice which could say *duty* and *justice* as calmly as you said *Good morning*. Did he want power clothed in duty and justice, or justice and duty clothed in power?

And Skrogg, who had no fear, who was sick and weak but strong as a lion for some inner fire? Were duty and justice the fuel for the flame, or were they the smoke from that fire?

And Davis, was it hate for those who had made him suffer, or love for duty and justice?

And Rowan—oh, he knew the story of that stained and devious life, what men said, the doubleness and trickery and unexplained passages and twisting corridors. Had Rowan founded Relief not for love of justice but as a last trick, Rowan who, they said, knew how to finger every stop and fret of poor human nature because he knew the secrets of his own so well? Or had Rowan founded Relief as a last attempt to redeem, or break from, the disordered past and stained self?

And he asked himself, had he had the history of any one of them, would he have been different from that one? Was his own conviction for Relief but the result of his own father's last poverty and defeat? The result of his memory of his mother, tired, leaning on a hoe toward evening in a scraggly garden patch by the edge of a field? What if he, Jeremiah Beaumont, had taken old Marcher's offer and had become Jeremiah Marcher? Then would he have been like the Duke, clothed in elegant black to rise and speak of duty and justice and the sacred bond of man to man in society?

But the justice and duty of the Duke were not those of Madison and the rest—whatever they were. And what was Madison's was not Skrogg's nor Davis's nor Rowan's. And what was his, Jeremiah Beaumont's, was not theirs. Yet each man would seize on all others and make his duty and justice theirs. They would seize on him, on Jeremiah Beaumont, to make their duty and justice his. But what would they offer him? What reason? Only the words, *duty* and *justice*?

At that thought, Wilkie was before him, as he had been in the dark street, saying, "Don't do what you will regret. Don't back the wrong horse."

So that was it, his mind replied, clear as a bell, and Wilkie had unmasked all the others, and what was their duty and justice was the horse that they thought would win, and if you did not win, what you had done was not duty or justice, for only those who won survived to say what was duty or justice. The joke was so simple, and it fooled all but Wilkie, good old Wilkie, honest old Wilkie, who told you the truth, to save you, and let you sleep.

But was that Wilkie's truth? Was that all Wilkie had to say? Was that the heart of the world, and of friendship and love? With the question a great desolation shook him, and he felt terribly alone. No, that could not be Wilkie. It could not be anybody, for with that truth no man could live, and Wilkie was Wilkie, and Wilkie had spoken thus but to make him free. Free? What had John Rowan said, with his curled, contemptuous lip? "For the fool who is bought still longs to be free."

So that was it. Duty and justice made you free. They were the words you used for what would make you free. The truth would make you free. But each man's chains were different, and you did not know your own chains but knew the need to be free and had to find your own duty and justice. And no man could tell you what they were, and when they tried, the best they said in the end was, don't back the wrong horse. You would have to find truth yourself and he would find his own. He knew where it lay.

He heard the watch call in the street, then, far off, shouting and laughter, then the watch call again.

He would be up early and would ride south to Rachel.

He rode south to Rachel, but also to old Parham, who said, yes, the project was good, but they could do no business yet, not till he knew what the fool Legislature would do, whether they would respect the law of the land and the Constitution or would break the Court. To which Jeremiah replied that the Legislature had been elected by the people and he trusted that it would execute the will of the people.

"Of a rout of blackguards and bankrupts," the old man rejoined. Then he looked sharply at Jeremiah, and said: "So you're for Relief, Mr. Beaumont?"

"I had told you that," Jeremiah said.

"You know if that Legislature goes Relief, we can't do no business?"

"Yes," Jeremiah replied.

The old man shook his head. "You're a queer one, Mr. Beaumont," he said, and laughed shortly. But he looked again, from his hard eyes, and said, "But you know, Mr. Beaumont, maybe we can do business, after all. I will let you hear from me."

So Jeremiah went back home, and waited. There was nothing to do but wait for the action of the Legislature and the word from old Parham, to push the work in making ready for the mill, and to enjoy Rachel. For in that period of waiting, in the middle of winter, they seemed to draw more deeply than ever before into a warm inner world of their own, leaving the hard frozen crust of the world outside, the way sap hid warm in the root of a winter tree or the furred animal curled in its warm earth to dream away the season.

In that time news scarcely penetrated to him, and he made no effort to get it. He was days late in learning that the judges had not been unseated. He felt no elation at this help to his prospects, and no distress at the set-back to Relief. And when he learned that the call for a constitutional convention had passed the House but had been defeated in the Senate, eighteen to eighteen, he felt nothing. Now he would hear from old Parham. Well, he would hear.

After some days the note came. Jeremiah laid it aside. Was this what he had hoped for most deeply? He did not know. All he knew was that now he lived in his winter dream. He would rouse himself from that some day.

It was late January before he rode to the Parham place, to discuss the terms of the partnership. The terms, he learned quickly, would be hard, if old Josh Parham had his way.

"I could hire me lawyers for chips and whetstones in these times," Parham said. "And surveyors, too."

"But you can't hire me, Mr. Parham," Jeremiah said quietly. "I am not interested in being hired. Only in a partnership."

"But what do you bring to it?"

"I bring myself," Jeremiah said.

"Yourself!" the old man snorted.

"Listen," Jeremiah said, suddenly surprised at his own cunning and boldness. "I know what you want. You do not want money. You have money. You are doing this for your son. And I know your son, Mr. Parham. He is a waster, Mr. Parham."

"I'd have you know, sir . . ." Mr. Parham began.

But Jeremiah interrupted: "I know what I know, and I know that you hope to make a man of him. To get him to the West, to a hard occupation, and you want me to take him. Well, if you don't want me, I bid you good day."

So he turned his back and got out the door. But the old man's voice called him back.

It was done. He and Josh Parham were partners. But it was a strange partnership, for the present a partnership only in waiting. It was the year for the election of governor, and Parham would not take serious action until he knew how the cat was going to jump. The best that Jeremiah could persuade him to was to finance a somewhat more ambitious expedition into the West for further exploration. After the return from the West, he sent Captain Marlowe, his neighbor, to Frankfort to file some patents at the registrar's office, and accepted, with what patience he could muster, the long delay. And the spring and summer passed with the old occupations, his work on the farm, his pleasure in Rachel's society, his games of Old Sledge with Marlowe, his dream of the day when he would be rich and stand justified before all men.

For a moment, in August of that year—it was 1824—that dream seemed ended for good and all, when Desha, the Relief candidate, was elected governor. Desha promised to break the Court of Appeals and set up a new Court. Josh Parham raged and swore that no penny of his would now go to open up land in Kentucky, for he spat on the state. But his fit passed, his old cunning returned, and he said, well, they'd just have to wait, wait till next year. He promised that in the spring he himself would go with Jeremiah to select town sites. The next spring they would begin in good earnest.

In the spring Rachel told Jeremiah that she was to have a child. His joy in that thought was enough to make him forget politics and land and all else. Then he remembered that land was money and greatness. He did not care for himself now, but he would make his son rich, rich and great. So in those nights of early spring he would wake to hear rain on the roof, and then, far off, thunder, and he would reach to take Rachel's hand and hold it in the dark. Ah, this was the end for which life was made.

Then he saw the news in the *Advocate*. Colonel Cassius Fort had returned from the East, after a long sojourn. He had rested a few days at his own residence in Pick County, where he had removed from Saul County, but was now at the Weisiger House, in Frankfort, where he had come to confer with the leaders of politics.

It was mid-morning of a bright day in March, with full sun streaming through the windows of the library behind the chair where Jeremiah sat. He had reached the end of the item before the meaning struck home. "My God," he said aloud, and rose from his chair, "My God, what am I? I read it and sat there!"

But he still stood in the middle of the room, clutching the paper. He stared at the slow fire on the hearth. Then out the window. A flock of robins hopped about on the lawn, pecking the dead grass. He counted them, and later he writes of the act: "I counted them, and there were seven, but even as I counted, I wondered why I should do so while I held that paper in my hand and knew that Fort was

184

alive and in Kentucky. Then I tore myself from the sight, and uttered again, my God, am I Jeremiah Beaumont?"

He went from the library, and across the hall and upstairs to the little sitting room where Rachel was.

She was sitting before a small easel, with her paint box by her side, and a big book propped in another chair before her. "Look," she said as he entered, and lifted her face toward him, bright with excitement, "look!" And she rose, and swept the skirts of her dark dress to one side, and picked up the book, and brought it to him. "There's just an engraving here," she said, "just an engraving of Downe Castle. That's where the Bonnie Earl of Murray died." She held the book before him, but so fleetingly that he saw nothing but the blur of black lines on white paper. "But I've copied it," she said. "I've painted it as it must be in Scotland." The big book drooped with its weight in one hand, and with the other she seized him and drew him to the easel. "Look," she commanded, "look!"

We do not know what he saw. Probably some trivial daub of a gray castle perched dramatically on gray rock, with a river, far too white and blue, below, and to one side two or three sheep, far too white, on a too green patch of meadow, with a kilted shepherd leaning on a staff. We know what they were like, those pictures. But there are few in attics or old trunks or Negro cabins now. And there are none in the museums where the "primitives" hang to show us the tavern or the quilting party or the severe face of the Merchant from Nashville, those things which were American, but were no more American than those things which were not American but the things which America dreamed it was, but was not.

We do not know what book she copied from.

But we know what Jeremiah Beaumont said. "It is very pretty," he said, and gave it scarcely a glance.

"But you haven't looked," she complained, bright-eyed, flush-cheeked from excitement, with her hair coming loose on one side.

"I must go," he said abruptly.

"What?"

"I must ride today," he said.

"West?" she demanded. "West? Are you—are you leaving me again—so soon?"

"Frankfort," he said.

"Will it take long this time? Will it take long?"

He took a step toward her and stopped immediately before her. "Long enough," he said, "to whip a villain in the public street. Until he shows fight."

"Oh," she breathed, "oh," and he saw dismay grow on her face.

"Look!" he commanded, and thrust the paper at her. "Look—Fort is in Kentucky!"

She lowered her face toward it, slowly, as though by an effort of will, while he held the paper before her.

"You see it," he said, and snatched back the paper and crumpled it and flung it to one side. "And I ride today. Now."

Then she reached to seize him by the wrist. "No!" she cried out.

"What?"

"Oh, it's different now."

"Different?" he demanded, trying to release himself. "My God, what is different? Am I different? Is Fort different? Are you different? And don't forget what you made me swear."

For an instant, she stared at him with a kind of terror in her face. Then she burst out: "Oh, that was because—that was only because . . ."

"Because what?"

"Because I was crazy then, I was crazy then and I did it because . . ." She drew back from him and stared at him.

"Because what?"

"Because you made me," she said very softly. "Oh, I see it now, you made me."

"I made you?" he echoed with a sudden cold constriction of the heart. Then sternly: "Don't be a fool. You did it because Fort betrayed you and you hated him."

"But I didn't, I didn't hate him, I . . ."

He leaned at her, fixing her with his glance. "You didn't what?"

"I didn't hate him," she said slowly, and shook her head. "Not before you came. But you came and you tortured me and you made me tell you, you knew all the time but you made me tell you to torture me, you made me show you the grave—the grave where he . . ."

She paused, and then her voice suddenly became a wail: ". . . where my baby was—he was dead and I had nothing, nothing —but I could have lived with nothing if you had not come and taken all my strength and made me crazy and weak, if you hadn't come . . ."

"But I came," he broke in harshly, "and I swore to kill Fort."

He turned toward the door, but she rushed after him and swung him to face her and slipped to her knees, clutching his thighs.

"My baby was dead and he is in the ground," she said, "but that was then, and now it's different, for he's alive, he's alive and he's in me, and he's ours, he's ours, and you can't ever go!"

No, he could not go. He would stay and sit by his wife and take joy in the thought of the son that he had, in his old rage, forgotten. But with that joy came speculation to taint it. Had he not, all the while, in some corner of his mind, really remembered the child? Had he not really known, therefore, that he could not go? Had there been a hollowness in his rage? Had the rage been, in its very violence, but an abstract rage, a false shadow? Could he never have peace with himself?

But he had peace on one point. Even if she now accused him of cruelty, it had been necessary for him to torture her to make her speak and tell him the old impediment to their love. That had been the only way to release her from the chains of the past. He had no regret there.

That night he had a dream. He dreamed that he stood at the edge of a big woods, a forest, toward night, and the forest was full of shadow. It was fall or winter, for the trees were nearly bare. He seemed to recognize the place as some place he had seen in the West, but it was different, too, from any place he had seen in Kentucky, and he did not know the names of the trees. That fact was terrible to him, and he struggled in his mind to know their names.

Then he saw the form on the ground before him. He saw it with no surprise because at the moment of perception he knew that he had already known it there. It was a strong man's form, naked, lying on the back, and bleeding from a wound in the chest. He could not make out the face, no matter how hard he tried, but he knew that it was the face of Cassius Fort. He knew that if he could only make out the face, he would feel the great joy that all had been done for, but when he looked, there was only a patch of grayness that swam in his sight and made him think of the gray growth on the eyes of the blind and made him fear that it was coming on his own. So he would look quickly away to be confirmed in his vision.

Looking up thus, he saw Rachel, more beautiful than in life. She was kneeling on the ground, beyond the head of the bleeding form, and was staring at him with horror and reproach. He was compelled to speak to her, to justify himself, and tell her that now they could be happy. But the words would not come, though he thought he would strangle with the effort of speech.

Then, as he looked, he saw that her face was changing. The brown spot on her cheek was enormous and each instant was larger and more devouring. It was Rachel's face and was not Rachel's face. It was Rachel's face but it was also the face of the old woman, her mother, peering at him, spying on him from the shadows. Then it was all discolored, but was still Rachel's face and the mother's face, but was another face as well, and he knew its name, but like the names of the trees it would not come to him.

Then she lifted her hands to her face, where the horror was increased by the fact that he saw Rachel's white bosom beneath. She said, staring above her hands, to him, "Look, what you have done to me."

At that he knew that there was something which could be said to make all clear, but speech would not come, though the agony of his effort grew greater. He felt cold, and a great desolation overcame him.

He woke at this point, with desolation still on him. For a moment he could not be sure that the dream was past. But there was a little moonlight in the room, and all became gradually familiar, and Rachel was beside him. He had the great desire to see her face, but he could not make it out clearly in the little light. So he rose from the bed and lighted a candle from the embers on the hearth. He leaned above her, shielding the light from her eyes with one hand, staring down at her. It was the face of Rachel, relaxed and young in sleep, younger looking than he had ever seen it, as it must have been years before when she was little more than a child, before anything had ever happened. There was such pathos in that thought, that he almost bent to kiss the spot on the cheek, which in the candlelight looked good.

A week later, mid-morning on a Sunday, Jeremiah was sitting in the library mulling over his maps when he heard a great halloo out front, and went to the porch. There was Wilkie, gracefully sitting a fine, restive bay gelding, and behind him Skrogg, gaunt and more sick-looking than ever, on a mount that seemed in little better health than himself.

As Jeremiah ran down the steps, Wilkie, smiling, swung from his saddle with the lightness of a boy, calling out, "Fill up the pot, open the cellar, rob the smoke-house! I told you I'd come. And I knew you wouldn't be at church, you old infidel."

Jeremiah took his hand, feeling happy and excited, then turned to Skrogg, who was painfully dismounting his rickety form. Jeremiah yelled for somebody to come for the horses, now tethered to posts at the edge of the drive, and led the guests into the house, saying all the while how glad he was, how Rachel would be glad, how he would run upstairs and fetch her. He established them in the library, and went for her.

"I told her," he says, "of the arrival of my dear friend Wilkie, and when I noticed nothing in her expression but apathy or a trace of displeasure, I repeated what I had said, thinking she had not understood, and added that it was her old friend, Wilkie Barron. She indicated that she knew him, and rose with an air of duty more than pleasure which puzzled me for the moment to make me think that she must be unwilling to be reminded of the past, who had seen no one but myself, her mother, the captain and Mrs. Marlowe, and the servants in all the long time since the dire event of her betrayal. For the first time it struck me what a strange life we had led, she and I, but it had not seemed strange to me before, for it had been what I sought. Or the truth might be, I thought as I followed her down the stairs, that she feared not only the past but also the future and resented these guests because, like my project in the West, they might call me forth into the world to leave her alone.

"But she greeted them with all properness and the good forms of hospitality, though Wilkie no more warmly than Skrogg. And he himself was somewhat more formal with her than I had expected, but I decided that this rose from his delicacy of feeling. His delay in coming to us, and his formality now that he had come at last, I took to be a way of saying to us both that he presumed on nothing from the past, and regarded her but as the wife of his good friend.

"We entered upon general conversation, and sat thus in the library until Rachel was called about her wifely duties to see that dinner was made for our guests. At dinner she was attentive to all, and took polite part in the conversation. Wilkie and I spoke most, and of old times in Bowling Green, as friends will who long parted speak of the past to assure themselves of what has bound them together. Wilkie told stories of that time with such good humor and wit that once or twice she smiled (though she was never much given to a lighter vein), and I laughed to split my sides as I had not done since the days when I frequented Tupper's tavern.

"Immediately after our repast, Skrogg, who had been silent and apart, was taken by a fit of coughing that brought blood, so we prevailed upon him to lie down in a chamber above to recover himself. Rachel brought a syrup for him, and then excused herself from the society of Wilkie and myself. We went down to the library, where Wilkie turned abruptly to me with a grave face to say that he feared for Skrogg, whose heart was iron but whose body straw, and that should he fall ill or die it would be tragedy not only for private friends but for the Commonwealth. I murmured something appropriate, but Wilkie cut in to say that I did not understand how bad things were. I could see that Skrogg was sick, I replied.

" 'Not that,' he said impatiently. 'It is an ill wind brings us here.'

" 'An ill wind?' I replied jestingly. 'I had thought it was love of me and my good larder.'

"But he smiled most fleetingly to acknowledge my poor sortie, then demanded had I heard the news. Before I could answer, he broke out feelingly, 'Oh, you were right, and read his black heart better than I.'

" 'Who?'

" 'Fort!' he said, 'the perfect Judas, consummate and complete. He

189

broke with us. Last week. But worse, he has betrayed us. He has betrayed Relief. Read this,' he commanded, and drew a handbill from his pocket and thrust it at me."

AN IMPORTANT COMMUNICATION
To the People of Kentucky
From Colonel Cassius Fort

Dear Friends:

We live in parlous times, and desperate diseases demand desperate remedies. Our dear land has been, and is sick, and I was among the first to support Relief though knowing it to be a strong medicine. I did this most prayerfully, and I challenge any man to discover to the public eye that I had any private interest to be served. I say this for what protection I can against slander, that crow which flies in heaven's clearest air, as the gold-tongued Shakespeare says, and which now gluts itself full on carrion under our distempered skies. But I do not say it in invidiousness or failing in respect for my late associates in Relief, whom I have known to be honorable men and to be named thus with no twisted tongue of sarcasm. I would pay them this due tribute, now at the moment when I must detach myself from them and disenthrall myself from the error into which I judge them to be fallen.

I judge it error, yea, grievous error, to strike down the Court which is the guardian of law. The people have the God-given right to make and change their laws, and I should not oppose the call of a convention to change our Constitution were that not coupled with the avowed will to destroy the Court. I oppose, and will do so with my last breath, any attempt to break a Court, though that attempt be cunningly concealed, for to break a Court or to threaten it with violence is to destroy the very idea of law and call old Chaos back to reign. We must find a medicine for the ills of our land, but that medicine must be under law, and it is no medicine to put a dagger in the patient's heart.

Therefore, I disavow the party of Relief, and shall bend my energies against it so long as it perseveres in its present course. I feel it my duty to announce myself even at this early date as candidate for the Legislature from Pick County, where I now abide, that my poor force may be exerted for what I hold to be right, for thought without action I deem disease of the will, and no virtue. And I feel it my duty, since my name has been long associated with Relief, to write this letter to whoever will deign to read, be he friend or foe.

Your humble servant,
CASSIUS FORT

That is what Jeremiah read, and then he looked up from it to find Wilkie's eyes narrowed and glittering, and to hear him say, "Villain and sophist. Oh, you were right, Jerry, long ago. Oh, you were right—and now—and now . . ."

Jeremiah, staring into his face, demanded, "What? What are you saying?"

"The time has come to act," Wilkie said calmly. "It is your duty, and you . . ."

"I'll not be told my duty. I'll not be played upon. I'll not be . . ."

"Easy, easy," Wilkie said, and lightly touched Jeremiah's arm. "You misunderstand me. I would have you do nothing rash. Only this . . ."

"What?"

"Do what Madison asked, what you would not do last year. You must run this year, in this county. Against Sellars." Wilkie was speaking rapidly in a soft voice, very rapidly. "You can win. And you must. But more than that, it is known you were the protégé of Fort. Were trained by him. And if you announce for Relief that will have its effect. It is another county, but I assure you it will have its effect. For we can see to that, I can assure you, and . . ."

"I will do nothing," Jeremiah said.

"Is it because you are committed to Parham? Have you signed a contract? Oh, I begged you not to submit to him."

"I'll submit to nothing," Jeremiah burst out. "To no man. Not to him. Or you."

"Why will you do it? With Parham? Why?"

"It is my affair."

"Oh, no, Jerry. Not yours. It is the affair of the whole world. Why will you submit to Parham, Jerry? Why?"

The man in Tupper's tavern was there before Jeremiah's face. "My God," Jeremiah said, "I'll tell you why. I'll not have it said I came here to live easy on my wife's land. I'll make my way, my own way. Do you understand?"

Wilkie ignored his words, studying him, repeating, "But why, Jerry, why? Why will you not run?" Then before Jeremiah could find words for an answer, he went on, fast and soft: "You are for Relief. Everybody knows that. And you know Relief is right. You detest Fort. You know he is a villain. And if you forgot and laid aside your former rash resolve . . ."

"I forgot nothing," Jeremiah cried out, and felt a fury come, but with it a great weakness so that he trembled. "What do you think I am?" he demanded. "To swear an oath, and cast it off like a dirty shirt. You do not know me. When I knew Fort had come to Kentucky, I rose to go to him. With my whip. To make him fight, to . . ."

"But did you go?" Wilkie asked, and smiled again.

The fury was gone now, but the weakness remained.

"But you did not go," Wilkie was saying, as though telling him a secret.

"Listen," Jeremiah managed to say. "Rachel begged me. She begged me, for—you see—she is going to have a child."

"Ah," Wilkie said, "ah!" And then: "And you are happy for that. Oh, I could see in your face when I came that you were happy at last. You were happy when you heard, weren't you, dear Jerry?"

"Yes, I was happy," Jeremiah said, and for an instant, even now, the happiness flooded back like quietness, here in the room.

"You were happy for that," Wilkie repeated, "like any man." He studied Jeremiah an instant, then asked, softly again: "But only for that Jerry?"

"What do you mean?"

"I've said enough," Wilkie said. "I've said too much. Forgive me, Jerry." And he seemed to withdraw, smiling.

"Say it, by God," Jeremiah commanded, and stepped toward him.

"No, Jerry," Wilkie said, shaking his head.

"By God, you'll say it!" Jeremiah exclaimed. "Say it, or I'll . . ." He had seized Wilkie by the front of his coat, gripping it hard together as though he would crush the body inside.

But Wilkie stood perfectly composed in the grasp, with his arms hanging easy at his sides, not resisting. "Oh, Jerry," he said quietly, almost pityingly, and shook his head.

"Say it!" Jeremiah cried.

"Jerry," Wilkie asked from his calm, "do you really want me to say it?"

"Yes, by God."

"It is only a question, Jerry. Only a question."

"Say it."

"When Rachel told you," Wilkie almost whispered, "when you knew, you were glad. Oh, you were glad for the child. But something else Jerry, something else. Were you glad, too, because now you did not need to go on? Because now you could escape from an oath which was a burden? Because now . . ."

Jeremiah felt cold at his spine. He heard the words, but they conveyed nothing to him. They seemed to come from a great distance. But they were coming yet.

". . . you could turn your back with good conscience and seek your private gain in the guise of pride? In the guise of duty? And now, when the man you know to be a betrayer has betrayed again, you would turn . . ."

Then all the words suddenly had their meaning. Jeremiah flung the body back from him, releasing his grip, so that Wilkie staggered back against the secretary.

"Get out," Jeremiah commanded in a voice that almost strangled him.

Wilkie stood by the secretary, looking at him from above his twisted coat and loosened neck-cloth. "Ah, Jerry," he said, "so I touched you there."

"Get out," Jeremiah repeated.

"It is your house, Jerry," Wilkie said, but lifted his eyes to indicate the region above stairs. "But Skrogg?"

"When he can ride," Jeremiah said, "him, too! But now, now I'll go. I'll go myself."

So he rushed to the door; turned there to catch a last glimpse of Wilkie standing in the middle of the floor adjusting his neck-cloth, as calm as though he stood before his mirror at morning; and then Jeremiah crossed the hall to the front door, and went out.

He went across the yard, almost running in his flight, then through the garden, over the stile and into the open fields. But he fled across them, too, they were so wide and open and the light so bright that there he felt undefended from the thousand eyes and a thousand enemies. He reached the woods by the creek, and plunged into them, afraid because the leaves were not out yet, there was not enough shadow and cover. He plunged on, deeper in, and when he stopped at last, there was no sound but his own wrenched breathing.

When he came back toward sunset, he passed by the stables and saw that the horses of the guests were gone. He felt relief, and then he was ashamed of the fact. By God, it was his house, he thought. It was his house, but he had had to run away like a beggar or a thief.

But as he let himself in the front door, he observed that his hand on the latch was light and that he was moving the door with stealth, and he felt the shame again. By God, it was his house.

Then he saw Rachel standing at the head of the stairs, looking down on him. She came down the stairs toward him, and even before she spoke he dreaded what she would say.

"What happened?" she asked.

"Nothing," he replied shortly, and half turned as though he would go to the library and leave her there in the hall.

"It was so strange," she said. "I heard him in the hall upstairs and thought it was you and came out. But it wasn't you, and he was bringing the sick man down. He said they had to leave, and had not wished to trouble me. I asked where you were, and he said you had been called away, that you would be back soon. Then they left, and I didn't know what had happened, where you were or why, and I was afraid, it was so strange."

193

She had come down the stairs now, and stood before him, with her hand laid on his arm. "What happened?" she asked.

"If you must know," he said, "we quarreled."

"I knew it. I knew something had happened. Oh, I don't like him, Jerry."

He looked sharply at her. "Well, you did once," he said.

"Once?"

"Don't you remember?" he demanded. "Long back—before . . ." He had almost said, "before Fort," but had stopped himself, and said instead: "Before I knew you."

"I scarcely knew him," she replied.

"Well, he liked you."

"I don't like him," she said, "and I never did, and . . ."

"Well, I like him. He is my friend," Jeremiah interrupted with emphasis which surprised even himself.

"But you said you had quarreled?"

"It is nothing," he said. "Nothing," and withdrew from her touch.

"What did you quarrel about?"

"Politics," he said. Then he stepped back from her. "I've got some work to do. In the library. I don't want any supper."

He went into the library and closed the door. He was certain, for a long time afterwards, that she was still standing in the hall.

That evening he wrote a note to Wilkie, saying that he would run for the Legislature, and that he would be advised as to the best time to announce his candidacy. Then he wrote another note, also brief. It was to Mr. Parham. He regretted, he said, to abandon a long-cherished project just at the point of maturity, but a change in his situation made it necessary for him to give over all thoughts of lands in the West. Since Mr. Parham might still be interested in the project, he was sending him all maps, plats and notes with full permission to use them however he thought best.

All of that material was in the secretary before him. He now began to sort it and put it in order for making a package. But that took him a long time, for he retraced his courses on the map, and read again the notes he had made, and saw again in his mind's eye those rich valleys lying in the quiet and shade of the untouched forest. "I thought of that country where man had not yet come," he writes, "and how I had stood in its silence, and I asked myself if in going there I had gone not for gain and pride, but for a motive perhaps more base, to flee from my obligation and forget. And I ask myself if all life was a flight, and had I always fled?"

Jeremiah rose to go up to bed, and to Rachel. At the thought of Rachel, he remembered what she had said, how she had scarcely

194

known Wilkie, had never liked him. He stopped all at once in the middle of the floor. But all women liked Wilkie. They always had. Had Rachel lied to him? Of course not, he told himself, and cursed himself for the thought. If Wilkie had thought that she liked him he had deceived himself. But Wilkie had loved her, or would have loved her had he dared. It was strange, he decided, it was strange but true that Wilkie's love for Rachel had in the end given her to him, to Jeremiah Beaumont.

He had the impulse to wake Rachel up and tell her that. He reflected that he had never told her exactly how he had heard her story, how Wilkie had railed against the betrayer and how he, Jeremiah, had felt nothing until Wilkie had accused him of being an intimate and confidant, even a kind of accomplice, of the betrayer. He supposed that he had never told her, and had answered her questions with evasions and half-truths, because he was ashamed of his own sluggish spirit that had only been aroused to justice by an unjust accusation. He reflected now that he should be grateful to Wilkie for the unjust accusation. Only through suffering injustice, he thought, do we grasp at the idea of justice.

There is little record of the next several months and the period of the campaign, at least in so far as Jeremiah himself is concerned. His candidacy, on the advice of Mr. Madison and Wilkie, was not announced until late May, when his crops were already in. But the late date was political strategy, and not a farmer's prudence: the candidacy would come as something of a surprise and the late announcement would give the Anti-Relief party less time to recover and plan its attack on him. There would be a bitter campaign he knew. Mr. Parham would never forgive him for dropping the land project, and already young Felix Parham had talked in the taverns of the county when he had his whisky in him.

It was a bitter campaign, but the very bitterness became a kind of intoxication for Jeremiah. He knew, he reports, that slander was abroad against him, but he had determined to make no reply unless it came direct to him. Then he would make the "only reply possible to manhood." Meanwhile, he discovered that his own partisans had a weapon against old Parham. The tale was afloat that old Parham had tried to buy him off with a rich partnership for land speculation but that he had spurned the offer when its full implications became clear. When he first encountered the tale, his impulse was to deny it, to explain the whole situation. But how could you explain it? It meant explaining so much, his whole life, really. So he had to suffer a sense of embarrassment and guilt at his silent conniving in the lie.

But he did ask Wilkie point-blank if he had set the tale afloat, and when Wilkie blandly accepted the responsibility, Jeremiah hotly reproached him.

"Why, dear Jerry," Wilkie said, "you don't understand the world. It takes the ground from under old Parham's feet. It draws his fangs."

"But it's not true!" Jeremiah protested.

"Oh, it is true, all right," Wilkie said. "I told you long back he was trying to buy you."

"But I took the idea to him, I initiated the whole . . ."

"What you thought does not matter," Wilkie said pityingly. "It only matters what he is."

So the summer wore on, hot and sultry, with tempers shorter and shorter, and the news of the outbreak of violence in one county fanning the outbreak in another. August was drawing on, and the elections. He was almost grateful for the last excitements and occupations. They took him out of himself and the heaviness of his thoughts at home. For the early happiness which had come with Rachel's announcement that she was to have a child had almost vanished, or it returned fitfully, not to be depended upon, no longer the climate in which he could move and breathe.

After his decision to enter the race, he had not told Rachel for two or three weeks. When he did tell her, she said nothing. She only nodded in assent, but the heaviness of her face touched him. A week later, he woke to find her weeping in the night. But he feigned sleep, and lay by her side quietly until the fit had worn itself out.

He had almost forgotten that event when the time came to announce his candidacy. One morning at breakfast he remarked casually that the next day he would announce. Her face went white, her lips trembled, and without answering she looked down at her coffee cup. For a moment he thought that she had had an attack of nausea from her condition, and rose and went to her and put his hands on her shoulders. But when she lifted her face to him, he knew the truth, even before she spoke. "They'll take you away," she said huskily. "They'll take you away from me. Oh, can't they leave us alone!"

He murmured something comforting, saying that she was overwrought, that her condition made her nervous, that he loved her and her alone and would do so forever.

But she twisted from under his touch saying, "Oh, you'll leave me, you'll leave me."

He tried to explain that during the campaign he would never be away long at a time, just in the county, and that if he won, he would take her with him to Frankfort.

At that, a look of real terror swept over her face, and for a moment she could not speak. Then she said, "Never—I'd never go. I can't go. I can't. And you—you'll leave me. I know they'll take you away."

He tried to soothe her. He said that she had been long out of the world, that their life had been unnatural and cut off with only the stupid Marlowes and Negroes for companionship, that a man had to play his part in the world, that they had to live in the world, for the child's sake if nothing more.

"I hate the world," she cried out. "And the world—it will take you away!"

He could do nothing with her, and in the end he left the room with a cold knot in his heart where there had been tenderness.

For some days she was distant and listless. Then he sent for Dr. Thomas. There was nothing wrong, the doctor said, and went away.

Then came the quarrel. It came upon some triviality. Later he could not even remember its occasion. They were quickly reconciled. He was sure that they were reconciled, and for a little he was happier than he had been for months. He left immediately on his political business, and for his two days of absence, he longed to get back to her. Within an hour after his return, which had been as perfect as he had hoped, they had quarreled again, and again for no reason which he could determine.

Suddenly he discovered that a pattern had been set. He found her bright and cheerful at morning and at noon distant and absorbed. Or at morning she woke sunk in some black, inner despair, unwilling to turn her face to him on the pillow, and if she took his kiss he felt that he was kissing a dead face. Then when he returned in the evening, full of foreboding, he might find her quick and smiling, full of questions about the business of the day, ready to read to him or play for him on the harpsichord in the parlor.

All at once he knew that these times were the worst of all. The smile was a mask ready to fall from her face. Her questions were hollow with the abstracted politeness of a bored stranger, and her eyes wandered when he attempted to answer. Two or three times, when she was reading to him, she read the same line over again without knowing it, and he knew that she had been reading with her mind far away in some desolate spot. Once, in the middle of a piece of music, she burst into tears and ran from the room and locked the door of the bedroom so that he could not come to her.

These times, which were a travesty of their old happiness, became horrible. He came to dread the brittle smile on her face more than her reproaches or desolation. At least, those things, the reproaches or desolation were real. They were the abyss, black and sure, but the smile was some thin crust, like ice, over a more terrifying mystery. He would wait for the mask to fall or the crust to break, and if that did not happen the waiting became intolerable, for he knew that it would happen. So he found himself, in the end, speaking some word or performing some act to precipitate the crisis. "For," as he was to write of that time, "it is what is not real that we cannot bear, who can bear reality no matter if it wear the Gorgon face to freeze the human heart to stone." But he adds: "I do not say this to excuse the evil I did to her, for it is the sadness of love that one who cannot find the reality of himself cries out most for the reality of her whom he loves and if he finds less than that truth in its fullness he feels himself betrayed, and one drop of that vinegar will curdle to foul whey the sweet milk of love more quick than a thunder-clap."

But even so, there came now and then, without warning, outside the pattern of things and beyond any expectations, the moments when she was completely the self of their old intimate life, when the smile she turned upon him was real, and when she stepped to a window in the morning and took the first sun on her face and laughed and turned to him to say, look, the day is beautiful, or when she held her chicks in her lap, sitting on the grass under a tree and leaning above them.

At those moments, all the disorder of the past would seem to have been an evil dream spun out of some darkness in himself. But the moment would pass, and when the pattern had reaffirmed itself more vindictively than before, he would wonder which had been the dream, the happiness or the unhapppiness, the good or the evil.

Or in the middle of the night she might reach over to touch his hand, and cling to it, thinking him asleep, as though her pride or her hopelessness would not let her take his hand in daylight or when he was awake. At those times he would lie as asleep, to avoid the shame of surprising her in the act or to cling himself to the illusion of trust evoked by her act and to steal this moment of happiness outside the whole circuit of their life. But one night the thought crossed his mind: "What does she seek from me?" Whatever it was, he knew that he had not given, and could not give it. And that thought robbed him of the last illusion, and left him lying panting and rigid in the dark.

Therefore he flung himself more ferociously than before into the life of the violent world outside. That, too, was an illusion, he began to think, a kind of "mock-show" or "play-party," he called it. Strangely enough, once that conviction had come, he could smile more readily into any face, the flattering, stale question or the hearty good-day sprang more blandly and falsely to his lips, good-fellowship came more quickly at the whisky barrel, and when he stood before a crowd to speak he found without effort now the warm phrases which inflamed passion or soothed vanity. He felt that he had stumbled on a great and comic secret: if you knew that the hurly-burly of the world was a mock-show, and a flight from another more dire mock-show, then you could play your part the better to win applause from all.

At Smileytown, just as he was about to mount the steps of the store to speak, an old man, whom he knew to be a Reliefer, plucked at his sleeve, saying, "I done been up to Frankfort, and a man ast me if I didn't come from down this-a-way, and give this to me. I thought you'd want to see it, about that son-of-a-bitch."

Jeremiah took the crumpled paper, and smiled, and thanked the man, and slapped him on the shoulder ("I slapped on the shoulder and thanked him who had given me that, not knowing"), and stepped to the porch. He thrust the paper into his pocket and began to speak.

Hours later, as he undressed for bed in a strange room in the house of a farmer near Smileytown, he found the paper. It was a campaign broadside:

THE TRUTH ABOUT
COLONEL CASSIUS FORT

One truth is known to all, that this man who now puffs and preens before us, and speaks for wealth and pride of place, though himself a hireling risen from the mire by arts of connivance, was once the king-pin and master of Relief, and captured hearts with his eloquent tongue that pled for Justice. Oh, be not deceived by him. Oh, hearken not to that eloquence now bought and sold for a price to plead for Injustice. Oh, know that he is a traitor, and betrayed for thirty pieces of silver and the flattery of the Pharisee. That truth is known to all.

But there is a truth not known, which should be blazoned forth to the general eye, that this Judas who betrayed Relief and lives a public lie had stooped in private to betray the precious trust and innocence of a female heart and all for foul appetite. Be it known that this seducer with smooth tongue and false fatherly kindness lured to his embrace a worthy lady of Saul County, by name Miss Rachel Jordan, and that when she had come heavy with the fruit of his lust he cast her off.

What shall we say of him who is traitor to both private oath and public trust? Who treads with equal ease upon the poor man's hope and the female's heart? Who is one mass of corruption through and through, and makes the sweet air of heaven stink?

There in the room alone, holding the paper in his hand, Jeremiah felt deprived and stripped, and the walls seemed to fall away to leave him sorely exposed.

He burned the broadside by the candle flame, then quickly blew out the light.

The elections occurred in August. There were the fifes and drums and fiddles in the square at Lumton, the shouting by the whisky

199

barrels, the cock-fights and the horse-run, the brawling and singing and scuffling, the Negroes playing Old Sledge and mumble-the-peg in the shade and drinking and whacking on gourd banjos, the ginger-bread and apple sellers screaming their wares, the young folks dancing in the glade·down by the creek and sneaking off in couples into the cover of the woods, the chaffing and guffawing, the drunkards lying on the pavement with wide mouths snoring, to be stepped over by the citizenry who could still stand. There was Sellars on his fine horse, bulging in a new black coat, with red-dyed goose feathers set around the band of his beaver, leading his parade with banners around and around the square, bowing and sweating and smiling to the sound of his music.

Jeremiah rode, too, to the sound of fiddles and the cheers of Reliefers, around and around the square, smiling and smiling, or stood by the whisky barrel and shook every hand. Oh, he knew what the world was.

But Sellars won the election. It was a sharp election, but toward the end of the second day, the result became clear well before the polls were closed. Jeremiah walked quietly about the square, thanking the men who had done most to further his campaign, and then found his horse and rode away. He was certain that nobody saw him go, or cared. There was some comfort in that.

It was over. He was not to know for three days that there had been a terrible fight in the square at the end, with blood freely let and one man dead with a knife in his belly. Well, that was part of the world. But he was out of it now.

It was late, long after dark, when he got home. He saw a light in the library as he rode up the lane, and wondered idly why it had been left there. It never occurred to him that Rachel would be waiting up for him. But she was.

She was lying on the couch now set with its back to the dead fireplace, her head propped on pillows, a branched candlestick on a little table at the head of the couch throwing the light down across her hair and bosom. He noticed the mound of her pregnancy and was about to ask how she felt, when she spoke.

"Were you . . . ?" she began.

He cut short her question. "You needn't worry," he said. "I wasn't elected."

"I'm sorry," she said.

"I'm not. It is probably all for the best."

"Do you want something to eat?" she asked. "I had something set for you in case . . ."

"In case I lost," he finished for her. Then: "So you expected me to lose?"

But the bitterness of his words was wasted, and when he had spoken, even before he saw that she would not respond to it, he knew that he did not feel the bitterness. He felt nothing. He had spoken thus simply as part of the old pattern in which he had been caught.

She regarded him soberly from her distance (he had not approached the couch), and then said: "No, you must not believe that. I could have no opinion of what might happen."

"I'm not hungry," he said, and sat down in a chair some distance from the couch.

They sat there for some time, not speaking, while the candles burned down to nubs.

That night defined a new stage for their relationship. The old tension was broken. But there was no return now of their former passion or affection. Each went through the day, respecting the distance between them, careful not to cross it, careful to speak only of the trivial affairs of the present without reference to past or future, speaking in even voices when there was something to say, capable of long silence when there was nothing. Jeremiah says that that time made him think of what old age must be like when two people have outlived all their love and their hate for each other, when they know each other's faults so well that the faults no longer have meaning, and old resentments are no more than the accustomed pain of a rheumatic joint, part of the nature of things, when they can live in peace because neither is more than a ghost to the other.

But he was to young to accept that peace without hope. He found that in some secret corner he was thinking of the time when the child should come. Life would begin again then. He did not try to prevision what that life would be like, but he and Rachel could share it. He tried to put the hope away, superstitiously dreading that if he acknowledged it, it would come to nothing.

Then it happened.

When he stepped into the hall, upon returning home one afternoon in late October, he saw Old Josie's face staring down at him from the stairs, and even before she spoke his heart was chilled.

"It's her," Old Josie said, "it's her."

And Jeremiah bounded up the stairs, past Josie without a word, and ran to the bedroom.

Rachel lay in the bed, on her back, with her eyes closed. For an instant, he thought that she was dead, but then, as he leaned over her, he saw that she was breathing. He called her name, twice, but she did not respond. Then he heard Josie, and turned.

"She yell out," Josie said. "She yell loud, and I come and seen her on the floor. She didn't say nuthin. She just moan-lak. Me and the kitchen-gal, we git her in the bed."

He kept staring at Josie.

She was shaking her head. "It done come," she said, and folded her arms across her breast. "A-fore its time. Hit warn't nuthin. Nuthin but a pore little piece of meat."

He could not speak, staring at that blank, wizened face of the old woman.

"The Lawd is agin her," Josie said.

"The doctor?" he managed to say. "Did you send for the doctor?"

She nodded. "Done sent a boy on a hoss. Long back." She looked at the bed. "I spect and pray Missie be all right. Hit is just the Lawd agin her. The Lawd and human kind."

"Please go," Jeremiah said. "Please go. Now."

She turned to obey.

"Thank you," he said.

He sat by the bed for a long time, while evening came on. Several times he spoke to her, but could not make her reply. But now and then she stirred and moaned. Just before it came full dark, he lighted the candles. Then he noticed that he let the fire go almost out, and suddenly he was very cold. He built up the fire to a big blaze and leaned over it, holding out his hands to it. She stirred and moaned, louder than before.

He leaned over the bed, and called her name, thinking it strange he should be using that familiar name to a strange face that was gray and sagging.

Then she opened her eyes and looked at him. But he could not be sure that she saw him or that, if she saw him, she knew him.

"It's me," he said. "It's me, Jeremiah."

He leaned and took the hand near him.

Then he thought recognition had come into her eyes, she gazed at him so fixedly.

But she said: "It was dead—he gave it to me—but it was dead—I would have loved it, but it was dead—he gave it to me dead—he . . ."

She was looking at him fixedly, but her voice was so weak that it seemed to come from far off, or down a well, not directed to him. It was saying: "He left me—he left me and—he gave it to me—dead—he gave . . ."

"It's me," he said, and pressed her hand hard to make her hear.

". . . it to me dead—and it was all I had—it was all he . . ."

"My God," he cried out, "listen. This is another time. This is now. And I'm not . . ." Then he said it. "I'm not Fort. I'm not Fort. I am Jeremiah, and I'll never leave you."

He saw the eyes widen in the gray face.

202

"It's me," he said softly. "It's me. Jeremiah."

The eyes were enormous, looking at him. Then the hand jerked back from his grasp.

"You," she whispered. "You! Oh, you gave it to me—and it was dead."

It was late when Dr. Thomas came. While he attended the patient, Jeremiah stood by the fire, staring into the blaze. Josie, who had conducted the doctor upstairs, waited in a corner, with her arms folded on her breast, her dark face impassive under the white headcloth. Twice Rachel cried out, a sharp clear cry of pain.

When he had finished, Dr. Thomas came over to the hearth. He said that he thought she would be all right. She was a strong, healthy woman, he said, but it sometimes happened to them no matter how strong they were. Any little thing might cause it. You couldn't tell about the future, he said. Maybe she'd be all right next time. But some of them, it looked like they sort of got the habit, not carrying them through right. Just like a habit.

He turned his eyes from Jeremiah, and looked into the fire. "You know," he said, "this being the second time it came this way."

And Jeremiah thought: *He means Fort.* And thought that he should strike him down.

After he had returned to the room from seeing the doctor to the door, Josie asked him if he didn't want something to eat. When he said no, she said she had it kept nice for him, he ought to eat. So he went down to the dining room.

When he had finished eating, Josie came in. A letter or something had come that afternoon, she said. A man had ridden over from Mr. Tupper's tavern to bring it. She didn't exactly know his name, but she knew his face. She had seen him in the country. She had taken the thing up to Miss Rachel, and then gone downstairs. It wasn't long after that she heard the racket and went upstairs to find Missie on the floor, like she said.

She fumbled in the pocket of her apron, and finally fetched out a piece of paper. "Here 'tis," she said, and laid it on the table by the dirty dishes. As he picked it up, she fumbled again in the apron to recover another piece and lay it down.

"Thank you," he said, and she went out.

We have no copy of what he read. We have only his paraphrase of it.

"It was a handbill which I saw, printed on a paper not quite white, of the sort passed about the towns and taverns to announce the sale of property or a public occasion or to persuade the voter at time of

203

election. It was addressed to men of judgment who would know the truth, or some such language. But could I forget its import, oh Israel, or pluck it from my heart? Nay, sooner should I forget the breast that gave me suck.

"It began by saying that the undersigned, while candidate for the Legislature, had been subject to foul calumny, that he was trimmer and traitor to Relief, which charge he had long since answered and to the satisfaction of the voters of Pick County. But another charge more foul and calumnious, and one that more deeply touched the heart of honor, had been made in print by cowards who dared not abide their words and had cloaked their names. This charge he had not deigned to answer while in the heat of public controversy, for it touched a private matter. But now that the good men of his county had expressed their faith in him, he owed it to them, to truth, and to his dear wife, and to himself to speak. He spoke with regret, knowing that his words might bring pain to one who perchance had already suffered to atone her crime. But the husband whom she had taken, who should have let the dead past bury its dead, had entered in politics (with results now known to all) and to gain sympathy had set slander loose.

"Therefore, he said, he spoke, and would have it known that far from having abused Miss Jordan, of Saul County, he had helped to raise the fortunes of that family, out of friendship for the dead father, an honorable man spared by death the sight of a daughter's fall. For she had taken to her bed a certain slave, a yellow man, Gabbo by name, who was coachman to the family, handsome and well-formed for all his taint of blood. When he, the undersigned, had learned, by chance, the truth, he had, without explanation beyond grounds of financial prudence, persuaded the good mother to sell the slave. This was done, and to a Mister Alstair, since removed to Alabama, but this came too late to save the erring maid (corrupted by wealth and idleness and the reading of the vile Voltaire and pagan philosophers, so that her itching blood was without Christian restraint) from suffering the public shame. For she had already conceived, and later bore a child which came black. Though the child was born dead (or such explanation was set abroad) and the poor creature huddled underground without bell or book, the facts are known.

"The thing was signed by Colonel Cassius Fort.

"I read the words, and read them once again, and let my eyes devour them as though a letter from my dearest love, and in a far country.

"Then all was clear to me, and the lost way I had come. Then all was clear."

VI

THE NIGHT WHEN JEREMIAH STOOD IN
the dining room holding in his hand the broadside with Fort's name
at the bottom, all was clear to him. At that moment he felt, he says,
like a man lost in the pitch dark in ground that should be familiar,
who suddenly sees in a lightning flash the old way before him, and
in the new darker dark while the thunder rolls, can rush forward with
sure foot. He was ready to seize horse, and ride, and on the instant.

But he could not, for Rachel lay upstairs.

There were the days and nights to sit by her bed, while she lay
with closed eyes and breath so shallow that the sheet did not stir on
her bosom, or while she stared at the ceiling, not speaking for hours
and apparently unaware that he held her hand. In those days and
nights if he did not rediscover love for her at least he rediscovered
tenderness. If she did not love him (and he could not think that she
did) there was all the more reason for him to protect her, who otherwise would have nothing. So every glass of water he could hand her,
or every spoonful of broth, became part of a ritual. It was a ritual of
tenderness, but more, a ritual of expiation. For he felt guilty for all.

When by the bed he had cried out to Rachel, "I'm not Fort. I am
Jeremiah," and she had jerked her hand from him and stared at him
and said, "You. Oh, you gave it to me—and it was dead," he had been

stung by resentment at injustice. But she was right. Fort's face and his face were the same. He and Fort were caught in the same web of guilt. Fort had had her in this house long ago against all right and had given her a dead child. And the printed paper that had felled her like a blow and killed the second child had borne Fort's name. But he was guilty, too. If he had not lost his mission somewhere along the way, all would have been different, and a child might now lie in her arms and her face would smile with life.

How had he lost the mission? Sitting by the bed, hour after hour, he turned that question over in his mind. He did not seek extenua-ation, but he had to know. He had an easy answer. The world had taken the mission away. The world had absorbed it, like a cup of fresh water spilled on the parched ground of August.

But what was the world? It was nothing. But the very nothingness was what absorbed and drew you in. And the nothingness had many faces, and many smiled. There were wealth and great place and ambi-tion and lust of the flesh and ease. He had been saved from them, and had passed them by, as easily as he had repudiated the estate of old Marcher, the tasty person of Silly Sal at Bowling Green and her kind, the patronage of Colonel Fort at the law, or the comforts of the com-mon life. But those things were not all the world.

There were more insidious traps, the satisfactions of work and the turn of the seasons to show the fruit of his labor, the vanity of self-justification in his attempt to become great and prove to all men that he did not live by his wife's lands, his gratitude to Fort for favor and kindness, the labor for a general good and the justice of Relief, his joy in the love of Rachel, his hope for the future and the child. He saw them for what they were, traps, traps baited with tainted meat.

And he had taken the bait every time. He loathed himself.

He had taken every time the "way of the natural world." And sud-denly, thinking back on the moment when Rachel had fallen to her knees before him to beg him not to go to Fort because she was to have a child, he saw her, in face and posture, as somehow merged with the foul dark-faced female creature in the woods beyond McClardy's Meadow clutching at his knees and whimpering before he struck her to snatch free and plunge toward the sound of healing waters. Now, by the bed, he dropped Rachel's hand and almost leaped from his chair to go, to go out now, to plunge into a stream, to kill Fort, to go.

But the face on the pillow was the face of Rachel, pale and lax and without its beauty now, but the face of Rachel, and the face he had loved. Could he blame her if he had loved her? Could he blame her if she had loved the child and had wanted him to protect it more than she had wanted him to protect her own good fame? Or his? He could not blame her, for that was "the world and the way of the

206

world." And the world was the enemy. It was the enemy of the "idea," and of "any truth by which a man might live, or die, who would not be the stalled ox drooling at a manger."

Ah, that was the trap, he thought. And thought: *I have not been vigilant, I have deceived myself.*

Then thought: *And I deceive myself now.*

For all at once he saw the truth. He had known the world as a trap. He had known that all his life, and he never would have taken its bait had he not taken the sweeter bait of another trap more cunningly concealed, concealed in the "dark run and footway" of his own heart. And that trap was the "idea"—the idea itself and pure.

It was perfectly clear. He had lived so long with the idea that that alone had seemed real. The world had seemed nothing. And because the world had seemed nothing, he had lived in the way of the world, feeling safe because he held the idea, pure, complete, abstract, and self-fulfilling. He had thought that he was redeemed by the idea, that sooner or later the idea would redeem his world.

But now he knew: the world must redeem the idea. He knew now that the idea must take on flesh and fact, not to redeem, but to be redeemed.

So all would be easy at last. And in that thought he was at peace with the world. He was at peace, strangely, with Colonel Cassius Fort. He was grateful to him, not with the old gratitude for favor and kindnesses which had pinched his heart, but with a new gratitude, more profound, like the gratitude of a good son to a father. He was grateful because Fort, with the last outrage, had showed him the truth.

Since he knew the truth now, all would be easy and he could wait out the last days with patience and without guilt at delay or fear that he now deceived himself in procrastination.

Who had sent the handbill to the house? Within a day or two after the event, when the first shock had worn off, he began to puzzle that question. He quizzed Josie again about the messenger. It was a man whose face she knew, she had seen him around, and he had come riding on a sorrel horse not too many hands high. That was all he got out of her, that and the fact that the messenger hadn't been "dressed too good." Jeremiah could not identify the man. He might be a well-wisher, some Relief man, who thought he was doing a favor. Or he might be some malicious scoundrel who took joy in bringing the libel.

So Jeremiah tore himself from the bedside for an afternoon, and rode to Tupper's tavern. Somebody had kindly brought a message to his house three days before, he announced casually, when he wasn't at home, and the messenger must have dropped his handkerchief, for one had been found on the porch. He wanted to return it, he said, and thank the man for his neighborliness. Did anybody know a man with a small sorrel horse? Then he exhibited a handkerchief, a big checked cotton handkerchief, rather worn and frayed. Or did anybody recognize this? They passed it from hand to hand.

Then one man said that Tim Adams had a sorrel horse, and turned to Mr. Tupper to ask if Tim hadn't been around the other day. Mr. Tupper said yes. But another man said, "Yeah, maybe he was here, but Tim Adams never had a snot-rag in his life, he has barely got pants, and if he takes a notion to blow his nose he don't hold with the foolishness of a handkerchief but does it the way God Almighty intended, right on his sleeve."

But he had been here the other day, Mr. Tupper insisted, handkerchief or no handkerchief, and he had a sorrel horse, not much bigger than a calf.

Yeah, another man said, and he had been talking to that stranger who didn't talk like folks around the section.

"Who was that?" Jeremiah demanded.

Just a stranger, a big fellow like a lot of others, wearing cowhide boots, and no marks, shot-holes, or brands.

"Marks," Mr. Tupper said. "Why, I saw a big white scar on his wrist, like somebody had tried to cut his hand off. I saw it when he reached out to pick up his glass."

"A scar?" Jeremiah asked, and showed his excitement.

One of the men laughed. "Mister," he said, "if you expect to find a feller just because he's got a knife-cut on him, you sure got a job. Hell, mister, this is Kentucky, and ain't many ain't earned him a mark some way."

"Where does Adams live?" Jeremiah demanded.

He got the information, and rode away.

But Adams had little to add. The stranger had given him the letter to deliver. Had paid him a dollar. Just a big feller that didn't talk like folks round there. The feller had ridden with him a way, and then had turned off on the Lumton road.

That was all Jeremiah discovered. Then the thought struck him that the messenger had been from Fort. Fort had wanted to be sure that word reached Jeremiah. He must have blamed Jeremiah for the campaign broadside against him, accusing him of the seduction of Rachel Jordan.

Jeremiah was not even angry at this last wickedness of Fort, or even at the treacherous means employed, the unidentifiable messenger.

It must have been Fort. Fort would have used the story about Gabbo, the coachman. He had been an intimate of the house, would have remembered the name. But Fort had made one mistake. Gabbo had been sold away more than nine months before the birth of Rachel's dead child. That would prove the story to be gross slander.

Then Jeremiah stopped that train of speculation. Did he expect to argue the case? God, no, he told himself. He would argue nothing, with no man. No, there was the better way.

Rachel improved. She could be propped in her bed to listen to him read romances or poetry, which spoke of "love and duty and faith and betrayal and death and the beauty of the world and the longing men had for what was beyond the world." He understood now, for the first time, he thought, what the poets and romancers tried to say, but since he knew already and better than they, there was nothing they could teach him, and he read, in so far as he read for himself, only as a child reads for "the tinkling pleasure and the tickle of curiosity." That did not matter, for he read that Rachel might "draw her mind from the depth and repair the sad hour."

Then the day came when she could sit by the window, with pillows behind her and a blanket over her knees, and look out over the yard and fields, where the season now swung toward winter. He was reading a book of Robert Burns that day, and records the very verses on which he stopped:

> Oh, wert thou in the cauld blast,
>   On yonder lea, on yonder lea,
> My plaidie to the angry airt,
>   I'd shelter thee, I'd shelter thee.

He put his finger in the place, and closed the book upon it. "I would shelter thee," he said.

She continued to look out the window, as though he had not spoken.

"I would shelter thee," he said. "I will shelter you," he said, "as long as I live, for you have suffered too much." And he was about to say how too he would shelter her "wounded name," how now he saw all things clear.

But suddenly she turned upon him, and with a low voice, but one edged with bitterness, said, "Oh, you—you never sheltered me."

For the moment, with the shock of her words, he could not speak. He could only listen to her repeat, "You never sheltered me. Oh, no one has. And least of all—you."

"I tried—I tried . . ." he burst out, but stopped as the truth of her words struck home.

"Oh, you tried," she was saying, with a weary sarcasm.

"I did try," he began angrily. Then more calmly: "I know my fault. I know that I failed. But grant me this. I would have gone to Fort.

When he came back to Kentucky. But you stopped me. You got on your knees to stop me. To beg me not . . ."

"Oh, you were glad not to go . . ."

"That is not fair. Not just. I would have gone . . ."

"I saw it in your face. Oh, I know your face, Jeremiah. You were glad not to go."

So she had read him, too, he thought in a flash. Like Wilkie. And he felt stripped and impotent. But from his very guilt he struck out at her, saying, "It was your fault. And if I was glad, it was for the child. But I would have gone. . . ."

"It was too late then," she said.

"My God, I had gone before. I went to Frankfort, but he would not fight. You know I went and . . ."

"Oh, I know nothing," she said, and turned from him to the window.

"Look at me, look at me," he commanded. But when she did not turn again, he went on: "I challenged him. But he was a coward, and he . . ."

"Challenged him!" She turned at him again, with life blazing back in her eyes. "What had challenging to do? Oh, if you'd struck him down—if you'd been a man—then this—then this"—she laid the tips of her fingers on the blanket at her stomach—"then this would not have happened."

He looked down at the fingers where they bluntly prodded the cloth, hard enough to hurt, and thought that all this was part of his guilt and part of his expiation and had to be endured. He had to watch those hands prodding as though they prodded a fresh wound in his body. He had to know his secret weakness exposed. And whatever in simple fact alone was unjust was in the end a crazy justice truer than truth.

He stood with bowed head, seeing the hands fall again to her lap, prone and empty, and knowing that she had turned again to the window and the bare country beyond.

He moved quietly to stand before her chair.

"You must listen to me," he began, "for what I have to say is important. I know I have failed, but now . . ."

"Now it is too late," she said, not looking at him.

"It is not too late to see at least some justice done. At least, it is not too late for me."

"But you . . ." she began.

"For me," he said, "let the event testify. As soon as you are well enough, I will go . . ."

"You will go," she said indifferently, "now that you are driven to it.

Now that you know you can't ever show your face again after what he has written. Unless you do go."

"All right," he said, trying to keep his anger down, and his voice level, for she was right, she was right in that wild way beyond fact. "All right," he said, "but I'll go and . . ."

"Oh, you'll go," she said, still indifferent. "And you'll challenge him, or try to whip him in the street. Oh, you will cut a fine figure and be a hero for your vanity. And he will shoot you like a dog."

"What are you trying to do?" he demanded, and the anger was on him now. "Frighten me? Well, I'll not be frightened. I'll take my risk."

"It will be easy for you," she said, with the bitterness back in her tone. "All you have to do is cut a fine figure and die. But me—oh, I wish I could die like that. Quick. Oh, it'll be easy for you." She jerked her head in dismissal, and again turned away. Then added: "But for me—oh, yes, you would shelter me."

"What do you mean? What do you want?"

"Nothing," she said. "It does not matter if you go or stay."

"Would you have Fort spared? Are you asking that?"

She turned to him slowly, and he saw the hands clench on her lap. But she spoke quite steadily. "Spare him?" she questioned, and for an instant he almost thought she smiled in the old way he had not seen for so long. Then the lips tightened. "I would kill him with my own hands," she said, "though he lay at my feet and begged for water."

He leaned to take her hands, and was about to speak, but she withdrew them from him.

"But you . . ." she said, and turned away.

He went to walk in the yard, full of his new thought.

For he saw now, he says, "that an obligation postponed and put away is like the serpent under the rock that in the new season brings forth its young. What had been easy once to scotch at a single blow was doubly hard now, for while I struck the elder the young would flee safe into its footless place. By which I mean, if I should die in my attempt on Fort, my wife were left unprotected in her new weakness and that obligation unfulfilled. And if I stayed by her as husband, my first obligation like the serpent-dam would bring forth generations of vipers, sired by justice like the sun.

"There was one way, and only one: to strike Fort down by stealth. That thought first stirred repugnance, for I had been bred by my revered father and my dear teacher Dr. Burnham to prize openness and honor, and I trusted that their counsels had not fallen in a rocky place. But reason drove me on, by the argument just stated. And I saw my honor in that light to be, however dear, but dear to me and

211

to my vanity. I saw it to be the last sacrifice I must make, and the last expiation. So I was determined.

"But one more thought I had, though not that morning, later when I mused upon the act. I had seen before, that the idea as but idea had been a vanity, too, and a deceit I practiced, and that it had to be redeemed by the world. But how could the world redeem the idea but by the flesh and way of the natural world? And the world was but the world, and its ways crooked and dark. Then I put the last question. If the idea could not wear the dark flesh and could not keep its foot firm in the crooked track, what was it worth, after all? I knew that that was the last hazard, and like the bold gamester I staked all on a card. I would submit the idea to the way of the world.

"So I set myself to the task with what coolness I could muster."

He set himself to the task, he says, with the same conscience, and almost with the same pleasure, with which he had once confronted a theorem of Euclid, a subjunctive of Cicero, or a paragraph of Coke or Chitty. "For there is always a pleasure," he says, "though that pleasure be the index of human pride, in the movement of mind beyond the appearance of things to their inwardness of logic."

His mind was never clearer, he reports, nor more at ease. He did not discuss the matter further with Rachel, though he spent long hours with her as before, reading to her or doing her small services. With her he was smiling and easy, as in the "happy and thoughtless period" after their marriage, but now and then he caught her eyes curiously upon him as though with unspoken question. Nor was there any talk of love or tenderness between them. That might come later, he hoped, after the event, when she could turn to him in full trust.

His plans matured. He built "what dykes were possible against the blind stream of circumstance." He picked the time for the deed, the night before the Legislature would convene. The date would give the color of political motive to the deed, for it was expected that on the morrow Fort would rise as the new champion of his Party. Jeremiah was ready to act.

First he went back to Tupper's tavern, where he had not been since the day when he had ridden there to investigate the handbill. Now he made his visit as casual as possible, nodding to the men gathered, passing the time of day ("but with no more affability than was my wont"), asking for news. He suffered the gossip of the neighborhood, and even had to suffer the question of the man who said he had heard that Mrs. Beaumont had "brung one off dead," and was it true?

Then another bystander, shaking his head in condolence, said: "Yes, sir, it is bad. Once they get in the habit, it looks like they can't carry them through."

Jeremiah felt the surge of blood and the tightening of muscles even before his mind framed the question: "The habit—the habit? Does he mean Fort's bastard? Would he insult me with that?"

But he steeled himself, kept his hands from the man's throat, and nodded gravely, agreeing without words and all the while studying the man's face. But the man's face showed nothing, and Jeremiah decided that Dr. Thomas had passed out the news, for the very words were the doctor's and this fool was merely trying to appear wise.

Then he thought that after the event to come he would never again have to cringe and fawn at some reference, however innocent, to the past, for then, even if he were never charged, or even if the court cleared him, people would know in their deep hearts that Jeremiah Beaumont had taken justice. The past would be dead.

Meanwhile, however, he said, yes, it had been a grief, but Mrs. Beaumont was bearing up well. So well, in fact, that now he was thinking of taking a trip about land business in the West, where he already held a tract, and he would like to buy a good draft horse, or swap a saddle mount for one, and did anybody know of one, or better, a team. If he got a team, he wouldn't have to worry about matching the one he already had with a new one. He would be beholden, he said, if the gentlemen present would pass the word in the community to anybody who might have some fair animals. With that he took his noggin, and left.

The next day, he rode early to the Barron place, spent the day in friendly visit with the old man, who was still hale though slower in his gait, told him of his plan for the West, and ended by buying a good wagon. He already had a wagon serviceable for such an expedition, but he wished to noise his project in that part of the county, too. Four days later, after he had concluded a trade for a team, he sent Captain Marlowe, to whom he gave a dollar for the job, to bring back the wagon. He knew that Marlowe was a great one "for blab and gab" and would stop every man on the road to advertise the news.

Meanwhile, he had made an agreement with the boy who had previously accompanied him, saying they might even go to Missouri, down the "big river," and that the boy should be ready for a quick start and a long stay. Then, to support that rumor, he discussed the possibility with Captain Marlowe that, in case he should go on to Missouri, Marlowe should take charge of the farm, and he and Mrs. Marlowe should move up to the Jordan house to be company for Mrs. Beaumont. Marlowe hemmed and hawed at this, and talked big about pressing affairs which might prevent, but Jeremiah knew he would agree in the end and knew he would boast about the

213

arrangement. ("I knew that he would relish nothing better than to live in a big house, though not his own, and drink himself drunk with a carpet to fall on, and bully the Negroes as he thought a gentleman would do. I had never been such a fool to leave my affairs in his hands, for my stock had been abused, my fields gone to weeds, and some slave had spilled his brain-pan with an ax and fled for the wilderness. I laughed inwardly at his demur when I broached the subject, and found comedy in his talk of his affairs while all the time he burned to agree. Ah, but the comedy was not for that poor clown.")

The time drew on. Marlowe had agreed to move up to the big house as soon as a letter came from Jeremiah, and meanwhile, Mrs. Marlowe would sleep there to keep company for Rachel. On November 3 he was to come early to the big house to help Jeremiah finish loading the new wagon, which now stood before the door as a public announcement of Jeremiah's trip west. But a few days before, Jeremiah went early to the Marlowe place to say that the departure had to be delayed. He had land patents at the office in Frankfort which were important to him and had tried to get some one to go and pick them up for him but with no success. (He had, in fact, made some inquiries at the tavern, but had been careful not to press them too hard.) Would Marlowe be able to go immediately to Frankfort? He would go himself, but he wanted to be with his wife as long as possible.

Again, Jeremiah enjoyed the comedy of Marlowe's squirming. Marlowe would have liked nothing better than to go to Frankfort at another's expense and dawdle in the common rooms of the inns and the bedrooms of the brothels, but, as Jeremiah knew, Mrs. Marlowe would not permit it. The last time the Captain had escaped her vigilance he had returned a "week late, wind-broke, string-halt, and with a look in the eyes like a dog that has been sucking eggs."

Now the Captain claimed that he was not well enough to travel, and coughed twice to prove it. Jeremiah offered sympathy, and then said, with an oath of irritation, that he would have to go himself, and postpone his real departure until his return.

After dinner that night, while Rachel went upstairs to their bedroom, he went to the plunder room off the kitchen, got his saddlebags, and then went to the cold library, carrying a candle. He unlocked the secretary (with the key which for days now he had carried on a string around his neck), took out his "accouterments," already prepared, and packed them in one side of the saddlebag. Then he went to join Rachel.

He found her sitting before the fire, already in her nightgown, wearing a wrapper and combing her hair. She held her head inclined to one side, and a little forward, so that the hair on that side fell almost to the floor, straight except for its rippling sheen. She did not turn or lift her head when he entered, nor did the comb pause in its motion.

He shut the door softly and stood there and watched her. "I watched, and thought of the times in the past when I had been thoughtlessly happy to watch that glossy motion of the instrument through her hair. Now I watched how it passed in a long, luxurious sweep downward for the length of her arm, and how in its track the fire set gold to glittering in the darker mass, as I had read once in a book how in the sea of tropic latitudes the passing of a keel at night wakes phosphorus so that stars seem to wink in that downward sky of dark waters. And even now I had the great impulse to go and pick her up in my arms, as I had done in the past once when I surprised her thus, sitting bemused with the motion of the comb in her hair, and carry her to the bed despite her protest of, 'No, no, I have not finished, set me down,' and hear her protest lost in a sigh as I took my will.

"Though the desire came great, I did not do so now, for I would not fall twice into the self-deceit of taking what I had not earned. Nor would she have accepted me, and without love it were only vile coupling in violence. But I stood and thought how it might have been, were all well between us and me going on a journey, how she might have sent me on my way with the comfort of her heart and her person. With that thought I was almost sick with sudden despair and it seemed that nothing could repair the twisted time. But I took command of myself, and came to the hearth.

"I addressed her, and when she raised her head, with the comb poised half-way in its stroke, I told her that I was prepared to leave, on the business about which we had spoken.

"She nodded in assent, and perhaps murmured something, and I said: 'I have taken all precautions, and should return in ten days or less. If anybody asks for me, say I am gone to Frankfort on land business to claim my patents and will hurry back as soon as may be to make my journey west and most like to Missouri.'

" 'To Missouri?' she asked in surprise, for I had told her nothing but that I was going about land.

" 'I have no plan to go. It is a subterfuge, and certainly I do not intend to flee and leave you. If I go, it will be when all is safe, and then not to Missouri, but on a short journey to guarantee my stratagem.'

" 'Your stratagem?' she asked, and began to question me.

"But I cut her short, and laughed, saying, 'Do not worry about it. I have done all possible. I shall come back. But now'—at this I held out the saddlebags to her—'act the good wife sending her husband on a journey and pack me some shirts and my necessaries.'

215

"She rose obediently and took the bags and went beyond the bed to the chest of drawers, turning to lay the bag on the counterpane of the bed. While I stood beside her, she took my things from a drawer, turned and laid them beside the bags, and started to open the bag which I had already packed.

" 'Don't,' I commanded, 'for that is my secret.'

"So she desisted and packed the other side. While she was doing so, I turned to shut the top drawer, whence she had taken my brushes, and saw there, with other loose objects, a dark red ribbon she had used as a sash or stomacher long before. I picked it up, and handed it to her, saying, 'Pack this too.'

" 'For what?' she asked in surprise.

" 'For your colors.'

" 'Colors?' she asked.

" 'Yes,' I said, 'for it is the color of blood and I go on an errand of blood and when you see it again it shall fly as a pennon for victory.' And I laughed, for the fancy pleased me.

"She looked at me strangely for an instant, looking up from her work, and then said with a twisted mouth, 'You have read too many books.'

" 'They tell us the nobleness of life,' I said, and laughed.

" 'Nobleness,' she echoed my word as she again twisted her mouth. 'What nobleness have I seen?'

" 'None,' I said, and my heart went heavy. 'None, poor girl, except your own.' Then I reached out to touch her shoulder. 'I know I am no Bayard. But I am the only knight you have, though unworthy.' I held out the ribbon to her. 'So take it,' I said, 'and pack it, for it is all I have to make me worthy.' "

She took it and packed it, with no other recorded word. He told her that he would now tell her good-bye, and sleep in another room, for he would leave long before day and did not want to disturb her. He took her in his arms, and kissed her on the brow. At the first, she stood with her arms hanging at her side, passively taking his embrace, then for one instant he felt her arms start about his waist somewhat timidly, as though she wished to draw him to her but were fearful. But her arms fell away again and he released her, picked up the saddlebags, and left the room.

He arose long before day, washed in water like ice, put on his greatcoat and hat, picked up the saddlebags, and went down to the kitchen, carrying his candle "stealthy on the stairs like a thief." In the kitchen he found some milk and some corn pone. He put two pones in the pocket of the coat to eat later in the morning, and began to take one now, washing it down with the milk.

216

He was almost through with the pone, when he heard the door open, and saw Rachel there with one hand on the jamb, regarding him.

"Why did you come?" he demanded. He was aware of anger and irritation in his voice.

"I could not sleep," she said.

"Go back to bed," he ordered. "You are not well. It is too early for you."

She hesitated a moment, and then came toward him, stopping several feet from him.

"Go back to bed," he repeated. He turned from her, took down a horn lantern from the shelf, and lighted it from his candle. He set the candle down on the table. "Take it," he said, "and go to bed. I am going to the stable now."

He swung the saddlebags across his shoulder, picked up the lantern, and made ready to go. He felt that he had to go now, on the instant.

But she came to him, and laid her hand on his arm. He drew back from the touch, but she touched him again, and he stood still.

"You do not have to go," she said.

"I am going," he said.

"You do not have to go," she said, with her hand timidly on his arm.

Then, before he could speak, she had put her arms about his body, saying, "You don't have to go. We could just be here. Just be here . . ." She was speaking rapidly as though to forestall anything from him. "Just be here, in this house. We could be kind to each other. Kind, like people can be. We could just be here. Away from everybody. From the world, from . . ."

"The world," he said harshly, and tried to pull himself free. "I have been away from the world too long."

She was clutching him tight now, saying, "We could just be here. In this house. We could just live and . . ."

"It is too late now," he said, and did not know exactly what he meant, what was too late, but he knew he had to go.

And he tried to disengage himself; she clutched him strongly and put her mouth up to his. He kissed her, and she pressed her lips against his, but he found them as cold as he knew his own to be.

Suddenly she released him and stepped back. "Have you ever loved me?" she said, but in a tone that expected no reply.

He moved toward the outer door. "Good-bye," he said.

"Good-bye," she said. But he saw that she was not even looking at him now. She was looking at the candle on the table.

He went out to the stable, saddled his horse, blew out the lantern, hung it on a peg, and rode up the lane that joined the drive beyond the front gate. As he passed the kitchen, he saw that there was still light there, but he could not see the figure of Rachel.

A hundred yards or so up the lane, he turned in his saddle and looked back again at the house. He does not say what prompted this, or what he felt. But he had lived in the house a long time now. He was leaving a piece of his life there, and it was gone forever and could not be changed. He had stood that morning in the kitchen, wolfing down the old corn pone, like a forward farmer anxious to get to the field before day. He might have been such a farmer, or a lawyer, ready to ride to court, and the woman there with him might have been any good and dutiful wife who had risen to make a pot of coffee to help her man on his way. But it was not that way, and he had taken the cold kiss and left in the way he had to go.

The road from the Jordan place ran south for some miles to strike the stage road from Bowling Green to Frankfort at a point below the settlement of Monroe and within sight of the Pilot Knob to the southwest. (Jeremiah says that the sky was hazy that day but that he could make out the Knob on his right.) At the junction he stopped for a moment. This was the place for him to take the left turn on the stage road for the direct way to Frankfort, but if he continued across the stage road and southeast, he would come into the country of his boyhood.

On impulse, against all his plans, he crossed the stage road and held southeast. He justified the course on sound practical grounds: he had the time and he could easily make Frankfort before the date set in his mind, and, besides, it would be well for his presence in the old parts to be remarked, for who would turn aside for a sentimental pilgrimage when bent on such a dire mission?

He did not define that need that led him from his path. He had no plan to see anyone. His sister had moved from the section long since, and as for Dr. Burnham, there had been no news or correspondence since he had left Bowling Green. Dr. Burnham might even be dead, for all he knew now. That thought set up an ache in him which merged with the "sweet melancholy" provoked by the flood of memories and the sight of old landmarks. Was it to this that all his life had tended all those years, like a blind river in one of those great caves of the region, and he had not known? Was this why his father had come into the strange country and struggled and died a bankrupt? Was this why Hettie Marcher had left the gentle life to follow the penniless Captain, in the end to hoe squash in a scraggly garden patch by the edge of a field toward evening? Was it for this he had spelled out the primer and felt the switch on his bare legs or later brooded over the great books while others took ease and pleasure? Was it for this that Dr. Burnham had turned him over to Cassius Fort, long ago in a cheerful room with a bright hearth? All that landscape of his past seemed distorted now in its very familiarity, as the real marks of the country he now entered on the second day—the curve of a road, the width of a ford, the shape of a hill—betrayed memory.

He came to the crossroads where the academy stood. The roof was out of repair, he saw immediately, and chinking gone here and there from the logs. He hitched his horse, and approached the structure. The greased paper that had served for windows had long since given way. He peered in, and saw that the benches had been removed and that hay was stored in one end. He went around the building to the spring. The water was still clear and fresh, though leaves and trash had nearly choked one side. He took a long drink from the spring, and resumed his way.

Down the road was the Mason place where Dr. Burnham had lived with his daughter. He turned in the gate, hitched his horse, heaved a stone at the dog, big as a bear-dog, that threatened to nip him, and hallooed as he approached the steps.

When the door opened to his knock, he saw Mrs. Mason. He greeted her by name, but though she responded in courtesy, he saw from her face that she did not know him. That fact struck him with despair, he did not know why, and he had the impulse to step back and get to his horse and flee, as though he had been detected in a shameful act. But he conquered it, and said, "I am Jerry Beaumont. Don't you remember me?"

At that her face broke into a smile, she said, of course, she remembered him, and Dr. Burnham would be happy.

"I was afraid," he said, hesitating. "When I saw the academy— what had happened there—I was afraid that . . ."

"Oh, no," she said brightly. Then more seriously: "Oh, no, thank God. He is with us. But a little broken. In good spirits, but a little broken. He is old."

So she led him across the hall to the big room and opened the door, calling out, "Father—Father—here is somebody to see you—he has come a long way!"

There was the old man, propped in his big home-made chair by the hearth, more bloated and bigger than ever to pop his black coat, smiling from a face that somehow looked small and seemed to be almost lost and absorbed in the fleshy mass of cheeks and jowls and neck. "My boy—my boy," the old man said, and lifted his swollen hands.

Jeremiah took his hands, hearing the old man say, "You bring bright light in the dark day," and seeing the weak eyes go moist behind the square spectacles.

"It's been a long time," the old man was saying, "and you'll stay long now to make up for it. And to make up for your wickedness in not writing. All we had was word from the road, how you prospered. But you'll tell us yourself now. You'll stay and . . ."

"I must go soon," Jeremiah said. "Tonight. Tomorrow morning. You see, I am going west and I . . ." He had decided before entering the house to explain his presence on some improvised business in the neighborhood, to make all seem casual, but the thought now flew from his head. He said: "And I had to see you. I wanted to see you before I left, for I may be gone a long time. I wanted to tell you how I have thought often of you. How I remember words you said that you have long forgotten. How I am grateful to you for things you know not, as you had unwittingly dropped morsels from your table to a creature. How I . . ."

"No, no," Dr. Burnham was saying, lifting his swollen hands in protest.

But Jeremiah's words came on in a rush, beyond any premeditation, and to his own surprise, with the sweetness of unburdening: ". . . how I owe you what is precious and of good report. How whatever has come or may come, I strive to be worthy of your precepts and of your honor and . . ."

"Sit down, my boy, sit down," Dr. Burnham said in a voice of sudden authority, which struck Jeremiah with an echo of the old schoolroom so that he expected to see the ash stick spring out to whack a shin for a bad recitation. His words stopped and he stood there feeling foolish before Dr. Burnham's chair.

"Sit down, my boy," Dr. Burnham said, more kindly. "You are tired. I can see you are tired."

Jeremiah sat, feeling suddenly will-less and drained.

"Martha," Dr. Burnham crossly ordered his daughter, who still stood at the door, "get this boy some refreshment. Can't you see he is tired? He has come a journey to see an old man."

Jeremiah stayed the night at the Mason place. He talked away the shank of the afternoon, and for a long evening, hearing how Dr. Burnham had had to give up the academy for his weakness in walking, how he had thought to build a school in the yard, but had given up the idea, for his remaining span was too short to merit the pain, how he still could read though his hand was too swollen for the pen-staff but how he dictated to his daughter the fruit of his meditation in the faint hope that some men might profit, for "nothing human

220

was ever to be lost, though burdened with error." And he heard the news of the community, what had happened to the other scholars who had "come to manhood and the world," the marriages, births and deaths, the successes and failures, the labors and the pleasures, and "all the unillustrious courses by which men weave their common life together and find it worth the days spent."

After he was in bed that night, Jeremiah remembered that Dr. Burnham had not once mentioned the name of Cassius Fort, which would have been most natural for him to do. So he surmised that Dr. Burnham knew the tale of Fort and Rachel Jordan. And of his own marriage. That was why he had said nothing, out of delicacy, waiting for Jeremiah to speak of the marriage. With that thought Jeremiah was suddenly angry at the old man. Was Burnham the fool to think it shameful? By God, he would leave the house now, and spit on the threshold.

The mood passed, but in the morning when the servant carried his dawn breakfast to a table beside Dr. Burnham's bed that they might have the last minutes together, he remembered, and said with studied naturalness: "I have spoken much to my wife of you, and have inspired in her the same sentiments I hold for you. She particularly asked me to pay her respects, though she is unknown to you."

Dr. Burnham said that he would be honored to make her acquaintance and that he trusted Jeremiah's judgment in all things touching worth.

"She is the soul of worth," Jeremiah burst out with more warmth than he had intended. "She is a very noble spirit, and I would not change her for the world."

"Jerry," Dr. Burnham said calmly, "I know you, and that is enough. I rejoice in your happiness."

Jeremiah rose abruptly from his chair. He felt rebuked and shamed. "I must go," he said.

From the region of his boyhood back to the stage road Jeremiah took a horse track which joined the main thoroughfare a little south of the crossing of the Green River and somewhat north of Monroe, bypassing that settlement, and then rode on to Summersville (which he gives as "Sommerville," and thus it is found on some old maps).

The road he traveled from Monroe to Summersville does not exist now. The main roads north from Nashville and Bowling Green now pass somewhat to the west near Mammoth Cave, Floyd Collins's Cave, and Hodginsville, where Abraham Lincoln was born in a log cabin, of obscure parentage. But in those days no tourist stopped at Lincoln's cabin, or at Mammoth Cave and wandered for twelve hours in the nightmare bowels of earth, in the absolute dark lit by electric torches, and shuddered with chill, with undefined memory and presentiment, and with admiration at the wonders of Nature.

Now the highways, 31W and 31E, glittering with concrete or asphalt, slash north across the Knobs, and in no time you can make it to Louisville (The Fall City), Bardstown ("My Old Kentucky Home"), Frankfort (Historic Frankfort), or Lexington (The Dimple of the Bluegrass). But in 1825 Monroe and Summersville were still on the main route north, and at Summersville the road forked. Both forks, however, could lead to Frankfort, the west fork, by way of Bardstown and Shelbyville, a little shorter than the east fork by way of New Market, Lebanon and Perryville, near Danville, where Dr. Burnham had lived and made his fame before he came to the southern part.

Just north of Summersville the road divided, one fork continuing north to Bardstown, the other more eastwardly to New Market and Perryville. Jeremiah elected the latter. He had, he thought, a good reason to choose the longer way. He had traveled the Bardstown road several times and was acquainted with various persons who lived along it. Also by that way there was the better chance of falling in with travelers who might know him. He was taking a rather slow pace, in order to time his arrival for the chosen date, and he feared that word of his journey might precede him. But he had little to fear on the east fork. People from his own neighborhood bound for Frankfort would scarcely take it, and he knew no one who lived along it.

He passed through the scrub country toward New Market, and spent the night on the floor of a miserable wayside cabin before he reached that settlement. (There was a sick baby in the cabin, and its "colic-squalls" kept him awake most of the night.) The next day he dawdled toward Perryville, and again stopped before reaching the settlement. At Perryville, he took a cut-off to miss Danville, forded the headwaters of the Salt River, and came to Harrodsburg (where the reconstructed stockade of the first Kentucky settlers can now be seen, true to the life). He slept beyond Harrodsburg, rose early, and took the last lap of his journey with some thirty-odd miles to go, a distance to which he could adjust his pace so as to arrive at Frankfort with the first autumn dark.

His going that day, however, was harder than he had imagined. Toward Lawrenceburg he found heavy brush fires along the way and even some patches of woodland smoldering so that a heavy smoke lay over the land, particularly in the dips and hollows. If he had had the time he would have waited, but for him there was no choice now. He had, he says, to "make a spoon or spoil a horn," and so he went on in the bad air. After a little his head began to ache violently. He stopped at a branch to bathe his forehead and get some relief,

and there discovered, as he first bent over the clear water, that his
face was grimy and streaked with fine ash so that at a few paces he
must have resembled a colored man. He washed his face for the refreshment, not to clean it, for he knew that after a little the dampness
would make him "look streaked and fearsomely worse than before."
Then he soaked a big green silk handkerchief he carried and bound
it about his forehead for what relief that would give. He was in
Lawrenceburg in the afternoon, and though he had stopped outside
town to clean himself at a ditch to avoid embarrassing notice, a man
on the street looked at him and called out, "Is all the world afire
down that a-way, and you the only one give Old Nick the sleight?"

Jeremiah made some reply in a tone as jocular as he could summon
up for the ache in his head, and rode on.

It was after dark when he took the last rise and saw beneath him
the long, dim swerve of the river by the flat land to the bluffs, the
lights of Frankfort backed by the black, solid escarpment of hill to
the north. He dismounted, tied his horse to a scrub tree, and clambered his way down to the water. He wanted to wash as well as
possible before going in. Then he rode on down to the crossing, went
over the river, and entered the town. As he entered the town he
heard the bells ringing for supper, far off, among the houses. He had
ridden nearly a hundred miles from Summersville.

He had planned to stay at one of the more humble inns, for he
had fear that at the Mansion House or at Captain Weisiger's he
might encounter some of the politicians or hangers-on who could
recognize him, or even Colonel Fort himself. But he was ill-informed
about the town, and had to stop a citizen. The man sent him to a
place called Mackey's Tavern. There the barman to whom he presented himself for a room (for the barman served as clerk in that
time and place) told him that there was no accommodation, that
the town was full of the "big men come to town for the opening of the
Houses on the morrow" and asked civilly was Jeremiah a member of
the new Legislature. Jeremiah replied that he was just a plain man
on business, and when the barman showed signs of pursuing conversation, asked him quickly to recommend some other hostelry.

He had no better luck at the second place, and at the third, he was
told that he might bed down on the floor with other latecomers in
the common room. Even at the Weisiger House, where he finally
screwed up courage to show himself, he would have to share a room
with two others, and perhaps more, for, as the barman put it, the
place was "fuller than a tick on a fat dog with all paws tied." Jeremiah
said that he was ill, pointing to his bound head, and chose not to
share a bed, or even a room, with others. The barman inspected him
and agreed that he did not look like a well man, then suggested that

he go to the home of a certain Caleb Jessup, who occasionally took in travelers and kept a clean house.

He found the Jessup place, on a back street, a brick house, the last good one before the shacks began, and was admitted into a dark hall by a very fat, dumpy woman whose gray hair strung down about a shapeless face that gleamed greasily and grayly in the light of the candle-stub she held askew. She allowed that they could take him in, even if it wasn't no palace for dukes and kings, and the bed was clean, she'd say that much, and maybe he'd like it well enough.

But after his horse had been stabled, and he came into the main room to get his supper, he knew that he would not like it at all. There was a close stale smell of old food and burned grease and of unwashed flesh, a smell that seemed to hang in the air like a substance, so solid that you expected to see it like mist, or feel its weight on your cheek. It was more offensive to him, Jeremiah says, than the odors of any "foul inn or cabin of the West," for what in those places seemed natural and to be condoned here seemed a degradation and insult in a room that had been designed for decency and order and some pretension.

A burly unshaven man seated by the hearth looked up when Jeremiah entered, and grunted some greeting. Two female children, with swollen gray faces and stringy hair, like the woman's, played on the floor; they looked up at Jeremiah but made no move to get out of his path. A handsome sluttish girl beyond the man gave Jeremiah a bold, contemptuous glance and resumed her changing of a baby on her knees, flinging the soiled cloth to the hearth where it steamed most abominably. A big boy was cracking hickory nuts on the hearth and picking out the meats with a nail.

Jeremiah was, for an instant, on the verge of turning without a word and leaving such a place, "where all seemed to hate you for no reason but that you were human, and to hate each other in resentment for their common misery," and would have done so had he had hope of another place that night, but he told himself that he was a little ill and his nerves overwrought, that the family he looked at were to be "pitied in the mortal lot," and that his business in Frankfort would not let him dwell upon niceties. So he took his place at the big table against the wall and accepted the food the fat woman set before him. It was no better than he had reason to expect, and its flavor was not improved by the discovery of the occupation that the man by the hearth now returned to. The man heaved a big bare foot over a knee and began to cut his toenails and pare his corns "with a clasp knife big enough to skin and butcher a bear."

The snap of the knife being closed signaled the end of that "wholesome entertainment," but Jeremiah's relief was short-lived, for the

man rose, stretched, and padded over on his bare feet to stand by
the table and play the courteous host. That he was a great talker was
immediately obvious, for he laid on without delay, and the subject
he chose was himself, how he had been a stout man in his time, could
heave up a whisky barrel to a cart, had licked to a frazzle Sull Tandy,
the biggest bully on the Ohio, and could do it yet if he hadn't strained
a "tennon," how he had been sheriff and laid 'em low when they
didn't behave, and, by God, would be yet if he hadn't been poli-
ticked out, how he had had lands and was rich as the next one, and
would have them yet if it hadn't been for bad times and thieving
lawyers, but no man could down Caleb Jessup, for yes, sir, old Caleb
would show them yet. Then he flexed his arm and invited Jeremiah
to feel his muscle. Jeremiah complied, muttered his admiration, and
returned to his meal.

Jeremiah interrupted the flow of conversation by asking if he could
have a glass of whisky, saying that he had a headache and thought
that it might help him sleep, but in reality wanting it to cut the cold
grease out of his throat. The man fetched a jug, and while Jeremiah
downed one drink, he disposed of three. Thus whetted, he was prepared to "embark again upon his predilected topic," but Jeremiah
rose and said that he had to go to bed, begging to be excused.

The man's ample jaw fell, and his whole face had the slack aspect
of one who has been stunned by a betrayal, but he collected himself
and took out his pique by saying in uncivil loudness to his wife to
look sharp and not keep a guest waiting. So the woman took a candle,
led Jeremiah out into the hall, and up the stairs to his room, where
the saddlebags had already been carried by a Negro boy.

The room was almost decent, and a fire had been lighted on the
hearth. The woman set the candlestick on the table and went to the
bed and turned back the covers. "Look," she said, "the bed is clean,
like I said. It is a clean bed."

"Yes," Jeremiah agreed, giving it scarcely a glance.

"It is clean," she said, and he saw that her face wore a beseeching,
wistful look, as though she begged for a favor she knew he would
never give.

He stepped to the bed and leaned over and laid a hand on the
sheets. "Yes, it is a clean bed," he said, "a very fine bed."

"I saw you didn't relish your supper," she said.

"I wasn't hungry."

"No," she said, shaking her head, "it just wasn't anything to brag
on. It wasn't any good." She shook her head again. "It looks like
nothing is any good around this house any more."

"I enjoyed my supper," Jeremiah said resolutely.

She looked at him, wistful again, and suspicious, as though he were not to be believed. So he supported his statement with an emphatic nod. She moved toward the door, but stopped just inside. "Things was nice here once," she said. "It was a nice house. My people was good people. They held their head up. It was my house. But he . . ."

She looked down at the floor with a sudden concentration of hate in her eyes so strong that Jeremiah thought it might pierce the boards to the room below.

Then she lifted her gaze again. "It was my lands he was talking about," she said. "You heard him, how he said bad times and lawyers took them. You heard him?"

Jeremiah nodded.

"Well," she said, leaning at him, "it was him. He gambled them off. Every acre. Every foot of ground." Then she leaned more closely, the eyes glittering, and her voice sank as though telling a secret. "This house," she whispered, "it's got a mortgage, and he can't pay." She said that with ferocious satisfaction.

Then the fire was out of her. She reached clumsily back for the latch of the door, and seemed ready to retreat from him as though she feared a blow. "It's a clean bed," she said, pleading or trying to offer him that bribe to avoid an inevitable blow.

She was gone. He would not have thought it possible for a woman of her bulk and clumsiness to vanish so quickly, and without sound. But there was the closed door, and he almost thought that she had not been there at all, that she was something conjured up, "or sent by the Powers for warning to show what the horror of life might be."

He had the momentary sense that nothing about him was real, that the people below, the man with his lies and the woman with her hate, and the very house were not real. They were shadows and emptiness. Then his glance fell on the saddlebags. Ah, that was real.

He picked them up, stepped to the door and bolted it, and came back to the bed.

First, very methodically, he took out his clean shirt for the morning, his nightshirt, his razor, other small items, and a book, and disposed them upon a chair. Then he took out the "accouterments," done up, except for one article, in a big, checked cotton handkerchief, quite old and faded and with a stain at one corner. He arranged the articles on the bed.

The article too bulky to be done up in the handkerchief was a kind of short surtout, of a dark color, very shabby and dusty and moth-bit. He had found it rummaging in the attic of the Jordan house, hanging on a nail. It had been tailed then, with brass buttons in front and two buttons at the small of the back, a coachman's coat he took it to be, probably once used by Gabbo before he had been sold off. Jeremiah had cut off the tails and brass buttons, had thrown the buttons in the creek and had burned the tails in the fireplace of the library, and had mistreated the coat further to make it unrecognizable—though who might ever recognize it? He would wear this tonight, for disguise, thinking, for one thing, that because it was too ample for him it would help conceal the build of his figure. He took some pleasure in the notion that thus unwittingly Gabbo, whose name had been used in the slanderous broadside signed Fort, would return and have some part in vengeance.

The articles unwrapped from the handkerchief were three pairs of heavy yarn socks, an old wool hat, very tattered and dirty, a mask of thin black silk, and a knife with a wooden brass-bradded handle and a narrow blade.

The socks were his own, but of a common color and stitch such as any man might have. The hat he had bought, but in a transaction never contemplated by the late owner. Jeremiah, riding down a track in the neighborhood of the Barron place, had seen the hat and a gourd water-flask hanging on a stake at the edge of a woods, and had heard, far in, the sound of an ax. Some Negro, he surmised, was in the woods at work, having left his stuff here. So he took the old wool hat, and stuck a silver dollar in the cleft of the stake, thinking how forever afterwards the poor darkie would superstitiously leave hats on stakes and turn his back and pray for a repetition of the miracle.

The mask he had fashioned himself out of an old skirt that had been in a trunk and had probably belonged to Mrs. Jordan. It was, in fact, more of a hood than a mask, made to cover the whole face tightly, and the throat and ears, with strings behind. He had made it himself, as his first adventure with the shears and needle, sitting up night after night in the library behind a locked door, using up most of the skirt in false tries before he got the thing right. He had burned all remnants of the skirt.

The knife had been a butcher knife. He had found it thrown aside with some old junk in the farm shop, rusty and obviously forgotten and untouched for years. He had retrieved it, and one Sunday when all the people of the place had gone to a "shout-meeting" on the next farm, he had put the knife to the grindstone to bring the wide blade down to the shape of a long narrow dagger, whetted halfway up the blunt back edge. When he got through, it was so keen you could shave with it. Then he had fashioned a crude leather sheath that could be strapped under a shirt-front.

That was his equipment, for he did not count the primed pistol in his pocket. That was only for some great and unforeseen crisis. He did not like to think on what such a crisis might be, for what he dreaded most was to shed "innocent blood." He had almost determined to die, if his mission were fulfilled, before he would do that. But did he have the right to die? He asked himself that, remembering how Rachel had accused him of vanity and selfishness in wanting to take the risk of a duel. He did not think the question through. It was too painful. He would let the moment decide, if it came, and meanwhile would pray that it would never come.

Now he put all of his equipment under the mattress of the bed and smoothed the covers. Then he unlatched his door to give an air of innocence in case someone should come to him from below, and sat to read by the candle. We do not know what book he had brought with him.

At last, he heard a stir below, heard steps on the stairs and knew from the tread that it must be Jessup himself and his wife. He waited a little longer for the house to settle down. Then he took his own long black cloak and his own hat, leaving his equipment, and went as silently as possible down the stairs and let himself out the front door. He had noticed when he came in that the latch was a simple bar that could be left drawn.

Now was the delicate moment of his design, the moment for which he had not been able to make proper provision. He knew, or thought he knew, in what house Colonel Fort was staying, for he had read in the *People's Hope,* an Anti-Relief paper of Frankfort, that Fort was to be with his wife's brother, John Saunders, a lawyer of the town, and he remembered from previous visits to Frankfort the situation of the house. It was, he was glad to think, a one-story house. But he did not know in what room the intended victim would lie. That information might be valuable. So now he was out to make a "scout."

"I passed casually along the streets toward the square and the black ruins of the recently burned capitol, knowing that the house of Saunders faced toward it. It was not late, but most houses were dark now, for it was Sunday night, and men retired early to rise for labor, or for the excitement the day was sure to bring, for then the Houses opened. But I guessed that Fort would not go to bed early, for I knew from old days that he was not one to early seek slumber, and I knew that tonight he would most like foregather with men of his party to perfect last plans for the morrow.

"If Fort came home alone, and late, I would waylay him near the house, barring the watch or a straggler to prevent, and that had been the happiest opportunity. I would play for that as my first choice, and the simplest, but it could not be depended upon, so I must have some way to summon him forth, and alone. For that I had to know in what room he would lie. I had struck upon the following expedient.

"The Saunders' house, as I have written, faces upon the square, and is built almost upon the street, with but a patch of yard before it, in which some big bushes of lilac stand behind a fence of low pickets. On the north side is a wide garden, fenced in, and beyond that a vacant lot, but on the south side is an alley, on which gives the side entrance of the house, set back but little from the alley and again screened by lilac bushes. Further down the alley there is a high board fence, not easily to be scaled, and in that enclosure another yard and the quarters of the servants. Across the alley stands the residence of the Allenby family, a most respectable connection.

"On an earlier visit to Frankfort I had seen an old Negro man playing a banjo on the street, and he played and sang so well and with the grace and comicality of his race that I had asked who he might be. I had learned that he was an old slave of the Allenby family, but with Mr. Allenby's indulgence was past all work and was allowed to play on the streets or in houses and inns for entertainment when he chose, though he had no need to earn money, for Mr. Allenby gave him a tight little house in the rear and fed and clothed him, and pampered him with much affection for old time's sake. My informant added, however, that Mr. Allenby had abated his kindness had he known that Uncle Samson owned less innocent sources of income than music and ready jest, that he loved money worse than a Scotchman, and would do anything to get it and swagger as rich among the other colored. (I have since learned that Uncle Samson did what he did for more worthy reason, to buy the freedom of a nephew, his only kin not dead or sold away, but he has not yet succeeded, by all report.)

"What would have offended Mr. Allenby, according to my informant, was that Uncle Samson would play pander for the white men of loose practices who relished some choice wench of color, and on occasion and for a pretty price would let his little house be used, for it was private and well back from the establishment and the other quarters, giving on the alley which went through to another street. Both wench and man could get at it with little risk of being apprehended by the watch.

"Now I had thought to play the part of a dissoluteness not my custom and use Uncle Samson. I knew that I could depend upon his discretion, for he had as much to lose as anyone if he should divulge his secrets. So I took a turn about the town, knowing that he sometimes hung about the doors of inns to play on the street and get change from guests whose potations had loosened pocket as well as tongue. I headed first for the Weisiger House, as the most likely location for Uncle Samson, and on the way passed what I now know to be the office of Sugg Lancaster. I mention this event, because it will show in one detail how the web of perjury has been woven, and on what little fact, to snare me.

"Before coming to the office I almost overtook two Negro girls walking hand in hand, but before I came up with them two men stepped forth from the shadow of a building and spoke to the girls, and one of the men made to seize a girl. But the girls jerked back and giggled and ran the way they had come. I passed the men and realized that they were drunk. Then three other men stepped forth from the shadow, and I knew them to be the patrol lying in wait for the girls, who had no reason to be out at the hour. One of the men was saying to the others that they would never catch them wenches now, that they'd be home in bed. Then two of the watch fell to talking with the drunkards and teased and fooled them for not getting any dark meat on that try, as I could hear as I passed for their loud voices, but the third patrol stood apart and looked at me as I passed. I did not worry about that, for I was but a respectable man and I knew that he could not see my face for my hat and the collar of my cloak.

"I passed on to the Weisiger House, where I did not find Uncle Samson, and by another popular place, and thence to the Mansion House, which I had held to the last because I knew it to be the haunt of Anti-Relief where complots were hatched and injustice bred. I approached the place cautiously so as to attract no attention, but maintained the manner of a citizen on a stroll. As I came even with the windows, I glanced within and saw toward the back of the big room a group of men sitting at a table, in close conversation around the bottle. I knew one immediately to be the Duke—Duke Wickliffe, whom I had seen when he spoke long before in the House—for he was facing my way. The others who faced me I did not know, but all at once one whose back was to me and who had been leaning forward lifted his head to speak in reply, apparently to the Duke, and by that movement and the lift of a hand to press down the unruly hair I recognized him to be Fort.

"It would have been easy, and in a flash it came to me that mine enemy had been delivered into my hand. I could fire through the window, and could not miss, for I am a confident marksman from my boyhood days in the forest, and could make good my escape in the deserted street and be abed before the tumult rose. I had already reached my hand under my cloak to the pocket where my pistol rode before I remembered and put aside that temptation. For if I set lead in him from the dark, he would die and never know, except by the voice of conscience, what will had winged that little stinger. No, if he died thus in ignorance, Justice would not sup her fill. I was determined, at whatever risk, to do my full obeisance to that unsmiling

230

goddess and glut her to sleep. Therefore with his last pang Fort must see my face.

"But the moment seemed not without significance for me, as I saw Fort sitting at ease with the great to whom he had betrayed his cause, and the sight was to me like the last gentle, loving whet a man gives a knife edge before he passes his finger along its edge to know that it should take no more.

"So I passed on and returned to the Saunders and Allenby establishments, but not to the street on which they faced. Instead, I came up the alley between them from the other end until I reached what I took to be the house of Uncle Samson. A kind of curtain was drawn at the window, or something heavy to kill light, but under one edge a little crept forth. I prayed that he was alone within, and tapped the door, and stepped back so that no light would fall directly upon me when it opened.

"When it opened, and the grizzled head popped out like an old squirrel from a hole when you tap on the tree trunk, I said nothing, but simply held a hand out with a silver dollar in the palm so that the ray of light fell on it. His eyes fixed upon the coin, and I knew he had taken the bait. He stepped immediately forth, and drew the door shut behind him.

" 'Who you?' he asked in a whisper.

" 'Never you mind, Uncle,' I replied in a disguised voice. 'But I am from Versailles, and the hostler at Weisiger's tells me you don't mind making a dollar.' Then, as he hesitated, I added to establish my credentials: 'He told me how to find your cabin. How else would I know?'

" 'What you want?' he asked dubiously.

" 'Oh, I don't want you to get me a slut,' I said to let him know I knew all. 'I have one picked and she'll take me in. If you'll just give me the lay of the land.'

" 'Who that?'

" 'One of Mr. Saunders' wenches,' I said, 'but I have to get in easy to the quarters. You know how he is about his gals cutting up. Just tell me how the folks sleep in the big house.'

" 'Mr. Saunders and his wife, they lay on the other side, and the boy, and . . .'

" 'Haven't they got some folks staying with them?'

" 'Yes, sir, that big Cunnel Fowt and his wife, she's Mr. Saunders' sister, one of his two sisters, the udder one . . .'

" 'Yes, yes,' I said impatiently, cutting off the Saunders connection root and branch, for if an old darkie starts to display his information it will go all the way to Omega. 'But where do Colonel Fort and his wife sleep?'

231

" 'They ain't laying tergither,' he said. 'She is porely, or they don't git along, or sumthin, and they ain't bin tergither, I hear tell from the other niggers, in a . . .'

" 'Where are they? On this side?'

" 'She bed down in that room off the little gallery down this side, and she sleep light, they say, and when you go down that side . . .'

" 'Where does Colonel Fort lie?' I asked, and held 'my breath for the answer.

" 'Aw, he—he lay in the room on the back side that little ell what butts off this side tow'd the alley. You got to go right by the winder, twixt it and them bushes . . .'

" 'Who is in the front room of the ell?'

" 'Ain't nobody,' he said, and my heart leaped with satisfaction. 'Dat the study-room Mr. Saunders use when he fool with his books and stuff. But Cunnel Fowt, now he use it and . . .'

" 'You heard him come home yet?'

" 'Naw, sir, I ain't heard nobody.'

"I gave him the dollar, and said good night. I knew that he would never betray me, though they put him to the rack, for if my deed were done and Samson suspected me that would be all the more reason for him to hold his tongue as my unwitting accomplice, for the Negro has a superstitious dread to mix in the business of the white folks."

(Thus Jeremiah, in his narrative, betrays old Uncle Samson. But apparently he had not in the end intended to do so, for along the edge of one of the pages dealing with Samson there is a scribbled note in the margin, an afterthought: "Cancel this? Do I have right to inform against the old darkie who acted in innocence and but to get money to enfranchise his nephew?")

After he left Uncle Samson, he realized that he had made a mistake. He should have brought out with him his equipment when he left the Jessup house, and hidden it in some secret spot, for that would have spared him the risk of a return trip to the house and would have given him more time to lie in wait for Fort should Fort return alone. But there was no help for it now. He made his way as quickly as possible to Jessup's, stealthily ascended the stairs, and came back out with the necessary rig.

He made his way west from the Jessup house to the bank of the river where it flows north again after making the western of its two bends. It was the deserted and shaded area to which he had lured Fort on his previous meeting with him at Frankfort. Now he divested himself of his cloak, hat and boots. He put on the wool hat he had found on the stake and the old coachman's coat, which he laced together in front, up to the neck to hide the white of his shirt, with a piece of string through the buttonholes and holes he now made with his knife. Then he put on the three pairs of heavy yarn socks to make a kind of soft boots in which he could run without sound and which would leave no traces in soft ground. He blacked the outside socks with dirt so that the light color would not be noticeable. With the knife in his shirt and the silk mask in the pocket of the coat, he was now ready.

He came up the alley again from the side away from the square, hugging the board fence for its shadow when he reached the edge of the Saunders property. There was no moon, but despite patches of cloud, some starlight. When he came even with the side entrance of the house, the street and square, as far as he could tell, were deserted. So he slipped inside the Saunders yard by the alley gate, and squatted in the lilac thicket on the west side of the gate. He reached inside his coat, through an opening in the lacing that he had left on purpose, to be sure that the knife was free to his hand. Then he removed the hat, adjusted the silk mask, tied his green silk handkerchief about his head and brow to help hold the mask, and put the hat back on. The hat was, fortunately, a little large for him, and the extra cloth now made it sit firm.

It was now nearly midnight, and he had some fear that in his absence Colonel Fort had returned and was now warm in bed. But he could take no chance on throwing away the simpler course in case Fort should yet come, and come alone. So he waited for what he took to be upwards of an hour. Once he heard steps on the street, and took the knife out ready, but the steps passed on. Once he heard a dog bark across the square, and had the sudden fear that one might prowl down the alley and smell him out, and with a sick heart he thought how all might come to nought by some cursed stray cur. He tried to devise some desperate expedient for such a case, but to no avail.

But even as he turned that problem in his mind, he heard steps. Then he realized that the steps were of two persons. They stopped at the head of the alley, and he made out low voices. He was sure that he recognized Fort's voice. The moment had come, he thought, and was perfectly calm. The discussion would end, the men would say good night there at the head of the alley, the stranger with Fort would go on his way, and Fort would come to the door, stop, and reach for his key. That would be the moment.

It did not happen so. The steps moved down the alley together, and stopped at the gate. The men were in some close argument on a point of law and the State Constitution. Finally Fort's voice said, very quietly and courteously, "We can settle nothing now, Fairfax, for we have not the text of the Bailey decision. I will hunt it up

233

tonight among John's books and bring word tomorrow early. Or would you care to step in with me now? You would disturb no one. All will be long asleep."

The man said that tomorrow morning would do, if they had a few moments in private before the opening, but he lingered as Fort got out his keys. Then the man said good night, but continued to stand, even after Fort had come to the doorstep. Jeremiah cursed him for a blackguard and saw the perfect opportunity pass.

There was another low exchange of good nights, Fort entered the house, and the man turned back to the street, whistling softly through his teeth.

After a moment a faint light showed in the study window below the curtain. Crouching, Jeremiah moved across the patch of brick walk between the door step and the gate, and lifted his head to peer in the study window. Then he heard from within the faintest sound of voices.

He saw Fort sitting at a table, with his back to the window, so that Jeremiah could not see his face, a book open before him under the candle. But Fort was not reading. He was speaking to someone beyond Jeremiah's range of vision. Jeremiah shifted his position, and saw, just inside the open door, a tall, thin woman wearing a night-dress and wrapper, holding a candle in her hand. It was Mrs. Fort, Jeremiah decided, waked by her husband's return. Or could it be Mrs. Fort? For the face looked so old and consumed, far older than the wife of Fort had any right to be. It was a drawn, ravaged face, looking thinner and sharper for the gray braids that hung straight down, one on each side, and for the candlelight that struck obliquely across it from below.

So that was Fort's wife, he thought. He had known that she existed, but he had never seen her, she had not been real. But now she was real, and for an instant he felt some shift in the center of his intention (he later describes it "as when the cargo shifts perilously in a ship at sea, from what I have read"), and he strained to make out the words she was speaking but could hear nothing. Then he thought: *She doesn't love him, I can see from her face that she does not.* And thought with a sickening fear: *but if she did, if she did love him, could I . . . ?* And could not finish the notion, even in his mind, and with a leap of release, and sudden certainty, thought: *but she does not.* She could not, not with that face and that dead gaze upon him. No, she came by night to him to stand like a ghost with the reproach of her presence to speak empty words which, by their very empti-ness, were an accusation. Seeing those gray lips move, in the room beyond the glass, he had the idea that they made no sound at all, or a sound too little and dry for human ears to hear, and that Fort,

234

sitting there and leaning forward, could hear them no more than he, and that was their terror.

Then he thought: *Ah, poor ghost, I will revenge you, too.*

At that she turned and went from the room, as though his thought had released her.

Fort continued for a little to sit as before, looking toward the closed door, paying no heed to the book open before him. Then with a slight but heavy shift of the shoulders, he bowed his head and devoted himself to the pages before him.

Jeremiah crept back to his place of concealment in the lilac thicket. He had received the last sign. If the sight of Fort with his cronies in the Mansion House had been the last whet to the blade, the sight in this room had been the caressing movement of the finger down the perfect edge to say that all was well.

He would wait, he decided, until Fort had gone back to his bedroom before summoning him. That would give time, too, for Mrs. Fort to get back to sleep.

He crouched there a long time, in the stillness of the night, feeling his muscles cramp and the chill grow in his bones. But that did not seem to matter. He scarcely troubled to make a slight shift now and then to get relief. He had the fancy that he was growing into the ground, was setting root like the plants of the thicket, was one of them groping deeper and deeper into the cold, damp earth with fingers of root and tentacles like hair. He let his cheek rest against a thick, dry stalk of lilac, but the silk of the mask came between. So he raised the silk to give his cheek that companionship. And he remembered how, on the morning of the great and glittering frost years before, when he had been but a boy, the morning when all the world was covered with brilliant ice in the sun, he had touched the bough of the ice-ridden beech and had felt his being flow out into the shining tree, as though the bough were a conduit, and into the sunlight from every lifted twig, and down the trunk into the secret earth so that he was part of everything. That memory was important to him now, for it seemed to verify him, to say that all his past was one thing, and not rags and patches, and that all had moved to this moment.

So he crouched there and relished the stillness of the night, straining into it until the stillness itself seemed to have voices and he could hear the snore of Jessup in his bed in the foul house across the town, or the tooth of a mouse on the wainscot in the Allenby house behind him, or the respiration of a worm in the earth beneath, or the tiny shift of a toad in its winter sleep under a brick of the walk, or the rustle of Colonel Fort's page being turned in the sealed room, or the beat of Rachel's heart, in a dark room far to the south.

Then the light disappeared from the window of the study, dimming for an instant while the candle was withdrawn, then cut off sharp as though a door had been closed. And Jeremiah thought that Fort would never enter that room again.

He waited a little to give Fort time to begin undressing.

Then he went to the window of the room. He could not see within, for the curtain was tight. But he tapped gently on the glass, then tapped again, waiting. Then he heard the voice, quite distinctly, and realized that the window was a little open to admit air. It said: "Who's there?"

"Grierson," Jeremiah replied, in a feigned voice, "William K. Grierson. I was benighted and late over the river and the town is full and I have no place to lay my head."

"I am coming," the voice said from within, and Jeremiah went to the door to greet him when it should be opened.

(He had used the name Grierson, he explains, because that family was a numerous connection in Bowling Green and the Green River country and many had been intimate with Colonel Fort in the past, in the south, and he had done much legal business for them. But there was no William K. Grierson, and Jeremiah had used that name to justify a voice which Fort might not recognize. Even if Fort did not recognize the voice, however, the name of Grierson would fetch him, because he would think it was some member he had forgotten, or if he did not attend too closely to the voice or the name he might think it William J. Grierson, who did exist and whom Fort, and Jeremiah, had known well.)

The door opened. Fort was carrying no candle. If Fort had had a candle Jeremiah would have struck it from him, with one hand, and have dispatched him with the other, and then have leaned over to announce his name. But Fort had no light, and so Jeremiah could pursue his other course.

As the door opened, he lowered his mask till it hung like a neckcloth, but the handkerchief still bound his brow and the hat was well down.

Fort peered out from beside the half-opened door, without his shirt now, and asked, "What Grierson is this, sir?"

At that Jeremiah shoved the door wide, stepped over the threshold, and seized Fort's right wrist with his own left hand in a grip not yet strong enough to intimidate, and said, in a firm voice, "I am William K. Grierson," and clenched the wrist suddenly hard.

On the instant Jeremiah was aware that Mrs. Fort had stepped into the hall from the room beyond, holding a candle, and was looking at them, and at the same instant, Fort, startled by the new violence

236

of the hand on his wrist, jerked back, exclaiming, "But I know no William K. Grierson, I only know William J.!"

Mrs. Fort, dropping her candle, which was extinguished by the fall, had turned in alarm at the violence of her husband's movement and his exclamation, and had fled up the hall to rouse the house. So the time was short.

"Oh, don't you know me, Colonel, sure enough?" Jeremiah demanded in an aggrieved voice, still not his own, slightly relaxing his grip.

"Your pardon, sir . . ." Fort began courteously.

But Jeremiah interrupted to say softly, "Come to the door, and I will show you my face." For there was a little starlight.

Fort took one step to comply, but then there was a noise within the house, and Jeremiah gave all his force to the grip and jerked Fort forward.

"Unhand me, sir!" Fort commanded in a strong voice, and reached with his own right hand to take the assailant's left wrist.

"Why, Colonel, don't you know me?" Jeremiah asked again softly, wheedlingly, and lifted his free hand to knock off the old wool hat and stand exposed but for the handkerchief binding his brow.

"Ah," Fort exclaimed, and Jeremiah knew from that breathed exclamation that Fort knew him, even before Fort said again, "Ah," and then, "Jerry!"

"Jerry!" Jeremiah cried out, and felt a strong shudder and tingle up the spine like (he says) the shudder of joy, for the knife was lifted, and fell even as he said, "Not Jerry to you, villain, but Beaumont!"

The blade sank deep into Fort's chest above the heart, with shocking ease, like a blade driven into a ripe melon. Fort staggered a little, breathed deep once, and did not even lift his free hand instinctively to defend himself but kept his hold on Jeremiah's left wrist as though to sustain himself a little longer, all the while staring into Jeremiah's face.

Then, as the blade lifted again, Fort breathed deep, with a kind of gasp, and said, "Ah, Jerry—so you had—to come."

"And come again!" Jeremiah exclaimed, and struck again with all his force.

Fort sagged against the facing of the door, and blood flowed from his mouth and down to mingle with that gathering on the half-buttoned undergarment. Jeremiah wrenched his knife free and stepped back just as he saw a light appear down the hall and the startled faces in its gleam.

He did not flee. He squatted again in the bushes, adjusting his mask, for he had to know if Fort would speak.

Mrs. Fort had flung herself by the body, lifting the head and staining her wrapper with the blood, crying out with a shrill voice but no words, while another woman stood behind and a man leaned over with a candle, demanding, "Who was it, Cassius, who was it?"

But Fort could not speak, and Jeremiah says that had Saunders not been a coward, for it was Saunders, he would have rushed out, half-clothed as he was, to pursue and know at whatever risk.

By this time someone had rushed out the front door of the house, making a great racket (it was the fifteen-year-old son of Saunders), calling and crying for help to raise the town, but Jeremiah still lingered, and he later remembered that the sound of the boy's voice calling sounded very hollow and thin in the bigness of the night, but it seemed to have a kind of free joy in it, like the voices of boys calling at their sport far off in a summer night.

People began to come. Two men ran out from the Allenby house and to the front door of the Saunders house, and then came back into the side hall. From beyond others came, and other voices were raised, shouting down the street, with the shouts picked up beyond, and beyond, as when news is shouted from hill to hill or as when the baying of one dog at night provokes answer, and that another, and so on in a chain of sound across a dark county. Three men rushed down the alley from the street, toward the light in the side door, and they passed so near that Jeremiah might almost have reached out to touch them as they passed. The little hall was thronged now, and there was a babel of voices, asking wild questions and uttering wilder opinions, some people even standing on the pavement.

But Jeremiah never felt safer, he says, as though he were hidden in the very ground itself, or were wrapped in invisibility, and he was full of a joyful contempt for them all who only fluttered and babbled foolishness about the candle-flame.

Fort was now dead, and had not spoken. He knew that much. But he lingered for another reason. (Or was there another reason, the real reason, a knowledge that once he left his thicket everything for him would be different from the fullness of this moment?) He told himself that it would be wise to let some see him beyond the rays of light, with the black mask on his face so that they might be misled and confused to think him a Negro and hold any story of Mrs. Fort about what she had seen or heard to be but the vaporings of her distress.

By this time they had picked up the body and were carrying it into the chamber where Fort was accustomed to sleep. So Jeremiah crept through the bushes around to the corner of the house, hoping to find a window that he might look in and perhaps let his face be seen. There was a window, and the curtain was not closed here. So he put his face near the glass and stared at the people that filled the room and milled about the bed. No one turned to the window, and so he played the game children play, to stare at someone hard to make them turn.

He was staring at a man beyond, when suddenly he heard a cry, and saw that Mrs. Fort was pointing at the window, exclaiming that she saw the murderer. So Jeremiah leaped back from the window. But instead of fleeing, he stepped to the corner of the house toward the side door and waited a moment that any coming out might have a fair look at his face. He was still sustained by his joyful contempt, and took no count of a risk.

Men did come to the door and turn toward the corner of the house where he stood. But when they saw him standing there as though waiting, they hesitated and did not come on, and Jeremiah says that in that moment he knew what he had always known, that that was the way of the world, if you stand and face it down without fear men will fall back and only yap like curs afraid to come in and join issue with bull or painter or bear.

They hesitated that moment, looking him full in the face at that short distance, then Jeremiah turned and ran across the back yard, past the quarters and across the side yard and garden, where old rose bushes snatched at his garments. He saw the pickets of the fence before him, and now heard the chase and shouts. He did not stop at the fence, or even vault it, but gathered his force and leaped, and in that soaring motion which seemed to free him from earth, he uttered a shout of "triumph and disdain."

His feet struck on the blind ground beyond, and he staggered for an instant as one of his feet, protected only by the socks, came down on a stone.

The pursuers were almost at the fence now. He turned and waited, and just as they came at it, he snatched his pistol out and fired a shot. He did not fire at them, for he wanted to hurt no one, but over their heads.

They stopped short at the fence, as he had guessed they would do with that warning.

So he ran on unmolested across the vacant lot, to another street, and was safe.

At the grove by the river, he put on his proper clothes, hat, and boots, and bundled the mask and socks in the coachman's coat, weighting the bundle with stones, and threw it into the river. The old wool hat he had dropped, he remembered, by the Saunders door, but that now seemed to him a fortunate occurrence. He buried the knife and sheath in the loose wood-earth by a stump in the thicket. Then he made his way calmly back to the Jessup house, where he found the door unbarred as he had left it, took off his boots, and mounted silently to his chamber. There he latched his door and examined himself for any stains or incriminating marks. He decided that he had best burn the big green silk handkerchief, for if he were apprehended on the morrow and if some sharp eye had detected the mask on his face, the handkerchief itself, being of such a dark color, might be taken to have been used as such. He regretted the need to destroy it, for it was fine and new, but he comforted himself by the thought that it might already be somewhat spoiled by the smoke and soot it had received on the trip hither. So he stirred up the last coals a little and consigned it to them.

He could detect no marks, but when he sat down to remove his socks, which he had worn under the heavy yarn ones, he saw that they were stained through with water and mud, for he must have trod in some mucky place. So he poured some water from the pitcher into the bowl, and washed them and hung them on the back of a chair near the fire to dry by morning. He was prepared to throw the dirty water into the jar for slops, but discovered that it was already full from the waste of some previous tenant. Thinking that that was no worse than you had a right to expect in such a slatternly house, he flung the water into the fireplace, finished his undressing, and got into bed.

The exaltation was suddenly gone. He felt nothing, nothing except a deadly weariness and emptiness. For what had he striven? For what did men strive? All dissolved into his weariness. Then he slept.

Next morning while he was dressing, he heard a commotion downstairs and excited voices, and guessed that news of the night had been brought to the Jessup place. Nevertheless, he made ready to descend to breakfast, thinking that the world was now agog with his deed and this was his first trial of facing it with a smooth brow.

His surmise was right. He had no sooner entered the room below than Jessup, so bursting with importance at being the bearer of great news that he did not even return a greeting, began to "void himself," saying, "A terrible thing, sir,—a terrible thing has happened, and you would never guess!"

Jeremiah agreed, no, he could not imagine, and took his seat at the table and steeled his stomach for the bad fare which Mrs. Jessup was bringing him.

"You'd never guess, sir," Jessup continued, but could not maintain his silly game of suspense and had to spill his news. "Some man came to Saunders' house last night, and stabbed him!"

"Stabbed Saunders? What Saunders? John Saunders, the lawyer?"

"No, no," Jessup burst out, impatiently, "stabbed Fort, Colonel Fort!"

Jeremiah let his fork drop against his plate in astonishment. "Good God!" he exclaimed. "You mean Cassius Fort?"

"None other," Jessup said, and reared back in what Jeremiah describes as the attitude of the tin-horn orator of the country hustings, remembering that Jessup had been a sheriff and had mixed with politicians. Jessup lifted his arm for a gesture. "Cassius Fort, sir!" he said, "none other, and he is dead. Struck down in the flower and the prime, like you say. Oh, 'tis 'bominable, and no man can say nay."

Jeremiah nodded judiciously, and agreed, yes, that it was abominable, and managed to get down another bite of the fat fried meat.

" 'Bominable, indeed, and him a great man. Why, he'd save the country. Why, he was great as old George Washington. Why, he'd put them Reliefers on the run today, he'd . . ."

"Was it some fanatic of Relief—some man who'd lost his property —that fought him?" Jeremiah asked, and was complacent to draw the thread of the question toward the political motive and at the same time subtly demonstrate his ignorance of the event by the notion of a fight.

"Maybe some Reliefer or New Courter," Jessup agreed, "for ain't nothing I'd put past 'em. But it wasn't no fight. No, sir. He killed him on his doorstep—yes, sir, his sacred doorstep and a man's house is his castle, like you say—the coward killed that great man. Oh, he'd a-saved the State. Why, he'd a-saved the country. They wasn't nobody like him, no, sir, and he . . ."

Jessup continued, while Jeremiah thought with sarcasm that it was right and proper that the eulogy of the traitor should be pronounced in this vile house by this bag-of-guts and blackguard braggart and mortgaged pauper who attached himself to Anti-Relief and the rich man's party out of vanity and the hope of some crumb.

But Jessup was saying, "Yes, sir, I knowed him well. Why, he was my kin you might say. Why, Fort married a Saunders, just like me. Why, me and Fort was pickers, I'll tell you. My old lady there," and he nodded toward the fat, gray-faced woman, "she's a Saunders, sister to Mrs. Fort and John Saunders. Why, I'm brother-in-law of Fort, in a manner of speaking . . ." So he began to tell how great the Saunders family was in all its connections.

But Jeremiah was scarcely listening to the foolish boasts. He was wondering, with a sinking heart, how he had ever got into this house, this house of all the houses in Frankfort, where Saunders' blood and Fort's connection inhabited. It came like a dire portent to him. But he knew he was a fool. It was nothing. So he politely excused himself as he rose from the table, saying that he had to go to the Registrar's office to claim some land patents now long since ready.

"I'll walk with you," Jessup said, "for I got to go to Saunders. The family will be expecting me. You know, me so near to the departed and all."

Jeremiah said that he had to go upstairs for some papers, and would not detain Mr. Jessup from such a sad errand. But Jessup waited in the hall, and resumed his discourse before Jeremiah was half down the stairs, and Jeremiah had to suffer his company as far as the square, where Jessup left him to join a group of men standing before the Saunders house.

Jeremiah proceeded to the land office, and asked for his patents. The clerk made a search, but came back saying that he could not find them ready. Jeremiah insisted that they must be ready by this time, for months had elapsed, and gave the date, saying that a man named Marlowe had filed the plats, certificates and warrants for him and that perhaps the difference in name had created some confusion in the records. But it was no use. Though Jeremiah waited for over an hour and insisted on another search, no record appeared.

Jeremiah was irritated but not unduly alarmed. He was caught here in Frankfort without a clear excuse for business, but Marlowe could, if necessary, give evidence that the claims had been filed and that Jeremiah had tried now to hire him to go to Frankfort to pick up the patents and had himself gone but unwillingly. So Jeremiah returned to the Jessup house, to prepare for his departure.

He had already paid Mrs. Jessup and thanked her and commented on his good bed, and had gone to his room to make ready, when he heard steps on the stairs and a knock on his door. It was Jessup.

Jessup said that he had hurried back from the sad, sad business at his kinsman's to be sure to say good-bye to his guest. Yes, sir, he always liked to treat his guests like friends, and have them come back just to have a noggin and pass the time with him. And he put out his hairy hand, saying, "I'm sure glad to make your acquaintance, Mr. ——" He hesitated, and repeated, "Mr. ——" Then he grinned, and said, "Now ain't that just like me, forgetting your name. But you know, all this sad affair, it just drove it out of my mind, Mr. ——"

Jeremiah took the hand. "My name is Beaumont," he said.

"Why, sure," Jessup said, wringing Jeremiah's hand and working his slack fingers over it, "sure, Beaumont, I recollect now. And where do you make your residence, like you say, Mr. Beaumont? Oh, I ain't prying, but I always like to keep track of my friends."

"I live down near Lumton in Saul County," Jeremiah said, and detached his hand.

He turned to finish packing his saddlebags. Jessup stood over him, watching, then said, "I hope you got your business done."

"Yes," Jeremiah said, not looking up, putting in the last articles.

Then he straightened, and put out his hand to Jessup, saying he had to go and had enjoyed his stay.

Jessup went with him to the stables, and stood paring his nails with his great knife while the Negro boy saddled the horse. "Riding far today?" he asked, when the job was done.

"I don't know," Jeremiah replied. "I am somewhat tired from the trip up."

They shook hands again, and Jeremiah took his leave.

As he rode out of Frankfort, he meditated on Jessup. Had Jessup returned out of suspicion? Or was all the elaborate falsity of Jessup's farewell just the "natural froth thrown up from his great falsity, like the bubbles that glitter on a puddle of horsestale"? It did not matter greatly, he decided, for he had always envisaged, and with confidence, the possibility of an investigation. If Jessup was suspicious, it could be at this moment only the general suspicion of any stranger. A dozen men in town must now be looking askance at strange faces.

He had taken the west road, by way of Bloomfield and Bardstown now, for that would take him more quickly home, and it was the natural route and the one least like to excite suspicion in retrospect. It was true that on this road he ran more risk of being overtaken by possible pursuers, but he would push on hard. He longed to be home, at least before called to account. He longed to see Rachel's face when she should, at last, know him for what he was.

But he would have to wait four days for that, or nearly. He could make no better time without harming his mount.

Meanwhile, for four days, he had to play his part, and he knew the difficulty. Coming from Frankfort, he bore the burden of the great news, and knew that it would be unnatural for him not to pass it along the way, for that was the custom. But he knew also that if he were ever accused, few men would have the firmness of mind to repeat without coloring or error exactly what his manner and words had been. Therefore he resolved to give his news only to a group where one man could be a check against another or to persons whom he held to be of integrity and strong mind.

Once during the day, he had the right chance to tell the news, to a certain Mr. Pembroke, whom he knew, and two strangers, whom he encountered at a branch where they were watering their horses. He rode down into the branch, and while he let his own horse water, told the story. It was brief, for he said he had had to leave before any particulars were known. Colonel Fort had been assassinated at the "front door" of the Saunders house, by some unknown assailant. He had decided that the fewer details he gave the better, for he had fear of making some slip. But he had cunningly decided to plant the idea

243

of the "front door" in all his conversation, in the "hope that that trifling seed would grow and shelter" him with its evidence of his "ignorance, and therefore innocence."

At Bardstown, where he spent the night at the inn, he gave the news to several gentlemen in the bar. Twice on the second day, he gave the news under promising circumstances, and to the family, named Holden, with whom he stopped the night. But the third day he approached the spot which he had dreaded all the way as the "Scylla" of his passage.

Scylla was the establishment of Jackson Smart, a rich, burly, full-blooded old man, given to liquor and notoriously gregarious, bullying, humorous, sly and rancorous, who had built his house smack on the road that he might sit on his porch with the bottle and pitcher by his chair and hail in poor travelers to his sometimes inconvenient hospitality. He never took no for an answer to his invitation, and report had it that once when a stranger had ridden past with a brief but polite refusal, old Smart had emptied a load of fowling shot into the rump of the withdrawing mount. The horse had leaped at the pain and had thrown the rider, breaking his arm and collar bone, and Smart had yelled, "Niggers, get that bastard in here 'fore he crawls off in the brush!" So the servants had fetched in the victim and stripped him and put him to bed in one of Smart's nightshirts big as a wagon sheet, and a doctor had been called to treat his hurt, and the poor fellow had been held prisoner for three weeks, gorged on ham, drunk on whisky, and stunned by conversation.

Smart was a great friend of Cassius Fort, and a fanatic supporter of Anti-Relief. And besides, Jeremiah could not know what motley outfit he would find assembled on the porch of the Smart house. He had even considered loitering that third day so as to pass in the dark, but his urge to get home and the fear that he might be pursued by riders from Frankfort overcame his prudence. He also had the faint hope that the weather might be bad enough to drive old Smart indoors (where he had to keep his watch from a window), but by afternoon it was bright and unseasonably warm and long before he came abreast of the porch he saw that it "accommodated a congress as numerous as a flight of wild pigeons settling in a beech wood."

The best he could do was to take the other side of the road, look straight ahead, and trust to pass unobserved if the tide of whisky and conversation was full enough on the porch. But Smart hailed him, "Hi-yah, Beaumont, get down and take a pull on Black Betty!"

He was trapped, and he got ready to tell his tale as pay for his drink and get away as soon as possible.

He was not more than half up the steps when Smart yelled out in a voice loud enough "to call hogs from t'other side of the mountain, for Mr. Smart's lungs were no respecters of short distances," and asked where Jeremiah had been, and where he was going, and what his errand was. Jeremiah had expected this, for he well knew that his host was as "hot for gossip and tittle-tattle as any widow-woman past the change of life." He gave his answers straight, he had been to Frankfort to claim some land patents, and he was bound home as quickly as might be, for his wife was not too well.

Even as Jeremiah was shaking his hand, and nodding to the other guests (a couple of waggoners, a well-dressed gentleman, two or three starvation farmers, a clabber-headed youth gone snickering drunk, a hunter, and some odd riff-raff), Smart was pumping him about his land business, had he got the patents, where the land lay, and so on. But Jeremiah cut him off, by saying, "A most dire and distressing deed has been committed in Frankfort."

"Hanh?" Smart demanded in irritation, for he did not like to be interrupted.

"A most dire and distressing event," Jeremiah repeated. (We can notice in the many instances in his narrative where he records his own description of the event that he seems to take relish in using terms of horror and condemnation—"dire," "distressing," "heinous," "reprehensible," "damnable"—as though he would cloak himself in the language of common report. Or did his motive lie deeper? Did that language cleanse his hands for the moment, and restore him to the society of men? Or when his own tongue condemned his act, did he relish the irony because at that moment he felt more free and secret in his inner self set off from the world?)

"What, what?" Mr. Smart demanded.

"Colonel Fort is killed. He was struck down as he entered the front door of the house of John Saunders, at night."

There was the babble of questions, and Smart's voice booming over all the rest "like a cannon over the rattle of musketry." But Jeremiah could tell them no details, he said, and stood there in the confusion calmly drinking from a bottle which someone had handed him.

"My God," Mr. Smart was booming, "they've killed our man. Our best man. Those damned Reliefers have killed our man."

"I abhor the crime," Jeremiah said, "and I respect Colonel Fort's genius, but I cannot admit that he was *our* man. For you know, Mr. Smart," and he smiled to take any sting from his words, "I am a damned Reliefer, too."

"So you are, so you are!" Mr. Smart boomed, and seemed to set his sights on Jeremiah.

"And so, too," Jeremiah said, enjoying, he admits, the boldness of the moment, "are a number of these gentlemen, I'll wager." And he surveyed the company. "If they will speak out."

245

"I ain't no damned Reliefer," the drunk boy shouted, and jumped up and threw out his chest and waved his arms threateningly to all the world, ignoring, Jeremiah points out, the moral of his patches and broken shoes.

"Let any damned Reliefer get off my porch!" Mr. Smart yelled out. "Black-hearted murderers to a man! Let them get off!"

"Mr. Smart," Jeremiah said, standing before him, smiling politely, "we have come at your invitation, all of us, to take a drink out of our respect for you, whatever our politics or yours. It so happens that I must go on my way to my home and my wife, but I would go as your guest and your friend." So he put out his hand, and watched Mr. Smart heave and puff, and then grudgingly take the hand.

"I thank you for your famous hospitality," Jeremiah said, and bowed.

Mr. Smart grunted something, and Jeremiah bowed to the company and wished them all good day, and went down to his horse and rode away. He turned once, and waved back, but even as he did so his lips curled to think how in that group of all cuts and classes not one man had had the courage to declare his principles and all had sat sodden and had sold honor for a few swigs of free whisky as though they were swine come to Smart's holler and swill. That was the way.

But on reflection he decided that things had fallen out well for his design. Had he been guilty, he would never have declared himself so boldly, and by saving his self-respect he had also saved his neck. For shame might later sting those men to speak the truth of his conduct.

Later on the fourth day he approached his house. When he was well up the lane, and in full sight of it, he reached into his saddlebags and drew out the red sash. He tied it to the butt of the little switch he carried, tying it so that the two ends flowed free. Then he grasped the switch in the middle, butt uppermost, and set spurs to his tired mount.

Near the stone gate, he raised the switch on high, and the ends of the sash streamed out on the air, and rising in his stirrups he uttered a great shout and in that moment recaptured the feeling he had had when he leaped the fence of the Saunders garden in the dark with the "rabble-pack" of pursuers behind him.

Then he saw the face of Rachel at an upstairs window, quickly withdrawn.

At the steps, he swung from the saddle, and started to the porch. He heard a call from one side and glanced back to see Captain Marlowe coming up from the stables, waving at him. But he did not wait.

Rachel was almost at the foot of the stairs, her eyes wide in the face which had gone white. He stood for an instant, while she approached him, staring into his face.

He flung the little banner of the sash tied to the switch at her feet. "It is done," he said, and took her in his arms with a strong embrace and kissed her on the brow.

She was passive in his arms for a second, then her shoulders began to shake, and he knew she was weeping. "The strain has been great," he said, comforting her. "I know it has been great. But all is over now. It is done."

She sagged in his arms, and he led her to the little couch beneath the bend of the stairs. "Lift up your face," he said, softly. When she did not obey, he took her chin in one hand and lifted it. With his free hand he wiped her cheeks with a handkerchief, murmuring, "Do not weep now, do not weep. It is all over now. It is done, but do not be afraid. Though the avengers of blood may be after me, they will have nothing."

At that, she ceased her sobs, and looked sharply into his face.

"That is good," he said, caressing her shoulder, thinking the news had stiffened her resolve. "I know you are my noble wife."

But she began to shake again, not with suppressed sobs but as though with a strong chill. So he commanded her to stop, saying that all was arranged, to have no fear, to trust him.

Then he was aware that Mrs. Marlowe had entered the hall from the back, and that the Captain was just behind her.

He turned to Mrs. Marlowe. "Help me," he asked, "she is not well, she is not strong yet. Will you help her to bed?"

Mrs. Marlowe came to Rachel, helped her to rise, putting an arm around her shoulder and clucking and murmuring in comfort. She led her up the stairs.

Jeremiah found himself facing Captain Marlowe, and his first thought was to ask about the plats and certificates and reassure himself that Marlowe had filed them in Frankfort. But he decided to wait, for he might offend Marlowe if he came directly to the question.

"How-de-do," Marlowe was saying, "how-de-do and welcome home. Everything is fine, for I saw to it. You can trust the Captain to drive a nail to the head or set the bullet in the pip. Yes, sir."

"Thank you," Jeremiah said, but he could scarcely find breath for that. All at once he was deadly tired.

Marlowe stepped across and leaned to retrieve the switch and sash. He examined it curiously, then lifted it, butt uppermost, and waved it lightly in the air, imitating the motion Jeremiah had made, scrutinizing its motion with the innocent, blank fascination of a child.

"You know," he said, "you shore come riding with a fancy switch."

VII

THE NIGHT OF HIS RETURN FROM FRANK-
fort, Jeremiah fell asleep as soon as he had finished his supper. But
he did take time to load an old musket with bayonet attached and a
rifle which had both belonged to Timothy Jordan, and his own pistol.
He had no intention to fight officers who might come after him, but
he had considered that Saunders, a man of violent disposition, might
make the matter a blood feud and pursue with some of his partisans.
In that case, Jeremiah had determined not to surrender, for to do so
might be, he thought, never to reach Frankfort but to be killed on the
way under some pretext. Nor would he even permit that party to
enter his grounds with impunity. He knew that such a course, however, would be a kind of admission of guilt.

What would he do then? Stand trial? Confess and justify himself
before men? Were he alone in the world he might do so. And he
thought, in his melancholy tiredness, how easy all would then have
been, how had he been alone all would have been different, and he
would never have killed Fort by stealth. But to stand trial or confess,
with the blood of Saunders compounding that of Fort on his hands,
would be to defeat the very reason for which he had committed the
act by stealth. No, if Saunders and his partisans came, he would have
to flee, out of the country, to the West, and hope to draw Rachel to

him later when he had settled in some wild part and all had been forgotten.

The vision then came to him, in the moment before he fell into deep sleep, of some place in the West, a silent, wooded valley where the great trees let only a green light down like the light under water when you dive deep and where everything is still.

He had the impulse to rise, now, and get a horse and start west and flee and leave all behind. But he was too tired. He was already asleep.

He was sleeping, partly dressed, on the couch in the library, with the weapons near at hand. He did not want to be trapped upstairs should Saunders and his men come during the night. But there was no alarm during the night.

He rose early, and started to go up to the room where Rachel lay, but he met Josie on the stairs. She told him that Miss Rachel was still asleep, and so he came back down, concealed the loaded weapons in a closet in the side hall, and had his breakfast. He would wait for Rachel to come down.

He took his own rifle, and went out in the yard (it was a fine morning), and made a pretense of adjusting the gear already loaded in the wagon on the drive. The rifle he laid in the wagon bed, where it might be ready to hand and not easily seen. Here he could keep a watch on the lane leading up to the yard.

About nine o'clock he saw the horsemen coming up the lane, four of them. He pretended not to see, and busied himself about the wagon, and continued to do so even after they had passed the stone gateposts and entered the yard. But he had assured himself that none of them was John Saunders (whose face he had memorized well while he lay in the lilac bushes and looked at the man with the candle leaning over the body of Fort). One of the men seemed vaguely familiar, but he could not place him.

One of the men called out the halloo common to the country, and Jeremiah called back a hospitable greeting, but waited by the wagon. They came up, and sat their horses, somewhat uneasily, looking down at him.

"Get down, gentlemen, and come in," he invited. "Have you had breakfast?"

They said they had breakfasted, and thanked him, then fell back into their embarrassment, exchanging glances covertly with each other.

Then one cleared his throat, the senior of the group and the one who looked most like a gentleman, and asked was this Mr. Beaumont.

Jeremiah acknowledged himself, and asked what he could do to be of service.

249

"If you are the Mr. Beaumont in Frankfort," the man said, "then you know of the murder."

"Yes," Jeremiah said, "if you mean the murder of Colonel Fort. I learned of it the morning I left. Last Monday."

"What made you up and leave so quick?" one of the men asked, the one whose face seemed familiar. Then with a show of guileless cunning: "Looks like a man would want to stay and see the Houses open and get all the news."

"Well," Jeremiah said, "I've sort of lost my interest in politics round here. After"—he hesitated and laughed a little ruefully—"I ran for office and folks didn't seem to want me. Besides, I had to get home on my business." He turned and nodded toward the wagon.

"What was the business?" the older man asked civilly.

"Oh, I was dickering in land," Jeremiah explained, "a time back, and I still have some hopes. I was planning on setting out west to make my fortune." He laughed again.

"When are you going?"

"Oh, I was planning to leave a time back. I had sort of set the third, but some business came up. So now I'm getting off as soon as I can get set."

The men again fell into embarrassment, looking from one to another. Then the familiar face began, "Well, now, Mr. Beaumont, I don't know as I . . ."

But the older man cut in. "Mr. Beaumont, we'll come straight to the point, and I hope you won't get offended. There is some suspicion of you in Frankfort, you being a stranger there that night and all, and we . . ."

"One moment," Jeremiah said. "Do you wish to tell me that you have come for me?"

"Yes, sir-ree-bobbin," the familiar face said, and the fellow made himself big in the saddle, "and we're aiming . . ."

"Stop," Jeremiah commanded. "I do not know who you are, or on what authority you come, but . . ."

The man patted his pocket. "I got heaps of authority right here," he said, and leered.

"I don't care what you have in your pocket, unless it is a warrant for my arrest. Which I gravely doubt, if there is any decency and justice in Frankfort. But unless you have a warrant, I will not submit to you as a prisoner. I am unarmed, but you will have to shoot me down in cold blood in my own yard. Do you understand?"

The man took out his pistol.

"Put that thing up," Jeremiah said. "You might hurt yourself."

"By God, I'll show you, you can't git uppity with me, I'll show . . ."

Jeremiah turned his back square on the pistol, and addressed the older man. "I don't know who this fellow is," he said, "but if . . ."

"Aw, he's Mr. Bumps, Mr. Carlos Bumps," one of the other men volunteered, a young peeled-faced fellow, not more than boy, and his voice had a tinge of reverence, as he added, "why, Mr. Bumps is on the patrol, up in Frankfort."

Then Jeremiah remembered in a flash why that fleshy raw face was familiar. The man was the third member of the patrol on the street in Frankfort, the one who had stared at him passing while the others jollied the drunks about missing their dark meat. But Jeremiah continued to address the older man. "It does not matter that Mr. Bumps —if he rejoices in such a name—can bully niggers and drunkards in Frankfort. He should learn better manners when he comes to Saul County and enters a man's yard or . . ."

"Ain't no man gettin funny about my name, by God!" the man behind Jeremiah exclaimed.

"Put up your pistol, Bumps," the older man said quietly. Then to Jeremiah: "We have no thought of making you a prisoner, Mr. Beaumont. We come in friendship and to . . ."

"A prisoner?" And at that word, spoken in Rachel's voice, Jeremiah turned to see her standing at the head of the steps, looking very pale but quite calm. His heart went full of a great pride in her, she was so clear and possessed.

She gazed from surprised face to face of the men below, then asked Jeremiah: "Who are these men? If they come in friendship, why don't you ask them in to breakfast?"

"They come from Frankfort," Jeremiah explained. "You remember I told you last night that Colonel Fort had been killed. Well, they come to tell me I am suspected and . . ."

"Suspected?" she echoed incredulously. She came down the steps and stood by her husband's side, laying a hand on his arm. "Jerry," she said (And he thought, *how long has it been since she called me Jerry, and her voice like that?*). "Jerry," she said, "why don't you ride to Frankfort with these gentlemen and clear everything up?"

"Lady," the older man said, "that's all we . . ."

"Listen," Jeremiah interrupted. "I have never said that I would not go to Frankfort. I am happy to go, and be sure that my name is not bandied about by every loose tongue. But I will not go as a prisoner. Is that clear?"

"That's all we come for," the older man said.

"Good," Jeremiah agreed. "And now if you will kindly tell me your names, I shall present you to my wife."

The older man's name was Crawford, the boy's was Showforth, the other man's was Jarvis. Jeremiah presented the three quite formally, passing over Bumps, and Rachel acknowledged them. Then Jeremiah feigned to discover Bumps. "Oh," he said to her, nodding at Bumps, "this man calls himself Bumps."

The boy Showforth snickered at that, and Bumps sat sullen and unhappy under the eyes of the other men, and Jeremiah felt that he had scored a point, for, as he records, "You can always turn the members of a group, however solid, against one of their own if you discover his weakness or comicality to them, for such is vanity that they will repudiate him to join you." *Dividere et,* Jeremiah writes and takes pleasure in his victory at the first little skirmish.

"Won't you come in for some refreshment?" Rachel urged. "I'll call a boy to take care of your horses." Then she let her gaze fall on Bumps. "Or," she said, as at a sudden inspiration, "perhaps Mr. Bumps would be good enough to do that."

The boy snickered again, and the men, even the older man, suppressed grins, so that Jeremiah wasted an instant of pity on poor, hulking Bumps, whose fleshy face had gone crimson. "Lady," he blundered sullenly, "listen, lady, I ain't no nigger."

"Why, Mr. Bumps," she said, with a voice full of contrition and surprise, "whoever thought you were? I knew you were white immediately I laid eyes on you."

The boy whinnied with laughter, like a horse on a frosty morning, and rocked in his saddle and slapped his thigh.

The others decorously ignored him. The older man thanked Mrs. Beaumont for her kind invitation, and said that they had to ride.

Rachel turned to Jeremiah. "That's right," she said to him. "The sooner you go and settle everything the better. I'll go and pack your saddlebags." She went lightly up the steps and into the house.

In the constrained silence, the older man, Crawford, passed some remarks on the fine weather, even if it was unseasonable, then gave up conversation. Then, just before Rachel came back, he asked if Jeremiah had a dirk.

Hearing Rachel's step, Jeremiah turned and said: "These gentlemen want to know if I have a dirk. Do you mind getting that dirk of your father's out of the secretary? I've been using it to cut paper."

So she dropped the saddlebags, and Jeremiah's hat and cloak, went again into the house, and shortly returned with the dirk. She gave it to Crawford. He thanked her, and put it in his pocket.

At that moment a colored boy led a saddled horse around the corner of the house to the drive. Rachel had sent for it, while in the house.

Jeremiah stepped aside with Rachel, and took her tenderly in his arms for the good-bye. He had expected, after her conduct of the moments just past, to find her melting in his embrace and to taste the full warmth of her kiss and to have the reward he had missed the evening before upon his return. But she was rigid to his touch, and the kiss was cold. "I love you, I love you," he whispered, "for you are my true wife." But his heart was sick in his breast.

He stepped back, and said aloud that he would be back in a few days, that she should take care of her health.

Then he mounted, and as he rode toward the gate beside Crawford, he explained that his wife had not been well, that not long before a child had come dead before its time. Crawford offered the appropriate sympathy.

A little way down the lane, Captain Marlowe stood beside some dry elder bushes, whittling a stick. He called out a greeting, and stepped into the road, as though getting ready for conversation. But Jeremiah did not return the greeting until almost abreast, and then, without reining in, did so in a way to discourage sociability. Marlowe fell back by the bushes, blank in the face.

They had passed a turn in the lane, when Bumps drew up even with Crawford, and said, "Ain't you fergittin somethin? Why don't you test it now?"

"It can wait," Crawford said.

"Look here," Bumps said petulantly, "I want to know, and I got as much right as you. I got as big a share as you. And I ought to have more by rights. It was me seen him that night. It was me remembered seeing him and . . ."

"All right," Crawford said, and drew rein.

Bumps and Jarvis dismounted, and handed their bridles to the boy Showforth. "Give it here," Bumps ordered Crawford, and Crawford fished a paper from his pocket, smoothed it out and handed it to Bumps, who now stood by Jeremiah's near stirrup.

"Lemme see yore foot," Bumps said to Jeremiah.

"Are you really a cobbler at heart?" Jeremiah asked, and elicited the whicker of appreciation from Showforth.

"Lemme see it," Bumps said doggedly, waiting.

Jeremiah ignored him and turned to Crawford. "Why should I do it for him?" he asked.

"You don't have to, Mr. Beaumont," Crawford replied. "There isn't any warrant. But folks found a boot track near the back window of Colonel Fort's room, where they saw the murderer looking in, and they took a measure, and Bumps just wants to see if it matches your boot."

Jeremiah laughed, remembering his good precaution of the socks, and took his foot from the stirrup, and said, "Anything for Mr. Bumps," and stuck the foot almost in his face.

Bumps applied the paper to the boot, studied it a moment, then exulted, "It's a fit, by God, and he done it! Boys, we are shore rich!"

And the word *rich*, as Jeremiah leaned over to look at the boot, grasped his heart like a cold hand. So there was money in it. But he suppressed his alarm, and studied the boot and paper. "Don't you see," he asked reasonably, addressing Jarvis, "that the boot does not match the outline?"

"By God," Bumps said, "it's the same length."

"It is near the same length," Jeremiah corrected, "but a tiny trifle longer. But any one can see that the heel is much wider, and at the instep."

Jarvis dubiously studied the match, but Bumps did not even bother to look. "By God," he cried in outrage, "you ain't gonna rob me that a-way. When Crawford drawed the pitcher here, I seen his hand woggle wide at the heel. Yes, sir, I seen it, and I said, look here, Tom, you air wogglin wide." He lifted his face to Crawford, with his look of stupid cunning. "Now ain't it a fack, Tom, like I said, didn't you woggle wide and didn't I say that?"

Jeremiah looked at Crawford, ready for his denial. Crawford did not return his look, nor did he look down at Bumps. He seemed to be occupied with something down the empty lane, and Jeremiah saw him swallow once, hard. He saw the Adam's apple bobble in the lean throat.

"Didn't I say that?" Bumps demanded, with wheedling voice and threatening face.

Crawford took out a plug of tobacco, bit off a chew, gave it a couple of preliminary grinds, spat, and still looking off down the lane, said: "Now, let me see. Maybe you did now. And maybe you didn't. It looks like I dis-remember exactly."

And suddenly Jeremiah thought: *Oh, I know you, Crawford. You will not tell the cold lie and say yes. Oh, I know you, for you are the kind will comfort your conscience with that, and take the pay for Bumps' lie.* He felt like bursting out to Crawford: *Don't be a fool. You know it's a lie. And I can prove it, for I wore no boots at all. I can dredge the socks up from the river and prove it!* And he went cold with terror at the thought that he might have cried out that confession only to confute a lie.

But instead, he leaned toward Crawford a little and said softly and insinuatingly: "Mr. Crawford, why don't you say yes to him? Would you deprive dear Bumps of the money—whatever money it is—he is trying so hard to earn by his lie?"

"Ain't no man gonna call me a liar!" Bumps yelled, and stepped back and yanked out his pistol.

Jeremiah laughed, looking down at him. "Shoot," he suggested, laughing. "Shoot and see what you can collect then of your bribe."

"It ain't no bribe!" Bumps screamed in outrage. "It's a reward for

254

catching the murderer. It's law, by God. The Legislature done voted three thousand dollars to catch the murderer, and Mr. Saunders, he done promised a thousand, and the Duke—the Duke two thousand, and . . ."

"A very tidy sum," Jeremiah said, "but you'll never see it. Unless, of course, you do shoot me and can forge a confession—that is, if you have ever learned to write—and can persuade Mr. Crawford to swear to it. The confession might stand then—even with your bad spelling. If Mr. Crawford swears, for I am sure Mr. Crawford bears the reputation of an honest man and a gentleman, and would be believed. Even without oath."

"You ain't gonna call me a liar," Bumps muttered, but did not raise the pistol.

Crawford was still staring down the blank lane. Not turning, he said, "Get on your horse, Bumps, we got a long ways to go."

"Gimme that dirk," Bumps said to Crawford. "That dirk of his'n."

"Get on your horse," Crawford said.

"Gimme that dirk," Bumps repeated, belligerently. "I got as much right as you. I want to see if it fits the cut."

Crawford handed over the dirk.

"I bet it fits—I'm shore it fits," Bumps said, handling the weapon.

Jeremiah knew that it would not fit. The dirk was Spanish, rather wide at the base of the blade, very sharp at the point but with unground edges somewhat rough from abuse.

"Did you bring the body with you to make the test?" Jeremiah inquired. "Or did you mark the cut on paper, and your hand woggled?"

"Oh, you think you're so all-fired smart," Bumps said. "You a lawyer trying to tangle folks up. But you won't be so smart, they put that rope around yore neck . . ." And he grasped his own throat with thumb and forefinger and dropped his head to one side and lolled out his tongue and rolled his eyes with what Jeremiah describes as delicious pleasure. Then he stopped, and said: "Yeah, and we got what'll hang you. We got that handkerchief you dropped by Saunders' door and never knowed. Yeah, and folks will swear it is yores and . . ."

"I now have no doubt," Jeremiah replied, "that some men will swear to anything."

But Bumps, not listening, had stepped to Crawford's stirrup, saying, "Gimme that handkerchief."

Crawford passed it over, and as Bumps waved it in mean triumph, Jeremiah saw that it was the old cross-barred, stained cotton handkerchief in which his "accouterments" had been wrapped, and sud-

255

denly realized that it must have been left tangled in the bedclothes of his bed in the Jessup house. Otherwise he would have seen it.

"Yeah," Bumps was saying, waving the handkerchief, "and you wiped blood on it and cut it with yore dirk."

Jeremiah could see that a corner was hacked off, and that it was stained. It was a bloodstain, he knew. He knew because the last time he had used it, long back, he had had a little nosebleed. He cursed himself for a fool. Why hadn't he known that one drop of blood, however old and brown, would be as dangerous as a spark in a hay barn? Why had he left the thing in the bedclothes? But, he checked himself, they claimed to have found it by the Saunders' door. Lies, lies, he thought with rage, and had the urge to scream out: *You liar, you know it was found in the bed. It was found in the bed, for I left it there, and I only dropped the old wool hat by Saunders' door, and that will prove nothing.*

He mastered himself, however, and asked calmly, "You say that is my handkerchief?"

"You're tootin, mister," Bumps said.

"And that that is the dirk used to kill Fort, and that I wiped the blade on it and hacked off the corner?"

"Yeah," Bumps said.

"Give me the handkerchief and the dirk," Jeremiah commanded. Bumps hesitated.

"Give them to him," Crawford said.

Jeremiah took them, grasped the handkerchief in a little loop at one corner, and inserted the dirk. "Now I will try to cut," he said, and exerted his strength. The cloth gave a little at one side, where a roughness in the blade caught, but it did not cut. "You see," Jeremiah instructed him, "the dirk has no ground edge. It will not cut cloth. It might tear it, but it will not cut."

Then he handed the articles back to Bumps, saying, "There goes your money, Bumps," and enjoying momentarily the gaped jaw and stunned gaze of his adversary.

But Bumps recovered himself, saying, "That's what you say," and made ready to try to cut for himself.

"Stop it," Crawford said, "you spile it for court."

Grudgingly Bumps desisted. But he glared up at Jeremiah and said, "Yeah, but it's got blood on it. Fort's blood, and you'll git hanged."

"Get on your horse, Bumps," Crawford said savagely. "Get on your horse, and let's go."

Bumps pocketed the dirk and handkerchief, and obeyed.

"Yes," Jeremiah agreed, "let's go. If Bumps has finished his little comedy."

They got a late dinner at a cabin on the road, about two o'clock. They had some whisky, while the woman was getting food ready, and the drink seemed to restore Bumps' low spirits. He began to boast darkly to the host how they had caught Fort's murderer, and how they would all be rich.

Jeremiah knew the host slightly, a man named Peck, a raw-boned, near-toothless, middle-aged man, shaggy and dirty, and when bad weather came on, near crippled with rheumatism, that curse of the frontiersman. The moccasin, even if stuffed with leaves or rags when the ground was wet, was just a "decent way of going barefoot," and Peck had been a hunter in his youth. But he was now half-farmer and half-hunter, worrying starvation out of a few gutted acres and the shot-over woods. Jeremiah had known Peck on his campaign, and knew that he was a Reliefer, as from his dire poverty he might well be.

Crawford shut Bumps up in the middle of his boasting, and the meal was taken in silence. Then the Frankfort men went out to get the horses ready, while Jeremiah finished his last few bites (he had found himself very hungry) and Bumps loitered just beyond the door, picking his teeth with a clasp knife and keeping an eye on his investment within.

Peck loitered near the table. In a low voice he all at once demanded: "They takin you back up thar to Frankfort? That what that feller was meanin?"

Jeremiah said that he was suspected and was going of his own free will to clear himself.

"Don't be doin it," Peck said grimly. "Don't git up thar with them folks. Them high-flyin bastards, they hates folks down here."

"They have no evidence against me," Jeremiah said.

Peck looked over his shoulder warily, then leaned closer. "Listen, I'll git some fellers round here. Won't take but one or two. I knows a cut-off through the woods. You hang back a little some way and make 'em slow. We'll bush-whack 'em. Afore Morfee's Station. We'll git you off. Ain't none of them bastards gonna come down here and take our folks."

"I'm going of my own free will," Jeremiah said.

"Don't be a durn piss-ant fool," the man said sourly.

Jeremiah rose, and put out his hand. "Thank you," he said. "I know the man you are and I thank you from my heart. But my mind is made up."

Peck took his hand, then dropped it. He looked around at Bumps, with a slow studious gaze. Then he shook his head mournfully. "See that-air mole or wart or whichever 'tis that feller's got?"

Jeremiah looked, and nodded. Bumps had a brown, hairy growth over the left eye, toward the bridge of the nose.

"I'd lay my sights right on it," the man said. "Then it wouldn't be thar no more."

Jeremiah laughed. "Save your powder for a turkey," he said.

"He's a lot fatter'n a turkey," Peck said, unsmiling, "but his meat would be pizen to a pole-cat." Then he spat on the puncheon floor, and for decency set his foot over the spot.

"Good-bye," Jeremiah said, shook hands again, and left.

He rode away very cheerful within himself, thinking that for every Bumps (or even Crawford) in Kentucky there must be a Peck.

He was so cheerful that he began to converse briskly with Crawford about harmless topics, how the country had changed since his boyhood, about the hunts he had seen, about early settlers he had known, like Jake Runnion. Gradually Jarvis and even Crawford, who had been gloomy since the episode in the lane, joined in. And from their talk Jeremiah began to piece together their lives, to know what kind of men he had to deal with. Crawford had been a farmer or small planter with two or three Negroes over near Versailles (Jeremiah guessed that he had lost his land) and now had some kind of little business in Frankfort (it turned out to be a harness shop, a hole in a back street) and wore a frayed black coat trying to be decent, and "suffered from a wounded self-esteem that bled inwardly and festered with the injustice done him by the world, though he tried to carry himself with the pride and manner of the independent man." Jarvis was a mechanic, and Jeremiah took him to be naturally honest, but so stupid that his honesty might come to nought in the company of corrupt men, "for virtue requires some soil to root in."

Jeremiah cultivated them carefully (he had no hopes of Bumps or the boy Showforth, who rode behind and took frequent nips from a bottle), and listened with respect to their tales and opinions, professing interest in their histories, flattering their high respectability and good moral character "as a man with a subtle hand lifts to the sun the green tendrils of a delicate plant of the garden in the hope that it may cling and grow strong."

So they passed the afternoon. They stopped late at a planter's house, and were all so tired that they got early to bed with little conversation with the family, but not before Bumps was snoring drunk. Bumps and Showforth slept in the room with Jeremiah, the boy on a pallet, Bumps in the same bed with Jeremiah, for the drunker Bumps got the more preciously he attached himself to Jeremiah as though he expected, Jeremiah says, to see him converted into cash at any minute and wanted to be ready to stuff his pockets.

The next day was without event until they came to Mr. Smart's big house on the road. Though it was early then, they put up there, lured no doubt by Smart's reputation for hospitality. Several hangers-on were still about the porch when they arrived, though the evening drew on cold, and it was not long before the liquor had opened Bumps and he told all how he would soon be rich and how Jeremiah had murdered Fort. Crawford was decent enough to set the matter in its true light, that Jeremiah came willingly to answer suspicion, and Jeremiah thought that he recognized already the fruits of his long conversation on the road. But Bumps was loud where Crawford was sober, and Bumps' story was the one the party seemed to want to believe. Smart expressed no opinion, but Jeremiah detected the pig's eyes peering out of the big face with a satisfied and rancorous gaze.

Then Bumps drew out the cross-barred cotton handkerchief and exhibited it to all, saying to look at the blood and the hacks on it, saying it had been found at Saunders' door and a dozen men would swear it was Beaumont's, for he had been seen to wear it bound on his brow. (So that was it, Jeremiah thought, it was the handkerchief bound on his brow. But he was sure somebody would remember the dark green one. He was sorry he had burned it.)

Then Bumps fumbled in his pocket, and said, "And yeah, I got right here the dirk he used—right here—just a minute, I got it right here." Then he lifted a face blank with elaborate surprise, "Fer God's sake, and I done gone and lost it. Now ain't that tur'ble!"

Crawford came and stood over him. "Hunt again," he commanded.

Bumps made another search, muttering all the while, "Now ain't that tur'ble?"

"If you didn't drink so durn much likker," Crawford said peevishly.

"Aw, Tom," Bumps complained, "I ain't had but a little nip now and then," and lifted his face to Crawford to exhibit injured innocence.

Then Jeremiah saw all. He saw that that bloating innocence was puddled and creamed with guile—to take his words. He was sure of everything.

He rose, stepped toward Crawford, tapped him on the shoulder, and turned to the group. "Gentlemen," he said, "I call on you all to witness. This man admits he has lost a dirk which I admit to be my own. I do not know whether he has lost it wittingly or unwittingly. You may draw your conclusion when I tell you that yesterday it was clearly shown that that dirk had unground edges and would not hack off the corner of that handkerchief. Further, I was anxious that the width of the dirk be tried by the width of the wound, if any record was made of that wound by honorable men, for I . . ." And in his fervor he had almost said that he knew that it would not match. But he caught himself: "For I would have—I would have . . ." He fumbled for a word, feeling his mind go blank for a moment. "For I would have all made clear, and . . ."

"Hey, Mr. Crawford," one of the men demanded, "is that right? About the dirk not cutting the handkerchief?"

Crawford turned his face, and Jeremiah saw the unhappiness on it. He cursed the questioner, for he was afraid for Crawford to be pushed now, he wanted him to stand alone to take a solemn oath, without Bumps and the others by his side. If Crawford spoke now he would be committed forever, beyond shame.

He saw Crawford wet his lips, and saw the suffering on his face deepen for an instant.

"Gentlemen," Jeremiah interposed quickly, before the stiff suffering lips could open, "with all respect I suggest that you should not question Mr. Crawford here, casually, on such an important point. A man's life—or at least his reputation"—he laughed, feeling confidence grow—"even Mr. Crawford's reputation—might depend on his words. Should you not let him wait, and speak in court, under solemn oath and before God?"

Jeremiah saw Crawford's face relax, and saw his lips go loose and let a breath escape, and saw the look of something near gratitude that Crawford flung him, and he knew he had won. Crawford would not speak now. He would cling to at least a rag of honor, however threadbare, to clothe him for another hour, another day, perhaps for always.

"Yeah, but a fact is a fact," the questioner was saying.

"Yeah," Bumps said, "and the fack is . . ."

"God damn you, Bumps," Crawford leaned over him with uplifted fist, "God damn you to hell, can't you keep your mouth shut!"

And Bumps slumped silent under the fist that would have glanced harmless off his tough mass of gristle and tallow.

"Now, gentlemen," Jeremiah said, feeling in full command, "I should like to request, for the sake of justice, that a thorough search for the dirk be made back by the way we have come. First, it is my property, and second it was consigned willingly by me to this gentleman," indicating Mr. Crawford, "that it might be presented at Frankfort in my defense."

"I ain't gonna go back and hunt nothing," Bumps muttered.

"Bumps," Jeremiah said soothingly, "I would never ask *you* to go back." Then added with clear irony: "Though I suspect that you could find it more readily than most."

Bumps leaped up, doubling his fists, shouting, "If you mean to be saying . . ."

But Crawford wheeled at him. "You fool!" Crawford uttered and leaned at him in an intensity of hate.

Bumps sank down again, working his big, raw fists in his lap, cracking his knuckles, glaring secretly at Crawford.

But no search was made. Crawford seemed undecided, and after making one more formal request, Jeremiah said quietly: "I do not insist, Mr. Crawford. I trust your testimony to establish the facts of the dirk when you come to oath, and I know that *you* will be believed. But"—and he turned to the group—"I request that all others present remember that I have done my best to have a search made and I hold that the dirk itself would support my cause."

He was sure that Bumps had thrown the dirk away. Bumps had waited until now, when they were out of Jeremiah's home county where friends might resent the injustice and insist on a search. And all during the supper (while a few men of the neighborhood came by to peer at him from the door, for word had got out), he berated himself for his behavior that first morning in the lane. He should never have demonstrated then that the dirk would not hack the handkerchief. He could see himself in the court of investigation, taking the dirk and the handkerchief and exhibiting before the eyes of all the fact, and then walking out a free man. He was like a green duelist, he decided, who fires too soon and sees his bullet plow the ground at the adversary's feet and must wait under the deadly muzzle leveled at his breast.

But he had learned his lesson. Next time he would wait.

Then, after supper, when they were shown to the room for the night, he had the idea.

There were other guests in the Smart house, and the party was to occupy one room, a big bare-boarded room, with two bedsteads. Crawford, who had been silent and preoccupied during the meal, professed to be tired and prepared himself immediately for bed. The others pulled up by the hearth, with one of Mr. Smart's jugs. Jeremiah said he was a little chilled, and asked for a drink, too. So he sat by, taking little while Bumps and Jarvis fell into a long-winded and well-likkered argument about a horse-run they had seen the summer before.

Each time the jug came to Jeremiah's hand it felt lighter and sloshed more hollowly. He blessed the jug, and blessed Bumps' thirst. Finally, he complimented Bumps respectfully on his prowess. Bumps flushed up with pleasure, and threw out his chest, saying, yes, sir, he had yet to find the man who could drink him down, yes, sir, he had drunk with the best, and he launched into a long account of a debauch he had been on some months back. Jeremiah kept him well larded with admiration tactfully applied, ably seconded by the boy Showforth, who punctuated the hero's narrative now and then by saying, "Yes, sir, yes, sir, Mr. Bumps can shore drink 'em down, ain't no man can put Mr. Bumps under." Once or twice he got up, lurching, to slap Bumps on the back.

Finally Jarvis got up and announced that he was going to bed. He started for the unoccupied bed, but Bumps turned and said, "Hey, Jarvis, you git in with Crawford. Fer me"—and he leered at Jeremiah— "I'm gonna sleep with baby. Case he gits restless." Then he bellowed and hooted with laughter, and Showforth whickered his relish in the jest.

Jeremiah had counted on that. Bumps had insisted on sleeping with him the night before.

A little later Jeremiah took off his coat, boots and breeches and got to bed. "It's getting cold," he announced, "and there's not much cover." So he spread his coat over the bed before he got in.

He lay pretending to be asleep, listening to the talk and the chink of the jug by the hearth. At last, he heard Bumps rise and yawn. He opened his eyes to the thinnest slit and watched Bumps make ready, and then pad over, in sock feet, shirt, and under-drawers, toward the bed. Jeremiah's mind was already at work on a new stratagem, when Bumps turned, picked up his coat, and said, "Might git cold." Jeremiah sighed his relief, and watched secretly as Bumps spread the coat and then heaved into bed.

In five minutes the whisky had done its work, and Bumps had begun to snore. Jeremiah waited. Showforth was still at the hearth, mumbling something to himself now and then. Jeremiah decided that Showforth had been ordered to sit up and keep watch. Or to sleep with his pallet across the door so that it could not be opened. Jeremiah smiled at that. He had no thought of escape.

After a little longer, Jeremiah rose on his elbow, seemed to rouse himself, and got from the bed and sleepily looked about until he had found his long cape. He brought that back and spread it over the bed when he got in, and drew it up to his shoulder. But lying on his left side, facing Bumps, he left his right arm on top of the cover but concealed by the cape. Then, after a little, he began the slow task of working Bumps' coat a little closer to him. It was going to be easier than he had thought. If Bumps' coat had been spread differently he might have had to make a pretense of rearranging all the cover before putting his cape over.

Within half an hour or so, he had succeeded. He had drawn from Bumps' pocket the big cross-barred cotton handkerchief. He stuffed it in the front of his shirt, and waited. From the occasional chink of the jug, he could tell that Showforth was still drinking. Then he began to get sleepy. He had the horrible fear that he would fall asleep with the handkerchief still in his shirt. So he decided not to wait for Showforth. Showforth might be under orders to wait up, or wait up a certain time and then wake another for a watch.

So Jeremiah got up again, muttering and grumbling about the cold, asking Showforth why he didn't keep the fire up. He himself put a chunk on toward the front of the fireplace, and poked the fire to make the chunk catch quick. He set another chunk, a big one, on end on the hearth between Showforth and the fire. Then he huddled over the hearth, spreading his hands to the flame, and still grumbling sleepily. Showforth, he had noticed, was blear-eyed drunk.

It was easy. In a little while, he leaned over to pick up the big chunk, and as he leaned drew the wadded handkerchief from his shirt. It was in his right hand, away from Showforth, and when he picked up the big chunk the mass concealed it. When he dropped the chunk in, holding it so long and so close, that the hairs singed off the backs of his hands, the handkerchief was beneath it and the chunk in front hid any edges that might be exposed. Jeremiah had "no fear that it might be smelt, for a fine piece of cotton goods as it was will make no smell burning, and as for Showforth, he was in no shape to smell even a gust of blazing brimstone from the Pit."

Then, after a decent delay, Jeremiah went back to bed and fell into a sound sleep. He noticed in the morning that Showforth had slept on a pallet placed as to block the door.

The loss of the handkerchief was not discovered until the next night at Bardstown.

When they arrived, it was past dusk, but a little crowd was already gathered in the street, for the news had come ahead. As they rode up, there was a confused babble, and somebody called, "Yeah, that's him and they got him! They got the man killed Fort!"

Then the crowd pressed up close, impeding the horses, staring at Jeremiah. He faced them down, then turned to Crawford, and said in a clear voice, "Does this"—(he almost said, "riffraff" but checked himself)—"set up as a court of justice?"

"Folks is right excited up here," Crawford murmured, almost in apology, not looking at Jeremiah, just straight ahead over the crowd.

But Bumps was enjoying himself to the fullest. It was a royal progress for him. He waved and grinned and yelled, "Yeah, boys—we shore got him."

Jeremiah looked at the crowd, loafers and drifters and ruined old men and pimpled boys and town Negroes and a few gap-mouthed wives from the back streets and a sprinkling of ribboned sluts, all swaying together, greasy-faced in the light of a couple of pine flares,

263

the eyes glittering like love or greed, their lips, where the light struck, bright with saliva. Then they roared with delight, when Bumps, rising in his saddle, grasped his own windpipe with thumb and forefinger, as he had done the first morning in the lane, and rolled his head and rolled his eyes and let his great tongue flap like a sick dog's.

So this was justice, Jeremiah thought, and the wild contempt that he had known as he leaped the fence that night from the Saunders' garden, flooded over him like a tide, lifted him on its crest and spun him giddily so that the scene swirled and blurred in his sight, and he felt like crying out, "I did it, I did it, make what you will of it, for nothing can ever touch me now!"

But they dismounted and entered the inn, where some gentlemen, not immune to curiosity, waited in that privileged place, while the rabble stared in through the door.

Crawford ordered drinks at the bar, and as they took them, Bumps waved his glass and began to hold forth to the spectators. Three of Jeremiah's acquaintances in town, one with whom he had spent the night on the way down and two others, made their way to him, and offered their sympathy. He thanked them, explained to them how he came of his own will, asking confirmation respectfully from Crawford, and told circumstantially of the episode of the lost dirk. But all the while he had an ear cocked for Bumps' discourse. Bumps was now telling about the handkerchief found at Saunders' door, and how men would swear it was Jeremiah's. Then he put his hand in his pocket for the handkerchief, then into another pocket, and another and another.

Jeremiah saw the first surprise and distress on Bumps' face pass into his flabby, puddled innocence, as he turned to Crawford, and said with a great air of casualness, "Hey, Tom, show these folks that-air handkerchief."

Crawford replied that Bumps had had it.

"I give it back," Bumps asseverated, and turned to Showforth. "Didn't I give it back?" he demanded.

"Look good," Crawford ordered irritably, "look in all your pockets."

"I give it back," Bumps said, "and you know it. Look in yore own pockets."

"I'll not look," Crawford affirmed. "By God, you had the handkerchief, and you'll find it!"

"I give it back!" Bumps cried, flushing with rage, "and you ain't gonna . . ."

Jeremiah took a step forward, toward Crawford. "This is too much," he said. "First that fellow loses the dirk. When he found it wouldn't cut the handkerchief. Now he loses the handkerchief. How much evidence will he be permitted to lose? Or suppress?"

"I never done it!" Bumps screamed, dropping his empty glass, waving his fists. "I give it to him." He pointed directly at Crawford.

Jeremiah turned again to Crawford and asked courteously, "Are you quite sure, Mr. Crawford, that he did not return the handkerchief to you?"

"Sure, I'm sure," Crawford said.

"Think carefully," Jeremiah softly urged, "for this is of great importance to me."

"By God, I'm sure," Crawford said.

"Mr. Bumps doesn't seem to take your word," Jeremiah said, even more softly.

"I give it to him," Bumps said sullenly.

"You see," Jeremiah said, soft, "he denies that you are speaking the truth."

Crawford's thin face suddenly streaked white and red, and his hand trembled so that the liquid sloshed in his glass. "Not him—or any man—is going to call me a . . ."

"A liar?" Jeremiah asked, and then before Crawford's rage would let him speak, he laid his hand on Crawford's arm, saying, like a friend: "Does it matter what Bumps says? I believe you implicitly. As all decent men will."

"By God!" Bumps bellowed, "are you sayin I ain't decent, are you sayin I'm a liar? Why, I'll . . ." He lifted his fists and made to plunge at Jeremiah, but two of the gentlemen standing by seized his arms.

"Bumps," Jeremiah said, "I should find it perfectly unnecessary to say what you are. What you are is perfectly obvious at a glance." Then he turned to the general group. "It is also perfectly clear . . ." he began.

But Bumps screamed, "Lemme go, lemme go, I'll kill him, I'll git him hung . . ."

"I hope, gentlemen," Jeremiah addressed the group, "you will remember these threats. They might cast some light on Mr. Bumps' testimony."

"Lemme go, by God!" Bumps screamed.

Jeremiah smiled. "Let him go, gentlemen," he said. "I think that he isn't struggling very hard to get loose. If he insists, I'll fight him later. What concerns me now is the handkerchief. I request now, as I requested when Bumps lost the dirk, that a search be made over every inch of our route. By responsible men. Mr. Crawford, I appeal again to your fairness."

"That's right," an elderly, black-clad man said with a tone of authority, a man who had stood in the rear, superior to the excitement.

Crawford hesitated, and again Jeremiah saw him swallow, hard.

"May I have your answer, Mr. Crawford?" Jeremiah asked.

265

Crawford turned to Jarvis. "Jarvis," he said, "in the morning now . . ."

"I ain't going," Jarvis said, "not and let you all git in there first and . . ."

Jeremiah turned to the group with a tone of patient explanation. "You see," he said, "Mr. Jarvis thinks of the sumptuous reward being offered. And he doesn't seem to trust friends to give him his share. But"—and he turned to Jarvis—"may I remind you, Mr. Jarvis, that the reward is offered for the capture and *conviction* of the murderer of Colonel Fort. It doesn't seem to be clearly established that I am your man."

Somebody laughed at that.

"I ain't going," Jarvis said stubbornly.

"Well," Crawford said, "I'll go myself. And I'll take Mr. Beaumont with me, and we'll hunt every inch and . . ."

"Naw you ain't," Bumps said, "he's as much mine as yores and . . ."

The black-clad old man stepped forward. "Enough of this," he said. "A search will be made. If he"—he indicated Jarvis—"does not trust his friends and will not go, we shall see that you," he addressed Crawford, "go with your prisoner. . . ."

"I beg your pardon, sir," Jeremiah said, "I am not a prisoner."

The old man bowed, begging pardon. Then continued to Crawford: "We shall see that you go, with Mr. Beaumont here, to make a search. I shall ride with you, and others, if necessary to guarantee that you go unmolested."

"I'll go," Jarvis said sourly. "All right, I'll go."

"In that case," the old man said, "two men will go with you. To help in the search and to testify to its thoroughness. We can show that there is some sense of justice left in Bardstown."

Two men offered themselves to go, and said they would be ready at dawn.

"In that case, I'll stay at home," the old man said. "My old bones creak a little after a day in the saddle."

Jeremiah stepped to him. "May I have the honor of your acquaintance?" he asked.

"Mr. Beaumont," he said gravely, "I am not of your political persuasion, and I was a friend of Colonel Fort. But I'll take your hand until the moment—which pray God does not come—when it is proved that it is stained with his good blood."

"Thank you, sir," Jeremiah said, and took the old man's brittle hand.

"My name is Bascomb," the old man said. "And may I invite you to stop to sup with me, with your friends?"

Before Jeremiah could reply, Bumps made a little stir and grinned and opened his mouth as though about to accept the invitation. But the old man turned toward the Bardstown citizens with whom Jeremiah had first spoken. "I mean, of course," the old man said, "your Bardstown friends. If they will be good enough to join us."

Bumps' jaw hung open, as proof of his past intention.

Jeremiah thanked Mr. Bascomb, but added, "May I ask Mr. Crawford to join us? I should like for him to be present wherever I am, and to hear whatever I may chance to say. And I am sure you will find his company as agreeable and instructive as I have found it on the road."

The old man formally invited Crawford.

Crawford flushed to the ears with his pleasure, and stuttered his acceptance.

Jeremiah looked at his face with its embarrassed pleasure, and all his own confident excitement drained away. *The fool, the poor fool,* he thought, *to be proud to sit at an inn and be seen at the table with this old man in his fine black coat and gold ring.* He thought with pity of that poor, bright moment for Crawford, and saw Crawford shabby and fumbling with the silver, and thought: *If that is his vanity, what is there in him for any man to trust, what is he but emptiness?*

His pride in his own triumph was gone. He felt dead tired. He wanted to lie down in a quiet, clear place (Did he think of the wooded valley, or of a high vacant plain in the West, under the glittering stars, or of his room at home?) where there would be no need to think of shifts and weaknesses and vanities on which he might play, where he could be alone and be himself. And then he thought: *Myself, oh, what am I?*

The country toward Frankfort was roused and all aflame. At every crossroads or little settlement on their way some people would be waiting to see them pass, and when they reached the edge of Frankfort, well after dark, a watchman by the roadside fired off a gun as a signal. By the time they reached the heart of the town, the street was lined with every loafer of the place. Bumps prepared again for his triumph. But now the response was mixed.

When Bumps rose in his saddle, and yelled, "Yeah, we got him and gonna hang him!" and grabbed his own windpipe and lolled out his tongue, somebody yelled back, "Yeah, and we'll hang you, you durned Anti-Relief, git the rope, boys!" And a stone hurled from the shadows bounced off Bumps' shoulder and somewhat cooled his enthusiasm. For Relief and New Court was strong in Frankfort, strong enough to give a cheer for Beaumont at one street corner, and at another the cry, "Death to the tyrants!"

It was the cheer naming him a hero that chilled Jeremiah's heart more than his earlier discovery of the web of greed and perjury being woven to snare him. That assumption by his friends was more deadly than any accusation by his enemies. His very denial of guilt would be to them a betrayal. What did they want? They wanted a hero and a martyr to make a ringing speech for Relief and step gaily to the scaffold, to save a mortgaged pasture or a leaky roof. The one thing they would never forgive him was innocence.

Then Jeremiah's distress crystallized into irony. He asked himself what the yelling crowd ever knew of its martyrs. Or what the men who wrote the histories ever knew when they gave the cold reasons. Was there always something deeper and darker, a need never to be told, that steeled the hand to action and the heart to contempt?

At that thought he had for a moment the vision of a throng of pale faces marked with blood, and uplifted manacled hands, and he felt like grinning at them in confidence and whispering, *Oh, I know you, I know you all, I know the secret you would never tell anybody.*

And in those musings, which liberated him from his case into the realm of his knowledge, he passed on.

He was not committed to the jail. Instead he was accommodated in the house of a Mr. Marton, just off the square. It was a pleasant room, with a fire on the hearth and a table laid for supper. Mr. Marton received him respectfully, like a benighted guest from the road. He inquired for his comfort, and then left him.

Supper was brought in by a colored man-servant, a good, solid meal, well prepared.

When the Negro was removing the dishes, Jeremiah said: "Will you ask your master if he can give me the recent journals of Lexington and Frankfort?"

The man shortly returned with them, the *Freeman's Advocate* (Skrogg's paper, Relief), the *Spy* (Aden Kilmore's paper, Relief), the *People's Hope* (Sabot Mickwell's paper, Anti-Relief), and the *Commonwealth* (John Potter's paper, ostensibly non-partisan but inclining strongly to Anti-Relief).

Jeremiah almost sorted the little handful of sheets to find the *Advocate* to read first, for that he was sure would be friendly to him and would give a true coloring of the facts. But he conquered that fleeting impulse as weakness, and spread the *People's Hope* on his table under the candle. The issue had appeared that very day, November 16, 1825. Under the heading, BEAUMONT APPREHENDED, there was the story:

> Intelligence has come to us that Jeremiah Beaumont, a citizen
> of Saul County in the south, has been apprehended by a party
> of Frankfort citizens who had the courage and initiative to

track down to his lair the man who it is strongly presumed gave the dastardly blow to Colonel Cassius Fort on the evening of Sunday fortnight. Beaumont was, according to our information, taken at his house as he was making preparation to leave the country. From his house was recovered a dirk whose description makes it not impossible that it was the fatal weapon, but unfortunately the blade was lost upon the road under circumstances as yet mysterious. But such a loss need not inspire the lovers of justice with the fear that guilt may not be established, for tracks of the assassin were discovered, as is well known here in Frankfort, and a handkerchief dropped by bloodstained fingers may be identified. Beaumont was seen to wear a handkerchief bound on his brow as he applied for lodging at several of our hostelries, and honest men can be found to swear to its description. A full account will be forthcoming in these pages when the worthy citizens of Frankfort return shortly with their prisoner.

Jeremiah saw it all. How Bumps (or was it Bumps? could Crawford have been guilty?) had called aside somebody at Smart's house (it must have been then, for the dirk had been lost) and started the rider ahead to Mickwell. How Mickwell (Jeremiah's fingers curled and longed to be at the throat of that man whom he had never seen) had scribbled out in haste that mixture of fact and falsity and innuendo worse than falsity. How the citizen of Frankfort, reading that, could believe in nothing but guilt.

He flung the paper aside. He could have expected nothing else from it, for it was Anti-Relief, and Fort had been the new god of that faction.

Then, like a hungry man reaching for bread, Jeremiah took up the *Advocate*. It repeated the bare news, but did not imply that Jeremiah was a prisoner. Then it discussed the crime, making no particular reference, however, to the evidence already available. It said:

It is well known that we do not agree with the policies promulgated by the late Colonel Fort, and it is well known that we hold him to be a betrayer, for whatever reasons, of the best interests of this Commonwealth. But we wish to make one thing clear to all men. WE DO NOT HOLD THAT RELIEF SHOULD THRIVE BY ASSASSINATION AND THE MURDERER'S HAND LIFTED IN DARKNESS. No, Relief thrives by the light of day and the truth in the hearts of men. As for Beaumont, we are not privy to his conscience, and know not his counsels, but if he, or whatever man, be guilty, for reasons of public policy or private vendetta, of this crime, we call for JUSTICE, for JUSTICE IS ALL THAT RELIEF HAS EVER HELD AS ITS GUIDING STAR AND ORIFLAMME.

Jeremiah laid the paper aside. It had not been bread, and, if not a stone, at least nothing better than a dry crust such as might be thrown to a stray cur. He was too dull in spirit to try to frame what he had expected, or hoped for, on that page. Then he decided what he had hoped to find—nothing more than a clear statement of facts cutting through all the tangle of suspicion and lies and innuendo. *By God,* he thought, and rose violently from his chair, *by God, I have given them the facts, let the facts speak, and I shall be clear.*

He did not even glance at the other papers.

He was pacing the room in his anger, when he heard a knock. It was his host, Mr. Marton, who said that a gentleman had come to see him and begged to be admitted.

A moment later, Mr. Madison entered, cool, dignified, smiling, and put out his hand as casually as though they met on the street on a summer afternoon. "My boy," he said, "it's an ill wind that blows me the pleasure of your company, but it will die down soon."

Jeremiah declared that he was confident, and asked Mr. Madison to have a seat.

The Negro brought in a tray with bottle, glasses and a pitcher of water, and slipped away. Jeremiah prepared drinks, and chunked up the fire.

Mr. Madison sipped meditatively for a few moments, watching the new blaze. Then he said: "I do not mean to intrude, but I have an interest in your case, an interest founded simply on what I know to be your talents and worth."

Jeremiah thanked him, and assured him that his interest could be no intrusion.

Mr. Madison waited again, then seeming to gather himself, said: "You are a lawyer. I suppose you know what the procedure will be. You will be summoned to the Court of Inquiry."

Jeremiah hotly declared that he had not waited to be summoned, that he had come of his own will to present himself to clear his name of suspicion.

"That little fact has been obscured in the press," Mr. Madison said sourly. Then he added that the country was in great confusion, that wild rumors had the status of truth, and that partisans had lost respect for honor.

Jeremiah touched the newspapers on the table beside him. "I find that easy to believe," he said.

Mr. Madison rose and stood on the hearth with his back to the

270

fire, looking beyond Jeremiah, fingering his glass. After a moment, still looking at Jeremiah, he said:

"I shall come to the point. You may want counsel and . . ." Then, as Jeremiah seemed about to interrupt, he lifted his hand and continued: "I have thought to offer my poor services. But I hasten to say that I would not consider this a business arrangement." He again lifted his hand, and continued: "First, I am strongly convinced that you are innocent, and I would not profit to defend the innocence of a friend. But second, another matter of some delicacy has emerged. Anti-Relief, as you may guess, has set abroad the rumor that the assassination was political, that Fort died by the hand of Relief. Our party must repel this accusation with all its force. Therefore certain gentlemen high in our circles have urged me against involving myself in your case, for it might imply an approbation of the murder of Fort."

Jeremiah leaped from his chair, saying, "In God's name, that implies that I . . ."

"Exactly," Mr. Madison replied, and motioned Jeremiah to sit. "But they do not mean to imply that. They are merely timid, and fear that your case, whatever the rights of the matter, will be used against the party. I have told them flatly that I will be governed by no such consideration. That justice comes first. But I will not fly in the face of what some seem to think the interest of my party, and then take money for doing so. Do you understand me?"

Jeremiah complimented him upon his delicacy of sentiment.

Mr. Madison, with embarrassment, waved that aside, but as he waited, not going on, his embarrassment seemed to grow rather than diminish. Then with an air of resolution he drained his glass, set it on the mantel shelf behind him, and said: "Much is at stake in this. Our friends are right that our party may sink or swim by this event. Now do not misunderstand me. I believe in your innocence. But I owe it to them to ask reassurance from your own lips. Can you give it to me?" Then he looked straight at Jeremiah with a sudden piercing gaze which he knew to practice, as Jeremiah reports, like the unsheathing of a blade.

Jeremiah's breath stopped for what seemed to be an eternity, and he had the impulse to tear his own throat to make it come. Then it came. "So you do not believe in me?" he asked quietly.

"I believe in you," Mr. Madison said, "and I shall believe your word."

Looking in that face, which was grave and severe but kind, Jeremiah had the terrible temptation to tell all, to unburden himself and justify all, thinking that there he could find the comfort of justification, that that face would understand all and would speak some

271

absolution. Then he thought: *Who is this man?* There was the thought that this man came to trick him into a confession, that an ear lurked at the door, that this was all part of the great web and snare of deceit. What made him think that this man was his friend? And he thought: *I have no friend. Now I have no friend.*

So he said in sudden calm: "I give you my word, Mr. Madison. I am innocent of Fort's blood."

"Good," Mr. Madison said, "now I . . ."

"Wait," Jeremiah interrupted, and got up. "I thank you from the bottom of my heart. But I must decline your offer. What I mean is this," he hastened to add, looking into that face, "simply this. I do not go into the Court of Inquiry as an accused criminal with his defenders. I wish to go as a free man who comes to answer questions to clear his name. Do you understand my position?"

Mr. Madison bowed, and said yes, and Jeremiah studied his face for some sign, of relief or of vexation. But he saw nothing. Mr. Madison was saying, "But I wish to help you as a friend, in that case, if not as counsel. If you wish to ask me any questions, to . . ."

"I shall ask you a question now," Jeremiah said. "Will Jessup be believed?"

Mr. Madison drew down the corners of his heavy mouth. "He will probably be believed on oath," he said.

"You mean he has never been convicted of perjury?" Jeremiah asked with sarcasm.

"He has never been convicted of perjury," Mr. Madison said.

"He probably will be," Jeremiah said. And then: "And Bumps?"

"He will be believed by those who wish to believe."

"On oath?"

"No more and no less," Mr. Madison said.

"And Crawford?"

"He is an unfortunate man, but he bears a good name."

At that Jeremiah gave a brief account of the journey up, the matching of the boot and the drawing, the lost dirk, the lost handkerchief, ending by the question, "Can I trust Crawford?"

"I can only say that he bears a good name," Mr. Madison repeated.

"There is money in it," Jeremiah said bitterly.

"There is a great deal of money in it," Mr. Madison agreed. Then he fell into a study, broken a moment later. "Do you know a man named Sugg Lancaster?" he asked.

"No."

"It is given out that he will testify against you. That he has heard you speak threateningly of Fort about a private matter. At Danville, at an auction, I believe."

"To my knowledge," Jeremiah said solemnly, "I have never laid eyes on the man. And, further, I have never been in Danville in my life." But he thought: *A private matter,* and knew that Mr. Madison referred to the old scandal and he was sick with the knowledge that he might have to sit in a courtroom with a hundred leering eyes upon him and hear the story mouthed and licked. He felt gripped by shame. But no, there was no reason for shame. For Fort had fallen by his hand—but would they know, would they know? By God they must know! He wanted them to know! But if they knew? If they really knew, he was lost. By God, he cared not for them. He had drawn the dirk for justice and Rachel. Not for those drooling swine or for his vanity before their eyes. For justice!

"Good," Mr. Madison was saying.

"Who is this Lancaster?" Jeremiah asked slowly.

Mr. Madison again drew down the corners of his mouth in that expression of heavy distaste as though ready to eject something from his lips. "He came to Frankfort some six or seven years ago. With some money. He is a lawyer, of a sort. He was, I have heard, driven from the bar in Alabama. I regret to say that he has become important, locally at least, in the Relief party." He drew the mouth down again. "In politics," he said, "you cannot always choose your own bedfellows."

"A pretty parcel of knaves," Jeremiah said.

"A pretty parcel," Mr. Madison nodded. Then he smiled heavily, and looked at Jeremiah. "Better a parcel of knaves, my boy," he said, "to accuse you, than a parcel of honest men." And with that he took his leave.

He had reached the door, after the good-byes, when he turned and said, "Oh, I almost forgot. I have a letter for you. From Wilkie Barron."

"From Wilkie?" Jeremiah echoed, and his heart leaped.

Mr. Madison produced the letter, saying, "He left this morning. For Lexington. He would have waited to take your hand, but some thought it better that he go. He could do you no practical good, and . . ."

Then Mr. Madison, apparently, caught the expression on Jeremiah's face. "Oh, no," he said, "he was not among those of Relief who would have stopped my coming. Quite the contrary. But in the light of his known intimacy with you, and his position in Relief . . ." His voice trailed off, and he handed over the letter. "Good night," he said, and left Jeremiah holding the letter, which was precious to him. He was shamed that Mr. Madison had detected a trace of doubt on his face.

"Dear Friend," the letter began, but we have no more of its exact

273

words, only the comment of Jeremiah: "It made clear to me, who could read between the lines, why he had not waited for me, and breathed confidence and implied that he was the man on whom I could depend to death, and all was couched in a language of sober affection which did good to my bruised heart and made my sleep the sounder."

In the morning Jeremiah was informed that the Court of Inquiry would meet the following day, November 18, so he set himself to rehearse the evidence accumulated against him as far as he could get it from the events of the road, the papers (by now he had gone back over them all, the earlier ones which he had not seen), and from Mr. Marton, who was willing to give *quid pro quo* in the way of conversation. He was somewhat encouraged by the diversity of rumors in the earlier papers. There was, for instance, the notion that a Negro who had been disciplined on Colonel Fort's farm had slipped into town for vengeance, or the notion of an assassin hired by Relief and brought in from another part, or the notion of someone who felt himself wronged privately by some case Fort had fought. Then, from Marton, Jeremiah learned that some held that a man strange to the town, as he was, could not have known the plan of the Saunders house, or probably might not even have known of the existence of a side door. This fact implied that the deed had been done by a local citizen, or was the result of a conspiracy. And he learned, too, that Mrs. Fort declared that the man used the name of William K. instead of William J. Grierson, and that this was held by some to imply the murderer to be a citizen of Frankfort. William J. Grierson came often to Frankfort and had visited the Saunders, and the error was natural for someone here who knew him only slightly or knew about him. He learned too, that Mrs. Fort had declared that she had heard the murderer's voice, and would certainly recognize it again though in the midst of Babel. All of this was to the good.

But Jeremiah also learned that as soon as the rewards were posted the suspicion had begun to crystallize about himself. He saw what had happened. He had been selected as the pay card by Jessup and Bumps. But, in that case, why had Jessup so early turned to him, for the rewards were not officially announced until thirty-six hours after the murder? He got his answer by fishing in Marton's conversation. The morning after Fort's death, John Saunders had sworn that he would give a thousand dollars to catch the murderer and had declared that if that Relief-corrupt Legislature did not want to be tarred with complicity in the crime it had better post money and bring somebody to justice.

Jessup must have heard Saunders and have gambled on that. He must have rushed back to the house, searched Jeremiah's room, found the handkerchief, and gone back to drop it conveniently at the door. Then he must have come back again to his own house to pump Jeremiah. Then he must have admitted his friend Bumps to the secret. Probably Crawford, and perhaps the others, were innocent of the conspiracy, merely tools. Crawford had probably been drawn in to give some respectability to the plot.

But what of Sugg Lancaster, the renegade lawyer from Alabama and the local pillar of Relief? Why would he swear to his lie? Then Jeremiah thought he had that answer. The answer was money. Lancaster had set the rumor afloat to stake his claim to a share of the blood money. Well, Mr. Lancaster had made one mistake. He had already specified Danville as the place.

Perhaps Lancaster had made another mistake. Jeremiah could not remember ever having seen the man, and it was possible that Lancaster would not recognize him. He began to develop the idea of laying a trap, of having Madison collect several young men unknown to Lancaster and trapping Lancaster into a false identification. He planned to send for Mr. Madison after dinner.

But Mr. Madison came that morning, accompanied by two or three other gentlemen, one, a Captain Hornsby, who was known as strongly Anti-Relief, and was introduced to Jeremiah in those terms. Jeremiah thought he appreciated his friend's cunning: Hornsby was brought along to kill the curse of Relief on the meeting. But Jeremiah was somewhat piqued by the fact of numbers. He did not want to discuss his plan to trap Lancaster except in perfect privacy. He was, in fact, debating the advisability of asking for a few moments alone with Mr. Madison, when there was a knock, and the door opened to admit the guest who had not waited for an invitation.

Conversation died on the instant, as all eyes, without warmth, turned upon the intruder. But the intruder did not seem to mind, standing there armored in self-assurance of "triple brass."

The guest was of little more than middle height, a little less than forty years old, and dressed in considerable elegance, from varnished black boots to white neck-cloth where the knot was fixed by a ruby pin. About his shoulders hung a wide black cape which almost swept the floor with its graceful folds. The face, at first glance, was strikingly handsome, aquiline, with a high pale brow beneath precisely curly chestnut hair brushed with gray at the temples. The eyes were dark brown and large, and should have been characterized by a "slow gaze and poetic meditation," but instead they had a "nervous, prying motion and glittered over-much." The flesh beneath them was slightly swollen and against the clear, well-molded, pale cheeks seemed unnatural, as though scarcely healed from bruising. The mouth, beneath a silky mustache, was full and flexible and remarkably red, "as though stained with berries, and when it opened you were surprised not to see the little seeds flecking his white teeth."

"Ah, gentlemen," he said, "I trust that I do not intrude." He spoke in a slow, very musical voice, which caressed the ear. But no one answered a word, and those lips which apparently were designed for "an expression of melancholy, almost female sweetness, drew back as from long practice into a twisted, thinning smile which made you think of new silk being ripped by a careless blade for wantonness or in hatred and contempt."

Then, very deliberately in the silence, the guest took two steps toward the group, saying, "Mr. Madison, I thought I might find you here. Mr. Skrogg tells me that he has word for you of some importance, and looks for you at your convenience."

But all the while his glance was flicking over Jeremiah's face.

"Thank you, Mr. Lancaster," Mr. Madison said heavily, as though he were tossing an indifferent stone from his hand, and did not rise.

Jeremiah got up. "Is this," he asked Mr. Madison, "Mr. Sugg Lancaster, the lawyer from, I believe, Alabama?"

Mr. Madison nodded.

Jeremiah stepped out of the group and confronted him, but Lancaster gave no ground and the smile of his face did not change. "Ah, Mr. Beaumont, so we meet again," he said, and, as Jeremiah puts it, staked all on that card.

"Will you swear that you have seen me before?" Jeremiah demanded.

"I think I called you by your name," Lancaster said, and smiled again.

"Any fool, coming into this room, could have selected me."

"I scarcely think I bear that name," Lancaster said, and with his fingertips flicked dust off his dark plum waistcoat.

"Whatever name you bear," Jeremiah said, "where do you pretend to have met me?"

"At Danville, of course. At the lot auction. Don't you remember, Mr. Beaumont?"

"Who introduced you?"

"Judge Pomfrey, Judge Lucius Pomfrey."

Jeremiah turned to the group. "I hope you have listened well," he said. Then to Lancaster: "I know no Judge Pomfrey. Produce him and he will so testify. And I have never been in Danville in my life. I can prove that."

"Danville," Lancaster said musingly and with no mark of embarrassment. "I had thought it was Danville. But you see, I have traveled so much."

"Yes, from Alabama, I hear," Jeremiah said, "and not always of your own free will. Take care that you do not travel again."

"Danville," Lancaster repeated in the same tone as before, ignoring Jeremiah's insult. "Perhaps not Danville. But I shall remember. And I shall remember who introduced us. I have a very good memory."

"Does the chink of coin rouse it?" Jeremiah asked.

"And I'll remember what you said to me when we met," Lancaster said, and smiled again, but this time a smile of pitying friendliness, so sweet and sincere that you took that face to be the face of your dearest other self.

For one instant, looking into that smile, Jeremiah felt a gush of warm gratitude for the pity. Then, with a wrench of nausea for his own weakness (*My God, do I want pity, and from that?*), he said: "Better remember what I say to you now at our first meeting: you are a blackguard, sir."

But the pitying smile remained on Lancaster's face, as he slowly shook his head. "Poor Beaumont," he murmured, and turned, and stepped to the door. There he looked back, said, "Mr. Madison, I shall tell Skrogg I have found you," bowed, and left the room.

There was silence, and Jeremiah heard his own harsh breathing.

Then Captain Hornsby said, as though to himself: "He is a black-guard."

One of the other men laughed. "Do you call him a blackguard, Captain," he asked, "because he winged you in that article he wrote for the *Advocate?*"

Captain Hornsby said: "He is a blackguard. But a clever black-guard. I am glad he is not of my party."

"The Lord uses strange instruments to bring on his just will," the other man, a Reliefer, said, and laughed.

And those words of idle jest twisted in Jeremiah's heart like a blade.

Thus Jeremiah Beaumont met Sugg Lancaster, the man to whom he was tied by a thousand filmy strands, and who was tied to him, as though they were two flies caught in the same web. And in the end, each struggled desperately to be free of the other and to climb upon him, like two swimmers drowning together. But the filmy web that held them together was stronger than steel, because each strand was a lie, and the element they foundered in was more suffocating than water, because it was a lie.

Sugg Lancaster. He had come from a Piedmont cabin in North Carolina, or South Carolina (we cannot be sure, for the most we have is gossip worn thin by a century), a sickly, big-eyed child spawned into poverty and dirt and short rations and the contempt of the burly and brutal around him, but with a contempt for them and their world to match any contempt they could spit upon him. Somehow he learned to read, probably from some Presbyterian preacher who saw in those deep eyes and that spiritual face the mark of the call. Then there is a gap in the story, until the morning when (he is about sixteen then) he is found lying sick with a fever on the street of a hamlet in Georgia and out of pity is taken to the house of a rich man named Maddox. He recovers, is made much of by the rich man's wife and is grudgingly tolerated by the old man himself, who probably saw little to admire in the delicate, princely hands and matchstick shanks of the stray youth who could tell no straight story but talked vaguely of being spurned and defrauded of his rights and driven into the world. And the Maddox son (we can guess what he was like, heavy-handed and red-faced, limber and tough as steel in the saddle, arrogant, ignorant, and profane, experienced before his time with the black wenches and the town sluts, the pride and joy of a back-country planter and the despair of a gentle mother) makes the boy's life a burden, until he leaves, driven out by the persecution of the son or the decision of the father.

Within a few months the son is dead of the fever, and the grief-stricken mother and father see this as a judgment on themselves. (It is no doubt this moral which put the tale into folklore and the pulpit.) They harry the country for a hundred miles seeking the lost youth with the pale face, deep eyes, and curly hair, and in the end find him and bring him back. For some years he lives in their house as a son, comforts the woman's grief and sings by her bed, the sad songs of his hill childhood, and even stirs some spark of pride in the old man by his aptitude for learning. So the old man, probably thinking to have a statesman in the house, puts him to the law with a judge in Macon. He does well there at his books, and moves in the best society. This until some insult, or perhaps even a casual, innocent overheard word, about his obscure origins. He returns home, robs the old planter's cash box, and disappears.

Somewhat later, a grown man now, about thirty, Sugg Lancaster reappears in Alabama (though some versions have it Tennessee) and prospers at the practice of law. But his taste for elegance and high living over-reach even his income, and the talk of crooked dealings begins to throttle his practice. He has his defenders, however, for he knows how to charm and is adept with middle-aged women, especially widows. His charm merely delays his ruin in Alabama (or Tennessee), or perhaps brings it on by flattering his confidence.

He becomes involved in a particularly sordid affair. The details are not clear, but he undertakes, presumably out of the goodness of his heart, to defend two manumitted slaves against the claim of an heir, and wins the case to the applause of the bar and all high-minded citizens. Then it is discovered that he has sold the two Negroes to an outlaw slave-runner, using the pretext that he is getting them out of the country for their own good. Then, after a blank period, Sugg Lancaster appears in Frankfort, from Louisiana, according to his tale, and makes his way into a position of some importance in the local life, especially in the Relief party.

At this time he enters the story of Jeremiah Beaumont, with his black cape, ruby pin, and twisted smile like ripped silk.

He survives the story of Jeremiah Beaumont, but only in his ruin. His part in the trouble destroys his reputation, and even his arrogance and charm cannot save him. He salvages what he can, seduces a widow (not even a very rich widow) and starts down the Ohio with her on a steamboat. At some point he abandons her, stripped of every-thing but the clothes on her back, and disappears.

No transcript survives of the hearings of the Court of Inquiry at Frankfort before which Jeremiah appeared. We have only his abbre-viated account of the proceedings in his narrative.

"I came before Justices McWhitty and Alsopp on the appointed day, accompanied by a great crowd of the curious who filled the streets outside. Mr. Madison would have been by my side, not as a counsel but as a friend, but I insisted on being alone.

"After the prescribed preliminaries, the farce began by a measur-ing of my foot, for which purpose we all went outside and I set my foot in the dust of the street while people shoved and shouted as at a cock fight. Then Bumps produced the paper with what purported to be the true picture of the track found beneath the Saunders win-dow, and they set to measuring under the eyes of the Justices. I had expected to see Bumps discomfited by this, but soon realized that the paper he now produced came nearer to fitting my track, and cursed myself for my innocence in not knowing that he would have by this time a new drawing with the 'woggling' more to his purpose. I was debating the advisability of telling the Court how at the test in the lane the drawing had not fit my boot and demanding that Crawford be sworn on the point (though I feared to push him too hard early, and meditated having some man of wealth and respect such as Madi-son put the matter to him flatteringly as one honest gentleman to another). But I was relieved of my problems by a young man who presented himself to the Justices, and was greeted most respectfully by the name of Hawgood (Hilton Hawgood, as I was to learn, a man of genius and excellent promise, and as true a heart as ever beat—ah, Hawgood, forgive me that I was not worthy of your best love and honesty, but take this tribute).

"He was sworn, and testified that he himself had been at the

Saunders house that morning of the murder, and had taken careful measurements of the track. Whereupon he produced a little book from his pocket, and offered it to the Justices, who called for a ruler and measured my mark in the dust and then the sole of my boot. They declared that the measurements recorded by Hawgood did not match my own.

"But Bumps cried out that that feller did not have nothing but 'figgers' and he had a true 'pitcher,' and others cried out, too, that a 'pitcher' was better. Then there was much swearing and counter-swearing, and perjury flourished like burdock by a dung-heap.

"Bumps, Jessup, and Showforth swore they had been present when Crawford made the drawing, and Crawford, unhappy in the face, swore he had made a drawing. Was it the same as that now produced? Crawford said he could not swear that, for it had been in the hands of Bumps, but Bumps swore and Showforth swore, and pointed to some miraculous little secret mark on the paper to prove it. I debated again whether I should call Crawford to swear to the measurement made in the lane, but decided to hold that. And Hawgood all the while stood contemptuously by, and then declared again most solemnly that his measurements were accurate and could not be my own. But some in the crowd cried that it was four against one and one man's word was good as another's or it was no democracy.

"Then the handkerchief was sworn to by several, and in various descriptions so that the instability of the human mind and observation was never more exhibited. But there was no object to confute the false descriptions, for Jarvis had just returned without it, and I began to regret that fact, for the handkerchief if produced would have discredited many.

"There was more swearing about the handkerchiefs to my hurt, before Hawgood spoke again and to the effect that when he had walked the grounds by the door of the Saunders house at an early hour, before the time when it was said the handkerchief was found (that was sworn to as seven o'clock), he had found no trace of a handkerchief despite his careful search for any marks. But Jessup and Bumps and others swore to finding the handkerchief, and there was much talk about it being still too dark when Hawgood looked to find it.

"I then accused Bumps of having wilfully lost it, and the dirk, but did not press that Crawford be sworn, but complimented him upon his honesty in forcing a search at Bardstown, though he had not done so without the support of old Mr. Bascomb, I was sure in my heart.

"Then I was asked what business had brought me to Frankfort, and I told how I had been interested in land speculation and had come for my patents but the clerk had not found them. The clerk of the

Registrar swore that none had been filed, and I pointed out that I had sent them by Captain Marlowe, who would swear to that fact and the time and how I had tried to hire him to come to Frankfort for me. There was some talk of postponement to send for Marlowe.

"But to my surprise, with little time for consideration, I was bound over for trial. I say to my surprise, for in common decency Marlowe and others whom I mentioned in my defense should have been called. I was not low in spirit, however, and thanked the Court for its courtesy, and expressed my willingness to abide the event, for I rested in my innocence and in the logic of circumstances when all should be sorted and brought to light.

"At my speech there was some cheering, but also jeers and hisses, for men were much agitated and confused in their hotness of blood and feebleness of mind, so that for both parties I had equal disdain.

"I went away with the Sheriff, Mr. Hubbard, a most decent man who treated me with courtesy, and took me back to Mr. Marton's house and not to jail, saying he knew I was anxious to stay for my good name and future and would not flee. Then he laughed and said that the gaming gentry would give odds on my acquittal and book was being made.

"So I said that was good news, for where a man's money lay, there lay the heart also."

That evening Hilton Hawgood called on Jeremiah. He was in a state of considerable excitement not entirely suppressed. He spoke with warmth of the disgrace of the hearings, and how he as a lawyer was shamed for the Commonwealth and had made no secret of his feelings. He went on to say that he had been a friend of Fort and a worker for Anti-Relief, for Relief as he saw it had tried to work for justice outside the holy bonds of law. But the same motive, he said, that made him work for Anti-Relief would now make him work for Jeremiah's salvation, if Jeremiah would permit him, and he asked no pay but a good conscience.

Jeremiah thanked him, and he left.

Jeremiah was almost elated. Hawgood, as Anti-Relief, could not be accused of partisan motive, and Jeremiah, as many men, had fallen under the spell of Hawgood's sincerity of purpose and purity of spirit.

For Hawgood had those things. They shone through his nondescript person and thin, sharp face. He had great abilities, and at a tender age was to become Attorney General of Kentucky and a member of Congress. The abilities are remembered at least in the two or three paragraphs allotted to him in the histories of the Commonwealth, but the legend of his integrity lived for a time on the tongues of men as well as on the printed page. But that is gone now, too, and all we have left is the engraving, preserved at Frankfort, of the thin, sharp, asymmetrical face, the face of a village schoolteacher, a little acid and impatient, for the light that shone through those features is lost on the paper.

Hilton Hawgood died very young, at Washington, during his first session in Congress. He died of a fever after but a few days of illness. When the physician told him there was little hope, and a nurse by the bed cried out, "Oh, he is so young!" Hawgood smiled and said, "Brief summons, but I go in God's will and the hope that He may find yet on a happier shore some small task for my hand and His glory."

If Jeremiah was encouraged by the odds given by the gaming gentry for his acquittal and by the support of Hawgood, he was also encouraged by the fact that now, without embarrassment, he could accept Mr. Madison as counsel. He would have a defender in each camp.

He reflected with satisfaction on another event of the day. Sugg Lancaster had not testified. He had frightened off that worthy.

VIII

JEREMIAH BEAUMONT SAT IN HIS ROOM IN
the Marton house (with a guard outside his door and another beneath his window) and waited for his trial. But long before the trial
the world outside that room was trying his case, and what was to happen in the courtroom was merely an epilogue to the action, a sum-
ming up of accounts already cast. Jeremiah Beaumont was a chip on
the tide of things, a tide shot through by sudden rips and twisted
currents.

But if Jeremiah Beaumont was a chip on the tide, he was a thinking
and suffering chip, and his dearest thought was that he was not a
chip at all but a mariner who had made calculation of tides and a
decision for his course. His calculation was that in the very confusion
of currents lay his hope, for once he had struck the right one he might
ride it through and thread past all dangers to his peace.

He thought he knew the world for which he had contempt, the public drifts and private passions. And probably he knew it as well as
most, for it was a world that did not know itself.

Old Court and New Court, each thought it was the world, and
justice.

Justice.

The Old Court said: The Law exists, The Constitution exists. They
exist by the sanction of Nature and Society. They are not Justice, for

Justice is a spirit never seen, but only through them can Justice speak. Untune them and all is jangle.

The New Court said: The Law exists. The Constitution exists. But they exist only by the decision of man and what man can make he can unmake. As for Justice, that is the name for the needs of man. Justice is man's Goddess but is also his slave. Let man seize her naked and make her speak.

As Tibbett Wyman said in a speech at Louisville, reported in the Frankfort Anti-Relief *Commonwealth:* "The Constitution is the temple of Justice established by covenant. Destroy that sacred fabric, profane that altar, intrude upon the privacy of that most secret room where burns the mystic flame to have your violent will, and nought can be found therein, for the unhoused Goddess shall have fled."

But as Ashel Hanks said after he was arrested for shooting the sheriff of Warren County, who had come to take his stock for debt: "The law may be the law, and I ain't saying it ain't, but a cow is a cow and I shot the son-of-a-bitch." So Ashel had broken into that "most secret room where burns the mystic flame," and had found, contrary to Tibbett Wyman's prediction, the Goddess of Justice, which, for him, at the moment, had the form of a slab-sided frontier cow.

So Jeremiah Beaumont had broken into that room in the very heart of the temple and had, like Ashel, found the Goddess and had seized her naked and wrenched the knife from her grasp and instructed her in her duty.

He had done justice, and it was not just that he should suffer for doing justice. But the world did not understand justice. He had gone alone to the secret room, and those who had not been there could never understand. Therefore, to do justice for Justice, he would have to save himself, alone.

To save himself he trusted in the confusion of the world, in the struggle between Old Court and New Court. The very identity of his victim placed the issue squarely there, for Colonel Fort was the champion of his party. The Old Court and Anti-Relief expected him to undo all that had been done, to destroy the pretenders and restore the Constitution. It was said that his prestige, after his sweeping victory in Pick County, where Relief had been strong, would count a score of votes in the House. It was said that he had a plan, to be divulged on the very day the Legislature met.

We do not know what the plan was. But we have the word, on oath, of John Saunders that Fort had come to him, very excited, one night, and roused him from sleep to say, "I have found a way to reconcile the differences in our unhappy country. I have found a way to reconcile all. I have found a way to save the Constitution and yet satisfy all in justice."

284

Fort did not tell Saunders the nature of his plan. He was a man to keep his own counsel, and all we have is the word of the brother-in-law and the report from several other men high in the Old Court party that Fort had questioned them closely on law and policy without divulging his main line of thought but had promised to reveal all in a conference the morning of the opening session.

But Jeremiah Beaumont's knife struck him down, and events followed their own blind, massive drift, with Jeremiah Beaumont caught up in them.

It was vanity that came first to Jeremiah's aid. It was the vanity of Stella Fort, the widow of Colonel Fort. Of Mrs. Fort, Jeremiah knew nothing more than was common report, that Mrs. Fort had been sickly in recent years and that she and her husband did not get along very well together.

Our own inquiries give us little more. Stella Saunders was one of the three children of the first John Saunders in Kentucky, a Virginian of good family who repaired his fallen fortunes in the West and built a house, later occupied by the Jessups, in Frankfort. But by the time of his death, in 1808, his affairs were again in confusion, and all he left to young John Saunders, Stella and Martha was the house in town and a small holding near Versailles. At that time the son was eighteen years old and reading law in an office in Frankfort, Stella was twenty-three, and Martha several years older. Both the girls were unmarried.

Within a year after the death of the father both girls had married. Stella married Cassius Fort and Martha married Caleb Jessup. Both girls married beneath themselves in family name, but the marriages must have seemed good enough.

Jessup was a burly fellow, several years younger than Martha, roistering and popular among men and reported to be sharp. It was assumed, no doubt, that he would settle down now, and a strong back, a gift for getting on with people, and a reputation for cunning made good enough capital in that opening country. But we have already seen Jessup and what happened to him, a shapeless hulk of a man paring his corns by the hearth of his ruined house. Martha had made a bad gamble.

But Stella had made no gamble at all. When she married Fort he was already a person of consequence, no longer the orphan boy of a stockade, but a famous lawyer and rich landowner. And he was the soul of magnanimity. He made his wife renounce her share of the Saunders estate, so that the Jessups might set up in the family house and John Saunders might have the land. He took John out of the office where he read law and made him his own assistant with such good effect that after a little the boy had a practice of his own in

Frankfort, after Fort had moved south to Bowling Green to be nearer his lands on the Green River. They said in Frankfort that to hire Saunders to take your case was just a good way to get Fort cheap. John Saunders no doubt knew this, but his pride was never hurt. He had gratitude to Fort, or rather what seems to have been a fanatical devotion.

There was nothing wrong with Stella's marriage except that it lacked love. Perhaps Stella had married for security and vanity in Fort's fame, hoping for love to come. Or perhaps there had been love, or what seemed like love in a situation so flattering. As for Fort, there is no reason to assume that he did not love her, at least in the beginning, and he may have loved her until the end. He had been faithful to her for years—at least there was no breath of rumor to the contrary —and after the relation with Rachel Jordan he came back to be the devoted husband in a joyless house.

There were no children. There had not even been that to hold husband and wife together. Stella could not, apparently, follow Fort's restless mind and lavish energies. The spoiled favorite child of a doting father could not find a new role, and Fort could not play the role she would have assigned him. So she lay in her shuttered room, and Fort spent his strength on the world outside, the great Colonel Fort with the heavy, swarthy face wearing the animal sadness and the blank question.

Then Fort died. The widow's health improved within a few months. She became active in all good works, and punctuated prayers and pieties with dishes of tea taken in the parlors of the more select Frankfort ladies. She always referred to her dead husband with the greatest reverence and affection and did not tire of singing his praises and bewailing his martyrdom. In the end, we can guess, she was perfectly happy. Her early wisdom was justified now and her marriage gave her everything she really needed. She always carried a little picture of her dear husband in her reticule, and showed it to all who would look.

But for the period just after the murder, she lay abed in an almost hysterical condition. According to reports in Frankfort, no doubt set afloat by Jessup, she was convinced that Jeremiah Beaumont was the assassin and, though she had never seen him, her reported descriptions fitted him like a glove. And his voice, she knew that she could identify that voice anywhere.

Madison and Hawgood kept Jeremiah informed of these rumors. "She has been played upon," Mr. Madison said. "She is not in a responsible condition, and she has been played upon."

"For profit," Hawgood added. "For I am sure that Jessup, who by family connection has access to the house, will claim a share of the reward if you are convicted.

"Will the word of a woman in her condition be given weight as evidence?" Jeremiah asked.

Mr. Madison said that it was impossible to predict.

"Fools!" Jeremiah exclaimed and rose from his chair and paced the room. "Fools!" he exclaimed again, "why don't they know that she could not possibly . . ."

He stopped.

"Could not possibly what?" Mr. Madison demanded, and Jeremiah suddenly saw that Hawgood's gaze was fixed curiously upon him.

He had almost said: ". . . could not possibly identify me—for she never saw my face, only the mask, and the old coat concealed my figure, it was so loose, and for my voice, why, I spoke in a false voice." But he stopped just in time, shuddering on the brink of the revelation. The words of Mrs. Fort, they were another lie. Lies were everywhere, in every chink and cranny and augur-hole. Lies were everywhere waiting to strike him. Or, more cunningly to trick him into self-condemnation to confute them. My God, if he could only tell the truth. My God, the truth would put an end to lies! The truth would come like a strong wind to blow down the fog and stinks of lies.

But Mr. Madison was saying again, in his even voice: "Could not possibly what, Mr. Beaumont?"

Jeremiah sat down. "Don't they know that a woman in her condition could not possibly be trusted?"

"Let us hope so," Mr. Madison said soberly.

He fell into meditation for a moment, then said, "I do not understand Saunders. I have known him long, and found him to be a sensible and honest man. But he is not himself now. He was devoted to Fort. Fort was his idol and God, and he is bent on blood for blood."

"But why *my* blood?" Jeremiah demanded. "When they have no evidence? What have I ever done to Saunders?"

(And Jeremiah reports that that question sprang unawares to his lips, and in all sincerity, so that he marveled at the words as though spoken by another through his mouth. In that instant he felt a great lightness and cleansing, as though he had had no part in all that happened, and *was* innocent and could trust his innocence. So to cling to that innocence, though unthinkingly, he demanded again, "What have I ever done to him?" But this time the answer lay in his bosom, a cold lump where his heart should have been.)

About this time help came to Jeremiah from a most unexpected quarter and contrary to the intention of the agent—from the Prosecutor for the Commonwealth, Nathan Gregg. Gregg was of the New Court persuasion, though more of a trimmer than a fanatic, if we are to judge from his subsequent devious career. In so far as he was a New Court and Relief man, he must have rejoiced to see Fort struck down, but at the same time the fact of his political difference from the victim made it the more necessary to push the case with energy to establish himself as a man of honesty above party prejudice. It was his great chance.

Within a few days after the Court of Inquiry he had laid hand on one of the handbills used against Fort in his recent campaign, the handbill accusing him of seduction and bastardy. No doubt he had known of the old gossip and of the new use it had been put to. But he also must have known that in the campaigns of that time no charge was too vile or baseless to find a place. So now he sought to establish a motive beyond question for the accused. He had the delicate mission of sounding out John Saunders and Mrs. Fort.

We do not know what passed at that interview, but we do know that at that moment the charges hurled at Jeremiah from Mrs. Fort's bed suddenly ceased. Her wifely vanity became more important than her vengeance. If the case should involve the liaison between her husband and Rachel Jordan, she would be branded as the despised woman. It was more than she could bear.

To support this vanity came another. John Potter, the editor of the *Commonwealth*, was a sympathizer with the Old Court under the guise of non-partisanship. But Sabot Mickwell, the editor of the official Old Court paper, the *People's Hope*, had not shared with him the early news of Jeremiah's arrest and the details of the case, and Potter was not committed to a view about Jeremiah's guilt. It was easy for him now to undercut Mickwell's prestige with the party, and to curry favor with the Fort connection, by taking a new line. Besides, he was a friend of John Saunders.

So John Potter published an editorial charging that Fort's assassination was purely political, "planned by some inner junto of the party that knows no law." He accused the Prosecutor of trying to conceal this fact by blowing up the flame of old gossip never substantiated, and of hastening to lay the guilt on "an unimportant young man who had the misfortune to be in Frankfort on the fatal night and who was noised to nurse a private grief against the great Fort, the Father of our Hopes." And he concluded: "No, Fort fell by no common hand! And for that bloodstained hand look among those that would profit most by his end."

So to Mrs. Fort's wifely vanity was added the vanity of being the widow of a savior and martyr. And for a time she would hear no word against "that unfortunate young man." John Saunders looked grave and said that he wanted only justice no matter where it struck, and friends of the family knew their duty and affection to take the same line in parlor or tavern.

Jeremiah could scarcely believe his luck when Mr. Madison brought him the copy of John Potter's *Commonwealth* with the editorial dominating the sheet. With beating heart he read it, then lifted his face to Mr. Madison. "This is good news for me," he said, "but not good news for you. It will embarrass you with your party."

"Son," Mr. Madison said, and laid a hand on Jeremiah's shoulder, "don't worry for me."

Looking up into Mr. Madison's face, Jeremiah felt the hand, he says, like a crushing weight that would bow him to the ground.

But the good luck was good luck, even if he had to pay for it with pain under Mr. Madison's fatherly hand. And the good luck grew. Before long Mickwell's paper was shifting ground, bit by bit; dark hints against high-placed New Courters ran the town, and the state; and a Negro coachman, glittering with teeth and brass buttons, and worth at least $1200 even in the bad market, delivered a basket of wine to Jeremiah's room. The wine was from Mrs. Docker, a prodigiously rich old dame who was prodigiously devoted to the Old Court and sound mortgages. Then cakes, jellies and sweetmeats came from other sources scarcely less elevated, and Jeremiah smiled wryly to find himself the darling of the enemy.

As for the New Court party, it was apparently split on the subject of Jeremiah's guilt; Aden Kilmore's *Spy* sneered at Jeremiah's new role and made much of the old gossip, but more to injure Fort's fame than to harm Jeremiah. Skrogg's *Advocate* violently repelled the accusation of a New Court conspiracy for the assassination, but in regard to Jeremiah maintained an Olympian impartiality, asking only that the facts be sifted to the last grain. Skrogg himself came to the Marton house on one occasion, in broad daylight, and paid his respects.

He was the same old Skrogg, wax-skinned and ice-eyed, with the thin lips scarcely meeting over the white teeth and sweat beading at the temples when he coughed into his dingy handkerchief. He sat by the fire and had little to say, nursing his sickness and his inner flame, staring at Jeremiah palely, without interest or calculation, "as at a page he knew the substance of already."

Then he rose, teetered crankily on his legs, and offered Jeremiah his cold, brittle hand. He wished him well, he said, "if well might be," and with that less than comforting phrase, took his leave.

Why had he come? Out of partisan feeling? Out of curiosity? Out of gratitude for Jeremiah's work in the old brawl at Lumton? Out of policy? It was none of those things, Jeremiah decided, and could not settle on the answer then. Later he was to decide that Skrogg had come to put himself, Skrogg, to a test, to know a truth about himself.

Skrogg found that truth.

Then a letter came from Wilkie. Wilkie was down in Bowling Green, where he had been called on urgent family affairs (his mother was ill) and where he would have to remain for some time. But his heart bled for Jeremiah's plight, and he personally was sure of Jeremiah's innocence, despite any color of circumstance to the contrary or previous talk. "I am sure," he said, "you had never been so cunning to do the deed in darkness and subterfuge and not in the blazing sun of honor. So when any here speak of the odds of your guilt, I repel indignantly the thought and affirm, no, that would never be Beaumont's way, for I know his manly spirit."

Jeremiah read the letter with a gush of warmth in his heart, gratitude for a steadfast friend like Wilkie. Then he looked again at the words, and knew that they were not for him. For one moment he had taken them for himself, and had been that Jeremiah Beaumont to whom Wilkie wrote, the Jeremiah whose actions were beyond cunning and lived only in the blazing sun of honor. So he had stood in the middle of the room, feeling confident and free.

But the letter was not for him. It was for someone else, some happy impostor who also bore the name of Jeremiah Beaumont and who knew nothing of the dark anguish of life. But he himself—the real Jeremiah Beaumont—was trapped in that anguish, was snarled in the thousand clinging threads of lies, was drowning in lies, and nobody could stretch out a hand to him, nobody would write him a letter.

There was the flood of winter sunlight in the empty room. He was alone. And he was what he was.

But before the despair could overwhelm him again, the rage came. By God, he was what he was, and he was not ashamed. What did they know, any of them, Wilkie or Madison or Hawgood, what did they know of what the world was like? By God, he had tried. He had tried to do all in the blazing sun of honor.

By God, he had tried, but they had not let him. The world had not let him. It was the world's fault that he had come by night with a mask on his face. For that was the way of the world. To drive you to a lie and then snare you by lies and false witness against all facts in the case.

No, worse, by God, they came and laid a hand on your shoulder, they looked in your face and called you a man of honor and took your word, they wrote you a letter to proclaim confidence in you, that you would do nothing not in the blazing sun of honor. For that was the world's last trick, to torture and snare you by honor, till you almost burst out with truth. To send the men of honor to smile at you with their clear eyes in which lurked the last treason.

By God, he hated them all, the Madisons, the Hawgoods, the Wilkies of the world. He spat upon them, for they knew nothing.

They did not know that the price of truth was lies.

He was suddenly calm in that thought. He was himself, and could not be otherwise. He would regret no more, and yearn no more. He would be strong enough to pay the price for truth. Rachel would understand.

And if she did not understand? If she did not?

Then, by God, he was himself. And the truth was his own truth.

He stood in the drenching sunlight, in the empty room, and heard his breath subside.

So he entered upon a period of great calm and inner confidence. He drank with relish the wine brought by Mrs. Docker's glittering coachman, and ate the sweetmeats sent by other great ones of the Old Court. Then, when whisky and venison came from families sympathizing with the New Court, for they were soon clever enough not to be outdone, to show that they trusted in justice, too, and would not have him killed to clear a party—for certainly the party was innocent—then Jeremiah ate and drank with impartial appetite, and nothing stuck in his throat.

Despite the hampers and platters and bottles from New Court and Old, Jeremiah knew that forces still moved against him in the world outside. Would Bumps and Jessup so easily surrender hope of the reward for their labors? They still got drunk and boasted in the taverns. They took men aside and whispered of new evidence that they saved for the trial. And Nathan Gregg, the Prosecutor for the Commonwealth, was still determined. He was gone now down to the Green River country and had sworn that he would bring back enough evidence to hang a dozen Beaumonts. He had had the trial, originally set for January, postponed. Madison and Hawgood had thought best not to oppose this. They rested in the certainty of innocence.

They were not even disturbed by Sugg Lancaster, who had begun again to proclaim that he had met Jeremiah Beaumont long before, and could produce witnesses to that fact, and that Jeremiah had made damaging admissions to him. Lancaster no longer named a place and time of that meeting. He gave only dark hints, and said, wait, they would see at the trial, for he, Lancaster, would be the man to put the rope around Beaumont's neck.

He was seen much with Jessup and Bumps, drinking with them, his elegance, his black cape and ruby pin and pale high brow and poetic glance incongruous beside their greasy coats and bloated faces. But he listened to them respectfully, and poured likker into their mugs, and slapped them on the back and laughed. Mr. Madison brought that news. "He must have made a deal with them," Mr. Madison said. "To divide the reward on good terms."

"Perjurers, blackguards and suborners together," Hawgood said bitterly.

Mr. Madison laughed. "Together like they belong," he said. "Give them rope and they'll hang themselves."

"Just so they don't hang me first," Jeremiah retorted wryly, and then they all laughed together at his joke.

They had no fear of Lancaster. Mr. Madison already was in correspondence with Alabama and Louisiana, assembling information about him. He was glad for the postponement of the trial. By that time he would have character statements about Lancaster from responsible men, and information of more than one scandal.

They were more disturbed about the Prosecutor, especially when they learned that Lancaster had visited him by night and had been admitted at a doorway with no light. And after Gregg's return from the Green River country, he and Lancaster were seen familiarly together at Versailles. "Gregg is honest," Hawgood said. "He is vain, ambitious and stiff in opinion, but he is honest. I wonder that he should believe and use Lancaster."

"Lancaster would use him," Mr. Madison said. "He is probably trying to betray Bumps and Jessup, and insure himself a larger share of the reward."

We shall never know if there was truth in Mr. Madison's surmise. Perhaps Bumps and Jessup did discover that Lancaster was trying to undercut them with the prosecution, and took their own measures. Or perhaps they decided that they would be fools to split with Lancaster, when they could get a conviction without him and when they already had the expense of Crawford and Showforth and Jarvis, and so devised the complicated plot that gradually emerged in the following months. Or perhaps there was no plot. Perhaps they merely improvised brilliantly at the last when the game was running against them and all seemed lost.

The clear facts are these:

In early February, at the height of Lancaster's intimacy with Bumps and Jessup, the *Commonwealth* published another editorial by John Potter, reaffirming his charge that the death of Fort was planned by an "inner junto" of the New Court party. He had new evidence, he asserted, which would appear when the hour was ripe. Meanwhile, he wrote:

There is a certain unsavory hireling of New Court in our midst who has already perjured himself to send to the gallows Jeremiah Beaumont, and who now gives out, unashamed by the detection of his former lies, that he will yet hang Beaumont. Why is he so anxious in this course? For love of Fort and Jus-

292

tice? Posh and piffle! It is known to me that he himself had grievously libeled that great man in the public press, though hidden by the name of "Candidus," and that Fort making discovery was meditating the only measure a man of honor can take against such vermin. And is "Candidus" a man of courage to stand against a Fort armed in righteous wrath? No, for he lacked courage to write over his true name. Therefore, I say, seek out this "Candidus" and make him give full account. Fort's blood cries out!

We know that Lancaster was the "Candidus" who had written scurrilous articles for Skrogg's *Advocate*. Did John Potter know this, or did he make a shrewd guess? Mr. Madison, who was of the inner junto of the New Court and a friend of Skrogg, did not know the identity of "Candidus," at least, not at this time. For when he brought Potter's editorial to Jeremiah, he said as much. And added: "I had not thought it wise of Skrogg to use the articles, for they slandered decent men. I told him as much, but Skrogg . . ." He hesitated, and shrugged his heavy shoulders. "But Skrogg," he continued, "you know him. His heart, his life, is New Court and Relief. They are wife and child to him, the image of justice. He will do anything for them. Put his hand in the fire, if need be. He is wedded to justice, and he will do anything for that good end."

So Jeremiah reports Mr. Madison's words, and reporting them, adds that he took a kind of joy in them. For if Mr. Madison could thus condone Skrogg's act because Skrogg served the good end of justice, then Mr. Madison would understand him, Jeremiah Beaumont, and how all he had done, however crooked and dark, had been done but for justice, too. And he was almost tempted to speak out, and tell all.

But he did not, and Mr. Madison was saying: "I do not know that Lancaster is Candidus. If he is, so much the worse for New Court, for he is a blackguard and I would he were not of our faction."

"You may keep him, and welcome," Hilton Hawgood said in amiable sarcasm.

"Politics, politics," Mr. Madison laughed, and shrugged again. Then he fell to brooding over the paper. At length he said: "It is possible. If Lancaster is Candidus, and if Fort knew. It is possible that Lancaster . . ."

"If Lancaster is not too much of a coward," Hawgood cut in.

"It was a coward's deed," Mr. Madison retorted, "to strike Fort unarmed, and in the dark."

And at that, Jeremiah's guts went cold and his head swam with a great giddiness as though he had been "Icarus and the waxed wings

293

melted in the sun's heat and he falling through the horrible emptiness of air."

Mr. Madison and Hawgood were agreeing to investigate Lancaster, if there was more to Potter's suspicion.

Potter promised more. Within a week he had reiterated his charge, still avoiding Lancaster's name but unmistakably indicating him as the assassin and tool of the New Court.

Frankfort buzzed with the talk. Lancaster did not show himself on the street for two weeks. Then he was out again in daylight, busily conferring in low tones with those he could catch on the corners or in the taverns, explaining, justifying, accusing, swearing he had evidence against Beaumont. But more than one important man in the New Court turned on a heel, and left him with the words on his lips. Desperation began for Lancaster.

Then the real blow fell. John Saunders stated publicly that Fort had threatened to challenge Candidus when he should know the true name, and Potter published the statement in the *Commonwealth,* and added that a "citizen of repute and a connection of Fort" had privately told him that Fort had guessed the identity and discovered it to him, and that the said citizen would swear to the fact. We can be sure that Jessup was the "citizen of repute." Was this a step in a careful plot, or an improvisation? It scarcely matters, for Jessup was gaining his end: he was cutting Lancaster out from the reward for Beaumont, and if Lancaster himself should come to trial and be convicted, then Jessup could claim a share in that—and with no necessity to take his confederates into account.

Lancaster twisted and turned in mortal agony. More desperately he waylaid men on the streets and began his explanations in that low, melodious, insinuating voice. More desperately he offered drinks in taverns, and the drinks were refused. More desperately he contrived new hints. His judgment forsook him. He compounded lie with lie. He had seen Beaumont on such a date and at such a place. Then at another place and another time. He had met him at Barker's Well and remembered the occasion perfectly. He had met him at a horse run at Bowling Green. He had not met him at all, he had merely the hearsay from a certain responsible man who later had confided Beaumont's threat against Fort. He sent a letter to Jeremiah and asked for an interview "to set all straight," and wished him health and good fortune. There was no answer to the letter.

The trial was postponed again. Rumor had it that Gregg was at last being forced to investigate Lancaster and that the case against Jeremiah would be dropped. Then that Lancaster had agreed to divulge a conspiracy against Fort, naming the great men of the New Court, as a price for immunity.

Then Lancaster left Frankfort.

He left by night, without warning. It was as good as a confession. Mr. Madison was jubilant. He predicted Jeremiah's release, without trial.

Then the letters came from Lancaster, a letter to the Prosecutor and to the editor of each of the Frankfort papers. He had gone, he said, into Saul County to investigate and clear his name from the "false aspersions and the whispers of malice," and could be found by any man at the inn of Melvin Tupper in that county, to answer any demand.

Perhaps Lancaster had left Frankfort with the intention of flight and at the last moment decided to try the turn of one more card. Perhaps he was tired of flight. Perhaps he felt he had to make a stand at last. Perhaps he thought in a crazy, wistful logic that if he could prove his innocence now for this, it would somehow prove his innocence in all things, would wipe out the past and still the whispers that had followed him from state to state, would restore him to the common body of men.

After all, he was now innocent. And we can guess the depth of despair and the bitterness of resentment as the toils wrapped him around. My God, he was innocent, he had always been innocent, he had just had bad luck, born a pauper and an outcast, to hanker and yearn after the great coach that whirled past him on the road, to yearn into windows when the firelight leaped and the fiddles began, to yearn after the soft hands of gently bred ladies, to yearn after the respect of men, to yearn after a black cape and ruby pin. He was the victim of a vile injustice and a horrid joke, to be deprived when his heart told him he was made for grace and greatness and his whole body twitched like a naked nerve at every calculated slight or casual insolence. He had asked only for what was his, and every time when it was almost within his clutch, it was snatched away again. He was innocent and wanted only his own.

He tried one more card. He was innocent, and it was hard to leave Kentucky. He had almost been a great man there. The troubled times had a place for his talents. Perhaps yet he could be himself. So he was in Saul County.

Bumps shortly followed him there, the day after the letters appeared, giving out that he was helping "to get stuff on that-air Beaumont." But, also, he went to keep an eye on Lancaster. Lancaster might be the pay card yet. So we can guess that he stuck closer than a brother, studying Lancaster's pale face for the shade of fear that might prompt flight. If Lancaster started to flee, that would be the time. And we can guess that Lancaster knew why Bumps was there, squinting at him from the cunning little pig-eyes, slapping him on the back, nudging him with an elbow, guffawing. And all the while Lancaster's spine tingled and the sweat gathered cold at his armpits and ran down his sides like ice.

By now it was April. The trial was set for June. There were two more months to wait in the room in the Marton house. To assess the past. To calculate the future. To talk with Mr. Madison about the trial. To stare out the window at the blackened ruin of the capitol among the leafing trees by the square (it had been burned in November of the previous fall), and think "superstitiously how the burning of our chief building had marked the time when the State seemed to be plunging to ruin." To sit late with a bottle and argue with Hilton Hawgood about philosophy, "if man has a soul and evidence thereof, if having no soul which is immortal he can be known to have a self and identity and how a man may know himself, and if the end of man may justify his means, and how the mind relates to the body as the end to the means." (In this last we catch an echo of Dr. Burnham and his speculations about mind and body.)

It was also two months more to wait and be lonely at night. He had not seen Rachel since the morning when he had ridden off with Bumps and Crawford and the others to clear his name. As soon as the Court of Inquiry had committed him for trial he wrote to Rachel and told her all in great detail, the episode of the boot pattern, dirk and handkerchief in the lane, the loss of the dirk and of the handkerchief, the quarrel with Bumps at the Bardstown tavern and the role of Mr. Bascomb in forcing the search. He feared to commit to paper the fact that he himself had burned the handkerchief. Perhaps instinctively he did not want even her to know, not from fear but from some motive hinted at later in his narrative: "I did not tell her, for man shrinks to admit that he tampers with the pattern of fact, even when his cause is good."

He did tell her how false witness and perjury were gathering head against him at the Court of Inquiry, but added that he rested confident in his "innocence." And he says later: "I wrote that word down, and looked at it and knew its doubleness of meaning. My motive was innocent though my guilt was in deed. Then I rose and paced the room and cried out in my heart against the world in which that happy word can ne'er be single."

He ended that letter by saying to Rachel that all distress and evil would vanish from the world if he could look into her eyes and know her love for him. He continued: "I ask this not for desert of mine, but in conviction of my unworthiness, as any sinner asks for grace and brings no bargain in his hand to pay."

He concluded his letter by suggesting that she take the Marlowes to stay in the house with her. She was not to come to Frankfort under any circumstances, for that would give her pain and serve no purpose. He could not face the thought of her moving in the street of the town under the eyes of the curious, followed by idle boys, shamed by the guffaws of drunkards. He did not, however, tell her his reason.

Her reply came after some days. She begged him for permission to come to Frankfort to do her wifely duty (the phrase twisted in his heart like a knife—was that why she would come, to do a wifely duty?) and bear with him what had to be borne. He immediately wrote commanding her to stay and be of good cheer and countenance.

She stayed. The Marlowes moved into the house, after Captain Marlowe had, of course, hemmed and hawed and hinted at the press of business. Sukie Marlowe, with her gabbling kindliness and slatternly competence, did what she could for Rachel, and Captain Marlowe strutted and swelled among the hands in the barn lot and grumbled at dinner about his responsibilities and at night sat by the fire with his wife and Rachel and spat in the general direction of the burning log and half the time fell short and fouled the hearth and after the women were in bed got dead drunk. "He is no doubt a good man," Rachel wrote Jeremiah, "and does us a kindness to come but I could wish that his habits were cleanlier and his conversation less given to foolish boasting. It is a pity to see large virtues discounted by small faults."

But all things, as she assured Jeremiah, went well in the house and on the farm. And Mr. Madison, who went down to Saul County in December to interview witnesses and while there stayed at the Jordan house, brought back the same report. Of Rachel herself he reported more guardedly. She was not in her best strength but was bearing up with fortitude. She brooded much upon her husband's plight and sank into fits of abstraction and sadness, but one could see, he said, the force of will and could trust her to overcome griefs and crosses. She was anxious to do all she could for her husband's release and the cleansing of his name, and on occasion had ridden about the countryside with Mr. Madison to talk with possible witnesses.

(Hearing that, Jeremiah had the thought that he had, at last, set Rachel free. He had restored her to the world. She had been out of the world for a long time, for years, the princess chained and enchanted, the pale sufferer bound by shame, but he had struck her free. Ah, all was justified, all fulfilled.)

Her presence had done Jeremiah's cause much good, Mr. Madison said. For she bore herself with such dignity and asked nothing but the truth, she begged no favors, but no man seeing the courage which shone through her pale demeanor could but be touched. Mr. Madison waxed warm in her praise. Such grace, he said. Such dignity, he said. Such devotion, he said. Such warmth of heart and amplitude of spirit, he said. Jeremiah was a man to be congratulated, he said.

And he said those things, and stirred his bulk in his chair. Jeremiah looked in his face, a full-fleshed, swarthy face beneath iron-gray hair, with sudden and shocking recognition. Madison was like Fort. The same breed. That heavy, arrogant breed that would seize the world and run it. That took what they wanted, for all their fine talk. Madison had come, like Fort, on an errand of courtesy. He had talked fine, and been in the house. He had been there, in the house. With Rachel, while Marlowe in a farther room snored like a drunk swine and Sukie Marlowe slept in her bed upstairs, and there was nobody to see. But he saw—Jeremiah saw—and what he saw made him sick. Then his muscles tensed and his breath came short with rage, and he gathered his feet under him as though to leap from the chair.

He would kill him. Fort or Madison, it did not matter. He would kill a thousand Forts. He would do it over and over again. He was doomed to do it, over and over again, and there would be no end. There was a flash of horror at that thought, and then, at once, a burst of clearest joy.

Then there was nothing. He knew he was a fool. That was only Mr. Madison before him, who had, perhaps, kissed Rachel's strong, not small, squarish hand in courtesy at his departure, nothing more.

He knew he was a fool. He loved Rachel, and had perfect trust in her. He was ashamed. His thought had made him forever unworthy. Could he ever make himself worthy?

He asked himself that question, in his mind, in the letters he wrote to her. And she replied that he was worthy of all esteem. But that did not satisfy him. He did not want esteem, he wanted her love. Had he ever had her love?

He asked himself that question, and waited her answer. She replied that she valued him more than the world. But he found that statement ambiguous. Had she not said long back that the world was not for her nor she for the world and that she valued the world as nothing? Then to be valued better than the world meant little, if the world was nothing, "for a farthing is valued more than an empty pocket by the count of arithmetic, but will purchase nought, or only a crust of dry bread." Would he have to be content forever with that crust?

He asked that question, and after many days her answer came back to say that what she was, was his. But he found in those words the fatal taint of equivocation. Did she mean to say only that he had had her body and her lands? That there was nothing else? Had he done what he had done only for a few acres of dirt lost on a continent and the quick pinch of pleasure?

He had to have her love in its fullness. He knew now that he had never had it. It was what he had hoped to have after all was done. He saw that he had always moved toward that hope, even when he wavered and forgot his purpose, "as a man at night in a broken country moves toward a far-off light sometimes concealed by wood or ridge, and not seeing it and stumbling from the way, moves toward it still."

He wrote her that.

It was a second courtship, stranger than the first, across the miles of country between the room in Mr. Marton's house and the lonely room in Saul County where Rachel sat. We have the record of that courtship, all the letters that she wrote him and many of his own, his protestations and solicitings, her equivocations, bitter or coy or gnomic.

Did she not believe in love?

She believed in what she had known.

Had she not known his love?

No man had ever served more faithfully, and she was grateful.

Not gratitude, not gratitude, did she not know he longed for her love?

She recognized his worth.

"Worth—worth!" he replied. "I know I am unworthy. But my worth is not at issue, for I am like the peasant who hears of the passage of the sovereign, and gathers a basket of his poor fruit, though the best he has, and comes to stand by the way to offer it in homage, and knows that the sovereign should not be grateful for the fruit, so wormed and warped, but hopes nevertheless for a smile in kind pity for the stained hands and humble heart. And that is my best hope."

To this she replied with a poem:

> Oh, yes, call me a sovereign
>   You speak the bitter truth,
> For I am queen of a wide land
>   And have been from my youth.
>
> Oh, yes, I have a kingdom
>   And hold it by my right,
> Wear regal robes of darkness,
>   Rule the starless realm of night,
>
> But here I have no subjects
>   Save for the tortured shades
> Who break the bread of shadows
>   And drink mist when daylight fades.

He would not take that answer, and said so in a poem of his own:

> I would not name your realm the realm of night,
> Who have found there the true demesne of light,
> Whose heart expanded in your genial rays
> And lifted forth green fronds to wave your praise!

More and more, in their correspondence, poetry triumphed over dull prose and cloddish earth. They assumed their perfect shapes, took their perfect roles for a drama enacted on a high and secret stage with no vulgar eye to leer. We can fancy them as high allegorical figures acting out their ritual. He puts his left hand on his heart and stretches forth his right to her to importune. She lets her arms fall at her sides and averts her face, shaking her head slowly, trapped in her own mysterious distress. He kneels before her, and she smiles down at him with wonderful pity, but cannot speak the word he seeks. He kisses the hem of her dress, and she covers her face with her hands, racked by grief. "Child of sorrow, child of pain," he calls her. "Soul-sister," he calls her. "Bright taper of the heart's desire," he calls her. "Fair Sphinx, whose smile is truth and pain," he calls her.

But what was she? She was an unfortunate young woman on whom life had played every trick. It had given her a clod for a father and a fool for a mother. It had given her a first lover but to snatch him away in betrayal. It had given her dead children. It had marked her for slander and shame. It had given her a strong young husband who came in nobility, but came too late. It had given her a high heart, clear aspiration, grace, and beauty, and had marked her for place and happiness, but all had come to nothing.

So now she was trapped in that lonely house, in winter, with stupid Sukie and the spitting and bragging Jake Marlowe, and the empty pillow beside her in the dark, and the night sweat of horror at the sight of the knife falling and falling on Fort's bloody breast. He was a villain, he had been a villain in the end, but the knife fell and fell. She cried out in the night.

Sukie Marlowe tells that much in her statement, that she cried out in the night and "made considebul racket, more than one night, and I went to her and she said how she was a ruint woman, how everything was ruint for her, but to be worse than ruint was to ruin other folks, everybody what come to you meaning no harm. Then she shivered and shuttered like she done had the chill, and cried some more ever time, and one time she grabbed holt me and ast me to teach her to pray the Lord, and would I git down and pray fer her. Whicht I done. But I don't know as it done no good."

By day she might be lost in the vast idleness of her despair, the embroidery in its basket, the paint brush dry, the novels on the shelf.

Time stretched away on every side, like the bare, gray fields and leafless woods, a landscape of emptiness under a sagging sky. When would she see Jeremiah Beaumont come riding again up that lane where now for weeks no hoof had stirred the mire? At least when he was there she was not alone.

So she would dress, and call out for her horse to be brought ("She'd git nervus and walk up and down the hall waiting with her face white and say, my God, ain't they come yet, ain't they got the horse," as Sukie Marlowe says), and mount and ride away alone to seek out some man whom she knew only by report, and pour out her tale to him, how they had raised false witness against her husband's life— and against her own, for she could not survive him—how he was innocent. She knew he was innocent. She said that.

What was her face like when she said it, that he was innocent? White and drawn, the brown mark on her cheek bold against the white, the eyes staring intently into the face of the listener? No doubt as she said it she believed it. The very intensity with which she denied the fact of guilt would wash away the guilt, make the lie come true, truer than truth. "Oh, you are innocent, and mine be all the guilt," she was to say later to her husband. Was that the reason she could now proclaim him innocent? Was it no lie she proclaimed, or even equivocation, after all?

So she poured out her tale to some local squire, who assessed her charms and no doubt in a flight of fancy calculated his own chances, or to some hairy frontier farmer, who scruffed the toe of his boot in the wet earth and squinted sidewise at her as from a thicket and thought with the sluggish stir and twitch of an old bitterness how it was them bastards like Beaumont—always them bastards in black coats and talking proud and fine—who got all them gals juicy and warm and the good land greasy to the plow, and he didn't blame Beaumont no way if he tuk her, spite somebody had done broke sod fer him fust and softened them titties a leetle, fer, hell, the second season and it all come sweeter to the plow, and hell, that Jordan land, it shore laid nice to the river, but—and the bitterness twitched again like an old wound—not fer the likes of him. Squire or hairy frontiersman, they listened, and studied that leaning face and the hot, intent eyes, and thought their thoughts, and said, yes, ma'am, yes, ma'am, they were sure Beaumont hadn't done it.

Then she would ride home, the passion spent, swaying with fatigue in the saddle, numb with chill, while the light drained away behind the westward woods and there was no sound but the creak of girth and the clop and suck of hoof in mire.

Then up the lane she would see the house, the brick dark and streaked with damp, the square structure blank and irrelevant amid

301

the bare trees set on the bare land, in the great emptiness, and the smoke from the chimneys raveled upward with imperceptible motion, absorbed into the empty, smoke-colored sky. It was a prison, set in a greater prison, and she was the prisoner being led back to the cell, and the key would turn coldly in metal. Beaumont was in a prison far away, and waited death, but she was in a prison here and lived her death. They were doomed together. No, not together. Alone. Alone.

There was no escape.

But there was an escape, an escape not by flight but by turning to embrace the very thing from which she would flee: despair. She could seize the quill, dip it in ink, lean in the candlelight, and write. Then rise and pace the room and come to write again. She could ascend the high and secret stage, join Jeremiah Beaumont there, and take her stance and make the gestures and speak the words that would transform the commonness of things. She could gather the waste and wreckage of her life, its vain furniture of old hopes and threadbare desires, its frustrations and guilts, and fling them all disdainfully into the flame to make it leap higher and higher and gild with light ruddy as gold and blood the dark landscape that in that combustion would leap to life.

So the prison became palace, defeat became victory, sorrow became joy in the secret she had discovered. She had discovered where reality truly abode, in the heart, the gesture, the word. Beyond applause or sneer she could act out the charade, which was the essence of truth. It did not matter how limping the meter or tawdry the phrase or strained the attitude. There was no one to criticize. And who can criticize the only truth?

She would fling herself into the flame of that truth, and embrace it. The fire would be faithful.

During those months Jeremiah Beaumont, too, lived on that high and secret stage. But he lived, too, in the room in Mr. Marton's house, in the world, surrounded by men, calculating the chances of the world. He had enacted his secret drama, masked and by night with the steel in his hand, as he enacted in secret the sequel with Rachel, but he was torn between that secret world and the public world. Where did he belong? He belonged in both.

The problem, however, was more than a problem of doubleness. If the worlds had been entirely different, with a gulf of unplumbed nothingness between, then all might have been easy. He could have lived in both untroubled, speaking different languages, abiding by different laws, worshipping different gods, walking different streets, admiring different landscapes.

But it was not so. The two worlds impinged, overlay and lapped, blurred and absorbed, twisted together and dissolved like mist. That was the trouble. You never knew when the doubleness you embraced might become simplicity, or when the single to which you looked or on which you laid your hand might divide like smoke, or to what strange corner the familiar street down which you walked might lead. The common word in your mind or mouth betrayed you. What did the word mean, after all?

But Jeremiah lived as best he could in that condition, longing for the singleness of life but trusting in its doubleness. He had to trust that doubleness, for in that, at last, he had come to his deed, and laid all his plans.

There was reason to trust it. More and more, all suspicion seemed to be passing from him, and every sip of wine or slice of fowl from the hampers that came to his room from the world outside seemed to comfort him with innocence.

But one thought grew. More and more it seemed that his own innocence was contingent upon Lancaster's guilt, and upon Lancaster's guilt was contingent the guilt of the New Court. When Lancaster fled, all seemed safe. The flight was confession. He, Jeremiah, was clear. He prayed that Lancaster would flee fast and far, into the wilderness westward where nothing mattered, or down the river that washed everything away to the sea, to lose himself in Louisiana, in the swamp-jungles or the stinking streets of New Orleans. That was the perfect doubleness of the world. Lancaster would flee and take his guilt.

So Jeremiah waited for news of his flight. But the news did not come. Bumps was there. Jeremiah cursed Bumps. He cursed Lancaster for a fool. Why hadn't he fled while there was a chance? Why didn't he flee now, set a knife in Bumps or brain him with a candlestick or get him dead drunk? Lancaster was a fool, sweating there in fear in Saul County. What was Bumps? Nothing. And Jeremiah thought with bitter relish how easily he had taken the handkerchief from Bumps' own coat and burned it under the very eyes of the guard. A child could give Bumps the slip, or cut his throat.

Jeremiah cursed Lancaster, for every day that Lancaster delayed, the fear grew in Jeremiah. It was not fear of his own conviction. He was confident on that score. It was fear that Lancaster would be seized, tried and convicted. Could he stand by silent, and let Lancaster hang?

He would wake at night and see Lancaster's face, the handsomeness all gone, the vanity all gone, the sweat pouring down it, the ripped-silk smile gone from the red lips that gibbered and swore to

303

innocence even while men set the rope under the ear. That was Jeremiah's nightmare. It was a nightmare in which the two worlds, the secret and the public, merged and overlapped and intertwined, their happy doubleness betrayed, betraying him. When they merged and their sharp distinction was lost, you were lost, too.

In the very moment of his victory he might be lost. He might be compelled to confess to save the neck of that prinking fool and butt-cut of cowardice that had tried to swear away his own life. That would be the final comedy, the final trick the world could play: to make him confess.

Then the letter came from Rachel, and reading it, Jeremiah laughed out loud, all was so comic. Here he had waked at night to dread the moment when he would have to confess his guilt to save Lancaster, and all the while Lancaster had been laboring for Jeremiah's ruin by searching out witnesses in Saul County. But Jeremiah had known that, and that was not why he laughed now. He laughed at his own guilelessness in thinking that Lancaster would seek only the legitimate witness or would seek to corrupt only some wastrel or gut-desperate lout on the fringe of the world. No, Lancaster had reached into Jeremiah's own house with his tickling finger.

For Captain Marlowe had come to Rachel one night, as Jeremiah reports, "much distressed and with anger on his face, to lead her into a farther room and say that a certain Lancaster from Frankfort, whom report accused of the murder, had come to him several times in a friendly way to visit and make talk and each time had led to the subject of the crime and had tried to pry out Marlowe's mind and poison his sentiments, all under the guise of smile and frankness. At last he had showed Marlowe a handkerchief somewhat soiled and blood-sprinkled with a corner cut off, and another of the same stamp but good and whole, saying that the first was that found at Saunders' door which had caused all the talk in Frankfort, and for the second leading with such meander and equivocation to a bribe that Marlowe should swear he had had it of me, Beaumont. He had some long-winded tale how the bloodstained one had been stolen by me and hid, but had been lately recovered, with good witnesses.

"So Marlowe, after his first anger, had struck an agreement with Lancaster and would see him later to be more fully instructed. But he came direct to Rachel to declare all, to say he would do what she commanded, even to rise in court and swear that Lancaster had tried to suborn him.

"And so I laughed for my late vaporish qualms at letting Lancaster go to the rope, and laughed again to think how now for a certainty he had put his neck in it and, like some foppish Rosenkranz or Guildenstern, did make love to that employment and go to it. By

304

God, I said, I would have let him do all that was natural to seek witness to save his life, except to come to my house, to reach his tickling finger under my roof to a friend to start an itch in that most dark and tender part of man where avarice dwells. By God, I would hoist him with his own petard. So I laughed that the poor fool had made it all so easy, and reached for the quill and smoothed my paper."

He wrote a letter to Rachel. Rachel was to instruct Marlowe to fall in with Lancaster's plan and to come to court as a witness for the Commonwealth, and testify according to the facts that Jeremiah would provide in an enclosed document. (He asked Rachel to explain carefully to Marlowe that as witness for the Commonwealth he could not be cross-examined by the prosecution or be impugned, even if his testimony defeated their purposes, and that naturally he need have no fear of the defense.) The document that Jeremiah enclosed was not to be delivered into Marlowe's hands, for Jeremiah had some fear of his discretion and his wit, but was to be read to him that he might make a copy in his own handwriting. Then Rachel was to drill him upon it until he was letter-perfect.

The document for Marlowe is preserved to us:

> Upon being called will say: "I reckon you want me to tell all I know about Mr. Beaumont going to Frankfort and what he did and said beforehand and when he came back." They will say yes. Then he will begin and use the words as follows, to wit: "We live—my wife and me—nearest neighbors to the Timothy Jordan place, where Mr. B. stays since he married Miss Jordan some time back. They are quiet folks and don't see anybody. But because we are neighbors we see the Beaumonts and my wife helps take care of her in a neighborly way. After that baby come dead Mrs. B. was low in her mind, and one time told my wife she could not stand to look upon the house she lived in or the country round, she was so sad. That must have been the reason Mr. B. began to think of going west somewhere. If he settled good he would come back for his wife.
>
> "All that time Mr. B. was getting ready to go west. He was getting all set to pull out, when one day he asked me for a favor if I would go to Frankfort for him to pick up a land patent he had laying in the Register's Office for some Kentucky land, him paying for the trip and my time. I would of liked to go for friendship, like I would do for a man, me and him on good terms, but I was in a press of business. But many a time since Mr. B. went and has been accused, I have wished that I had gone so no blame had come to him. That is the wish of friendship.

"There is a little misunderstanding comes to my mind now and I will clear it up. I hear that when Mr. B. went to the Register's Office they told him there was no patent laying there for him and people have said he lied about having a errand and mission in Frankfort and had come to kill Fort. But there should of been a patent there in his name, and there was as far as he could of known. A long time before, it was when Mr. B. was fooling with land in Kentucky at first, he asked me when I went to Frankfort would I take some paper to register for him and I said yes. He said he would bring the paper to my house toward sun that evening. I waited till past sun and when he had not come I stepped down the road on some business. When I got back I did not see anything of a paper, and went to bed. But you know what happened was he brought that paper when I was down the road and my wife was feeding the chickens in the back and he laid it on the table. He must of reckoned I would see it when I came in.

"But my wife came in first, and put the paper away, not thinking it was anything, for her eyesight is not what it ought to be. And not long ago, she was cleaning up some old papers and showed me one and said is this anything? I looked and it was the plat and paper that Mr. B. must of left and me not knowing. I did not know what to do then, for Mr. B. was already in jail in Frankfort and I figgered he did not want to be bothered with toys and trifles and I would tell him when they let him out. At that time I had not heard the talk how he had gone to the Office and found no patent and people therefore claimed he was a liar. But when I heard that talk I knew I must speak and uphold the truth for my honor and a man's innocence."

☞ (*Attention:* provide him with an old plat and paper not filed, some of which you will find in my desk.) ☜

"Anyway, Mr. B. went to Frankfort himself and was gone more than a week, I never kept track. Then he come home late one evening and run in the house to see his wife, him being mighty partial to her and her not well. I come in the hall and they was hugging and kissing for him to be home. But she was sick that day, and she had to go upstairs, leaving him and me in the hall. Then he told me how Colonel Fort was murdered the night before he left Frankfort, and I said, my God, can such foul murder be true, and he said, yes, in a fight at his front door on his sacred doorstep, where he died or maybe died in bed later, he did not have the facts straight from common talk."

☞ (He is to emphasize this and make much of it.) ☜

"The next day they come for Mr. B. from Frankfort. I seen

306

them ride away, and he was bright and cheerful in the face and talked to the men like it was a party.

"I knew no more but the gab and lies that go round till a man name Lancaster come to our section from Frankfort. He stopped me on the road the first time I laid eyes on him and asked was I Captain Marlowe. Then he fell to talk and come to Mr. B. Then he taken out a barred handkerchief dirty and with some blood and a corner cut out or tore off, and said it was found on the doorstep where Fort was killed and everybody knew it was Mr. B.'s because Mr. B. had stole it from one of the guards and thrown it by the way, in a sink-hole, but a boy had seen him throw it and had picked it up and Lancaster had tracked it down and had good witnesses to prove it. Then he looked me in the eye and said *Anybody who swears this is Mr. B.'s handkerchief will get a cool $100 bill.* I looked stern at him and must of showed my dander, but he said quick he was not offering a bribe, he was seeking out men as knew the truth.

"Then he said how he himself was accused unjustly of the crime and a man had to save his life, and how he would stop at no expense for his innocence. So he looked me in the eye like he would wink or something and he jingled money in his pocket, and my blood boiled like any honest man's. But I held my tongue, and let him talk, and he then pulled out another handkerchief like the other, but good and new, and said how it was found in Mr. B.'s saddlebag, but it would be better if somebody swore it was give him by Mr. B., and it would be to tell no lie because it was indeed Mr. B.'s handkerchief, and it would all serve justice. And I saw he had a bill in his hand sort of crumpled up, rolling it betwixt his fingers.

"At that I let fly, I cursed him with what I laid my tongue to, and ordered him to *clare out*. Then he begged me, and declared he meant no harm or bribe, and would pay me to say nothing about our conversation, and he thrust the bill into my pocket. It was a $100 bill."

☞ (He will reach in and produce a bill and hold it to the court for all to see. *Attention:* provide him with a bill, you will find four in my desk in the black box. Then he says: "I do not want money for blood, and here it is for the Court, pleasing Your Honors, to take from me." Then he returns to his story.) 🌱

"I nigh threw the bill to the ground, but then I had a notion to lay low, for it looked like God's will and my blood boiled to think how Mr. B. was being made to suffer and was sworn against falsely. So I said to him that I would tell nothing of our talk. He smiled in that way he has which is mean, and said thank you, sir, thank you, sir, and I heard his breath come.

"Then I said, would he swear to all he had said of the handkerchiefs. He swore. Then I looked him in the eye like there was more in my mind than in my words, and said that I would swear the truth if I was called to court and hoped what he told me was true. So he pertened up. And I said for him to give me the handkerchief. Which he did and there was another bill in it."

☞ (He gives another bill to the Court.) ☜

"Then he said I would be called to court, and I have come. If I done wrong to him to lead him on and to come here I apologize, for I done what my conscience says, and if I gave a lie to him—to Lancaster, I mean—I done it for the right as best I could figger. God judge me.

"That is all I know about this sad business."

☞ (He may step down now, for the Prosecution cannot examine him, being a Commonwealth witness, and the defense will not. *Attention:* Drive this point home to him that he may feel secure and not fear the tangling tricks of lawyers.) ☜ .

So Jeremiah prepared the document, a speech for the drama he had contrived, in the idiom of Captain Marlowe, with stage directions complete. It was done with great cunning, and with great understanding of Marlowe, who was to speak the lines, the emphasis on his "business," on his kind neighborly heart, on his good conscience and honor. How Marlowe would relish the stance it gave him, the great gesture as he surrendered each $100 bill to the Court!

And on the practical side the document accomplished three things. First, it established a reason for the visit to Frankfort. (And this called for the dramatist's greatest subtlety: Jeremiah knew that Marlowe had lost the original plat and application in some tavern or brothel, and then had lied to him about it, and now he had to devise some explanation that Marlowe could utter without gagging and that would carry with it no implied condemnation. Happily, he had, in fact, left the plat and application on the table in Marlowe's house.) Second, it put his account of the murder on his return home in the proper light. Third, it set the rope firmly under Lancaster's ear.

All that remained was to see that the document safely reached Rachel. He was afraid to trust it to a common messenger. Here luck played again into his hand. Mr. Madison announced that he was soon again to go to Saul County. Jeremiah gave him the packet, saying that it was an intimate message to Rachel, and would he deliver it to her and to her only. Mr. Madison promised, and his promise was his deed.

It was now late April.

It was April, moving into May. He knew how the swollen creeks had now receded, leaving slime rings on the tree trunks and rich new soil in the bottoms and the muskrat track was perfect in the silky sediment at the water's edge. He knew that the sky was washed and pale and pure, its blueness flecked with gold, and in that air you could see the last hill as clear and small as something held in your hand, and the distance ached. He knew that the corn had broken through and its pale-green flecked the brown field like regular bright sprigs on a rich brocade he had unrolled long ago in Mr. Harrod's store in Bowling Green for some lady's inspection. He knew how the winged seed of the maple released the bough and fluttered luxuriously down. He knew how, at the edge of a glade in the knobs, the bear stood reared like a man, and blinked in the brightness, then dropped with a grunt and nuzzled a rotting log for grubs, and then lifted his head and yawned like a baby with the tongue lolling pinkly innocent over the terrible tushes as white as milk. He knew how the wild pigeons had passed and left the sky empty and the silence new. He knew there was a valley in the West where the sycamores glimmered white as bone beyond the cane and the tulip trees stood grave and straight to offer their blossom in the green bloom. He could hear the murmur of a riffle beyond the cane.

But he was here in Frankfort in the room in Marton's house. Hawgood and Mr. Madison came and went. The letters from Rachel came. Munn Short, the jailer, with a game leg (a tendon clipped by a bullet long ago), came to take him out for air (this privilege had been granted him since January), and Jeremiah walked down the streets of Frankfort now, smoking his cigar, as soberly and as unremarked as any citizen. People no longer stared at him. The boys and riffraff no longer trailed him. He might have been here, in this town, forever. This might go on forever.

It did not. One afternoon, past the middle of May, Munn Short knocked on Jeremiah's door, and entered. Jeremiah rose from the table where he had been writing, and said, "Well, Mr. Short, we're a little early today, but I'm ready for a walk any time, such a day as this."

Munn Short scratched his chin whiskers with a thumb, and hawked once or twice, and clumped across to spit in the dead fireplace. Then he wiped his lips with the back of his hand, not looking at Jeremiah.

Meanwhile Jeremiah had put on his coat—he had been sitting in his shirt for the warmth of the day—and had turned to say, "Well, let's go, let's walk down to the river."

"We ain't walkin," Munn Short said, and looked at the carpet.

"Well, have a seat," Jeremiah invited.

"I can't take no cheer," Short said, "fer we got to go. But we ain't goin walkin."

"Well, pray, where are we going?"

"To the jail, God-durn it!" Short burst out. "I got orders, God-durn it, and we got to go."

"Well, I'm damned," Jeremiah exclaimed in pure surprise. Then he laughed. He felt excited and almost pleased, he did not know why. He noticed Short's blank amazement, and stepped to his side, and slapped him on the shoulder. "Courage," he exclaimed, and laughed again. "I'd be honored by your jail. Unless, of course"—and he laughed—"your bugs bite bad. How are your bugs, Mr. Short?"

"My bugs—now my bugs . . ." Short grinned sly and slow in his whiskers, with a kind of conniving comradeliness, and cocked his head, and thumbed his chin to make a rasping sound. "My bugs," he said, "I don't want to brag, Mr. Beaumont, but I got the most perlite bugs ever et off you, or air man. They drag it sweet and slow, Mr. Beaumont. Ain't no man ever complained bout them bugs. They drag it so sweet and slow, lak a baby lovin on his mammy's tit. You'll plain love them bugs, Mr. Beaumont. You'll plain set up nights, Mr. Beaumont, singing them bugs songs, lak you was they mammy, and namin 'em love-names, ever one."

So they moved cheerfully down the street and across the square to the jail, followed by a Negro boy carrying Jeremiah's effects.

The "dungeon cell" where they put Jeremiah was a kind of cellar, with a trap door above and sloping ladder. It was commodious, some four by six paces, with a little alcove. The floor and walls were rough brick, the ceiling of board supported by hewed cedar beams. There was a decent table, about which the three chairs had been formally set and on which a candle burned as though in preparation for an honored guest.

Short stood by the table and eyed the place critically. "I done had it cleaned good as I could," he said in a mixture of pride and apology. "They's a pot in the corner you kin use fer nay-tur. A boy will git yore slops. As fer victuals, Mr. Beaumont, you'll git 'em off my table, not fancy but good as me, and no leavins. I done the best I knowed, Mr. Beaumont. I allus done the best I knowed for them as was put here."

"I'm sure it will be fine," Jeremiah said, and meant what he said, and shook hands quite ceremoniously with Short, and watched him ascend the ladder-stair, slightly favoring the game leg. "Come again," Jeremiah called gaily, "you're always welcome!"

Then the trap door fell shut, and the candle flame leaped into sudden significance in the new darkness. Jeremiah heard a bolt thrust home, then the limping gait of the jailer across the boards above.

He stood before the table, when the last sound had died away, and leaned and stared into the small unflickering tip of flame that speared upward into the dark. He stared at it as though he were the first man, ages back, ever to confront that mystery.

Some two hours after he had had his supper, plain though decent enough, when he was sitting at the table with a book before him, he heard steps above, the jailer's gait and another, then the rattle of the bolt. Then a pair of spindly legs came groping down the ladder, in a comic mixture of haste and uncertainty, and the door slammed above, and the man turned from the ladder into the light. It was Hawgood.

"It is an outrage," Hawgood affirmed, stepping forward, thrusting out a hand, his askew face white and intense.

"It's nothing," Jeremiah said.

"An outrage!" Hawgood repeated. "I have just heard. I came as soon as I heard. Rather I went to Nathan Gregg as soon as I heard. I demanded if he had done it. He said yes. And I would have known why—why, even if he is the prosecutor—why, when they have no case, and they know it. Oh, he was evasive and sly and gave some talk about a movement among friends to deliver you by force before trial. I pressed him on that, but got no satisfaction. None. I asked him why you would be delivered when you were innocent and sure of acquittal. Oh, I told him my mind straight, then came here."

Jeremiah was smiling at his intensity. He himself felt very calm. "I don't mind," Jeremiah said. "I don't mind at all."

"I don't understand it," Hawgood was saying fretfully. "I don't understand why they do this now—put you here—I don't understand —what could they have—they could have nothing . . ."

"I don't mind at all," Jeremiah said.

And he did not mind. After Hawgood had gone and the trap had slammed and the bolt had been thrust home, Jeremiah undressed, blew out the candle, and lay on the clean, decent bed that Short had provided. There was no sound. He thought of all the night sounds you could hear if you were above ground, even on the quietest night, all the rustle and murmur and twitch of darkness. But there was nothing here.

And the darkness was absolute. You could lie and be lost in that darkness. So he thought of how he had crouched at night in the dead lilacs by the Saunders door, waiting for Fort to come, and how on that occasion he had had the fancy that he was growing into the earth, setting root like the lilacs of the thicket, groping deeper into the dark earth with roots and hairy tentacles and his life was retreating there downward like sap when the cold comes. And he thought

311

of that morning in his youth, long back, when all the world glittered with ice and sun and he had touched the bough of the ice-ridden beech and had felt all his being flow into it, into the tree, and into the earth downward, and upward from every twig into the glittering air. He had forgotten those things, but now they came back.

But this moment, now, was not like those. This was deeper, truer. What was it like? Then he remembered how, when he was a boy, he had explored some of those sinks and caves that riddled tortuously the soft stone beneath the land of his home section, and how once he had crawled back a long way, through winding, cranky gullets that constricted breath, how he had come to great chambers and stood (he knew their size despite the blackness because when he shouted his voice bounced back from high unseen ceilings and farther walls), how he had felt along the wall, inch by inch, to another aperture, how he had crawled again, deeper, deeper and narrower, and had come at last to a place where he could crawl no more, it was so close. "So I lay there, and breathed the limey, cool, inward smell of earth's bowels, which is not like any smell common to the superficies, though in spots dank and unvisited by sun. It is a smell cleanly and rich, not dead and foul but pregnant with a secret life, as though you breathed the dark and the dark were about to pulse. And while I lay there, I thought how I might not be able to return, but would lie there forever, and I saw how my father might at that moment be standing in a field full of sun to call my name wildly and might run to all my common haunts to no avail. I felt a sad pity for him, and for all who ran about thus seeking in the sun and shade. But I felt no terror. It was like a dream of terror with the terror drained away, and the dark was loving kindness.

"Thus it was now as I lay on the decent bed in the dungeon cell. No, it was different, too, and more inward in its truth. It was dark, and in that darkness you could lie and not know the perimeter and boundary of your being if you did not lay finger to your face, for the darkness entered into you and you dissolved into the darkness and were absorbed like a body thrown into the sea to sink forever and flow away from itself into the profundities of no intrusive light.

"Then I thought: why should man fear aught, for there is always this truth, whatever its name."

There was always that truth.

IX

THE TRIAL BEGAN ON JUNE 6, 1826.
It was a brilliant, sweltering morning, unseasonably hot, and the courtroom was jammed, and the crowd—a restless, uncertain crowd streaked with violence and guffawing humor like fresh butchered bear meat with gristle and sweet fat—spilled out into the yard and into the street, waiting.

At ten o'clock the clerk said: "Jeremiah Beaumont, hold up your hand!"

And as Jeremiah lifted his right hand to admit identity, a man crouching on a window ledge, a small, knotted sort of man, all whiskers and elbows and patched homespun and squinting red eyes, yelled out, "It's him—Jeremiah Beaumont—and he ought to killed a million them bastards—Hooray fer Jerry!"

The gavel crashed. The Judge shouted, "Arrest that man!" The sergeant pushed toward the window, blocked by the crowd. There was shouting out in the street. The little man on the window ledge gathered his feet under him, crouching like a mangy cat, squinting with baleful glee at the sergeant's struggles. Then, as the sergeant broke through and lunged toward him, the man stuck his tongue wickedly out at the Judge, spat on the floor in front of the sergeant, gave a sudden crazy cackle of laughter, and dropped lightly beyond the ledge and was lost.

All the while, in the tumult that followed, Jeremiah Beaumont had stood quietly and soberly, as though the confusion did not concern him, as though there had been no confusion, as though he were alone. Then there was silence.

"Jeremiah Beaumont," the clerk began again, "I will read you the charge."

Then he read: "The Grand Jurors of the Commonwealth of Kentucky, empaneled in the County of Franklin . . . in the name and by the authority of the Commonwealth of Kentucky, upon their oaths do present . . ."

Jeremiah says that he listened intently, but that the words came to him strangely as though the tale they recited had no meaning for him, and could never have:

". . . and two inches below the breast bone one mortal wound of the breadth of one and one half inches and of the depth of five, of which said mortal wound so given as aforesaid . . . and so the Grand Jurors upon their oaths aforesaid, do say that the aforesaid Jeremiah Beaumont in manner and form aforesaid, feloniously and of his malice aforethought, did strike, thrust, stab, kill, and murder the said Cassius Fort . . ."

And all this against the peace and dignity of the Commonwealth of Kentucky, it said. It was signed: Nathan Gregg, Attorney for the Commonwealth.

Nathan Gregg, very clean, scrubbed, handsome, razored and pomaded, sat there rolling an unlighted cigar in his fingers and staring at the floor, studying justice.

The clerk finished, looked up, and demanded: "What say you—are you guilty or not guilty?"

Jeremiah replied: "Not guilty."

The clerk demanded: "How will you be tried?"

Jeremiah replied: "By God and by my country."

And the clerk: "God send you a happy deliverance!"

"Amen," Jeremiah said clearly, and straightened his waistcoat. It was a buff-colored waistcoat ornamented with little tufts of black wool and pewter buttons.

We have a full record of the trial, the transcript itself, which was later published and hawked about the streets of Lexington, Frankfort, and Louisville, the reports in the newspapers, a few letters by observers, and, of course, Jeremiah's own narrative.

The first two days passed in the selection of jurors. On the third day the long procession of witnesses began, the barman at Mackey's Tavern, where Jeremiah had first applied upon his arrival in Frankfort, the barman from the Weisiger House, and some man who had been talking with the barman—or claimed to have been—when Jere-

314

miah came. They all testified stoutly that Jeremiah had worn a hand-kerchief on his brow, a handkerchief with a cross-barred design, and the Weisiger barman was so far carried away by his zeal that he de-scribed Jeremiah as "a fellow looking like he was all worked up to devilment and murder, with his eyeballs rolling but him trying to be sly all the same and wanting a room secret and private." At this point Mr. Madison protested the opinion, and his objection was sustained.

The drift was clear: Jeremiah had been seen wearing a cross-barred handkerchief, and a cross-barred handkerchief had been found at the Saunders door, hacked and bloodstained. And so the trial began with a lie, a lie to be compounded.

"A lie," Hawgood said, leaning to Jeremiah, "another few lies like that and there will be no case. We can handle the handkerchief." And he smiled sourly to himself.

Jeremiah smiled, too, but inwardly. Yes, they could handle the handkerchief.

Then Caleb Jessup was called and sworn.

But Mr. Madison was on his feet: "I object, Your Honor," he said, "that this witness is incompetent in this case. He has publicly ad-mitted that he expects a share in the reward—in the"—Mr. Madison hesitated for the flicker of an instant to relish the word—"*lavish* re-ward that is offered for the conviction of the murderer of Colonel Fort. And he has publicly affirmed that he holds the accused to be guilty."

"Look here now . . ." Jessup began, but the Judge's gavel cut short his words, leaving him heavy and uncomfortable before all the eyes.

Nathan Gregg was up, he deferred to his learned opponent, he said, rolling the unlighted cigar in the fingers of one hand, touching his pomaded locks with the other. But might he remind the learned opponent, and humbly call the attention of the Court to *Phillips and Swift* to show that such a witness was not rendered incompetent.

He had expected this, Jeremiah thought. Gregg was more than a fop, he decided, grudgingly giving the admiration of the professional.

Mr. Madison was replying that he was acquainted with the cita-tion, but he would appeal to justice and the general principle of the law that rejects the interested witness.

Gregg returned to his citation, and while he argued, Hawgood leaned to Jeremiah and said: "Does he think, that fool, to instruct Madison? Madison could quote it to him. We will carry the point. Look at Judge Cooper. He is flushing up."

Judge Cooper, a big, slow, leonine man, white mane and intricate looped jowls above his black, was leaning forward a little, watching

Gregg and blinking sleepily, speculatively, at him. But the color was mounting in his face, and one of his big scarred, knotted hands—a hand that seemed scarcely uncrooked from ax-helve or plow-handle —was slowly working the gavel in its grip.

Hawgood whispered: "See, he doesn't like it. When he flushes like that, you may know."

Judge Cooper spoke. He was definitely opposed, he said, to admitting interested testimony, on principle and in common sense. But the authority was stronger than he had reckoned. He reckoned he would think about it while he ate his dinner, it being near his time. But was the witness truly putting in for the reward?

Mr. Madison asked permission to address the witness. Then to Jessup: "If the defendant is convicted do you expect a share in the reward?"

Jessup shifted his feet and moved his heavy shoulders under his coat as though he itched and could not lift a hand to the spot.

"I don't expect nothing not mine by rights," he said sullenly.

"I shall repeat the question," Mr. Madison said. And did so.

"Like I said," Jessup began, and wiped gray tongue out over his lips, "like I said now . . ."

Judge Cooper's gavel crashed. "Man," he roared, "can't you say yes or no in God's name? And"—he leaned forward a trifle, fixing on Jessup's unhappy face—"if you lie I'll see you rot for perjury." Then to Mr. Madison: "Ask it again."

Mr. Madison repeated the question.

"Yes," Jessup said, and the sweat beaded out on his forehead.

"Do you expect a considerable share?"

"I done much as air man," Jessup said.

"Thank you," Mr. Madison said, and turned contemptuously away.

During the noon recess, while he sat at dinner with Mr. Madison and Hawgood, Jeremiah got his idea. "Will Judge Cooper admit Jessup?" he asked.

Mr. Madison shrugged, but Hawgood said: "He may. But for one reason. Judge Cooper was strong for Relief and inclined New Court. Even if he never went whole hog, being too good a lawyer for that . . ." he said this blandly with a sidewise glance at Mr. Madison.

"I don't hear a human word," Mr. Madison remarked. "I just hear the weasel in the cane and the wind down the chimney."

"Yes," Hawgood continued, "Judge Cooper knows too much law to go whole hog for New Court, even if he did learn it sitting on a stump at the end of a corn row while the beast plowed. But since he is known Relief, he will lean over backward. He will not have it said against his honesty that he did not seek all justice for Fort because Fort was Anti-Relief. So he may admit Jessup after all."

"Isn't Jessup's word poisoned now?" Jeremiah asked.

"He did not make a good impression," Hawgood said.

"Well?" Jeremiah said.

"Well, what?" Hawgood demanded.

"Ah," Mr. Madison said, "I think I read your mind. You mean we should retract, should admit Jessup. We should suffer less that way in the public eye than if he were forced over our objection. And he may be forced on us. By Cooper's conscience. Ah, what an inconvenient conscience!"

"I do not like to toy with the law," Hawgood said. "And if the law forbids that Jessup . . ."

"It is my neck we are toying with," Jeremiah said softly.

"And," Mr. Madison said, "if Jessup swears what I think he will swear, we have him. We have him in the lie. It is better to prove the lie on him than to have him silenced before."

Hawgood impatiently pushed back the plate of beef and green beans he had been finicking at with his sick man's appetite. "Lies," he said with sudden disgust as though the food had gagged him. "Lies, all lies! Is there nothing but lies around us? Men will lie for a shilling and kill for a crown."

Then he fell into silence, brooding inward. After a moment, he said: "Do what you will. I trust your judgment."

Jessup's testimony was what Jeremiah had expected. He swore that Jeremiah when he arrived had worn on his brow a cross-barred handkerchief, dirty with smoke and sweat. That he had been very insistent to get a private room. That late he had gone out of the house as quietly as possible, but the stairs had creaked. It had been some time after midnight, for the watch had just cried. (*Oh, the liar, the liar*, Jeremiah had exclaimed bitterly to himself, for the stairs had not creaked and at that hour he had been far from the house. He had been far from the house and could prove it. He could prove the lie on Jessup. He could get a witness—why, at midnight or near he had been talking to Mr. Allenby's old colored man in the alley— he could prove it! And his heart froze: yes, he could prove it, and if he proved it, he would prove that he had stood in the alley by the Saunders door.)

Jessup was going on: That Mrs. Jessup had heard the stairs, too. That next morning Jeremiah had gone white and shaken like a girl when they named the murder to him, and couldn't eat his breakfast, though "it was a good mess of vittles and fit fer any honest man," and that Mrs. Jessup had had her feelings hurt for the slight. That when he, Jessup, reached the Saunders house he found a cross-barred handkerchief lying in the bushes near the door and that started his suspicion so that he returned to his own house to question the stranger.

("The handkerchief," Mr. Madison whispered, "the handkerchief —he has sworn it. We have him there!")

That the stranger had said he had finished his business in Frankfort and had received his land patents, when everybody knew now there were no patents at the office. That he, Jessup, had not detained the stranger, not wanting to suspect anybody wrongly and without good advice, but that he had ferreted out his name and place. That he, Caleb Jessup, always undertook to do his duty, like when he was sheriff, and that his heart was full of grief for Colonel Fort, for Colonel Fort was his brother-in-law, and like a brother to him, God bless him.

Mr. Madison rose for the cross-examination. The hush fell on the room. Mr. Madison stood solidly in the space before the witness, for the moment not noticing him, looking back over the crowd, out the windows where the late afternoon light now slanted in, out the windows at the sky, as though he had been alone.

Then he turned to Jessup, almost with surprise, or as though recollecting an unpleasant duty.

"At what spot did you find the handkerchief?" he asked quietly.

"Right on the south side that biggest lilac bush near the Saunders door on the back side the walk."

"At what hour did you find it?"

"Not before a quarter past seven, and not later than seven-thirty."

"How do you know?"

"It was seven o'clock when I left my house to come walking over. I seen the clock just before I left."

"If the defendant is convicted will you claim a share of the reward?"

Nathan Gregg was up, livid with rage. "I object!" he cried.

"Objection sustained," Judge Cooper said.

Mr. Madison bowed to the Judge. Then turned to Jessup: "Your heart is full of grief for Colonel Fort?"

"Grief!" Jessup began, "why Cass was like a brother—he . . ."

"I object!" Nathan Gregg screamed.

"Objection sustained."

Mr. Madison bowed again, murmuring, but murmuring quite distinctly, "I beg your pardon—I was not sure I had heard the witness aright, on the point of his love."

Then he stood, waiting, while the laughter and the catcalls flared over the room like a grass fire in August, and the Judge's gavel punished the desk to splinters, and Jessup's face exuded oil like a chunk of tallow in the sun.

When the silence had returned, Mr. Madison flicked one glance over Jessup, from head to heel, a glance like a flick of spittle from the side of the mouth—so Jeremiah describes it—and strolled to his seat.

There was no re-direct examination.

Mrs. Jessup was the last witness of the day. She had been sitting there all those hours, waiting to say what she knew she would have to say, sweating in her good black dress—it had been a *good* dress once, even if it was too tight for her now and popped the seams, even if there were stains like oil on the black, even if her hands were raw and hangnailed and red against the black.

She rose, and with an incongruous rustle of the silk, moved across the open space, footing the boards timorously like bad ice, stealing a glance from face to face—the faces of strangers, of enemies, where wrath or contempt might suddenly flash forth. But she did not look at Jeremiah.

She gave her testimony in a dead, flat voice that carried only a few feet. Yes, that man had worn a barred handkerchief on his head. Yes, he had gone out of the house just after midnight. Yes, she had known the hour, she had heard the watch cry. Yes, she had heard him come in later. Yes, at breakfast he was queer-like when he heard the news. And after he had gone she had started to set his room aright and on the hearth, in the ashes, she had found what was left of a dark green, almost black, silk scarf or handkerchief. It must have got put out before it burned, for some water had been thrown on the coals. Maybe because the slop jar was full. She had to admit it was full. Anyway, the scarf or whatever it was had a knot in one corner and toward the other end of what was left was a hole cut out nice and neat about the size of your eye. She hadn't thought anything about it then, but had thrown it back. But later her husband, Mr. Jessup, he told her how the murderer wore a mask or something on his face, so she said how she had found this, and he got excited and she ran upstairs and grubbed in the ashes and found it. But she must have flung it on some hot coals in the corner where the water didn't get, because it had now smoldered some more and part was gone. But she had saved the rest.

At this Nathan Gregg produced the remnant of Jeremiah's green silk handkerchief, wrapped up in a piece of paper, the handkerchief he had worn on his brow on the ride to Frankfort and later had flung into the fire. Now Nathan Gregg gave it to the jury. The men passed it from hand to hand. All the while, Mrs. Jessup stared devotedly at the floor. She had never taken her eyes from the floor during her testimony.

On the cross-examination, Mr. Madison focussed his attention on the matter of the hole in the handkerchief. He produced a paper and requested that Mrs. Jessup draw the size and shape as true as she could of what she had originally found. Then the hole in its proper location. Was she sure that her sketch was about right? Would she swear it?

She answered yes, in a voice not above a whisper.

(Jeremiah leaned to Hawgood. "She is lying," he said. "You can tell she is lying. That blackguard of a husband made her lie." Hawgood nodded.)

Had the very corner of the unconsumed part of the handkerchief shown the twist and pressure of a knot?

She answered yes to that. And the jurymen inspected the corner.

Mr. Madison picked up the sketch, and with the edge of his own handkerchief measured the distance from the corner to the indicated hole. He moved across to stand beside Jeremiah. He stood there a moment, while the room went dead quiet.

Then, in the quiet, he leaned, placed the corner of his handkerchief at the back of Jeremiah's neck, and brought the border forward toward the left eye. His thumb marking the distance to the hole according to Mrs. Jessup's sketch struck Jeremiah's head just at the forward edge of the ear.

"Look, gentlemen," Mr. Madison said, very softly. "I beg you, look. A strange eye-hole it would have been, gentlemen, to fall here. Perhaps it was an ear-hole. Though, of course, a trifle too small for this apparatus." He touched Jeremiah's ear.

The jurymen were leaning and staring, shuffling and snickering.

"Come," Mr. Madison invited, "won't one of you make the experiment?"

So the foreman came, measured from the chart on Mr. Madison's handkerchief, and applied it to Jeremiah's head.

Mr. Madison returned to Mrs. Jessup. When he spoke he had the constrained, patient air of someone dealing with a child, or an invalid. "My dear madame," he said, "my dear madame, you have seen where the hole . . ."

"Oh, I don't draw so good," she wailed. "I don't draw so good . . . I drawed the best I could but . . ."

"My dear madame," Mr. Madison repeated, more soothing than ever, "I am sure that you drew it very well. I am sure it was very true. Why, a lady who makes the nice calculations of sewing and household tasks would have an eye trained true and . . ."

"Oh, I drawed it the best I could!" she wailed, her head drooped on her chest, her shoulders shaking.

"Now, madame, now, madame," he murmured over and over, waiting for the fit to pass.

It was over at last, and he leaned at her: "Just one more question, and I apologize to impose upon your sensibilities. But just one more. You said that the hole had been cut out?"

She nodded, not trusting her voice.

"The handkerchief is very dark," he said, "a very dark green. Could it not have been burned out by contact with a coal, and you might not have noticed the char at the edge, for the fabric is so dark in color? For you did not look too carefully then, did you madame? For there was no reason to look carefully then? To you then it was just a rag on a hearth?"

She did not reply.

"Might it not have been burned?" Mr. Madison asked again, in his enormous patience.

Mrs. Jessup flung up her head as at a sudden stab of pain, and showed her fearful, tortured, gray face, and fixed her gaze on him.

Then Jessup coughed. He coughed twice. She looked at him. Then flung her wild, despairing gaze over the room. Suddenly she fixed on Jeremiah's face.

He writes of that moment: "Her eyes were upon me, and I have never seen greater anguish. Her gaze implored me. She was swearing my life away, and yet she implored me, in pain and humbleness, to save her. She implored me as if I were the only person in that throng to understand and forgive. It was the look of humbleness and beseeching she had turned upon me by the rented bed long before when she had wanted me to say it was a good bed, at least a good bed in her ruined house. And now I was struck by pity for her despair, and I found myself unawares smiling at her, as if to say, Courage, courage, in her need. Then Mr. Madison spoke again."

Mr. Madison recalled her to the question. He asked again if the hole might not have been burned.

Jessup coughed.

She swung to face Mr. Madison.

"No!" she cried despairingly, twisting her weight in the chair, clenching her raw hands on the black silk, "no—it was cut—the hole was cut!"

Mr. Madison waited, while her head sank again to her chest and her gaze fixed on the floor.

Then he said: "Thank you. That is all."

She tottered to her seat. And as she sat there, shapeless and sunk and heavy in the black, Jessup kept staring at her, gnawing his nether lip like a chunk of gristle to get the juice.

Jeremiah meditated that he did not envy her that coming evening in the privacy of her chamber.

321

The following day John Saunders took the stand to give his account of the night of the murder.

Then Mrs. Fort was called.

Jeremiah had not known that she was in the room. She had not been present on previous days, and this morning he had not noticed the gaunt figure in black, with the black veil, which Nathan Gregg now escorted like a queen to the stand.

She raised the veil to show the bony and ravaged face that Jeremiah had seen in the candlelight of Fort's study, long ago. And now when she spoke, the fact was shocking to Jeremiah. That night, seeing her beyond the glass of the study window, he had had the fancy that no sound came from her gray moving lips, or nothing but a whisper too dry for any ear to catch, that whatever sound it was came as a ghostly accusation to the husband who had wronged her. And he remembered how he had thought: *Ah, poor ghost, I will avenge you, too.*

But now her voice was an ordinary voice, and that fact was shocking. She was real, and no ghost. She was real, and was telling how she had heard her husband come in late on the terrible night, and had gone to his study to speak with him on some domestic matter of no importance but to husband and wife and to know if she might bring him a glass of milk and some food, or a cup of tea, for she feared for his health, he worked so hard in times of stress.

A cup of tea—she had asked if he wanted a cup of tea. Now as she said that, in that ordinary voice, it was horrible to Jeremiah, as though the earth had shivered beneath his feet. That truth was more fearful than any lie, that she had asked if her husband wanted a cup of tea. That husband had betrayed her and had lived lovelessly with her, but something had bound them, not love, not hate, something else—some commonness of the world, some thousand wispy bonds of their common lot and common hours, stronger than steel—and she had come late at night, not like a ghost to accuse but to ask if he wanted a cup of tea.

And Jeremiah felt like crying out, *But nobody told me, but nobody told me, how could I know.*

He had been betrayed.

She was telling how when she had entered the hall, after hearing a noise, she had seen the assassin seize her husband by the wrist.

Then Nathan Gregg: "Did you see the assassin's face?"

She hesitated a long moment. Then she looked, for the first time, at Jeremiah. She peered at him, as though from shadow, ambush, or cranny, all her face sharpening at him.

And in a foreshortening and fusing of time, he knew her face: the old face peering with envy and hate from the shadows of the Jordan

322

house, the gray face, sallow or gray, floating bodiless in the shadows, the face of old Mrs. Jordan—no, not hers—the face of the world. You could not escape it. You saw it die, you saw it buried under the ground, but it came again and peered at you. It peered secretly, though here in a throng of people. It peered from its inevitable shadow, though here in the flood of day.

She peered at him, and he was sure that she was going to say, yes, she had seen the face of the assassin, and that was the face. And her finger, stiff and dry as bone, would point at him.

She would tell that lie. That was the lie the world would tell. She would say it.

But she did not say it. "No," she said, "I did not see—the murderer's face."

That was a trick, it was bound to be a trick, she was telling the truth to trick him.

"But I heard his voice," she said.

But not my voice, Jeremiah thought, *for my voice was disguised.*

"I heard his voice," she was repeating, "and I would know it anywhere, it rings so in my ears."

"Have you heard that voice since?" Nathan Gregg asked.

"Yes," she said.

"Will you please relate the circumstances?"

So she said that one day in May she had come with her brother, Mr. Saunders, to the Marton house, and Mr. Marton had conducted them to the door of the prisoner's room, which was ajar of a purpose, for all had been arranged. She had heard three men speaking within, and had picked out the prisoner's voice immediately. All had been arranged for the test. Mr. Marton had asked two gentlemen to call on the prisoner at a certain hour and talk with him. She had wanted this, though for a long time she had not believed the prisoner guilty, but that voice had been ringing in her ears, and she had known it.

He knew she was lying. She could not have known his true voice that night.

Then, looking at her, he knew that she was not lying. If what she said was a lie, it was a lie that she believed. It was her truth.

Ah, that is the thing to fear, he thought, *not the lie the world tells as a lie, but the lie the world holds as its truth.*

He was afraid. For the first time.

In the cross-examination, Hawgood concentrated on one issue, that of the voice.

Had she known what men were in the room with the prisoner?

No.

Did she now know?

Yes.

Who were they?

They were Mr. Sims Motlow and Mr. Amos K. Puckett, citizens of Frankfort.

Was she acquainted with either of the gentlemen?

With both.

How long had she known them?

She had seen Mr. Motlow around ever since he came to Frankfort, perhaps ten or twelve years. She had known Mr. Puckett for three years, more or less.

How well did she know Mr. Motlow?

She had a speaking acquaintance.

Ah, a speaking acquaintance?

Yes.

Did she have a speaking acquaintance with Mr. Puckett?

No.

Had she ever heard him speak?

Yes, but she had not known his name at the time. He had come to her brother's house and asked for him. Later her brother had told her the name.

How long ago?

Perhaps five or six months.

Who had chosen the men to go talk with the prisoner?

Her brother.

Might she not have remembered their voices and guessed that the third voice was that of the prisoner?

No. No. That would have been impossible. The voice rang in her ears.

Jeremiah was covertly watching the jury during the cross-examination. He was sure that they were impressed by Hawgood's attack. How could they fail to be impressed? But when he looked back at Mrs. Fort, he found nothing but certitude in her face. She was sure of her lie.

On what day of the month had she gone to the Marton house? Hawgood was asking.

She had gone on May 17, she said.

On May 17, Jeremiah thought. And: *Why, that was the day before they came to take me to the jail.*

So that was it. Mrs. Fort's identification had been strong enough to make Nathan Gregg sure that he could convict. But why had not Mrs. Fort identified the voice sooner? It had been ringing in her ears, she said. Why had she waited?

Jeremiah did not have the answer. But we have it. She had not done so because she feared that to accuse Jeremiah Beaumont would be to define his motive as revenge for Fort's seduction of Rachel

Jordan, would be to cast her, Mrs. Fort, in the role of the unloved wife. She could not bear that thought.

But now she had changed her mind. Or circumstances had changed. Jeremiah sensed some change in the drift of things. Behind all the words and the waiting, some force was operating that he could not identify.

The words went on. They were the words of Jackson Smart, the "Scylla" that Jeremiah had tried to skirt on the way back home, the rich, fat, old bellowing man who snatched in every traveler to his gossip and lethal hospitality. According to him, Jeremiah had said that he had been to Frankfort and had received land patents, Jeremiah had reported Fort's death but, when he fell to drinking, had cursed Fort and said he was better dead as damned Anti-Relief.

Was Smart lying? Jeremiah asked himself. No, he was not lying, Jeremiah decided, he was simply telling his own truth.

Then, with the next witnesses, the testimony took a new tack, started by Smart: Jeremiah had been a violent partisan of Relief.

There was the fight at Lumton, five witnesses, the first two of them men Jeremiah had fought that day. The whole event unrolled in the shambling speech of the men, but all the violence and fury was nothing now, nothing but empty words. It was so long ago.

The last witness was Skrogg, paler than ever, sicker, more remote, more dispassionate, more racked by the cough. He told his story.

Then Nathan Gregg asked if Skrogg had been a friend of Jeremiah before the fight.

No, he had seen him for the first time the night before.

Did he know why the prisoner had fought?

Skrogg assumed that it was for Relief.

You fool, you fool! Jeremiah thought. *Don't you know I fought because you were weak and sick and one against many! Relief, what did I care for Relief?*

Then came the incident at Tupper's tavern.

Old Squire McFerson, windbroke and bloated and shabby, oozing his rancor and defeat, rose to tell how he had found treason on the wall of the tavern, and had quarreled with Tupper, and how then for no reason but politics and spite, Beaumont had leaped upon him. "And me an old man," he said, "me an old man, as had fought for my country—an old man . . ." And his eyes swam with tears again, pity for himself and all his ruin and defeat and wasted years.

All at once tears were gone, and the bleared, red old eyes were staring at Jeremiah across the space with a horrible, unrelenting hate that would never die.

Then more of the tavern hangers-on, a wandering confusion of talk, half-truth and half-lie, but neither truth nor lie big, a sluggish eddy without drift or direction, with the aimlessness of dream. And, all at once, that was the sinister thing, the eddy, the lack of direction, the thought that that was all your life was—a dreamlike confusion that stunk like a rotten backwater when the creek went down.

Then Old Josh Parham, the great man of the county, swollen in his arrogance, rose to tell of the partnership with Jeremiah, and how they had quarreled over politics because "that Beaumont was so strong for Relief and ruination that he was a desperate fool to throw away a chance for good money from land in the West." He produced all Jeremiah's maps and notes, and the last letter breaking off the partnership.

Then young Parham, Felix Parham, the wastrel son, the weak-chinned, likker-rotted dandy, finicking with his cuffs. He told of the trips to the West. And Jeremiah thought of the West, not hearing the words, thinking of the woodland gloom and the rivers, noble and raw with flood, brooding back over that time. Until he heard the words: ". . . and told me how Cassius Fort was the enemy to the people, and a traitor, and hinted at a private spite, and said that some man who was a man would do justice at any cost."

All lies, all lies! Jeremiah thought. Then knew that it was not all lies. It was lies and truth, and lies told for truth and lies told for gain or vengeance, all twisted together. But Felix Parham had lied, he had lied the lie complete. But for a moment, Jeremiah could not even be sure of that. Had he himself not said those things to that fool? He could have said them, every word, for they had been in his heart. He could almost see himself sitting by a campfire at night, far in the West, leaning into the little glow and heat in the middle of the great darkness, saying those things to the slick face that glistened corruptly beyond the flame.

But he had not. But could he be sure that he had not? Lies and truths had blurred so together and interfused.

And before his eyes, in the sunlit room, among the forms and voices, all things for a moment seemed to waver and blur as in darkness. He thought of what he had heard an old boatman of the Ohio say, and felt like that boatman. Jeremiah describes that moment: "So I remembered the old man who had worked the broadhorns and the keelboats, what he had said. How at night on the wide Ohio, in a darkness without moon or stars, you look to the shore but cannot know it. You see only the denser dark rising from the dark water, but it may be but the shadow of a bluff or cliff where the darkness thickens to make a false shore, and the true shore beyond, and you look up and cannot be sure of a bluff against the sky, only darkness. So I looked into that darkness of men's hearts and words and could not be sure where lay the shore of truth. But that brought not the fear. That comes when you look into your own heart, and in that darkness the shadow and shore confound. Where was my truth? Where was my truth? And for the moment I did not know why I had come here, or what need had brought me, for the idea by which man would live gets lost in the jostle and pudder of things."

They were testifying to his candidacy and campaign now. How long ago that seemed!

Then Lancaster:

There was the ruby pin, the frilled shirt, the haunted, restless eyes that never ceased their flickering over the faces in the room, over every face but Jeremiah's, contemptuous and imploring, while the red, twisted lips moved and moved, convolved and contorted, to utter the words.

It was a vague and wandering tale, full of hints and prinkings and sentences that found no end and a self-assurance as glittering and thin as skim-ice on a puddle. (So Jeremiah describes it.) Lancaster had met Beaumont long ago, he said. After the murder, he had first remembered the meeting as at Danville, at a lot auction, and had freely said as much. He had recognized the prisoner in a group at the Marton house, but the prisoner denied ever having been at Danville. Later he had thought he might have met the prisoner at Barker's Well, but could not be sure. And perhaps at Bowling Green, at a horse run.

But he would have it known, he said, that in all those instances of which he was unsure as to place and circumstance he referred only to his *first* meeting with Beaumont. But he was completely sure as to place and circumstance of the *second* meeting.

"And where was that *second* meeting?" the prosecutor asked.

Sugg Lancaster touched the frill of his shirt, below the throat, as though that fleeting caress of fine linen gave him courage and proved all. Then he said in a clear voice: "On his own property, in Saul County."

Jeremiah tightened and leaned as though ready to leap from his chair. But Mr. Madison's hand was on his arm, hard. "Steady," Mr. Madison whispered, "steady." Then: "What is one more lie from a liar?"

The prosecutor was asking: "Do you mean his farm in Saul County?"

"I do," Lancaster said, "or the farm that was"—and his silky melodious voice edged with a sneer, so gently—"that was his wife's before marriage."

Oh, for that I'll kill him! Jeremiah thought, and the act flickered in his mind, a knife falling, falling, falling. It would be joy. It would be joy. He grasped the edge of the table.

Lancaster's voice was going on. He had been passing through Saul

327

County and got the wrong road and stopped to ask a stranger the way, but it was no stranger, the man he remembered from an earlier meeting, and the man had remembered too, and called him by name and asked him to enter his gate and sit under an oak—a great white oak—for shade and a drink from a spring there, and the man had a bottle and they drank together from the bottle, washing it down with water from the spring, and the man, who was Beaumont, talked with him and asked him news of the state and then expressed deep disdain and hatred for Anti-Relief, and especially for Colonel Cassius Fort with a violence which made one recoil, and also hinted at darker wrongs unnamed. It was two years back, just before election time.

The prosecutor asked if the meeting had been observed.

Happily so, Lancaster replied, and happily he had lately met the man again, one Sut Prosper, of whom he had asked the way before seeing Beaumont by the spring. That day Sut Prosper had passed as they sat by the spring, and greeted them and called Beaumont by name.

The cross-examination shook Lancaster. Mr. Madison was ready with the questions as to Lancaster's past, the slave-selling in Alabama, a scandal in Louisiana, disbarment in Tennessee, or near-disbarment. The prosecutor's objections were sustained early, but not before an effect had been made. And not before Lancaster was soaked with sweat and the frill of his shirt was twisted to a rag in his fingers. But he clung to his words.

Then Sut Prosper confirmed Lancaster's story. If any word of a Sut Prosper could confirm anything, the word of a creature "so obviously marked by misery and sloth to be bought for a farthing and spat on for boot."

It was late in the seventh day of the trial. The sun struck in long, leveling rays across the heads of the crowd in the room. Judge Cooper lolled massively back, like a gorged bear, easy in the somnolent last wash of the afternoon. But his eyes blinked brightly under the shaggy brows.

But Nathan Gregg called one more witness. It was Carlos Bumps, his pig's eyes confident and cunning in his great slick face, a kind of animal grace in his movement despite the excess flesh and slovenly posture.

After the usual preliminaries, the prosecutor asked that he tell his tale in his own way.

"Me and two of the boys on the patrol," he began, "we was on Washington Street that night and it was gettin late, long past curfew, and we seen two nigger gals coming down the street. But bout the time they come close, two men what was drunk, like you could tell, come round the corner and seen them gals. One of them fellers grabbed a gal, but she squealed that kind of nigger-gal squeal and jerked back, and she and that-air other gal, they run up the street. Them boys with me—they was Ike Serle and Tom Postum—they started to talk and joke with them drunk fellers, but I was standing back some and seen another feller come along . . ."

Then Nathan Gregg interrupted: "Can you identify that man?"

"Yeah," Bumps said, "yeah, I shore can."

"Who was it?"

Bumps rolled his head easy on his shoulders, letting his glance slide along the row of faces. Then it stopped, and without even turning his body, lifted his left hand and jerked the thumb contemptuously over the left shoulder. "Him," he said, "that-air Beaumont."

"What time was this?"

"Late. I know, fer eleven o'clock had done been called."

Nathan Gregg flashed his quick look of triumph over the jury, then turned again to Bumps. "And now, Mr. Bumps," he said, "at what hour did you go to the house of John Saunders?"

"That's sort of gettin ahead," Bumps said, and lolled back easy and squinted at Gregg. "I seen something else, long afore."

"Well?" Gregg demanded, irritation flickering in his tone.

Mr. Madison was leaning toward Hawgood, whispering. "Look, look," he whispered, "that blackguard is making a fool of Gregg, he has deceived him somehow."

And Hawgood, intent on Bumps, nodded.

"Yeah," Bumps was saying. And then with the faintest shade of insolence: "Don't you want me to be tellin *all* I seen?"

"Yes," Gregg said. "Yes, of course. Tell it!" And Gregg stiffened in his fine clothes.

"Yeah," Bumps said, "I seen that-air Beaumont come past, his collar up and his hat pulled down, but it warn't that cold. And he stopped of a sudden, just afore he got to the corner."

Bumps paused, shifted easily in his chair like a man relaxing for pleasure, and waited for a second, to relish the silence all around.

"Yeah," he said, "he stopped. Then he went over to the door, and stood clost like he was knockin soft—but I couldn't hear nuthin—and the door opened up, and it was dark inside. The door opened up quick, like somebody was waitin in the dark . . ."

Mr. Madison spoke sharply: "I object! The comments are not relevant."

And Judge Cooper: "Objection sustained!"

Bumps looked up at the Judge with easy innocence. "I'm shore sorry, Judge," he said plaintively, "I was just aimin to tell the truth."

"Then that-air Beaumont," Bumps was continuing, "he slipped easy in the door, in the dark, and the door shut."

Bumps paused again, and shifted luxuriously in his chair. The chair creaked in the stillness.

"It was the third door off the corner," Bumps said. "Yeah," he repeated, "the third door." Then he sat up straight in his chair. "It is the door of the office what belongs"—he pointed—"to him."

His finger was pointing like a pistol at the heart of Sugg Lancaster.

It might have been a pistol, for Sugg Lancaster's face was white and sick with fear.

Mr. Madison leaned across Jeremiah to Hawgood. "My God," he whispered harshly, "I see it all. It's a trick to pin it on the New Court, to make the murder a conspiracy, to . . ."

And Bumps had eased back in his chair now and was saying ". . . and that-air Beaumont muster gone to git the lay of the land, to find out how the house was, and Colonel Fort's room and . . ."

Madison was up. "I object! The witness is . . ."

"Objection sustained!" Judge Cooper said.

And all the while Gregg stood there, stiff and stunned, swallowing hard.

"I see, I see it all," Mr. Madison was whispering, "it's a . . ."

And Jeremiah saw it, too. It was a plot, brilliant and simple, to tie him and Lancaster together in the same package. Whatever had pointed to the guilt of one now pointed to the guilt of both. The argument would be simple. Lancaster by his own admission had known Jeremiah. Lancaster, close to the inner circle of New Court, had played on Jeremiah's prejudices and made of him a willing instrument. He had spied out the house for him. He had given him the last information and instructions. And Lancaster and Jeremiah would hang together.

Jeremiah now saw it all. Bumps and Jessup had everything. They had a stronger case than the single case against Jeremiah. They had cut Lancaster out of any share of the reward. They had drawn Mrs. Fort and Saunders into their plan by making Fort's death appear the result of a New Court conspiracy. That had flattered Mrs. Fort's vanity and soothed her fears of being named the unloved wife, and so she had been willing to identify Jeremiah's voice.

Had Gregg been party to the project? Clearly not, Jeremiah decided. Gregg's shock and Bumps' insolent relish had been too real. It would have been easy for Jessup and Bumps to point out to John Saunders that Gregg was, after all, New Court in sympathy and would naturally prefer to treat the crime as one of personal vengeance and not partisan fury. So they would keep their secret and spring it on Gregg in court. Then he would be forced to follow that line. If he wanted a conviction. And Gregg wanted a conviction above all.

We can accept Jeremiah's guess. It accounts for all the facts.

Gregg had rallied and was continuing with the direct examination of his witness. Bumps was telling all the dreary and predictable lies, the handkerchief at the Saunders door, the boot pattern, the dirk, how Jeremiah had stolen both dirk and handkerchief to destroy the evidence.

Mr. Madison's cross-examination was cool, savage and protracted. To take one section of the transcript:

Mr. M.: Where did you first notice the loss of the dirk?

B.: At Mr. Smart's house.

Mr. M.: You have testified that Mr. Beaumont had stolen it from you?

B.: Yeah, he done it.

Mr. M.: How do you know?

B.: Well, a man just knows.

Mr. M.: How? Did you see him? Did you feel him? Did you smell him?

B.: I just knowed.

Mr. M.: Are you sure, Mr. Bumps, that you did not lose the dirk? After you had found that it would not cut the handkerchief, after you remembered that the wound in the victim was made by an edged weapon, after . . .

Objection.

Objection sustained.

Mr. M.: Well, Mr. Bumps, let us accept, for the purpose of discussion, that you did know by your mystic intuition that Mr. Beaumont had stolen your precious and incriminatory dirk. You say that you knew the fact at Smart's house?

B.: Yeah.

Mr. M.: When did you notice the loss of the handkerchief?

B.: At Bardstown, in the tavern.

Mr. M.: You have testified here that Mr. Beaumont had stolen it from you.

B.: Yeah.

Mr. M.: In the Bardstown tavern, when you discovered the loss, did you not first accuse Mr. Crawford of having lost it?

B.: Now look here, I ain't gonna be . . .

Mr. M.: You will answer the question. And may I remind you of the law of perjury?

Objection.

Objection sustained.

Mr. M.: Did you accuse Mr. Crawford of having lost it?

B.: Yeah, but it was afore I knowed that . . .

Mr. M.: You have answered the question. You have admitted

331

that you first accused Mr. Crawford of having lost the handkerchief.

B.: But you ain't sayin I . . .

Mr. M.: When Mr. Beaumont insisted that hunt be made for the handkerchief, you opposed such a plan?

B.: I didn't oppose nuthin. I just knowed that that-air Beaumont had stole it.

Mr. M.: How did you know it?

B.: I just knowed it.

Mr. M.: Like you *just knowed* he had stolen the dirk?

B.: Yeah.

Mr. M.: You were the custodian, Mr. Bumps, of two very important pieces of evidence. According to your account, you discovered that a dangerous and subtle fellow had stolen one piece of evidence, and then the next day you allowed him to steal the second. Don't you feel that you were a—a trifle—careless, Mr. Bumps?

Objection.

Objection sustained.

Tumult in the court.

It was a sad day for Bumps. Nothing could protect him—the objections of Gregg, his arrogance, his powerful hulk or the great hands that worked and knotted emptily in his lap with the knuckles glistening with sweat. Nothing could protect him against that cold, grinding savagery.

It was a torture and an exhibition. Jeremiah knew that it was an exhibition. He suddenly knew that Mr. Madison had long since finished with Bumps for all practical purposes. He was staging an exhibition. For whose benefit?

And then Jeremiah knew. It was for the benefit of Mr. Crawford. For Crawford's turn was to come, and now he could watch what might be in store for him. Oh, it didn't matter about Bumps, he would squirm and sweat and then it would be over. But it would matter for Crawford, to be shamed before men, to be proved a liar, a dupe, and a fool, to be proved the companion of louts and knaves, to suffer the barbs and ironies of a gentleman like Mr. Madison, high-fronted, correct and severe in his black, confident in rank and power.

And Crawford knew, too. You could know that he knew, for he sat there streaked white in the face, gnawing his ragged mustache, staring with the fascination of horror at Bumps, his brother in abomination, the index of his last ruin. He had had land and servants—not much land and not many servants, but enough, enough. He had held his head up, and men like Mr. Madison had acknowledged his grave bow. But now he was stuck in a stinking harness shop in a back street, and all that was left him was his black coat and his honor, and in an hour, a day, Mr. Madison would flay his honor from him, and that poor, threadbare black could never huddle him warm against the chill of disgrace.

So Crawford came to the stand, with the gaze of Jessup and Bumps, on one side, fixed upon him, and on the other, the gaze of Mr. Madison. So he could lift his eyes to neither side. At first, after the oath, he looked at the floor, and then, out of some last strength or desperation to escape, out of the window, over the heads of the people, into the glittering sky.

His tale was halting and confused. Gregg fretted and fumed under his professional calm, as Crawford blurred the answers to his questions. Yes, Bumps had tested the boot of Beaumont against the pattern. Had it fit? Yes, but in a manner of speaking. Had it fit? A man might say so if he made due allowance. Allowance for what? Well, the pattern wasn't drawed too well. Who drew the pattern? He himself had drawn the pattern. Had he known that the pattern wasn't drawn well? He had drawed the best he knew. How had he known it wasn't drawn well? Bumps had said it woggled, but for himself, he didn't know. Did woggling mean a mere wavering of outline? You might say so. Aside from the wavering of outline, the pattern had fit the boot? Yes— yes, if a man made due allowance and wanted to say so in a manner of speaking and—

Hawgood leaned to Mr. Madison and whispered, "Poor Gregg, he is breaking down his own witness for us."

Mr. Madison nodded, and studying Crawford, whispered back: "I never saw a more unwilling liar. If we nurse him, he may tell the truth in the end."

"Yes," said Hawgood, "and have his throat cut in an alley. Look at Bumps!"

Jeremiah looked at Bumps. Bumps was leaning forward, and baleful cunning glinted in the pig's eyes. "Yes," Jeremiah said, "there's murder there." He laughed. "And why shouldn't there be murder? With every word Crawford utters, Bumps loses a dollar."

And so it went on for the whole dreary tale. Crawford gave and took back, took back and gave. As Jeremiah puts it, he "spoke in riddles and shadow, gagged on *yes* and retched at *no*, and sought to conceal himself in the dusk of circumstance." And all the while Gregg suffered and fumed to fetch him out into the light.

"I'll fetch him out," Mr. Madison whispered grimly.

"He'll come to one bait," Jeremiah replied.

"What?"

"Your implicit belief in his honor."

Mr. Madison snorted. "Honor!" he whispered, "honor—that poor boggler!"

"Yes, honor," Jeremiah said. "For he will come to the lure of your belief that he will speak the truth."

"He will be afraid," Madison said.

"Yes," Jeremiah said, and studied Crawford again, "but he might risk it."

"And die for it," Mr. Madison said.

Hawgood, with his gaze fixed curiously on Crawford said, "Yes, yes, and die for it." Then he added, still looking at Crawford: "But men have died for truth before."

In the early afternoon, the dreary tale was over. And Mr. Madison took the witness. He took him with a massive courtesy and profound respect. He wished to compliment the witness, he said, on the love for the public good and attachment to justice that had inspired him last December "to leave the press of business and his thriving affairs" (at this the witness visibly straightened and looked about with a pitiful air of pride and vindication) and seek to "bring an assassin to book." Mr. Madison appreciated, he said, the difficulty of setting forth with perfect certainty small events of the past. And he more deeply appreciated the scruples exhibited by the witness in refusing to commit himself to statements on which he could not be perfectly clear before God and man.

At this point Nathan Gregg was on his feet, objecting.

But Mr. Madison interrupted him. "Am I to understand, sir," he demanded of the prosecutor, "that you do not share my belief in the scruples of the witness?"

Judge Cooper's gavel came down. "Will you proceed to business and question the witness," he ordered.

Mr. Madison bowed.

Crawford's answers were still larded with *disremembers* and *manners of speaking*, with evasions and confusions, but question by question he moved in an imperceptible drift, like a chip on the tide of Mr. Madison's certainty. He eddied and shifted, but the tide was sure. He looked into Mr. Madison's face and found there his strength, the illusion of strength. To Crawford, as Jeremiah says, Mr. Madison was a staff for the hand and the shadow of a rock.

The result, substantially, was that the pattern had not fitted the boot, that the dirk had torn rather than cut the handkerchief; that Bumps had lost the dirk and refused to search for it; that Bumps had lost the handkerchief, accused Crawford of having done so, and opposed any search; that the pattern produced at the Court of Inquiry might not have been the original pattern of the track under the Saunders' window, for he could not remember any identifying mark.

334

Then it was over, and as Crawford rose to go back to his seat, he found the eyes of Bumps and Jessup upon his. His knees gave and his hands trembled.

It was the end of the day.

"He may save his soul yet," Hawgood said.

"Wait till tomorrow," Mr. Madison replied. "They have not finished with him."

They had not finished with him. For the next morning, Crawford, sick in the face, sat for the re-direct examination by Gregg. Crawford remembered better now. He remembered that there had been a mark on the original pattern, a curious whorl in the paper, and that same whorl appeared in the pattern used at the Court of Inquiry. Many things came back to mind now. And he said them in his sick voice and never lifted his eyes from the floor.

"He lies, and all know it," Madison said savagely.

That seemed true—that all knew Crawford lied. And all knew that the trial was good as over and Jeremiah would walk out free. All seemed to know it except Gregg. Why didn't Gregg know it?

Then Jeremiah remembered: Gregg was depending on Marlowe and Marlowe's lie. Jeremiah remembered that with wicked glee, thinking how Marlowe would come on the appointed day to confound him. Then, with a stab of fear, he remembered one more thing: he, Jeremiah Beaumont, was also depending on Marlowe and Marlowe's lie. *Well, lie for lie,* he thought grimly, and the fear was gone. He knew which lie Marlowe would tell.

That night Munn Short, the jailer, came clambering stiff-legged down the ladder with the basket of supper, set out the food, and then settled himself, as he sometimes did, to talk while the prisoner ate. "You air gittin off," he said.

"Do you think so?" Jeremiah asked politely, reaching for the platter of peas and ham.

"Everybody says you air, and I says so, too. I done hear'd me lots of lawin twelve years I been here. Yeah, lots of lawin, fer you know"—he leaned and pointed his pipe-stem at Jeremiah—"you know I takes a pow-ful interest in folks comes to stay in my house here. I go to all the lawin fer 'em, *pro* and *con, sub peney* and *haby corpiss,* and may God have mercy on yore soul. Hell fahr, I bet my head is so swole with law I oughta be jedge and make them lawyers yore-honor me all day long, till cows drop coon-hounds stid of calves and bulls grow tits. Yeah, lak I was sayin, I hear'd me lots of law, and I says you gonna git off."

"You ought to be a judge, Mr. Short," Jeremiah said. "You have a fine legal mind."

"I knows when folks is lyin," the jailer said, "and that-air court is full of lies lak a dead dog with maggots and July bearin down."

"I recognized a few," Jeremiah said.

"Yeah, you let 'em lie enough, and you won't have to do nuthin. Jest let 'em lie you out. They done tole too many lies on you. One or two leetle lies—now that might hang you. But all them lies—hell fahr, you git so many lies and hit jest biles down to truth. Lak renderin lard."

Jeremiah had the tin cup of coffee halfway to his lips. But at those last words the cup stopped in mid-air. A chill ran down his spine and rippled tingling out into his limbs, like ripples spreading on a pond from a stone thrown in. *Truth*, he thought, *truth*.

Over the poised cup he stared at the dirty, hairy old man, and hated him.

Then, with enormous care he brought the cup to his lip, and set it there. He was fearful, he says, that it might shake. It might shake, and those bleared, old, squinting eyes might know all.

But the old man knew nothing, and was saying: "Yeah, you gonna walk out here, in God-a-Mighty's sun. But I tell you, ain't all laid down here has walked out to joy and rejoicin. Ever kind has laid down on that-air bed." He pointed the stem of his clay pipe at the bed in the dark alcove. "Ever kind—the wickit and the pure of heart, mean ole gristle and them so young they nigh ain't sprung beard, them as had blood on they hands and them as had prayin in the mouth. That-air bed is a mortal place to lay down, and they is ever kind as had laid thar. And rose up to what was their'n. The glory and walkin free, or the pain and the angrish. When the rope taken holt. But you now, you is innocent, and I am shore glad fer . . ."

Jeremiah rose abruptly, jarring the table, so that the candle-flame danced and shuddered.

Then he found the old man's eyes curiously upon him.

"My God, my God," he exclaimed. "Can't you see? Can't you understand? I want to be quiet. To be by myself. Can't you . . ."

The old man got up slowly, favoring the game leg, still looking at Jeremiah. And with his gaze still on Jeremiah, he began to assemble into the basket the objects of the table and the broken food. Then the old man swung toward the ladder, and took two paces.

"Wait!" Jeremiah called. "Wait!" He suddenly felt lost and abandoned.

The old man turned.

"I want . . ." Jeremiah began, "I want to beg your pardon."

"It ain't nuthin," the old man said.

"You have been kind to me, and I want to beg your pardon. I do not want you to be angry. Are you angry?"

336

"Son," the old man said, "I ain't angry. Not with you ner no man."

He turned and began his laborious ascent. Then the door dropped and the bolt slammed home.

"I want to be quiet," Jeremiah repeated, to the empty cell aloud. "I want to be by myself." That was all. To be by himself. To hear no voices. He had heard so many voices. That was the trouble. He was not afraid. There was no fear. It was just that he wanted to be quiet.

It was just that he wanted to be quiet. Quiet now. With no voices. But the voice now was the voice of Mr. Madison. Of Hilton Hawgood. And the voices would not be quiet. Mr. Madison's voice would not be quiet. It was saying: "And I took this case because I had confidence in you. In your innocence. Mr. Hawgood came because he had confidence in you. But you—you have lacked confidence in me. In him. You have betrayed us, betrayed . . ."

And Jeremiah felt like crying out: *Betrayed, betrayed, it is I who am betrayed.*

He could cry out with justice, for he had been betrayed.

That morning, two days after the testimony of Crawford, Captain Marlowe had appeared in court, shaven and scrubbed and wearing a new blue coat with brass buttons and a new neck-cloth, arrayed as for a wedding and grave and self-important in the face as for a funeral.

But Marlowe was not called.

Late in the afternoon Nathan Gregg took from his satchel a packet of papers, rose, and addressed Judge Cooper. "Your Honor," he said, "I am in possession of a most interesting and significant—yea, heinous —document. It is prepared by the defendant's own hand. It is a bold and bare-faced attempt to suborn a witness and corrupt justice. Had the subornation not been attempted upon an honest man"—and Gregg bowed toward Marlowe—"it might have . . ."

The terrible truth struck Jeremiah like a blow in the belly, and his breath went out. He could hear no further words, and the room reeled and swam. All but the face of Marlowe. That face, yellow and larded with self-esteem above the new brass buttons, was fixed. It was the entire world.

Then he heard the weight of Mr. Madison shift and his chair grind on the floor. And Hawgood's withheld breath escape with a hiss. He did not dare look to either side.

He stared at Marlowe. He could at least do that. As Marlowe could not look at him, he could not look at Mr. Madison or Hawgood.

Judge Cooper now held the document in his hands. Words were being said, but Jeremiah could not understand them. But he did see Marlowe rise and twitch his coat and move toward the witness chair.

But he could not follow Marlowe's words. But he could see Marlowe's lips move.

Then Mr. Madison was up. Enough had been said, he affirmed, to show that the document was of a confidential and privileged nature entrusted to the hands of the defendant's wife, from whom it had been improperly obtained. Therefore, he protested, the document was inadmissible as evidence, as was any allusion to its contents.

Then Nathan Gregg was speaking, and the room began to stir and rustle. The gavel crashed. In the new silence, Judge Cooper declared that on the morrow the Court would rule on the admissibility of the document.

The court was adjourned. Jeremiah was led back to the cell. Neither Mr. Madison nor Hawgood had spoken to him. Nor had he seen their faces.

He saw their faces that night, in the cell, by the light of the candle. They stood before his table.

Mr. Madison's voice was saying: "And I took this case because I had confidence in you. In your innocence. Mr. Hawgood came because he had confidence in you. But you—you have lacked confidence in me, in him. You have betrayed us, betrayed us and withheld information and tried to go behind us and hoodwink us, your friends, in no honest sort . . ."

Jeremiah stepped forward to the edge of the table and laid his hands upon it. They would have trembled, he thought, if he had not done so.

"Gentlemen," he said, and was happy to find his voice clear and calm, "you have a grievance. But you must believe me when . . ."

"Believe?" demanded Mr. Madison, in some asperity.

Jeremiah bowed slightly in acknowledgment of the tone, then corrected himself. "You must *try* to believe me when I give you the circumstance. You must try to understand . . ."

"Understand what?" Mr. Madison demanded. "I understand that you . . ."

Jeremiah lifted his hand. "Have you ever been ringed round by false witness?" he asked, and leaned earnestly at them. "And seen every fact perverted from nature to your hurt? And then seen subornation enter your own house by a crevice and seen the chance to turn the invention upon the inventor—what would you do? What would you do?"

Before an answer came, he said sharply, "Wait!" and stepped into the alcove and fumbled with a brick in the floor and drew out papers wrapped in a handkerchief. He flung them on the table, and extracted one. "Look," he commanded, "look!" and passed it to Mr. Madison.

It was Rachel's letter giving Marlowe's visit and his account of Lancaster's approaches. The two faces bent above it, in the candlelight.

When the eyes lifted, before either mouth could speak, he said, "I grant you there is a lie in my document." "Yes," Mr. Madison cut in, "about the bills—the money Marlowe was to produce in court."

"No," Jeremiah said, "that is not a lie. At least not a lie in one sense. For money was offered him by Lancaster, and . . ."

"A lie is a lie," Mr. Madison said.

Jeremiah fixed him with his gaze. "My God," he demanded again, "should I hang for that?"

"No," Mr. Madison said, heavily. Then: "No, not for that."

"For what then?" Jeremiah demanded fiercely, thinking to detect sarcasm in the words. "For what, then, pray? For if you do not believe me . . ."

"Believe?" Mr. Madison echoed.

"Yes—believe! And if you do not believe me, you say . . ."

Mr. Madison seemed about to speak, but Hawgood stepped forward and laid a hand on Mr. Madison's arm, and looked earnestly at Jeremiah. "We believe that you are a man much abused," he said, "and sworn against for gain and rancor. We will prevent that if we can."

He turned to Mr. Madison, and lifted his hand from the arm and clapped him on the shoulder. "That's true, isn't it, Madison?"

Mr. Madison stirred again, as to shift the weight, paused, and said, "Yes. Yes. That is true." Then lifting his gaze somberly to Jeremiah, he added: "but I would that you had told me."

"I was in error," Jeremiah said, "and I am ashamed. But I thought— I thought that the Lord had delivered them unto me—and I could do it. One stroke, and be safe. But I could not tell you. Involve you. You could not tamper with the course of truth. But I—the temptation was great, gentlemen—and I—I pawned a bit of my truth—my honor, if you will—for"—he wanted to stop talking, to stop explaining, but he could not stop, for the words kept on coming and his tongue wagged and his lips convolved against his will—"for my safety—for my neck— but also"—and the words kept coming out—"also to serve justice— to serve . . ."

Hawgood cut in sharply, his thin, schoolmasterish face sharper and thinner for the candlelight striking it from below, and his tone was like the tone of the schoolmaster that interrupts a halting and inept recitation: "It is done now. Now we will do what we can. To redeem it."

He picked up Rachel's letter from the table, and turned to Mr. Madison. "If we can present this to the Court—if we can have it entered— it might do much . . ."

Mr. Madison leaned and struck the table with his fist. "That Marlowe!" he exclaimed. "That blackguard!" Then his fury seemed to strike him wordless.

And so it was over, and Hawgood and Mr. Madison were gone, and the candle was low in the socket, and every nerve in Jeremiah's body was tingling and twitching, and the words kept coming into his head and his mouth, and he said them out loud. He walked up and down on the uneven bricks and said the words out loud, carefully and logically, explaining how everything was, how it had all come about.

Then, all at once, he knew that there was one thing he could not explain. How had Rachel let the document into the hands of Marlowe? He had warned her. To read it to Marlowe. To dictate it so that it would be in Marlowe's own hand. My God, had she betrayed him, too?

He flung himself at the table, seized his quill and paper, and began to write. He was writing a letter to Rachel. She should know how she, with her own hands, had knotted the rope, how she had betrayed him, she for whom he had done all and risked all.

At two o'clock the next afternoon Munn Short came to the cell. "Hit's time," he announced. "The Jedge done made up his mind and et."

Judge Cooper had decided to admit the document and have it read. The document, he granted, had been come by in a peculiar way that did no man credit, and it had in it some things not bearing on the case. But it must be read, for it was in the prisoner's handwriting, and the delivery to the witness Marlowe had been voluntary.

So it was read, and Jeremiah had to sit and bear a stony face as best he could, and hear his words come alive in Nathan Gregg's voice to shame him, and know that now, no matter how things ended, the best he could hope would be pity and not the respect due a man. He had done all for honor, and it had come to this.

The reading was over. Gregg addressed the Court, saying that one important witness could not appear because of sickness. But that witness was mending fast, and could come within a few days. Might he then be introduced? If so, the prosecution would rest.

It was an amazing request, Judge Cooper remarked. It might be granted only with the consent of the defense.

Mr. Madison asked if, under the peculiar circumstances, the defense might know the name of the witness.

Gregg declined to divulge the name. But added that, if the request were not granted, legions of witnesses were yet available whose testimony would fill in the time until the unnamed witness should be able to come. He, Gregg, merely wished to spare the patience of the Court.

Mr. Madison, after a short whispering with Hawgood, rose to say that the defense would consent. That the defense would trust in the fullness of truth.

When Nathan Gregg bowed his thanks, and preened his razored and perfumed vanity, his face wore a sneer like oil.

Could they not have fought it? Jeremiah asked himself that. Insisted that the trial be continued, fought any delays or postponement, driven it through, and held off that mysterious witness?

He leaned to Mr. Madison. "Could we not have fought?" he asked.

Mr. Madison turned his heavy, brooding gaze upon him. "Fought it?" he echoed. Then shook his head. "We are in no position to fight it. If it is a lie, we must try to brand the lie. If it is the truth, we must make the best of it. We must not appear to fear the truth. That is our only hope. After . . ." He hesitated.

"After my document to Marlowe? Do you mean that?" Jeremiah demanded.

"Yes," Mr. Madison said. "That is what I mean." And turned away.

And Jeremiah thought: *My God, does he betray me, too?*

As the witnesses for the defense came and went, Jeremiah's heart rose steadily. The story that came forth was so clear, so simple, so logical. So many lies were exposed, lie after lie.

Two witnesses declared that Jeremiah had worn a dark green handkerchief on his brow when he appeared in the Weisiger House—and no cross-barred one as others had sworn—and declared, to the best of recollection, that its color was the color of the burned bit on the Jessup hearth. As for the cross-barred handkerchief, and the tale that it had been found by the lilac bush at the Saunders door, a certain Powell Hancher, "an eminent and Godly gentleman and a friend of Fort," swore that he had made a tour, inch by inch, of the area shortly after six o'clock and had found nothing, and so, if any handkerchief had been found toward seven, it had been placed there. Hilton Hawgood's own little black book in which he had recorded the measurements of the track under the Saunders window was produced by gentlemen into whose keeping he had entrusted it the morning of the Court of Inquiry, and measurements were made again under the eyes of the jury. Two men who had been present at Tupper's tavern at the time of the trouble with old McFerson gave cool and unprejudiced accounts of that event. Mr. Bascomb gave the story of the tavern at Bardstown, declaring that Bumps had opposed all search for the lost handkerchief until forced. Several persons of good reputation swore that they had frequently heard Jeremiah refer to William J. Grierson and had never heard him mistake "K" for "J," as the assassin had done and as some witnesses for the prosecution (two shady and shifty characters) had sworn was Jeremiah's practice. William J. Grierson

341

himself, though infirm, came all the way from Bowling Green to declare a good acquaintance between him and Jeremiah and to say that Jeremiah had correctly written in his name on many legal papers.

And so on, witness after witness. Nathan Gregg could not shake a single one. They were men strong in their honesty and in their good name, and they knew what they knew. So the joy grew in Jeremiah. "I began to feel," he writes, "that I should walk out free, but the joy I felt was not the mere joy of that success, but a joy to find all good men and true gentlemen ranged on my side to strike down lies raised against me. It was as though their very trust and truth had done more than make me free, had made me innocent of all blame and in their bright contagion I was as reborn. I did not then probe the depth and reason of my joy, but breathed in that sweet illusion and sustained by it walked firmly to the witness chair when my name was called."

That sweet illusion sustained him well. He was a good witness. We have that from the record, the clear, unwavering answers, the precise phrases.

Jeremiah's self-command did not waver even before Nathan Gregg's attack, before his nagging, innuendo and virulence, and more than once Jeremiah turned the tables to bring guffaws from the spectators and grins from the jury. Even when the subject of his instructions to Marlowe was presented, he was firm. He confessed his fault and weakness, he said, but ringed round with false witness (here protests from Gregg and confusion in the court) he had been foolish enough to take the bait offered by Lancaster through Marlowe (protest and confusion) and to trust to subterfuge and an old friend's loyalty rather than to the justice of his own cause. In the confusion, Jeremiah asked permission to present the letter from his wife which had led to his action (Mr. Madison had planned it thus), that his action might be explained if not condoned. (Over the protest of Gregg, the letter was admitted and was read into the record.)

At the end, Jeremiah asked permission of the Court to make one comment: he wished to say that, whatever he had done in the transaction with Marlowe, it should be clearly understood it was done without knowledge or connivance of his counsel, and the full blame was his own.

The day was clearly Jeremiah's, and when he came back to his seat, Hawgood took his hand. The clasp of that hand seemed to seal the sweet illusion that sustained him. That night he slept like a baby. ("We can sleep but in innocence, or the dream of innocence. Why did I ever wake!")

He woke to go into the courtroom and find there his dearest friend. Wilkie Barron sat somewhat toward the far side of the room, immersed in a book and seemingly oblivious of his surroundings. Jeremiah's impulse was to rush across and greet him, but even as he took the first step, order was called in the court.

Wilkie did not lift his eyes at the sound, and that struck Jeremiah as queer. Why did not Wilkie look up, at least look up to greet him? He was studying Wilkie's face across the distance. It seemed thinner than before, and paler. Or was that a trick of the light? Or had he been sick? Even as that question struck him, he remembered that the mysterious witness had been delayed for sickness. But that witness could not be Wilkie.

Even at that moment Nathan Gregg was saying that the witness whose appearance had been delayed for sickness was now present and with the indulgence of the Court would speak. And Wilkie rose to his name.

Pale from sickness? Jeremiah thought. *No, pale for shame!*

But Wilkie was coming across the little open space with his head held high and in all proper dignity. He took the oath that he would speak the truth.

He spoke the truth:

Had he known Jeremiah Beaumont?

Yes.

Well?

Very well. Jeremiah Beaumont had lived with him in the house of his mother, Mrs. Girard Barron, in Bowling Green. For two years. They had been close friends.

Friends, friends! The word rang in Jeremiah's head.

Had the accused known Colonel Cassius Fort?

He had been employed in his law office.

Why had he left that office?

He, Wilkie Barron, feared that he had caused this break.

How so?

By revealing something to Jeremiah Beaumont that did Colonel Fort no credit.

What?

The talk that Colonel Fort had fathered a child of Rachel Jordan of Saul County.

How had this caused the break?

Jeremiah Beaumont had felt the call of honor to take Miss Jordan's cause as his own.

How so?

And then began the long account—question and answer, question and answer—leading to the moment when Jeremiah had confided his resolve to avenge Rachel Jordan, to the pursuit of Fort from Frankfort to Lexington, to the marriage, to Jeremiah's candidacy ("undertaken at my suggestion to divert him from more private thoughts, for politics and policy never lay close to his concern").

And then it was over, and Wilkie had not once looked at him, and the speeches began.

Gregg talked all day, weaving the lies, all the lies that Bumps and Jessup and the others had told, and then, then at last, the truth told by Wilkie Barron. And he rested there: the private spite, long brooding aggravated by political difference, or political difference aggravated by long brooding, the deed. He touched on Lancaster, but lightly, hinted that Lancaster had not corrupted the accused and conspired with him to the deed, but that the accused had corrupted Lancaster, using him as spy and tool, perhaps a tool unwitting of the dire stakes played for.

Jeremiah says that he heard little of all this. He felt that all the words could mean little now. He was like a man caught in a black flood and being borne down and down, and all the words spoken now would be but bubbles and froth on that blackness. Wilkie had cast him off, and cast him in. What if Wilkie had spoken truth? My God, could he not have told one lie, one little lie, to save a friend and all that friendship meant? My God, he knew the deed was done for justice.

Even the words of Mr. Madison and Hawgood were but bubbles and froth on the dark flood. He did not listen to them. But others listened and were impressed. And we can read the speeches now on the yellow, flaking pages of the old newspaper, Mr. Madison's "grinding logic and powerful sarcasm," and Hawgood's "flights of fervid fancy and impassioned appeal to justice."

Mr. Madison dwelt on all the contradictions and distortions of truth. He rehearsed them all. Then asked, "Shall we believe that this deed was done for vengeance? No. This is not to contradict the testimony that when the news of that poor unfortunate woman's plight reached the defendant he did not feel the pulse of rage. Why should he not? I ask any man who is a man if he does not feel sympathy with the sentiments of that romantic youth. But think! At that time he had never seen the lady. His rage was but the abstract rage, a dream of honorable anger. I ask you, has heart e'er been thewed or steel lifted by such? No, for action comes when the quarrel strikes nearer home and twists our vitals to pain and not our mind to dream. What if, long after, that romantic boy had loved the lady and won her love? Love mellows, happiness mellows, and time grows over the old scar like moss. The boy becomes a man, with manhood's prudence. Think of the years that had passed, the years of love and peace in that sylvan retreat where . . ."

Bubbles and froth, and Hawgood's eloquence, too, was bubbles and froth, too, on the black flood.

After an hour and thirty-six minutes the jury returned a verdict of guilty.

There was some disturbance in the court, hoots and cheers and exchanges of blows. There was brawling in the yard, and, as the evening wore on, in alleys and taverns. In the morning one of the jurors was found beaten unconscious in a vacant lot, but since his purse was gone, it could not be settled conclusively whether the deed had been prompted by cupidity or an outraged sense of justice. All that is certain is that early in the evening the man, with several other jurors, was seen drinking with Bumps.

"Boys," Bumps had shouted to the jurors, as he made for them and began to wring their hands and slap them on the back as soon as the verdict was announced, "boys, you shore done yore duty, by God and you didn't, and I want you boys to come git yore likker with me, and I'll shore pay . . ."

While Bumps continued in this vein, Jeremiah was shaking hands with Mr. Madison and Hawgood, and thanking them. Then an officer led him away. He was resigned, though strangely cheerful in his resignation, cheerful because now nothing, somehow, seemed to matter. He felt like nothing, light as air.

He came out into the yard. It was a beautiful, calm evening, drifting toward sunset. A few bull-bats whisked low and whimpered in the light. He lifted his eyes to the high sky, and thought how beautiful it was, crossed and threaded by the darting birds, and how, light or dark, it was always there. "I lifted my eyes to the sky," he describes the moment, "and dwelt on its solemnity and beauty, and thought how beneath it, all men and things, and I among them, appeared and passed away. Then I felt like the man in the tale told of the great earthquake which in 1811 shook the Mississippi so that the waters ran north for three days, and which ravaged the country, striking down cities and men. A man sat in an upper room in Louisville on that night, gaming at cards for large sums, and he had just received a hand and was inspecting it to know whether he should answer a heavy bet, when the quake struck so that chimneys fell and walls, and people began to shout in the street that the end of the world was come. The man looked once at his cards, in that tumult, then laid them down and smiled and said, 'Gentlemen, it is sad to think that such a beautiful world shall be destroyed.'

"So I looked into the sky and felt a resigned sadness that its beauty and all things should soon be, for me, blotted out forever."

Jeremiah proceeded across the yard to the jail. Munn Short was standing in the room above the cell, by the open trap door. He came to

345

Jeremiah and took his hand. "I done hear'd," he said, "and I am shore sorry."

"Thank you," Jeremiah said.

"Don't think cause I warn't thar in court I didn't keer," Short said. "I keered and yearned to know. But I got called off fer my business."

"That's all right," Jeremiah said. He took a step toward the opening. He wanted to go down, down into that quietness and dark and hear no voices.

"It was fer my business," Short was saying, plucking at Jeremiah's sleeve, "but fer yore'n, too. They is somebody . . ."

"Thank you," Jeremiah said, disengaging himself, and starting his descent.

"I'll lock the door outside," Short was saying, "and leave the trap open fer air, bein she is . . ."

"Thank you," Jeremiah called back wearily.

Then he set his foot to the floor, and turned.

Beyond, by the table, Rachel stood.

X

WHEN JEREMIAH TURNED FROM THE LAD-
der to discover Rachel, he felt, as he records for us, a sudden distress.
Looking into the beautiful evening sky, he had experienced a sad
peace, and in that peace was prepared to go down into his cell and be
alone with his fate. "Now that all was over," he says, "I had thought to
go down into my private darkness, and in the privacy of that darkness
beyond voice or tread, had thought to embrace my peace. I had
forgotten—though I shame to say it—even my dear wife, for whom
all had been done. So now that I saw her thus without warning, I
felt a distress, and no glad cry rose to my lips and I stood at the
ladder."

The distress must have shadowed his face, for Rachel paused in
her step toward him as though rebuffed and confused, and stared
mournfully at him.

Then she cried, "Oh, Jerry, oh, Jeremiah, I have heard—they have
told me!" She rushed to him and seemed about to embrace him, but
when his arms did not rise to greet her, she sank on her knees before
him, and seized one of his hands, kissed it two or three times, and
laid her cheek against it, while she murmured, "And all for me—all
for me."

Her words echoed in his head. *And all for you—no! All by you—for if you had not given the letter to Marlowe* . . . And he felt the muscles tighten and tingle in his arm to snatch back the hand she kissed.

But she was murmuring: "All for me . . ."

He felt the tears on his hand, and thought that if he did not love her, what was there for him? That all had been blind butchery and lies. So he stooped to raise her, and as she lifted her face and the light from the open trapdoor fell across it, he saw how the heavy hair was in disorder and the flesh was chalky white so that the freckles stood out and the brown spot on the left cheek was no index of the warmth of her blood like the russet bloom on fruit, but a blotch. *She is not beautiful,* he thought, *she is not beautiful now,* but in the recognition of that fact he felt an overmastering pathos and warmth flood his being. "I do love you," he said. And repeated: "I do love you." Then suddenly the words wrenched out of him like a cry: "For if I do not love you, oh, what am I?"

"You are my poor Jerry," she said.

"Poor!" he exclaimed. "Poor! Not poor, for I have the richness of life. You have given it to me. Long ago!" So he raised her, and kissed her soberly on the brow.

Then she offered him her lips. As he kissed them, he noted how they felt dry and parched and cracked to his own, but that seemed to make the kiss more precious.

That was how she came to him. Or to be more exact, that was how she was brought to him. For officers from Frankfort had brought her. They had come to bring her before the Court of Inquiry to answer the charge of being accessory to the murder of Colonel Fort. They had appeared at dawn, and one had beat on the front door and hallooed, while others went to guard the back door and side door as though she were a common criminal who might take to the woods and hide out like an animal.

Sukie Marlowe had answered the racket at the door, standing there in her night-dress and wrapper, with bare feet. When they demanded Mrs. Beaumont, she asked what news—was her husband saved?—and before their answer, she said, thank the Lord, for it would make that poor sweet lady well again.

"If'n she waits fer that she won't never be well," one of the men said, and laughed.

"Yeah, fer they aim to hang him," another one said.

And the first: "And hang her, too, and she ain't keerful. Fer we done come fer her, sick or well."

So they forced their way into the house, and against Sukie's protests and tears, upstairs. They flung open one door after another, until they struck on the right one and saw Rachel, alarmed, sitting up in bed, clutching a sheet to her bosom.

All the while Sukie stood by the door and wept. Poor slatternly, stupid Sukie. She had lived in the house and been what comfort she could. She was not privy to Marlowe's treachery, and when she did learn of it, fell out with him and stayed bitterly at home in Saul County while he did his whoring and swaggering in Frankfort. But when the bribe was spent (as well as the two hundred dollars received from Rachel to be turned over to the Court according to Jeremiah's instructions—though Marlowe denied having had this money), he came back home, diseased, old, finished, and whining, and she took him in and nursed him to the grave.

But all that was to come. And now Sukie weeping at the door could do nothing to save Rachel.

On the road Rachel was so sick that the officers had to put up for a day at a farmhouse, and the first night in Frankfort she tossed all night with a fever, while Jeremiah sat by the bed and held her hand and heard her tell in broken sentences how she had ridden out day after day to seek witnesses for him, how she had wept at night, how she had fallen sick, and in her sickness had betrayed him.

That sickness accounted for Marlowe's possession of the document. He had played his game deep. Once he knew that Jeremiah had taken the bait and put instructions in writing, he knew that he had to have possession of the document. When Rachel sat him down to take the dictation, he would claim that his eyes blurred, that he had a headache, that he had forgotten some pressing business on the farm. Once he took to his bed for several days. He must have thought, for a time, that he might have to steal it in the end, or take it by force. But Rachel fell sick and was too weak from the wild pain in her head to read it to him. The appointed day was coming on, and she was no better. At last in desperation, she gave it to him. She had undone Jeremiah, who loved her. She said that, over and over, and tossed her head on the pillow, in the alcove, beyond the fraying candlelight.

The next morning, in full daylight, she fell asleep, and when Jeremiah was called for the Court, he did not wake her. So he went alone to stand at the bar and hear the Judge declare to him that according to the law of the Commonwealth he had been indicted, tried, and found guilty of murder, and then asked if he had anything further to say why the sentence of the law should not be pronounced upon him.

"Yes, Your Honor," Jeremiah replied calmly, "I have something to say."

"You may speak," Judge Cooper said.

"I have this to say," Jeremiah said in a deliberate voice. "I have been convicted here by false witness and testimony perjured for gain, as all honest men now know and as all men shall recognize in the future time when passion and cupidity shall be withdrawn from the occasion."

It is interesting to remark here that Jeremiah did not affirm his innocence, only that he had been wrongly convicted. Was this merely an accident of phrasing, an emphasis caused by his own training in the law, or had the word *innocence* stuck in his throat at last to leave him with only a deep equivocation by the card? In any case, he spoke the words and then stood there while the Judge pronounced sentence upon him to be hanged by the neck until dead.

The execution was to take place on Thursday, August 30. The trial had run three weeks, ending on Saturday, June 24.

When Jeremiah was brought back to the cell, he found Rachel awake and sitting at the table. The jailer's wife had brought her water to wash, some hot food, and a little later, out of kindness, a pot of tea to give her strength. Rachel's face was still drawn and white, the brown spot was still a blotch on her cheek, and her eyes still stared with a preternatural intensity, but her hair was combed and coiled and the fever and restlessness had been replaced by a deep calm. The light from the open trap door fell across her face.

He told her that sentence had been pronounced, and the day set.

"Yes," she said, "yes," with a listlessness that made him think at first that she had not understood.

So he repeated his words.

"Yes," she said with the same listlessness. But now that show of indifference stabbed him so that he was about to burst nastily out that she should think nothing of the matter, that it was only his neck.

Before the angry thought had taken words, however, she said, "Yes, and I shall be with you. They will hang me, too. If they do not, I shall find a way to die on that day."

He was filled with shame for his resentment and pettishness. *Will I never be worthy—never be worthy?* he demanded of himself.

He leaned and took her face between his hands and looked searchingly into it, so long that the familiarity of those lineaments seemed to drain away and leave him staring into strangeness, even as he murmured, "My wife—my poor brave wife."

He suddenly released her, and straightened up. "No," he said, "you must live. To show the world the pattern of a true woman."

He took a few paces, turned, paced again.

She was shaking her head. "I shall die. That is all I ask. It is all I have ever asked of life. At least, for a long time. For as long as I can remember. To die."

Her words startled a peculiar irritation in him, he could not tell why. *Die—die,* he thought. What did she know of dying? She used the word, that mouth in that face he scarcely recognized made a sound, but she did not know what the sound meant. It was only a sound, a movement in the air. But there was something, some reality, behind the word. What was it? Did he, did he himself, know what it was?

The flesh along his spine began to twitch inwardly and tingle.

She was saying: "I'll confess. At the court. How I knew. How I made you do it. Then they'll have to hang me. They'll have to put a rope around my neck—and . . ." She lifted a hand to touch her throat, and began to turn her head gently from side to side, ever so slightly.

"Don't be a fool!" he burst out. "You'll confess nothing."

". . . and they'll do it—around my neck . . ."

He stepped to seize her by the shoulders, shaking her. "Listen to me. You'll confess nothing. For there's a chance. For me. For us both. Of having a mistrial declared. The document to Marlowe was wrongly admitted, it was privileged and should not have been admitted. There will be an appeal, for I'll make Madison and Hawgood appeal and . . ."

She studied him as he spoke. Then asked, interrupting him: "Do they—Madison and Hawgood—do they think you innocent?"

"Innocent, innocent!" he exclaimed savagely. "How do I know what they think? But they know I have been lied against and sold for a price, and they will appeal, and you will confess nothing. Do you hear?"

She nodded humbly.

"I will be cleared," he affirmed, and she nodded again, and as he watched the terrible humility of her bowed head, even as he spoke the words, he felt how sweet it would be to confess and be done, like closing your eyes and slipping into blackness.

He braced himself and started back from her, as from a dire contagion.

The next day was Sunday. Rachel was to appear at the Court of Inquiry on Monday. Saturday afternoon and evening she was sunk in a lassitude, sitting by the table or lying on the bed in the alcove. Whenever Jeremiah tried to talk to her, or even when he took her hand, she would say, "No—no—please—I am so tired."

So he paced the room, and at last, late at night, long after Short had come to bolt down the trap door, he lay down on the bed, carefully apart from her, and listened to her slow breath until he fell asleep.

On Sunday with some appetite she ate the breakfast brought by Short, and then, having washed herself, she sat by the table and began to comb her hair. She sat with her head bowed as though by the weight of the hair that fell in heavy folds almost to the floor, and moved the comb down through it in a slow, bemused motion. But the comb sometimes paused in the middle of a stroke, buried in the fold of hair, and then, after a long time, resumed. Jeremiah paced back and forth, and she sat there, cut off from him, shrouded in the inner shadow of the dense fall of hair, like a tent.

In the afternoon she lay on the bed in the alcove.

Quite late, toward five o'clock, steps moved across the room above, there was a rapping on the open trap door, and Munn Short's voice called down that Mr. Madison and Mr. Hawgood would like Mr. Beaumont to come up, please. Jeremiah ascended and greeted the guests, and the jailer withdrew, locking the door of the room behind him.

"You have sent for us?" Mr. Madison asked.

Jeremiah replied yes, that he had sent to impose upon their courtesy to discuss his situation to ask about an appeal, an appeal on the grounds that Marlowe's document was not admissible, to know if they thought well of such a course.

Mr. Madison was sad and heavy, and Hawgood abstracted. And for a moment after Jeremiah had finished speaking, neither answered. Mr. Madison was intently tracing the whorls of a knot in a plank of the floor with the point of his stick, and Hawgood's wry, distorted face inclined to watch that operation as though out of it would come the answer to a momentous question.

Jeremiah suddenly said: "I do not care much for myself. I am resigned. Follow what course consideration or conscience dictates in my behalf. But I beg you one thing. My wife, you know, has been brought here. They bring her here to persecute her. She is in despair for me, and is sick. They seized her from her bed, like savages. Can you do something for her? Why should she suffer more?"

Mr. Madison immediately agreed that he would do what he could. Might they go down to speak with her, he asked.

So Jeremiah went down to rouse her, and called back up the ladder when she was ready.

Mr. Madison greeted her, and Hawgood was introduced. They begged the honor of assisting her, Mr. Madison said.

"I thank you most heartily," Rachel said, "and do not think me ungrateful if I decline your offer. I can go in alone. Somehow—somehow I feel that I must go in alone. I have been alone. So long. So long. I must go alone."

"No," Mr. Madison said warmly, and said that he would never

permit it, no honorable man could permit it, to see a gentle and beautiful lady badgered and persecuted without a friend, and said more of that kind.

Jeremiah watched the stirring and the growing warmth in Mr. Madison's heaviness, the increasing animation of his face, the masterful lift of his arm in a gesture when he said again, no, that he would not permit it. And there flickered in his mind again the old thought how Madison, too, Madison like Fort, had been in that dark house with her, how Madison was like Fort, that same dark, heavy, full-fleshed breed with fine words but strong, blunt hands to seize the world and take what they wanted despite all the fine words and all the *dear sirs* and *by your leaves*. He had been in the house with her.

She must go in alone, Rachel was saying, and Madison was leaning toward her over his firmly planted stick, towering over her, insisting with fine words, while a flush grew under his swarthy skin.

Then, at the very instant when his rage tightened the muscles of his body and his breath came short, Jeremiah heard Rachel say faintly, "Yes—yes . . ." And murmur thanks for kindness.

So she had betrayed him, too. Not in the darkness in far away Saul County. But now. Just now. When that flushed, dark face leaned at her, she had betrayed him, too. Damn her, damn her—and he would hang for her.

With that his rage was gone. There was merely a great loneliness, and nothing mattered. And he found himself thanking Mr. Madison and Hawgood in phrases that were like ashes on the tongue.

Then Mr. Madison was saying to Rachel: ". . . and for your husband, do not despair. We will work for him. I swear it." And turning to Hawgood to lay a hand on his shoulder: "We'll save him, won't we, Hawgood?" And again to her warmly: "We believe in him, and we'll save him. If man can."

Then they were shaking Jeremiah's hand.

Then they were gone.

"They will save you," Rachel was saying.

"Save me," Jeremiah echoed. *Save me!* he thought, and his heart leaped. *I shall be saved!* The sweetness of life suddenly flooded him.

She was saying: "I know they will save you." And she reached to touch his arm.

He looked into her face, where the faintest flush now came through the chalky white. For an instant he recognized the old beauty.

He jerked back from her touch. For he suddenly thought: *They will save me because of her. Madison will do it for her.* And thought: *And was that why I brought him down? To show her to him? To make him flush and lean? To warm him. To show him my wife, like bait?*

Had he done that, lying to himself that it was all for her?
She touched him again, and under her hand he shivered.
My God, he thought, *my God, am I that vile!*

Jeremiah was permitted to attend the Court of Inquiry on Monday, to sit and watch the case against Rachel coil round and round her. Gregg had planned well. There was the old mysterious handbill used against Fort in his last campaign, accusing him of the seduction of Rachel Jordan. There was an affidavit by Sukie Marlowe that she had delivered Rachel Jordan of a dead child in May, 1821, and had buried it, a statement that Gregg's men had got from Sukie by wheedling and lies only four days earlier. There was new testimony by Marlowe about the return of Jeremiah from Frankfort, how he had waved a red ribbon like a flag, and how his wife had near fainted when she saw him and had to be helped upstairs by Mrs. Marlowe, and how later, after the arrest of her husband, she had spoken darkly of being to blame for all. And much more. Again the old tangle of lies and truths that blurred out all distinction.

Jeremiah had to sit and watch Rachel suffer under the words, surrounded by the prying eyes, the nudges, the whispers, the suppressed snickers. But she never flinched. She sat erect and cold, beside Mr. Madison. (Hawgood was not in court. Hawgood, Mr. Madison told Jeremiah, was busy preparing the appeal.)

Gregg had done well. When Mr. Madison escorted Rachel back to the cell, he maintained his air of confidence, and when he kissed Rachel's hand in parting, he said that all would be well. But Jeremiah was sure that he detected a shadow on his face.

And that night, after the candle was out, Rachel sat up in bed and called, "Make a light."

Jeremiah was still sitting by the table, in the dark. Now he fumbled to make the light, asking, "Are you sick? Are you sick?"

The candle caught, and she was crouched on the bed, staring at him. "I can't do it," she said.

"Do what?"

"Go on. Go on with—with the trial."

"There will be no trial," he said, with all the assurance he could muster. "You will not be indicted."

"Oh, it's not that. Not that. It's tomorrow. To go in that room and lie. To have to lie. I tell you, I'll confess. I'll confess, and it will all be over."

"Over," he said, and started up from his chair. "Over, and they'll hang you. Do you hear? And hang me. My God, I killed him for you, and now you'd hang me!"

She lifted a hand to her head and drove the fingers distractedly into the mass of hair, lifting its weight from her scalp. "Oh, you killed him," she uttered in a terrible, small voice.

"And for you," Jeremiah said, savagely.

"And for me," she echoed in the same voice.

"Yes," he said, and stepped to the edge of the bed, and stood leaning, "for you."

She reached out toward him weakly, fumbling to seize his hand. "You killed him," she said, "and you never told me—you never told me what he said. What did he say? I've seen it. I've seen it at night. In the dark. How the knife went in. How the knife came down and came down and came down and . . ."

"Twice, I tell you it was only twice," he cried out. "It was only twice I stabbed him."

She pulled herself up to her knees, dragging on to his hand for support as to a rope end. "Where?" she demanded. "Where?" And with her other hand she prodded at her own breast. "Here? Was it here?"

"Yes. There."

"I've seen it," she said. "I've seen it. In the dark. And I see his face and his mouth moves. But I never hear what he says. I've tried—I've tried to hear—but I never hear what he says." She pulled at Jeremiah's hand. "What did he say? If I only knew what he said . . ."

Jeremiah stiffened. "I will tell you what he said. He saw my face and called me by name, Jerry. And I replied, 'Not Jerry to you, but Beaumont,' and named him villain. So I struck him, and he gasped from the blow, and said, 'Jerry, you had to come.' I said, 'Yes, and come again,' and gave the second stroke."

He looked down into her staring eyes, trying to make out what was in them. Then he said: "The blood came from his mouth at the second stroke, and he spoke no more."

She tugged at his hand, like a child wheedling. "Was that all?" she asked, pettishly. "Was that all he said? Tell me what he said."

"My God, didn't you hear me tell you?" He snatched his hand from her clasp and she groped again for it.

She stared at him, and asked, whispering: "Tell me the truth. He cursed me. Didn't he name my name, and curse me?"

She tugged at his hand.

"Didn't he?"

"No!"

She released his hand, and sank back from him. "He did not curse me," she whispered. "Oh, he did not. If only he had done it—had cursed me—if . . ."

She suddenly let her head fall forward and shoulders slump. Sobs began to shake her.

"Stop it!" he commanded. "Stop!"

". . . if he had cursed me—then—then I wouldn't see—his face and . . ."

He leaned above her. "You love him," he said. "Is that it?"

She shook her head. "No," she said, "no—but I have seen his face."

"I saw his face," Jeremiah said, and straightened up. He was not looking at her, not speaking to her but beyond, to the cell of candle-light and shadows. "I saw his face, and I drove the knife in, and I took joy and I am not ashamed. He was a villain. Do you hear?" And he leaned over her, seizing her by the shoulder and shaking her. "Do you hear? A villain. Listen"—he leaned confidentially as to tell a secret—"do you remember—remember how he wrote the handbill? To say you had a child by the black man, by Gabbo? Do you remember?"

The sobbing stopped.

"Ah," Jeremiah whispered, "so you remember that?"

"Yes," her voice came very small and distant, for she still slumped forward with her head almost touching the bed and her face concealed.

"But you love him," Jeremiah insisted, and waited intently, with a kind of fierce and joyful expectation that she would say yes, that she loved Fort, for such words would fulfill some truth, complete some terrible logic.

But she did not say that. Instead, without lifting her face, she reached out her hand toward him along the surface of the bed, and said, "No—no . . ."

He leaned to take her hand. There was nothing else to do. He took her hand and sank down on the chair by the bed.

After a little, still holding his hand, she stretched her body out, and lay face down. Then after a little, she began again to sob, but very quietly.

"Hush," he urged softly, "hush."

"I see him," the voice said, muffled by the bedclothes, "I see his face."

"Hush," he said, and pressed the hand he held, "hush, for I love you."

"Oh, I have ruined you," the muffled voice said.

"Hush," he said, "hush, you have given me all I have."

What did he have? He sat there by the bed a long time, holding her hand while she slept.

What did he have? He had the face of Fort, and the knife falling. That was strange, for it had never happened before.

"It had never happened before," he writes, "and I could not understand that it should happen at this time. I did not regret my deed, not even then, for I had acted only to be avenged on a villain and to defend one defenseless. But the deed was enacted again in my mind and before my eyes, and it would not stop. It was as though I had caught some contagion from her who lay on the bed, like a fever or disease, and I wiped my hand before my eyes but the event would not stop. And in its repetition there was no meaning, and not even a horror, for even the horror was drained away, and I could not think why it had been done, which was a new horror. I could not recall the reason for anything that had happened. I tried to think back on all my life that had led to the deed, and what came after. I could remember the events, but the reason that held them together seemed to have fled away, even though I could say words to explain. So I sat there in that room, and could not be sure how I had come there and the form on the bed of my beloved wife seemed strange to me as though I had never seen it before, and the room where I sat, and I myself strange so that I said to myself, I am Jeremiah Beaumont, I am Jeremiah Beaumont. But I marveled even at the sound of my name. And all the while I saw before my eyes the face of Fort and how the knife fell, and it would not stop."

The next morning Mr. Madison was late beyond the time appointed for the Court. At last the upper door creaked on the hinges, then there were quick heavy steps across the planks above, and beyond the open trap door Mr. Madison's voice calling, "Beaumont, Beaumont!"

Jeremiah answered, and Mr. Madison asked if he might come down.

Even as Mr. Madison turned from the ladder foot to speak, Jeremiah saw the excitement in his face. "I bring good news," he said, and moved quickly across to take Rachel's hand and kiss it. He straightened himself, and said, "The proceedings have been dropped. You are free."

Rachel sank into a chair heavily, as though all strength had failed. She shook her head slowly, saying, "I do not believe it."

"It's the truth," Mr. Madison declared. "I swear it. I have just come from the Court."

Tears began to roll down Rachel's cheeks.

"Thank God," Jeremiah said.

"Thank God," Mr. Madison echoed.

"And my husband," Rachel demanded of him, "what of my husband?"

"Have hope," Mr. Madison said. "The appeal is prepared. This is a good omen. Have hope."

Rachel let her head sink to her breast, and wept.

357

Jeremiah stepped to Mr. Madison's side. "I don't understand," he said. "Why—why was it dropped?"

Mr. Madison's face sobered. "I cannot be sure," he said, "but I have been thinking. As I hurried here. Why did they send officers for her so late? The answer must be that they did so only when they became confident of your conviction. And when the weight of motive was to be shifted from a political assassination to a personal vendetta. Gregg sent for her late. After, shall we say, he was sure of the testimony of Barron. That would fit the time. Then . . ."

"I see, I see," Jeremiah broke in. "But why, now that they have me, do they not pursue with the final malice and torture her, torture me through her? It's not the soft promptings of Gregg's nature. He'd hang his mother to advance himself, and count it a deed in God's name."

"Gregg is of my party," Mr. Madison said, "but you are right. No, I'll tell you why he did it. The way she"—he inclined his head toward Rachel—"bore herself in Court yesterday, it touched every heart and . . ."

"But not Gregg's!"

"No, but Gregg feels the slightest breath of opinion on his cheek. Like a sick man, and he's sick from vanity and ambition, he feels the change of weather in his bones. And he'd not risk it, the chivalrous sympathy for beauty and gentleness"—he bowed again toward Rachel —"the shift of opinion . . ."

"I see."

"And one thing more. Gregg knows there will be an appeal. To indict your wife and bring her to trial would stir so many hearts— oh, Gregg is deep—that you . . ."

"That I might escape?" Jeremiah demanded, and a strange confusion of feeling coiled and twisted in his bosom.

Mr. Madison nodded gravely.

Rachel rose abruptly from her chair, leaned back and braced herself with one hand to the table. "I see," she said. "I see, but I'll not have it. Oh, you mean that my safety puts my husband in danger? I'll not have it. Do you hear, I'll not have it. . . . I'll go to them— I'll not have it—I'll . . ."

Jeremiah had stepped to her side and seized her, saying, "Hush, do you hear! Hush!" For in his mind was the thought: *The fool! She'll say she will confess.*

"Hush," he said to her, "hush!" Then turned to Mr. Madison, shaking with his suppressed fear and fury: "You should not have told her. Look, how you torture her!" And he put his arm around Rachel's shoulders.

Mr. Madison's head was bowed in shame. "Madame," he mur-

358

mured, "madame, I beg your pardon. For I was a fool—a fool to put it thus—an idle speculation—you must forgive . . ."

"Mr. Madison," Rachel interrupted him, "it doesn't matter, what the Court does to me. You can tell them one thing—and tell everybody. If they kill my husband, I'll die, too, the same hour. I'll find a way."

Mr. Madison lifted his head and studied her. "I believe you would," he said slowly. Then added: "For you are Roman, madame."

"Yes," Jeremiah said, and drew her more closely to his side, "she is Roman."

"I congratulate you," Mr. Madison inclined his head slightly. "Few men find such devotion. But, madame"—and he looked at Rachel, and lifted his head confidently—"you may be a happy Roman. For we'll save him. I promise you. Beaumont will never hang."

So he laughed, and stepped to take Rachel's hand and bid her good-bye. And Jeremiah good-bye.

Beaumont will never hang, the words tingled in Jeremiah's mind, as he watched Mr. Madison ascend the ladder, and disappear. *Beaumont will never hang, Beaumont will never hang,* like the refrain of a ballad or old song forgotten but for those words, the dire story lost, all but the rhythm forgotten from some desperate violence of long ago, the identity of the hero lost.

He released Rachel from his embrace, and stepped from her side. He took a few paces, and stopped, hearing the words in his head.

But I am Beaumont, he thought.

Then: *I am Beaumont, and I will never hang.*

The appeal was refused. Mr. Madison and Hawgood brought the news, said all the things they could find to say in the emptiness of the moment, swore that they would yet find a way, kissed Rachel's hand, and departed.

It was evening, just after dark, when they came with the news. Jeremiah and Rachel had just finished supper. They heard the departing steps, the clatter of the bolt in the outer door, and then stood in the absolute silence, while the candle shed its light on the dirty dishes and fragments of food on the table.

Jeremiah lifted his gaze from the broken food to meet Rachel's eyes. She lifted a hand, and took a step, and seemed about to come to him. "Go to bed," he said sharply.

She moved toward him around the table, her hand still lifted, approaching him, about to touch him.

"Go to bed, I said go to bed," he commanded more sharply. And, as she paused, with the hand still lifted: "Can't you see, I want to think, I want to be alone!"

359

He heard her move into the alcove. Then he began to pace the cell, but stayed at the farther end, in the shadow, and never looked toward the bed. The rhythm like the refrain of the ballad or old song was in his head, *Beaumont will never hang,* defining the rhythm of his striding, back and forth. *Beaumont will never hang, Beaumont will never hang,* three paces back, three paces forth, three paces back, three paces forth. He clung to that rhythm, which in its pride and certainty seemed to promise all, past all accident or logic. It was all he had to cling to.

Then he knew. There was a way. He stopped in his stride. The rhythm was dead.

But he could not take that way. It would rob him of something. It would be to throw something away. Something that he had to live by.

Live by, he thought. Then thought: *die by.*

He thought: *die.*

Die: it was only a flicker in his brain, nothing.

He said the word out loud, fearfully, as though the sound might suddenly by terrible magic define a reality. But it was only a sound, the touch of his tongue tip to the forward roof of his mouth, and the exhalation of breath. It was only a sound.

He did it again. He touched the tongue tip to the position, and made ready to release the breath. But the breath would not come. It was stuck in his throat, and would not come past that constriction. He felt its pressure mount, but he could not will it to come.

He put his hand to his throat. He felt it swelling, and the beat of the blood there.

Then the breath came back. He almost sobbed with relief. But he had not said the word.

I am not afraid, he thought. *I have never been afraid*—and he finished the sentence quite firmly in his mind—*to die.*

He had taken his chance when he did the deed. He had put his life to pawn. He had been willing to die. But they had lied, they had snared him with lies, and it was not fair. It was not fair, for he had acted in justice, and justice was all he wanted, it was not fair to make him die for doing justice.

Justice: ah, that was it. His heart took a great leap. The way he had almost rejected was the way, after all. It would rob him of nothing, after all, for it would make justice clear.

He moved quickly to the alcove, leaned, and seized Rachel by the shoulder. "Listen," he urged, "listen," shaking her till she woke and stared up at him with startled eyes.

"Listen," he said, quickly, "there is a way!"

In her confusion she only stared up into his face.

360

"There's a way, I tell you," he said, shaking her. "Don't you understand—a way?"

"What? What is it?"

"I'll confess!" he exclaimed triumphantly. "Don't you see? Don't you see?"

"Oh, God," she breathed, "oh, God."

"Don't you see?" He shook her again.

"Thank God," she breathed, and went limp. "Confess—confess—and we can die—and it will all be over—I can die and it will be over and . . ."

"Are you mad?" he demanded, and straightened up and stepped back as though she had struck him or spat in his face.

". . . we can die . . ."

"Die! We'll not die. Don't be a fool. Listen to me." And he began to explain very carefully how once the truth was known they would live, they would be pardoned, the Governor would pardon them, for he would not stand against the will of all good men, who would know how he, Jeremiah Beaumont, had acted in justice, how Fort had betrayed her and in the end had printed the handbill laying fatherhood to the black man and how no husband could suffer that. He explained how he should have done it at first, in broad daylight, killed Fort in the street, and would have if she had not prevented.

"Oh, it's my fault!" she cried.

But he broke in. "No, I did not mean to blame you. But I should have done it. And would have earlier, even at the first, if he—the villain—had not refused my challenge. He tricked me—he tricked me and brought me to this—oh, he was clever, to catch me like this. But I'll trick him, I'll confess. I'll show the handbill."

She had covered her eyes with her arm. He looked down at her and saw that.

"Why should you be ashamed?" he demanded. "It is his shame, not yours. And you'll confess nothing. Do you hear? It was my doing, and I'll declare it, and prove that it was justice."

He had to prove to the world that it was justice. It would have been so easy once. To stand up, with the hot knife still in his hand, and say, "Look, this is the blood of a villain!" But now justice was the bright needle lost in the haystack of lies, it was the coin tarnished and thumbed by lies till the minted face was gone, it was swallowed in a fog of lies.

Before he could cry out to the world and bring forth truth again, he would have to stand before Mr. Madison and Hawgood and confess himself a liar. That was not easy.

They sat in chairs by the table, the lighted candle beyond them,

361

for it was night. Rachel was in the alcove, and had not come out to greet them.

Jeremiah stood in the open space of the cell, and said: "When you two gentlemen came to me in my need, you came at a sacrifice of your personal and party interests. New Court and Old Court—you came, and it was beautiful to see men who put justice beyond party."

Mr. Madison stirred in his chair, and his big hands knotted and unknotted on the head of his stick.

"You came," Jeremiah continued, "because you believed me innocent."

Mr. Madison leaned forward, and the ferrule of the stick scraped sharply on the floor. "Are you . . . ?" he began.

But Jeremiah lifted his hand. "Innocent?" he completed Mr. Madison's question. "Innocent?" he repeated. "Gentlemen," he said, slowly, "from my heart I declare that I wish I could answer your question."

"If you can't," Mr. Madison angrily demanded, "my God, who can?"

"Who can?" Jeremiah echoed, and the question, *who can? who can?* rang in the great hollowness of his head till he thought he would reel. Nothing was as he had planned it. He had not planned that question. He steadied himself, and looked at Mr. Madison, then at Hawgood, then back at Mr. Madison's darkening face. "You can," he quietly said. "You can," he repeated, and felt that his voice was small and pleading.

"How do I know the facts?" Mr. Madison demanded.

"The fact is, gentlemen," Jeremiah braced himself and straightened. "The fact is . . ." and he poised for an instant that seemed endless on the brink ("on the brink of myself," he was to put it for us, "and I was frozen in fear or exaltation, and did not know which, nor do I know now, for the moment when a man falls into himself, into the past which is himself, is like the moment of love or death and is terrible to think on").

The fact was, he said, that he had killed Colonel Fort.

The words seemed so simple, and the silence so absolute.

Then Mr. Madison kicked back the chair and heaved up, saying: "By God!" And lifted his arm, with the stick clutched: "I knew it! I have known it for a long time. Since Marlowe. For you lied and you led me by the nose and you used me and you made a fool of me—oh, you lied and I believed you innocent and you made me a fool before all men and I thought you innocent and . . ."

"Innocent," Jeremiah said. "You must believe—you must try to believe—that I clung to a hope of inward innocence—for all men—

362

I believe that all men must cling to innocence to live—that is all a man can have to live for—innocence . . ."

What had he meant to say? That was not what he had meant to say, and the words were coming strange on his tongue.

"Innocence!" Mr. Madison pronounced in his shattering irony. "What do you know of innocence? When you stabbed a man in the dark and smoothed your face and caught me in your tangle of lies and . . ."

"Madison!" It was Hawgood's voice, not loud but with an authority that fell across the violence and left Mr. Madison standing there with his stick upraised and unspoken words on his lips.

Hawgood did not rise from his chair. He only straightened his rickety form a little, and turned his face farther toward Mr. Madison so that the candlelight lit up more fully the sharp, dry, pedantic features. "Madison," Hawgood said, in a voice that sounded sad and tired, "it does no good to talk so."

"No good," Mr. Madison said, "but I'll say it. And you—you've been bit, too. You've been bit. And you sit there!"

Hawgood shook his head. "Madison," he said, "we've come a long way, and by paths not all of our choosing. But when you go a journey, you never know the end. When a man starts home in the evening, he doesn't know that his hand will crook to the old accustomed latch." He paused and studied Mr. Madison's face. "We've both lived long enough to know that. Haven't we, Madison?"

"But . . ."

"And he," Hawgood pointed at Jeremiah, "he has come a long way, part of that way with us, and no man knows at what point on the road the darkness may fall. We must hear him, Madison."

Mr. Madison turned and sank slowly back into the chair. He did not look at Jeremiah, but stared at the shadowed bricks of the floor.

"Thank you," Jeremiah said to Hawgood. "You do me the last goodness. And I want to tell you—to tell you both—all there is to tell."

So he told them, the dead facts of the past. How Wilkie Barron had told him of Rachel Jordan's betrayal, how he had been shamed for his own coldness before Wilkie Barron's generous anger, how he had left Fort's office, how he had gone to live near the Jordan place and had sought the wronged woman's acquaintance, how pity and love had conspired in his breast as he came to know her worth, how he had challenged Fort and been refused and how Fort had fled the country, how he had overcome Rachel Jordan's scruples after the death of her mother and married her that she might not be alone, how he had finally put aside thought of vengeance in his happiness and the occupations of the world, how he had been drawn into the political troubles of the time, at first not from principle but

363

from sympathy for poor Skrogg knocked down by a bully, how after Fort's betrayal of the Relief party he had been whetted by Wilkie to run for office, how he had seen the handbill accusing Fort of bastardy, and later how the handbill by Fort had come to his house, the handbill naming the coachman as the father of her dead child, and how this had struck her down and brought a second child dead from her womb.

He told the facts, and they seemed dry and spare and very distant from him, not the story of all those years, just a few words uttered in five minutes to two men, almost strangers, who sat there in the candlelight and stared at him.

But he omitted one fact: that Rachel had ever known of his plan to kill Fort.

He finished his account, and suddenly felt drained and empty. That was all a man's life was, those dry words uttered in five minutes in the air of this cave.

Mr. Madison rose, took a pace toward Jeremiah, and looked into his face. "If that is Fort," he said, "if that is Fort—to betray her and then publish the black man as father—if that . . ."

"If?" Jeremiah demanded hotly.

Mr. Madison looked dubiously at Jeremiah. "Mr. Beaumont," he began, "I knew Fort. I knew him well. He might have done the first, in human weakness. Even in villainy. But the second—the second . . ." He shook his head heavily.

"I've told you the truth!" Jeremiah declared.

"The truth," Mr. Madison repeated, still staring Jeremiah in the face. "You've told me the truth before, Mr. Beaumont."

Jeremiah almost leaped upon him. Then stopped, and let his arms drop. "You are right," he said. "I have told you the truth before. I have no right to resent what you say."

He stepped beyond Mr. Madison, past the table and to the alcove. "Rachel," he called.

She came out from the shadow of the alcove, and before the guests could greet her Jeremiah said: "Rachel, you have heard what I have told them. Is it the truth?"

She looked at him for a moment, then turned to the others. "No," she said, quietly. "It is not the truth."

"Ah!" Mr. Madison exclaimed, and the blood rushed to his face, "So I . . ."

"It is not the truth," Rachel said, "because I was guilty, too. Before I promised to marry, I said to him, 'Kill Fort.' I do not know why I did it, but I did. And I knew all, later."

Mr. Madison stepped directly before her. "Are you a religious woman?" he demanded.

"No," she said.

"Do you not believe in a God?"

"I have seen no working of His will in this world, and I grieve for it."

"Do you hold nothing sacred?"

"Yes."

"What is it?"

"My duty to my husband."

"Will you swear by your duty to your husband, that such a hand-bill as has been described, naming the coachman father of your child and signed by Fort, was brought to you?"

"I swear it," she said.

He looked searchingly at her from under his heavy brows, then at the floor, prodding the floor with his stick. Then he lifted his gaze to her, and to Jeremiah, struck the floor once with the stick, and said, "It was great provocation." He paused. "But . . ."

"But it was done in secret," Jeremiah finished for him.

Mr. Madison nodded.

"And that was my doing," Rachel said. "I was afraid. I could not bear to be alone and I was afraid of being left alone. Do you know what it is to be alone, Mr. Madison? Truly alone?"

He seemed about to speak, but she broke in: "No, Mr. Madison, you do not, for you live in the world. You are at home in the world. But I was afraid of being left alone. So I made him do it in secret." And she added: "For love of me."

"Madame," Mr. Madison began, "for such a cause . . ."

She thrust her hands from her in an awkward desperate gesture, saying, "No! No! Do not make compliments for a miserable woman. That he did it for me is my misery." She sat down and looked into the candle flame. "That I was born," she said, "that is my misery. And the misery of others."

"Madame . . ."

"I wish I had not been born," she said.

"Then we had been deprived," Mr. Madison said.

"Oh, stop," she said wearily, "stop."

And let her head sink until her brow was against the edge of the table.

The three men looked at her bowed head, then at each other.

"There is one course," Hawgood said. "We can present the facts to the world. To Governor Desha. And ask for pardon."

"I don't understand one thing," Mr. Madison said. "The hand-bill, why have we never heard of the handbill? It must have been distributed in Fort's county, and that is near."

"I can say why it didn't appear in the trial," Jeremiah said. "Why

365

should I introduce it, when my plea was innocence? And why should Gregg? He would have feared an acquittal with that provocation known."

Mr. Madison nodded somberly. But said again: "The handbill." Then: "We must have some handbills. And establish that Fort had them published. If there is no handbill . . ."

Jeremiah leaned and struck the table with his flat hand. "Enough!" he exclaimed. "My God, you can drop the whole matter. If you do not believe, I'd not have a pardon by your doing. I'd rather hang and be done."

Hawgood got up, and came to Jeremiah's side. He laid a hand on his arm, a feeble, match-stick hand with bitten nails. Jeremiah looked down at it.

"He believes," Hawgood said. "He believes." He looked at Mr. Madison.

Mr. Madison met his eyes, then looked across at Rachel's bowed head. "Yes," he agreed, nodding, "I believe."

He believes, Jeremiah thought, *but not because of me. Not because of me.*

So they went away. Rachel did not raise her head, even to their farewells, and they went out cautiously, as from a sick-chamber.

Jeremiah crossed and laid his hand on her head, on the mass of her hair. "You must go to bed," he said, but she did not stir. He lifted his hand and looked down. He thought that he saw some strands of gray, but could not be sure. Perhaps it was a trick of the candlelight. But what would that matter?

"You must go to bed," he repeated.

She lifted her face, and he saw how chalky-white and strained it was, how the flesh sagged a little at the throat, how the brown blotch stood out on the cheek, and he wondered how Mr. Madison found beauty there now or found whatever it was that made him flush and lean. And made him believe. *Well, let him believe her,* he thought, *and it will save my neck,* and with the thought was too tired even for shame.

He reached out again to touch her hair. "You are very beautiful," he said, feeling that he had to say that, he owed it to something. To her? To himself? To the past? To Mr. Madison? To his neck? He did not know.

"Go to bed," he said, "and sleep."

She moved to the alcove.

Jeremiah stood and waited for the silence. It would come and engulf him. He would have that, at least! He had expected peace. He had thought that after a confession there would be peace. But there was only silence, which was the absence of sound, of voices, as

366

dark was the absence of light. But peace would be a presence, not an absence, a light and not darkness, a state of being and not a defect of being. He wondered why peace did not come.

The confession had given hope. It might save him. Was that the reason why it could not also give peace? Because it had been made for a reason?

He remembered how long ago, when he was a boy, he had not been able to find God as long as he thought to bring some price in hand for his soul. Now he had given the confession as a price, and it was therefore as nothing, like water thrown on the dry ground and gone. It had been made as a bargain for hope.

Hope for what? For his neck, was that it? For life? He sat down wearily in a chair by the table, and tried to think what he might hope for. He named over "the occupations and pleasures of men and their joys and labors by light and dark, and none seemed to justify the rising and going forth. But men do rise and go forth, therefore they must find sweetness and live in hope. But where was the sweetness and hope for me? When all the works of men seemed but a plague to the flesh? Something had been subtracted from my heart. I stretched forth my arm and knew it to be strong. I felt my body and it was firm and sound. But I knew it to be a dry husk, fit to be cast aside with the kernel drawn."

He had lived in the dark hole too long, he thought, alone. But, he suddenly remembered, he was not alone. Rachel was there.

So he rose and tiptoed to the alcove. She was asleep. He might find hope in her, he thought. She was willing to die for him, therefore could he not live for her? He leaned to straighten the sheet over her breast. "I love her," he said out loud. Then: "Oh, God, help me to love her, help me to love her." He prayed God for help to love her, but he knew that he had ceased to believe in God years ago.

He had believed in something else. But what was it?

Mr. Madison and Hawgood rode into Pick County, where Fort had last lived and had made his last campaign. After three days they returned to announce that they had found no copy of the handbill by Fort, though many of the handbills attacking Fort for bastardy, and had found no man who admitted to having ever seen one. So Jeremiah had to watch the old doubt flicker on Mr. Madison's face.

But Hawgood said: "There is one more hope. To find the one in your house."

So it was arranged that Rachel should go with them to make the search. Hawgood promised that his sister would accompany her. The ladies would go by coach, Mr. Madison and Hawgood by horse.

They could not hope to return before ten days. By the time of their return it would be middle July. Jeremiah paced the cell and nursed his hope, or, as he puts it, his "hope beyond hope," the hope that if he should live there would be something to live for. "For I could never cling," he says, "to the mere fact of life without inwardness, for that were but music without melody and the color of flame without heat, and the trampling of cattle in the stall's dung." So the summer wore on, as he paced the cell.

"Hit is a season fer fair," Munn Short said, and propped back in the candlelight. (Since Rachel's departure, he had taken up his habit of lingering for conversation in the evening.) "A season fer fair," he said, "lak God-a-Mighty done made it to fill the mortal belly. Cawn— Lawd, you ain't ne'er seen sich cawn. Hit come bustin outa the ground, sayin, Lawd, sayin, Lawd, lemme grow, you send the rain, Lawd, you send the sun, Lawd, and I'll do the growin. I'll grow till they ain't no man hungry, Lawd. And the rain come. And the sun come. Fer the Lawd done sent 'em, rain and sun, and the Lawd . . ."

Rain and sun, Jeremiah thought. Was that enough, he thought, was that enough? To see the miles of rain coming down gray over the fields? To see the sun? A great sweetness welled up in him, and he felt tears come into his eyes. *Will I ever see it again,* he thought, *ever again?*

". . . and the Lawd sent 'em, rain and sun . . ."

"Stop," Jeremiah commanded. "I want to tell you something."

"Hanh?" Short asked, and canted his hairy face farther into the candlelight.

"Listen," Jeremiah commanded. Then he said very carefully: "I killed Colonel Fort. I stabbed him twice."

"You?" Munn Short said, "you?" He drew back a little from the light, and shook his head. "I looked in yore face," he said, musing, "and I never knowed."

"I killed him," Jeremiah said.

"I done looked in the face of all 'em as has come here, and hit seemed lak I always knowed."

"I want to tell you," Jeremiah said. And so he told all. An inch of the candle was gone, and he had told all. He told how he had clung to innocence, how he had hoped for innocence in the midst of blood and lies. "Do you understand?" he asked, and leaned toward that dirty old hairy face beyond the candlelight, asking.

That face was squinting at him from the shadow.

"Do you understand?" Jeremiah demanded.

"One time I lived in a settlemint," Munn Short said, not looking at Jeremiah now. "Place name of Morgan's Ford, and they was a gal thar, name I don't rickerlict, belonged to the Deep-water Baptists what didn't hold with jubilation. But that-air gal, she went to a dancin and break-down, come what may or Jesus grieve, and taken her pleasure. So they called her in church fer to church her, and named how she had done danced and cavorted. But no, she said, it warn't dancin, not what she done. You was on the floor and was seen, they said. Yeah, she said, she was on the floor. They said, was they dancers thar. And she said, they was dancers thar, fer as I could tell, if'n you aim to call 'em that, but me, I warn't dancin. And they ast, pray what was you doin thar with a man for partner? Hit was a man, she said, and a partner if you name him that, but I never crossed my feet fer dancin. And they wanted to know, pray what was she doin then, out thar cavortin. Cavortin, she said, what if a gal and she walk backwards and forwards and turn and bow, and no man nigh, and no music, do they call hit dancin? They said, no, they did not call hit dancin. But what, she said, if a gal happen to walk backwards and forwards and turn and bow, and a man happen to do hit too, can she stop him, and the music, can she stop the music and make the fiddles to cease, and the man and the music, is that her fault, and her never crossin her feet to dance?"

Munn Short squinted into the candle flame. He said: "And she never crossed her feet. Was she dancin?"

He waited. "Was she innocent?" he asked.

He waited, then said: "Innocent. Hit ain't the crossin of feet or the sound of fiddles. Hit is the kind of music in his heart a man steps to. Hit must be the music thar, fer the steppin is always mortal steppin and thar ain't no innocence to hit. Innocent only is the heart music, be hit that kind."

Munn Short got up, standing stiff on his good leg, the bad leg loose. He leaned to pick up the basket of dirty dishes and broken food, and straightened again. "Ain't no man," he said, "kin ast what kind of music is in his heart. No man kin tell him. He has to hear hit hissef, and know in his heart."

He swung away from the table, and made for the ladder, favoring the game leg.

"Good night," he said, at the ladder, and went up. He bolted the trap door now, as he had always done since Rachel's departure.

Jeremiah had confessed again. He had confessed without hope, not as a bargain for hope. He had confessed because of a sudden swelling of sweetness in his heart when he thought of rain and sun and saw them in his mind.

But peace did not come.

He thought of Munn Short's words, how no man could tell another, and pressed his hand hard to his chest, above the heart. He stood there and breathed the flinty, dry, cool air, like the air of a cave, and felt the strong pounding of his heart. That was its only music.

He felt that steady beat and thought that that was what you lived by. He asked if that was his best hope, to keep that beat up night and day. That thought was horror to him. But when, standing there, he tried to think of the beat as still, as absolutely still inside him, that was a horror, too.

Well, he thought, *well.* Then: *well what?* He took that question to bed with him, and rose with it the next morning. It was always there, as the days passed, as Munn Short came and went, as Munn Short's dry, nasal voice went on in the evenings by candlelight, telling how his life had been and the men and things he had seen, as the heart kept beating. But there was a hope, too. There was nothing Jeremiah could name that he hoped for, but the hope was there. "It was as though the heart in my bosom hoped, but could not tell me why."

The hope was there as he heard the feet on the planks above, and knew that they had come back from Saul County.

Then the hope died when he saw Rachel's face, and the faces of Mr. Madison and Hawgood behind her, at the foot of the ladder.

"You didn't find it," he said quietly.

Rachel shook her head. Then she came to his side, and he kissed her on the forehead.

They had made a thorough search. They had been over the house, inch by inch, every cubbyhole and drawer. Old Josie remembered the man on the little horse, with the letter. She remembered all that had happened, how Rachel had cried out and fallen, with the paper on the floor by her, how she herself had saved the paper and given it to Jeremiah. That was the last time she had seen it. As for Jeremiah, all he could remember was leaving it on the table in the dining room that night when she had put it into his hands.

Mr. Madison had hunted up Tim Adams, the man who had come riding to the Jordan place on what Josie called that "leetle ole sorrel hoss not too many hands high." But Adams could tell little about the man who had originally given him the letter and paid him the dollar to take it to the Jordan house: a big man in his full strength, with a cut-scar on his left wrist like somebody had tried to hack a hand off, and another scar crossing it.

Jeremiah remembered that Tupper had said the man carried a scar on his wrist.

"We'll do the best we can," Mr. Madison said wearily. "We'll go to Governor Desha. I can swear to him on my soul, as can Hawgood, that we believe such a handbill was brought signed Fort. But there is no saying what line he will take. Without a copy we can do little to convince the public, and Desha. But Desha likes to bend with the popular breeze. And things go badly for him now. Relief and New Court—well, it seems he had backed the wrong horse. Relief and New Court"—he shrugged—"well, I haven't thought much about those things lately, but it looks like the rich man will have his pound of debtor flesh, after all."

. "And his pound of my flesh," Jeremiah smiled grimly. "For if there had been no partisan passion . . ." He stopped, finding their eyes upon him. "No," he said quietly, "no—if I had trusted you—if I had trusted the world—if I had not lied . . ."

Hawgood laid a hand on his shoulder. "What is past, is past," he said. "We'll do our best."

But their best was nothing. Desha refused to act. So the last hope was gone.

It was gone, but nothing seemed changed. Jeremiah could not believe that it had gone. The cell was the same. The world outside was the same. The beat of his heart was the same. The faces before him were the same, Mr. Madison's face and Hawgood's, those faces saying what they had to say, the words you would say to a dead man.

For I am a dead man, Jeremiah thought. So he said to them: "Gentlemen, do not disturb yourselves. It is no shock to me. It is not as though hope had died at once, and with violence. No, it has died slowly, over a long time, like growing old."

"There may be . . ." Mr. Madison began.

But Jeremiah lifted his hand. "I am no child," he said, "so give me no toy of hope to play with, or no sugar-tit to suck. I trust that I can die as well as the next man, and not shame you. But I want to tell you one thing. I am sorry to have imposed upon your generous hearts. I am sorry to have robbed your lives of this time that you might have given to one more worthy. Or to the world's profit. I am sorry that I lied and tangled you in my lies, that I gulled you and was not innocent."

Mr. Madison looked heavily at him. "I would you had not lied," he said. "For all our sakes."

"For your sakes," Jeremiah said.

"No!" Hawgood burst out. "Don't think of us. If you had lied a thousand times—if you had been guilty a thousand times—it would not matter. For innocence—it is an accident. It is always an accident. We did not do it for accidental innocence. No—we did it for—for truth. For truth, Beaumont."

"For truth?" Mr. Madison demanded, leaning his bulk slightly toward Hawgood's meager brittleness, leaning almost like a suppliant. "For truth?"

"What else is there to do for?" Hawgood asked. "That's all there is, and nothing can hurt it. Not our lies or guilts, for it is bigger. It is higher. And we know it is there. Even if we cannot see it. Nothing can hurt it. Not even our innocence can hurt it!"

He stepped forward to take Jeremiah's hand. "I believe that, Beaumont," he said. And asked earnestly: "Will you believe that I believe that?"

"Yes," Jeremiah said.

And so Hilton Hawgood passes from our story with those words on his lips. We, too, must believe that he believed them, whether we can believe them or not. For he lived selflessly by them, through the brief time as a lawyer in Frankfort, his term as Attorney General of Kentucky, and his one session in Congress before the fever struck him down and he was called to "some small task" on the other shore for God's glory. And in all that time, when to be in politics was to court the vilest calumny, there was never a whisper against him.

So Mr. Madison and Hawgood leave. They had been a focus of light in the dark scene of our story. Mr. Madison, experienced in the world, with a strong grip on the world, had taken up, late in his time, the cause of the deprived and debt-ridden. He had fought well in the new cause. Was it ambition? It is easy to say so. Perhaps it is too easy. We know that he could have made his peace with his class, which he had betrayed, but did not. He died solitary and poor. Did he remember Hawgood's words, "For truth!" Did he find some truth at last? And we know that he had come to Jeremiah Beaumont's side prompted only by decency and honor. He had not come prompted by Hawgood's high truth, but for that moment the worldly decency conspired with the unworldly truth. For once they stood together, the heavy-fleshed, full-blooded, seasoned campaigner, and the Platonic student with the thin, sharp, asymmetrical face, a little acid and impatient, like the face of a village schoolteacher.

They were gone, and Jeremiah stood there alone.

Alone, he thought.

Then he turned. There was Rachel. She was sitting at the table, looking fixedly at him, holding in her hand a letter.

"I found this," she said. "It had come after they took me away, and Josie kept it."

"What is it?"

"It is your letter."

"My letter?" He could not think what letter.

"The letter you wrote after"—she hesitated, seemed to take strength and proceed—"after Marlowe."

Then he knew. It was the letter he had written the night after Marlowe presented the document in court: . . . *nor can I understand how you, after my full instructions, have been so careless, or worse, as to give that document into the hands of him, for he has betrayed*

372

me and knotted the rope about my neck. Nay, you—you have knotted
the rope—you for whom I have done all . . .

"Well?" he demanded. "Well?"

"Could you not have trusted me?" she asked sorrowfully.

"Trust you!" he burst out. "I did trust you and . . ."

"And it came to this," she said, and shook her head. "Oh, God," she
cried out, "has it all come to this—that you could write this!"

"And why not? After your botching?"

"I told you," she said, softly again, "I told you how I was sick, how
I had ridden the country, how . . ."

"You were sick," he cut in, and the old bitterness of that night when
he had written the letter surged back over him, "but it was my life,
and you threw it away. Yes, you were sick, but I was sick unto death."

"I killed you," she whispered. "You are right. I ruined you." And
she added in a whisper he could scarcely hear: "I ruin all the world
I touch."

"You ruined me," he said with tight lips.

"I can die," she said calmly. "At least, I can die with you."

"Die with me!" he cried. "I can die alone. Do you hear—alone?"

"I will die with you."

"Because you think that would make it up! Well, I tell you . . ."

"No," she said. "Because I love you."

Her voice, as she said it, was completely quiet and passionless, and
it left him, suddenly, foolish with his violence, staring at her.

"Love me?" he said then, like a simpleton, mouthing words he did
not know the meaning of.

"Yes." She looked down at the table, at her hand holding the letter.
"If there isn't that, there is nothing. That is all there is left."

"There is not much time left for love," he said bitterly.

"Love doesn't need time," she said. She was still looking down at
the table.

"Or heart?"

She looked up at him, raising her head slowly, and studied him sadly
across the distance, as though she were leaning after something that
withdrew across the width of a plain toward the horizon. (He describes her look that way.)

Then she said: "I thought you loved me. Once."

And looking at her across the great distance—for suddenly time
seemed to him like a distance lying between—he thought: *I loved her
once.* As those words came into his mind, he felt an enormous sadness,
and a pity. It was a sadness and pity not for her, not even for himself, something darker and deeper that seemed to well out from and
flow from their poor story and wash over the entire world. They themselves seemed merely caught up in it, lost in it, tossed together in its

blind flood. That was the image he had—an image of them tossed together and clinging in a desperate embrace while the flood rolled them and spun them.

His head reeled in a vertigo, as though, quite literally, they were caught and spun.

He steadied himself, and moved toward her, stopped before her, and looked down into her face. He dropped to his knees before her, and buried his head in her lap. "I love you," he said, "I love you," against the cloth over her thighs.

But he knew that it was not love. He did not know what it was, or care. Whatever it was, it was enough.

"Jerry, Jerry," she was murmuring, and he felt her breath upon his head as she leaned above him.

He reached his arms up to take her waist, and drew her down to him. For an instant the thought of rising and going to the bed flicked at his mind, but he rejected it. This seemed right, to lie here, to be together here on the dry, hard, trodden brick of the floor, where the feet of the despairing and condemned had pressed, to be here as on the floor of a cave. And she did not protest.

At last she had said she loved him. He had labored a long time to bring those words to her lips. Now they came, unsought, at the moment when he had cast her off and found his only strength in the bitterness of self. Had she spoken them out of her own guilt as an expiation? Or out of pity for the very loneliness which made him reject her? Or had she spoken the truth when she said that she loved him because love was the only thing left, and you must have something, even to die? Or because the unwritten text of the drama that she and Jeremiah Beaumont acted out on their high and secret stage demanded this in the end? Without it there would be no climax, no noble gesture to fulfill all the rest, no unveiling of magnanimity to lift the heart and redeem error.

Or perhaps we can take her word simply: she did love him at last. For the word *love* will comprehend all the speculations just made, and all the things that were to come after, from the uncouth, unexpected violence on the bricks to their highest sentences yet to be spoken or suffering yet to be endured.

At any rate, now that hope was withdrawn, they discovered a new passion, a blank and absolute passion, as blank and absolute as the face of death that they now confronted. It was as though the passion reflected like a mirror the features of that death. "Not even in the first days when she had become mine," Jeremiah writes, "did I learn such rapture, for then my joy was part of the world and was mired in the common life, like a wheel that can scarce turn in heavy earth, and the purity of that joy was murked by the shadow of my oath and obligation unfulfilled, so that the joy itself was stolen. The joy was not able to snatch me from the commonness of things and therefore was not true joy. But now that death was upon me, and in my very strength I might be called dead, the joy was truly a rapture, for I was rapt and seized out of the world, as the word means from its Latin. It was a kind of dying out from the world, and a glorious martyrdom, for in that death as we fell into the central blindness of its flame we held the world in all contempt. It was as though we practiced over and over what death we had to die that we might be perfect in it and taste a keener bliss with the end. Our practice was the last of life and the first of death, and which was its greater sweetness, we could not say. But then I felt I had defined a truth I had known but darkly, that only when life and death shake hands do we know what is real, and in that acquaintance find our being. Or is that a madness?"

Whether or not that notion was madness, they lived in a kind of madness, a kind of wordless exaltation, without memory or expectation. "We clipped and clung, and had not strength to surfeit our need, and that was our sadness, that desire leaps beyond appetite and the poor flesh. So past the function of appetite we hung to one another's hands and practiced tenderness while yearning for the divine frenzy and the sweet blackness to return upon us. We did not speak with one another, for there was nothing to say, and we remembered nothing. Day and night passed over us, but in our cave we did not distinguish, though we saw the light wax and fade at the trap door, nor did we care. Sometimes we took food and sometimes we did not and the kind jailer carried it away untouched.

"We slept much, and often while Rachel slept I stared into her face and thought how it had changed from its former bloom, and how in sleep it changed from waking, and how in the strain and trial of passion it was not the face I now saw, and I wondered how it would look after death when all was spent, and sometimes, even as I looked, the face was strange to me, as though she had been another person never before seen, and at that a terror would come on me as I thought how a man never knows the true face of his beloved and is alone.

"Sometimes out of my terror grew a pitifulness for her, that she was also alone, or if not alone, there was only myself and the poor thing I was. Oh, what was I that she should cling to me and take comfort? Had she not deserved better than this, a condemned creature who had dragged her to this pit? And what comfort could we be to each other, I might ask myself, but to fan our appetite so that in the end neither knew the other but only the hot blackness of self, and a blindness like death of self, and then a sleep? No, I would say to myself, we had striven, and strove, for more, for any brute could have as much.

But if nothing else, at least that much, I might say in my distress, and turn to her and lay hand upon her. There was at least that.

"And sometimes when I embraced her I was aware how thin her body had become, and how the ribs were scarce sheathed by the skin and were like small brittle sticks bent to hoop about and protect her inner being with that weak cage. But that frailness, though a mark of sickness and time, could stir me more than the earlier ripeness of person or the fullness of her breast which had somewhat withstood the general wasting. The very pitifulness of her falling away, even as I wished to weep for it (how much had been for my sake!), might still fan the lust that we cultivated and the blackness we longed for. Should I say lust? No, for our rage deserves a better name. Or call it what you will, it was our all."

It was not quite his all. Another passion came to compete with it. Even as he plunged more deeply into the "divine frenzy and sweet blackness," and discovered its blankness and absoluteness, he felt the need to tell his story. It was as though the passion itself, whose very meaning was its meaninglessness, its blankness and absoluteness, would lose that meaning unless he could trace the steps by which he had reached it, unless it were put in the context of the very world that it repudiated. Jeremiah was aware of the paradox: "For what is absoluteness if not set round with the shadowy moil and clutter of the world? Else how would we know it absolute and speak its worth? Else how can man justify?"

So he seized his pen, and sat down to "justify." How would he justify? By telling the truth, he said, "for the truth will justify." But he came to know how hard it was "to know the inwardness and truth of things, for a man remembers what was the fact, but even as he remembers he knows the fact to be a fleeting shadow of something that passed, as when he looks at the ground and sees the swift shadow of a bird's flight and lifts his eyes, but the hawk, or whatever bird it was that had swooped thus low, is gone." The truth would justify, for "if we can truly know the truth we know that it could never have been otherwise, and what we know to be true we can accept, for that is all the heart yearns for in the end." But it was hard to know.

He struggled to know it, to live back into the past time and know it as he had not been able to know it when caught in the toils of its presentness. During the first days of the passion that he and Rachel now discovered, he had slept much, not caring for day or night, courting a dreamless oblivion. Now that passion had not waned, but in the long periods between its manifestations, he scarcely slept. He would hump over the table all day long, or all night long, driving the pen forward, word after word, in its race. Or rather, this, too, was a kind of sleep, a kind of oblivion of the present world, but "a sleep with a dream, the last dream a man must make, the dream of himself and the way he has come and how things came to be."

So he lived in the two worlds, the world of the present passion with its lust for blankness and oblivion, a kind of crazy, black honeymoon with Rachel and with death, and the world of passion for the past, of the dreamful sleep. The pen raced forward, against time, and the dream expanded, unfolded, sought its definition. Across a vast distance, the two worlds moved toward each other, two lines converging across all space, and he knew that at some last moment they would coincide, the world of blankness and the world of dream, the present and the past, and at that moment he would die. Then men would come for him, and he would die. But a man could die then, at the moment when the two lines, across all distance and accident, had converged to make the perfect point. About such a point, "the universe with its great stars and the unnamed dark beyond might swing."

Moving toward that point, he re-lived the past, the world of boyhood, his mother and father, Grandfather Marcher and the loss of inheritance, his conversion and falling away, Dr. Burnham ("sitting on the bullhide under the maple, intoning the hexameter"), the introduction to Colonel Fort with his swarthy, sad face ("as though he grieved already what would come"), the years in Bowling Green in the attic room of the Barron house, the bright years of friendship and poetry, the first time he heard the name of Rachel Jordan, then the moment when Wilkie reported her betrayal and with his noble indignation shamed Jeremiah's cold and lethargic heart.

At that moment, the moment when he came to that moment, Jeremiah laid down his pen. His hand shook. That was the moment when all had begun, he thought. Wilkie had begun it, had leaned at him, rebuking him, accusing him of connivance with Fort, of being Fort's creature: ". . . and is that why you felt no honorable rage? Because you are his friend? Because he pays you? Because . . ."

And he had struck Wilkie in the face. The muscles went taut now, as if he were to deliver the blow again, and again, for that cruel injustice. Had he struck to avenge injustice? He asked himself that, torturing the question. But he was glad he had struck Wilkie's face, that handsome, smiling face, had brought blood to the lips. For Wilkie had betrayed him in the end, had betrayed all friendship and the memory of those good years, had come to the court and offered his testimony. He would strike him again if he were here, and would not stop till the smile was gone for good from the puffed, bloody lips.

Then, with a sadness, he remembered that Wilkie had rebuked him because Wilkie had loved Rachel Jordan, had loved her but had not dared to aspire so high, had had nothing to offer and had kissed her hand in farewell and, looking up, had seen tears in her eyes. Wilkie had loved Rachel. His rage drained away. After all, it had all happened so long ago, and now it was only the dream of rage.

Wilkie had loved Rachel, too. That thought revived fleetingly the old warmth of comradeship. So he looked toward the alcove where Rachel lay. "Rachel," he said. And when she answered, he said: "I have never told you how I first came to you. I came because Wilkie had loved you, because when he told me your story his anger rebuked my coldness and I caught fire from his outraged love, though his love had been put aside and . . ."

"Love?" her voice demanded from the shadow.

He rose from the table and went to her. "Yes," he said, "love, Wilkie's love."

She sat up and looked at him. "He never loved me," she said.

"Never loved you! Why, he loved you and gave up hope, for he was poor and you were too high. Don't you remember—how he told you good-bye, kissed your hand and looked up and there were tears in your eyes—for you must have understood—for you . . ."

She shook her head. "No," she said.

"But he told me. And that was why . . ."

"He lied," she said. "It is nothing but a lie."

It was nothing but a lie. By her words he had been robbed of something. It was like the ground shaking beneath the foot, like stepping over an edge. "But he told me that he . . ." Jeremiah cried out, gasping.

"He lied," she said, "and I do not know why."

So all had been based on a lie. The rage came back, full and real. For this, somehow, was the great betrayal, the great lie, the thing that had tricked him in the beginning and he had not known. If Wilkie were here, now!

But there was only Rachel, and he looked down at her white, strained face, as she leaned toward him, propped on an arm. Pity came over him. "It is all right," he said softly. He sat on the edge of the bed and took her hand, that squarish, strong hand. "I am glad he lied," he said, and leaned to kiss her hand. "I am glad," he said, looking up at her face, repeating the gesture that Wilkie had not made, "for his lie gave me my truth. For you are my truth."

He went back to his task, to the pursuit of truth, and then pen drove on, page after page, day after day, its pace broken only by a little sleep, by the greeting and brief conversations with Munn Short, by the hurried and scarcely tasted food, by the interludes when they plunged into the blank and black oblivion, which seemed to be enough, but was not enough. For he woke from that passion into the other, and returned to the table where the unfilled page and all the past waited for truth.

378

Rachel would lie in the alcove, waiting, or sometimes come to the table and sit there near him, sometimes leaning her head sidewise to the surface, watching him as he wrote. And one day she reached across to touch his hand and take the pen from his fingers, and the sheet on which he had been writing. She struck a line beneath his words and began to write.

We can see what she wrote on the old sheet, in her precise, copy-book hand, interrupting his narrative:

> Stone walls that bind to me are boon,
>   The prison grate to me is naught,
> For in this trammeled space I find
>   The whole great world for which I sought.

It is signed: *R.B.* It cuts across Jeremiah's narrative at the point where he surprises Rachel in the arbor and takes the Plato from her hand. That seemed to him a sign, their end and their beginning juxtaposed. He wrote beside her verses: "What love is more?"

That night, when Munn Short came with the supper, Rachel asked him for another pen. He brought it. Her poems begin again. She goes up again to their secret stage. She has showed her face to him in love at last. All that remains is to celebrate the end, to make a victory out of defeat, to translate some shameful wrench and contortion of the flesh into a noble gesture at the end. "All, all is nothing," the poems proclaim, "but for the steadfast heart." "The tattling world is naught to me," the poems say, for Truth needs no word. The world's "prospect dear and charming hope" are nothing to one who has glimpsed the "radiance of Love's pure Idea." Jeremiah becomes "Bright Angel of the noble brow" and "Stripling of a seraph's might," who stooped at Honor's call to put honor aside and "In darkness do a deed of light."

Poor Colonel Fort—he becomes "Dishonor's thrall," whose "high mien was mask to treachery." There is pity for him, but only the pity spared for the "fanged worm we tread upon." We hear no more of the nightmare vision of the knife falling and falling, nor of her cry, "If he had only named my name, and cursed it!" She has put all that aside. Fort must be the villain in the end. For the drama calls for that. It must be a simple drama of great wrong, of righteous vengeance, of love unto death. There is no place in it for subtlety and complication. It must be pure, for that purity is her last escape.

She will die with her martyred love:

> And wedded to his side my form shall lie
> Encircled by his arms; for naught but fate
> Could move my stubborn purpose, free, to die
> With all my soul calls dear, or good, or great.

She declared her purpose over and over again, in the poems and to Jeremiah. She would brook no protest. Her mind was made up.

She declared as much to Munn Short, as he was to report: "Many and a time she said to me how she was aimin to die, and I'd say to her, now lady, it ain't right fer a sweet and pretty lady like you to die, but she said how she would not live past her husband and own true love what would die for her and hang fer all to see. And I said how it was not the Lawd's will fer a human to kill hisself, and she said she did not believe in the Lawd, and where was the Lawd to let the world be so? She swore she would die, and ast me to git her a double coffin made to lie with him in the grave, she would pay my expense and troubel. And I aimed to joke her and take her mind off, so I said, lady, you ain't goin to die, you make me take all that troubel fer that double coffin and then you don't die and I have to knock you in the head to keep it from goin to waste. Then after they had done gone, I found all them pomes writ out to say how she was fixed to die."

But meanwhile the days and the nights passed—it was well into August—and the two lines converged across infinite space toward the moment of thrilling conjunction, and Jeremiah and Rachel lived in the only way left to them, acting out the noble drama in the dark hole, piling up the manuscript that was to "justify" all, clutching and straining together in their last violence of life or the first of death.

"Dyin," Munn Short said, and pivoted on his good leg, the dirty platter tilting from his hand. "Yeah, dyin," he said, and let the platter sink back to the table, among the clutter of dishes. "Yeah," he said, "hit ain't lak they say, something of angrish and moan. Hit ain't to be feared of."

"What makes you think I am afraid?" Jeremiah demanded angrily. "And want your comfort?" He shoved his chair back from the table.

Short shook his head, and peered down at Jeremiah. "I knows you ain't a-feared," he said. "Air-man could look at you and know, and I has seen 'em feared and not a-feared, and knowed their faces. Ain't no call to be a-feared. Why, Lawd, the graveyard, hit is the cheapest boardin house. Don't cost nobody nuthin, not the man nor the worm neither. Why, Lawd, ain't but one thing more natchel than breathin and that is not breathin. Hit comes easy, and don't take much sleight nor practice. Come the end, and ever-body learn hit. Ain't no call fer a man to be a-feared, and he knows how to come to hit."

"If you mean salvation," Jeremiah said, "what's that to me? You know I am not a believer."

"A pity you ain't, and I'll say hit," Short said. "Fer believin is a help in the dark when the fear comes. But they ain't no call fer the

380

fear, no way, believin or not. Not of the dyin. The angrish and moan is of the livin time, not of the dyin. I knows. Fer I died once."

Jeremiah leaned a little forward, peering at that innocent, old, hairy face, with snub nose and watery-blue, quizzical slit eyes. "You died?" he asked.

"A long time back," Munn Short said. He sat down, and stretched out the bad leg before him like a stick. "Time I got this here," he said, and tapped the bad knee.

"How?" Jeremiah asked. "How did you die?"

"How old you reckin I am?" Munn Short demanded.

Jeremiah studied him. "Maybe fifty-five, fifty-seven."

"Naw, I am seventy, goin on seventy-one. Been forty years since I died. A long time ago, after I come to this here country. Fer I warn't born here. I was born in Virginie, nigh Ca-lina, in them hills. I knows the year, but I done fergot the day. My mammy tole me, but I done fergot, hit is so long. But I rickerlict she said hit was fodder-pullin time and they taken me outa a punkin. Hit was the way she talked to me and me leetle, not much outa swaddlins and hippins. She talked to me by the fire while I come on. She taught me head-countin and tole me about Jesus when I got big to hear. Hit was all the learnin I got, what you might call a fireside eddication. When I learnt to read, hit was later and me growed, after I had done died and I yearned to read the Holy Word how hit is writ.

"But my mammy died when I warn't naught but a sprig, and left me, and hit is hard to see her face, the time is so long. Then my pappy died. They was good folks, my foreparents, but they never had no money and the world's goods to any extreme. They warn't nuthin fer 'em to leave me, but I made hit and growed. Growed to be big and I fit them British the fust time. Virginie and Ca-lina. I was at the Mountin. King's Mountin, and I seen men die, but nuthin tetched me, lead nor sharp steel, and I says to myseff, like a man will and him young, hit ain't fer me, the dyin, fer I ain't gonna die.

"Come over the mountins, into Kaintuck. The war warn't over, but folks was movin and goin a-ready. They hear'd how the land laid sweet over the mountins, and they moved toward hit. Folks moved toward land layin sweet and new, lak water down hill. Hit is nay-tur. And me too, and I lived in the new land.

"Lived lak a man will, and labored fer bread. I seen the belt tight and I seen the gut full to plenish, in the change of time and the seasons, how they come. I taken what come and ne'er give thanks, fer hit was my strenth I laid trust in. And I taken my pleasure. I drunk likker and laid on the ground lak a hog. I fit with folks fer no cause, and cut men to let the blood come out. I stole, and I grieve to say hit. A man layin drunk, and I taken what he had. I laid out with women

381

in the bresh. I done all the meanness of man. But a man comes along and he falls in the world and the mud lak a man will. Ain't nuthin to tell him, if he don't harken soft, fer the world, hit is a quagmire and don't hang out no sign.

"One time I was at a station west of here. Tubb's Station, they named hit. We was forted thar agin the Injuns, nineteen folks, ten of us men and the rest women and some chillen. They was a man named Perk, but his last name I fergit, had a wife not more'n a bitsy gal looked lak, sixteen year, maybe. Her hair was dark to night and plenty, and her eyes was blue and she walked the ground light nigh to dancin. Lottie was her name, but we called her Sis fer her littleness and bein so big-eyed to look at you. Perk was old, gittin on to sixty, maybe. He had taken Sis when her folks got kilt nigh Lexington, and he loved her fer a wife, and she loved him and done her duty.

"We made one crop at Tubb's Station, and laid in fer the weather, close but fer the huntin. They was Injuns that fall. We seen their signs, but ne'er hair ner hide. But we hear'd 'em call in the night. Call lak a owl. We laid close, and Sis moved amongst us. I seen her, and I was nigh thirty but my sap was green and she come on my mind. I done hit. Tuk me nigh all winter but I done hit. Made eyes to her and helt her hand, and she jerked hit away, and then time comes she didn't jerk hit away, and one time I put my hand in to lay holt on her sweet leetle titties, and she just stood thar in the dark a minute and shaken lak a chill, then she run away. She never tole Perk nuthin, so I knowed hit was a-comin.

"Come sugar time. We was gittin sap outa them sugar trees, and I tolled her off in the bresh and done hit. Warn't no trouble, she ne'er strove none, but she cried, and I ast why, didn't she lak hit? She shaken and said how she cried fer Perk. And I said, Perk be damned, and laughed, and said how I had done Perk a favor.

"We laid up close in the Station and hit was hard to git a gal off. Then full spring and they was no more signs of Injuns and folks moved out to make a crop, and hit was more easy. Then she said how she was gonna have a baby, and hit was mine, but Perk never knowed and he was glad. I said to her how I had done Perk a favor, and she cried agin, lak the fust time.

"The cawn was in and folks worked in the crop. They taken the rifles, and some stayed in the Station to keep watch, but we taken no good keer. One day I said to Sis how I would slip off from the fer field and go down the branch and fer her to come. Hit was berry time and she could go to git berries, but hit would not be berries she would git. Hit will be sweeter'n berries, I says to her, and she looked at me big-eyed and her breath come sharp. So I laughed, and went my way. I knowed she would come.

"She come. I was down by the branch, scrouched down in the green bresh, and seen her comin. I whistled low, and she harkened, but never seen me. She come long the branch, footin slow and light on the ground, and lookin all round her, big-eyed. I never stirred, but just lay fer the joy of watchin her come so, lak a pretty critter, shy-lak and touchous and wild. Then I stood up, and put out my hand.

"We had done hit, and laid in the green shade fer breath. Then I hear'd hit. Hit was a man yellin, fer off. Then a rifle, fer off. I lept up to listen, then I knowed, fer thar was the horn from the Station, blowin the sign. Come on, I said, and started, fer I had left my rifle agin a tree towards the field. Come on, I yelled agin, before I got to my rifle, and looked back.

"She had done riz up in the green and whilst I seen her the arrow come. Hit went in, in the chist under the neck, and she didn't make no sound. She just throwed up her arms lak she was liftin 'em up to somebody to hug 'em maybe. Then she fell down.

"A arrow missed me, and I made hit to my rifle. I grabbed hit and dodged behind the tree, and behind another tree, gittin toward the Station. I knowed that Injun was in the woods a-comin, but I did not see him. I never seen him till I got towards the nigh field to the Station, and I seen him and give hit to him. I started to run agin, totin my rifle and hit not loaded now, when the bullet come. Some them Injuns had rifles. The bullet hit me in the leg and I come down. I was tryin to load my rifle, but did not make hit. A Injun come out the woods and run towards me. He grabbed me by the hair and thowed me back. He lifted up his knife, and I knowed I was dead. Hit seemed lak hit taken ferever, me thowed back to look up towards the sky, and that Injun's face and paint dabbed on hit lak hit was floatin in the sky and that-air knife high in the sky ready to come down on me, but hit looked lak hit would never come.

"Hit come. Hit taken me in the chist, towards the left side. I knowed hit was in me, but I never felt hit, just a lettle push lak.

"That Injun thowed my head back holding my hair, and I felt that-air knife tetch my head, fer he was startin to take my scalp. I knowed I was dead. Hit was the last I knowed, fer I was dead and gone.

"Night and I come to. Knowed I was dead and did not know whar I was. I laid a long time not knowin and my eyes shet. Then I hear'd a stir, but hit was fer off and nuthin, lak hit was a dream. Then somethin tetched my mouth, and hit was water, and I opened my eyes. They was somebody thar, but I was too weak to keer. I taken the water, a sup, and shet my eyes.

"I laid long, hit was days and nights, and knowed leetle or nuthin, just layin, and they taken keer fer me. Then I opened my eyes, and hit was toward evenin, and somebody was settin thar. I looked at him,

383

and seemed lak I could not rickerlict nuthin, who hit was setting thar. Hit looked lak time had done gone and left me. Then I knowed. I knowed hit all, how hit had been. Hit was Perk settin thar.

"I studied on him and he was lookin at me. I said to him then, how I had been dead. And he said, you was more nigh dead than you knowed.

"Hit was Perk had shot that Injun fixin to scalp me. Perk had been in them woods and not in the field ner the Station. He shot the Injun and he toted me to the Station, and him a old man, while them Injuns was shootin. They started fer him, but them fellers in the Station hit one and skeered 'em back. He got me in, and hit was him taken keer fer me most. He done fer me when he could and would not let other folks. Hit was lak I was his blood-kin, they said. Fer all his grievin fer Sis he done hit. They tole me how Sis was gone.

"My strenth was comin on, slow but hit was comin. Perk would set with me and he would watch me. Sometimes I would shet my eyes lak I was asleep, but squinch-eyed I would be a-watchin him, and he would still be lookin at me and never stop. I studied on hit.

"One day I ast him why he taken keer fer me. And he said, because you air mine. And he looked at me lak he done.

"I was much obleeged, and thanked him kindly fer savin my life. And he said, I never saved yore life. So I tole him what folks said, how he brung me in.

"He said, I brung you in, but I ne'er saved yore life, hit was that Injun saved yore life. And I said, that Injun, why he nigh kilt me. And he said, that Injun nigh kilt you, but me, I'd a kilt you.

"Then I looked at him stidy, and he looked at me, and I knowed that he knowed. I did not say nuthin, but he looked at me and then he said, yeah, I knows, I knows all hit, and I was in the woods, fer I knowed Sis never went fer no berries and I had found you I'd a-kilt you and ne'er said by yore leave.

"I studied on him a minute and I said, why didn't you let me lay and that Injun had kilt me. And he said, I nigh done hit, but hit come on me sudden, how you was mine, and that Injun had no right on you, fer you was mine.

"He looked at me, and a skeer growed in me. Hit was not lak the skeer when the Injun lifted up the knife. Hit was another kind, and more deep. My lips was dry, but then I said, what you goin to do?

"Nuthin, he said. And I said, nuthin?

"God damn you, he said, I caint do nuthin, I caint do nuthin I aimed to do and studied on, fer I done brung you in and laid you down and I done give you water to sup, and I set here and aimed to, when you got yore strenth and could know, fer you was mine, but God damn you, I caint, fer I done give you water and they is just us here and them woods, and we air togither, but God damn you, fer I give you water to sup.

"He got up from his cheer, and laid a curse on me, sayin fer God to damn me to hell, fer hit had not been fer me Sis would ne'er left the Station and gone in the green woods and ne'er been taken by them Injuns.

"And I said, taken by them Injuns, did you say taken? And he said, yeah, they taken her, and men done trailed them Injuns, but they never seen 'em. And I ast him how they knowed she was taken, and he said how they had looked good in all them woods whar she went in, and it was the part them Injuns come through and they must of taken her.

"Then I almost bust out and said how Sis was dead and the arrow in her chist, but I could not say hit fer fear and my tongue stuck in my mouth hit was so dry. So I laid thar, and he went away. I laid thar all night, and sweat fer the fear. But ever time I shet my eyes, I seen Sis layin on the ground in the green bresh, and I could not sleep. Then it come so when I laid with my eyes open, I seen Sis layin on the cold ground and the arrow in her leetle chist.

"Hit was nigh day when I called out loud. I yelled, and they come, and I said to git Perk, which they done. He come and I taken his hand and said, the Injuns ne'er taken her, she is dead, and a arrow in her chist. And I told him the part of the woods and the green bresh.

"He did not say nuthin. He looked at me clost, fer the light was comin on, and he went out the door. After sun he come back. He come in and looked down on me whar I laid. Scalped, he said, and looked down on me. Then he said, varmints, varmints and birds, they been at her. They done et they fill of her, and her layin thar. And I thought he was not goin to stand, fer he called out loud, Oh, God, she laid on the cold ground.

"But he stood and looked down on me. Then he said, you had not tole me and I had come thar, I'd a-kilt you, had I given you sup or not, I'd a-kilt you, fer oh, God, I seen the place in the bresh whar you laid and her layin on the cold ground.

"He beat his hands togither, and said, you done kilt her, but I caint do to you lak I aimed, and go yore way, but never fergit you air mine and my name and my mark, they air on you, fer I saved you and brung you in, and you air mine.

"He run out the room, and I never seen him agin. He left the Station. Back towards Lexington in that country, but whar I ne'er knowed.

"I got my strenth, and went forth. But hit was ne'er the same. I knowed how I had laid dead, and come alive, and walked with folks, but inside me I was dead, fer Perk had put his mark on me. I could not rickerlict how it was to be alive lak a-fore, fer last year's hot spell cools off mighty fast in December. And I cried out why I had not been let lay dead on the ground and fergot. Body-dyin was easy when I laid on the ground, but dyin ever day when you walk in the sun, hit is hard, and I cried out fer the mercy.

"Long time, and hit come. Come in the night when I laid and seen how them varmints had come and Sis on the cold ground, and they et on her while she lay, and I cried out how Perk had laid a curse on me and I was his'n and could not git away. Then hit come, how I did not have to be Perk's and his mark on me. I could be Jesus', and the mark plum washed away, lak I had hear'd tell. And I cried out, Oh, kin hit be! I was layin in the night.

"I found the way and the promise, and Jesus come in my heart. He is hung on my heart lak a cow-bell and a cow-bell caint keep no secret. I move and I got to tell about Jesus, how he come. I know you ain't no believer, but . . ."

Jeremiah shoved his chair back sharply on the bricks, and grasped the edge of the table as though about to rise. "But what?" he demanded.

Munn Short looked at him across the dirty dishes under the candle. "Body-dyin," he said, "hit ain't nuthin. I done hurt worse, stubbin my toe in the dark when I was a sprout and runnin. Fer a fack, fer I been dead. But the dyin what ain't body, hit is different. Hit begins and hit don't stop. Till Jesus come in my heart. Red rose don't brag in the dark, but hit shore smell sweet, and Jesus lays in my heart in the dark and is sweet-smellin. I smells Jesus in the dark. Hit ain't lak hit was when I laid and I smelled all night how them varmints had come and Sis a-layin on the bare ground all that time with the weather and that place a-smellin. I smelled hit in the dark, nigh to puke.

"Hit was bad to lay and smell hit, but worse to lay and think how I had laid with her that time in green bresh and taken my pleasure, and her her'n, fer she had a relish, and her good as dead a-ready and not knowin, and me good as dead, and that-air Injun a-squattin in the bresh, lak as not, and a-watchin. Squattin thar and watchin us do hit, and paint on his face and a-pantin to watch us, and waitin, and us good as dead and . . ."

The chair fell back as Jeremiah suddenly rose. "God damn it!" he said. "Why don't you stop?" He stood there on the floor and breathed heavily.

Munn Short said quietly: "I was just a-tellin . . ."

"Telling!" Jeremiah exclaimed savagely. He stepped quickly around the table and stood over the jailer. "Listen," he commanded. "I don't have to hang. Do you know that?" He shook Short by the shoulder. "Do you know that?"

"God's will, and you don't," Short said.

"God's will! Listen," and he leaned confidentially over him. "I could kill you. Now. Right now. I could kill you. With my hands. I am strong and I could kill you and escape."

Short peered up at him. "Naw," he said, "naw."

"Because the door is locked outside, you think because the door is locked outside? But I tell you, I could kill you and go up and knock for the door and your fellow would come, and when he opened the door . . ."

Munn Short peered up at his face. "I ain't a-feared," he said. "I done died one time, lak I said. But I ain't a-feared, no-way. I kin look in yore face and I know you ain't goin to kill me."

"By God, I could, I'll show you." His hand tightened on the shoulder.

Munn Short straightened his game leg a little, but otherwise did not move. "Naw, son," he said, looking up. "You ain't. I kin look in yore face, and, son, I know you done done all yore killin."

Jeremiah tells us that then, for one wild instant, he thoroughly intended to kill the man. He stood there, willing it, but it was as though all strength had been drained from him.

He released his hold, and stepped back. There was a great nausea in the pit of his stomach, and he thought that he would be sick. "Please go," he managed to say, mastering himself.

Munn Short got up, pivoted on the good leg toward the table, and methodically began to assemble the dishes and scraps into the basket. He finished, and turned to face Jeremiah. "I didn't mean no harm," he said. "I was just tellin how . . ."

"Please go now," he said. He braced himself with a hand on the back of the chair, and watched the old man go up the ladder.

He sat down at the table, and propped his head in his hands. After a while, he reached for the pen and ink and his papers. That much was left, at least that. He tried to write, but the words would not come. All that he had put down seemed useless. It was a horrible joke, all the words ever written or said.

After a time he blew out the candle and went to the alcove, where Rachel lay. He disposed himself as carefully as possible so as not to wake her. She stirred and murmured his name and reached out her hand to him. But he did not respond. It was a warm night, but he lay there shuddering in the dark as with a chill.

Death had become real to him. He tells us that. It had been a word before, but now it was suddenly real. "I had lived all my life and had heard the word," he says, "and I had seen my father and mother die, and I had put a man to death and had seen him die with the blood on him, but it had never been real to me, the fact of death. I had thought of death as the absence of life, as dark is the absence of light, but it is not so. For death is a thing in itself, and has its being. As the believers say, it is with us in the midst of life. It is the mote in the ray of sunshine. It is the shadow we cast in the bright sun and moves with us. It lies beneath the blossom and is like salt in the bread on our tongue, and it is like blood in the meat we take from the skillet and the hot fire will not kill it. It rises like mist in the evening, and in the morning it lies in the bed with us and its breath stinks, and all night it was there, and I knew it. I knew that it had always been with us, even in the time of rapture and our straining for joy, and it had squatted with its painted face like a savage hid in the brush to spy upon us no matter how deep the dark and feed its lust on our own.

"Then I remembered it is said that when a man is hanged, in his twisting and agony, his manly part is extended as for lust and his seed are spilled. I lay there and shuddered like a strong chill to think on that horror which made the dying more horrible and made life horrible, too, and infected all pleasure in the past, so that I could not bear to think back upon it. It was horrible to think that the poor body of man is so blind that it does not know life from death or light from dark, or love from hate, and spends and spills itself always in such ignorant spasm. It was as though until that moment my way in the world had been lighted, albeit by a feeble ray, and I had known where to put the foot, but now the flame had been blown black out as by a strong gust that made the marrow go cold and the darkness had rushed upon me with the noise of a wind. I lay there and shuddered that all man's life should be but the twisting and contortion of a cat hung up strangling in a string for sport of boys.

"At length I fell asleep, though fitfully and troubled. In my sleep it seemed that the day of my execution had come and they dragged me out amid cheering and laughter and foul jests. They would not let me walk, but dragged me by my arms and legs like a sack. It was not fear I felt so much as shame to be treated thus. Then all the crowd was silent while they put the rope on my neck. They let me fall. My neck did not break but I hung there struggling and strangling, and for all my agony in a blind lust, and all the people laughed and pointed at me and jeered for the obscene jest. Then the agony was too great and I knew I was dead.

"I awoke from the nightmare, and for a moment was happy and peaceful like a child and tears of gratitude came to my eyes to know it was but a dream and I was safe. Then I knew that I had befouled myself, and all the shame and despair of the dream returned upon me.

"I got up from the bed and stood in the room and longed for light to come. I felt nothing now but a numbness and the knowledge without even despair that my life was nothing and all I had ever done was nothing and meant nothing, it was no different from any man's life. Except that I had come to the knowledge."

He had come to the "knowledge," he says. He says that, but we can scarcely believe him, for if he had come truly to the knowledge, would he have sat again the next day at his table and written down the account of all that Munn Short had said, and all that he himself had said, and the horror of his nightmare? With that knowledge what would have been the meaning of that act of recording? But he did write it, and the words are all there before us on the yellowing, curling sheets. Or is there the paradox that even in that knowledge, even when it is truly had, man must put down the words, must make the record? For even when that knowledge of blankness comes, he is still man and must "justify?"

XI

ON THE MORNING OF AUGUST 27, TWO MORN-
ings after the talk with Munn Short, Jeremiah woke to a far-off, rat-
tling, rolling rhythm. In the moment of confused waking that distant
undefined sound stirred his heart to excitement and hope. Then he
recognized it. It was the sound of drums.

At that he thought, with a sudden fear, that today was the day of
his execution. Else why the drums? Had he miscounted the days? He
leaped up and ran to the calendar he kept on a sheet of paper stuck
to the wall. There were three days left.

The militia had been mustered three days before the date set for
execution, from Lexington and Louisville. Wild rumors ran the country. That friends of the condemned would seize him from the scaffold. No, that the condemned had prepared a statement to be given
on the scaffold incriminating some of the great of the Commonwealth,
and therefore he would be murdered as soon as he was led forth,
before he could speak. No, the Old Court men had picked that day
to seize the government and set up a junto of the rich to tyrannize
over the land. No, New Courters were organizing for a march on
Frankfort and would burn the town. There were a thousand rumors.

After Fort's death the Legislature of the State had proceeded with
its business. The House had had a majority for the repeal of the

Reorganization Act, which had set up the New Court. It voted to undo all that had been done and restore the Old Court and make a contract a contract again in the land. But in the Senate the repeal was defeated, and the New Court survived.

It survived, however, on borrowed time. The little revolution that would have set up the "unerring majority" against Constitution and court and contract and the sheriff's writ had failed. Hunger and ambition, need and cunning, idealism and calculation had conspired—in what proportion we can never know, for it was all long ago, and men's hearts are always sealed, even to themselves—to make the revolution in "justice."

But where was Justice, after all? In the sacred obligation of the debtor and the words of the Constitution? In the bargainer's calculation and the creditor's confidence, in the daily work of the world? Or did she, "planted on the isthmus between conflicting elements, dispense her impartial awards, unawed by the storms that rage below, and unshaken by the waves that break at its base?" That was where she was, according to George Robertson, LL.D., member of the House, who had spoken for the Old Court long ago, in December, 1824. Perhaps Mr. Robertson, LL.D., did see her there, but most men were far below, shaken by the storms that prowled the base of that high promontory, and had not time to lift their heads to see if the clouds of the summit had, for a moment, rifted.

Even the borrowed time of the little revolution and the New Court ran out during that summer of 1826. While Jeremiah sat in his dark hole, the candidates made their rounds of crossroads, courthouses, and barbecues, and uttered their denunciations and made their promises, fiddles scraped, the bungs were knocked out of the barrels and the free whisky sloshed like water, eyes were blacked and blood was spilt in high argument on principle, and the young men lured the girls off into the thicket by the beech glade. The climax came with election under the broiling August sun. And when the votes were counted it was clear that the New Court was dead. The obsequies would take place when the new Legislature met in November.

But the last twitches and spasms were there in that hot month. Sullen and bitter, New Courters drew aside in small knots after the market or church meeting. It was not over. There would be blood. Votes had been bought. They would take the state. By God, they would not be deprived. Then they scattered to the lonely houses or hovels, the space of bare ground before the door, the tumbling litter of children in the dust, the hound asleep, the hen panting under the elder bush, and beyond, the scrub patch of corn browning in the merciless sun. And some young lawyer retired to his office and nursed his ambition like a sucking babe, while dusk came on: words had inflamed the general heart before, men had ridden the crest of violence to greatness, the world was far away over the mountains, Kentucky was here, and was herself, who could say nay?

So the militia paraded Frankfort, in their grand uniforms—when they had them: tight breeches with fringes on the outside seam or hip-length soft leather boots, gartered above and below the knee, long square coats with gaudy facing on the lapels and great side pockets swollen like saddlebags (bottles of likker, hunks of corn pone and sow-belly, handkerchiefs, dice, cards, knives, spare socks), broad-brimmed, oval-crowned hats with the brims rolled back or pinned up on one side, and feathers in the band for officers. They shambled along in their finery, in slovenly files, toting the musket or rifle, squinting sidewise at the citizenry on the street, shifting the quid to the other jaw and taking a sly spit. They were the men who had driven the Indian from the glade and the canebrake and who had butchered Pakenham's redcoats before the cotton bales at New Orleans. They could not keep step, but they knew their worth. And they aimed to have some fun. They'd drink this town dry. And pappy better lock up his gal tonight.

About four o'clock on the afternoon of the twenty-seventh, Munn Short came to the trap door and asked Jeremiah to ascend, that somebody wanted to see him, somebody who wasn't able to make it down. Jeremiah went up.

At the door of the room above, he found a couple of militiamen leaning against the wall, seeming to be half asleep, their rifles propped beside them. "An extra guard," Jeremiah said to Short. "So they're not taking any chances of my skipping out and spoiling the fun."

"Town full of sojers," Short said. "A durn army, and you jest one pore man."

Jeremiah followed the jailer down the hall, and one of the guards fell in behind, his rifle cradled in the crook of his arm. He still seemed to be asleep, tottering along in his drowse, but Jeremiah knew that those sleepy eyes saw everything, that that slouching form was keyed up, like a cat.

Jeremiah thought: *this is my chance.*

Not his chance to escape. But he might make a break. When they had reached the outside door. And the man might use the rifle. A little lead would cheat them, after all.

There was another militiaman at the outside door. He fell in beside the other, at the same sleepy pace.

I'll do it, Jeremiah thought, *in the street. Where there's space to run.*

They turned the corner of the building to the street. There, under the shade of a big white oak, was a cluster of people, town loafers, boys, Negroes, idle, half-tipsy militiamen, and a couple of solid citizens, black-coated, who stood a little back from the others. And there, in the middle of the group, elevated above them somehow, was a great bulk of a man. For a moment Jeremiah merely glanced at the figure, thinking that it had nothing to do with him. Then, with a clutch at the heart, he knew. It was Dr. Burnham.

He stopped still and looked at the figure propped there on the big special chair that was lashed to the bed of the wagon—enormous, swollen, black-swathed, the big head set on the shapeless shoulders like a boulder on a hill, gawked at and gaped at by the scum around like a captured bull buffalo or a circus elephant, detached, above them, not even contemptuous, sunk in his heaviness, somnolent and regal and sick.

Then the head turned, and the eyes opened, blinking in the light.

"Dr. Les!" Jeremiah cried, "Dr. Les!" And ran toward the wagon, shoving his way, knocking men aside. He leaned hard against the side of the wagon, reaching up to take the big, swollen, trembling hands that were extended to him.

Dr. Burnham's bulk inclined slightly. His head leaned over Jeremiah, the sparse gray hairs sticking to the skull with sweat, the face more swollen and pasty than ever, more than ever the color of the belly of the dead catfish, the pale, baby-blue eyes lost in the swollen expanse. "My son," he managed to say, then his mouth began to twitch.

"You came," Jeremiah said, marveling in the happiness that engulfed him. "You came all that way," he said.

The old mouth was twitching. Then it said, "I had to, son."

"For me," Jeremiah whispered, and pressed the bloated hands, and thought of the wagon on the road, lurching on rut or stone, the Negro man hunched motionless over the reins, the hoofs of the team stirring heavily the slow dust, the wagon creeping hour by hour beside the fields, along the edge of a woods where the leaves hung limp, under the blazing sun, the enormous old man propped in the lashed-down chair that was big as a bed, the wagon creeping on, hour by hour, forever, across the land.

One of the crowd, a raw-faced youth who was practically leaning into the wagon beside Jeremiah, plucked Jeremiah's arm, and said: "That yore pappy?"

Jeremiah released Dr. Burnham's hands and wheeled so violently on the youth that their faces were only inches apart. "Get back!" he commanded. He lifted his arm. "Get back, or I'll kill you!"

The youth stumbled backward a few steps, into the safety of the crowd.

393

Jeremiah turned to Munn Short, who hung on the outskirts. "Mr. Short," he said loudly, "this old man is a scholar and a great physician and healer. He is like a father to me, and I love him. He has come many days to speak with me. Won't you insure us some privacy? If not for my sake, at least for his dignity, whose spit would honor this crew. Will you clear this rabble?"

"Rabble!" a burly fellow said, and thrust forward, "you ain't callin me no . . ."

"Your true name would be fouler," Jeremiah said.

"I'll . . ." the man said and took another step, lifting his arm.

But the butt of a rifle had chunked him in the ribs. "Get back," the militiaman commanded.

"Git 'em all back!" Munn Short commanded, and the other guard came forward.

The crowd fell back raggedly, clearing a decent space. Munn Short himself retired some paces, out of earshot, and one of the guards with him. The other guard crossed the street, and stood there, leaning on his rifle.

With a sense of victory, Jeremiah turned back to Dr. Burnham. The sense of victory mingled with the happiness in him. "So you came all that way," he said again. "For me," he added, and the thought was sweet to him.

"I had to come," the old mouth was saying. "It was stronger than me. It drew me out of my bed. And Zebulon brought me. He took care of me."

"All that way," Jeremiah said. "How long?"

"Twelve days. We couldn't go fast. We lost two days and . . ."

"You were sick!" Jeremiah exclaimed. "On the road. With strangers."

"I had to come," Dr. Burnham said.

Jeremiah studied him. Then he asked: "Why? Why did you come?"

Dr. Burnham hesitated, blinking down at him. Then he shifted his mass a little and seemed to stiffen inside the bulging flesh. "I had to look at you, son. Seemed like I had to look in your face. So I could know . . ."

Again he hesitated.

"Know what?"

The old mouth was twitching again. It did not seem able to make the words. Then it managed: "Know—know that you were—were still Jeremiah."

Jeremiah reached up and took one of the bloated hands. "You were afraid I had shamed you," he said, and was filled with pity.

"No, son. No. I didn't care what they said. But it was done in the dark and . . ."

"By God," Jeremiah flared up, "I had challenged him, I had . . ."

"I heard, son. I heard, after the trial. But Fort, Cassius Fort was a good man."

"Good enough to betray a young girl, and then slander her name. To publish that the father of her child was a slave."

The mass of flesh shifted uneasily. "I heard it said. But how they never found one and . . ."

"Look!" Jeremiah commanded. "Look in my face, and believe me."

Dr. Burnham peered down at him, squinting as though trying to make out a difficult page. "I believe you," he said then. Then he heaved his bulk in a kind of painful, despairing effort, and said, "Oh, God." Then: "But Fort, he was my friend, he was a good man."

"Good!" Jeremiah exclaimed.

"He was good, but, oh, God, a good man is good by the barest, his good is mixed up with his foulness and he doesn't know. I've lived a long time, and that's all I know, for I've looked in myself and I've prayed and striven, and I knew Fort." He paused, and lifted his head and swung his weak gaze around. Then he said: "Cassius Fort was my friend, and I loved him."

He looked down at Jeremiah. "And I loved you, too, son. I never had a boy of my own, for all my praying, but the boys that came to me for learning, I loved them. But I loved you best, and, oh"—he swung his gaze again around the hot street—"and oh, is this what it comes to!"

"They will hang me," Jeremiah said, very quietly.

The old man looked down at him. The mouth was twitching, but no words came.

"They will hang me, and they will stand all around and watch and laugh—that scum that was here to watch you and gawk. Would you have me hung up for their pleasure?"

"Oh, God," the old man breathed.

Jeremiah suddenly laid a hand heavily on the old man's knee. "Well," he said, almost whispering, "you can prevent."

"Prevent? Oh, God, what can I . . . ?"

"You are a physician. You would know a way."

Dr. Burnham peered dumbly at him. The thought was growing, puddling, in his face. He suddenly shook his head.

"But you will," Jeremiah repeated, leaning and whispering.

"No, no."

"I am not afraid to die. But would you have me kick in the air for their sport?"

Dr. Burnham's head was still shaking, almost automatically, and he was saying, "No—no. It would not be . . ."

"Right?" Jeremiah finished for him.

Dr. Burnham nodded.

"I am not a believer," Jeremiah said. "And I know you believe in a God. But you believe, too, in the nobility of man, and would your God hold less? And I swear to you, if you do not do it, you cannot stop me. For I will die, and not for their game."

"I cannot, I cannot," Dr. Burnham was saying, the words barely forming on his lips.

Jeremiah grasped the knee hard, and thrust his own face up. "Listen," he said, insistently. "You owe it to me. For it was you that planted the seed of all. If it had not been for you, I would not be here."

Then, as pain and confusion grew on the big, gray, sweating moon-face that swayed above him, he said: "For you sat on the bull hide and read to me. Under the maple tree, and read me the Greeks and the Romans. You taught me the nobleness of life. And I swear to you, if I have botched and blundered, all began in what you taught. For I yearned to do a thing noble and worthy, and all began in that thought. And it was you . . ."

"Oh, God," the old man said.

"And would you have me die less than Roman?"

"Oh, God," the old man breathed.

"You will do it," Jeremiah insisted. "You owe it to me, and you will not let me die like a dog." He grasped the knee hard, driving his fingers in, feeling the mass of soft flesh give and spread with his force. "You will do it," he said.

"I will do it," Dr. Burnham said, but his words were scarcely audible.

Munn Short and the guards took Jeremiah back to his cell. He made jokes with them, then thanked them for their courtesy. He was very cheerful, hugging his secret. That night he wrote an account of his conference with Dr. Burnham, and afterwards he paced the cell in a kind of exaltation, and in his mind, in the rhythm of his steps there were the words, *Beaumont will never hang, Beaumont will never hang*, like the refrain of a ballad or an old song.

All the next morning, the morning of the twenty-eighth, two days before the date set for the execution, Jeremiah was in a fever of anticipation. When, by two o'clock, he had had no word from Dr. Burnham, he began to despair. But before three, Munn Short called him.

As before, Dr. Burnham sat in the chair in the wagon, under the white oak, the Negro driver drowsed over the reins, the horses drooped their heads in the heat, and a few loafers hung about the wagon. But now Dr. Burnham was not propped sleepy and detached. His bulk was upright, his face was animated and glistening with

396

sweat, his head turned nervously from side to side as he harangued the loafers, and now and then he refreshed himself from a brown bottle and waved it in the air. He was assuring the little crowd that he had been a physician more than fifty years and had wrought many a miraculous cure but that in his considered opinion there was no medicine like Black Betty, there was no potion brewed as sovereign as a drag on the brown tit, that rebuke to Hippocrates, that counterblast to Aesculapius, that envy of Paracelsus.

For a moment, watching, Jeremiah was touched by shame. Then he understood.

Jeremiah turned to Munn Short. "Can't you clear them back?" he asked.

"No!" Dr. Burnham declared. "They are my friends, and I give them wisdom. Yea, I give them better than wisdom." And he passed down the bottle to the nearest fellow. "Drink!" he commanded, "drink and praise God. *Deum laudemus!*"

He picked up another bottle from beside him, wiped the sweat from his brow, heaved the bottle on high, and cried, "*Laudemus!*" And drank.

"Oh, drink, what they lay to thy charge!" he cried, and waved the bottle. "Oh, soreness of eyes, dropsies, and gouts they say are thine! Oh, empty dishes, naked brats, scolding wives, shrunken purses, bloody noses, weedy corn fields, broken fences, hollow-horned cows, spavined horses, bruised brain-pans, fallen pricks, and bad reputations—all, all are thine, they say. And truth, they say! But"—and he tried to heave his bulk to stand, but failed and fell back—"but drink and *laudemus!*"

He drank amid the guffaws, spluttered for breath, went from pasty to purple. Then he caught his breath, and lifted the bottle and waved it. "Oh, oriflamme, oh, legion's eagle, oh, blower of trumpets and signifer of joy!" he addressed the bottle, and shook it until it sparkled in the light. "Oh, what you are—oh, annoyer of modesty, oh, enemy of learning and spoiler of wealth, oh, bringer-on of puke and ruiner of reason, oh, my rod and my staff, oh, comfort me!"

He drank again, thrust the bottle down to Jeremiah, saying, "Drink, my son, drink, and let not thy heart be troubled, for God gives to drink and we drink the God, oh, *Deum bibamus!*"

Jeremiah felt the hot, whisky-stench of the old man's breath upon him, seized the bottle and drank.

"Let them drink," Dr. Burnham commanded, pointing to the guards and Munn Short with a sweeping royal gesture.

Jeremiah passed them the bottle.

Dr. Burnham fished up another bottle, took a swig himself, and passed it to Jeremiah. "Drink, my son, drink!" he said, "for we drink

God in his mercy, and what is man, my son, oh, what is man"—and
Jeremiah felt the bloated hands on his head as he tilted to drink, laid
there in benediction—"oh, what is man, oh, what is God that man
should be mindful of Him . . ."

Jeremiah lowered the bottle.

Dr. Burnham thrust another at him, saying: "Oh, *Deum bibamus,*
oh, *Deum laudemus, laudanum laudemus, laudanum laudemus,* for
what is God but a sleep, *laudanum laudemus!*" He was leaning over
with his hands on Jeremiah's head, and Jeremiah saw that he had
begun to weep, the tears exuding painfully from the baby-blue eyes
and running down the vast sagging cheeks to mix with the sweat.

"Drink!" Dr. Burnham said, and straightened up, and Jeremiah felt
under his fingers a knot of string about the neck of the last bottle.

Dr. Burnham had produced another bottle, had drawn the cork,
and was tilting his head back to drink, the bottle high, his big face
sweating under the sun. Then he righted himself, waved the bottle,
cried, "Drive on, Zebulon, drive on!"

And as the Negro picked up the reins and clucked to the horses,
Dr. Burnham waved the bottle and cried, "*Deum bibamus,* oh, what is
man!" He drank again, and began to sing, waving the bottle in time
so that it glinted in the sun:

> There is a fountain filled with blood
> Drawn from Immanuel's veins,
> And sinners plunged beneath that flood . . .

He drank again, waved the bottle, and resumed the song, his hulk
swaying with the motion of the wagon, weeping as he sang, while the
sun beat down.

> Lose all their guilty stains,
> Lose all their guilty stains.

The wagon moved slowly off down the street. The creak of the
wheels was lost in that cracked and quavery voice that filled the afternoon silence of the street. Then the wagon turned a corner, and was
gone, and the last notes were lost.

Jeremiah, dangling a bottle in each hand, stood and stared down
the street where the wagon had gone.

"Now warn't he a sight?" one of the guards asked, still looking down
the street, and shook his head, and spat.

When the militiaman said that, emotion filled Jeremiah. It was
"a gratitude and humility that such a force existed in the hearts of
men as had drawn that sick old flesh out of its bed and over all the
weary miles to me, unworthy as I am, for old affection's sake. And had
made him make his dignity and age a drunken motley to the common

view, and debase himself thus to easier give me what I had demanded of him, that it might not be observed. For in his drunkenness was method, and when he put into my hands the last bottle, he mixed in the word *laudanum* with his drunken Latin, trusting that the vulgar ear would not know that he had said, 'Let us praise *laudanum.*' And it touched my heart that in the moment when he gave me the instrument of death, he still played upon the words, as had been his custom in happier times to make such jests, now on *laudemus* and *laudanum*. And I recalled how the great Paracelsus to make his master remedy had mixed in flakes of gold and the poppy-gum and was said to have given it the name *laudanum* from the Latin word for praise. But his medicine with its floating gold deserved less praise than that in this bottle on the table before me now. For this medicine will cure all and rock the night to sleep. Soon health steals o'er me, and I am made whole."

This is what Jeremiah wrote late that afternoon, with the bottle marked with string on the table. He was to wait until evening to use it. Otherwise there was the risk that Munn Short might suspect when he brought the supper and call in a doctor.

So Jeremiah spent the time before supper putting his manuscript in order. After supper he wrote two letters, both to Mr. Madison. One was to go outside the packet of manuscript, one within. The first simply consigned the manuscript to him, and was innocent enough to be read by any eye. The second runs:

Dear Madison:

I shall make a final imposition upon your genial nature and your time. And you may rest assured that this is the last claim I shall make, unless in after times the claim of a passing thought touched with some kindness.

To be brief: I am leaving for you this narrative, in which I have tried to set down my story with what truth is in me. But whose heart does not recoil and go cold before Pilate's jest? What truth is in me, I do not know. But I have felt the need to set all down that I might try to know the truth of my own coming hither. A time comes—and that time has come for me—when all the heart asks is truth. Long ago the profound Lucretius wrote that the terror of life and the gloom of the mind could not be routed by the lucid arrows of day, but only by the face and law of Nature. *Sed naturae species ratioque.* So have I tried to dispel the terror and gloom of my lot by seeking that face and law.

Have I seen it? I cannot answer. It may be that my poor story begins—as I beg you to believe—in a dream of honor only to end in a dream of truth, and only a dream in beginning as in end. But here is my story.

Read it, and give it to the noble Hawgood to read, if such suits your several pleasures. Destroy it, if you will. Or if you find it to have some interest and worth, you may, if you will, bring it to the popular eye. But not until such time as it can do no harm to any person mentioned therein. Do not think vanity would prompt me to ask that it be published. Would I, whose fingers have not firmly seized the fleeting skirt of Honor or of Truth, now seek a boon from Fame? No, believe me.

My time draws in. Shorter, indeed, than even the stern law suspects tonight. So farewell, and all my thanks to you and Hawgood—noble pair.

Y'r ob'd't ser't,
Jeremiah Beaumont

Mr. Madison never saw the letter, but we have it.

After supper, after Munn Short had cleared away the dishes and said good night, Jeremiah wrote a brief note of instruction for the burial of himself and Rachel. They were to be buried in the same coffin, with her head upon his left arm. Her hair was to be loose and laid across his face that he might go to his last rest "in that fragrant shadow." Once shrouded, they should not be exposed to view, not even to the eyes of those who wished them well. The burial should be in Frankfort, and a modest stone should be erected. Upon the stone should be carved an epitaph composed by Rachel that very night:

Here lie two lovers, in last embrace interr'd,
Who rather than Life's shame have thus preferr'd
To seize the forelock of Death's hideous face
And drag him prisoner to th' appointed place.

At the end of the note of instructions there is a line straight across the sheet, and beneath it:

It is now twenty-one minutes past eleven o'clock. We have just drunk the entire contents of the bottle. The liquid is brown of color, slightly thicker than water, and has a bitter taste, but it was sweet unto our tongues. Good night.

J. B.

Jeremiah and Rachel lay down, side by side, on the bed in the alcove and composed themselves, and waited. After some time they fell into a stupor. Before dawn Jeremiah revived a little, conscious of a growing nausea and a great lassitude. Because of his torpid senses he was not aware of Rachel's breathing and assumed that she was already dead. He himself relapsed again into the stupor.

Later, the stirring of Rachel brought Jeremiah to semi-consciousness. She was moaning and trying to get from the bed, but being on the side near the wall she could not easily do so. Jeremiah tried to quiet her, and drew her down beside him, but she pushed free and mumbled something he could not make out for the thickness of her tongue and his own confusion. As she feebly shoved at him, he conquered his own weakness, and struggled to a sitting position.

At that moment a gnawing, burning nausea seized him, and he voided the contents of his stomach. Then he writhed in the grip of spasms of retching. He managed to get as far as the table and fell into the chair, with his forehead propped against the edge of the table. Sweating and exhausted, he sank again into a bottomless stupor. When he revived, a little light was coming in at the trap door.

He could not rise, but managed to turn his head to look toward the bed. He thought that Rachel was dead. But after a time he saw her stir, and with the increasing light he made out that she had in her sickness fouled the floor and the hanging coverlet of the bed.

Dr. Burnham had not deceived Jeremiah. As far as we can judge from Jeremiah's description of the potion, and the results that followed taking, Dr. Burnham had given him the laudanum compound most readily available in that time and place. But, it was not the true *Vinum Opii:* in such a dose, that would have been fatal. Dr. Burnham's potion was probably what was called "Brown Mixture," officially *Opii et mistura glycyrrhizae composita.* This concoction contained a considerable proportion of opium, mixed with antimony (tartar emetic), spirits of nitre, and water or wine. It had appeared in Philadelphia in 1814 and had immediately become a popular remedy for colds, coughs, consumption and even malaria. It was so popular, in fact, that any apothecary or physician would have had it sitting about in jug-lots, and Dr. Burnham would have had no difficulty in procuring any amount desired.

The laudanum in the huge amount of Brown Mixture drunk by Jeremiah and Rachel would certainly have been a lethal dose, as Dr. Burnham well knew. But what Dr. Burnham apparently did not know was that, taken in any considerable quantity, the mixture would prove self-defeating for Jeremiah's purpose because of the emetic action of the antimony. This property of the mixture, in the ordinary dosages of 4 cc. (about one teaspoonful), would never have appeared. Perhaps Dr. Burnham did not even know that antimony was one of the ingredients.

So after the fine speeches and the tragic stance, the grand exit was muffed. The actors trip on their ceremonial robes, even at the threshold of greatness, and come tumbling down in a smashing pratt-fall, amid hoots and howls from the house, and the house gets its money's worth. For that is what the house has paid for, after all: the smashing pratt-fall. It never really believes in the fine speeches and the tragic stance. Even when it surrenders momentarily to the noble illusion and sheds a sympathetic tear, it wipes that tear away in furtive embarrassment, or it titters at the peak of intensity. It knows that the speech and the stance are only an illusion, a dream, a somewhat embarrassing dream. It knows where reality abides: in the femur cracked and the buttocks black and blue.

So Munn Short came down and made the discovery, and sent back a colored boy to clear the mess. Then, a little after, a guard was stationed in the cell to prevent another attempt. But everything, that morning, seemed far away and meaningless. Once or twice Jeremiah tried to talk with Rachel, to give her some comfort, but she was still in a dazed condition, and finally, in his apathy, all that had passed between them seemed meaningless, too.

When in the middle of the afternoon Munn Short came to announce a visitor, Jeremiah had no curiosity. He nodded to indicate that he had understood, but said nothing. He was not even surprised when, in the bad light, he recognized the visitor. It was Crawford.

Crawford stood at the foot of the ladder, more gaunt than ever, his mustaches more frazzled and stained, his respectable black coat more threadbare. He stood there, timid and embarrassed, shifting his weight, unable to find words to say to the man whose life he had sworn away. Jeremiah regarded him dully. He could not find anger, or even contempt.

At last Crawford took a step forward, and managed to say, "Mr. Beaumont—Mr. Beaumont—I got something—something to say. But it's private." And he cleared his throat and nodded significantly toward the drowsy guard who sat propped in a chair against the wall.

"I cannot control my circumstances," Jeremiah said, "if you have anything to say, say it."

Then Crawford took another step or two toward Jeremiah, inclined his head a little, and wiped his mustaches with the palm of his right hand, with a humble, apologetic, downward motion, as though he had just finished drinking and had dirtied them. "Mr. Beaumont," he said, and studied the bricks at his feet. He seemed to draw some strength from that contemplation, enough to lift his head a degree or two and say: "I reckon you know I did not tell the truth. Leastways, what I said was not the truth good and proper."

Jeremiah merely nodded. He could think of nothing to say. All he wanted now was to be alone.

"I reckon," Crawford continued, "I reckon you might say I lied." At that he managed to lift his head straight and look Jeremiah in the face, tense and strained, as though waiting for a blow he was powerless to avoid.

Jeremiah nodded.

"I done it, it ain't to be denied," Crawford said. "It looked like I had to, Mr. Beaumont. I come of good folks, Mr. Beaumont, over the mountains. My father was lettered, he was a rector and lettered and sat at any man's table, rich howsoever, and they give him respect. But he died, Mr. Beaumont, and me young and nothing to go on. But I made my way, Mr. Beaumont, I come out here and made my way. I had me a place, nigh three hundred acres, Mr. Beaumont, and some niggers. Not many, but some, and I held my head up. Then"—he paused, swallowed air, wiped his mustaches, resumed—"then, Mr. Beaumont, they up and taken it from me. And me getting on, Mr. Beaumont, not young any more. So you see—so you see"—his voice rose, cracked into a kind of wail—"don't you see, Mr. Beaumont, don't you see?"

Jeremiah nodded again.

"They promised me money, yeah, money, Mr. Beaumont, and I said I'd swear. Reward money, Mr. Beaumont. But the time come— the time come, and you know—you know I nigh couldn't swear to a lie —don't you remember, that day how I nigh told the truth?" He looked beseechingly at Jeremiah, found no response, and continued: "And that night they said they would burn my shop down—all I got now, my shop—they said they would beat me, said they would kill me. And next day—you know how it was next day?"

Jeremiah nodded. He knew how it had been.

"But I wouldn't have done it, Mr. Beaumont, not even then, Mr. Beaumont"—he came close, timidly, peering into Jeremiah's face— "not even then, if I hadn't believed you was guilty, had done it and killed him. You got to believe that, Mr. Beaumont, you got to . . ."

He suddenly stopped, and looked desperately into Jeremiah's face. Then cried: "But you ain't saying a thing, you ain't saying nothing, ain't you going to say, Mr. Beaumont?"

There was nothing to say. What had this miserable creature with the agonized face and the hands that plucked at each other and the miserable story to do with him? With Jeremiah Beaumont? With Jeremiah Beaumont, who was about to die?

But the agonized mouth was saying: "I wouldn't done it, I swear it, if I hadn't knowed in my heart you was guilty—for you was—they say how you said you done it—Mr. Beaumont, tell me you done it— you done it—didn't you do it?"

"All right," Jeremiah said, without passion. "I did it. If that makes

403

you feel better. I am a murderer, and you—you are a liar. You lied a man's life away. For money."

The face flinched as though the expected blow had been delivered. The eyes closed, the mouth twisted, the head jerked to one side. Then the eyes opened, and the face showed nothing but an innocent, tired surprise, as though surprised that now, afterwards, nothing had changed, he still stood and all was the same.

The mouth began to speak again: "Money," it said. "Part of that reward, but not what they promised. Not what they ought. Last month, when they give the reward. Then I had the money and folks said how you had confessed, and I ought to felt good you had confessed, but it was not so. Before you said how you done it, I was nigh easy, for I believed you was guilty, but once I knowed you had confessed it was worse for me and I cannot say the reason, and the money —I ain't even got the money—for they taken it from me, we was drinking and carrying on, me with them fellows, that Bumps and that Jessup and a fellow named Lilburn Jenkins, me drinking with that kind of folks, what once held my head up, but it looked like they was the only kind left for me, for folks on the street didn't pass the time with me no more, not folks that had knowed me once and made a bow for politeness, and I was drinking with them and we got to playing at cards, and I was drinking for it looked like I had to drink and I thought if I had some more money then everything would be like I wanted, for they had not give me my share. Well they taken it from me. Every cent, and they took it."

It was all said now. He stood there drained and dry, eyes sick, the yellowed mustaches drooping.

Jeremiah looked at the man, and felt his nausea come back, and a great weakness. He sank into the chair by the table. Then he controlled himself and said: "Well, what am I to do? Pay you the reward again?"

Crawford shook his head. "No," he said quietly and sadly. "No, Mr. Beaumont. I don't want money now. It was a judgment on me."

"I would gladly pay it to have you go," Jeremiah said wearily.

"No, Mr. Beaumont," he said. "I can't go yet."

"Can't you give me peace?" Jeremiah burst out. "Can't you even give peace to a man about to hang?"

Crawford came close and leaned down. "Maybe you won't hang. That's why I come, Mr. Beaumont. Maybe to keep you from hanging."

"I suppose you have Governor Desha's pardon in your pocket."

"No, but I got something to tell." He came closer. "Lilburn Jenkins, he has a brother, One-eye they call him, One-eye Jenkins. Them as worked once for Skrogg. You seen him round town here. One-eye is mad with his brother because Lilburn wouldn't give him money, which he got lots of somehow of a sudden. I don't know exactly how 'tis. So One-eye had a fight with Lilburn in the street, and got put in jail. He got out of jail this morning and come to me and said how me and him was against Lilburn, for Lilburn had done him wrong and taken my money at cards, too. And he had something, he said, what would get us money, would I help him. He said how them lawyers of yours was trying to find a handbill Fort wrote against your wife, for maybe it would get a pardon, and for the right price he could show a handbill, and would I swear how it was true and all, for two men's word was better than one and he would pay me. But I told him I was through swearing and . . ."

"Why shouldn't you swear?" Jeremiah demanded. "Why should you bury your talent?"

Crawford bowed a little, and his eyes closed for an instant. Then they opened, and he said: "You can say it. I don't mind, for you got the right to say it. But I done come to help. To tell you. Maybe it would help to know. If them lawyers could . . ."

"Help!" Jeremiah said bitterly. "With Hawgood in Lexington, and Madison over near Versailles, and it near four o'clock now and the gallows built."

"I could go to Versailles. Get me a horse and ride hard and get Mr. Madison. Leave word for One-eye I had gone and to wait."

"If you wish," Jeremiah said, listlessly. If there had been a flicker of hope, it was gone now. What was there to hope for?

"I'll go," Crawford said. "I'll do what a man can."

"All right," Jeremiah said.

Crawford waited, looking at Jeremiah.

"Mr Beaumont," he said. And when Jeremiah looked up: "Mr. Beaumont, will you do me a favor? Maybe I ought not to be asking, but if you will do it . . ." His voice trailed off.

"What?"

"If"—Crawford stiffened himself, then continued—"if you could let me shake hands."

Jeremiah looked at him for a moment. "All right," he said then. Without rising from the chair he put out his hand.

Crawford took the hand, gave it two or three formal jerks, and released it. "Thank you, Mr. Beaumont," he said.

"It doesn't matter," Jeremiah said.

Then Crawford left.

After Crawford had gone, the guard got up, stretched himself, shook like a dog, and climbed to the head of the ladder. He yelled a few times, then another guard came and took his place. The first guard did not come back.

There was nothing to do but wait. Munn Short brought the supper. Jeremiah took a little and persuaded Rachel to a few spoonsful of the soup and a morsel of bread. She lay back down, and he sat by the table for a while. He even considered opening the packet of his manuscript and adding an account of Crawford's visit, but that scarcely seemed worthwhile. That was Crawford's story, not his. And what was his own story, anyway?

Then he considered burning the manuscript, sheet by sheet over the candle. There might be some satisfaction in that, in removing all trace of himself from the world, in plunging totally into the blackness. To burn the manuscript would be almost like the suicide that had failed. But that impulse faded, too.

About ten o'clock he heard steps above, and thought for an instant, with a little start of hope, that it might be Madison. But it could not be, Versailles was too far. It was only a militiaman coming to relieve the guard. He was ashamed of that start of hope, as of something unworthy.

He lay down on the bed beside Rachel. He wondered if she were asleep. Then he wondered if she would kill herself as she had sworn. Then he was sure that she would, and he wondered if, were their roles reversed, he would do it. He thought that he must talk to her. He even rose on his arm to rouse her. But as he looked at her face, he knew that he had nothing to say. They had said all there was to say, they had used up everything.

He took her hand and lay back down. He pressed it lightly, fondling it, thinking that such a weak, wordless pressure was, perhaps, all anybody ever had to communicate to another in the end. There was no response. So he wondered if she were awake, and was conscious of his act. Perhaps she merely feigned sleep because she, too, knew that there was nothing to say. If she was awake, what was she thinking? Then he thought of all the time they had lain together and he had never known what she was thinking.

He wondered if Madison would come. And if he came, would he be able to accomplish anything with Desha. A reprieve, a pardon. He did not hope, he merely wondered. But there was one hope. He hoped that his neck would break tomorrow at the drop. That was something to hope for. Strangling would be bad. But he felt no horror now. He was too weak for that. Or was it weakness? It was as if he thought about somebody else whom he had heard about but never seen. Then, because he could not muster up the horror, he felt a queer sense of loss and deprivation. The fact that he could not summon up the horror made him feel sorry for himself.

Then he slept.

He woke, heard steps overhead, sat up and looked around the

edge of the alcove. Someone was descending the ladder. For an instant he thought it was Madison, but then as the man reached the bottom and moved into the light of the candle, he saw the dress of a militiaman. It must be another guard come to relief.

The guard rose from his chair by the wall, and greeted the other, but apparently with some surprise. The new man mumbled something, stepped in front of the guard, and suddenly flattened him with one blow to the face, leaped on him, and cracked his head soundly two or three times against the bricks.

Then he rose, quick as a cat for all his bulk, and whistled softly. Another figure moved down the ladder, burdened by a bundle. The figure stepped to the table and leaned to deposit the bundle. Then as it straightened and turned, Jeremiah saw, in the candlelight, the face of Wilkie Barron.

The face was smooth and handsome, the teeth showed a glint of white under the mustache, for the lips were drawn back a little as they always used to be when Wilkie was excited, the eyes glittered and darted from side to side.

Then Wilkie detected Jeremiah in the shadow and came quickly toward him, hand outstretched, smiling. "Ah, Jerry," he said, "we've come for you."

"Come for me?" Jeremiah asked dully, for he had not yet grasped the reality.

"Of course, you fool," Wilkie said, laughing. "Do you think I'd let them string up my good old Jerry?"

He swung to the table, picked up the bundle, and flung it to Jeremiah. "Get these on," he commanded, "and be quick." He turned toward the other man, who was now stooping over the fallen body and fumbling at its throat.

For a second Jeremiah had the impression that he was strangling the man, or cutting the throat, and leaped up, and said, "Look—look —don't let . . ."

Then he saw Wilkie grinning at him. "Shut up!" Wilkie said. "He's not slicing his pipe, he's just undressing him. We need his clothes for your wife. And for God's sake wake her up. And make her dress. We haven't got eternity."

Jeremiah, dazed, dressed himself as quickly as possible. Then he woke up Rachel and began to fumble with her clothes. She was too weak, or confused, to help much. Suddenly Wilkie came into the alcove, flung the guard's clothes down, and leaned over Rachel, and his fingers leaped expertly to the business of buttons and laces. "No time for modesty," he laughed. Then: "My God, Jerry, you are damned clumsy for a married man. Here, let me show you!"

They got Rachel into the guard's trousers and coat, rolled up the trousers, which were too long, and tried to set the hat on her head. But twice it fell off. Her hair was too heavy. All at once Wilkie pushed her to a sitting position on the edge of the bed, seized her hair in a great mass with his left hand and held it up and back, so that her head was back. And almost in the same moment his right hand had plucked his knife—it was the Spanish knife, Jeremiah fleetingly recognized—out of his tunic, and had set its edge to her hair.

"Don't!" Jeremiah cried in a kind of terror.

But the knife's razor edge was deep into the hair. It made a faint, gritting, silken sound, and the hair parted, stroke by stroke, while Rachel's head bent farther back with the tension and her eyes stared wide at the ceiling. Her throat was exposed in a strained, white arc. It seemed to invite the knife. An instant, and the knife would be there, would flick across with its silken sound.

The last lock of hair parted, and Rachel's head jerked forward a little as the tension was released. The knife was back in Wilkie's tunic. He snatched up the hat from the bed, and put it on her head, squinted fleetingly at it with a critical air, then touched it to an angle with the finesse of a milliner. "Ah, madame," he breathed, "how fetching!"

He stepped back, serious. "Hurry," he commanded, "hurry. Start up the ladder with her." Then he turned to his companion. "You got him tied?"

"He can't budge," the man said, "nor squeak neither," and gave the fallen form a solid kick to prove his point.

Jeremiah leaned to gather a handful of the mass of hair on the bed, and shoved it awkwardly into a pocket. Then he helped Rachel toward the ladder. But he delayed a moment to pick up the packet of manuscript that he had prepared for Mr. Madison.

"Well, Jerry," Wilkie said, with satisfaction and surveyed the scene behind, "I haven't had as much fun since we fought the bastards at Lumton."

XII

WILKIE HAD REASON TO BE PLEASED WITH himself. The jail delivery was a brilliant piece of improvisation, simple and daring. With Lilburn Jenkins and another fellow (whom we know only as Finger), Wilkie had taken the uniforms off the backs of four militiamen. There had been no protest, as Wilkie said, for they were most obliging fellows, they'd give the coat off the back. In each instance, the donor had been soundly unconscious at the time. By playing pimp, Finger had lured two drunk militiamen to a deserted cabin near the bluff north of town. There Wilkie and Lilburn had quietly stepped from behind the bushes and simultaneously tapped the victims on the back of the head. Then, Finger and Lilburn having rigged themselves out in the borrowed finery, the three went back into town and waylaid two other militiamen in dark alleys and accumulated two other costumes for their little charade. "We could have had a wide selection," Wilkie said. "This town is as full of drunk heroes tonight as a graveyard of ghosts."

Wilkie changed into a militiaman's coat, cocked the hat on his head, and led his companions to the jail. They engaged the outside guard in conversation, backed him into a shadow, and knocked him unconscious. Finger took his position, and Wilkie and Lilburn went in. The guard at the door to the room above the cell received the same treatment. They bound him and gagged him and laid him inside the door. Then Wilkie waited until Lilburn had disposed of the guard in the cell. Munn Short, asleep in his quarters, never heard a sound.

Once outside, the deliverers and the delivered were simply five more drunk militiamen prowling the town at a late hour. Rachel was so weak that she had to be supported—a task that Wilkie undertook —and Jeremiah himself staggered now and then without feigning. Halfway to the river they passed the watch, and Jeremiah was sure, even in the faint light, for the moon was almost down, that Carlos Bumps was one of them. Wilkie greeted them with drunken gravity, and as they passed, broke into uneven song.

They passed through the sleeping town, and the moon went down over the river, and very far away some drunken night-walker shouted, and Wilkie's voice sang, and Jeremiah managed to move down the street, feeling nothing, and the whole thing was but a dream. He might still be lying in the cell, dreaming this. It was the dream of a world he had long ago forgotten. He felt that he was moving off into a dream, had faded through some film into another dimension, and nothing would ever be real again.

Wilkie was telling him now, with evident zest, how he had seized the uniforms and had managed the escape, but Jeremiah scarcely listened. And he scarcely listened as Wilkie began to explain why he had testified against him at the trial. He was saying that he had done so only because he was already sure of conviction, he had come to Frankfort only when he was already sure, he had testified to the personal motive because that might gain sympathy, because it had been necessary to save the New Court, for the charge of conspiracy for political assassination might have ruined the party—ah, it now seemed ruined anyway, since the August election—and more and more in that urgent, controlled, compelling voice. Jeremiah heard the words, but did not attend to their meaning.

Then Wilkie was saying again how Jerry, dear Jerry, need never have worried, for Wilkie would never let him hang, not Wilkie, he should have had faith in Wilkie.

They came to the river. Wilkie halted them, and Finger went ahead down the bank toward the shadow of a keelboat moored there. He tossed a stone over to the deck, then another, and a sleepy voice answered. He turned and motioned and Wilkie led the way down, supporting Rachel with great expertness. Had it not been for Lilburn Jenkins, Jeremiah himself could not have made the descent.

Two men on the keelboat had laid a plank to shore, and Wilkie escorted Rachel aboard. The others followed. Wilkie turned to Jeremiah. "You are going on a journey," he said. "Jenkins will go with you all the way. Trust good old Lilburn. He will love you like a brother." Then he leaned, took Rachel's hand and kissed it. "Good-bye," he said. He shook hands with Jeremiah, saying, "Good-bye, dear old Jerry!"

Lightly, with arms slightly lifted for balance, with a finicking dancer's step, Wilkie had run down the plank to shore. He wheeled, poised for a moment, his body above the waist rising from the shadow and mist as from water, and lifted an arm in farewell. "Good-bye!" he called softly, "good-bye, my dillies, my darlings, good-bye!"

Gruffly, a voice behind Jeremiah spoke: "Git down, git out of sight."

So Jeremiah turned, and climbed down as the boatman indicated. Rachel was already down.

They were put under the deck, forward, in a black space of rough timbering, a kind of cubby with a smell like a latrine. They lay down on the boards, exhausted. The smell was almost overpowering. Then Jeremiah identified the smell. The boat had recently had a cargo of hides.

There was some stirring above, and suppressed voices. Then Jeremiah felt the boat swing sluggishly, then lurch forward. There was new movement above, and the grinding of wood. The boat was shoving off. Then Jeremiah felt it caught in the slow yaw and suck of the current. But the poling continued. The boat gathered speed.

Jeremiah lay in a daze between sleep and waking, breathing the foul air, incuriously hearing his heart beat in some vast emptiness that was himself, not feeling anything, not even the boards beneath him. In his weakness it was as though his blood and his being flowed perpetually out of him, leaving him lighter and lighter, floating in a dense, dark atmosphere. Or as though he were not separated from the river by that sheath of plank beneath, but were himself in the river, in its dark inwardness, being drawn on and on, absorbed into the water, just brushing luxuriously in that blackness, the black velvet mud of the bottom. He had a vision of his own body, naked and faintly gleaming in the depth, flowing on with the inner current, on and on. It was peace.

Then, before he slept, he remembered with a dreamlike marveling the time, years before, when he had wandered the country back of his Grandfather Marcher's place and had come to this very river and had swum in it and had lain on the sand spit drowsing in the sun to wake to the sound of music and to see the keelboat round the greenery of the bend, and how the boat had moved past him with the deliberation of the river and he had risen naked to watch it and the man on board had waved the fiddle and burst into a wild, crazy tune, and the boat had gone on with the river and he had run into the water as though to plunge in and follow, but had only stood there leaning after the boat until it was masked by the next bend, and how, as he stood and leaned, there had come the sound of the boat's bugle over the emptiness of the river, summoning him.

And now it seemed that that time and this time were the same time, foreshortened and fused in the dream, that he had plunged into the river to the call of the silver notes, and had surrendered, and the river had sucked him in, away from the empty sunlight, into the darkness, with the notes still ringing in his head forever, and this was it, and this was it. So he slept.

Even the next day, Jeremiah and Rachel were not allowed out of their hole. And just after dawn, to make matters worse, the boatmen had set some kegs across the entrance and piled some sacks of something, leaving only a little space for air and for handing in some water and bread. The heat was intolerable in the hole, the air was bad. Jeremiah was faint and sick. Rachel lay in a semi-conscious condition, only rousing now and then to take a sip of water.

In his sickness Jeremiah tried to decide why Wilkie had saved them. Why, after he had betrayed friendship and old affection, after he had knotted the rope, did he take this way, full of every risk, to save them? Well, this was Wilkie's way, and he saw the mouth draw back under the mustache to show the close-set white teeth, and saw the eyes glitter with excitement, and heard Wilkie say gaily again, "Well, Jerry, I haven't had as much fun since we fought the bastards at Lumton."

He had never understood Wilkie, what was inside Wilkie. All he had understood was that Wilkie was at home in the world, was made for the world and the world for him. But the world was not made for Jeremiah Beaumont, nor he for the world.

Then Jeremiah remembered that he had not even thanked Wilkie. He supposed that you should thank a man for saving your life. Even if your life was nothing. He supposed that he should have thanked even Lilburn. Whoever Lilburn was, brute and cut-throat or whatever. But he was a creature of Wilkie, and Wilkie has said, "Trust good old Lilburn. He will go with you all the way." Wilkie and Lilburn, he did not understand. But the wondering was lost, for he fell off to sleep again. It must have been the middle of the afternoon.

The grating of the keel on gravel roused him, and he felt the boat swing heavily as the current tugged the stern. Then the swing was caught, as the boatmen set their poles. It was dark now: he could tell that through the chink between the sacks.

Then the boatmen heaved some of the sacks away, and a voice ordered them to come out. Jeremiah helped Rachel through, and followed.

The boat was grounded on a patch of gravel under a steep wooded bank that blacked out the stars. Lilburn Jenkins was already on the spit below. For it was his voice that called urgently, in little more than a harsh whisper, "Git on down, git on down!" And it was he who helped Rachel down the plank.

They stepped back into the deeper shadow of the bank and waited while the keelboat was poled off and around the spit, and then was caught in the current. Finger had not come down. There were only the three of them, Jeremiah, Rachel and Jenkins, abandoned here at night on the dark shore.

They scrambled up the bank into a woods thick with undergrowth, then, scratched and torn, through the brush to a glade. Jenkins left them here, was gone about an hour, and returned to order them to follow him. After another couple of hours of travel by a faint trail in more open woods, they came to the edge of a cultivated field, the first sign they had discovered of human habitation. It was scarcely a field, merely a shirt-tail corn-patch, half taken by late weeds, the scraggly stalks now silvered by moonlight.

"Moe Sullins," Jenkins said, as though the name would communicate something, and nodded in the direction of the woods beyond the patch. Then he left them. A little later they heard a dog bark in the woods beyond. Within an hour Jenkins was back, leading two horses, and behind him another man leading a third. The man, whom Jenkins did not introduce, was the lanky, stooped, whiskered, half-lazy, half-lethal figure that might have risen from any back-country corn-patch by moonlight. The horses were the scrawny and indestructible animals of the frontier, hard-mouthed and mean-eyed.

"Hold 'em," Jenkins said, and passed the rope reins over to Jeremiah, and Jeremiah caught the gust of whisky breath. That, Jeremiah considered, must have caused the delay. Then Jenkins retired for a last conference with the man who must have been Moe Sullins. Sullins gave him a substantial sack. He came back, nodded at Rachel, and said, "Git her up."

Jenkins held the reins now, while Jeremiah helped Rachel to mount. Then he mounted, and then Jenkins, and Jenkins led off at a walk down the open space between the corn-patch and woods. The knees of the animals ripped with a weary deliberation through the tangle of weeds and looping vines. Once Jeremiah's mount stumbled, caught in a hobble of vine. Jeremiah looked back once, to see Sullins, or whoever he was, standing in his enormous, sad inertia, like a post or a scarecrow by the moon-drenched field.

They rode all night along some sort of trail or track that bore roughly west and north. Once or twice they passed a cabin in a clearing, and once a dog came out to bark at them. Long after they were out of sight, Jeremiah could still hear the dog barking in a doleful and unforgiving iteration. When, after a little, he could no longer hear the dog, he felt deprived and alone. What it was he had lost, he could not say.

Shortly before dawn, Jenkins stopped and dismounted and handed his reins to Jeremiah. He scouted off in the woods to one side, returned and ordered them to follow. He led them a half mile down a declivity into a constricted valley, then up the stream where the valley narrowed like a gorge, with dank stone walling each side. Then suddenly, there was a little open space, with grass and a few trees like great blobs of denser blackness. From the shape, Jeremiah decided that they must be beeches. Beyond the space, the gorge resumed.

But Jenkins stopped here. "Git her off," he ordered Jeremiah, who dismounted and went to Rachel. She could scarcely move from fatigue. She simply slid off into his arms, like a sack. He set her on the wet grass, propped against a stone, and following Jenkins' example, hobbled his horses, and let them free to graze.

Jenkins rummaged in the sack and produced some food. When Jeremiah bit into corn pone and cold side-meat, the mess was clammy to the tongue. He managed to work it down. But Rachel could not eat. She sat propped against the stone, and held the food decorously in her hand, and stared straight ahead at the night. Then Jeremiah realized that she was shuddering with a chill. He took his coat off and put it around her, but she got no relief. He turned to Jenkins: "She's cold, we've got to have a fire."

Jenkins' jaws continued for two or three strokes their steady grinding on the mouthful he had, then he swallowed, reached a finger into his mouth and extracted a chewed string of meat rind, looked at it, and flung it aside. "Fahr," he said.

"Yes," Jeremiah said, "she's cold."

"They ketch you and hang you," Jenkins said, "and thar'll be fahr in hell."

"But she's got a chill."

"You be a durn fool," Jenkins announced, and restuffed his mouth with pone and side-meat, and the jaws resumed.

After he had finished eating, by the time dawn was well on, Jenkins ordered them back under the beeches. "You kin sleep," he said. Jeremiah smoothed a spot of old beech husks, laid his coat out, and made Rachel lie down. Jeremiah himself was not sleepy. He found a natural seat in the roots of a tree and leaned back.

Jenkins unbuckled his belt, swept a spot smooth with a stroke or two of his hand, laid out a couple of pistols from his pockets, and composed himself. Jeremiah watched him, thinking that the whole procedure reminded him of a dog turning around three times before lying down. He studied Jenkins for a moment, as Jenkins twisted and settled himself.

"Sullins," Jeremiah said, "who is he?"

"Feller I knowed when I was on the river."

"You're afraid of a fire," Jeremiah said. "Aren't you afraid Sullins will talk?"

"Sullins talk," Jenkins repeated slowly, as though the idea had struck him as new and marvelous. "Naw, he won't talk," he stated, finally.

"Why?"

"Mister," Jenkins said, "Sullins knows he talks and I cut his thote. Follow him fer as the brimstone, and cut his thote."

At that, Jenkins stretched his arms and gave a prodigious yawn, dismissing Sullins and the world and the whole preposterous idea. Then he collapsed upon himself, and was asleep, like a brute or a baby.

Jeremiah stayed awake for a long time, propped against his tree. But finally, staring at the glittering stream beyond the low beech boughs, for the sun was well up and bearing down into the gorge, he fell asleep, too.

That was the beginning of the journey. At dark they began to travel again, then camped at first light. The fifth night, shortly before dawn, they crossed a good, well-traveled road. Jeremiah decided that it must be the road running south from Louisville, and he thought how, in broad daylight, a coach would pass here, and people talked and laughed on the journey, how men rode along on horseback, and met other men, and lifted the hat and gravely bowed, or stopped in the shade of a tree together, or at a branch to water their mounts, and passed their civilities and news, how people came and went here about the business of the world, driven by something inside them that would drive them on and on, miles and miles, years and years, while their faces changed and their bodies changed and sagged, and their hair went white, hair by hair, and they finally lay down in a bed and people stood around and wept and then they were dead, and those who had wept went away and forgot the names of those for whom they had wept, except for a moment in the stillness of some hot afternoon or at night before drowsing off, and waited, too, for the time when they themselves would lie down and others would weep for them. A sweet melancholy rose in Jeremiah's heart. The weeping or the being wept for, the forgetting or the being forgotten: which was sweeter, he could not decide.

Jenkins crossed the road, looked sharply left and right, even though it was night and there would be no travelers, and plunged into the shadow of woods beyond. They pushed on hard till a little past dawn, then made camp. Once, in the late morning, Jeremiah stirred from his drowse and thought he heard the horn of a stage. But then he remembered that they had come too far from the highway for the sound to carry.

A little later the country began to get rougher, and the clearings sparser, the cabins more poverty-bit. They had long since left the region where big houses were. They began to travel by day. But when business was to be done at a cabin, Jenkins always went alone. He dickered for food, once swapped his horse, which had gone lame, and finally bought a rifle. "Mought need it for pot-shooting," he said. The next day he got an ax.

"Where are we going?" Jeremiah asked Jenkins one day.

"Place I know," Jenkins replied.

"Where?"

"Yander," Jenkins said, and nodded ahead, west.

"Where?"

"A place nobody keers what yore name is or what you done."

Nobody cares what your name is or what you have done, Jeremiah thought, and thought that that would be peace, would be like being born again, would be like the joy of grace and salvation, as when he had gone to the meeting when he was a boy, and Corinthian McClardy with his pocked face and yellow, red-rimmed, flashing eyes and terrible voice, had loomed above the people and shouted how God was like a bear treading the earth and breaking the thicket and the fawn exposed its throat, and how McClardy had shouted to the people, "Oh, lie down in your weakness and bleat, bleat to call forth the bear!" and how he, Jeremiah, had fallen to earth smitten by grace, and there was peace.

Why had he not been able to hug that peace forever? Why had he risen from the ground? How had he lost that peace? It was all so long ago. But he gazed at the back of his conductor ahead, the greasy hair matted on the neck, the broad bulky shoulders that seemed to dwarf the animal beneath, and thought how this man, this brute with the blunt, hairy, clay-colored face and slit-eyes and yellow teeth streaked with a gray-green like fungus, was now his guide to peace, was now the vessel of his grace.

The woods by which they rode now were in full color. We know how it would have been then, for the same species grow there now, in the woodlot, in some bend by the creek, on the hill too rough for cultivation, disinherited remnants hanging to the waste fringes of a land they had once possessed in full right. The black gum would have been scarlet and black, each leaf shining like enamel, the sweet gum yellow, the oaks tawny and russet, the maples red and gold, the hickories yellow, the sumac and buckberry wine-red. By the water-courses, among the cane now streaked yellow, the trunk of the sycamore would be white, and the great brown and gold leaves would drift down to float on the stream.

In the glades the vine of the wild grape would loop and festoon the trees, even to the upper branches, and the fruit by now would be turned dark. Once, as they rode along the edge of the woods, Jeremiah saw Lilburn reach up and spread his fingers and shred off a handful of clusters and cram them into his mouth. All afternoon, every time they rode under a vine, Lilburn repeated the action, even when he had to rise in his stirrups to reach. Late, when they stopped for camp, he turned his face to them for the first time in all those hours, and Jeremiah saw it. He saw the face shockingly smeared and stained, as though bruised and beaten pulpy, as though savagely painted for ritual, or as though it had fed on dripping flesh and the waste blood had caked about the muzzle. Jeremiah had, for the instant, forgotten the grapes.

Day after day they rode on, Jeremiah and Rachel, behind that man about whom they knew nothing, who never spoke except to give a command or a grudging answer to a question, who told nothing about himself, who, Wilkie had said, would love them like a brother, who led them now through the brilliant autumnal land toward some destination he would not define.

Jeremiah recognized the beauty of the land and the season. "It was that time," he writes, "when Nature arrays herself most gloriously and spares no pain to be splendid. If she is to die, and the dark winter come, she will die as a queen clad in gold and scarlet who steps gaily into the flame. Once my heart had been lifted by the display of Nature, not only this of the autumn, but by the beauties proper to each season, and when I had lain prisoner in the house of Mr. Marton or in my cell, I had sometimes whiled away the heavy time by closing my eyes to summon up some spot I once had seen that had snared my fancy, a place homely and familiar, like the bank of the creek on the Jordan place where I had thought to build my mill, or some wild valley in the forests where I had hunted in my youth. Now, in very fact, I saw the open land I had never thought to see again, and moved freely across it, and it was a fair land. My eyes saw, but my heart did not, and was not lifted up. This was strange to me, and the cause of sadness.

"We were moving into the western part, and though it was not a region I had seen before, I remembered how long back I had gone into the west seeking land for a speculation. In that time I had thought to gain wealth, to open the land to others for my profit and bring in the uses and works of man. But that had come to nothing, for in the end I had pursued not wealth and the esteem of the world but an idea that I placed above all, and now I was coming into this western land

417

not to open it to the world but to hide myself from the world and to lie in secret in the pathless woods and dark entrails of America. Ah, I thought then, the land is the same, and its beauty, and is voiceless, whatever our errand, whether for wealth or peace, to open or to close."

They went on. They forded streams. They passed beyond settlements, and worked through new country. They hoarded the dry bread and lived on what fell to the rifle. They killed a deer and gorged on the meat that they boiled scarcely before it had ceased to quiver. They carried what they could with them, the best parts, and ate it until it began to taint. They came to a patch of settlement on the Ohio, and Jeremiah and Rachel lay out in the woods for a day, while Jenkins went to cabins to buy bread and salt and powder. Then they struck again to the southwest, for a time by a trace, and then across the wild country, by the stars.

Jeremiah saw it first, on a late afternoon, through the drizzle. Twice lately they had come to a "great river" and had had to build a raft for themselves and swim the horses across. Now, just beyond the second river (the Tennessee) they had come into a low country of creeks and slews where the rain prickled grayly the dark, unflowing surface of the water, a country of rank cane and water oaks and tangled vine, with a matting of vegetable rot like black scum over a pale soil, slick to the foot. Jenkins had followed confidently a winding alley in the cane. He had not warned them that they approached their haven. He had gone on ahead, in his sullen silence. Until they broke from the cane into an open muddy patch, by a slew, and he turned to them, and pointed across the water, and said, "Thar, thar hit be."

"I looked across the water," Jeremiah narrates, "which widened here to some twenty-five yards, and saw the strip of flat on the farther side, set with patches of cane and beyond that the rising ground where scrub timber, going leafless now, rose in the mist and rain. At the first glance I saw no trace of the works of man, for all there, the water, the cane and timber, and the sky, seemed dissolved into the common grayness. But upon my closer inspection I observed in the flat part certain shacks set upon stilts as to avoid flood water, and behind them, where the ground rose, what looked to be the remnants of a stockade, and farther still, half concealed in the timber, two or three cabins. Then I saw some strands of smoke, which was absorbed into the mist and subdued to its color.

"I turned to our mentor and asked who lived here, in such a desolate spot, and he replied in his common surliness, that had I ever been on the river I would know. I said sharply that I had not had the privilege of being on the river and would he instruct me. To which he replied, the Gran Boz, or what sounded thus and conveyed naught to me. I asked again, and he said sourly that there had been many a man on the river who was sorry he ever found out.

"At that he turned from me and halloed two or three times. Then I saw that on the farther shore were several pirogues and skiffs drawn up, one of them large, but all of such a color that they were scarce to be distinguished from the gray mud of the bank. A human figure emerged from one of the shacks and without regard to the ladder dropped to the ground, and peered in our direction. At that Jenkins put his hands to his mouth like a horn and called the strange jargon, Reverend set and heave-oh! (This I later learned to be a river language, for when they would set the iron head of the pike on a firm bottom or sunk log, the boatmen named it a reverend set.) This seemed to be a password, for thereupon the man across asked a name, and Jenkins gave his and said he would speak with the Gran Boz.

"The man waved to us, as though to counsel patience, and started up the little rise behind. He passed the ruin of the stockade, and was lost to our sight. We stood there in the rain, huddling upon ourselves to keep the cold from our bones, and stared across at the dreary prospect of our haven, and waited. Even those shacks or cabins would be better than the wet earth, on which we had lain the night before in our undefended state.

"At length he came back to the flat and shoved a boat off from the mud and began to paddle toward us. It was the large boat and moved but heavily in the water. When he had reached our shore, he stared curiously at us, saying nothing, then motioned us to enter. Jenkins took the saddles off the horses and flung the saddles into the boat. So we crossed over, making the horses swim on their halters.

"We reached the farther shore and stepped out into the mud. We hitched the horses to a tree, and put the saddles there for a little shelter. Then we moved into the open, following the native of the place, who all the while had said not a word. Now in the open Jenkins turned to us, and ordered us to wait. We looked about for some shelter and started to move toward the tree where the horses were, but at this the native exhibited some faint instinct of common humanity and hospitality by motioning us under the shack from which he had descended. It was elevated some eight or nine feet from the ground, on stout piles or stakes, and was floored with boards and walled with light board and cane matted together. As we approached it, after making our thanks, we saw a face that seemed to be female spy out at us fleetingly from the curtain that covered the doorway.

"We stood under the shack for a long time, and waited. I saw from the grayish staining of the lower part of the stakes that flood water had here come up some five feet from the ground. I looked down at the ground and the objects of filth and waste that had accumulated

419

there. In the area near the front of the ladder the ground was blackened by old fire and pieces of burned sticks lay about. At first I thought that here they must cook, but then I surmised that fires were put here in the evening in the warm months to repel the insects natural to such a swampy and miasmal habitat. Scattered about were two or three fish heads in various stages of decay, and several bones of small animal or fowl half trodden into the earth. A twist of rotten cloth, once some bright reddish color but now faded out, lay near one of the stakes. Fragments of a fire-blackened pottery container lay about our feet and to one side the handle of a broken knife, the short remnant of blade flaking to rust. A lean hog slouched out of the cane and began to nuzzle one of the fish heads.

"In the midst of all this trash I saw something that sparkled, and leaned to pick it up. It was the piece of a comb such as gentlewomen may put in the hair for ornament, and in the heavy part that would be exposed from the hair some bright stones or glass had been set. One of them remained and yet had some glitter. The thing was broken and muddy and twisted and had the sadness of an object fashioned for pleasure and vanity that has been cast aside. I turned it in my hand and wondered how it had come here so far from any haunt of elegance and laughter. As I held it, I heard a stir in the shack above us, then the place was quiet again, and there was only the sound of water, drop by slow drop, tapping a stiff leaf nigh where we stood. Meanwhile I felt that I had previously lived that moment and its fear of the mysterious life or death that might be in that place, and one knew not if the life or the death was more fearful. Then I knew what echo had risen from the hollowness of memory. I had felt thus on that day long ago when I had first entered the house of my Grandfather Marcher, where all seemed sodden and bemused past the human hope. And with that recollection that made one moment of those two so disparate, I had the fear, deeper than the mystery of the place, that a man might live his years and end but where he began."

Lilburn and the man came back finally and led them up the rise, toward the cabins past the broken stockade, and some hundred paces north up the island (for it was a sort of island, Jeremiah was to learn, cut off by a slew on the other side). Rachel was so exhausted that Jeremiah had to support her as best he could with one arm. With his other hand he carried the bulky packet of his manuscript under his coat to keep it from the wet. Days before, he had wrapped it in a piece of sacking and had tied it with heavy cord.

They came to a cabin, set at the extreme end of the high ground, and the man led the way in. A very dirty woman, barefoot, swarthy, and with uncombed hair, squatted on the puncheons, assembling some household gear in a blanket. Beside her on the floor was a smaller bundle done up in some sort of coarse cloth and sacking. At second glance, Jeremiah saw that it was not a bundle at all: it was a tiny baby trussed up in the rags. The gray, wrinkled face stared up at the ceiling. It made no sound.

As they entered, the woman looked up at them from under the tangle of hair with a naked hostility. Jeremiah surmised that she was being evicted to make a place for them, and he was right. Within a few minutes she had made her pack. She picked up the baby, heaved the pack to her shoulder, and went out the door. There she turned, gave one last look at them, and calmly spat on the threshold.

The native made a gesture to say that they were to remain, then he and Jenkins followed the woman out into the drizzle, and Jeremiah and Rachel were left in possession.

The last strength which had supported Rachel through the wilderness flight seemed suddenly to go. She sank down by the clay hearth, where a few chunks smoldered, and began to sob. It was a dry, choked sobbing, without tears. Jeremiah went to her, and found that she was shivering with cold. He threw more wood on the fire, fanned up the flame with a turkey wing flung down by the hearth, and then went to the bed in the corner to get something to put about her. He almost took the bear robe, for it was warmest, but then thinking that it was probably flea-ridden, picked up one of the two blankets.

Later, when she had ceased to shiver, he got the damp clothes off her, wrapped her in his own coat, which he had meanwhile dried by the fire, and put her on the deerskins on the bed, or what passed for a bed—a frame of poles built out from the corner of the cabin and supported by a stake at the outer corner of the structure. He covered her with the blankets, and drew the bear robe up as high as her middle.

Then he put a couple of deerskins on the puncheons before the hearth, and himself lay down. He was too tired even to think of food. All he could think was that now he could sleep.

So he and Rachel came into their new home and new life.

The next day, Jeremiah woke to a cold hearth and stiff bones. At first he thought it must still be early, for only a little gray light seeped into the cabin from the ill-hung door. He stumbled to the door, opened it, and looked out. Over the whole place there was only the gray light that itself seemed heavy and sodden. He could see the muddy track leading up the rise, and there one of the cabins beyond some brush. There was no sign of life anywhere. But his woodsman's sense told Jeremiah that it was late.

He went out to forage for some wood, and found a few cut pieces more or less protected by a tree. He had carried those in and was leaning over the hearth trying to blow up some coals dug from the ashes when he sensed someone behind him. He turned quickly and saw a small figure, black against the light of the open door, the figure of a child, a boy about ten or eleven years old.

"Who are you?" Jeremiah demanded, but the boy said nothing, only held out a basket.

Jeremiah went to the door. The boy retreated a step or two, still holding out the basket and looking up with a wild animal's wariness. The face was dark, with the darkness of some kind of half-breed, the black hair matted down over the forehead, the body was clothed in what seemed to be a cut-down deerskin hunting shirt, tied around the waist with a piece of rope over ragged homespun pantaloons, the bare feet that stuck out below were mud-splattered and horny-looking. He held out the basket, and waited.

Jeremiah looked into the basket. There was a pot with what seemed to be corn meal, a jug and three fish loose in the basket. He received the basket, and the boy retreated two steps, never taking his eyes off Jeremiah's face, waiting for some sign of threat.

"Thank you," Jeremiah said.

The boy made no reply, retreating another step.

"Listen," Jeremiah said. "Who is Gran Boz?"

The black eyes sharpened a little, but there was no answer.

"Gran Boz—who is he?" Jeremiah repeated.

"Beeg—beeg," the boy said then, and lifted his arms wide.

"Who is he?"

The boy let the arms sag, and leaned forward as though he had a weight on his back, still peering up at Jeremiah. "Eel—eel," he said, and that is the way Jeremiah transcribes it for us ". . . eel bow-sue."

"And what the devil is that?" Jeremiah asked sharply.

He had spoken too sharply. The boy stepped back, gave one searching look more, and turned and ran up the track.

Jeremiah went into the cabin, built up his fire, cleaned the fish and patted out corn pones, and made a meal for himself and Rachel.

Then he went out to explore their situation. He went down some paces northwest to the low ground, encountered the slew on that side and turned south, along the edge of the water. Willow and cane grew along the edge for some distance, then there was an open space. Here a keelboat was partly drawn up on a mudflat, or had been left there by high water. A rotting rope still reached across to a water oak on the bank. The keelboat, he saw, had been partly broken down, apparently stripped for plank and timber; the decking was all gone, and great gaps were in the sides.

Jeremiah tried to make out the movement of the current in the slew, wondering how the keelboat had been brought in from the river. There seemed to be a slight drift northward, to his right. He now surmised—and later learned—that this was a sort of creek that merged with a swampy backwater of the Ohio. One day, some weeks later, he was to go down the creek in a skiff. The channel, he was to discover, narrowed sharply within a few hundred yards of the island, and veered west. Where it debouched into the Ohio, several miles on, it was quite narrow and would have been scarcely discernible from the river, the growth hung here so heavy. Mud and silt, he saw, had now begun to accumulate at the mouth, spawned there by the river. It had been a long time since a keelboat had made the passage.

Today, however, he had only his surmise. He left the ruin of the keelboat and continued south. A little farther, in a kind of cove, he found several skiffs and a sort of raft drawn up to the shore. Beyond the cane, across the spread of water to the west, he saw sycamores and timber, and beyond, a little thread of smoke. So the settlement was not confined to the island.

Back of the cove a track wound toward the high ground. He took it, passed among the scrub oaks, passed one cabin, then another. From the doorway of the second, two children peered out at him, then quickly withdrew. He entered what had been the stockade. There were several cabins here, two small, and one unusually large, a double cabin with an ell. All were occupied, for smoke showed from the chimneys, but the doors were closed.

He passed on, and took the track to his own cabin. Far down the river, he saw some men in a skiff.

Except for the same child, who in the late afternoon brought a batch of food, he saw no other inhabitant of the settlement until the next day. Then Jenkins appeared and said abruptly that Jeremiah was to bring the woman and get her some "clothes fitten and proper." They followed Jenkins back to the stockade, where eyes peered out at them from doorways as from ambush, and around to the ell of the large cabin. There, beside the door, a man waited for them, a gaunt, tall man, a bundle of powerful bone and dry tendon, for the flesh proper to such a frame must long since have withered away. His long face was yellow-streaked, mean, and sick. Jenkins addressed him as Jack.

Jack inserted a key in the hole of an enormous iron lock attached by a chain run through a hole in the heavy planking of the door, opened it, and admitted them. It was a room some twenty by twenty feet, with no light except what came from the open door. Old chests, traveling cases, and boxes were stacked about the wall, and clothing hung in great festoons from pegs on the walls, along with bridles, saddlebags, ropes, hanks of yarn, a couple of swords that looked

423

rusted into their scabbards, a short cutlass without scabbard, two or three bear-traps, and other odds and ends, including a rosary in black jet with a cross and a soutane. On a trestle were some pieces of china, several broken, a heap of silver utensils long since gone black with tarnish, and a couple of gilt cups. Some books and papers were rotting into a corner. The place had a still, dense air that smelled of damp and decay and old leather.

Jack drew out one of the chests and opened it and exposed a jumble of feminine garments. On top lay a tangle of colored ribbons and sashes and stomachers, all streaked and faded. He reached in his bony claw and pulled out a dress and flung it over Rachel's arm. It was some sort of gray wool with black stitchings and braiding. He inspected it critically, fingering it, then rummaged again in the chest. He dug out another dress. Then he came up with something that was white, or had once been white, for now it was yellowish and splotched from time. This seemed to satisfy Jack better.

"Git somethin else, if'n you need hit," Jack ordered.

Rachel began to search among the clothes. While she was thus occupied, Jeremiah turned to the corner where the books and papers were piled. He picked up a book. When he opened it, the leather cracked in his fingers. It was a New Testament in Greek, much fingered and marked, the ink of the marginal notes faded to gray. He put that into his pocket. The next book was "Paley's book on the evidences of the Christian religion," another was Hume's *History of England*, another was Euclid. The fifth that Jeremiah glanced at was a "book by Shaftesbury the great philosopher, much torn and abused."

He heard Rachel say that that would be all, and turned. She had taken some other things from the chest and was now adjusting them over her arm, with the white dress on top. She looked down at the dress. "Whose was it?" she asked the man.

Jack plucked it, then said: "Ain't no tellin, hit was so long back."

"What was so long back?" Jeremiah demanded.

The man looked across at him in dull astonishment. "Whatever 'twas," he said then.

The man leaned down and picked up a couple of ribbons from the tangle, and slammed the chest shut. He dropped the ribbons over the other things on Rachel's arm. "Put 'em on, too," he commanded. "He laks a tetch of brightness."

"Who?" Jeremiah asked, and came across the room.

Jenkins stared at him with a profound contempt, worked his jaw slow, twice, over his quid, and said: "Don't be a durn fool. The Gran Boz."

So, Jeremiah reflected, they were to see the Gran Boz.

It was not until late in the afternoon, however, that Jenkins came to the cabin and said: "He's waked up now. Come on."

They made a procession up the rise, Jenkins first, with his long, bent-kneed stride, then Rachel wearing the white dress, which was too long for her, trying to hold up the dress from the mud, the red ribbons tied at her waist, then Jeremiah, all moving up the rise, through the slippery mud, under the half-leafless scrub oaks, while the sun lowered over the woods and swamps to the west. Jeremiah looked ahead at Rachel, at the white dress, and thought how strange a sight it was under the trees, and how strange it was to see her hair cut short. He had not thought it strange before. He had scarcely thought of the fact. As long as she had worn the militiaman's clothes he had not thought about it. But now, with the dress, it was strange. But what did it matter, he thought now. He reached into his pocket and fingered the lock of hair that he had picked up from the bed in the cell after Wilkie had hacked it off. That had been so long ago, he thought. *What does anything matter?* he asked himself, and trod the mud.

Eyes were upon them as they passed into the area of the compound. The secret life of the shacks and cabins divulged itself a little, like something that protrudes partly from the earth, though still undefined, after the wash of rain or flood water. Two women stood by the door of a cabin, barefooted, dressed in some dun-colored shapeless garments, and stared at the procession, at Rachel. One of them was the woman who had been evicted from the cabin to make room for them. In her arms she held the bundle that Jeremiah knew was the gray-faced baby. There was something strange about her now, Jeremiah remarked idly to himself. Then he realized that she had smoothed back the tangle of her hair and wore a ribbon around her head, a red ribbon like those sad bits of finery in the chest of the treasure room. He looked at her again. She was young. She stared back at him and her dark eyes glittered in the fading light with their unremitting enmity. Or so he thought.

A little farther on, some five or six men were assembled. Two of them sat on the trunk of a fallen tree, staring. The others, staring too, squatted on their heels, or leaned against saplings. As Rachel came even, each jaw, as at a signal, stopped working its quid, and the head swung slow to follow her as she passed on. At the end of the second cabin, several children peered from around the mud-and-wattle chimney. But as soon as Jeremiah looked directly at them, they snatched back out of sight.

Jenkins knocked at the main door of the big cabin, and waited while the door swung slowly inward with a grating sound. Iron hinges, Jeremiah judged, and was surprised to find them here in this

425

last outpost in the swampy wilderness. He remembered that the hinges of the treasure-room door were iron, too, though earlier the fact had not struck him as remarkable.

He followed Jenkins and Rachel into the room, and as his eyes adjusted to the dimness, the door creaked shut behind him. He felt the presence of the person behind him who had shut the door, and the flesh prickled along his spine, but he did not turn.

The light from a fire on the hearth at the left fell across the room toward a great canopied tester bed of mahogany, and a grease lamp stuck in a chink of the wall beyond the bed supplemented that illumination. "I stared," Jeremiah says, "to see that elegant furniture in such a place, for even in that room all other objects were the crude make of the backwoods. But I stared again, as my eyes accepted the dimness and flickering, and as I saw the creature who was the master of that bed and of the land. He was propped in the bed. I saw a large head, bald and of a swarthy, oily color, the face very wrinkled, and seeming more so for the uneasy cast of shadow across it, and on the shoulders beneath it a scarlet coat with some gold braiding, very tarnished, which I took to be the coat of a British officer. I say on the shoulders, for the coat could not be brought fully across the chest, having been cut for a smaller person, and I saw some of the chest (the coat was spliced in the back, I was to learn), which was sagging and creased like the flesh of an old man.

"But I have not mentioned the aspect of the creature most worthy of note. The shoulders were very large and the head was thrust forward from the pillows by a swelling or hump, not unlike the hump of the bull of the buffalo that roamed Kentucky before civil men had conquered the country. Seeing that hump, I suddenly knew what was the name of the creature, what Jenkins and the other had meant by the name Gran Boz. I remembered from my days with Dr. Burnham that in the French tongue the word for hump is *la bosse*, and therefore knew that what they meant to name him was The Big Hump, and that what the child had said was not gibberish but *il est bossu*, he is hump-backed, the defect of understanding being in my ear that did not well know the language in the living mouth. He was humpbacked, but in such a way that, by all report, his great strength had never been impaired.

"Now he leaned forward from the pillow, and blinked at us as though in drowsiness. On the far side of the bed stood a woman of dark complexion, but with hair straight rather than kinked, wrapped in a red shawl about the shoulders and with several gold rings on her fingers, which seemed to indicate some position of privilege. She was of middle years, and extremely ill-favored. Near the fireplace a very large man, also dark, sat on a stool, and stared at Rachel. On the floor, by the head of the bed, an old Negro man was squatting with his arms hung forward between his knees. He, too, stared at Rachel.

"All at once, the eyes of La Grand' Bosse ceased to blink, as though he had come full awake, and he lifted his right hand a little in a sign, and said, 'Viens.' The word was to Rachel, but she did not understand, or stood back from fear. Then he said, 'Come—come,' in a husky tone and with a voice not well tuned to the English, and motioned again.

"Again, she did not stir, and Jenkins said: 'Git up thar, he says git up thar.'

"So she slowly approached the bed, and stopped a little back from him. He inspected her in his bleared and drowsy fashion, and I saw that his eyeballs were large and yellowish, streaked with red. He motioned again for Rachel to come closer, and she obeyed by a grudging step. I saw how white her face was and how set as from the strain of the moment.

"Again he motioned, and again she obeyed by a step. He reached out his hand very slowly. It was a large hand, swollen and crooked with age, and it moved out with enormous slowness, like something that moved under its own drowsy volition. It came into contact with the cloth of her dress, fixed on a fold and clutched it, and began to draw back, with the same heavy slowness, pulling at the dress. As the strain increased, she again moved a little forward, then stopped, with the fabric straining, for there seemed great strength in that hand. His face blinked up at her.

"The man on the stool by the hearth stirred, and said, 'Il veut you come.'

"Rachel turned her face to him for an instant, like one making an appeal in despair, and he said: 'Attendez! Il veut you bend—you bend over.' This he said, too, with a tongue unaccustomed to our language.

"Thereupon Rachel leaned over. La Grand' Bosse continued to blink at her for a moment, then, not releasing the dress, lifted the other hand, a great gold ring and diamond stone glittering on it, and with the same weighted slowness touched her cropped hair and felt it. Then he drew his hand away. 'Tête de brosse,' he said in his husky voice.

"La Bosse still clutched her dress with one hand, and she still leaned. I saw the other hand move again, but could not be sure of its intent, for the position of Rachel's body somewhat between. Then I saw her jerk a little, then stiffen, and I realized that she had submitted herself to that hand that had entered the bodice, which was low-cut, and had tried her breast.

"At that realization, I started forward to defend her, but Jenkins

427

grasped me strongly by the wrist and twisted my arm back of a sudden and leaned at me. Just as I made to jerk from him, he leaned closer and said in a low voice, 'Durn fool—you be a durn fool,' and I caught the stench of his breath on my face.

"I would have struck him, come what might, but then I saw that Rachel had straightened up, and the gross hand was withdrawn, the diamond glittering on it, though the creature still clung to the fold of the dress, even as he said: 'Va donc, sans-nichons!'

"Then, with that insulting word, which would be like naming her Little Tits for the shrunkenness of her breasts, his hand released the dress, and Rachel stepped back. As she turned her face to one side I saw that it was white and she looked to be sick. I stepped forward, and supported her with an arm about her waist, for I feared she would fall. Thereupon I found the eyes of La Bosse upon me. So I stood there and held up my wife, and stared back at that wrinkled and evil and greasy face, and thought how I should have struck it with my fist.

"And the face was speaking to me, saying, 'Tu—tu—on me dit que tu—que tu fais du meutre.'

" 'Murder!' I cried, for I had caught his words. 'They lie to say I murdered—I did not murder—I . . .' And I stumbled for speech, for what could I say to such a creature?

" 'Rien,' he said, and made a gesture with his hand, then let it fall on the cover. 'Rien, ce n'est rien,' he said, and blinked at me.

" 'But I . . .' I began.

"But he lifted his hand. 'Quelquefois,' he said, 'c'est nécessaire.' And he repeated: 'Some time.'

"I began to speak, against my will and common sense, to explain to him, to say I had not murdered, that it was done in justice, but he lifted up his hand, and said, 'Autrefois—autrefois—you tell me autrefois—how you keel—maintenant j'ai sommeil.'

"Whereupon he let his hand fall, and his eyelids shut to hide the big, bleared old eyes."

La Grand' Bosse—known on the river as Ole Big Hump or Gran Boz—had the legal name of Louis Cadeau. At least, that seems to have been his legal name, if he had any legal name. And one report has it that that name, too, was merely a nickname, and was not Cadeau at all, but Caddo, Louis Caddo, with the name derived from the Caddo tribe of Indians, and that his father was some sort of half-breed Frenchman. All reports agree that his mother was of mixed Indian and Negro blood, with a dash of Spanish or French, probably a slave. In any case, he had been spewed up out of the swamps and jungles of Louisiana, or out of some fetid alley of New Orleans—out of that dark and savage swill of bloods—a sort of monstrous bubble that rose to the surface of the pot, or a sort of great brute of the depth that swagged up from the blind, primal mud to reach the light and wallow in the stagnant flood, festooned with algae and the bright slime, with his scaled, armored, horny back just awash, like a log.

When we first hear of him, he is a trader with the Creeks in Alabama. Ferocity and cunning had already made him a name—if the rumors concerning a certain Cadeau pertain to him. Then he appears among the Cherokees in the towns of Chota and Settico, in the late 1760's, when that able people was disputing the passes of the mountains and the waters of the Tennessee with the push of immigration from Carolina. And he stays with them, or at least appears and reappears among them, until near the time when Major Ore's Tennesseans struck them by surprise at Nickajack in the fall of 1794, and broke them forever. During that long period of ambush, treachery and counter-treachery, valor, torture and endurance, La Bosse survived and prospered. He dealt with the French. He dealt with the British during the time of the Revolution and seems to have acted as their agent to whet the tribes (his tarnished red coat must have dated from that period). He dealt with the colonists. And always during this time he is a friend of chiefs—Double Head, Bloody Fellow, The Breath, Little Owl—a strategist advising in their councils, a diplomatist, a torturer delighting in the sound of the ritual rattle the prisoner shakes before he is put to the post and the flames rise. He supports and encourages the irreconcilables of the party of Dragging Canoe, for what would peace and the penetration of civilization mean for him? He arranges at least one truce with a white outpost, and then, when it has been lulled by his gifts and has bought corn from him, he sits under a tree, at night—a beech tree, according to the story— and watches the flames and hears the screams of the massacre.

In the end, he betrays the Cherokees, too. Or was there any bond, any allegiance, for him to betray? He was merely La Grand' Bosse, and himself. Whatever the name for his act, he threw the Indians off guard, promising to lure the whites into an ambush, then sold the whites information about the trail over the mountain to a village fastness guarding the river, himself led the white party, saw the beginning of the bloody work, when squaw and babe died beside the warrior, and then pocketed his profit and faded westward into the wilderness. He had, presumably, foreseen the end of the Cherokee resistance, and had cashed his investment while the market was still good.

The Cherokees became peaceful farmers, Christians worshipping the white man's God and aping the white man's ways, waiting unwitting for the white man's last great betrayal that would drive them west. But La Grand' Bosse set himself up somewhere in the wilds south of the Tennessee, gathered about him a few runaway slaves, some of the white scum of the frontier, and outcast Indians, tribeless outlaws no longer fighting for their land and their villages but robbing a cabin or cutting a traveler's throat for the poor loot to be swapped to La Grand' Bosse for a few sips of whisky and a pinch of powder.

La Grand' Bosse found himself, however, in a kind of backwater here. So he moved on into the country of the Natchez Trace, lingered briefly (for the heyday of profit in that section had not come), and struck north. According to one tradition, he built himself two great "batteaux" on the Tennessee, loaded on them the choicest of his cutthroats, his several families (black, red and white, with fine impartiality), his most portable plunder, a few horses, and a small brass cannon. He drifted down the river toward the Ohio, where a rich traffic was moving now, broadhorn and ark and galley and keelboat, where there was no one to say nay to a strong or cunning hand, and a dead man rotting in the cane or floating slowly toward the Gulf, naked and swollen and faceless, nibbled by fish, told no tales.

Well before the turn of the century his presence is felt on the river. Men who start down to New Orleans with a cargo never come back. Cargoes are bought in New Orleans with no questions asked. Possession is ownership. Isolated river settlements are raided. Tales begin of the bald, big-headed creature, with the great shoulders and humped back, more deadly than any chute or snag, an ogre of the swamps terrible enough to give bad dreams to the stoutest bully of the keelboats. Few have seen him and lived, and many have seen him. He is Ole Big Hump. He has a citadel back in the cane, armed with a dozen cannon (so the poor single piece had spawned in the legend). He has raised up a nation out of the mud back there to do his bidding. If every man's hand is against you and you have no refuge, if you are bold-hearted and black-hearted enough, if you are desperate enough to risk your life on Ole Hump's whim when you reach him, you may find safety there back in the cane, and a new life.

Then, one day late in 1811, when La Grand' Bosse is, we can guess, about sixty-five, Nicholas Roosevelt runs the falls at the settlement of Louisville with the *City of New Orleans* and starts down-river to the Gulf. In the weeks of waiting before high water allowed Roosevelt to run the falls, had rumor of the contraption reached into the swamps? Or did one of La Grand' Bosse's sentinels, lolling in a skiff under the frost-bitten willows, turn bug-eyed and drop his jaw when he saw the preposterous, nightmare thing round a bend above, puffing the black smoke and creaking and clanking? In any case, it was the end of the great day of Ole Big Hump.

Age was already creeping on him. More and more he had been

430

content to lie at ease in his mud and let the younger men, his sons, slaves and bullies, venture out for the kill on the river or on the tracks farther east. Civilization, with its rules for making profit, rules too complicated for him to understand, was creeping on him, too. With the increase in river traffic, the prizes had become richer, dangling there before his eyes, but the risks had increased. He had already lost two sons and six men, trapped by one keelboat while they were plundering another. But it was not age or civilization that undid him in the end. He was simply the victim of technological unemployment.

More steamboats came. There was no end to their coming. They are loaded with richness, all things the heart can desire, bright cloths, shining gewgaws, money, women, drink, but he cannot get his hands on them. It is outrageous. It is an outrage, a profound injustice, against him, against La Grand' Bosse, and he will not abide it. He will take a steamboat. He will take it and cut every throat and burn it in the river. No, he will not burn it, he will take it to New Orleans himself, La Grand' Bosse. Then they will know that he is still La Grand' Bosse. They will know that they cannot flout him, for the river is his. He lies in the swamp and plans. He will make a big barge, will set up his cannon on it and anchor it in the middle of the river, and his men will be in ambush in skiffs along the shore growth. No, he will build a keelboat, no, a galley with oarsmen, the biggest ever seen, with thick walls above water, and set the cannon in that (had he heard of the armed galley that George Rogers Clark had used on this river in the Revolution?) and go out and take the steamboat. He has a thousand plans.

He goes down to the river and lies in his skiff, day after day, spying, waiting for a steamboat to come, that he may study it and perfect his plans. One comes, sweeping down the broad water under its black plume of smoke, passes him, strides imperiously away and is gone. It has not even given him contempt. It has not even known he is here. And he is wild with rage. His heart will burst with rage. He strikes his hands against the edge of the skiff until they bleed. He bites his knuckles until they bleed.

"*Je me mords les osselets*," he says to Jeremiah, and leans forward from the pillow and gnaws his knuckles to show the old passion. "They are *de sang*," he says, "see," and holds up his hand, with the diamond glittering, to show the blood that is not there. "*Je ne peux pas respirer—mon coeur*—my heart—he *se crève*—he break—I am *insulté* . . ." He heaves on the pillow and gasps, and the old chest swells until it seems that the red coat of a British officer will split off his back and his big, muddy, red-rimmed eyes start from the old face. "A stimbotte," he says, when he can get his breath back. "I weel take heem —I weel burn heem—I am La Grand' Bosse . . ." And he beats his

431

chest, where the old flesh and muscle sag like shrunk tits, and the diamond glitters on his hand. Then he goes to sleep, and even the shadow of old rage is gone.

He had never taken a steamboat. He had never even tried. Perhaps if he had been a little younger he would have tried. But he had watched the steamboats pass on the river, and had always come back to his stronghold in the mud, raging and bitter, to nurse plans that came to nothing, to lie in his big mahogany tester bed under the rotting canopy and drink himself drunk and take one of the women there with him—what woman he did not care, what tint or what relation, for tints and relations had long since become confused in his tribe— and fondle her and have her, if drink or anger or age was not too much for him, and then sleep.

It had been fifteen years now, almost to the month, since Nicholas Roosevelt passed with the *City of New Orleans*. It had been years now since La Grand' Bosse had even seen a steamboat. He had prowled the island, or lain there, torpid or glaring, steeping himself in the outrage, nursing the old passion, revolving the old plans, tyrannizing over his people. The stockade had fallen to ruin. The little cannon was sinking into the earth, rusting away. Some of his nation, even some of his sons or nephews or grandsons, had defied him and fled, or had merely slipped away, not even doing him the respect of defiance. But he remained, lying with his massive stupor and dark twitches amid the massive stupor and dark twitches of the wild land, while the slew steamed in summer or crusted a leprous white with skim ice in the shallows when winter came, and to the north the river, where he went no more, where he was forgotten, slid past, red or green according to flood or low water, and in his treasure room the loot rotted away, the dresses and ribbons intended for vanity and joy, the silver plate, the rosary and soutane, the books he could not read—all that poor plunder of a world he had never seen and could never have understood.

It is Jeremiah Beaumont who leaves us the last record of Ole Big Hump and his nation. He was there in the last days, and put down the record in his narrative, which now became a sort of desultory journal. What happened to Ole Big Hump and his people after Jeremiah's departure there is no knowing. He could not have lived much longer, for he must have been near eighty when Jeremiah saw him. He must have been buried there on the island. Some of his people remained there and no doubt fathered some of the breed of later river-folk, malarial, wistful, vindictive, inhabiting shanty-boats or shacks above the mud-flats, scorned by the world and deprived. Some, no doubt, were caught up into the westward sweep of the world that had, in the end, destroyed Ole Big Hump, and entered that world, and raised

432

up sons who learned the rules and tricks of that world, who read the books and wore the clothes of the world, and voted and paid taxes and owned tidy houses with green lawns or subdivision palaces and went to the field or factory or office, and became farmers, storekeepers, statesmen, heroes, mechanics, insurance agents, executives, bankers.

So Ole Big Hump was forgotten, but more than a century later, lying under the earth of his island, he might grin to think that the joke, in the end, was not on him but on the world, for those most respectable descendants, who did not know him and would have denied him with shame, still carried under their pink scrubbed hides and double-breasted sack suits (cunningly cut to redeem the sagging paunch) the mire-thick blood of his veins and the old coiling darkness of his heart.

Now, as Jeremiah left the door of La Grand' Bosse for the first time, and started down the hill with Rachel and Lilburn Jenkins, he could scarcely contain his anger and disgust. As they passed the last cabin, he plucked at Jenkins' arm, and said, "Wait, I want to tell you something."

Jenkins stopped, turned to him, and said, "Huh?"

"This," Jeremiah said. "It does not matter to me who that old half-breed ruffian is, but I'll not have him lay finger again on my wife."

Jenkins studied him in some astonishment, then said, "That's Ole Big Hump you talkin about."

"I don't care what he is," Jeremiah retorted.

"Listen," Jenkins said, "this-here is Gran Boz's place fer a fack and ever thing in here, but looks lak he ain't honin fer hit lak he used to. Last year now—they tell how that woman they thowed out the cabin fer you and her . . ." He nodded toward Rachel down the trail. "She was layin up with Ole Big Hump and he must made out pretty good, fer he swelled her up and that kid of her'n come. But he ain't lak he was, they tell me, and if'n he taken a fancy fer yore woman, lak as not all hit would be would jest be layin up thar and he would'n do nuthin, not to mount to nuthin, jest grab holt a leetle for a squeeze and . . ."

"God damn it!" Jeremiah burst out. "What do you take me for?"

Jenkins looked at him again. "Mister," he said, in an aggrieved fashion, "I'm jest tellin you how hit is. This-here is Ole Big Hump's place. But hell"—he paused and spat—"hell, looks lak he don't fancy yore woman no way. Don't lak her hair all chopped off that a-way. Put his hand in to her bubbies, then shove her off. Warn't nuthin to 'em fer him, all shrunk down. She's peak-ed. Hell, mister, Ole Big Hump laks 'em sort of juicy . . ."

Jeremiah stepped back from him. "I'll leave this place," he said quietly. "We will leave. A place like this where . . ." And he gazed

433

suddenly around, as though seeing it all for the first time, in its sudden blankness of being, the slew, the mud, the cane, the sopping sky.

"Leave," Jenkins said. He studied Jeremiah. "You be a durn fool," he said, without heat. "Leave," he said, "hit ain't easy to up and leave here. Not less Gran Boz says to."

"I'll go, and no man shall stop me. Do you understand?"

"Gran Boz," Jenkins said, "he has stopped lots of folks. Stopped 'em and they stayed stopped fer a long time."

"He'll have to stop me then," Jeremiah said grimly.

"Listen, mister," Jenkins said, in patience. "You try to git away, and they ketch you. Afore five miles. Looks lak ain't nobody watchin here. But they's watchin all the time. And they knows you done kilt a man. Knows you was to git hung. If'n you left and I tole 'em I bet they was big money to ketch you and git you up-river to the law, would you git fer? Naw, mister. Ain't nuthin to me, mister, but I tole Mr. Wilkie Barron I'd watch out fer you."

"I'm going," Jeremiah said. He felt that he had to go. The air that came into his body seemed to choke him. He could not breathe the air.

"Maybe you could," Jenkins said. He looked at him appraisingly. "You bin right stout. You bin in the woods and the wilderness. You ain't lak some as live always in settlemints and don't know nuthin. Luck, and maybe you git away. But . . ." and he nodded again down the trail, where Rachel was now waiting, some twenty yards off.

"But her," Jenkins resumed, "she done peaked and puled way to nuthin. Nigh never made it here. She wouldn't git nowhars. You have to leave her on the trace to lay and they ketch her. Or leave her here. Yeah, leave her here. Ole Big Hump don't hanker none fer her. But they's them here would take her lak a bait of fresh. Lak fresh meat fer a change. Chopped hair and leetle titties or no. Ain't nuthin to me, I'm jest tellin . . ."

Jeremiah turned abruptly away. He could not bear to look at that face any longer, or hear the words. He walked rapidly down the trail, not looking back. For a moment he had the irrational thought that Jenkins might leap at him and strike him from behind, and his spine prickled with cold fear. He suppressed the impulse to run, and resolutely did not look back. But there was no sound behind him. Jenkins had not even followed.

He reached Rachel. She looked curiously at him. "Is there—is there something wrong?" she asked.

"No," he said sharply.

"I saw you back there, talking with that man, I thought there must be something!"

"I said no," he burst out. "Didn't you hear me say no?"

For an instant, as she stared at him, pain flickered over her face.

434

Then there was nothing there, not even surprise. He looked into that strained, numb, chalk-white face, with the brown splotch now sharp on the cheek, and thought how ugly it was. How ugly that chopped-off, disordered hair was. He looked down and saw how the fabric of the white dress hung loose on her bones, she had shrunk so, and how her bosom, which had once been full and rich, was now nothing. She was an old woman in a stained and draggled white dress, with a twist of miserable colored ribbons about her waist in a kind of horrible vanity, standing in the mud under a half-leafless scrub oak, its boughs black with wet and the last light faded and she stared blankly at him and her shoulders drooped in a humility that started a blind anger in him, and he did not blame that stinking, villainous old brute in the bed for rejecting her with contempt—my God, he himself would have done so—my God, he would leave her and leave this foul place, and he did not care if one of these ruffians did take her for a bait of fresh, take her and welcome if he was such a fool, for he, Jeremiah Beaumont, would be gone.

Then, as he looked into her face, a wild anguish swept over him: *Was it all for this, was it all for this!*

But even as that despair gripped him, and he spat out all his past life like a tainted morsel that had made his guts rise, he reached out a hand to touch Rachel and say quietly that they should go down to the cabin. For such, he says in his narrative, is the doubleness of life.

He did not go away from the island. He did not desert her, after all. He had done so in his heart, that evening on the trail, and admitted his crime. But in fact he stayed. Sometimes, in the weeks that followed, he turned over projects of flight. Flight alone or flight with her. He thought of fleeing with her and making a stand, a last fight, against pursuers and dying with her in a skiff on the river or in some trampled corner of the trail through the cane. Why did he not flee? Because he was afraid? Why did he stay? Because, in honor, he wanted to protect her? Or did he stay merely because he had sunk into the brute torpor and mire of the place, because he had accepted the place and the place had accepted him, as a quagmire accepts and sucks in whatever offers itself to that black peace?

He asked himself those questions, and more, torturing the possibilities.

And he had found here a kind of peace, a peace which he called the "black inwardness and womb of the quagmire." It was a peace with no past and no future, the absoluteness of the single, separate, dark, massive moment that swells up fatly like a bubble from the

435

deep mud, exists as a globe of slick film housing its noxious gas, then pops and is gone, and then, with the regularity of the pulse of the blood, is followed by another that goes, and then by another, forever.

He stayed, and found there a kind of life. He could go out with one of the men on the slew to fish, and drift down the imperceptible current, waiting somnolently in the sunshine (for the first rains of the season's turn were over now), with no talk (for what could he find to say to that thatch-headed, louse-bit, yellow-skinned creature lolling at the other end of the skiff?), not thinking, not stirring, feeling the diminishing warmth of the sun, waiting for the twitch or tug on the fish line, like the twitch or tug of a memory from the dark depth. He could go out with them on a hunt for deer in the higher wooded land to the southwest beyond the cane bottoms and crouch in the thicket and wait for the deer to come footing delicately down the run, and could set the little lead pellet in its breast and see it leap and fling its antlered head with a "sudden sweet and desolate nobility" (for he describes it thus) before the knees buckled and it plunged to earth, ready for the knife. He could go with the men to chop wood for winter and take a kind of bitter hypnotic joy in the rise and fall of the ax, and caught in that rhythm would wish that it could go on forever. He could go, as he went twice at the summons of Ole Big Hump, to the cabin and listen to the old brute's wandering conversation, to the tales of the triumphs among the Cherokees and looting on the river, to the boasts about the vanished glory ("Me —me—I am La Grand' Bosse—I make *la peur*"), to the outrage at the steamboat, and the threats. "And you—you keel, too," the old brute said. *"Pour un homme,"* the old brute said, "eet is what he do—*c'est naturel."*

Or he could find a sunny patch on the high ground south of the stockade, and lie on the fallen leaves and read the Greek Testament he had found in the treasure room of La Grand' Bosse, another piece of detritus among the pieces of detritus in that midden of junk that had sifted down here from the world. Years ago, with Dr. Burnham, he had learned that language. He had studied it, night after night, by firelight, in his mother's cabin, and she had gone silently to another room so as not to disturb him. He had studied it in the twilight, in summer, after a hard day in the field. He had seen Dr. Burnham lie on the bullhide, under the maple on a Sunday afternoon in August, and had heard his voice utter the words. Now, seeing the words, he remembered that voice: ἐν ἀρχῇ ἦν ὁ λόγος, καὶ ὁ λόγος ἦν πρὸς τὸν θεόν, καὶ ὁ θεὸς ἦν ὁ λόγος.

"I remembered Dr. Burnham's voice," he writes, "as he lay under the maple, reading from the Greek of the Gospel of John, where it says in the beginning was the Word and the Word was with God, and I

remembered how my own heart had then swollen with a kind of joy
hearing those words, not from piety, for my days of young piety were
past then, but because they seemed to speak a truth to my heart and
in the world. And now as my eyes fell on those words, I felt like laughing out loud. I thought how men had written that book long ago,
almost two thousand years, in passion and hope, and how men had
all those centuries read it for comfort and had believed that in the
beginning there was the Word, and how I myself had lifted up my
heart at the sentence. Then I thought how I had come to this strange
place, after the years of my life and the darkness, and had found
this book rotting in the corner of a hovel amidst the junk of mankind's vanity and hopefulness, and I did laugh. I laughed as I lay on
the leaves and looked down at the slew, and I said out loud, in the
beginning there was the Word and the Word was with God, but in
the end there is the mud and the mud is with me.

"At which, I put the book into my pocket and went down the hill
to the shack of one of the men with whom I had had some dealings
on the hunt and otherwise, and we drank the whisky he had, which
was a foul drink, and we lay drunk until the next morning long after
dawn, when I returned to my cabin to find Rachel much disturbed
for my safety. But when she practiced a gentle remonstrance with
me, I spoke sharply and flung from the house and was away most of
the day, and passed the evening with some of the men and two
women who drank and caroused in one of the cabins till we reached
soddenness."

All these weeks he was keeping the narrative. He had made a pen
from the quill of a wild-turkey wing and had brewed himself ink
from oak balls. With his packet of manuscript he had brought some
sheets of paper. We can see how sparingly he used them, for there
is writing on both sides, the lines run from margin to margin, the
letters are small and cramped together, and the lines have no space
between. When these sheets had been filled, he got permission to
go to the treasure room. There he tore out blank pages from books
and gathered the scattered papers on the floor in the corner. The
last of his manuscript is on these, on the end pages and title pages,
on the reverse of sheets that had been used for a sermon (by whom
we do not know), for a legal document, for a land patent, for a map.
So we may indulge ourselves with the fancy that this is appropriate,
that his story, the personal and secret story, is properly on the back
of those sheets that document the public and practical life.

His record now becomes a kind of journal. Sometimes there is not
more than a date and a bare statement:

Oct. 3. Hunted deer with Jack and Jenkins in country southwest of settlement. One buck.

Oct. 5. Heavy frost in morning. Hot sun all day. Read Greek.
Oct. 19. Took skiff and went down slew toward Ohio. Thought myself alone, but one of the men had·followed in canoe. When I passed him on return he proceeded as though on another errand, but I am not deceived.

Then there is the most laconic of all his entries:

Oct. 20. Drunk.

But other entries are fully rendered accounts of events or elaborate analyses of his emotions, of his state of mind, of his relations with Rachel. He had begun now to fear for her reason. The first expression of this fear comes only a few weeks after their arrival at the island: "Came in late this afternoon from cutting wood. Upon entering my cabin I saw Rachel sitting by the hearth, bending forward a little as for the warmth, but the fire was out and had been out for some time, for no coal or spark showed. She had sat there and let it die, though much wood lay on the hearth ready stacked and the room was very cold. I spoke to her but she did not turn. So I went and took her hands, which were very cold, and chafed them to restore warmth. I chided her kindly for letting the fire die and risking her health for damp and cold, then she stared at me with great intentness and said, 'They took it away, they came and took it away.' I asked what she spoke of, and she jerked her hands from me and drew herself as far on the chair from me as she might and stared at me with accusation and said, 'It was you, you took it away.' Whereupon I was much puzzled, and turned to repair the fire. That done, I brought a blanket to put about her shoulders, but she paid me no heed and stared straight before her, now into the new fire. I tried to speak with her, but she ignored me until of a sudden she said with wildness in her voice, 'He will never see the bright fire, he will never see the bright fire!' I demanded who, but she moaned and pulled the blanket over her face and bowed forward and would not look up.

"At that I remembered how more and more often of late she had sat and stared at the floor or wall and had not spoken with me, even to answer a question. I had thought that behavior but a sullenness engendered by my own abstraction or sharpness with her, or her awareness that my heart had turned cold in its despair, but now, for the first time, I suddenly thought that her reason was threatened.

"I thought how this woman once beautiful and delicately nurtured and my own wife once dear to my heart and flesh, had been dragged through misery and despite, and into the wilderness among uncivil men viler than beasts, and had come to this state. She was precious to me in that moment, as of old, and I stood by her chair and pressed her bowed form against my body, and her name was wrung from my lips, several times. But she only sat there sunk in her own darkness,

438

and I thought how all was useless, for each person was but himself and reaching out the hand across distance did not avail."

That entry is the beginning. More and more often he notes the symptoms of her condition. She would sit long hours staring at wall or floor or hearth, not making a sound. Or she would refuse to rise from her bed in the morning or take food, lying there on her back with her eyes closed tight shut. He might sit there half the morning, watching her thus, knowing that she was awake.

He records it all, and how for hours he might sit by the bed and look at her: "Sometimes she lay with eyes closed, and that for hours, and sometimes thus, when the eyes were closed the face was smoothed like windless water at evening and the old beauty returned to stab my heart. But sometimes I looked at her and would ask myself, who is this, who is this, and how did I come here? For it seemed that I did not know her, and even the name. Or I would know who she was, Rachel Jordan whom I had married and lived with and enjoyed and for whom I had done violence, and I would know these facts but know that I had never known her truly. I had longed after her, but had not possessed the subtlety of sympathy to know why she was as she was and had done what she had done and had asked what she had asked from life. Or what had she asked? I did not know. I had never entered into that region where her soul abode and kept its house. Oh, might I have done so! And had I done so, I might have followed her glimmering as through the maze of a dark forest and come upon her at last in some sunlit glade and sat with her calmly there upon the grass, holding her hand. Then all might have been different."

But there were the few mornings when she tried to seize on life again. These were the worst times. There was, for example, a morning when he had slept late, heavy with the evening's drink, and woke to find the fire going briskly on the hearth and Rachel busy with breakfast. He lay and spied on her through scarcely opened lids. She had dressed herself with care, he noted, the white dress, which she had not worn since the visit to La Grand' Bosse, and a ribbon to bind her hair.

She turned suddenly as though summoned by his gaze, and cried, "Oh, Jerry!" in a tone that stabbed him with memories of mornings long before, and smiled, and came quickly to him and took his hands and tried to draw him up, saying, "Up, you lazy-bones, up!"

His heart leaped for joy. It was as though, at a stroke, some fresh morning long forgotten had returned in full innocence and nothing that had come after it had happened at all. He pushed himself up on an elbow, and thought that he might faint from happiness and relief. The room seemed to glitter and spin around him, he was so happy. "Rachel," was all he could say, "Rachel!"

She gripped him with a hand on each shoulder, shaking him a little. "Oh, Jerry," she said, "it will be all right, everything will be all right!"

He looked up into her face. It was smiling. He was still in the confusion of the new happiness.

She was gripping his shoulders, saying, "I love you, Jerry, I love you, you must believe I love you."

As she spoke, he was looking into her face. All at once, he saw that the eyes were too large and bright, that the lips were drawn back too tight in the smile so that it was almost a grimace of agony. Then he heard his own voice saying, "Yes, yes, and I love you, too," as part of the parody, the charade.

He rose with enormous care, and dressed himself. He made every motion with care as though he moved among precious objects delicately balanced, as though he walked across ice, as though he himself were brittle and might break. And all the while, Rachel's voice was going on in a kind of thin precarious gaiety, saying how they would be happy, how they loved each other, how beautiful was the day, and his own voice was saying, "Yes, yes, yes," while he felt a band tightening slowly around his skull until he was sure his eyes would bulge from their sockets.

She made him sit down. She brought him food and leaned over him like a mother over a sickly child, murmuring to him to make him eat. He ate dutifully, mouthful by mouthful, forcing each movement of the jaw, listening to her voice. She sat down, and watched him. Then he had in his mouth a morsel of meat that had crusted so hard in cooking that he could not chew it. He tried to remove it secretly from his mouth, but she spied the act. "What is it?" she demanded.

"Nothing," he said.

"Tell me, tell me," she insisted.

"Nothing," he said, "just a piece that got burned a little."

He reached for a piece of bread, then looking up, saw that the smile was gone from her face. Rather, the grimace and strain that had been the smile was still there, but they were no longer a smile.

She was holding her hands just above her lap, not touching each other, and the fingers, spread tensely out in different directions, moved slowly in some complicated secret pattern. Then the tears began to show in her eyes.

"What's the matter?" he asked.

"Oh," she moaned, "oh—oh, I never do anything right—nothing is ever right for me—whatever I do is wrong."

"It was just a piece of burned meat," he said, feeling the band tighten on his head. "Anybody can burn meat."

"But I burned it—I was just trying to wake you up and tell you how

440

everything would be different, how I loved you—but I burned it—I never do anything right—I am always wrong—I . . ."

"In God's name!" he cried and stood up.

He saw her shrink back from him, shock and pain in her face.

"I'm sorry," he managed to say, and stepped toward her and stretched out his arm as though to put it about her shoulders. She rose from her chair, thrust her hands at him, palms outward in a gesture of repulsion, and cringed against the wall by the hearth. "Don't touch me," she whispered, "don't touch me!" And all the while her eyes were glittering at him, with the whites wide.

"I'm sorry," he said again. But he was not sorry now. He was not anything now. He went and found the Testament, and sat by the hearth and tried to read it, but the Greek characters crawled and spawned before his eyes like, as he says, "a congress of vermin."

Yes, the times when she tried to seize on life again were the worst. They were the worst because they were a trap. They were a trap to make him think that happiness was possible. Just as he had found that last peace which was neither happiness nor unhappiness but darkness, that trap was set and baited again. But he had learned. He was as wary as the old bear that has lost two toes to the steel, or crushed a paw in the deadfall. He would not be deceived. He would not come to that rich, tainted smell of happiness. For he knew now what was possible, and if there was not happiness, there was at least knowledge. At least knowledge, he would say. At least knowledge, he would write on the old scrap of paper, with the quill from a wild turkey's wing.

There was at least knowledge, and there was at least drink, and that, too, was a kind of knowledge. He could sit with the men of this place in their brutal silence and drink, drink from the jug that passed from hand to hand and mouth to mouth, that was smeared with the common spit, that was lipped by every mouth, that was their bond and communion. That jug made them all the same. It was his ticket, his password to their being and their world. "For when we had drunk from that jug we were the same, the same heat in the gut and flame in the head, and the same blackness to come after, and in that thought was my peace and my salvation. If I could become one with them I should reach the end of a journey, and nothing more would matter."

So he spent as little time at his own cabin as possible. He would come in late, reeling with his drink, and lean back against the door after he had closed it, and hear her breathing in the shadow of the corner where the bed was. Or she might be sitting in a chair by the dying fire, and not even turn her head when he came in. And he began to think that she was going, too, on a journey, toward a goal, toward her kind of peace, too, and she was faster than he, and slyer than he, and she would get there first. It was a race, and she would win the race. Perhaps she had won it already.

One night he came in earlier than was usual on occasions when he had been drinking with the men. They had stopped early because they had decided to go on a three-day hunt to the southwest, for deer, and would start the next morning. Besides, he was hungry. He had had enough liquor to whet his appetite, but not enough to make him drunk, really drunk.

He opened the door of his cabin to find Rachel sitting by the hearth. That did not surprise him. What surprised him was, first, that the fire was blazing brightly and the hearth was swept, and second, that she turned to him when he entered. She turned with an abstracted, serious smile, and put a finger to her lips, and shook her head a little as though to caution him.

He leaned back against the door and looked at her. Then he saw that she had a bundle in her lap. For a moment he puzzled over the sight. Then she turned from him, gathered the bundle up to her breast, and began to rock back and forth, with a crooning murmur. His heart was stabbed at the sight, that she should sit here in this hovel, at night, in this savage place, and croon and sing to a bundle of filthy rags, that her arms had been so empty all the years, that there was now nothing for her, nothing in all the world for her but that bundle of rags.

Ah, this was a trap, this pity, he knew that this was a trap, the most deadly trap of all, but he could not help it. He stepped toward it even as he recognized the fact.

He stepped toward her, and she turned again to him, again putting the finger to her lips, saying, "Shh, shh."

"Rachel," he said.

"Shh," she whispered, "you'll wake him."

He came closer and stood a few feet from her, looking at her.

"Oh, Rachel!" he said.

She looked up at him with a smile of profound peace. "You have to love him," she said. "You have to love him. Because he is so beautiful."

She shifted the bundle a little.

"Look," she commanded in a whisper. "Look, how beautiful he is."

She held the bundle out from her breast, and he looked down at it. It stirred. Then, in the bad light, he saw that it was not merely a bundle of rags. In the rags was the child of the woman who had lived in this cabin and who, leaving, had spat on the doorsill. It was the child she had had by Ole Big Hump.

He looked down at the wizened, earth-colored little face cramped under a forehead that bulged baldly and horribly with its wisdom. A shudder shook him. Then the baby wailed. It wailed once, thinly, and then stopped, and the silence left seemed choking like invisible feathers, or dust.

"Give it to me," Jeremiah commanded her.

"No," she said, "no," and shook her head.

"Give it to me," he repeated. "I'll get it out of here."

"No."

"Give it to me. Give it to me now," he said. "You've stolen that woman's baby—hers and that old halfbreed cut-throat's and . . ."

"It's mine," Rachel cried, and clutched it to her breast.

In the end he had to take it from her by force, while she screamed at him. He ran out the door with it, and into the darkness and some yards up the path. Then he stopped. He had the impulse to take it by its heels and brain it against a tree. The way an Indian might do. The way Indians had done the children of settlers. And fling the body into the slew.

But he went on up the trail, gingerly holding the bundle out from his body as though it were contaminating.

He reached the cabin where he had seen the woman standing in the door with the ribbon in her hair. It was a two-crib cabin, and he could not remember in which door she had stood. So he knocked on the first, and waited. He knocked again. Then he heard some stirring within, and, he thought, a murmur of voices.

The door opened a little. Against the firelight from within he saw the head and shoulders of a woman leaning cautiously into the aperture, one hand clutching some garment at the breast to cover her. He could not be sure that it was the woman he sought. And he did not know her name.

He stammered for words. Then he thrust the bundle out, and asked: "Is this—is this yours?"

"God-a-mighty," the woman said in mild surprise and came forward a little. Then, peering: "Reckon 'tis. Never noticed when I come in. Jest figgered he was layin quiet fer a change."

Jeremiah held out the bundle. "My wife"—he tried to explain —"my wife—she—she borrowed it—she meant no harm—she . . ."

"God-a-mighty," the woman said, "she could kept hit fer all of me. Till hell done froze. Ain't nothin but a pukin botheration."

Jeremiah thrust it toward her. "Here it is," he said.

"God-a-mighty," she said, and reached out one arm and tried to take the bundle. She could not manage with the one arm. She had to release the garment bunched at her breast, and Jeremiah saw that it was not a garment at all, but a blanket or something of the sort flung about her shoulders, and saw that as she reached for the bundle it fell loose. For an instant, in the shadow, he had a glimpse of her body, before she had caught the bundle against her and drawn the blanket back into place.

Then he lifted his eyes and found her staring at him. Her eyes glittered in the shadow. Again he heard the stirring in the room beyond her.

"What they name you?" she was demanding.

"Beaumont," he replied, "Jeremiah Beaumont."

"Beaumont," she repeated, as if meditating the strangeness of the syllables. Then, all at once, she had withdrawn, and the door was shut.

He stood there staring at the blank wood, and again heard, or thought he heard, the murmur of voices, then a man's short laugh. Then there was the wail of the infant, quickly cut off.

About a week later, coming down the trail in the dusk, Jeremiah saw a movement in the leafless brush near the woman's cabin. At first he thought it must be one of the hounds or half-wild bony hogs that roamed the island. Then he saw that it was a human form, a woman's form. Then he knew that it was Rachel. And knew that she was lurking there in the cold evening, in the brush, waiting for the woman to leave the cabin so that she might again steal the child.

He went to her, took her by the arm, and led her to their own cabin. She came meekly enough, without a word.

Then, three nights later, he came home late, to find her, as he had found her before, sitting at the hearth, the hearth swept and the fire made up, with the child in its hippings and swaddlings of rags on her lap. This time he let her keep it. That woman up the rise in the cabin would not care. She had probably not even missed the child. She would be lying up there in the cabin with some stinking, drink-sodden brute. Why should she care?

He said nothing to Rachel. He lighted his lamp (he had made a grease lamp out of baked clay some time before), and sat down to read. But after a little he gave up. His head was too thick with drink, the murmuring and crooning that Rachel made distracted him, he was tired. So he lay down and went to sleep, leaving her there with the child.

When he woke up the next morning, she was in a deep sleep. Even the fretting of the child did not wake her. So he had no difficulty in taking the child back to the other cabin to restore it to its mother.

"God-a-mighty," the woman said, and not another word, and stared sullenly at him from under the tangle of hair, and took the bundle, and closed the door.

For a date shortly after, November 9, we find the entry in Jeremiah's narrative: "Went to corn husking at place southwest of island. Proprietor said to be a son of La Bosse and somewhat like him in brutish aspect, but without hump. However, leads a life more like that of civil men in that he has a farm and holds some blacks to work upon it, and the women to bed with him to judge from the color of skin of some of the young I saw there. Blacks I take it stolen from Tennessee in some earlier raid up the river by that name, or up the Cumberland into the Tennessee country. Many from island, some women, went to husking.

"We worked at husking some before dusk, then roasted venison and gorged ourselves thereon and drank much. Then with aid of drink fell again to work by light of bonfires. As night wore on more drink and dancing to fiddles, and much wildness, with fighting among some, and one man cut with knife to his hollow and by my judgment will not live. But none seemed to care, for he was laid in a shed on old shucks and forgot, in the vile merrymaking.

"I was drunk with others and gave myself to the vileness, and took my joy to be part of it. Lay with the woman whose child my wife had stolen and tasted her carnally for she made herself agreeable to me and I was hot with drink. We lay behind shed where wounded man had been put and been forgot, and to judge from the evidence of my ears a man and woman were in shed with him and took their pleasure there near him while his life bled out. We heard them as we worked our lust, and took added relish thereby and profane delight.

"I record the fullness of my shame and my joy in the foulness thereof, for there is that in man's soul which seeks his own shame and glories in it. Or am I different from all others and most accursed? I do not longer ask. I am what I am, and what is man that he should know his journey?"

This first time he lay with the woman was not the last. On several occasions during the following weeks, he went to her cabin. The child might be down in his own cabin, on Rachel's lap, and Rachel would be crooning to it. Rachel had the child much of the time now. She no longer had to steal it. The woman would give it to her, would bring it down to the door of Rachel's cabin and hold it out and say, "Take hit, hit's done pestered me to death." So Rachel might have the child and cuddle it and murmur while he was up here with the woman. But once or twice the child was in the cabin with them, and once woke and wailed and fretted while he lay with the woman so that she cursed it. But it would not stop its wailing, so the woman, cursing it again, had to rise and take it and hold it in her arms to quiet it. Meanwhile, Jeremiah saw her in the

445

firelight holding it and thought with bitterness how that scene might have been in "any humble room at night where the mother rises to quiet her child in love and give it suck by the fire and the father looks on in the plenitude of his joy."

But he was not the father, Jeremiah Beaumont was not the father, Ole Big Hump was the father, Gran Boz, La Grand' Bosse, and the mother was not Rachel, who now waited down at her cabin and rocked her body back and forth with empty arms and stared at the dying fire, or even now lurked mournfully in the winter-raddled brush outside this cabin in the cold night, no, not Rachel, Rachel Beaumont, she was not the mother, but this woman, this swarthy slut with the lank hair who now leaned and gave suck to the child she had cursed, this swarthy creature with eyes that glittered in the shadow, with the slick skin and hot breath, who gave him his delight, his wisdom, and his peace.

But it did not matter who was the father, Jeremiah Beaumont or Ole Big Hump, or who had lain with that greasy old ruffian with the red coat in the big bed, whether the swarthy slut or Rachel Beaumont, or who had carried that humped little clod of a body and earth-colored, wizened, sad face in her belly and dropped it forth into the world, or who had planted it there in the belly, for it did not matter and nothing mattered, and as he lay here in the cabin with this woman, he found a surer communion with them all than he had found in the drink from the jug lipped by every mouth. With Ole Big Hump, Jenkins, this woman, Rachel, the flea-bit rabble of this island, his mother, his father, Wilkie, and everybody he had ever known. Even with Colonel Fort. Perhaps this was the end of the journey, the wisdom, the peace.

There was, however, to be another stage to the journey: "Sore worse this morning. As I looked at it this morning, I knew what it was. Why had I not guessed before? I should have known at once. I should have known because it is right that my blood should take on corruption from the corrupt blood of that woman, which corruption she herself had had from some man whom I have never known, as he in turn from another, like a rich legacy coming to me in this far and secret place across the thousands of miles of the deep ocean and across the dark land and forests and down the passage of years and the buried channels of the corrupt blood of all those who have labored to nurse and pass on this heritage to me. Ah, let me be grateful to them all who did so much in my behalf in this future time and lost island. Let me regard this canker with reverence and amaze, like a jewel fit for a royal diadem. It proclaims me one of them, and of their great descent."

446

It was past dusk, well into first dark. Jeremiah had cooked some corn pones in the ashes and broiled some meat, had persuaded Rachel to eat a little (she had been lying abed when he came in), and had finished his own meal. He was leaning over the hearth to put on another stick when he felt a slight current of cold air strike his back and saw the flames bend. For an instant he thought that the latch might have slipped on the door, for he had not yet bolted it, then he had the cold prickling sensation of eyes upon him. He let the wood drop to the flame, and rose, and stepped aside with the greatest casualness in the world, and still not looking, moved toward the table where he knew a knife lay. Then he heard the voice, low and urgent: "You—you Beaumont!"

He saw, in the crack of the door, the in-thrust face, bearded, the eye glinting under coonskin.

The man slipped inside, and lightly shoved the door shut behind him, and straightened up. A rifle hung from one hand, muzzle a little down. The light from the fire fell clean now upon the empty eye-socket of the bearded face. Then Jeremiah remembered. It was One-eye Jenkins.

"What do you want?" Jeremiah demanded.

One-eye did not answer. With a quick, long-legged, bent-kneed stride he stepped to the hearth, to one side of the fireplace, propped the rifle, and reached his hands diagonally toward the flame. He wore cowhide boots, muddy with the pallid mud of the region, a blue coat with brass buttons that seemed to be an old greatcoat hacked off short for the liberty of the legs, and under the open front a leather hunting shirt, very greasy. As he worked his fingers at the flame, he held his head cocked sidewise at Jeremiah, fixing him with the eye.

"What do you want?" Jeremiah repeated.

"Ain't what I wants," One-eye said. "Hit's what you wants. I done come a fer piece to bring you what you wants."

"What I want?" Jeremiah echoed him. And thought: *What do I want in the world?*

"You rickerlict," One-eye was saying, "how that Crawford come to the jail? How he tole you I had a printed paper signed Cunnel Fort saying how yore woman's baby was a nigger baby and was black and not by the Cunnel nor no man and him white, but you was gonna give me money to put hit out to the Guv'ner and swear how hit come so they would let you walk free?"

The eye squinted and probed at Jeremiah. Then the man said: "You rickerlict?"

Jeremiah nodded.

447

"Yeah, I was aimin to help you, yeah," the man said. "To make you walk free, but they knowed, they knowed. Fer that sojer down thar in the jail, he went and tole 'em. Yeah, I knows he tole 'em. And then what they done to me. What my own brother, my own Big Bubber, what he done to me. You know what he done, my own Bubber, my own Bubber Lilburn?"

Jeremiah shook his head. He could scarcely listen. What had this to do with him? Why couldn't they leave him alone? Let him alone? But the eye kept fixing on him.

"Yeah, you know what he done, my own Bubber?" And the man suddenly stepped away from the hearth, toward Jeremiah. He stopped directly before him, and said: "Yeah, he stobbed me. Because Crawford come and told you. Stobbed me in the back. Two times, and left me to lay. Layin in the alley that night in Frankfort. And him my Big Bubber Lilburn."

He came closer a step, and leaned insinuatingly. The eye was closer, squinting with cunning now. "Yeah," he said, "hit ought to be worth more now. More money fer me. Cause he stobbed me." He leaned closer, so close now there was the smell of his breath. "What's hit worth, mister? Mister, what's hit worth now?"

"Worth?" Jeremiah said.

"Yeah, worth. Fer you got money. Back thar in Kentucky, and a big farm and niggers and hosses. You jest say what hit's worth. To git back and be free. Jest say ten thousand dollars maybe, and I'll git you out of here. I'll take you back. You want to go back, mister, don't you want to go back?"

Go back, to go back, Jeremiah thought.

"I kin git you back. Git you off this place. I brung two hosses, they is back in the cane crost the slew. Two days I been layin and watchin, and I seen you and whar you went in at, and I made me a raft and laid down on hit and come raftin down in the dark to the t'other end of the island and I brung me some meat fer them hounds to toll 'em and to keep 'em quiet-lak, and I come on here, and nobody seen me, and I kin git you off. Yeah, I kin git you back."

Back, Jeremiah thought. Back to all that had been, all the faces he had known, all the life he had lived, all he had been. *No,* he thought, *no,* and was struck with terror. Why wouldn't they leave him alone? Leave him here?

"I kin git you back and git you free," the man was saying, and fumbling in his shirt. He held out the paper. "Yeah, jest lak I tole you," he was saying, "and the Cunnel's name to hit. See!"

He held out the torn paper, and on one piece, under the bitten, blackened, crusted nail of the finger pointing, Jeremiah saw the printed words CASSIUS FORT, in big letters, and he lifted his hand to

448

his head as though trying to remember. Oh, he knew, he knew, but it was all so long back.

"Yeah, look," the man was saying, "fer I got hit, and I knows how hit come. Yeah, I knows a lot, and I'll tell 'em. That Guv-ner, that Jedge, and hit will surprise 'em, and they will set you free to roam. But . . ." and the eye winked in cunning, "you gonna pay me. Once I git you out here. I ain't gonna tell 'em till you pays me. And the paper won't do no good less I tells how hit come. And I got 'em as will swear, and swear how this-here paper was come by and what was done with hit and all."

Swear, Jeremiah thought, *swear*. And burst out: "Swear! I don't care what they swear, for I . . ."

"They'll swear you free, they'll swear . . ."

The man was saying they would swear and he would be free, but Jeremiah could not stand the thought of all the swearing and counter-swearing and all the lies and truth and truth and lies, all over again the way it had been and the truth became a lie and the lie became truth and it was like a quagmire, deeper and deeper and darker and darker, and the truth was the worst, or it was when you had to swear to it, but he had the truth now and did not have to swear to it, and why would they not leave him alone with the truth that needed no swearing, no, it was not the truth, it was peace, and peace was not truth and was not lies, for it was itself and was peace, it was darker and deeper, and why would they not leave him alone?

The eye was looking at him and the voice was saying: "Yeah, we got to move fast. We caint"—he turned and nodded toward the bed, where Rachel lay—"we caint be takin the woman."

Jeremiah looked at the bed where Rachel lay. She lay on her side staring at them, or not staring at them but beyond them, across the space they occupied as though they were not there, through them into the distance beyond them and beyond the closed wall.

"If'n yore mind stays set on her," the man was saying, "maybe you kin git her after. But now we got to go. Now."

"No!" Jeremiah exclaimed.

"Now look here, mister," the man wheedled, "I done come a fer piece fer you, and you got to go. And her"—he nodded toward the bed—"a woman lak her, mister, jest laying thar, hell, she's nigh a old woman, you ain't gonna let her stop you."

"No!" Jeremiah repeated.

"Look here, mister, a woman lak her to stop you, a woman lak that to . . ."

The rawhide hinges of the door had made no noise. Nor did a cold draft warn Jeremiah this time, though an instant later he became aware of the draft. He saw the eye suddenly leave him, saw the cunning squint leave it, saw it widen and fix on a spot behind him. Then from behind him, he heard the voice. "Naw—naw, a woman like her won't stop him," the voice said, "but I will."

Then One-eye's mouth, which had dropped open with astonishment, closed, the tongue came out and licked the lips once, and the lips opened again to utter: "Bubber—Bubber Lilburn!"

Jeremiah turned. It was Lilburn Jenkins, standing at ease inside the door, the firelight playing over the slick, blunt, grinning face, and glinting on the pistol in his right hand.

"Bubber," One-eye repeated in a whisper.

"I thought I done fixed you," Lilburn said. "I was a durn fool to stob you and not cut yore thote. But I warn't a durn fool lak you. I stob you good and you git well and durn if'n you don't come ast fer hit agin. Come all the way here to git hit agin. Come to Ole Big Hump's cause you figgered I was here."

"I—I didn't know," One-eye said in his whisper, "I didn't know you was here. I thought you'd be done gone."

"You knowed Ole Big Hump was here and you come raftin in and ne'er ast Ole Big Hump by-yore-leave. I seen you. Lucky I seen you. If'n some these boys seen you, you ne'er got to shore."

"Listen here, Bubber," One-eye said, "listen here. Had I knowed you was here I had done come to you. To say how we could git money. Off'n him here," and he pointed at Jeremiah. "To swear 'bout this paper. How hit was fixed. You'd swear, Bubber, wouldn't you swear, Bubber, how 'twas, and I'd give you half, Bubber, half fer you, Bubber . . ."

"Half," Lilburn said, and waggled the pistol and grinned to show the big, square, fungus-streaked teeth. Then he stopped grinning. "Ain't gonna be no half," he said.

"You kin have more'n half," One-eye said, leaning and coaxing and loving. "Cause you my Big Bubber. Yeah, more'n half."

"Ain't gonna be no half. Ain't gonna be none," Lilburn stated.

"Listen, Bubber, listen," One-eye said. "You ain't skeered of that Wilkie Barron. He caint stop you. He ain't got nothin on you. You kin swear . . ."

"Ain't gonna be no swearin."

"Hell, Bubber, you ain't skeered that Wilkie. Or if'n he got somethin on you and you skeered to go back, thar's them will swear and I bring you yore share, Bubber, ever bit and you don't do nothin, jest take hit, you don't have to swear."

The pistol waggled, then stopped.

"Bubber, listen, Bubber . . . ," One-eye insisted.

"Right now," Lilburn said.

"Naw—naw," One-eye cried. "I'm yore Bubber—yore lettle Bubber—don't you remember?—yore lettle Bubber what loves you. . . ."

"I'll leetle-Bubber you, all right," Lilburn said, and his hand stiffened directly at One-eye's chest.

At that instant, Jeremiah had flung himself on Lilburn's arm and had grasped it and ridden it down, and strangely, the pistol did not explode. Even in that moment of struggle, Jeremiah thought how quick and cunning of Lilburn not to fire from surprise and waste the shot. Then he knew that Lilburn was fumbling in a pocket. For another pistol, he knew. Then he saw a shadow between him and the firelight, and heard a slight chunking sound, and the sound again, and a single scream from Rachel, and then Lilburn gave a long, tired sigh and sank back against him, like a friend. One-eye danced back, the bloody dirk in his hand.

Lilburn's body sank to the floor, propped against the table, with Jeremiah still grasping his right wrist, holding up that arm as though in benediction or victory. The pistol, still unexploded, was in Lilburn's hand, hanging limp.

Jeremiah took one hand from Lilburn's wrist and lifted the pistol free. Then he saw the wrist that was now thrust forward from the sleeve. There was a great silvery scar on the wrist.

He stared at the scar. He stared, and tried to remember. Then he knew.

"It was you," he said to Lilburn, almost whispering, "you."

Lilburn rolled his head toward Jeremiah, very slowly. His face was petulant and pale now, and suddenly smaller, like a sick child's.

"It was you," Jeremiah repeated. "You carried that paper to Tupper's tavern. You sent it to my house. It was you. Answer me!"

Lilburn stared numbly at Jeremiah's face, and said nothing.

"Damn you, answer me, or I'll"—and Jeremiah seized him by the shoulders—"or I'll . . ." He stopped, released the shoulders. There was no threat he could make.

But Lilburn spoke, in a weak, careful voice, as though any word might slip and fall and break. "Yes," he said. "I—done—hit."

"Who gave it to you?"

A film seemed to be coming over Lilburn's numb gaze.

"Who? Who gave it to you?"

Then Lilburn said: "Skrogg—and . . ." He stopped.

"And who?"

Lilburn stirred. He looked laboriously down at the left hand on his chest, where the blood came out. He managed to lift his hand a little, and gazed at the blood on the fingers. "Look," he said, marveling, "hit—keeps—on—comin."

"Who—who besides Skrogg?" Jeremiah demanded, and shook his shoulder.

451

Lilburn rolled his head again toward Jeremiah, and stared at him from a great distance. Then he said: "Wilkie—hit—was Wilkie."

Jeremiah leaped up, shoving Lilburn aside as he rose.

"My God," he cried, and stared wildly around, at One-eye with the bloody dirk, at Rachel sitting on the bed. "My God," he repeated, and knew their eyes on him.

There was a terrible constriction in his chest, and a lightness in his head.

"It was all a lie!" he cried out. "Everything was a lie. They betrayed me. Everybody betrayed me. Even Wilkie, even Wilkie betrayed me. They used me, they betrayed me, Skrogg and Wilkie and Marlowe and all . . ."

His eyes suddenly rested on Rachel. "And you!" he cried. "Even you, you betrayed me to Marlowe, betrayed me, when I—when I . . ."

He stepped toward her, leaning at her.

". . . when I had done all for you!"

She rose slowly from the bed, under his accusing gaze, and stood there swaying. Then she stiffened, staring into his face. Then she said, very low: "No. No. Not for me."

"For you," he said, "and then you . . ."

"Oh, for yourself!" she exclaimed suddenly. "Not for me. For yourself. You came and you used me. You made me hate Fort and you used me. Oh, I didn't hate him, I loved him, and you used me, you used me to kill him, you used me, you ruined me, you used me, used . . ."

"Stop!" he commanded.

"I won't, I won't, for I know the truth now."

"I'll make you," he said, and lunged at her, to seize her. He had forgotten the pistol in his hand.

She swung to one side, under his arm. "You won't have to shoot me. You don't have to kill me," she said. "Like you killed him. And like you killed Fort. Oh, no. For I . . ." She had seized the knife on the table, the old hunting knife he had used to eat with. She had turned toward him. "For I . . ."

He fell back a step, and lifted an arm in defense.

"Oh, don't be afraid," she said. "I won't hurt you."

Then she took the hilt of the knife in both hands, and set it cleanly in her own breast. She stood there, both hands still on the hilt, and looked at him, and shook her head slightly in a distant and weary commiseration. Then, the hands still on the hilt, she took two steps toward the bed.

Jeremiah fell back from her.

She sat on the edge of the bed. "Poor Jerry," she whispered.

She sank heavily to one side, and lay down, still clasping the knife

452

hilt. The blood was darkening the gray wool of the dress. "Forgive me," she whispered. "For you—you could not—help—it—Jerry."

"Rachel!" The name wrenched up from some depth inside him that suddenly opened, like a wound.

He leaned over her, and said her name several times. Then he saw that she was dead.

He was still staring down at her, when he heard One-eye's voice behind him. "Be durn," the voice said, "and she didn't go and do hit."

Jeremiah rose, and turned.

"Caint tell bout them women," One-eye said. "Caint tell what they'll up and do."

One-eye had finished wiping the blade of his dirk. He had used the lining, near the bottom, of his cut-off greatcoat. Now he put the dirk inside the front of his hunting shirt.

"One thing," One-eye said, "we kin go now, and not bother. Not bout Big Bubber"—he gently prodded with his boot-toe the leg of Lilburn—"ner her." He nodded toward the figure on the bed. "You kin go now, and not have yore mind set on her, fer worriment."

"Yes," Jeremiah said.

"He tole you," One-eye said, "bout Skrogg and all, and how he taken that paper. But won't do no good less'n I swear. You got to pay me if'n I show the paper and swear."

"You may rest assured," Jeremiah said. "If I have you swear for me, I shall pay you. What you ask."

"Les git," One-eye said.

Jeremiah went to a shelf on the far wall. He took down his manuscript, laid the pen with it, and made it into a parcel. Then he went to the bed. He arranged Rachel's body and covered it with a blanket. He took another blanket for himself, made it into a roll with a rope, and hung it on his shoulder. He picked up his parcel and the ink-horn, and turned.

One-eye was rising from beside the body of Lilburn. He chinked the purse in his hand. "Jest gittin his money," he explained. And added with a trace of apology: "Looks lak hit ought to come to me, count of close kin."

"Yes, of course," Jeremiah said, and followed One-eye out the door.

They got a skiff, lay down in the bottom, and drifted down the slew. They did not use pole or paddle until they were well down from the island. They had reached over the side and paddled softly with their hands to help the drift.

They landed well down the slew on the far side, in the cane. Then One-eye took the lead and worked inland. Finally they struck the trace. Near dawn they reached the spot where the horses were hobbled. There they mounted, and rode. As they rode, they munched some stale corn pone provided by One-eye from a sack hung on his saddle.

Just before dark, they camped. As they lay there in the dark, Jeremiah heard One-eye tell how he had come by the copy of the broadside signed Fort. Back in Frankfort, One-eye, jug by his side, had been lying on his pallet one night in his usual corner in Skrogg's print shop when Skrogg and Wilkie came in and Skrogg began to set up something from the type box. This was not too unusual, to have Skrogg, or Skrogg and Wilkie, break in on his slumbers and potations. What was unusual was that they kicked him out. Even in his drink-fogged state, he calculated that their business was secret and of special importance. When a couple of hours later they left and he was readmitted to the room, he smelled smoke, and noticed that some papers had been burned in the fireplace. There, buried under some other papers, smoldering at the edges but otherwise unharmed, One-eye had found the broadside. (It must have been a proof sheet of Wilkie's and Skrogg's broadside and the other papers, we can guess, were the rough drafts in script.) "I taken hit," he said. "I ain't lyin, I caint read so good, but I knowed that name of Cunnel Fort, and I figgered they try and burn hit, hit must be worth a leetle, some time, maybe." Next morning, Skrogg and Wilkie had had a long conference with Lilburn, and Lilburn had gone on a journey for almost two weeks. At the time One-eye had not connected the two facts, but he had hung onto the paper. Then, when he heard the rumor that the lawyers were making a search for a broadside signed Fort, he took it to Crawford. Crawford could read. Crawford needed money. Crawford was angry at Lilburn and Bumps. Crawford, everybody knew, had sworn for money. Crawford was his man. And so all had followed. The guard in the cell had reported back to Lilburn. Lilburn had stabbed One-eye and left him for dead in an alley. Wilkie had delivered Jeremiah.

But there were many *whys*. As he lay there, at night, under the winter trees, Jeremiah turned them in his mind.

Why, oh, why, had Wilkie betrayed him? Why, long ago, had Wilkie lied to him about loving Rachel Jordan? Why had Wilkie feigned his noble rage at her plight and shamed Jeremiah to his desperate purpose? Why had he used him in politics? Why had he published that broadside against Fort, in Pick County, in the last campaign, reviving the old scandal? (For Jeremiah was sure now, perfectly sure, that Wilkie and Skrogg had done that, too.) Why had Wilkie tricked him with the second broadside and sent him to kill Fort? Why had Wilkie, in the end, sworn away his life? Was this Wilkie's return for all youthful friendship and trust?

But Wilkie would have an answer for every question. He would always have an answer. Wilkie would lean at him and smile pityingly and say, "Good old Jerry, poor old Jerry, don't you understand?" And the answer would be so true, so noble.

So true, so noble, and he lay there and thought blackly how all he wished was to have that smiling, pitying face before him, under his hand. Whatever its answer, whatever its answer! But the fury passed —he had so little strength and place for fury now—and only the questions remained.

And there was the strangest question of all: Why had Wilkie delivered him at last? Why had he not left him there for the rope next morning? One-eye was dead, or was thought to be dead. But Crawford knew something. How much? And Crawford had gone for Madison, and Madison might get a stay from the Governor, he was strong with the Governor, and then nobody could predict what would happen. How much did Jeremiah himself know now?

But why not shoot Jeremiah down in his cell, or cut his throat? Why take all the trouble to deliver him? Was that the last flicker of boyhood affection, a last sop to conscience? Or was it just Wilkie? Just Wilkie's way? What had Wilkie said, there in the cell, at the foot of the ladder? He had said: "I haven't had as much fun since we fought the bastards at Lumton."

Was everything, the whole world, fun to Wilkie?

Since we fought the bastards at Lumton: and he saw Wilkie's face, the eyes glittering, the lips curled back, as he balanced to drive the toe of his boot into the kidney of the Old-Courter at Lumton, he heard Wilkie's exhalation as he drove a fist against the man's mouth. And he saw Wilkie's face, that night in the Barron house at Bowling Green, as he dandled his clean little old chirrupy mother on his knee— and not cool yet from the arms of a Silly Sal. And Wilkie's face, in that same room, as he read one of his poems, and tossed back his locks, and lifted an arm to the swelling rhythm. And Wilkie's face, lit with noble rage and contempt, speaking of Rachel Jordan, Rachel Jordan and her betrayer, saying, "My God, but I knew her! Could any man know her and not feel the disgrace of this? Could any man with a spark of manhood not itch to give justice with his own hand? Don't you understand? Don't you understand?" And Wilkie's face leaning then, saying to him, "And is that why you feel no honorable rage? Because you are his friend. Because he pays you? Because he will make you? Because you are his creature?" And Wilkie's face, sober and statesmanlike, as he sat by Mr. Madison and Skrogg and Rowan and the makers of destiny. And Wilkie's face above the coiling mist at the river's edge, Wilkie's arm waving to them in the keelboat, Wilkie's face saying, "Good-bye, good-bye, my dillies, my darlings, good-bye." And Wilkie's face . . .

For what was Wilkie's face but the mask of all the world? And everything it spoke was true, always true, and what Wilkie did was always done for affection, for calculation, for interest, for conscience, for honor, for noble rage and contempt, for the cold flicker of pride, for the public good, for the sweetness of cruelty, for the joy of magnanimity, for the warm tear of pity, for fun, for fun, for fun . . .

For the fun of what?

For the fun of being Wilkie, Wilkie Barron, with the warm voice and quick smile, and the arrogant lift of the head.

For the fun of being Wilkie Barron, who was all the world, or rather, was the mask of the world and was, therefore, nothing.

But Wilkie Barron was something, was somewhere. His face was the mask of the world, but he was not his face and a mask, but was real, he was a cold, bright, terrible seed in the dark, somewhere in the darkness behind the world, beyond the world, and it sprouted forever and grew, and the world was the mask of it, the world was its terrible leaves that grew from the stalk.

He would find Wilkie. No matter where he lay, he would find him. And then. And then. The fury came back. It filled him. It lifted him high among the winter trees, in the dark.

That was almost enough. But it was not enough. For too much had happened. He knew too much now. For he knew too much. For the fury was gone, and he would have cried out: "Oh, why am I the bleeding sore of all the world? Oh, who will stanch me, rinse me, wash me clean?"

He did not know. But he knew what he would do. He remembered how Rachel had said, "Poor Jerry," and had asked his forgiveness. So he thought: *poor Wilkie*. And again: *poor, poor, Wilkie*. And that was a sad and pitying good-bye to Wilkie, who meant nothing to him now, for love or hate, good or evil.

He had known, from the moment of Rachel's death, what he would do. He had known it without knowing it. It was a knowledge beneath knowledge, the "kind of knowledge that is identity." (He puts it that way in his manuscript.) So next morning, he took the first step to do what he had known he would do.

He waited until One-eye had risen, stretched, relieved nature, taken a drink of water, and munched a corn pone. Then he said: "Look here."

One-eye lifted his head and found himself looking into the muzzle of Lilburn's pistol.

"Lay that paper on the ground," Jeremiah ordered.

For a long moment, One-eye stared at Jeremiah with his mouth open and the little lump of chewed corn pone lying damp and yellow in that orifice. Then he managed to swallow, then said: "What?"

"Lay that paper on the ground."

"Won't do you no good," One-eye objected. "You can't do nothin with hit, less'n I swear how hit come. You won't git no pardon less'n . . ."

"I don't want a pardon," Jeremiah said.

"You out yore head?"

"Do what I say. Quick."

One-eye hesitated. "Won't do you no good, less'n . . ."

"I do not want you to swear. Either lies or truth. I want that paper." For a moment longer, One-eye hesitated.

"I have killed one man," Jeremiah said. "With my hands. I stabbed him twice. He was a man. A great man. He was my friend and benefactor. He loved me like a father, and I killed him. I did that. Do you think I would shrink to kill a creature vile as you?"

One-eye laid the paper on the ground.

Jeremiah flung a length of rope to him. "Tie your legs up. Good and tight," he commanded.

One-eye obeyed.

"Roll on your stomach," Jeremiah said, "and put your hands behind you."

One-eye did so, and Jeremiah drew his legs up and tied his wrists with the same length of rope.

"It is not tied very tight," Jeremiah said. "You can probably work it loose in half a day, if you are lucky. If you can't work it loose, somebody might find you. If you can't work it loose and nobody finds you, then you aren't lucky. I'm sorry, but it's the best way I can think of."

"God damn you," One-eye said.

"It's the best way," Jeremiah said musingly, "except, of course, to shoot you. I do not want to see more blood. I've seen enough. But if—"

"Naw—naw," One-eye said.

Jeremiah picked up One-eye's purse, and counted out ten silver dollars. "I'll take this," he said. "I might need it on the way. I won't touch the gold or paper. This is just part of what you took from Lilburn. After all, I helped you kill your brother, even if I didn't mean to, even if I was just trying to keep him from killing you. So I ought to have a share. In simple equity."

One-eye said nothing.

So Jeremiah pocketed the coins, picked up the paper, tucked it into his shirt, took the rifle, mounted One-eye's horse, the one with the food sack, and rode away, leading the second horse. He could not leave a horse here for One-eye to use.

He had taken a turn in the trace, beyond a dead thicket, when he heard One-eye's voice calling, very thin for the distance: "You—won't—git—no—pardon!"

Pardon: was pardon what he sought? Certainly not the pardon that Governor Desha, or any man, could give.

He knew what he would do, but he also had to know why. So on this second flight, not the flight to but the flight from the wilderness, he huddled by the shirt-tail full of burning sticks, in the winter woods, at night, and scrawled on what were to be the last sheets of his manuscript. He had to say it that he might know.

"Pardon," he wrote, hearing again the distance-thin voice of One-eye calling from back up the trail, beyond the dead thicket. "I do not seek pardon," he writes, "for who could give me pardon? I do not flee toward pardon but toward expiation."

Expiation for what?

"I killed Cassius Fort, in darkness and deceit, and that was a crime. But I do not seek expiation merely for that. Nor for what I did to Rachel, greater crime as it is, to go to her not for her sake but my own and to defile her mind, and torture her until she cried for Fort's blood, and lead her into ruin for my vainglory. Nor that I willed the death of my mother, and sent her into the farther and colder room, that I might be left alone to my advantage. Nor that when I struck Wilkie, that night long ago in Bowling Green, when he was my friend, I struck not in proper indignation because he accused me of being Fort's creature but in hurt pride and fear that it might be true, and for that inner reason killed Fort. Men have laid low their fathers only because they were fathers. Nor that I entered upon politics and fought for New Court, not for conviction and love of justice, but for a black need within me. Nor that I deceived the honest hearts of Madison and Hawgood. Nor that I did not trust truth in the world and would have lived by a lie and named it truth. Nor that I have played on the heart of Dr. Burnham, that good old loving man, to break his duty as citizen and healer and give me poison. Nor that I had committed a thousand particular crimes. I do not seek expiation for them, for each of these crimes is particular, and is lost in the detail and flux of time.

"No, that crime for which I seek expiation is never lost. It is always there. It is unpardonable. It is the crime of self, the crime of life. The crime is I."

The crime was himself, and that crime was worse than the crime of Wilkie Barron. Far worse, for Wilkie was but the world, either seed of the world or mask of the world, and it did not matter which, and would justify himself only by the world. Far worse, for Jeremiah would justify himself, not by the world, which he would deny, but by the idea. *The idea is all,* he had thought.

"For," he writes, "it is the first and last temptation, to name the idea as all, which I did, and in that error was my arrogance, and the beginning of my undoing and cold exile from mankind. And now I remember a passage I once read by the ingenious Mr. John Locke in his book on our Understanding, in which he says that we are wont to regard any substance we meet as being a thing entirely by itself, and having all of its qualities independent of all other things, and that in doing so we neglect the operation of those invisible fluids which compass the substance about and spring from all other substances. Take a piece of gold, Mr. Locke says, which is of a tawny color, and is heavy and malleable, and has great worth, and put it aside in some place beyond the world, and the influence of all other substances. Then it may lose that color, and the weight become nothing that it may float as a feather, and the malleableness be changed into a perfect friability, and that worth we put upon it—ah, what becomes of that worth in the cold and silent dark beyond the stars? So, I ask, what becomes of the idea, if we place it apart from our warm world and its invisible fluids by which we live?"

He had thought that the idea in and of itself might redeem the world, and in that thought had scorned the world. But that thought, he tells us, had led to a second error, which must always follow from the first when we find that the idea has not redeemed the world: the world must redeem the idea. "Then in this thought," he writes, "man will use the means of the natural world, and its dark ways, to gain that end he names holy by the idea, and ah! the terror of that, the terror of that. So Skrogg for his idea of justice had, in the end, sent Fort to my knife, and me to the rope. So I, no better than Skrogg, and in the same error, had put the mask on my face and lurked by night in the dead lilacs."

But there is a third error, he says, that follows from the second: to deny the idea and its loneliness and embrace the world as all, or, as he puts it, "to seek communion only in the blank cup of nature, and innocence there." He had taken that step, at last. "For I had sought innocence, and had fled into the brute wilderness where all is innocence, for all is the same in that darkness, and even the shameful canker is innocence. But that innocence is what man cannot endure and be man, and now I flee from innocence and toward my guilt, and bear my heart within me like a bleeding sore of self, as I bear the canker on my body. And if I can clasp my guilt, then both may become the marks of my triumph, as of my shame."

What was his way?

"There must be a way I have missed," he says, and looks mournfully back on his story. "There must be a way whereby the word becomes flesh. There must be a way whereby the flesh becomes word. Whereby loneliness becomes communion without contamination. Whereby contamination becomes purity without exile. There must be a way, but I may not have it now. All I can have now is knowledge. But if we can have knowledge, if we can know the terrible logic of life, if we can only know! But at least I know now that life tells no lies in the end, for all the lies, single and particular, will at last speak together in a great chorus of truth in many voices. Thus all the lies and false witness against me told truth, but in my anger and betrayal I did not guess that that is all we need: knowledge. That is not redemption, but is almost better than redemption. I go home through the wilderness now and know that I may not have redemption. I no longer seek to justify. I seek only to suffer. I will shake the hangman's hand, and will call him my brother, at last."

He never got to shake the hangman's hand.

But, for the events that followed Jeremiah's escape from One-eye, we must make inferences from scanty evidence. We know that Wilkie Barron had left Frankfort some time before, in company with the boatman Finger, who had been his accomplice in the jail delivery, and had ridden hurriedly to Louisville. There they had taken a steamboat as far down as Paducah, had bought a stout but light boat and equipped it, and had started down-river, alone. Presumably, Wilkie had discovered that One-eye was on his way to bring Jeremiah back, and presumably Wilkie had found Finger as his guide to Ole Big Hump's stronghold. Did he intend now to kill Jeremiah, or rather, arrange for his death, and close the books? Or did he have the notion of luring him to some new refuge, where One-eye could not follow? What he intended to do, once there at the island, we cannot know.

Whatever it was, he arrived too late, to find Lilburn and Rachel dead and Jeremiah gone, presumably for Frankfort, with One-eye and the evidence that would ruin Wilkie and Skrogg. We do not know whether One-eye escaped from his bonds and returned to the island, or whether Wilkie and Finger set out in pursuit and found One-eye on the way. In any case, One-eye now threw in with Wilkie, and, well horsed and equipped, took up Jeremiah's trail. One-eye had, no doubt, learned from Wilkie that the amount of the new reward for the cap-

ture of Jeremiah after his escape had been raised again. The Legisla-
tors, in December, had voted one thousand dollars in addition to the
thousand previously offered by the state and the thousand offered by
John Saunders and other friends of Fort. And perhaps One-eye made
other arrangements with Wilkie. The proof-sheet of the broadside
must have had a value.

Wilkie would now have a difficult decision. He could wait here in
the wilderness until he had word of developments at Frankfort—
whether Jeremiah had arrived to ruin him or whether One-eye had
overtaken the quarry. Or he could return to Frankfort, hoping to
arrive before Jeremiah, if Jeremiah had escaped, and settle matters
there, one way or another. He took the bold course, and returned to
Frankfort. He caught an up-river steamboat at Paducah.

Wilkie now had with him a piece of baggage. It was a crude box
in which lay the blanket-wrapped body of Rachel Beaumont. The
box was sealed with pitch, the weather was very cold, the box was
transported on the outside promenade of the saloon deck to take
advantage of the temperature. The body arrived in what one of the
Frankfort papers called a "remarkable state of preservation, thanks
to foresight and the rigorous season." The paper also congratulated
Wilkie on his humanity in bringing back "the body of that erring and
unfortunate young woman that it may lie in civilized soil and receive
the meed of generous tears."

Two days after the arrival of Wilkie, One-eye reached Frankfort.
In a sack, swung from his saddle-bow, was the head of Jeremiah
Beaumont. Some four or five days west of Frankfort, One-eye had
overtaken him, surprised him in camp, and killed him. One-eye had
hacked the head off the body with his hunting knife, and had neatly
encased the neck with clay to prevent its soiling through the bag.
There was no question of identification. Half of Frankfort came to
the jail yard to gaze upon the trophy and proclaim it genuine.

Then Wilkie, in piety to old friendship, and no doubt in considerable relief, claimed the head to give it decent interment. Meanwhile,
he had sent back a party, with One-eye as guide, to recover the body.
Well before their return, however, the weather turned warm. So the
body of Rachel was removed from its box and placed in a casket,
with the head of her husband, cleansed of the clay, propped against
her left shoulder. The casket was buried in the back of the cemetery.
Subsequently a small stone was erected at Wilkie's expense, with
the epitaph that Rachel had composed.

The party that had gone for Jeremiah's body came back. All they
had for their pains was a few bones corded up in a bundle of sacking.
Wild hogs, as they had been able to determine from the trampled
earth at the spot in the woods, had been before them. The bones,

461

without ceremony, were consigned to a hole beside the new grave.

One-eye received the reward for the capture of Jeremiah, and very probably received a token of appreciation from Wilkie Barron in return for Jeremiah's manuscript. After a sensational spree of ten days, which revived the best traditions of the heyday of the keelboat, One-eye disappeared toward the west. He is never heard of again. Wilkie's luck had held.

Wilkie's luck always held. With the collapse of the New Court, he dropped out of the public notice, but he improved the time by making his fortune. In partnership with old Josh and young Felix Parham, he entered upon a notoriously successful speculation in lands in the western part. With the capital thus gained, he established himself in the esteem of his elders among the rich, conservative and well born, and at the same time cut a dashing figure in the eyes of the young and impressionable persons of fashion. He married a rich, handsome widow, not too much his senior, Casselbury by name.

It is a pleasantly ironical reflection to think that the foundation of Wilkie's fortune was the old maps and descriptions that Jeremiah had made for western lands and had sent back to Josh Parham when, at the instigation of Wilkie, he dissolved that partnership. Wilkie, of course, had not planned it that way. But the Wilkies of the world never have to plan. They need only to be themselves, to be Wilkie, and the world plans for them.

The world continued to plan well for Wilkie Barron. It gave him fine sons and beautiful daughters. It gave him a wife who grew quickly fat and comfortable and thought more of furbelows, fabrics and trencher than of her husband's vagrant glances. It gave him thriving herds and solid investments. It made him a Senator in the end. For Wilkie, when the time came, allowed a friendship with Henry Clay to cool, and re-emerged upon the political scene as a stalwart Jackson man. Radicalism was in again, and he was again a radical, but now a rich one. He acquitted himself well in Washington, for a year and a half. He was still handsome, he was eloquent, he was at the height of his powers and in the prime of life. So one morning he stepped into his bath, in his Washington house, and shot himself tidily through the heart, without a single spatter of blood on the floor. Nobody knew why he did it.

We do not know why. But we know that, all those years, he had carried about with him the manuscript of Jeremiah, in a locked leather case. The case, with all his papers, remained in a trunk for two more generations, and then found its way, unread, into the store-room of a library. It remained unread for a long time. For who was Wilkie Barron? A man of no historical importance.

462

Why did Wilkie not destroy the manuscript? He knew that the truth in it would ruin him if it ever came out. He did not destroy it, but he could conceal it. Something in him prevented him from destroying it. Something in him made him keep that truth and carry it, year after year. He destroyed himself, not it, in the end.

The House to which Colonel Fort had been elected in 1825 had a majority for the repeal of the Reorganization Act that had broken the Old Court and established the New, and voted thus. But in the Senate the Old Court could not yet command a majority. So the New Court lingered on for another year, on borrowed time, in a twilight world, the judges already ghosts on the bench, speaking words that the living ear could not catch.

The elections of 1826 returned a majority in the Senate as well as the House for the repeal of the Act. In November, while Jeremiah Beaumont lay hidden on the island of Ole Big Hump in the west, the new legislature assembled. The cock crew, the ghosts fled, full day dawned.

What powers had summoned up those ghosts and made them seem, for a brief time, real and solid? Political chicanery, ambition, the despair of the debtor, the laziness of louts, the cunning of speculators, and, even, a crazy dream of justice. But daylight came, the ghosts fled, and a mortgage was again worth more than the paper it was written on, laziness was no longer put at a premium, the laborer was worthy of his hire, and the rich man did not bury his talent but put it out at twelve, or fifteen, or even twenty per cent. For daylight, too, brought its own crazy dream of justice.

For all men believe in justice. Otherwise they would not be men. But there is the world and there is the idea, there are the flesh and the word, there are the Old Court and the New.

Cassius Fort had risen in the night and gone to John Saunders' bed to wake his kinsman and say that he had a plan to "reconcile all in justice." But he did not divulge his plan, and the steel of Jeremiah Beaumont found him soon, and things went on their way as though he had never lived.

Things went on their way, and the Commonwealth of Kentucky has, by the latest estimate, 2,819,000 inhabitants, and the only Shawnee in the country is in a WPA mural on a post-office wall, and Old Big Hump and his brass cannon are lost in the mud of the swamps, and tourists occasionally visit the grave of Daniel Boone and the log cabin in Larue County where Abraham Lincoln was born and the log cabin in Todd County where Jefferson Davis was born and the Old Kentucky Home at Bardstown in Nelson County, and some 400,000,000 pounds of tobacco are grown annually, and in a good year over 60,000,000 tax gallons of whisky are distilled, and the State University now has 8000 students and a championship basketball team, and the literacy rate for the state is one of the lowest in the nation, and the thoroughbreds untrack to the roar of the crowd and the dainty galvanic legs flash like a blur of scimitars and the sun is on the colors and the parimutuels do a $40,000,000 business, and the Negro is emancipated and can vote and if he is smart he can even get paid for voting (just like white folks), and anyway he is free and can die of tuberculosis in a Louisville slum if he wants to and nobody will stop him (for it is his legal right and is damned near the only right the white folks will let him have) and as long as any man is not free, all men are slaves (and even the President of the Junior Chamber of Commerce of Louisville is a slave, but he probably doesn't care whether he is a slave or not), and from the white-columned portico you look across the gracious sweep of meadow to the sunset beyond the blue knobs and your heart almost breaks because it is so beautiful (and you love beauty), and there are 31,788 miles of improved highway and some of it passes through the little towns where if it is Sunday you can ride by the white gingerbread or lace-scrollwork houses or the new bungalows and see the old folks sitting under the maples, and some of the highways go back into the mountains (and you had better go there if you want to see it really quaint and old-timey and maybe pick up a hickory basket or patch-work quilt for a souvenir), and the teeth of the stalwart children of the hills tend to rot out by the age of thirty-five, but things are improving as all statistics show and civilization is making strides, and we can look forward to a great future for our state (if we accept the challenge, if we carry on our great tradition, if we pass on the torch), for it is a fair land and some people who live in it are happy, and many have the strength to endure without happiness and do not even think of the word, and only a few are so weak and miserable that they give up before their time, and in this fair land there is little enough justice yet, heart-justice or belly-justice, but that does not make Kentucky different from other places.

In the days before the white man came, the Indians called the land of Kentucky the Dark and Bloody Ground. But they also called it the Breathing Land and the Hollow Land, for beneath the land there are great caves. The Indians came here to fight and to hunt, but they did not come here to live. It was a holy land, it was a land of mystery, and they trod the soil lightly when they came. They could not live here, for the gods lived here. But when the white men came, the gods fled, either into the upper air or deeper into the dark earth. So there was no voice here to speak and tell the white men what justice is.

Unless Cassius Fort heard that voice in the night. That, of course, is
unlikely, for Cassius Fort was only an ignorant back-county lawyer.
But men still long for justice.

"I had longed for some nobility," Jeremiah wrote on the last sheet
of his manuscript, by some huddled flame at night beside the trail
back, "but did not know its name. I had longed to do justice in the
world, and what was worthy of praise. Even if my longing was born
in vanity and nursed in pride, is that longing to be wholly damned?
For we do not damn the poor infant dropped by a drab in a ditch, but
despite the mother's fault and tarnishment we know its innocence
and human worth. And in my crime and vainglory of self is there no
worth lost? Oh, was I worth nothing, and my agony? Was all for
naught?"

Was all for naught?